Metaphorosis

2016

Also from Metaphorosis

Score – an SFF symphony

Reading 5X5: Readers' Edition
Reading 5X5: Writers' Edition

Best Vegan Science Fiction & Fantasy
Best Vegan SFF 2018
Best Vegan SFF 2017
Best Vegan SFF 2016

Metaphorosis Magazine
Metaphorosis: Best of 2018
Metaphorosis: Best of 2017
Metaphorosis: Best of 2016

Metaphorosis 2018: The Complete Stories
Metaphorosis 2017: The Complete Stories
Metaphorosis 2016: Nearly Complete Stories

Monthly issues

by B. Morris Allen
Susurrus
Allenthology: Volume I
Tocsin: and other stories
Start with Stones: collected stories
Metaphorosis: a collection of stories

Metaphorosis

Nearly Complete Stories 2016

edited by
B. Morris Allen

ISSN: 2573-136X (online)
ISBN: 978-1-64076-074-5 (e-book)
ISBN: 978-1-64076-075-2 (paperback)
ISBN: 978-1-64076-076-9 (hardcover)

from
Metaphorosis Publishing

Neskowin

Contents

From the Editor

SFF magazines (esp. *Analog* and *SF&F*) were an important part of my introduction to speculative fiction. Around the same time that my uncle introduced me to Barsoom, a substitute middle school English teacher gave me her boyfriend's old pulp magazines – with such stories as "The Screwfly Solution" by James Tiptree, "The Cold Cash War" by Robert Lynn Asprin, "Ender's Game" by Orson Scott Card, and "After the Festival" by George R. R. Martin. Those stories amazed and astounded me. At that age, I was soaking up every book I could find, but once I spotted Burroughs, Martin, Zelazny, and the rest, I took a sharp turn toward science fiction and fantasy. Not only could these folks write, they wrote about fascinating stuff!

Once I found I could buy this stuff in actual books – a habit strongly encouraged by my parents – my magazine reading slowed. I'd pick them up in school libraries, and I subscribed to *Omni* for a while, but mostly I read books. A decade or two later, I flirted with pulp reading again, but I couldn't afford to sustain the habit, and the market had changed – I wasn't as taken with the then-new SF&F.

With age and responsibility came even less time to read, but I started to to feel guilty – the pulps had helped start me on my reading path, and I wasn't repaying my debt. By the mid-2010s, I started reading actively in the new online magazines – *Clarkesworld*, *Beneath Ceaseless Skies*, *Strange Horizons*, *Tor.com*, *Lightspeed*, *Nature*, *Daily SF*, *Apex*, *Subterranean Press* – I read all sorts of things (and put together a much-ignored best of the month list at free-sff.metaphorosis.com).

It was exhausting – I kept it up for less than 6 months. But it was also a welcome reminder that there was all sorts of great new SFF being published that I hadn't previously seen. However, while there was a lot of good writing, there wasn't as much as I'd hoped of the kind of thing I wanted to see – not just good ideas, but beautiful, stylish writing to go with them. And while the new magazines were impressive, they didn't have the breadth I looked for – they each, naturally, tended to converge on a single editorial style, with each of the stories starting to sound a bit the same.

Around that time, the obvious solution occurred to me – put my money where my mouth was, and start my own magazine. As one does, I mumbled "Mm-hmm" and put the idea away for the day I won the lottery.

It nagged at me, though, and in the back of my mind, I developed my plans – pro-rates, commissioned art, a terrific website. I made up budgets – yes, I'd definitely need to win the lottery to make it work.

But then, in late 2014, I found myself (voluntarily) unemployed. I caught up on my reading, walked a lot on the beautiful Oregon coast, wrote a heap of stories, and even got a fantasy novel done (*Susurrus*). Every now and then I'd think about that magazine, and tell my spouse about how someday I'd start it up. Practical person that she is, she said "Why not now?" and why not start slow, with rates I could actually afford? I made my calculations, and told her "It's still going to cost a lot of money." Because she is who she is, she just answered "We can manage. If you want to do it, do it."

So, by 2015, I found myself doing it. I spent months learning simple things about how put together websites, doing a lot of design and planning, and figuring out how to work around my weaknesses (no artistic skills, no interest in promotion). It was frustrating and fun. By September 2015, I was ready to launch – uncertain whether I'd get any submissions, whether they'd be any good, whether I'd really be able to make it work.

Planning, in this case, paid off – the administrative side worked about as I thought it would. Luck made the rest of it work. We got plenty of submissions – about 5 per day, a number that remains steady today – and they were plenty good. Sure, we only buy 5% or so of what comes in, but there are good stories even in what we turn away.

We (I tend to use the royal we in talking about the magazine) were paying only $.01/word, so I knew from the start that we'd have to distinguish ourselves in some way. I focused on things under my control – we'd respond quickly (because I was annoyed with magazines that took 6 months to say no), and we'd give feedback (because I was always so pleased when I got some from magazines like *F&SF*, *Beneath Ceaseless Skies*, and *Shimmer*). We've been able to keep that up.

So, has it been a success? For me, there's no doubt. As the stories in this volume prove, we've published a lot of great stuff. Part of the reason this volume exists is that when I selected stories for the *Best of 2016* anthology, I had such a hard time. I realized then that I'd missed a trick – that I wanted a *Complete Metaphorosis* for my own selfish purposes, and that I'd completely failed to secure the rights for one.

I fixed that in late 2017, but for 2016, I needed to go back and ask each author individually for additional rights. I'm pleased and humbled that virtually all of them agreed. The result is not only this volume, but monthly issues from 2016 that will be available as e-books.

So, that's a brief history of how we got here. Now, find a comfortable spot, sit back, and enjoy 52 great stories.

B. Morris Allen
Editor
1 April 2018

January

The Demon in the Page

Joshua Phillip Johnson

"Ochre!" Mahj's tired shout was the crunch of autumn leaves underfoot, and the densely packed tomes of the library devoured the sound.

"Ochre!" She tried again, her voice straining, tempting another coughing fit. Running from place to place was a student's game.

"Coming!" came the faint reply, wafting through the archives like a shallow breath.

While Ochre's footsteps grew from light pats to insistent thumps, Mahj looked again at the open journal in front of her, at her frustrated attempts at translation, each word and letter splitting apart into seemingly infinite variations and meanings, infinite attempts at connection and understanding.

Mahj ran the soft pad of one finger over the page, over the crisscrossed chaos of her pen strokes, trying to trace the force she saw there, the opaque, shifting demon, at times frustrating and clarifying her work, lurking just behind the inky nettles of text.

"I see you," Mahj whispered to her demon.

As a younger scholar, Mahj had been mocked for her tendency to talk to herself or the books she studied. That had all changed, though, when she had been the first of her peers to successfully translate an Old World Göthelian text during her 3rd year working at the Languages Institute. Since then, the same evidence used to malign her in social and professional circles was used to support titles like "athrylith" or "genius" or "عبقري"or Olive Drab#7.

Ochre raced into the room. Ochre raced everywhere. He had the candle-at-the-end-of-its-wick look worn by graduate students everywhere: tired eyes surrounded by great pillowy masses of discolored skin, hair that had seen neither pillow nor comb, and days-old clothing. He looked a mess.

"Yes, Mahj?" Ochre's deep voice still shaped words with the thick tongue of Grißla, a dulcet chromatic language that played on the soft palate.

"How is your High Caste Illysial coming?"

Ochre held himself a little straighter, his sixth student sense detecting an exam. Ochre had been a student for a long time, and he could sense an exam, formal or not, from a great distance. And he did not fail exams.

"Very well, Mahj. I have memorized the primary, secondary, and tertiary indents along with successfully mastering 43 of the 55 writing implements."

Mahj raised an ancient eyebrow.

"Edmund took the rest and hid them," Ochre said, his confidence slipping away in the face of his annoyance.

Mahj frowned, making a mental note to speak with Edmund, who was the Institute's (admittedly) brilliant but (just as admittedly) immature head curator. Ever since Ochre's arrival three years past, torturing the new graduate student had seemed to become a regular part of Edmund's job. Mahj suspected it had more than a little to do with Edmund's crush on Ochre.

"Very well. What do you know of the language itself?" Mahj rarely gave these kinds of impromptu quizzes for her mentee, who had arrived from a Very Serious school where Very Important tests were given frequently in order to separate the Great Students from the Good Students, and the Brilliant Students from the Greats. Ochre was not used to gaining validation from his superiors from simply doing good work, and he often wished Mahj would quiz him more, if only for the sake of his own sense of self worth.

Ochre spoke with robotic accuracy, as though he were citing from a book, which, in a way, he was. His photographic memory pulled up the correct page and he simply read it from his mind.

"High Caste Illysial, a purely written language, is comprised of indents pressed into soft, medium thickness paper. The indents, based on their width, depth, and shape, communicate a series of increasingly complex subjects. A series of 55 intricate, specialized tools are used to create these indents. Ink is then applied to the area surrounding an indent or, in rare cases, inside the indents, to articulate the predicate."

"Good—" Mahj began, but Ochre was on a roll and would not be stopped from putting forward his argument.

"Because of the intrinsically exclusionary nature of the language, and based on its historical usage, it is my contention that High Caste Illysial is the precursor of several modern languages, most notably Lark's and the Silent Tongue. Although certain scholars disagree with High Caste Illsyial's impact and historical importance, one only has to look at—"

"I yield!" Mahj cried, wheezing out a laugh and holding up her hands in mock surrender. "Very nicely done," she said, smiling at Ochre, who fairly glowed with the praise.

Mahj handed him a book of High Caste Illysial.

"What do you make of that? Just general impressions."

Ochre felt a thrill of anxiety. Mahj was asking about his overall thoughts, but he could sense an urgency pulsing behind her words. She was after something else, something she wanted to see if he could or would find on his own, something secret. This was the real exam, and Ochre did not fail exams.

"Paper is standard synthetic vellum. Cover is surprisingly soft reinforced Estin leaf."

Mahj waved a hand to move Ochre on.

"The text. What about the text itself," said Mahj, her voice easy, the light in her eyes belying her casual tone.

Ochre blew a spout of air up from the corner of his mouth, causing a frazzled thatch of hair to puff up and settle again. He opened the book and scanned through a bundle of pages at random before quickly and systematically working through and commenting on each chapter. His eyes moved often to Mahj's face, and his happiness of only a moment earlier dimmed a little each time he saw no spark of recognition or praise there.

"Standard index with class-specific gerunds integrated into an otherwise typical syntax," he finished, knowing that he had failed. He passed back the book, defeat plain on his face and in the slump of his shoulders.

"That's just fine, Ochre," Mahj said, taking the book. Her words were a blow to the graduate student, who was not used to being *fine*, not used to having his work be *fine*.

Mahj opened her mouth to say more, perhaps to reassure her pupil that he'd done a wonderful job, perhaps to lie and say that he'd found exactly what she was looking for. Perhaps to tell him the truth and to ask him to look again for the demon lurking there.

But she erupted into a coughing fit, and Ochre, his motions practiced and routine these days, passed her a handkerchief before placing firm hands on her shoulders, holding her upright. If her coughing fits were a storm, Ochre was the sturdy foundation Mahj huddled under.

It ended slowly, the coughs crumbling away into nothing, leaving Mahj red faced and short of breath and Ochre concerned and uncertain how to help. It was an uncertainty he'd come to know well.

"Are you alright?"

Mahj nodded and gestured for Ochre to sit. While he did, Mahj ran a finger over the closed cover of her journal, thinking again of the demon.

"What," Mahj began, her voice thin atop her shallow breathing, "is the purpose of translation?"

This was a cherished and well-worn conversation between them, a debate relished by both the teacher and the student.

Ochre leaned forward and sent another spout of air to unsettle the hair falling into his face.

"Translation is the process of shifting content from one medium to another. The goal of translation is to preserve content as perfectly as possible, to maintain meaning and syntax in the face of linguistic barriers."

He grinned, knowing his next statement would be met with rolled eyes.

"Translation is mathematics. The translator balances the equation. The good translator balances the equation *elegantly*."

Mahj disagreed, as she always did during these discussions, though she struggled to articulate why. Ochre presented a theory of translation held and taught by every expert in the field, a theory so widespread as to be thought a certainty.

"How robotic and rigid your translations must be," she said, smiling at her student. "What of the moments when perfect translation is impossible? What of the moments in translation when a text proliferates in meaning, one grapheme splitting into three or five or ten possible and viable meanings?" She held up a book Ochre had become increasingly familiar and annoyed with in his time with Mahj.

Translators the world over called it *The Blank Book*: a private joke celebrating their failure, lessening the blow to their collective ego. A text as old as the written word and filled with a monolithic language, but it was still devoid of meaning for all their attempts at translation. And so it remained *The Blank Book*. The author, as best they could guess, was someone with initials that translated to EY. Or perhaps VC. Mahj had published several papers arguing for a female author named EY, and this many years later, she had almost no idea if she had been right.

Ochre, the dogged optimist and rule-abiding absolutist, glared at the book in Mahj's hands and said, "No more than obstacles to be overcome by the talented and clever translator."

Mahj reached for her journal.

"Take Grißla for example," she said, pursuing her point despite Ochre's defense. She pointed to one of her entries on an ink-filled page. " 'Hooker's Green'. A color whose meaning, when translated, splits into several related but distinct possibilities. One does not arrive at *the* meaning through context; one arrives at *several* meanings through context. Even if that one were, as you say," Mahj arched an eyebrow and leaned forward, "a talented and clever translator."

Ochre laughed and offered his rebuttal. And the student and teacher talked late into the night, interrupted only once more by another coughing fit.

Journal Entry 38

Hooker's Green; Hex triplet: #49796B; sRGB[B] (73, 121, 107); CMYK[H] (73, 36, 59, 15); HSV (163°, 39.7%, 47.5%):
>   Noun: 1. Password, passcode, secret word; 2. Shibboleth
>   Adjective: 1. Secretive, covert; 2. Clandestine
>   (An adjectival Hooker's Green is often found juxtaposed with a subjective Carrion Red or an indirectly objective Chartreuse. Interestingly, a nominal Hooker's Green often begins an expression and undertakes the chromatic modifier without leading to or necessitating an adjunct. Another worrisome example of a linguistic unit or phrase multiplying its meaning through translation. Could this be the work of the demon?)

Mahj walked along the table, an overly long slab of repurposed wood that had once comprised part of a ship's hull. Edmund had acquired the wood at a sale and spent the long, laborious hours straightening the slab and refinishing it. It was a beautiful piece, elegant and impressive in an old-world kind of way, as though it should have stood in the middle of a grand and wonderful mead hall, weighed down by heavy gauntlets, thick drinking horns, and the viscous consonants of dead languages.

It was an impressive table, but in the few weeks following Mahj's debate with Ochre, it had become increasingly hard to see the wood beneath the thick layers of overlapping texts it had accumulated. Books from myriad cultures and in myriad languages covered the table in a mesmerizing bricolage of attempts at communication.

And in the middle of all of these, the only text on the table given its own space, like a sacred relic, hallowed and venerable, was *The Blank Book.*

"You asked for me, Mahj?" Ochre stood in the doorway, surveying the textual proliferation spawning across the room. Scrolls and books covered the table, yes, but there were also piles congregating on the floor, each one with mountainous aspirations.

"Well?" Mahj turned to look at her student, her eyes questioning. A rill of anxiety ran through her, as though she were a first-year student again, nervous to receive her grades. She'd given him a draft of her most recent article, a lengthy academic argument about translation and the demon. It was the first draft she'd given out to anyone at all, and his would be the first reaction.

Ochre reached into his bag and removed the bundled papers.

"A Demonic Tangle: Discourses on the Intrinsically Problematic and Entangled Spirit of Translation," he read before looking at his teacher. Mahj nodded, her enthusiasm bubbling away beneath the surface of her eyes.

"Yes, yes. I am sure our colleagues at other institutions will call me a fool or a heretic. But what do *you* think?"

Ochre felt a little part of himself break into pieces at that. His brilliant teacher cared for his opinion, not as a student but as a peer. He considered his next words carefully, wanting to hold and cultivate this newfound relationship as best he could.

"It is certainly *ambitious*," he began, emphasizing the word with raised eyebrows and softening it with a smile. "Your argument regarding the spreading of meaning through translation is brilliant, Mahj. Easily some of your best work."

Mahj nodded, flapping her hands, pushing Ochre onward. She'd experienced enough professional praise in her lifetime to be able to brush it away as flattering but more than a little useless.

"What of the rest, though? What of the demon?"

Ochre felt more of himself shatter as he spoke next, knowing he was disappointing Mahj. This was not a simple disagreement between two peers, a debate filled with sly grins and well-intentioned criticisms. To truly respond to Mahj's article would be to call her faculties and her sanity into question, and this was not an endeavor Ochre could imagine a loyal and loving student undertaking.

"I am not so sure, teacher," he said, hoping she still was his teacher, still would be. "It seems, perhaps, too great a leap you make." He flipped through the draft, stopping on a page adorned with his comments, marginalia composed of curving question marks and statements that dribbled off into ellipses.

"Translators," he read from the article, "offer the metaphor of a mathematical equation, but I instead offer the metaphor of a woman on a horse. This woman is clothed in resplendent garb, and her horse clip clops proudly. The woman rides into the thick, dark wood of translation, a place never touched by the light of a sun, and when she emerges from the other side, she is very nearly the same. Her clothing is still impressive, though the colors have shifted somewhat. And she no longer rides a horse, or perhaps she does, but this horse has a long, leathery tail and wings made of ash. And the woman's hair has grown and turned curly where it was once straight."

"You can accuse me of purple prose if you like," Mahj said, smiling, her enthusiasm preventing her from seeing the anxiety and worry in her student's face and voice.

Ochre, instead, continued reading.

"Translators today spend their days examining this new woman and this new horse, categorizing and codifying the changes, questioning their meaning. But we have missed a very important question. Whom did the woman meet in the wood?"

"The demon," Mahj whispered, sweeping a hand over the books on her table.

Journal Entry 51

willað hy hine āþecgan/ gif hē on þrēat cymeð:
1. They will rip him apart if he approaches their pack.
2. They intend to serve him if he comes toward their band.
3. They desire to feed him if he brings their peril.

(A fragment of the famously untranslatable ancient poem *Wulf and Eadwacer*. The line is rife with proliferations of meaning. For instance, 'willað,' an anomalous verb, implies a sense of futurity, though it is unclear whether that futurity is a hope, desire, or certainty. Further, 'āþecgan,' a class one weak verb, oddly translates to both "serve/feed" and "kill," with even more figurative readings possible. The line writhes beneath my hands like a snake. The demon is here, a shadow behind the words, pulling them out of true, poisoning them with endless and opposing meanings.)

"These books are becoming my tomb," Mahj mumbled, her words as dry and flimsy as the pages in the texts surrounding her.

She sat amid her books and felt herself dying. It was not an immediate thing, not the all-body constriction of a seizure or the thunderclap terror of a stroke. Mahj felt herself going gradually, her mind and body putting everything back into its right and proper place and giving one final look around before turning off the lights on a mind once filled with glister and sharp edges.

"Just as well," she told herself. Her article had been published purely, it seemed, on the strength of her name and the absurdity of her claim. It had been published to nearly universal criticism, every scholar and translator hastening to join the mob intent on panning Mahj's most recent work and questioning her past works. She was back where she had begun, just Mahj, no longer the eccentric genius.

She leaned forward and stared into *The Blank Book*, her tired eyes searching around the hooked angles of letters for the demon, striving to see that which had so confounded and frustrated her. It was there, she knew, hazy and indistinct, just beyond seeing. Just beyond knowing.

It was her obsession, her fascination. This beast convoluting and confusing language. Even now, so far into her career, Mahj felt the fire of discovery burning through her veins again. She had found something, something that made her past work seem insignificant by comparison.

She saw Ochre and Edmund arrive together for Ochre's lesson. They had been doing that more and more in recent days. Ochre pecked Edmund's bearded cheek before playfully pushing him away and walking into the library. The joy drained from his face as he saw Mahj sitting in her chair, *The Blank Book* on the table in front of her.

"Hello, teacher," he said, stepping into her line of vision. When the criticism began to arrive in response to Mahj's article about her demon, Ochre had been one of the few to defend her, despite his inability to see her work as anything other than the product of a failing mind. She was still his teacher. She was still his friend.

"Ochre, good. Sit, sit," Mahj waved a limp hand at the chair next to her. "I have been thinking of *The Blank Book*. That and the demon."

Ochre drew in a deep breath and released a sigh.

"Teacher, I'm worried that this has begun to get the better of you. *The Blank Book* is simply untranslatable, an impossible text. There is no—"

"Yes, yes. You're right," Mahj said, intervening in his words smoothly, with no resistance. "Untranslatable. Absolutely."

She nodded at Ochre as though he had said exactly what she was hoping he would say, but he felt no joy in it this time, no victory. Only confusion and worry.

"I have realized now what this demon represents. What it is. The demon, the being in the woods, does not merely exist in language; it *is* language."

Mahj held her arms aloft, encompassing the texts embedded in the walls around them.

"How long have we spent translating these texts, poring over pages covered with ink and color, rippled with indentations? And in each one, obscuring meaning and twisting language, is the demon."

Ochre nodded, not because he agreed but because he didn't know what else to do. Here was his teacher fallen so far, her mind filled with things Ochre could neither see nor believe. This was no coughing fit, and he could not shelter Mahj from herself.

A great wave of sadness filled Ochre as Mahj continued to speak.

"It is troublesome, I agree," Mahj said, turning to *The Blank Book*. "But I am no closer to translating this, to understanding what EY wanted to tell us all. I feel so close to her but still held at a distance, held back by the powers of this demon. I feel I can see her so well, can see her in my mind and feel her words floating on my tongue, but I am stopped, prevented from more. I feel as though we have only brushed one another in darkness." Tears filled Mahj's eyes.

Ochre put a hand on his teacher's hand and, not knowing what to say, simply sat in silence.

Journal Entry 59

$240189_{4n}/3433-22.2*23x(-75i/r^2512)$:

1. She wrote about the lecture with great attention to detail.

2. She speaks on these formidable topics with sharp accuracy.

3. She will leave behind a powerful semblance of herself that is both herself and not herself.

(This phrase, found in an old diary dredged up in a recent haul by the *Titania*, highlights the true difficulty of translating Göthel. Several arithmetical nouns in this phrasing interact too situationally with the directional verbs around them, which leads to a greater need for subjective clarification. A single meaning for this phrase is simply impossible to offer; if anything, translation to any given language multiplies the possible meanings, which is troubling. Even in a language of mathematics, I can see the demon's influence. Equations spawn other equations, meaning grows rampant. And behind it all, the smoky leer of the demon.)

Mahj died ten days later. Every major translator in the field attended her funeral, many of them the critics who had excoriated her recent work as useless and nonsensical.

Ochre wanted to turn the sharp edge of his tongue on them, to let his sorrow explode into rage, if only to give it purpose. Instead, he sat with Edmund and, in silence, missed his teacher.

After the funeral, Ochre left the apartment he'd begun sharing with Edmund and walked to Mahj's office. He went through her things: to organize, to conclude, and to grieve. Next to *The Blank Book*, he found her journal. He spent the afternoon reading it, feeling as though he was seeing her for the last time, the real her, feeling as though he was doing with her what she had never been able to do with the author of *The Blank Book*. He was seeing the true Mahj: his clever, funny, and kind teacher.

Her last entry was a clearly failed attempt at the opening passage of *The Blank Book*.

Journal Entry 82

|_ _ _--_ -|_ _ _| |_ _ - - _ _ --:
   1. In time (age?), a community (populace? family?)
must/will/does...

(What a fool I've been. The demon in the page is no demon at all.
Or perhaps it is. But if it is a demon, it is also an angel. If it is a thorn,
it is also a rose. If it is chaos, it is also peace.

For so long I have seen our communication as a Sisyphean task,
something truly impossible. My debates with Ochre, each of us
speaking at length, with fervor, each of us trying desperately to deliver
a message to the other, each of us failing.

My life has been a study in metaphor. Metaphors about
language and metaphors about a life studying language. And so it is
fitting that I end with one more.

We each stand alone. A dense, swirling fog surrounds every
person in the world, a fog inhabited by this demon. To communicate
with another is to pass a message, a message that is you.

But this fog is thick, too thick for any fully formed message to
get through it, and the demon is too sly to allow something so pure to
pass by him. So you must reshape your message, your self, in order to
make it through the fog, through the hands of the demon.

And perhaps you move about, you seek the place where the fog
is thinnest, where the rays of day are just a little brighter. Where you
might better see the other.

Even after all of this, though, the message you pass is not what
you truly hoped it to be; it has been corrupted, changed by your
attempts to pass it through the fog, changed by the person to whom
you are passing it. The meaning is lost or shifted or split infinitely and
irrevocably, and the demon in the fog smiles at his good work.

But there is victory here, too, and it has taken me all this time to
see it. Even as you changed your message, your self, you have also
worked to see just a little more clearly through the fog, to better see
the other. The demon that has held back your message has also been
the angel encouraging you to understand one another.

You have reached, and I have reached, and though the message
you pass is not what it might have been, we still brush hands for a
moment, and that will have been enough.)

It came from Joshua Phillip Johnson

The idea for "The Demon in the Page" showed up at the most inopportune time. My
graduate program in English-Literature required me to pass a foreign language translation
exam; it consisted of a relatively short passage in your chosen language (German for me), a
bilingual dictionary, and a time limit (an hour or so, I think). To call my German rusty at that
point would have been an insult to rust. I hadn't spoken or written or read German for

something like six years, and the test wasn't going to be easy, even with the dictionary to aid me.

I made it to the tiny room on time, was given the passage and left alone to work. And just as I began to scan the passage (an intro to a literary edition of fairy tales), I had this incredible vision of a face staring out at me from behind the text. It was long and thin, with gaunt eyes and horns, and it simply stared and stared. So, like the good and dutiful student I was, I spent most of the next half hour staring back at that face, imagining it to have thoughts and beliefs and words, all of which were caught in the barbs and lines of the text, and if only I could decipher this damn German, I could understand it. I imagined the two of us reaching through these layers of text, brushing fingers and almost touching, and there was something so sad and poignant about that image for me. Once I came back to the real world, I only had 30 minutes left of the test, and I frantically translated (well enough to pass apparently, though I suspect the bar for success on that test isn't especially high) until my time ran out.

But that face in the page (a demon, I'd decided, and an angel, too) stuck with me, and that night, instead of doing my homework (did I mention I was a dutiful student?), I spent the night thinking about translation, between languages and idiolects, and I imagined a person who had dedicated her life to reaching through the tangled barbs of words in order to find the person on the other side. I thought about how sad her life might be, but how powerful and important and valuable, too. And there was Mahj. Story ideas, though, are slow things for me. The demon and Mahj and Ochre germinated in my mind for several years before I set about writing the story, but once I did, the levies broke and it poured out all in a single sitting. And in the writing, I had the chance again to see my friend in the page, buried in my words now, still reaching, still hoping.

A question for Joshua Phillip Johnson

Q: What hero (of any gender) would you name your child after, if we lived in a society with names like that?

A: Princess Eilonwy! As a boy, I would sit in the corner of my hometown's public library in the summer and read and reread the Prydain Chronicles, always wishing I could be as brave and creative and self-knowing as Princess Eilonwy of Llyr.

About Joshua Phillip Johnson

Joshua Phillip Johnson writes, reads, and teaches in a small town in Minnesota. His house is 100-years-old this year and probably doesn't have any ghosts in it.

He can be found online at thelastworldfair.wordpress.com

Cat Play

Mari Ness

When the girl moves almost next door – across the way in our apartment complex – I lose my breath. Literally. She's – well, gorgeous doesn't begin to cover it. Long, incredibly rich black hair that you know just from looking at will feel like silk, and extraordinary eyes that I've never seen before – large, green, tilted, kinda cat shaped, really. The eyes are the first thing you see in the face, which is incredible enough on its own, with the perfection I've seen on film, but never in real life. Not too thin, either – she's got cleavage that I'm trying to keep my eyes off, but failing. And young. Probably still in high school, maybe a bit older. A few years younger than me, but with looks like that, we can deal.

She's moving in boxes and furniture, and even in this heat, she's not sweating at all. I don't question that. Instead, I gulp. The right thing to do, of course, is to go and offer to help. To pretend, for a moment, that she might actually want to be my friend. She won't, of course, but I could have a few seconds of that before the word gets around, before she starts hearing about me and how I don't really have any friends. Not here, anyway. On the internet, and a few hours away, sure. But not here. Assuming she doesn't blow me off in the first place.

I watch her struggle in with a box. Oh, screw it. I'm just being chivalrous, that's all. Which automatically means she's going to put me into that "nice guy" category and we'll never be more than friends, but, you know, just being friends with someone that good looking is something, right?

Right.

So I head over. "Need help?"

She's so startled, she drops the box. I don't know if it's that she's unused to talking to people, or expects she won't get help, or what, but it lands, and the tape on it rips, and the stuff inside starts to slide out. Nothing much – I see what looks like towels and a few pots and pans. I bend down to help her stuff it back into the box, but she waves me away.

"Sorry about that," I mutter, although I wasn't the one that dropped the box.

"No, it's cool," she says, standing up after she's sort of repacked the box. I'm staring into her eyes, thinking that I've never seen eyes like that, and I really haven't – not anything that brilliant. Contacts, maybe? Man, I hope I don't say something stupid about them.

"I'm Javier," I say. "Almost a next door neighbor," I add, waving towards my apartment, so she won't totally think I'm just a freak who walks up and terrorizes women carrying boxes into their apartments.

"Oh," she says.

I wait to think of something brilliant to say, but I can't think of anything. *Come on,* I tell myself. You got past the introduction part. Now say something smart.

But I can't think of anything smart to say, so I just repeat my first question. "Need help?"

It's pretty obvious that no one else is helping her move things in, which suddenly strikes me as odd – usually, when people move in and out from these apartments they've got a few friends to help them out. I glance towards the parking lot and the rental truck sitting there. It's a bit difficult to see, but it does look as if she's got furniture inside.

"No, I'm ok," she says.

"Sure?" I ask. "I'm not doing anything."

She seems to consider for a moment, then holds out her hand. "Not sure," she says.

I take it, and surprisingly, even though it's August in Florida and she's been moving boxes, it's not sweaty or anything.

So we start unloading her truck. It doesn't take long, and I realize that she was probably right when she said she was ok. Everything, from the bed to the couch to the boxes, is remarkably, incredibly light, easy enough for one person to handle. My mom and I have moved our couch and chair enough so that I know. I want to ask her how she found such a lightweight couch.

"Thanks," she says, as we slam down the back of the truck. She wipes her hands on her jeans.

One of those awkward silences arises that I never know how to handle. I should say something, I know, but this is the part with girls that I always screw up, and knowing that is clamping my mouth shut. Luckily, after a few seconds that probably seem a lot longer than they really were, she says, "So, you live around here?"

I don't bother to point out that I've already pointed that out. "Yes," I say. "Over there," waving my hand. I don't mention my mother. For some reason, I don't want to let her know that I'm still living with my mom. It's just temporary, until I graduate from community college, but right now I only have one of those part time, sucky retail jobs, which isn't enough to pay the rent. The only good thing is that it lets me work around my school hours. And it's keeping me from ringing up the kind of debt some of my friends are getting from a full four year school. Sometimes I wish I'd just gone straight to a regular job, like Andy, but I can make more money with a community college or four year degree. Money. It's an important thing, money. You realize that when you haven't got any.

"Cool," she says, as I try to think of something hot to say. Something that will jump me out of the "friend" category and into the "interesting" category. It's hard, because I'm suddenly all too aware that I'm sweating, right through my T-shirt, even if she isn't. Luckily, before the silence gets too awkward, a large black cat saunters up, and sits near her, staring at me. It's a little unnerving, the way a really intense stare from a cat often is.

"Huh," I say. I remember reading something, somewhere, about how one way to get a girl to like you is to get her cat to like you. Of course, that depends on the cat. I kneel down and put out my hand. The cat just continues to stare. Feeling weird, I stand back up. "I'm not sure your cat likes me," I say.

"But she isn't my cat," says the girl smiling. "She's my sister. My twin."

Great.

I don't say this out loud, of course, because the girl's hot, and I'm not about to let her just put me on. "You have a twin sister," I say, trying my best to imitate Darth Vader's voice, and when that's clearly lost on her – she's probably not a Star Wars fan – "A biological miracle."

The girl smiles down at the cat. "Well. I don't know about biological."

The cat just continues to stare at me, in that unblinking way that cats have. The silence grows. But it's not an uncomfortable sort of silence, yet, the sort where you know you're just going to have to break it by saying something unbelievably stupid.

"So," I say. "Do girls with cat twins drink Starbucks?"

She grins at me. "You can try to find out."

The Starbucks is just a couple miles off. We go there. She doesn't say anything about my car, which is about one mishap from falling completely, but does have a kickass sound system, which I demonstrate for her. She grins. At Starbucks, I try to pay for us both, but she grins and hands over cash, and for some reason I don't feel like continuing to push. Oddly enough, she gets plain, straight black coffee, while I end up getting the chocolate raspberry latte with extra whipped cream. It doesn't seem, I don't know, overly masculine or whatever, but she doesn't say anything, and I like the thing.

And we talk. It's awesome. She's listening to me, Javier, and I'm not saying anything stupid, the way I usually do around anyone I don't know well, or most girls, for that matter. And she's laughing at my jokes. Not polite laughter when you realize that someone wants you to laugh, but really laughing. She's doubling over and pulling her feet up in the chair. She's got me telling more jokes and funny stories. I've never been this funny.

It's all going so well that I don't even realize the cat has followed us. I blink. I don't remember the cat even getting into the car, much less following us in. In my experience – not much of it, I admit – cats don't even like cars, or travelling, so how and why did this cat walk into the car in the first place? It must have been in the car; it's too long of a walk for even a cat to run here this quickly.

And why the hell is Starbucks not chasing the cat out? They've got signs on their doors saying that the only animals allowed in are service animals for the blind and deaf. Sure, I've seen a couple women sneak in anyway with those little toy dogs stuffed in a shoulder bag, but at least those dogs are up in bags, only their eyes blinking. This cat is walking around the furniture, slowly, looking for the best place to nap. She finds one, by the girl, and curls up in a ball. And nobody in the Starbucks says a word.

Maybe this Starbucks just has a lot of animal lovers. I don't know.

It's probably a couple hours – maybe a little more – when the girl stretches and says that she'd better go home. We aren't getting any looks from the place, but I offer to get more drinks anyway, just to stretch out my time with her. She shakes her head. She still has some unpacking to do, she says. And other things. We walk out and get into my car, still chatting. It's not until we're about a block away that I realize it.

"Crap," I say. "I think we left the cat back there."

The girl smiles a little. "Nah, she just wanted to stay a bit longer. Maybe pick up a guy later on, or something."

"Um," I say, not sure how I should respond to this.

"Don't worry," she says. "She can find her way back."

"It's three, five miles," I say. Not to mention, I think, but don't add, over a couple of busy roads that are not going to be too cat friendly. I make a U-Turn. "It's no big deal. I mean, other than having to admit that we own the cat –"

"Nobody owns her."

That shuts me up.

When we get back to Starbucks, the cat's just waiting outside, sitting on the curb calmly. As I pull up, it walks up to the car. I open the back seat, and the cat jumps in and curls into a ball on the back seat.

"Smart cat," I say, getting back in. "I'm almost tempted to ask it to put on a seat belt."

The girl doesn't answer that.

Once we get back, the girl and the cat head to her – well, I guess, their door. The girl turns to look at me. The cat doesn't. "Thanks," she said. "I had – it was a great time."

I'm grinning. That might not be cool, but I can't help it. "So did I."

There's a dead bird at our doorstep in the morning. *Gross,* I think. Already, a couple bugs are hovering over it, buzzing, along with the usual tiny moths in the air. I start cleaning the thing up.

When I look up, I see the cat staring at me. It – she – puts a paw up towards her mouth.

I find myself feeling a bit sick.

I'm even less happy when I find five dead lizards on the doorstep the next day. They're carefully fanned out, in a pattern that I guess is supposed to resemble a star or something, and I've gotta tell you, it's totally gross. *"Fuck,"* I say, out loud. I groan. I don't want to clean this, but I know damn well that once my mother wakes up, she'll make me clean it anyway, so I might as well get going.

While I'm scooping up the lizards, I look up, and see that cat watching me.

"Scram," I say.

The cat just stares.

I don't see the girl, or the cat, for another couple of weeks. When I do see the girl heading into her apartment in the afternoon, I hurry up. "Hey," I say.

She doesn't even answer me, or look in my direction, before slipping in. I see the cat at the window, looking out, but that's it.

Well.

You'd think I'd have gotten the message, but somehow, I keep trying to see her anyway.

Maybe it's because of all of those dead things that keep appearing at my doorstep – feathers, lizards, other things I really don't want to identify. I've heard that cats do this sort of thing to show affection, and even though this is beyond stupid – I mean, I've never even seen the cat leaving the dead things there, and certainly when I have seen the cat, it hasn't been particularly friendly – I'm letting myself hope.

It's early in the morning, not quite hot, and I'm cleaning up some lizards when I hear her voice again. "Hey there."

I cringe. Because as bad as it was to have a hot girl like that blowing me off, it's even worse to have her see me trying to pick up dead lizards from my doorstep. "Hi there," I say, trying to hide what I'm doing, which never works. "Just trying to clean something up," I finally say, lamely.

"Oh," she says.

"You're probably used to this kinda thing," I say. "Being a cat owner and all."

She grins. "I told you," she says. "I don't own a cat."

"Right. Right. Because the cat owns you and has convinced you you're twins."

She just grins.

I've got the remains of the lizards in a bag right now; I tie the bag and stand up, getting ready to throw it in the dumpster. She looks at the bag, and then looks at me, and something seems to darken her eyes. Disappointment, maybe, although it's not like I'm good enough with girls to tell. But maybe she's disappointed because she's expecting to hear something from me.

"Say," she asks. "Want lunch?"

I hesitate. "What is it?" I say, a little ungraciously.

"Tuna fish," she says, and she runs her tongue across her lips.

That does it. I immediately agree, and we head out to the little park right next to the complex. It's not much of a park – really small, and the playground equipment's all rusty, but it's got a couple of old picnic tables, and now, midweek, early afternoon before the schools let out, it's pretty much deserted. She hands over a tuna sandwich and a Coke, and grins.

And for some inexplicable reason, I start talking. Really talking. Telling her, really telling her, about everything. About wanting to be a musician, a really good one, only the only instruments I was able to practice on for years were the crappy ones at the school, and sometimes a friend's guitar or something. The way I'd first saved up money, bit by bit, for a guitar, a really good guitar, and the way I'd come home to find that my mom had taken the money, all of it. For rent, she'd said, but I'd seen the look in her eyes. It wasn't the rent. The way I'd snuck out to a second job at Subways, not telling her about it. They way she'd looked at me when Subways had called to see if I'd work another shift for them. What I felt when I'd finally gotten a guitar, started to play, terrified that I'd started too late, that all the other musicians were already ahead of me. And how, after all that, last year, Mom had bought me Guitar Hero for Christmas, and given it to me, expecting me to smile and be happy. The way the guitar felt.

She nods.

I don't know why I'm telling her any of this. I mean, it's only our second date. Or, hanging out.

But there's more to it. I swallow. This is as bad as not having an instrument, as not knowing how to get the tunes I hear in my head down on paper or on a computer, not knowing how to get the different sounds in a band to work together and sound *right,* knowing that I'm going to be taking all of these practical computer courses at Valencia instead of music classes because they're, well, practical. This isn't as bad; it's worse. It's the way I look. The way I am. The way -

She's been listening, up until then, but she cuts me off right there.

"Most musicians aren't good looking at all."

"You kidding me?" I say bitterly. "I mean, Tori Amos, the –"

"You think they honestly look like that? Or that they started looking like that? Come on. It's all Hollywood. All makeup and surgery and shit. It's not real. You wanna look like a rockstar, you can look like a rockstar."

"But –" I swallow. I don't want to say it.

"Sure," she says. "You're fat and ugly now." Well. That hurts. I've got tears in my eyes. Whatever people might say, honesty isn't always the best policy. "But that's changeable, I'm telling you. Surface shit. Nothing more. What's important is what's *there.*" And she hits me in the forehead and on the chest.

"You been watching American Idol?"

"It's a really stupid show."

I can't exactly argue with her there, so I take another route. "Every person –"

"You telling me that American Idol is the only way to go?" she asks. "How bout just recording your stuff and putting it up on the net and seeing what happens?"

I have to admit, the thought makes me feel chilled.

"I don't have -"

"Oh, forget it," she says.

I don't know why that pisses me off, but it does. I forget that this is the first hot chick I've talked to, like, ever, forget that we're actually friends. "How the hell would you know what it's like?" I shout at her. "Being ugly and fat and all that. I mean, god, you stop people dead in your tracks. You haven't a fucking *clue* what it feels like."

Her face changes then. I can't exactly explain how, but it does, *shifting.* Suddenly, she looks a lot less perfect, a lot less pretty. Those eyes glow, even more than they usually do, and I could swear that they actually swirl, the way they sometimes do in a horror movie, or something.

"You think I was always like this?"

From nowhere, that cat pops up, and arches its back, hissing.

It's an absolutely gorgeous cat, as cats go.

"Yeah," I say. "Yeah. I do. You've always been pretty, ever since you were two or three years old. You've always had people come up to you and offer to do things for you, or give you candy, or pay attention to you just because you're pretty. You've had teachers smiling at you. You've had friends. You've had –"

It's all choking up in me. It's coming out, and yet I'm not really saying what I want to be saying.

"You've always had it," I manage, although that's still not really what I want to say. "You've always been gorgeous. You don't have a clue what it's like."

Those eyes can't possibly tilt up any more, but they do.

"You think so?"

Her hands extend out; for a second her nails look more like cat claws than anything else. She almost snarls.

"I wish," she says. "I *wish*." And then she really does snarl. I can't explain how she does it, but it's exactly like the shriek of an angry cat. Even her hair is standing up.

"You don't know what we did to make ourselves look this way," she hisses. "But I'm telling you, it wasn't just Hollywood shit. That's the stuff you can do. We didn't have –"

But at that the cat is standing up, hissing. Well, more growling, and then it lets out a shriek, the sort you might hear from fighting cats, only this one is even worse than that, piercing, raw, actually painful. I slap my hands over my ears without thinking about it. The girl, too, seems startled. She opens her mouth, then shuts it again. The cat shrieks again. The girl nods. She looks back at me.

"Look, all I'm saying is you can change all that. Just – just don't go to extraordinary lengths to change it, ok? Nothing wrong with Hollywood stuff. Stick with that. Not what we –"

And then she's gone. Just like that.

It can't be just like that, of course. I must have put my head down for a second or something – more than a second – long enough for her and the cat to run off.

Or so I tell myself.

And that's it. I don't see her, except in the distance, again, and whenever I do see her, and wave, she never waves back. The dumb thing, the really dumb thing, is I don't have her number, or her email. Or even a name, to try finding her on Facebook or something. I have nothing except a couple of conversations, and her face. And knowing where she lives, and what her cat looks like. And hoping she'll come by again, just to talk to me.

But she doesn't.

Sometimes I see her on her porch, looking out. That's when I wave, only to be ignored. Once, just as the sun was almost slipping beneath the horizon, just at that moment when light plays tricks on you, I almost thought I saw two of her out there, both lightly leaning against the porch screen, fingers raised up against it, almost as if she – they – were trying to claw their way out. It's nonsense, of course. I wave again, but whether it's the light, or something else, she – they – don't wave back.

And then they're gone, just like that.

You can't always tell when an apartment is empty around here – most people keep their blinds down for privacy anyway, and behind closed doors, who knows? But I knew. I could sense it. Her apartment was empty.

"So, looks like those twins just hightailed out of here, huh?" It's another neighbor, looking at the door, an older guy I nod to on occasion. He's got a wife, or rather, had a wife, we think; we haven't seen her around for awhile.

"Twins?" I say, a little shakily.

"Yeah," says the neighbor, giving me a really odd look, as if I should know this, because I've supposedly been hanging out with the girl so much. Or, maybe, girls.

"I just knew one of them," I say.

"Well, I'll say that you didn't often see them together. Just early in the morning, or real early in the evening, sunset, you know. I guess they had really different schedules or something."

"Or something," I agree.

"Anyway, they were a lot quieter than the last group."

"Yes," I agree, although honestly I can't remember the last group.

She didn't even say good-bye. Or, I guess, they didn't say good-bye.

I don't sleep well that night. I keep thinking I see a cat at the window, or something, but every time I look up, nothing. I wake up really late the next morning, after some weird dreams about cats and guitars and some unrelated stuff I can't remember – pineapples, maybe. My mom's still passed out, so I move around pretty quietly, feeling like shit.

She could at least have said good-bye, or something.

I make some coffee, decide to throw away the trash, and open the door, clutching the trash bag in my hand, see a pile of black feathers on the doorstep.

Shit.

I head back inside, come back out with a small dustpan and some paper towels. I'm about to just start sweeping the whole thing up when I realize that the feathers are perfectly, completely dry, and something's under them.

It's a picture of two girls, identical twins. Maybe ten. Black haired.

Incredibly ugly. To the point that, if I'd passed them on the street, I might have averted my eyes. And yet – and this is the weird thing – even though they don't look anything like the girl, I can somehow tell that one of them is the girl, grown up. Maybe it's the nose or something.

Even if the girls in the picture have perfectly ordinary eyes.

I'm so involved in looking at the picture that I don't see what's below it for several seconds – minutes, really. When I do see it, I blink a little, and move the feathers that have drifted back on top of it away. I pick it up.

Sheet music.

Pages and pages of blank sheet music.

When I pick them up, I can actually hear music dancing in my mind. And – the most amazing part of all – I think I know how to write it.

It came from Mari Ness

I don't really remember much about the actual writing of this story, but I suspect that I wrote it in part because although one of the cats that I live with seems convinced that I too am a cat, just a rather overlarge and clumsy one. (The other cat is well aware that I am a deeply inferior creature who can in no way claim to any of the glory and beauty that she can.) And because I once had a dog who could not quite grasp the difference between "people" and "dog," but seemed pretty sure he was people- which made some sense, given how terrified he was of dogs. What if my cat and dog were right- that is, I am, on some level, part cat, and the dog was, on some level, part people? That was part of it. The other part was that if my Excel spreadsheet is correct, I wrote the story during a period when I was sick, and bored, and considering choices, and possibilities, all of which I can now see bled through the story. Along with those thoughts about cats and dogs.

A question for Mari Ness

Q: Are titles easy or hard for you? Do you start with the title or the story?

A: I hate writing titles, primarily because I am just terrible at it. It's always the very last part of the process for me. I can't even imagine the idea of starting with a title and writing a story, although I realize others do just this.

About Mari Ness

Mari Ness spent much of her life wandering the world and reading. This, naturally, left her only able to eat chocolate, snark about popular culture, and occasionally write. She lives in central Florida, with a scraggly rose garden, large trees harboring demented squirrels, and two adorable cats.

... and now He erases

Rhoads Brazos

He calls me the Motorcycle Man. One word? Possibly. I've never seen it in print. Certainly never needed to scratch it on paper. The Boy knew my proper name up until last week, when he forgot. I forgive him. Besides, I like *Motorcycle Man* just fine. It says all it needs to.

I'm forever wearing a white jumpsuit crossed with Dixie stars. My helmet appears on my head whenever I ride, but it's gone when I hop from my bike. When I wink at the camera and let the audience soak up my chiseled chin savoir-faire, I am the apple pie perfect ideal.

It's what the Boy knows, so it's who I am.

The Boy's with me now, with the last of us as things wind down. The others just sit, biding their time, but that's not how I roll. My hands are wrapped in fringed white leather that squeaks when I ball them into fists. I'm in the fray. Nothing and no one's going to touch him. I'll knock them flat and shout victory. That's how a man does it.

I recognize this carousel with its peculiar steeds. It burned to the ground back in '78–close to it, or thereabouts. No horses, though the zebra is an almost. There's a dragon, a buffalo, a lama, even an oversized chicken, all shiny and perfect and chasing each other in a forever-circle. I hold myself steady on the deck as if I were striding a catamaran through deep swells. The Boy rides next to me, daring the ostrich.

"Motorcycle Man?" The Boy bounds up and back down, his little hands tight on the bird's skewering pole.

"Yeah, kiddo?"

"I don't think I can wake up."

"Things like this happen. You get laid out on your back? Hey, been knocked out myself. Many times."

"Am I knocked out?"

"Yeah, sure. In a way."

We make another two circuits.

"Want to do a stunt on my bike?" I ask. "Gotta full tank."

It goes without saying that it never runs empty.

"I dunno. What'll we jump?"

"This whole merry-go-round, if you want. Bet everyone'll be surprised and clap loud."

"Can we drive up the roller coaster? That'll kick 'em in the pants."

I can barely see the coaster through the mists. Its hump breaches the fog like a whale of white bone.

"Now that would be a hell of thing! Kiddo, like how you think."

He grins and it warms me.

A stir of motion distracts me and I notice Photo Girl. There used to be thousands like her. She's the only survivor so she gets the lone title. It doesn't surprise me she's here; she's never been far away. She and the Boy play together sometimes. Cute little gal, but always thirsty. It's because of all of that Polaroid sun.

Photo Girl struggles to climb the gazelle. I give her a careful boost and she settles atop with a smile. At her age she shouldn't have such sparkly even teeth, but in the photo–the one where she's drinking a too-big-for-her glass of ice water–you can't see any gaps, hence the perfect string of pearls.

"Thank you," she says.

"Anytime, miss."

Always be a gentleman, no matter how small they might be.

I stand between them, two paces back where I can make sure they won't tumble. I'm still on guard, still keeping him lively. I won't let it take him.

The carousel's clockwork keeps time.

The Boy reaches over and she takes his hand. Neither of them is very tall. When the animals crest and trough, fingertip to fingertip is all the kids manage.

I watch the scenery spin by.

The coaster is gone. I clench my jaw tight.

Down at the outdoor tables with the others, the Dad scowls at me. He's jealous, you see. He doesn't understand the Boy the way I do, and never will. Despite this he has my respect. He was the one who introduced the Boy to me thirty years past. I owe him like no other and forgive him his flaws.

A slow whirl.

The Wife checks her watch. Soft brown curls and cheeks slippery with tears–that's how she looked when the Boy closed his eyes. She's a quite pleasant lady and sometimes we talk. The Boy knows us both well so our conversations always are vivid. The Wife brushes a curl from her face and looks about quickly. I spot it too. During the last revolution the Brother sat on the bench beside her. He's nowhere now, gone and forgotten. According to the Boy, the Brother liked me too, just not as much.

Around again.

The Twins share a sundae under a green and white umbrella. They're too old for the Boy and a little young for myself, though I wouldn't think twice. A gentleman's panache has a time and a place—an expiration date, if you will. I remember when those two girls hopped off their poster, both in half-missing bikinis, each one oiling the other. At his tender age, they were a scandalous whatnot he shouldn't have seen. Since they're still here they must have made a powerful impression. Ponytail winks and Braids blows a kiss.

A slow spin, always back to the start.

There's that Wolf, birthed from a cartoon, now panting in the tableshade. Back in the day it used to chase the Boy without mercy, until I showed the kid how to stand up swinging. On my bike doing sixty, we crunched over the cur and cracked its back like a pretzel stick. Though the Wolf had recovered by the following night, at the moment you wouldn't know it. It's forsaken walking on two legs and never speaks. Sad, in a way. I miss our old battles and the way it snapped at our heels.

We turn.

The Wife buries her face in her hands and I know that I've failed him. I thought there'd be a chance to hold tight, a knuckle-on-bone tussle. I would have done anything, fought anyone. He's the only reason I live.

I help Photo Girl to the wooden-planked deck. With the calliope slowing, plunking out a languid non-tune, we hop to the ground.

"Well," the Dad says. "Just us, looks like."

The Twins hug each other and shiver. The Wife scowls at the back of their heads.

"Don't guess he woke," I say.

"He sank deeper," the Dad says. "Told him that a man's got to pull himself up."

I don't disagree. The Dad and I share a few philosophies.

"This won't last," Photo Girl says. She pets the Wolf on the head. It smacks its lips, but seems more thirsty than hungry.

She's right. The carousel already is peeling. Its colors snowflake upward and crumble into the mists.

"We don't want to die," the Twins say together.

"You won't," the Wife says. "You just won't be."

The girls weep and whisper and hold each other's face. They're always this way—waiting to be rescued.

The Wolf trots away at a stuttering limp.

"Huh, where's he off to?" the Dad asks.

No one answers. We trust the Wolf's nose and follow.

We travel empty stages of the Boy's life, stepping lightly so they don't collapse beneath us. Some are easy to recognize: Grandma's house, an empty lecture hall, a restaurant where he and his parents used to go. No other actors though, just us.

There used to be a spot where the light always shone–a lush, vibrant place, where the shadows couldn't help but fall coincidentally perfect. When the Boy was young I'd play with him there, riding my cycle alongside his own. We'd hit a plywood ramp and overlap. I needed his joy and he needed my purpose. In many ways we are the same person.

Whenever he wished it, I'd pop in to that place. I've been with him in boardrooms, threading in a sly witticism here and a shock of brashness there. Once, though the Wife doesn't know it, the Boy and I were in a barroom fight. Our side won. During his preteens I even helped at a spelling bee, though that's not my forte.

At the Boy's wedding, when he felt up-at-the-altar jitters, I stood beside him. Best Man, naturally. It fit me to a T.

"A real guy takes charge," I said.

Even with the Dad sulking in the pews and not approving of this–not at all, not at all, not one bit–I performed my greatest stunt. I pulled the Bride close, like a sashed Miss Idaho after my '67 jumbo-jet jump. With the crowd's eyes upon us and the rocketsled smoldering and her in my arms, I could do no wrong. She gave the green light–I do. I kissed her hard, twice as long as seemed decent.

The Wife giggles.

"What is it now?" the Dad asks.

Again, she brushes away a curl, a willfully coy gesture she learned in her youth. After so many years it's now a habit. Our practiced lies become little truths. She looks from the Dad to me yet says nothing. I was thinking too loudly, but I'm not ashamed. Even back then she knew it was me.

The Wolf steps onto a back patio, cracked stone mortared with weeds and an aluminum picnic table with a plastic pitcher upon it. It's a hot day in June, one where the whole sky seems jaundiced and sweaty sick. I hate this place. The Boy and I never come here.

The Dad shuffles his feet. "Well?" he asks. "Let's get a move on." But the Wolf has lain down.

"He looks so bad," the Twins say. They both kneel and offer comfort through petting and coos.

"Maybe he needs water," Photo Girl says.

"He only ever wanted meat," I say.

The Wife raises an eyebrow. "This is your fault."

I think at first she means me. Truthfully, I'm to blame for many a fuddled scrape, but she's glaring at the Dad.

"Me?" he says. "We used to live here. What of it?"

"You made him choose," the Wife says. "He told me. Right here. God, I wish he'd think of something else. Anything."

"Bah. He's a tough kid. Isn't that right?" The Dad looks to me.

I give a single slow nod.

A weak fist tugs the tassels along my sleeve. Photo Girl has found a waxed-paper cup. I fill it for her from the pitcher.

"Thank you," she says and drinks deeply.

"'Sides," the Dad says, "court ordered it. Child's wishes, heard of it?"

"It wasn't right," the Wife says.

"That's all it was, and by the book too. Maybe it'll please you to know he picked her."

"Oh, I'm aware."

"But don't see her around." The Dad gives a smirk. "We see who matters most, don't we? Proved by the pudding."

He has stated the boldest of truths. We all fall quiet. Out of an entire lifetime, an accumulated world, we've made it farther than any of the others. It's a cross-continental record, a twenty-bus jump on an XR-750.

Eye meets eye and each of us wonders. The Wife watches me. The Dad grimaces at her. Even Ponytail and Braids appraise one another. They can all think what they want. They can believe they'll be last if they find that soothing. I don't begrudge them. But the Boy and I have been together more than any can guess. In daydreams and nightmares and hopes and desires, I'm always there.

A soft whine comes from the patio stone. The Wolf curls up tight and whimpers. He withers and twists into lintlike nothing. He's gone.

The Twins squeak. Photo Girl drops her drink.

"Damn," the Dad says. "Will you look at that?"

"Never seen one go," I say.

"It means he's not afraid anymore." The Dad looks from each of us to the other. "He was always afraid of that mutt. You see that! My boy's not–"

I cry out as the Dad blinks into motes.

"He's right." The Wife gathers herself in short order. "It won't be long now."

"Was hoping he wouldn't clock out," I say. "I once pulled out of a thirty day coma. It's true. A man never gives in."

"Oh, they all do, eventually," the Twins say as one. They hug each other close and mumble last-minute apologies. They weren't meant to be angry and can't maintain a distance.

The Wife moves her frowning scrutiny from them to me. Of course I'm watching the gals with great interest.

Photo Girl presents her cup to me, tapping it on my sleeve. I wipe it dry and refill it.

"Got some pepper in it," I say. "See?"

"That's dirt."

"Pretend its pepper."

"Okay." She drinks slowly.

Our surroundings have crumbed into a gritty vapor. We huddle in a ten-by-ten stone-pavered world.

Do they realize I'm the only guy here? Do they know what that means? They're nurturing figures: innocence, passion, love. Wanted by the masculine in different ways at different times. I can't be fooled. A 100% man perceives them with ease. Now look at me, the everything else. The totality of Motorcycle Man is the core of the Boy. I'm his soul.

"Shh," I say. "Listen."

Each of us stills. Even the wind holds its breath. Around and through us floats a delicate murmur.

"Angels?" Photo Girl asks. She sets down her cup.

"Maybe," the Wife says. "I'm not sure."

"Can we–somehow–" I grasp for the proper expression. "Cross? Leap the chasm? You know, with him?"

The stones feel soft, as if I'm standing on a mattress. The Wife looks amused. "Scared?"

"No, I–" I look left and right. "Where are those girls?"

"They went a moment ago."

"You should have said!"

The Wife brushes her hair back in place. "Popped like a soap bubble, both of them at once. Smelled a bit like cocoa butter."

"It's all that oil," I say. "I'll miss them."

"Yes, I'm sure you will."

Photo Girl plays with the hem of her dress. The Wife watches the fuzzy sky. "I hope he's not hurting," she says.

"He's tough as nails." I rub at my eyes. "Ugh. Need a smoke." I rifle through my pockets.

"That's very final," the Wife says.

"Not at all," I answer. The Wife's scrutiny is palpable. I know how relieved she is to outlast the Twins and I don't blame her for sizing me up too. "Didn't want to do it while the Boy was around."

"He knows you do."

"Well of course, otherwise I wouldn't."

I find a pack and tug a cigarette out with my lips. Photo Girl approaches the Wife and whispers at her ear. The Wife smiles softly and rests a hand on Photo Girl's cheek.

"There's nothing in the dark," she says. "I promise."

Photo Girl looks unsure. She gives me a questioning glance.

"S'true," I say from the corner of my mouth. I find my lighter. "I always told him that. You know–" I point up at the mists. "You know he used to be worried too?"

"Really?"

"Sure. Know what I told him?" I inhale a slow drag. "I told him to pretend."

"Like pepper."

"Just like that. Pretend it's daytime and your eyes are closed, then it's all easy. Sissy bar safe."

"It really works?"

"Worked for him. Bet it'll work for you too."

The Wife smiles at me. "I see why he loves you so much."

I shrug.

"He does, don't deny it. Thank you for what you've done." She leans forward, strokes my sideburns once, and pecks me on the cheek.

I'm left stunned for two missed breaths. The cigarette slips from my lips. I struggle with a response while I scoop it back up–and then I recognize a goodbye.

She's gone.

For a moment, I'm wounded. But I've broken every bone twice: no tears will fall today. I inhale another unfiltered lungful and brush the ashes from my jumpsuit. I've just jumped Snake Canyon–yet *another* ultimate stunt with me as the conquering king. I'd give a double Nixonesque vee if cameras were rolling. But against a woman? No, that's not proper. Not what a man would do.

Instead I stand and stretch my back. Photo Girl watches me with unabashed curiosity.

"Won't lie," I say. "Wasn't sure I'd outlast her. "

"Who says you did?"

The Motorcycle Man never, but *never*, comes in second. I mean to argue this simple truth but the words won't come.

Photo Girl brushes a loose curl away from her eyes.

And then–

–she sits quiet and still with her knees to her chin. She watches her feet and tries not to think of the white nothing around her. The floor has melted away. She may be falling, but without landmarks to mark her descent it's so hard to tell.

"It's daytime," she says.

She turns out the light.

It came from Rhoads Brazos

With "and now He erases ..." I was striving for the ultimate apocalypse, one in which the whole world quite literally crumbles away. It turned out to be a rather bittersweet tale, though still amusing in small parts. The aforementioned "He" is never named, and his demise isn't explained. The main character, clearly Evel Knievel, isn't given a proper name either. In a person's final moments, names aren't of that much importance. It's what each person represents in another's life that carries weight. I've always wanted to get Evel into a story. All of that swagger and recklessness impossible to contain, it's rolled up in a character who simply can't be forgotten, and he knows it. As the world disintegrates, he realizes what his presence means, and sees it all as one last contest. He's already sized up the competition and found them lacking. I thought it was something that Evel would do (if in such a fantastic situation) and, in all of this, really strove to make him as sympathetic a character as possible. He's impossibly vain, but in many ways he deserves that honor. This one figure makes so much of an impression on another life, that he changes its entire course. It's difficult to say how much of this story is autobiographical. Sometimes an author can divulge too much. I was definitely hounded by that accursed wolf until an age I will not admit to. I saw it on TV at the age of three and distinctly remember hiding behind the couch when it came on. (Thank you, PBS!) As mentioned in the story, aggression was the key to escape. And Knievel was a character from my formative years. I used to have the motorcycle toy of him on his bike and still remember cranking the guy up to dangerous speeds on his red ramp launchpad. Like any kid from the 80s, I did more than my share of plywood ramp jumps on a Huffy. Maybe on my last day, that sense of courage will be my own final thought, but as I hope I've shown here, there are other choices.

A question for Rhoads Brazos

Q: How do pets/children/significant others help/hinder your process?

A: Almost all outside forces conspire against me. My son barges into my office, as nine-year-olds are wont to do, and tries to read my on-screen words. I'm a perfectionist by nature, so no one is allowed to see the first draft, but with him especially, I can't shrink the screen quickly enough. I don't want him to drink in the horrors of my writing and develop some sort of neurosis. As a parent, I feel I'm already doing unspoken psychological damage. I have to avoid anything blatantly scarring. This job is really hard. At the same instant, my wife has been pestering me to continue a novella series I started for her amusement. I had bragged to her that I could craft a regency romance that would knock her socks off, providing I could give it my own unique twist. She doubted me, so of course I wrote it to prove how right I was. (This is standard husbandly behavior.) I'm not sure what genre the piece falls into. Picture a fusion of P.G. Wodehouse, Clive Barker, and Georgette Heyer. It's charming in its lunacy. I could write five short stories in the place of a new novella, but just thinking about it now … perhaps I'll build my daily wordcount and add another escapade. I suppose the housecat is the only one who lets me work. He preferred my old boxy monitor, which made a toasty perch for him in the winter months, but he seems satisfied with the bench I've set up next to me. He has developed a habit of snoring, which I've never heard of afflicting a cat, but clearly it happens. It's funny for ten minutes or so, until I find my breathing syncing with his own. That just feels weird to me, so I bump him to make him stop. Lord of the manor, and all that.

About Rhoads Brazos

Rhoads has written stories across the entire spectrum of speculative fiction, from light fantasy to the most decrepit tales of horror to quirky sci-fi. He currently lives in Colorado with his wife and son.

The Machinery

Julia Warner

"I want you to know your options," Dr. Foss said, handing the card across the table. The paper was crisp; the edges bit into Adelaide's fingers.

"Thank you." Her voice seemed to come from the walls around her rather than her throat. Adelaide dropped the card into her purse and returned to the PET scan results. Her skeleton glowed before her in 3D, a ghostly smudge of purple, grey, and the traffic cone orange of radioactive glucose. She drew a hand through the hologram, tracing the disease through her body. When she'd gotten the call she had ordered herself to stay calm, but her body had trembled ceaselessly. She couldn't speak. It was like someone had ripped a hole in her throat.

The cancer has metastasized, Dr. Foss had said gently, like a mother speaking to a child. Months ago they'd slit her pancreas and scooped out the tumor. For months she'd danced with the fantasy of branding herself a survivor. She'd imagined herself striding out of the office after the oncologist declared her cancer-free. She would have called Nick first, then her parents and friends, then—heck—posted cliché Facebook prose about how grateful she was to be alive and how she would forevermore live every day to the fullest because she was Adelaide Fox, conqueress of cancer.

"Dr. Viande offers free consultations to people in your situation," Dr. Foss continued, scribbling something on her clipboard. Her eyelashes were sheathed in mascara, so thick and curly they almost looked like feathers. "It may put you at ease to speak to him now even if you never end up needing the Operation."

Adelaide digested this. "I want the chemo as soon as possible."

Dr. Foss looked up from her clipboard. Her thick brown ponytail reeked of hairspray and bounced every time she moved her head. "We can give you your first round this Thursday."

"Perfect. Give me the highest dosage you can." She'd had a taste of chemo before the surgery, and while it wasn't fun, she could muscle through the main course if it meant her life. She stood. "I want to blast the hell out of this thing."

"Noted, Mrs. Fox," Dr. Foss replied. "The receptionist will be in touch."

The wet clay felt good between her fingers. Adelaide inhaled the strong, metallic smell and pressed hard around the neck of the vase she was creating. This was what she loved about wheel throwing—making art with nothing but earth, the physics of rotation, and the force of her own body. Every piece started as the same lump of mud and then her hands coaxed out a form. It was rhythmic and pure.

Marylise sat on the floor drawing a rainbow with Crayola markers. "Mama?" she asked, shaking mousy brown bangs out of her dark eyes. "What are rainbows made of?"

Adelaide splashed more water onto her vase. "They're not really made of anything the way you and I are," she said. "We see them because water reflects and refracts light."

"What does refract mean?

"To bend."

Marylise drew some purple flowers at the base of the rainbow. "What is light made of?"

"Streams of photons."

"What are photons?"

Adelaide knew where this rabbit hole led. "A photon is a tiny, tiny particle. So small you can't see it—not even with a microscope."

"What are photons made of?"

Adelaide slowed the wheel to a stop. Her hands were gloved in clay, and a few wet traces snaked down to her elbows. "I think that's as basic as it gets. Or as far as we know."

"Where do photons come from?"

At that moment the door to the studio swung open. Nicholas entered, still dressed for work. He crossed the room in long strides, newspaper crunching beneath his feet. When he reached his wife he crushed her into his arms. He didn't say a word, just stood there and held her.

Adelaide's phone rang so frequently in the next few days that she began glaring at it every time the screen lit up with an incoming call. Yes Mom, they found some spots. No, not just in my pancreas. In my liver too. Yes Dad, I'll send you the scans. Yes, those days work Dr. Foss. I'll mark my calendar. Thanks for the casserole Ashley—that was so sweet of you. Could you watch Marylise after school this Thursday?

Trips to the hospital. Medical records, physical examinations, blood tests. Drug disclaimers and informed consent papers. A whirlwind of white smiles and firm handshakes. Oncologists, nurses, assistants, nutritionists, even psychologists.

Thursday afternoon, Nicholas and Adelaide sat in Dr. Foss's room, listening to the final speech. "The chemotherapy agents will target cells undergoing cell division," Dr. Foss said, repeating information that Adelaide had heard fifty times. "We can take out the big guns against your cancer cells, but the drugs don't act preferentially. They will disrupt the cycle of frequently dividing cells all over your body. This means your hair, skin, the lining of your gastrointestinal tract—"

"I understand. I'm gonna get sick."

"Probably. And you understand that the five-year survival rate is 25%?"

"Yes."

"If these drugs fail, there are others we can try. However, should chemotherapy prove completely ineffective, you know that you will become eligible for a Spare."

"We'll cross that bridge if we come to it," Adelaide said, but Nick leaned forward. Another one of those crisp, little cards changed hands.

"If you have any interest whatsoever in the Operation, I would advise you speak with Dr. Viande now." Dr. Foss finished writing on her clipboard and gathered Adelaide's paperwork into a file. "Now let's get you hooked up." She led the way out of her office with quick, clickety-clack steps, brown ponytail swinging behind her head like a pendulum.

The chemo nurse was tall as an Amazonian warrior and looked to be as strong. Adelaide couldn't help staring, bewitched by the luster of her golden curls, the hills and valleys of muscle beneath her flesh, and the unnatural green iridescence of her eyes. She winced as the needle sank into her arm, but when she opened her eyes the catheter was in place. "You're all good to go, hun," the nurse said. She must have detected the anxiety brimming beneath Adelaide's fight face because she touched her shoulder gently and said, "I've been in your position before. I was scared too. But one way or another you're going to be fine." She flashed a porcelain smile and turned to leave.

"Five hours to go," said Nick, handing her the television remote. He evaluated the selection of magazines cluttering the bedside table and reached for the *Sports Weekly*. Adelaide leaned back into her pillows, her mind engulfed by wonder. She painted a mental image of who the nurse had once been—a willowy sixty-five-year old with long silver hair, maybe—as poison began to drip into her veins.

When they got home, Adelaide went upstairs to her studio, where Marylise was abusing a sheet of paper with crayons. The little girl squealed when she saw her mother and leapt up to hug her. Adelaide paid the babysitter and then sat at her wheel. The sun was sinking in a gold-stained sky; there wasn't enough time to actually start and finish a piece, but the routine of the wheel soothed her. Feeling the power of it turning beneath her hands made her think of her heart pulsing blood through her circulatory system. Around and around and around.

By Saturday she was vomiting. Adelaide spent most of the day in the bathroom crouched over the toilet. Nicholas took the day off from work. He held her hair and rubbed her back while she retched.

Two weeks later she was in her studio, preparing to start a piece. She pulled her hair back with her hands to put it up and a silky black clump drifted to the floor.

The biweekly chemo rounds became routine. The days blurred together and the weeks bled into months. Nausea was her new baseline. Dr. Foss prescribed some anti-nauseants. They made the room stop spinning but they didn't keep the food down. Her belly caved in. Bones she'd never felt before poked out of her hips.

Many nights she would stand in front of the bathroom mirror, naked, and drag her hands across her stomach. She'd pinch the skin over her pancreas and liver and imagine she could feel her cancer squirming beneath like some sort of parasitic worm. She'd pretend that she could suffocate it if she just squeezed hard enough. "Leave my body," she'd whisper. "You have no place here."

"Can I kiss your pancreas better?" Marylise asked sometimes. Adelaide let her kiss her surgery scar.

At first the cancer responded to the chemo. "There's been shrinkage here, here, and here," Dr. Foss said, pointing out the areas on her most recent scan. "This is good progress."

Then gravity reversed. "The cells are replicating again. This is not abnormal; it just means they've begun to resist the effects of your particular regimen. We need to get you on new drugs."

She got on a carousel of new drugs. Each time one stopped working that familiar numbness seeped from her bones.

A call from school came one day. "Mrs. Fox? Yes, hello. This is Ms. Becker, your daughter's home room teacher. Marylise tried to take all the Band-Aids from the medicine cabinet today. I found her backpack full of them. I don't mean to intrude here but I hope... is everything ok?"

Adelaide's throat was dry. "Thank you for letting me know."

Time flowed through her fingers, washing away more and more of her with every wave. Finally she was sitting in Dr. Foss's office again, hearing words she had once refused to consider hearing.

Dr. Foss removed her glasses. "I'm sorry, Adelaide. It's time to face reality. Chemotherapy is not eliminating the cancer from your body. It may be impeding the growth of tumors, and you may buy yourself time by continuing your regimen. But it's time to think about quality of life. You can stay on chemo or you can end it. It's your choice."

Adelaide wore a face of stone. Her hair had long since abandoned her body. Hair, eyebrows, even eyelashes. "Are you saying in your professional opinion I will never be cancer-free?"

"Your body won't, Mrs. Fox. But you can be, if you want." Dr. Foss reached for a card.

"I already have one," she said quietly. It lay crumpled at the bottom of her purse along with loose change and grocery store receipts.

"There is grant money, Mrs. Fox. Charities. The Board of—"

"I'll stick with the chemo for now. Thank you." Her eyes were glassy with tears as she strode out of the office, her breathing punctuated by involuntary shudders.

Her car recognized these signs of distress. "Are you okay?" chirped its computerized voice as she buckled her seatbelt.

"Home please." It dutifully backed out of its parking space and fed into the network of AI-controlled traffic flow.

In the bathroom, facing the mirror, she surrendered to her sobs. She looked so old. Maybe she'd never been conventionally beautiful, but she had loved her body and cared for it well. She'd loved her crooked, little nose and her almond eyes and her thin lips. But now her chest swelled with revulsion. She was infuriated by the ludicrous incompetency of her body, by the way her own DNA was trying to destroy her. What a way to die. No airplane crash. No snakebite in the Amazon rainforest. No gunshot, no stab wound, no broken bones. Not even a last exhale of breath in the night at old age. Just a self-destruct button. A flaw in the machinery.

Was that all the body was? A piece of equipment humming inside a case of flesh, driven by mechanical processes, disguised as life? She scraped her fingernails down her cheeks, wondering what she would find if she peeled back the layers—a soul or a computer? Perhaps everything could be slashed down to the tiniest bits; every part of her, every organ and bone, every muscle, every thought—perhaps it was all just an ocean of particles, slamming into each other and reverberating in endless, mechanical chaos.

"Adelaide?"

She turned and saw Nick standing in the doorway. The defeat in his eyes made him look almost as broken as she was. He reached for her. "I want to talk with this consultant," he said.

She looked at him as if he'd just proposed treason. "You can't mean it," she said, closing her eyes. "We organized protests against this shit in college, for Christ's sake."

"It's your only chance. And even then, maybe we felt squeamish about the Operation but we always knew fighting it was a hopeless cause. The Spares aren't people. They aren't competent enough to survive. This business—it makes sense."

"It's not fair. I—"

"Please listen to me, Adelaide. Your body is dying. I am begging you to call the number on that card."

"Let's talk about it after dinner," Adelaide said, pushing herself to her feet.

She got her body up the stairs to her daughter's room. She wiped the wetness from her cheeks. "Marylise?" she asked. She pushed the door open and gasped. "Oh God, what—"

Her little girl sat on the floor, hacking off her hair with a pair of craft scissors. The blades were blunt so she was having a hard time of it, but piles of brown hair already littered the floor. Marylise looked up with another *snip*. "Mama!" She grabbed a handful of the hair, bounced to her feet, and barreled into her mother's arms. "I wanted to surprise you. Since you don't have any more hair we can share mine."

Adelaide stroked her little girl's head. "I wish you hadn't done that," she said. "But that was a sweet thought. What do you want for dinner?"

"Can you make pasta?"

"Sure. I'll start it now."

She left and went back to the bathroom, where her purse lay on the floor. She dug around the bottom until her fingers brushed a small piece of cardstock. She retrieved it and stared at the number and pulled out her phone. And she dialed.

"A pleasure to meet you, Mr. and Mrs. Fox."

Dr. Lawrence Viande was a human skyscraper. Adelaide had to tilt her head up to look him in the eye. His face was dominated by a bulbous nose and a mane of silver hair. He gestured for them to sit in large leather armchairs. Everything about his office boasted class, from the chairs to the mahogany bureau to the Persian rug and the velvet curtains.

"And you as well," Nicholas said, shaking hands with the doctor before sinking into his chair. Adelaide sat down stiffly.

Dr. Viande gazed at her like an owl. "I can only imagine the pain which you and your family have been going through," he said, his forehead crinkling like a sheet of paper. "You don't have to suffer anymore, Mrs. Fox. I can save your life."

"With a Spare," Adelaide said. Her mind registered the crispness of her words, but she couldn't think of anything charismatic to pull from her throat.

"Are you familiar with the Operation?"

"It's a body transplant."

"Essentially, yes. There will be some preparatory analysis and then once we find a good match for you, it's five hours in the Operating Room. When you wake up you'll spend eight weeks in Rehabilitation, adjusting to your new nervous system and refining your motor skills. In the beginning you will experience difficulty speaking, walking, and eating—a consequence of scarring of the nervous tissue—but with a daily supplement of neurological growth factor, physical therapy, and the care of our highly trained employees you will regain every function you currently enjoy."

"As good as new."

"Better than new." Dr. Viande took a sip of water. "Mrs. Fox, our Spares are genetically engineered to approach physical perfection. They have higher muscle mass, denser bones. Their cells harvest 20% more of the chemical energy in food. They resist a range of diseases and contain genes for the production of antibiotics that are activated by the detection of foreign bacteria. They have enhanced mechanisms playing roles in cell repair, cell communication, homeostasis—Mrs. Fox, you don't ever have to be sick again."

Adelaide inhaled. The thought was beautiful and it terrified her. She felt a door inside her open just far enough to let a crack of light through. "What about the souls that inhabit these bodies?"

"The Spares aren't natural, Mrs. Fox. They're biochemical machines assembled in test tubes and gestated in tanks. Without us they would never exist. That being said, we take pride in the humane treatment of our Spares."

Adelaide's eyes narrowed.

"The Spares enjoy more luxury during their existence than most people see in a lifetime. Caretakers see to their every need and nutritionists design a specialized diet for each individual. They have intense exercise and enrichment schedules, with daily opportunities for social interaction. Our clients are welcome to tour the facilities, if you would like to see firsthand the quality of life we provide for our Spares."

"And what about consent? Do they consent to the Operation?"

"Mrs. Fox, due to the artificial nature of their existence, Spares are not recognized as humans and are not inherently entitled to the same rights as you and me. Consent has no technical applicability to this situation. However, speaking from personal experience, no Spare has ever voiced a word of opposition to the system."

Adelaide was incredulous. "Truly? They show no emotion at all when you tell them they are born to die?"

Dr. Viande wove his fingers through his beard. "We don't use such abrasive language with them... the consensus within the scientific community is that their brains would be unable to process the complexity of their purpose. For all their physical superiority, the Spares show a pattern of intellectual incompetence. They have limited emotional capacity and often require assistance to complete the most menial of tasks. They panic in the absence of structure. They are utterly incapable of taking care of themselves on their own."

"What exactly *do* you tell them? When you're leading the sheep to the slaughterhouse, what do you say?"

Dr. Viande did not falter. "Merely that it is time to sleep," he said calmly. "The nurses hold their hands and administer anesthesia. During the Operation the brain is severed at the spinal cord. It's the quickest, gentlest death possible. Absolutely painless."

Nicholas turned to his wife. "What are you thinking?"

Adelaide saw the quiet hope in his eyes. "I think... I need some time to think."

"Take your time, Mrs. Fox," Dr. Viande said, reaching to shake her hand. "I realize this is a powerful decision. I want you to know that I have only your best interest in mind."

"How much time do I have?"

Adelaide had quit chemotherapy one week ago, when the pain had become so relentlessly consuming that surrender had finally seemed like relief. Her cheeks were hollow, and the whites of her eyes were not white at all, but the color of mustard.

Dr. Foss clasped her hands. "Your disease is aggressive, Adelaide. You probably have a few months."

In her studio, Adelaide watched the wheel spin round and round. She wanted to create, but her touch no longer commanded the power it once had. The clay seemed to wilt instead of grow. She looked at her hands and imagined them rotting. Skin blackening and softening until it slid right off, exposing the meat, which itself would wither and wash away until all that was left behind was pristine white bone.

Nicholas's study was littered with bottles and Operation literature. Adelaide felt tiny next to him, as if she were his child rather than his wife. Long gone were the days when his eyes had looked on her with desire. Now they roamed the pictures of dollish Spares, feeding upon any material they could find—pamphlets, books, web sites. She wondered if he found that manufactured perfection beautiful, if he imagined touching her through one of those flawless bodies. He toiled whole nights away clicking through articles and message boards, searching for some crucial piece of information which he had not already read. Adelaide, who had months ago taken to sleeping in the guest room to sequester the stench of her sickness, wouldn't know until she'd go to the study for their morning coffee and find him typing away, exhausted and bleary-eyed.

"I'm scared," she said one morning, staring into her mug.

"We're running out of time, Adelaide." Nicholas's voice was never cruel, but veins of frustration invaded it every now and then. He reached out and swallowed her hand in his, his grip so strong it was painful. "I know you're stubborn and idealistic and you hate admitting defeat. But this operation... it wouldn't be that. It's our chance to win. To reclaim your life."

"But the Spares... I just... you used to say—"

"We didn't understand what we were talking about then."

The preparations were in place in two weeks. A computer program incorporated blood test analyses and trait preferences into an algorithm to identify optimal matches. The results were ordered in the form of single-page profiles, with photographs and basic statistics about physique, proportions, and internal physiology. During a second consultation with Dr. Viande, Adelaide chose the Spare which most closely resembled her healthy self. 5'5, fair skin, brown eyes, straight black hair. #2706.

"Your new body will, of course, be sterile," said Dr. Viande.

"Excuse me?"

"Copyright issues. Furthermore, testing on the matter of whether the body of a Spare can successfully reproduce with a human remains inconclusive. Studies suggest that insurmountable complications arise from the extensive differences between the two genomes. Your body will, however, be fully capable of carrying an implanted embryo to term. You may wish to harvest some of your eggs before the operation, if you and your husband plan on having more children. We can do this for you for an additional fee."

On the third consultation, Dr. Viande had nurses bring #2706 into his office. She moved like a doe, stepping lightly and pausing frequently. She fit the computer's description and looked like the girl in her photographs, but she had a beauty and vitality in person that was impossible to communicate on a piece of paper. Her skin was white and luminescent as moonstone, her hair dark and glossy as onyx. Her figure itself looked cut from crystal, though the soft roundness of her features promised femininity. "Hello," she said, big brown eyes gazing vaguely in Adelaide's direction. Her voice was strangely lyrical.

"Hello," Adelaide replied, blinking rapidly. Panic blossomed within her; what did this creature think of her? What had she been told? She desperately wanted to leave the room, and yet at the same time fascination flickered amidst her unease. She didn't move.

A silence sprawled between them. "Feel free to ask any questions you have," Dr. Viande prompted. "Anything at all."

Words tangled up in her throat. At first she had no idea what to say, and then questions swarmed in her brain. There were a million things she wanted to know, without knowing why she wanted to know them. They clogged up her thoughts, each vying for her voice. The ones which actually made it past her lips seemed utterly random.

"What's your favorite color?"

"Blue makes me happy."

"What time do you go to bed?"

"When the light disappears."

"Do you like the smell of rain?"

This question seemed to trouble #2706. She struggled with it, her luscious brows curving into Roman arches.

"You've never felt rain?"

#2706's eyes darted to her nurses for guidance. One of them signed something with her hand. "No," she said.

Adelaide was leaning forward now. "What do you live for? What do you dream of? Do you feel wonder, desire? If you could have anything—anything in the entire world—what would you have?"

#2706 clutched the arms of her chair. Each question seemed to physically wound her, like a needle prick or a flash of light right in the eyes. Adelaide saw no comprehension there. She saw nothing at all.

Adelaide's hesitations did not vanish in the days leading up to the Operation. She worried about what people would think and how she would explain everything to Marylise. She ruminated on #2706. The thought of extinguishing that simple creature made her gut squirm. But now that the door had opened, she couldn't bear to close it. Hope bloomed in the chaos of her mind like a wildflower reaching up through cracked concrete, and each day when she looked in the mirror it grew stronger. Whenever the pain was crippling, whenever the cloud of despair settled around her as she thought about the End, how could she not bask in the light of that seductive salvation?

As time drained away that hope grew brighter. Fiercer. She woke each day inside a cage of skin and bone, impatient for the freedom which dangled in front of her. Her moral scruples became less problems and more inconveniences. When she sifted through the photographs of #2706, she didn't see a person; she saw an animal. She hungered for the vibrancy of health, the softness of that hair, those breasts, those firm legs, that power. The thought of spitting in Death's face filled her with ecstasy.

The day arrived. Adelaide's parents came in the morning to watch Marylise. Adelaide, who had not eaten anything in the past twenty-four hours, had to be helped to the car. *This nightmare is going to end,* she repeated over and over inside her head.

She wasn't really aware of the nurses taking her vitals and connecting her to monitors, or of #2706 lying placidly on the surgery table beside her or of Dr. Viande entering the room and shaking her hand. She didn't feel the needles. Everything in the world had smeared together. It was only when she was under the mask inhaling general anesthesia into her lungs that she felt the urgent need to speak with #2706. She had something to say, something... But her voice slumbered in her throat and her lids were suddenly made of iron. The need slipped from her mind as she floated out to sea. Her last conscious thought before sleep claimed her was that she would not awaken inside this ruined body. She would molt it like an outgrown shell.

"She's awake now."

Nicholas sat in the waiting room with Adelaide's parents and his daughter. At the nurse's words they all stood. As they followed her back to the Recovery Room, Nicholas took Marylise's hand. "Marylise, Mama is going to look different, remember? And she's going to be weak for a while. But she's still herself."

"She's going to have hair again, right?" Marylise's own hair had recently been fashioned into a short bob to remedy her last haircut.

"Yes, sweetheart."

"Right through here," the nurse said with a manufactured smile.

Dr. Viande greeted them on the other side of the door. "Hello Mr. Fox. And Adelaide's parents I presume? And you are..."

"Marylise."

"A pleasure, Marylise."

"Can I see Mama now?"

"Absolutely. At the moment all she can do is open her eyes and move her fingers, but—"

"Why can't she do anything else?"

"Her range of movement will improve with time," Dr. Viande continued. "Your mother is going to live a very long, healthy life." He stepped aside and gestured for them to enter.

Adelaide lay in bed, staring at the ceiling and wiggling her fingers. The body she had lived in for thirty-eight years and which one year ago had begun to fail her was gone. It had been designated for Disposal and wheeled away, along with the irrelevant tissues of #2706. As Nicholas approached, he could see her lips moving slightly, begging to form words that wouldn't come. "Shhh," he said, placing a hand on her shoulder. "You're safe now."

The bed was too high for Marylise to see her mother. She stuck her arms out. "Daddy can you lift? I made a card for Mama."

Nicholas reached down and hoisted his daughter into the air. When Marylise looked down and saw her mother's face—the huge eyes, the straight nose, the full lips and the perfect, unwrinkled skin—her body went rigid. "That's not Mama," she said, wriggling to free herself from her father's arms. He set her down and tried to calm her but she wrestled away from his touch and turned to Dr. Viande. Amusement crinkled the tall doctor's face. She started to tremble. "What have you done to Mama?"

Dr. Viande gestured at the body on the bed. "She's right here, sweetheart. She's much better now."

Marylise's eyes were glassy with the onset of unbidden tears. "But... but that's not Mama." She turned to her grandparents, who were reaching for her hands.

"Yes it is, Love," said her grandmother. "She looks different, that's all."

"That's not Mama!"

Nicholas saw the anguish in his wife's new eyes. "Everything is going to be okay," he assured her. He caught sight of Marylise's card, which she'd dropped upon seeing her mother's strange face. He bent to pick it up and held it open for Adelaide to see. "Look what Marylise made for you, Love."

Inside the folded piece of paper were the words, "I love you Mama" and the drawing of a rainbow. Bright blue puddles of water lined the bottom and an orange sphere burned in the upper right-hand corner. Bits of glitter fell from it and filled the blank spaces. Leading away from one particular streak of glitter was an arrow to the side of the card, where Marylise had scrawled in big, five-year-old writing, "THE FOTONS."

A question for Julia Warner

Q: What's an idea you're dying to write but haven't, and why?

A: I have a deep fascination with ancient history and the myths and stories which have been passed down in some cultures for hundreds and even thousands of years. I've always wanted to write a fantasy story set in ancient times and draw inspiration from these literary fossils. Maybe the Chimera laid an egg before she was slain by Bellerophon. Maybe the children of Anubis could shapeshift into dogs. I think the reason I've never fleshed out any of these ideas is that writing in a time period which happened so long ago feels much more difficult than writing in the one you are experiencing for yourself or in a world of your own creation where you get to make up the rules. It sounds like a fun challenge though!

About Julia Warner

Julia Warner is an undergraduate student at the University of Virginia from Nashville, Tennessee. She loves running, writing, and playing guitar. She cannot live without books and spends more time in Westeros and Middle Earth than she does in this world.

In the Belly of the Angel

Henry Szabranski

It was Full Night, the climax of the two-week Festival of Threll, and the narrow streets of Thranrak heaved with the devout, the curious, and the avaricious. Freya Adinyan plunged past the torch-lit processions and the bustling market stalls, her heart pounding in time to the drums. Tonight she was determined to leave Thranrak and the world of man behind.

She forced her way through the mass of festival-goers crowding Ascension Square, towards the tower at its center. Wooden barricades and, eventually, a balding, pot-bellied guard blocked her way. He eyed her suspiciously as she strained to catch a glimpse of the Angel's Nest over his shoulder. She bit her lip and turned her fresh-bruised cheek from his gaze.

The gnarled remnants of the Ascension Tree could barely be glimpsed through the corroded metal tower encasing it. Twin staircases spiraled around the outside, identical save for their destinations. White-sashed ascenders, elderly and frail, inched their way up the rickety-looking High Stairs towards the Angel's Nest, the splay of wooden platforms and gantries that crowned the tower. Meanwhile on the Low Stairs, pike-wielding guards shepherded a ragged line of convicts up to the less accessible decks beneath. These were the scum of the City Justice's dungeon: the sorcerers, the murderers, the thieves and the insane. Tonight, only the blessed or the cursed would be allowed up.

Almost halfway up, a commotion broke out on the Low Stairs. A prisoner leaped, heedless of the chain binding him to his fellows. He screamed obscenities down at the crowd as he dangled over the railing. The line of black-sashed convicts staggered, the chain pulling them under his weight. The crowd roared.

The pot-bellied guard turned to look up at the disturbance. Freya didn't hesitate. She ducked beneath the wooden barrier and sprinted across the cobblestones towards the tower, vaulting up the steps of the High Stairs two at a time. She glanced quickly over her shoulder, but the guard was too busy trying to hold back the suddenly surging crowd to notice her.

Her luck held until just beneath the Nest. At least a dozen grim-faced guards congregated on the arrayed platforms there, settling in the last of the white-sashed ascenders and enjoying the elevated view of the city whilst they could. These were the Justice's best men, hard-bitten and loyal; she wouldn't get by without challenge. For a moment she hesitated, uncertain what to do. She couldn't go back down, yet neither could she stay put: the guards would soon descend past her.

To her left loomed the dark bulk of the Ascension Tree. Ignoring her rising fear, she scrambled over the stair rail and leaped onto a protruding branch. She slipped as she landed, the impact knocking the breath from her lungs. Bark peeled beneath her fingers as she scrabbled for purchase. Tonight she sought death, but this was a little too soon! Gasping for air, she edged from the stairs and the garish light cast by the paper lanterns strung around them.

She rested against the leathery bark, breathing in the tree's sweet floral smell. No reek of fungus and slow decay here, but the familiar, heady scent that brought back so many memories. Lightning flickered across the dark horizon. The great trunk vibrated against her cheek. Freya craned her neck. Overhead, the full disc of the moon Threll stuttered above the gathering clouds. Her stomach cramped. For a moment, her determination wavered. The angel was supposed to fling the unworthy to damnation and lift the rest to an afterlife on the gardens of the moon. What would it make of her?

"Clear the scaffold!"

Her heart jumped. A cry rose from the ground. In the square below, the crowd began to cheer and the drums to pound. The relief was almost palpable. Despite the best assurances of the Temple authorities, in recent days fears had grown the angel would fail to appear. It came back every year, but there were all those rumors of it acting oddly recently: smashing houses, snatching cattle, scooping fish from the sea. Who knew if it would return?

One by one, the remaining guards retreated to the ground. Freya pressed against the tree as they climbed past, the whole trunk seeming to thud with her heartbeat. But the guards' attention was on the square below. The last one down strung a chain across the Stairs to prevent further access.

Freya climbed carefully back out onto the stairs. Feeling as if the whole of the crowd below were staring up at her, she quickly scurried up to the Nest. None of the elderly ascenders seemed to take any notice of her as she reached the highest platform; they were too busy rousing themselves from their huddled positions, exhausted after their long climb. The more capable supported those who could no longer stand. Consumed by old age, most had only a few days or weeks left to live; this was their last and only chance to achieve paradise, and they knew it. Freya was suddenly conscious of being an impostor amongst them. What right had she to be here, a young girl amongst the elderly and frail, those so near the end? But then she remembered her new stepfather leering down at her. The City Justice himself, the man who had condemned her real father to climb the Low Stairs a year before, the man who had made her life unbearable since. *You're a very pretty young girl, Freya Adinyan. Just like your mother.* The sting of his palm striking her face. The stink of his breath.

No. She couldn't stay in Thranrak one day longer.

Thunder cracked. A hush fell across the square. Only the prisoners could still be heard, segregated on the lower reaches of the Nest, howling and rattling their chains in protest. Freya wondered how many of them were innocent like her father, victims of the Justice's cruelty and ambition.

She looked up. Her breath caught.

The angel of Threll was directly above.

Spiky, multi-jointed legs dangled from a central inverted dome that breached the underbelly of cloud. Globes, gathered in great clusters like eggs, dotted the underside. The visible portion of the angel could easily encompass the whole of Ascension Square, but Freya knew the vast bulk of it lay still hidden in the clouds above. On her upturned face she felt the caress of the angel's tears, tiny droplets of moisture, their familiar floral smell. The glowing sky seemed to ripple as she breathed in their heady scent.

She felt, more than heard, a long, low ululation. The sound rolled across the city, vibrating doors and windows in their frames. Down in the square, the crowd burst into applause; drums pounded with renewed vigor, a string of firecrackers exploded. This, at last, was the culmination of Full Night, of the whole two week festival.

She heard a shout from below and glanced down. A guard at the base of the High Stairs had spotted her. Moments later he ducked under the chain and began to sprint up towards the Nest. With growing panic Freya strained on her tiptoes, arms outstretched, swaying on the platform as it rocked beneath her.

Take me, angel.

She heard a gasp beside her. An elderly ascender hung suspended in mid-air, a tentacle curled tight around his waist. She glimpsed his look of terror just before he accelerated up towards the angel.

Another shout. Freya looked down. The guard was almost at the Nest. And he wasn't alone. In desperation Freya squeezed her eyes shut and stretched up her arms as far as she could reach.

She was knocked off her feet. She reached out to stop her fall, but grabbed only air. Opening her eyes, she realized she was falling *up*, not down. A dark coil circled her waist. Cold, hard and slick, segments interlinked like a worm.

She saw the guard looking up at her, his arms outstretched as if he had only just missed her dangling feet. And next to him — despite all that was happening, Freya still felt a moment of shock — was her mother. *How did she find me?* She was shouting, reaching up, her face contorted with fear.

Freya's mind whirled, thrown by the unexpected sight: her mother present, so upset. So *sober.*

A sickening lurch. Freya rose with dizzying speed. Thranrak spun below, lights whirling to create a thousand glowing circles. Countless other tentacles curled up towards the angel, each loaded with a white- or black-sashed figure. She looked up and saw the belly of the angel approaching.

Leathery flaps slapped against her head. She tried to lift her arms to shield herself but the fibrous canopy forced them down. Like a submerged buoy released from the ocean depths, she shot up through the opening and was tossed into the dim and cavernous space beyond.

She landed heavily on a taut surface. It vibrated like stretched canvas beneath her. Hard objects skittered across the slanted floor. Far above, an oval-shaped roof divided into sections by rib-like supports emitted a pale gray light. She groaned and turned her head. Jagged silhouettes surrounded her: rocks and boulders, and further away, up-rooted whole trees and even what looked like a fishing boat lying on its side, nets tangled around its mast and fractured planks fanned out like fingers. She had landed some distance from the lowest point of a large, circular bowl filled with debris and junk; she had been lucky to avoid the rocks.

A nearby shriek. Instinctively she rolled behind one of the nearby boulders. Only a stone's throw away, a group of large apes hooted, snarling and snapping at each other. Narrow-set eyes glinted in lean, savage faces; elongated snouts bared fanged teeth. The white-furred creatures pulled at a flank of red meat.

A tentacle thrust up through one of the rents in the floor and uncurled a white-sashed ascender from its grasp. He crashed onto rocks not far from the apes and gave out a wail of pain. Immediately, a group of three or four of the beasts broke off from the ongoing tussle and bounded through the jumble of debris towards him. Freya watched in horror as he was torn this way and that, like a toy fought over by demonic children. She heard a sickening crunch and dark fluid spouted as one of the apes clamped its jaws around the ascender's throat.

Freya ducked back down behind the boulder. Her breath came in short, sharp gasps. This wasn't what was supposed to happen. The angel was supposed to take the white-sashes up to paradise, on the surface of the god moon Threll. Not... this. Not *this*.

A growl. She looked up. Atop the boulder, above a bloodied snout, a pair of hungry red eyes stared down at her.

Before she could react, she heard a sodden *thwack*, a grunt, and a heavy weight collapsed on top of her. Strands of coarse hair filled her mouth as she struggled to breathe, crushed beneath a mass of warm fur.

The weight and darkness lifted from her as suddenly as it had descended. She was grabbed and pulled upright; a hand clasped around her mouth. She began to struggle, but an arm tightened around her chest. "Shhh. Quiet! Or you'll get us both killed."

She went limp at the urgent whisper. A male voice. A Thranian accent.

The hand withdrew. She looked down at the great white ape at her feet. A dark gash scarred the side of its bald head; hair tangled its still snarling face. Ribs protruded from its sides, and Freya noticed bare patches on its scrawny limbs. It looked half-starved.

"Follow me. Be quiet. Be quick."

In the dim light, Freya tried to make out her rescuer. He wore a torn canvas shirt and knee-length shorts. Patchy stubble hazed his chin. Gaunt and wiry, his dark hair cut close, he looked to be only two or three years older than her; the lack of light and the dark hollows beneath his eyes made it difficult to tell his age for sure. She followed as he scrambled over the rocks and debris, away from the center of the bowl-like arena. A coil of thick rope netting dangled over his shoulder, and on one hand he clutched a hooked gaff stick, the kind used by fishermen to haul in and kill heavier catch. Neither item slowed his progress as he dodged between the boulders.

Freya struggled to match his pace. She kept slipping and sliding on the yielding and uneven surface. Half-seen obstacles bashed her fingers and grazed her arms. She tried to concentrate on the boy bounding ahead and not on the screams and snarls from behind. Eventually they reached the edge of the chamber, where the rocks and debris thinned out and the slope rose to become a wall.

The boy pointed at a vertical slit in front of them. A series of similar gill-like openings ran along the curved side of the chamber. "Through here," he said.

Freya wavered. The gap looked too narrow, even for her.

"This way." The boy knelt down and pulled the taut fabric aside. He pushed first a hand and then his whole head inside the hole. The gaff stick went next. The sides sprang together as he disappeared inside. Freya realized it would be impossible for any pursuer to know, by sight alone, which of the slits he had gone through.

She still hesitated, turning to look down into the cavernous bowl. The angel's tentacles continued to rise up, looping black fountains that withdrew after depositing their human load. Growing gangs of albino apes descended upon the ascenders, who were too frail and too shocked to resist. The convicts, shackled at hand and foot, were even more helpless. Freya's throat clenched with horror and disbelief.

This isn't how it's supposed to be.

With distant hoots and screams echoing behind her, she stifled her tears and thrust inside the opening, deeper into the angel.

She pushed into a dimly lit passageway. Circular in cross-section, it undulated into the darkness. Her rescuer squatted on the floor, some way up the tunnel, silhouetted by pale, glowing material that drooped in long ribbons from the walls.

He gave her a weary look as she made her way towards him across the spongy floor. "Full Night in Thranrak?"

Freya nodded and sat down next to him, exhausted and disorientated. All her plans, all her preparations, all her naive dreams lay in ruins, and now she didn't know what to do.

"I was supposed to be down there," the boy said. He had unslung the rope netting from over his shoulder and was busy untangling it. "Ma had arranged for us all to stay in one of the fancy inns beside the square. We'd look out at the celebrations from the balcony. Cost her a small fortune, it did."

Freya forced herself to focus on the boy. "Freya," she said.

"Gathan." He didn't look up from his net.

"You saved my life."

Gathan frowned. "I couldn't help the others. The ascenders. Most were half-dead already. And the prisoners were shackled."

"You were waiting for us?"

"Knew the angel was due for Full Night. I could feel it maneuvering. Thought I would see if I could get down the tentacles somehow..." He shook his head. "No way." He hefted the net. "Got this from the *Vokran*, though. We'll be needing it."

Freya remembered the smashed hulk of the boat lying on the boulders. And the rumors that had circulated about the angel before Full Night, about its strange behavior. "The angel lifted your boat?"

Gathan nodded. "Came out of the clear blue sky and picked her clean up out of the water; anchor, sails, nets'n'all." He shook his head, as if he still couldn't believe it. "We held on as the boat tilted and heaved — it felt just like a huge wave had hit us." He frowned at the memory, and Freya watched as his hands clenched. "The angel gobbled us up and wrecked us on those rocks... in there." He waved in the direction they had just come from.

"Cap'n kept saying it was a great honor, that we had been chosen by the gods. But then those apes came at us. We tried to fight 'em off... but there was just too many, and Cap'n had already hurt his leg bad when we was lifted." He reached out and touched the gaff stick nestled against his knee. "I managed to brain a few and get away. Been rummaging about in the darkness ever since."

Freya couldn't decide if she should believe the gaunt boy's story. It sounded incredible. Yet... here he was. And so was she. "How long for?"

Gathan pursed his lips. "Seems a long time. But it's probably only been three or four days."

Freya rubbed her bruised face. Her hand trembled. She couldn't stop images tumbling through her mind: the stricken expression on her mother's face as she stared up at Freya rising towards the angel; the looks of confused and still hopeful disbelief on the ascenders faces, even as the snarling apes descended upon them. She kept shaking her head, as if the motion would detach the memories from her mind.

Gathan returned to untangling his net. "What're you doing here? You're far too young to climb either Stairs."

"I had to escape Thranrak."

Gathan raised his eyebrow. "Why?"

She shuddered. *You're a very pretty little girl, Freya Adinyan.*

She said, "My father was forced to take the Low Stairs, last year. My mother... hasn't coped. I thought... I thought..." She thought Father would be waiting for her. She thought he would tell her that everything would be all right. That the angel had recognized the good in his heart and that she would be allowed to join him in paradise on the surface of Threll, away from the City Justice. Away from his corrupt power, his leer and grasping fingers, his stinking breath. She had meant to escape it all. Escape even life itself, if she had to.

She hung her head. "I don't know what I thought."

Gathan looked up from the net. He hesitated, then reached out, resting his hand on her shoulder. His fingers were rough and callused, but his touch was gentle, almost timid. "Look, I don't hold much with all the Temple talk of gardens of paradise and all that. Come from a family of fisherfolk, and what we know is the wind and the tides and the moods of the sea. Some say they've seen the faces of Ueldu moving in the depths, or angels and dragons fighting each other in the storm clouds, but until the *Vokran* was taken I never saw anything like that. All I've seen here, inside the belly of the angel, is that it's just a big critter. A great floating whale."

"Don't say that!" Freya said, angered by his skepticism. She had never before seriously questioned the teachings of the Temple. It wasn't a matter of faith: she had seen the faces of the gods with her own eyes on many occasions, striding twelve-feet tall through the festival crowds. Her entire focus this past year had been to reach the Angel's Nest on Full Night, be chosen by the angel, join her father...

But this wasn't how it was supposed to be, was it?

Gathan shrugged. "Who knows? There could still be some way to Threll in here; this thing's huge and I've only crawled through a small part of it. But I'm more interested in getting back to Thranrak and my family." He leaned forward. "And I think I've found a way."

She looked at the ragged boy in surprise. The possibility of leaving the angel, so soon after her hard-won arrival — it hadn't even occurred to her. And what did she have to return to, after all? A drunken, half-mad mother? An abusive stepfather who was one of the most powerful men in Thranrak?

Gathan seemed perplexed by her silence. "What? You want to stay in this stinking place?"

"What if we're just being tested? What if we're supposed to find our own way to Threll...?" She trailed off, her justifications sounding unreasonable even to herself.

"Little Freya. You've got it so wrong. The angel isn't all-powerful. In fact, I think it's in trouble."

"What do you mean?"

Gathan re-slung the untangled netting over his shoulder, picked up the gaff stick and stood up. He stooped to avoid his head sliding along the top of the passageway. "Come on, I'll show you. It's on the way to the seed bay."

Without waiting to see if she would follow, he set off up the corridor, into the darkness.

Freya lost her balance and stumbled as the angel rocked beneath her.

"Goodbye, Thranrak," Gathan announced. He was already well ahead of her.

"What's happening?" Freya could not hide the concern in her voice.

"We're rising. Your ears will start to hurt, and it's going to get a lot colder." He disappeared around a bend in the tunnel. "Keep up."

Freya let out a shriek as the floor dropped out beneath her, and then, just as suddenly, seemed to rise. Gathan did not turn back. Swallowing hard, she gritted her teeth and concentrated on moving forward. She was concentrating so hard, moving one foot in front of the other, ignoring the awful swaying sensations, that she didn't notice Gathan stopping ahead of her. She almost collided with him.

"Shhh," he warned her. "We have to be quiet here." He took hold of her hand. Together they emerged into another dimly lit chamber.

This new cavern was much smaller than the one they had escaped from, but still sizeable, at least thirty yards in diameter. Here again a bowl-shaped floor, but much shallower, and flooded with a clear liquid; the surface of the pool swirled with faint rainbow reflections, visible even in the gloom. The curved walls glistened with moisture. Huge interlocking teeth formed one entire wall, bowing deep into the chamber; each tapered from a wide circular root to a vicious-looking needle tip. A series of dark cavities pockmarked the wall opposite, openings to further passageways and chambers. To Freya it seemed they stood on the grotesquely stretched lower lip of a giant mouth.

She wrinkled her nose. The chamber stank. Saliva-like liquid trickled into the pool through narrow gaps between the teeth. Side channels, fissures and half-hidden recesses drained the overspill away. The intensely sweet, rose-like scent that filled the chamber made Freya's head ache. Even Gathan seemed unsteady, his face flushed.

"We can't stay here," he said. "We'll start having waking dreams."

"What is this place?"

"It's where the angel's tears are made." He crouched and pointed across the pool, towards the lower set of teeth. "Hush, now. I don't think they've seen us."

Freya suddenly realized they weren't alone in the chamber. A pair of shapes squatted beside the teeth. One was humanoid and human-sized, but Freya wasn't sure it was human. So many distended sac-like growths and tumors weighed the creature down it seemed it could scarcely move. Dark tendrils grew like snakes from its head and disappeared into the ceiling above it. The deformed figure swayed from side to side in a slow rhythmic dance; its twisted hands moved as if conducting an invisible orchestra.

At the feet of the swaying conductor sat a second, hulking, shape: one of the white-furred apes, but much larger than any of the others Freya had seen. No protruding ribs on this specimen; it was meaty and heavily muscled. A mound of cracked bones, skulls, and scraps of bloody hair rose out of the shimmering pool beside it. The ape loudly sucked and chewed on what looked like a human rib.

At first Freya thought the beast sported a strange, lop-sided hat, a comical-looking beret worn at a jaunty angle, and she couldn't quite believe her eyes. Then she realized the covering was more like a grotesque fungal infection, bulging out of the sloped skull. Delicate, root-like tendrils ran back to the conductor who swayed behind the ape.

"Who... *what* are they?" Freya stared at the malformed couple with horror.

Gathan shook his head. "I'm not sure. But you know how the Justice likes to haul sorcerers up the Low Stairs. He's terrified of them. I reckon most are frauds or plain crazy... but what if one had real power? What do you think they'd do once they were inside here?"

Freya shrugged. The idea had never occurred to her. Sorcerers were just bogeymen in stories. Although Gathan was right: the Justice had a terror of them.

"Well, I think this one is trying to take control of the angel."

Not much sign of any sorcerer remained, if Gathan's theory was true — but was that a stray clump of white hair she glimpsed amongst the pulsating mess atop the swollen head? And the tattered remnants of a black sash?

And if a sorcerer, and Gathan, had survived this long inside the angel, then perhaps other people had too. Freya felt a sudden squirm of hope. Like her father...

Gathan pointed. "That collection of... things, back in the belly of the angel. That isn't normal. Rocks, houses, uprooted trees — boats — I've never heard of angels picking things up like that before. Those apes, I'm pretty sure they were brought inside accidentally when the angel grabbed up part of a forest. I've seen plenty of the monsters dead, starved or diseased, or killed and half-eaten by their own. They're no more happy here than we are."

Freya stared at the shuffling form of the sorcerer. "But the angel still returned for Full Night."

Gathan shrugged. "Maybe he hasn't got complete control. Not yet. Maybe he can only take charge at certain times. Maybe all this grabbing things is just him practicing. I don't know." Gathan placed a hand on her shoulder. "Let's go. Before he stops concentrating on the angel. Or that ape of his runs out of bones to crack. This isn't what I wanted to show you, anyway."

Freya shook his hand off. "But we need to stop him."

"Believe me, you don't want to attract his attention." He looked at her pointedly. "This isn't a place where being noticed brings good fortune, in case you hadn't realized."

Freya ignored him. She began to edge towards the giant mouth.

Gathan pulled her back. "Not that way. Our way out, it's just past here." He pointed to the openings on their left.

"We can't just leave him here," Freya insisted. "This isn't right. This isn't what Threll would want. The sorcerer's a... a *leech.*"

"I'm sure Threll can sort His own matters out without our help. We need to get out of His angel, that's what we need to do."

"You're wrong. This is up to us." Freya was suddenly convinced this was the test of faith Threll has set them. It was the only thing that made sense.

"We have to go!" Gathan hissed. "Or that big ape will brain the both of us. And who knows what other tricks the sorcerer's got up his sleeves? I'm telling you: the best thing we can do is get out of here. Before these damned fumes poison our brains permanently."

Freya didn't agree, but she didn't see what else she could do on her own. She glanced at the gaff stick in Gathan's hand. She didn't think she could grab it from him. And besides, he was right; the ape would shrug off any attack by either of them. Reluctantly, Freya followed Gathan as he crept around the edge of the pool, away from the tooth wall.

Gathan peered into the first couple of side-openings before deciding on the third one. Freya briefly glanced into the rejected passages — it was like looking into a pair of giant nostrils, she decided, and shuddered at the thought of moving through them.

The third opening was more appealing, but only in comparison. A short passageway opened into another chamber, smaller and darker than the mouth chamber. Freya immediately noticed the rounded, egg-shaped objects, each twice her height, dangling from the ceiling like huge, obscene fruit. The floor sagged towards a central, sphincter-like opening, a circular hole large enough for a person to fall through. The air was so cold her breath fogged.

Gathan half-walked, half-slid towards the hole in the floor, beckoning Freya to follow him. "Don't slip," he warned.

She eyed the large shapes crowding the narrow space. Each was an elongated, pear-shaped bulb. Veined, paper-thin wings, slick with moisture, sprouted from flukes and furled tightly around each seedpod. Like everything else inside the angel, they gave off the same pungent, sweet smell. She remembered the scent of the Ascension Tree as she had gripped it. Had it grown from a seed like these? She had never heard of a tree turning into an angel... but then, it hadn't really felt like a tree, had it, up close?

Gathan stared down into the hole at the center of the floor. He motioned Freya towards him. She approached as close as she dared. An icy cold blast swirled around her. Through the opening, she saw a ragged carpet of cloud or mist, barely visible in the dark. There was no sign of Thranrak's festival lights.

"This is our way out," Gathan said.

Freya eyed the hole uncertainly. "It's a long way down."

Gathan crawled over to the seedpod closest to the hole. It had separated from its stalk and sagged on the floor. "These have got wings — see?" He peeled off a gossamer section. "You ever watch those chute-gliders above Throndak Head on calm summer evenings?" He tugged at the translucent material. "This stuff is strong. I reckon we can ride one of these all the way down to the ground."

Freya grimaced. "You're crazy."

"Look — I've been searching for a way out for days. I've thought about sliding down the tentacles, or jumping out over open water, or even asking the sorcerer to bring the angel down to land... trust me: this is the only way." Gathan eyed Freya with growing exasperation. "You want to stay here and grub around like those crazed apes? We don't belong here. The angel doesn't know or care about us; we're like stowed away rats. We have to find a way off."

He drew a small knife from a pocket in his shorts, hefted the net he had retrieved from his wrecked boat, and began to saw at it. Freya watched as he fashioned a makeshift harness. He strung the net around the fallen seedpod, taking care not to snag the wings. He checked and tightened the knots, his face furrowed with concentration. He hummed a shanty as he worked. Eventually, he stood back to admire his handiwork. He grinned at Freya. "There. We're ready to fly."

She pointed back in the direction of the chamber with the teeth. "We can't just leave the sorcerer in there, doing whatever he's doing to the angel."

As Gathan had worked, she had grown increasingly agitated. She couldn't understand why the angel had allowed itself to be harmed by the sorcerer. Surely the divine entity had some means of defense? Was it even aware it was under attack?

Gathan's smile disappeared. "There's nothing we can do about it."

"But he's damaging the angel! He's... he's the cause of all this. He's ruined what's supposed to happen!"

"What? You think we were supposed to go to heaven? Live forever in the lush gardens of Threll?" Gathan snorted. "Grow up, Freya. Whatever the sorcerer's done, he hasn't changed that outcome. Face it. The angel is just an animal. Like a fish, or a bird. Just bigger."

"You're wrong."

A thought kept racing through her mind, something Gathan had said earlier. *This isn't a place where being noticed brings good fortune.*

"I don't get it," he said. "Don't you want to return to Thranrak? To your friends, your family? I've rigged the harness for both of us."

Instead of answering, Freya reached down and grabbed the discarded gaff stick. She turned and bounded back towards the chamber of teeth.

Maybe the sorcerer had evaded the angel's attention for so long because he was like a blood-sucking insect, numbing the skin near its bite until it had drawn enough sustenance.

But if that was the case, all she had to do was bring the sorcerer to the angel's attention.

She approached as close as she dared to the guardian ape. The great beast glanced up at her with disinterest before returning to sucking the marrow from a splintered rib. The sorcerer continued to conduct his invisible orchestra, oblivious to her presence.

She hefted the gaff stick and stabbed its metal hook into the chamber wall. Again and again, she wrenched the hook free and then stabbed it back into the grey flesh. Clear ichor oozed from the wounded tissue.

There was a splash. The ape had dropped the rib and risen out of the pool. It now lumbered towards her. Freya turned her back on it and continued to hack into the chamber wall.

A deep and resonant sound filled the chamber. *Aaaaaah.* It grew louder. With a hiss and a clang, the huge teeth unlocked and began to part. A blast of moist, fetid air almost blew Freya off her feet. The sorcerer staggered as the cavern shook.

"What have you *done?*"

Freya turned. Gathan stood in the entranceway to the seed chamber, his eyes wide. He wasn't looking at her.

A huge wet bulge of pink, fleshy material pushed from behind the opening teeth. Freya made a last vicious stab and then let go of the gaff stick. She backed away as quickly as she could. The sorcerer's ape, oblivious to the threat behind, splashed through the pool towards her, its fangs bared and its muscular arms outstretched.

The ape did not get far. The tendrils that connected its skull to the sorcerer did not stretch far enough for it to reach Freya. Realizing this, she couldn't help but give a triumphant laugh.

The sorcerer turned to see the huge tongue emerging from behind the teeth. He staggered back; the cords trailing from his skull and upper body stretched taut. Some of them snapped and tore, but the thicker, older connections refused to separate. The sorcerer twisted, tethered to the angel he had sought to subvert, and Freya heard him mewl in panic as the immense tongue oozed towards him.

She ran towards the seed chamber, past Gathan, who had strode out and stood knee-deep in the saliva pool.

"Get back!" she cried.

But Gathan didn't move. "Look at that," he said. He stared towards the opening jaws.

Freya didn't wait. The chamber shook. The sound emerging from the angel's throat grew louder and higher pitched. She dived back into the seedpod nursery and saw that here, too, the hole in the floor was widening. The entire inside of the angel appeared to be reconfiguring itself, with flesh stretching and huge bones and muscles shifting and re-arranging themselves.

"Look!" Freya cried. "I think I see land."

She twisted round when she received no reply. Gathan still stood in the mouth chamber. He stared in the direction of the opening maw, although Freya could no longer see it from her position. The interior of the cavern was bathed in light, and the young fisherman's face, still registering shock, was turned towards the source.

"Gathan! It's time to go!" She had done her bit, released the angel from the sorcerer's malign grip. Perhaps Threll would show His gratitude once she was safely back in Thranrak.

Freya tried to heave the seedpod towards the hole. The pod hardly moved, much heavier than it looked. Her feet struggled to find purchase on the slippery soft floor. By rotating the seedpod back and forth, she eventually managed to position it near the rim of the hole. She paused, still panting from the effort, and looked back to check on Gathan.

She couldn't see him.

For a moment she considered climbing into the harness and jumping without him. Then she cursed loudly, using words she had heard her mother use when drunk and angry. Gathan had saved her life. And this escape route was his idea. She couldn't just abandon him. Besides... he seemed nice.

"Gathan!"

She ran back into the mouth chamber. The air inside vibrated with the sound of the powerful exhalation from between the opened teeth. She wrinkled her nose in disgust as another wave of humid, sickly sweet air belched out. The chamber jaws were closing now, the huge tongue withdrawing.

There was no sign of Gathan, the sorcerer, the ape, nor the mound of discarded bones. The tendrils that had linked the sorcerer to the cavern walls were gone. The floor, walls and ceiling shone with a pearly iridescence, scoured clean. A long smear of bright red streaked the tongue's surface, a jellied mass mixed with crushed bones and dotted with bloodied white fur. Freya couldn't tell if there was more than one body in the carnage. She suddenly felt light-headed and dizzy, the cloying fumes in the chamber overwhelming her.

"Gathan! Where are you?"

Freya thought she heard a faint answering cry from behind the closing teeth. Cursing again, she slogged through the saliva pool towards the mouth. Another blast of sweet, moist air hissed around her, and her dizziness grew. She shielded her eyes from the glare as best she could and peered into the long throat.

The tunnel beyond the teeth started in similar fashion to the mouth chamber, but quickly narrowed and sloped upwards. The retreating tongue also thinned, and displayed regular horizontal creases further back.

Steps. Those are steps.

Freya squinted against the intensity of the light... but then her eyes widened in wonder.

There were clouds, deep in the back of the throat. And open, star-scattered sky. And the full round face of Threll, a gleaming silver disc, suddenly and inexplicably so large that for the first time in her life Freya could make out patterns on it — silver traceries of concentric circles, canals, complex interlocking circuits... the breath caught in her throat. It was beautiful... and so close! The disc rippled, as if distorted by a heat haze. She had but to jump over the teeth and make her way up the stairway... just the same way she had climbed the High Stairs. These steps were just an extension of those, she realized. These were the Highest Stairs.

And there was Gathan! A tiny figure, impossibly far away now. He was climbing towards Threll itself, to paradise. His movements were odd, she thought, jerky, like those of a marionette. But it was definitely him.

"Wait for me!" Freya was seized with a sudden fear she would be left behind. She splashed through the remnants of the pool, but the bottom was slick; she slipped and fell face forward. She spluttered out mouthfuls of oily liquid and scrabbled back to her feet. The jaws were closing. They were almost shut.

"Father!" she shouted. "Are you there?"

She grasped the ivory-colored enamel of the lower teeth and tried to vault over, but the upper teeth bore down upon her hands. She barely got them away before the teeth locked shut with a loud, wet clack. The seal was tight, airtight, and the light and the noise and the wind were gone.

The chamber spun around her. She leaned over and threw up. Her head pounded. Her eyeballs felt gritty and too large for their sockets. She had once drunk half of one of her mother's hidden bottles of spirit, just to spite her. This was how she had felt the morning after — only much worse.

She groaned, suddenly filled with relief she hadn't succeeded in hurdling the teeth before they closed. The glimpsed vision of Threll must have been nothing more than a mirage, induced by the vapors flooding the chamber. There were no stairs up to Threll — of course there weren't: it had just been an illusion. Hadn't it? The intoxicating fumes had overwhelmed Gathan, led him to who knew what grisly fate. She had only narrowly escaped following him.

She trembled with sudden guilt. They could have jumped already and been free, had it not been for her. She stood and battered her hand against the slick wall of teeth. "Open up!" Perhaps she could force them apart again. Perhaps —

The angel lurched, this time for real. The remaining liquid in the pool slosh wildly. Grunts and snarls came from what seemed like a newly opened passageway into the chamber. Apes approaching. She didn't have much time.

Still feeling nauseous, head throbbing, she stumbled back into the seedpod chamber. She couldn't stay here any longer. Her father must be dead, she knew that now. Gathan too. She should concentrate on the living, on those she could still help. On her mother. She had to return to Thranrak, try and free her from the grip of the City Justice. The old tyrant no longer scared her now — nothing could be worse than what she had faced here. Freya burned with sudden anger: at the angel, at the lies of the Temple, most of all at herself, at her weakness in running away, giving up, praying for escape at any cost. The least she could do for Gathan was let people know he had been right — there were no answers up here. Only death. Even for those who didn't seek it.

The angel rocked and bucked beneath her as she scrambled towards the seedpod. She tugged at the net, checking it wouldn't slip once the pod started to fall. She climbed into the harness and prayed Gathan's skill with knots was better than her own. Her feet dangled free of the net and she used them to inch the seedpod closer to the hole.

Without warning, the floor tore and gave way. The seedpod lurched and fell.

Freya screamed as she plunged, as the seedpod tumbled end over end. The air tore at her like a thousand furious hands. For a brief moment the angel tilted into view, and she had an impression of an enormous cyclopean eye on its underside, blinking open to stare down at her. Then it was gone.

Below, glittering water, wisps of cloud, golden desert. Lands new and totally unfamiliar. The great dome of the ground rushing towards her, faster, faster.

The seedpod's wings snapped open.

And Freya held on for dear, precious life.

It came from Henry Szabranski

I'm a visual thinker. The inspiration for "In the Belly of the Angel" came from a single, sudden, unbidden image: of a large orangutan-like ape, squatting atop a pile of human bones, its wispy hair stirred by a strong breeze as it contemplated an opening in the floor of a vast, bird-filled chamber floating far above the ground. The birds didn't make it into the final story, but most of the other elements of this image did. The setting is the world of Othasu, with Thranrak one of the seven cities of the Heptatheon, a society ruled by the seven god moons that orbit above the planet. Quite a lot of world-building for a single short story, but Othasu is the milieu for several of my other published stories ("Dance of the Splintered Hands" and "Against the Venom Tide"), and also my first novel attempt. Speaking of novels,

"In the Belly of the Angel" could easily be the first two chapters of one. I've even written part of the third chapter: Freya's crash landing, her discovery by the inhabitants of the strange land she finds herself in, her reluctant recruitment to the cause of the gods, and the start of her perilous journey back to Thranrak on a quest to set free her mother and bring justice to the City Justice... One day I may even find the time to write it.

A question for Henry Szabranski

Q: Does a nameless horse make you more or less nervous than a named horse?
A: All horses have names, even if those names are not known to humans.

About Henry Szabranski

Henry Szabranski was born in Birmingham, UK, and studied Astronomy & Astrophysics at Newcastle upon Tyne University, graduating with a degree in Theoretical Physics. He lives in Buckinghamshire with his wife and two young sons. He doesn't believe in angels.

February

Heard

Elise Forier Edie

When Dr. Paulson Kurtz clones the mammoth Sukari, the whole world gushes. Blog posts, interviews, TV spots, websites, opinion pieces, essays, tweets, and podcasts, the message is always the same: everyone's enchanted, everyone's in love. YouTube viewers thrill to her image: Sukari chases a big red ball; Sukari bathes in a plastic pool; Sukari sucks from a bottle, held by a comely grad student. Everyone agrees that her name, taken from the Inuit word for "sweet," suits her perfectly. Her golden eyes, her shaggy fur, her obvious intelligence make her as popular with adults as she is with children. Sukari mouse pads, Sukari iPhone skins, even Sukari backpacks pop up at fine retail stores everywhere.

The most popular video online is one of Sukari learning to grab a tuft of grass with her trunk. Kurtz shows this clip over and over on talk shows and it is played again and again online. In it, Sukari gambols in a field, adorable and furry. She grabs for the grass, but aims a little too high. She tries again, but dips a little too low. Finally, she curves her tiny trunk around a tuft and pulls. Success! She rocks back, carefully attempting to propel the blades to her mouth. The trunk advances ... her mouth opens... but darn it! She hits her cheek instead. So funny! She's such a star! How can you not fall in love with Sukari?

Of course, everyone also asks, over and over, if she's lonely. She's the only one of her kind in the world. Doesn't a baby mammoth miss her herd?

Dr. Kurtz's answer is always the same. He says, "Quarantine is necessary, for Sukari's safety. But she doesn't know she's alone. How can she miss a herd that she's never even seen?"

School children write Kurtz letters, asking for a mammoth of their own. Jesus freaks write too, and condemn him for a heretic. Women send him naked pictures. Meanwhile, corporate investors publicize the construction of a five thousand acre compound in the Pribilof Islands, off the coast of Alaska. The acreage will be for Kurtz's exclusive use. Everyone waits breathlessly for a whole herd of mammoths to manifest.

On her second birthday, Kurtz releases another Sukari video. In it, bearded and tanned, he kneels under a perfect blue sky. The summer green grass of the Pribilofs ripples around him. Sukari's trunk, hairy and pliable, explores his wrist and then his forearm. She seems to be laughing as she tickles his shoulder, his neck, all the way up to his face. She gently pats his cheeks, his lips. She seems to be saying, "I love you. I love you." Kurtz strokes her head, rubs her neck. Sukari closes her eyes.

"You're very fond of her," an interviewer prompts, after being thoroughly charmed by the video.

Kurtz clears his throat. "It's more accurate to speak of attachment," he says, "which is a biological imperative, as opposed to a poetic construct. Baby mammals behave in a way that releases hormones in their caregivers. These hormones cause pleasant sensations, and insure they will continue to be cared for. What Sukari and I feel for one another is merely attachment. But we both enjoy it."

On Sukari's third birthday, Kurtz does not release a video. No more extinct mammals have appeared in the Pribilof compound. Reporters inquire about Sukari's welfare, about the future of the mammoth-cloning project. But Kurtz does not reply.

A Twitter account surfaces, one purporting to be from Sukari's handlers. It says there's a problem with her internal organs. A subsequent grim picture is painted in a series of 145 character reports. Sukari is in pain. Kurtz is keeping her alive anyway. Kurtz is Mengele. Sukari is a victim. Hash tag SaveSukari rises to the top of Twittering Trends, even though the account disappears, just as mysteriously as it began.

Public outcry intensifies. People demand a statement from Kurtz. The President receives a flood of outraged e-mails, begging for an intervention. Finally, a White House press spokesmen, balding and beleaguered, emerges from the West Wing to wearily explain that, though the President cares deeply about Sukari, the White House has no jurisdiction over extinct animals, especially ones manufactured in a laboratory.

In retaliation, several Congressional critics of the President attempt to draft bills to save extinct mammals. But since such legislation would also encompass the protection of certain endangered species, and possibly infringe on key oil and timber company holdings, the bills die before reaching the floor.

Meanwhile, a lone woman raises half a million dollars on GoFundMe, and pilots a boat to the Pribilofs. She braves perilous Arctic seas, only to have armed guards turn her away when she tries to dock at the compound. Undaunted, she sets up a streaming cam from a distance, on the mast of her ship. Fuzzy images transmit along with breathless narration. "Someone walked across the compound. I think it's Dr. Kurtz." "I saw a tractor." "I'm sure that truck is carrying Sukari." "There goes another person on the dock."

A colleague from Texas A & M University attempts to defend Kurtz. "Cloned animals usually don't have long life spans," she explains in an online piece. "Especially if they are cloned from elderly animals. And health problems are not uncommon either." She goes on to say, "But whether or not Sukari lives, whether or not Dr. Kurtz is able to repeat his success, the cloning procedure is a great leap forward for science, and for the preservation of endangered species. There is hope for the black-footed ferret. We can bring back the Balinese Tiger. We mustn't lose track of what Kurtz's achievement means to the future of science."

The subsequent deluge of hate mail, sends her into a suicidal depression. Missives such as, "If I were a Balinese tiger I'd eat your fucking heart out, you bitch," appear daily in her e-mail inbox.

Nothing is said of the messages Kurtz receives. But lab techs and grad assistants flee the Pribilof compound. Corporations withdraw their sponsorship. Association with Sukari is bad for public relations. Also, the mammoth industry has proved not to be as profitable as anticipated, although Toy Directory Online reports stuffed animal mammoths are still a very popular item in stores.

The last videos of Sukari appear to be from a crib cam. They are clearly pirated and transmit on an anonymous website, grainy and rippling, through an untraceable address in the Philippines. In the videos, Sukari lies in a lab, chained to a pallet. Tubes feed her intravenously. Sometimes her eyes open and close. She paddles her chunky limbs. She tries to raise her head. Latex coated hands administer sedatives. A faceless tech combs and washes her fur.

At one point, Kurtz steps into view. His beard is shot with gray. He looks pouchy and depleted. He stands by Sukari. She pats his arm weakly with her trunk. He scratches her head. He rubs her neck. She closes her eyes.

But in much of the footage, Sukari is alone. While she sleeps, the skin around her cheekbones flutters. A zoologist postulates that she hums to herself then, as elephants do, in a frequency too low for human ears to hear. Sukari hums like an elephant, and the earth beneath the lab vibrates in tandem. Her transmissions can be heard over long distances. The message will always be the same. "I am here," it says, "I am here. I am here. Are you there? I am here. Please, come back to me."

It came from Elise Forier Edie

"Heard" began as an experiment in trying to write shorter fiction. I tend to write long pieces, and it's really a challenge for me to keep things in the 3,500-word range. For "Heard," I set the super tight goal of about 1,000 words, and it was very tough going, for quite some time. I kept wanting to delve deeply into character motivation, and linger on environmental details, and all that "writerly" stuff. Needless to say, I failed my word count again and again. At some point though, I gave up trying to tell the story in a traditional way, and landed on the idea of telling it thought social media transmissions. Only then did I find my way through. I still went over my original word count goal, so I have yet to write a piece of true flash fiction. But I learned some nice lessons about how less is more, and I look forward to rising to the challenge again.

A question for Elise Forier Edie

Q: Do you have any pets? Do they influence your writing?

A: I have two dogs, Krypto and Jubilee. They are named after super heroes. They absolutely influence my writing. For one thing, they don't give two shits about it, and this helps enormously, especially on bad days, when I think my work sucks beyond belief. My dogs always remind me that life is not about achievement, and that beauty and love can be found everywhere, even in old tennis balls and saggy bags of dog food. I like making their tails thump on the floor after I've been wrestling with metaphors. I substitute their names and the word "puppy" in poems and song lyrics. It always makes me feel better. "Shall I compare thee to a summer's puppy? Thou art my Krypto and my Jubilee." They wag their tails and I feel like a genius.

About Elise Forier Edie

Elise Forier Edie is a playwright and author. She lives in Southern California and writes mostly about monsters. She teaches writing and theater arts at West Los Angeles College. She is a proud graduate of the Odyssey Writing Workshop.

You can visit her at her website: www.eliseforieredie.com

Rowboat

K. G. Anderson

I've never seen an ocean, but I grew up playing "Rowboat" in my family's cramped living module on level C of Xinxin Colony. The worn blue carpet was the water, the concrete floor beyond it, a sandy shore. With a broomstick as an oar, I pretended I was Gramma Jen, rowing hard against the tide to get us home.

"They'd restricted travel by then, but Gramma Jen wanted us to know about beaches and the sea," Mom said. "One afternoon we found an abandoned rowboat and she took us out on San Francisco Bay. A government patrol nearly caught us."

Mom paused. Sitting in a faded chair, propped up by a thin pillow, she looked exhausted. Dad had told me she'd be gone in a matter of days. Like many of the colony's pioneers, she'd ignored the dangers of radiation to build our station on Ceres.

I closed my eyes, as if that would shut out the sour air of the sickroom. Then I finished the story Mom had told me so many times when I was a kid. The one that had always been my favorite.

"Gramma Jen hid the boat behind an abandoned freighter," I whispered. "By the time the patrol passed, the tide had turned against you. But she rowed you back to shore and beached the boat just as the sun went down."

When I opened my eyes, Mom was nodding.

"Thank you, Maya. I hope you'll always remember that story. Remember Gramma Jen."

With time running out, Mom was telling us all the stories again. How she'd volunteered to come to Ceres on an Early Migration mission. How our Gramma Jen had encouraged her every step of the way.

"Your Grampa Peter didn't want me to go, but she told him she believed I had it in me to be a pioneer," Mom said.

My half-sib, Dad and CeCe's son Rikki, 10 in Earth years, was hearing some of the Gramma Jen stories for the first time.

"So, did Maya's," Rikki hesitated, looking for a word we didn't use much on Ceres, "—did Maya's *grandmother* want to someday live here with us?"

Rikki was playing soldiers on the floor using my old "armies" of hex nuts and bolts. He sounded doubtful.

Mom and the other pioneers were the only ones who talked about Earth. Our teachers always told us to focus on the future.

"Rikki, there was a time when we thought we'd finish all the asteroid colonies in time for our families on Earth to Migrate," Mom said. "And, maybe we could have. But no one expected the Last War— or at least how terrible the Last War would be. Everyone who stayed on Earth, including Maya's grandmother and grandfather, died."

Rikki shrugged and went back to advancing a line of hex nuts toward a regiment of bolts. I knew how he felt. In spite of Mom's stories, and the pictures they showed us in school, for those of us born on Ceres so much of the Earth stuff seemed unreal.

At Earth-16, I was long past my days of playing "Rowboat." I'd moved from my family's living module into the First Gen dorms, five levels down. The Xinxin families had agreed that their children should be weaned away from them, taught to focus on the long-term survival of the colony, and prepared to be assigned to other colonies on other asteroids. We'd form families and have children there. My assignment could come any day now, as soon as the next freighter arrived. My throat tightened when I thought about how I'd never see Ceres, or my family, again.

Mom was asking Rikki a question about school.

I wanted to tell her that I dreamed about Gramma Jen and Grampa Peter. My battered tablet had a copy of the one picture we had of them, taken when they were only a few years older than me. I look at the picture almost every night. In it, they wore the bright, sleek clothing of the 2070s. They were picnicking with friends in a park. She, dark and lively; he, tall and thin. A bridge—the "Golden Gate," Mom called it—spanned the sparkling blue water behind them. I'd seen it in Earth movies.

In my dreams, I was Jen's best friend. We drove a vehicle, a car, with the windows open, across the Golden Gate Bridge, the blue water rippling below, and green forests rising beyond. Because of Mom's stories I could imagine it all: Trees. Oceans. Rain. Earth gravity. The wonders of atmosphere. I smiled to feel the pull of Earth all the way out here on Ceres, tugging me towards the planet where my parents and CeCe had been born.

But Earth wasn't just millions of miles away. Thanks to the Last War, everything on it was rubble. The Earth they showed us in pictures and videos existed only in my dreams.

Voices from the living room told me that Dad and CeCe were back. Rikki jumped up and ran out to greet them. Mom had drifted off to sleep.

I could hardly stand to look at her, slumped in her chair. I knew she was getting weaker. I'd heard CeCe say she'd reached the point where there were more bad days than good. Yesterday a glass bottle filled with a pale green liquid had appeared on in our refrigerator, labeled with Mom's name. I'd changed the subject after CeCe told me what it was. Mom would be confronting death as fearlessly as she'd confronted everything else. She expected us to, as well. I didn't dare disappoint her.

A hesitant knock on the bedroom door. Another one of the pioneers wanted to say goodbye. Edison Kang and I nodded a silent greeting as we exchanged places. I tried not to shudder as his arm brushed against me.

Mr. Kang had many of the early signs of radiation sickness— limp gray hair, creased and wrinkled skin, and ugly lesions. I dropped my gaze. Raised in the safety of the Xinxin compound, I could not imagine him and Mom working for years on the asteroid's surface in the original flexsuits. But they had. All to make Xinxin our home.

That night I dreamed I was rowing a boat through space, searching for a shore. Earth shone bright in the vast emptiness, impossibly far away. I had to get there—Grandma Jen was waiting for me.

I woke soaked in sweat and burning with curiosity.

After morning classes I went looking for Mikel Clark. Mikel was smart, but not well liked or trusted. I usually avoided him, but I'd overheard him bragging about hacking into the inter-colony databases and I knew he'd be eager to show off his skills.

"Is it true they've found more Earth data?" I asked.

Mikel's eyes lit up. He pulled me into an alcove where we wouldn't be overheard. "Two of the other colonies had it all along. They weren't sharing. But now the Xinxin Council has it." He grinned. "The security guys haven't opened up general access yet, they say they have to 'review' it, but people like me can get around that."

"I want to look for some images. Family stuff. Nothing classified."

Mikel flipped his braid over his shoulder.

"You came to the right man. I could get you in through a workstation in the admin section," he boasted.

"Tonight?" I swallowed hard. I'd never broken the rules before.

Mikel glanced down for a moment, as if weighing the risks. "Sure, why not?"

That night I followed Mikel through a maze of hallways. He used someone else's override codes on the doors. We were leaving tracks, but someone else would get blamed. By the time we entered the cramped office deep in the admin sector, I felt sick to my stomach. But it was too late to stop now. Mikel pulled an old data pad from a drawer, connected it to the system, and attached my data card that held the image of Grandma Jen and Grampa Peter.

Sure enough, Xinxin Colony's network now had the Earth archives we had been told were lost or held in secret by one of the other colonies. With Mikel's help, I searched several of the databases with facial recognition software. My first hit was a low-res image of Grampa Peter. He was older—handsome but worried looking. Just as Mom had said, he'd been an official in a California city called Palo Alto. But the matches for Gramma Jen's face were an Elisabeth Washington, a music professor in Georgia. I frowned. I was pretty sure Georgia was nowhere near Palo Alto.

Where was Gramma Jen? I searched for Grampa Peter's name plus "Jen," "Jennifer," and "Jeanne." Nothing. Real estate data from Palo Alto paired his name with a Margaret Dempster. His sister? His mother?

Mikel fidgeted at my side, not as confident as he'd seemed before.

When I typed in "Margaret Dempster," a news story appeared. I saw the words "arson conviction."

Before I could read more, an orange bar flashed at the top of the data screen. Mikel grabbed my arm.

"We gotta go. We've been spotted."

In the distance, an alarm shrilled.

Mikel yanked out my data card, logged out of the pad, and shoved it back in the drawer. Following him as he retraced our path, I saw him toss my data card into the corner of a dark stairwell—figuring, I guess, that I'd be the one blamed for the break-in. I stopped to snatch up the card and nearly missed catching the door he'd keyed open. I'd been stupid to trust Mikel.

Sure enough, there was trouble.

"You went looking for Gramma Jen."

It wasn't a question. Mom beckoned to me from her narrow bed.

"I'm sorry."

Mikel and I had been caught on the admin network and they'd told not just Dad, but Mom. I'd hoped I'd find something to make me feel better, but all I'd done was make my mother feel worse.

"I'm sorry," I said again.

"No, Maya," Mom said. "It's my fault."

My eyes went wide. This didn't sound like my mother.

"I hoped you'd never find out," she said. "So many records were lost in the Migrations and the War. But I guess they're finding some of that data can be recovered. I should have told you."

"Mom, I didn't find anything," I lied. "Just a picture of Grampa Peter from his job."

Mom gave a clipped laugh, devoid of humor. She reached for a cup of tea from the bedside table and took a sip. I watched her trembling hand and tried not to show my confusion.

"Maya, you didn't find anything because there's nothing to find. There is no Gramma Jen. Never was."

"*What?*"

Mom, sitting on the edge of her narrow bed, flinched.

"If there's no Gramma Jen..." my mind spun with possibilities. Was I adopted? "But you're still my mother?"

She reached out her thin arms and I knelt beside the bed to be hugged.

"Oh, Maya, of course I'm your mother."

Relief poured through me. After a minute I felt Mom square her shoulders. I settled cross-legged on the floor and waited, shivering. Mom was getting ready to tell me—once again—that things weren't as frightening as they sounded.

"Maya, I invented Gramma Jen. I need to tell you why."

Mom hugged herself as if she were cold. I reached for a blanket to cover her, but she waved me away.

"I'm afraid the story starts with Margaret Dempster," Mom began.

"She was my..." she stopped, worked her lips, and continued. "She was the woman people would say is my mother."

Her tone turned as grim as I'd ever heard it; my stomach twinged. Margaret Dempster, the arsonist, was my grandmother?

"Margaret was ..." Mom sighed and shook her head, casting about for words. "I know now that she was mentally ill, but when I was a child, all I knew is that my brother and I seemed to get punished no matter what we did and my father...well, he loved us but he just couldn't admit that there was anything wrong. He couldn't protect us. We left home as soon as we finished high school."

"I thought that simply by coming to Ceres—as far away as anyone could get during the first Migration—I'd solved my problems," Mom said. "And, in a sense, I had. Our work building Xinxin was important—far more important than anything I could have done on Earth. I met CeCe and your father, we all were in love, and—Maya, we were so happy."

A smile lit her face and eyes.

"I don't think you can even imagine what our lives were like," she went on. The smile faded.

"Then, the Last War—only six days, but when it ended, everyone on Earth was gone and we were alone in space: six colonies on three asteroids. Two of the colonies failed—one from starvation."

I nodded. They'd told us this, over and over again, in school. But what did this have to do with Gramma Jen?

"We were focused on mining, agriculture, manufacturing, and production of everything we needed to survive—including children. With no more Migrations from Earth, it became crucial for the colonies to have children before we got too much radiation. That's when I began to have nightmares. I dreamed that I'd had a baby and when I took the baby in my arms, I turned into Margaret. I dreamed that I hated my baby. Once I dreamed that I … was lighting a fire."

I shuddered. Mom didn't know that I knew about the arson. Tears rolled down her skeletal cheeks. Her head fell forward. Her thin, lesioned hands covered her face, then fell to her lap.

"Maya, I would wake up from those dreams knowing that something was terribly wrong with me. My friends were having children. They loved those children! I saw Edison Kang holding Leah when she was born, and I couldn't imagine ever feeling like that. I was a sick, broken person. I didn't want anyone to find out."

I turned my head so Mom wouldn't see the tears rolling down my cheeks. "Mom, why didn't Grampa Peter help you? Why didn't he divorce her and take you away?"

"Maya, I've asked myself those questions a thousand times. We'll never know."

Mom put her ravaged hand on my arm and gently shook it, as if to wake me up.

"Let me tell you about the picture."

Mom stretched out her hand for the battered data tablet on the table by her bed. I handed it to her, and with a few taps she brought up that picture of the young couple at the Golden Gate, the two I thought of as Gramma Jen and Grampa Peter. I stared at the striking young woman. *Elisabeth Washington.*

"This photo saved me," Mom said. "I found it in a digital album my dad had given me years before, when I left Earth. I'd never bothered to look at it. I thought he'd given me a lot of images of nature and landscapes, in case I never came back."

"After the Last War, when it was all gone—then, of course, I looked at the album. I came across this picture, recognized him, and I looked at the metadata. It was taken in 2071, two years before he married Margaret. I realized that my father had wanted me to know about that beautiful moment in his life. He wanted to send that woman, whoever she was, with me into the future."

I sat on the bed beside Mom and saw the picture as I never had before. The woman looking at the camera while Grampa Peter held her hand and gazed at her as if she were the most precious thing in his world. What had happened to separate them?

"That's Elisabeth," I said. "Mom, I found her."

Mom frowned.

"I found her. Facial-recognition software. She's Elisabeth Washington. She taught music in Georgia. What do you know about her?"

I'd thought I knew all Mom's stories, but now there was so much more to know and so little time left.

"Elisabeth..." Mom stared at the picture and shook her head. Then she dropped the tablet onto the bed and lay against her pillow.

"Maya, all I know was that my father had loved her. When I saw that picture I realized I could rewrite history, for him and for me. I could make *her* my mother. The mother I'd always wanted. A wonderful mother.

"I named her Jen after the neighbor who'd given me the art lessons Margaret refused to pay for and who told me I had talent. Her courage came from the ship captain who mentored me on the First Migration. Her generosity is from CeCe. I got all those great recipes—and the story of the rowboat—from Nina, my first roommate on Xinxin."

While Mom told the story, my dad and CeCe had slipped into the small room. Dad caught sight of the tablet with the photo of Grampa Peter and Gramma Jen.

"Gramma Jen is one of your mother's finest creations," he said, sitting carefully on the bed beside Mom.

So he had known. Mom leaned her fragile body against him. Her dark eyes were bright with tears.

"Maya, for me, your Gramma Jen was not just real—she was essential," Mom said. "She changed my life. She made yours possible."

The room spun. I didn't know what to think. Gramma Jen had become a stranger. My real grandmother—I opened my mouth to ask about the fire. But I closed it again. Mom was falling asleep. I tried to slip out of the room, but CeCe stopped me.

"Maya...tomorrow," she whispered, squeezing my hand.

I pulled away, mumbling that I needed to study for an exam. That was true, but instead I took the long way through the corridors that led back to the dorm. I walked close to the grimy, familiar walls, afraid that the artificial gravity I'd grown up trusting might prove as unreliable as my ties to Earth. Fearing, as I never had before, the cold and airless world where I'd been born.

The next evening, my mother asked for the injection. With all of us gathered in the room and a recording of her favorite Beethoven sonata playing, Dad slipped a hypodermic into a vein. She took three, perhaps four, shallow breaths and then Mom was gone.

We gathered again a few days later, to watch as her ashes, wrapped in fragile Earth-made fabric, were taken out onto the frozen surface of Ceres and placed in the colony's communal grave for pioneers.

"Maya, you can refuse," Dad said. "I asked them not to tell you about this when your mom was so ill.

He sat on the bench beside me, looking over my shoulder as I opened the tablet and read the message.

I gasped. They were offering me a permanent assignment to Charboneau Colony on Vesta. This was out of the blue. I'd always thought they'd send me to Pallas or Hygiea, never imagining I'd qualify for the agricultural engineering team at Charboneau.

"Mom would have been thrilled." I felt tears start to well, but shook them away.

"I think it's too soon for you," Dad said. "But the freighter will be packed and ready to go by the end of the week. And this is the closest Ceres will be to Vesta for 17 years."

I nodded, my eyes fixed on the message. Permanent assignment. Charboneau. I'd have only three days to pack and say goodbye to Dad, and CeCe, and Rikki and nearly everyone I knew on Xinxin. Three of us from Xinxin First Gen would leave on the freighter *Sunrise* and travel 930 million miles to join the agricultural engineering team at Charboneau. We'd live on Vesta for the rest of our lives.

I thought of Mom again. She'd left Earth to build the first colonies. She'd understand. And Gramma Jen. She'd...but there was no Gramma Jen. Confused, I shook my head. So I think it surprised Dad when I turned my face to him and said "I'll go."

The words sounded so small, so flat and empty. But once I said them they set in motion a whole new story.

Dad and I hugged without words.

I walked slowly back to the dorm, trying to imagine my life on Vesta. Living with strangers—and eventually creating a family with some of them. New foods. A new religious system—some of the parents were worried about that. A quasi-military system of government, stricter than the democracy we'd maintained in Xinxin. I frowned as I recalled that data access on Vesta was rumored to be far less liberal than on Ceres. If I wanted to find out more about Elisabeth or Margaret, I'd have to do it now.

To my surprise, Dad got me official access to the Earth files. I read the news story I'd glimpsed before—"Palo Alto Woman Convicted of Arson." Margaret Dempster had set her family's house on fire. Everyone had escaped unharmed. A small, blurry photo showed a pale, frightened woman. To my relief, she looked nothing like my mom.

I would never know why Grampa Peter had married her. But now I understood why my mother had replaced the broken world of her childhood with the fantasy of Gramma Jen.

I found real estate records for Elisabeth Washington in Atlanta, Georgia, and a review of a concert performance. One of the pieces she'd played I recognized as Mom's favorite Beethoven sonata. I pressed my fingertips to the screen, as if I could reinforce that connection between the two of them—but it was as thin and as wishful as my own ties to Earth.

Had Elisabeth Washington married? Had children? My searches came up empty. I knew as much as I would ever know.

The inside cabin Leah, Jinx and I were assigned on the *Sunrise* proved to be cramped and stuffy, the bunks narrow and hard. We complained at great length that first night so none of us would be tempted to talk about home and the families and friends we were leaving. At last I crawled under the thin blankets, exhausted, but too excited to sleep.

I thought of Mom, and the many times she'd soothed me to sleep with her stories. In the dark cabin, I began to tell my own tale.

Like Gramma Jen, I'm rowing a boat. I'm not alone. There are people in the boat with me. My friends. And someday, my children. I envision a small boy and an even smaller girl, their faces pale with worry, who sit facing me, their hands gripping the seat.

To pass the time I tell them stories of Ceres and Earth and their families, both real and fantastic.

I feel the polished wood of oars against my palms. Each stroke I take sends the light of the stars around us rippling through the black of space.

"Almost home," I murmured as I drifted off to sleep. "Almost home. I'll get you there."

It came from K. G. Anderson

I've often wanted to rewrite parts of my own life story, so it was natural that I'd write fiction about a character who attempts it. Fiction is filled with characters who reinvent themselves. This used to be true in real life, as well — people who emerged from war zones, or who turned up on the frontier, where no one could check identities. (My parents had a friend, born in 1913 to a working-class immigrant family in Boston, who changed his name, became an acclaimed artist and adventurer, and successfully passed himself off as a European blueblood.) But with today's fingerprinting, DNA identification, and rapid communication, creating a new history for yourself is increasingly difficult. In my story "Rowboat," the asteroid dweller who invents a false family history takes advantage of the unexpected extinction of life, and destruction of records, back on planet Earth. Of course, something eventually occurs to unravel her deception... I enjoyed collaborating with my character to invent the stories she would then pass on to her daughter, Maya. We had to figure out how to replace all the tragic elements of her childhood with empowering ones. As you'll see in the story, she creates her fictitious mother (Maya's "Gramma Jen") using the stories, recipes, and characteristics of other women who were mentors in her life: an artistic neighbor, a glamorous spaceship captain, a beloved friend. My protagonist's initial inspiration to rewrite her life comes from a photo she discovers — one that reveals that her father had his own secret past. I've discovered a number of old family photos that hint at my family's own secrets. I'll never uncover them — everyone who might have helped me is long dead. I wrote "Rowboat" to watch Maya achieve, and grapple with, the discoveries that I will never make.

A question for K. G. Anderson

Q: What kind of non-fiction do you like to read and how does it affect the fiction you write?

A: My nonfiction reading is mostly autobiography and biography. I'm interested in the ways that people shape their life stories, and how and why they tell them — to themselves and to others. In my fiction, I like to explore trickster characters for whom lying is an art form; characters who delude themselves (often for self-preservation); and people who create stories of the future that serve as roadmaps, often for the organizations they lead. Many of my stories, including "Rowboat", involve family secrets. I was deeply influenced by Russell Baker's Pulitzer Prize-winning autobiography Growing Up. Baker's stories about the Depression era helped me understand my parents and grandparents, who didn't want to talk about those hard times. As the child of a Jewish parent, I was fascinated by Art Spiegelman's ground-breaking graphic novel Maus: A Survivor's Tale.

About K. G. Anderson

K.G. Anderson is a Seattle-based journalist, arts reviewer, humor columnist, and technology writer. She worked on the launch of Apple's iTunes Music Store, wrote a book about the iPhone, and served as president of the board of Northwest Folklife. She shares a house full of books and cats with bookseller Tom Whitmore and lives for the warm summer months and gardening.

writerway.com/fiction-by-k-g-anderson

How to Survive a Fish Attack

Kato Thompson

[From the memories of Sample AH537272. Transcript created using the extended Mahala method.]

I remember tracing words in the memory mat with my mother. She showed me her favorite passages and we repeated the words together, sonicating the tiny algae into alignment and preserving the ribbon of knowledge for our future.

I sang for the mat once. It was a great honor and I am proud. Our mat is not so large, so we can only record what is important. One day, the tenders will probably consolidate my story with others about surviving a fish attack, but for now it is my voice imprinted there in the mat, telling the story.

Our mat grows very close to the thermal vent. If the vent caves in, the only memories we will have will be the ones we carry in our own heads. My mother tells me if the vent caves in, we will all become wanderers in search of another vent. The memories in our heads will be enough to get us there.

I have sisters and brothers. Our generation is special that way. My parents said that there was a period of time when the water became too salty and the microbes wouldn't grow, so there were no shrimp to eat. Nobody could lay an egg and the oldest generation died off without replacement. When the water finally cleared and the shrimp came back, everyone felt that it would be okay for parents to lay more than one egg. My mother felt that it would be okay to lay several.

I read about the salty era in the mat. What my parents don't talk about are the giant crabs that came with the salty water. The crabs attacked us, ending many of our lives early. It was Old Crehar who figured out the right way to zap the crabs, stopping them cold and drifting. So, in the absence of the shrimp, my parents survived on crab meat. My mother doesn't like crab meat, but here she is and I have sisters and brothers.

Old Crehar was a wanderer before he set down at our vent. He claims to have traveled all the way to the upper boundary. He says that if you rise very slowly your head will not explode. This was recorded in the mat, but some of us wonder if it is true. Old Crehar can carry two conversations at once. My sisters and I sing, "Of Old Crehar take heed, the love he flashes you, the same he flashes me." Not that Crehar flashes to me in any special way, but I have seen him proposition two or three of my sisters at the same time. He flashes chemiluminescent images of monogamy to each, the old fool.

There is no one flashing at me in a special way. It may be because of my lack of symmetry, but it is true that I have always been a drifter. When we gather together over the mat and groom our memories, the smell of contentment permeates the water and the warmth of my sisters and brothers becomes too much for me and I can't help rising to the fresh coolness above. Perhaps it is hard to flash at someone who is always on the verge of drifting away.

To survive a fish attack, don't become distracted by the teeth. Instead, grab the fish with your strongest legs and squeeze until the gills pop open. Quickly slip the tips of your delicate legs deep into the gills. Then, zap its tiny brain and feast upon your enemy. That is what I learned and what I sang for the mat.

Old Crehar says that the world goes on forever in every direction except up. He says that the mat at his first vent was so large that everyone must be a tender, and everyone must lay an egg. The entire history of the world is recorded there. Or so he says. He also said that my missing leg would grow back after the fish attack, but it is still short and stubby.

Sometimes when we are gathered together and the water becomes too warm for me, I drift up and up and I wonder if I could make it to the upper boundary. I wonder if I could drift all the way to another vent. I know it is dangerous to wander out there, but I am missing a leg and I know how to kill a fish.

[From the memories of Grover Benoit. Transcript created using third person extended Coi method in conjunction with secondary sources.]

Grover glanced at the chemical signature of sample AH537272 and then wished he hadn't. He wished the samples sent back from the Lemnosa probe network had never been collected. He wished the Lemnosa probe network had never been deployed. He wished he had never noticed the tiny orbital blip that had revealed Lemnosa's frozen face to the elemental hunger of Benoit Mining Venture. He wished he and his brother Reuben had never founded the Benoit Mining Venture. He wished Reuben were here.

At that moment Reuben was little more than information. His last checkpoint in life was recorded on Earth, where an atomic imaging machine had recorded the location and relationship of his every atomic connection to the world, and in the process reduced his physical body to an insignificant pile of carbon.

Reuben's information was now traveling across the vacuum of space to Sedna Way, where a nonillion nanobots were waiting to reassemble him in a molecular printer. Even at the speed of light, it would be seven days before he lived again. And the first tribulation of his continued life would be Grover's message following him, explaining that their risky venture had just become significantly riskier.

So risky, Grover thought, that perhaps they should fold. Perhaps they should announce to the world that life existed on Lemnosa and settle for the minor fame, though not fortune, associated with the discovery. But they had invested everything they had in the mining expedition. If the venture folded there would be no resources to pay for another atomic shuffle across space. The brothers would be separated indefinitely and very possibly forever. And it wasn't like it was the first alien ocean discovered to have something strange swimming in it.

If the venture succeeded, Lemnosa would become the next big way station. If the brothers were correct about the elemental composition of the moon's mantel, their mining expedition could support the creation of the newest node in the Interplanetary Light-speed Transportation system. They would be united on Lemnosa, in possession of one of the new economy's most highly sought charters and all of the mineral wealth needed to exploit it.

But all of their data and statistical models had predicted a barren moon, and the charter Reuben was on his way to apply for might not be granted if life existed on Lemnosa.

And exist it did. The earliest samples imaged on Lemnosa and transmitted back to BMV headquarters on Earth had revealed a wide variety of microbial life forms living in and under the ice at the moon's equator. Further samples captured an array of multicellular organisms swimming in the ocean. And now, here was another unfortunate organism that had been reduced to carbon dust and an image file. Grover turned his attention to sample AH537272. It had a significant mass compared to the other Lemnosan organisms, but was not the largest the probes had discovered. He twirled the 3D image on his display. It was kidney shaped, with no discernible sense organs. It didn't even have a mouth. Grover frowned. He examined a cross sectional view and saw a diverse group of internal organs, several of them highly complex. Well, he would throw it in the Box and see what happened.

Grover's Box AI read the atomic image of Sample AH537272 and simulated the organism. Then it began to run through the most basic of stimuli. Did it respond to electromagnetic radiation? Did it respond to pressure? Did it respond to magnetic fields? Did it respond to thermal radiation? Did it respond to chemical gradients? Once the sense organs were established, the AI set about establishing optimal parameters for each sense, fine tuning the simulated environment for further interactions. Again and again, the box AI initiated the sample's simulation a billion times simultaneously, each existence stressed in a slightly different way, then terminated. All of this happened so fast, that before Grover had time to message the future existence of his brother, a simulation of sample AH537272 was drifting in a dimly lit, slightly salty simulated ocean, unaware of the sensory horrors her fellow iterations had experienced to place her there. Grover watched curiously as she cautiously unfolded her legs, her kidney shape blooming into a flower of billowing tentacles. He dropped an avatar into the simulation and picked up the Box controllers.

[From the memories of Sample AH537272 v1.1. Transcript created using the Mahala method.]

Impossibly, I was drifting near the vent of my childhood. Everything was slightly wrong, but not in a way that was easy to sense. I was near the vent. The warmth, the pressure of the water, the shapes and smells drifting just over the horizon all told me I was, but the vent was not reachable.

A shadow in the distance began to worry me. Unlike the familiar things that hovered at the edge of my perception, this shadow grew. It scuttled through the water using long legs like a crab, but as it approached I could see that it had no shell or pinchers, and it had only four legs. It had soft skin like mine but it looked forward like a fish and I could hear hard teeth around its mouth. It swam toward me with its strange, pulsing leg movement. As it came closer I saw that on top of what must be its head there were thousands of incredibly thin tentacles, waving in its wake. Was it a shrimp eater? Or a fish?

I drifted toward the unreachable vent. My heart began to race. The creature never stopped coming and the vent never came any closer. I flashed the colors of the water. I am not here, I said. I am just a shadow on the edge of your perception, drifting by. But the thing could see me. It tracked me with its bulbous eyes and it was much too close. It began to smell of excitement. I unfurled my longest legs. It kept coming.

I was swift. I propelled forward and back, my legs were fast. It was strangely un-ferocious. It tasted like crab.

[From the memories of Grover Benoit. Transcript created using third person extended Coi method in conjunction with secondary sources.]

Grover dropped the controllers of the Box simulator and gave himself a moment to adjust to the real world. The attack had been so vicious. He had only wanted to make contact. Apparently he was not going about it the right way. After a few minutes he thought of an alternative approach.

[From the memories of Sample AH537272 v1.2. Transcript created using the Mahala method.]

Impossibly, I was drifting near the vent of my childhood. Everything was slightly wrong, but not in a way that was easy to sense. I was near the vent. The warmth, the pressure of the water, the shapes and smells drifting just over the horizon all told me I was, but the vent was not reachable.

A shadow in the distance began to worry me. It drifted closer and its shape emerged. I could hear the familiar form of many legs. I began to drift toward it. Was it someone from the vent? Someone I knew?

It was one of my sisters! No. No it was not one of my sisters. I unfurled my longest legs and she mirrored my every move. She was not intimidated. Strangely, she and I were missing the same leg. My heart began to race. I could not smell her in the water, but every smell of mine seemed twice as strong.

Hello, we sang at each other.

Of who are you? We sang at the same time. My fear in the water was suffocating.

I was swift. I propelled away. Away into the fresh water. Away as far as I could go.

[From the memories of Grover Benoit. Transcript created using third person extended Coi method in conjunction with secondary sources.]

Grover watched Sample AH537272 v1.2 interact with herself and then picked up the Box controllers to try again.

[From the memories of Sample AH537272 v1.1.1. Transcript created using the Mahala method.]

... Was it a shrimp eater? Or a fish?

I drifted toward the unreachable vent. My heart began to race. It never stopped coming and the vent never came any closer. I flashed the colors of the water. I am not here, I said. I am just a shadow on the edge of your perception, drifting by. But the thing could see me. It tracked me with its bulbous eyes and it was much too close. It began to smell of excitement. I unfurled my longest legs. It stopped and drifted in place, a body's length from my reach. Its longest legs drifted down but its shorter legs remained up. I paused to give it time to consider the greater reach of my legs, then I mirrored its gesture, my legs drifting down. But not all the way.

Hello, it sang through its mouth.

Hello, I sonicated back, startled.

The skin around its mouth receded, the teeth flashed. It was a fish.

I didn't wait. I propelled forward and back, my legs were fast. It was strangely un-ferocious. It tasted like crab.

[From the memories of Sample AH537272 v1.1.1.1. Transcript created using the Mahala method.]
... Its longest legs drifted down but its shorter legs remained up. I paused to give it time to consider the greater reach of my legs, then I mirrored its gesture, my legs drifting down. But not all the way.

Hello, it sang through its mouth.

Hello, I sonicated back, startled.

It pressed the skin around its mouth together tightly. It seemed to be waiting for something.

Of what you eat? I sang.

Of shrimp, it replied.

I eat of shrimp as well, I said.

I was swift. I propelled forward and back, my legs were fast. It was strangely un-ferocious. It tasted like crab.

[From the memories of Sample AH537272 v1.1.1.2. Transcript created using the Mahala method.]
... Its longest legs drifted down but its shorter legs remained up. I paused to give it time to consider the greater reach of my legs, then I mirrored its gesture, my legs drifting down. But not all the way.

Hello, it sang through its mouth.

Hello, I sonicated back, startled.

It pressed the skin around its mouth together tightly. It seemed to be waiting for something.

Of what you eat? I sang.

There was a long pause.

Of fish? It said, as if it weren't quite sure.

I eat of shrimp, I said. We can be friends.

[From the memories of Grover Benoit. Transcript created using third person extended Coi method in conjunction with secondary sources.]
Grover and Reuben disagreed about Sample AH537272. Grover, who had spent Reuben's transit time twiddling his thumbs over the controllers of the Box simulator, was rather cautious. Reuben, being the one potentially stranded at Sedna Way, was feeling more opportunistic. Their conversation was choppy, separated as they were by space.

"Think about it, Grover, she's the first truly intelligent being we encountered and we killed her. How is that going to play out when we need permission from these squid-things to mine their ocean floor? What if she could be our ally... our ambassador...?" [seven weeks ago]

Growing up, it had always been like this. Reuben saying what if, what if, while Grover clung stubbornly to the plan. If Grover said first person to the fence wins, Reuben would say what if the first person over the fence wins? If Grover said let's build a telescope and look at the moon, Reuben would say what if we build a bigger telescope and look at Saturn's moons? If Grover said lets send an expedition to Lemnosa and establish a mine, Reuben would say what if we could get a charter...

"We don't need an ally, Reuben, we need a charter." [six weeks ago]

"What we'll get is a provisional charter. What if the squid-things object to our mining operation? Would the charter be renewed? All of this is new, there is no precedent for placing a way station on an occupied territory." [five weeks ago]

"We only have enough raw material on Lemnosa to print the mining bots." [four weeks ago]

"So we reduce the initial number of mining bots we print. We'll have enough. Think Grover, we can't begin our relationship with the squid-things by killing one. Our probe imaged her, now we need to return her." [three weeks ago]

"But even if we bring her back into being, it's not likely she'll be our ally. In the simulations I end up as her lunch more often than as her friend." [two weeks ago]

"What if, instead of printing Sample AH537272 on Lemnosa, we print Sample AH537272 v1.1.1.2? Give her the best impression of us you can, then upload her to the printer." [one week ago]

Grover frowned. There was no precedent for bringing a simulation into being either. He sent his response.

"I don't want to do it." [today]

In a week he expected a message would arrive from Reuben convincing him that he should.

[From the memories of Sample AH537272 v1.1.1.2.9. Transcript created using the Mahala method.]

...Grover said goodbye and the world changed. I was floating in the dark, then a great whoosh of current pressed me up against a smooth rock. The rock shifted and I was washed into the frigid, bright water of the upper boundary. My legs contracted involuntarily while I drifted, adjusting to the sudden change. The blue and white contours of the boundary glowed painfully above me, speckled with algae and skirted by fish. Emerging from the icy boundary was the rock that had just spit me out, which I could now see was one of Grover's machines. I listened to the hollow chambers inside of it and the gentle humming of its entrails. Below me, currents traveled deeper than the light. I was a wanderer again.

Before meeting Grover, the ice seemed so hostile. Where it glowed, the light was blinding, and where it didn't glow, lurked the hungry fish. But now the very threat was comforting. What is a fish to me? I know what to do with a fish. I listened to the ice groan and pop above me and tried to imagine that another world existed on the other side, a world like the one Grover flashed for me. How did Grover flash an entire world?

When I could extend my legs, I drifted up to Grover's machine and explored its surface. Once I found the hinge and edge, I popped it open like a shell. At the very center was a small chamber that hummed. The guts of the machine were acidic in places and there were many long tendrils radiating out from the noisy chamber.

I zapped the chamber until the humming stopped. It tasted terrible and I didn't eat it. Then I began the long journey home.

When I get there I will sing to the mat about how to kill a machine.

[From the memories of Grover Benoit. Transcript created using third person extended Coi method in conjunction with secondary sources.]

Grover watched the simulation of his ninth attempt to send Sample AH537272 v1.1.1.2 home with despair. She didn't trust him. She destroyed the printer every time. They would never be able to return her to Lemnosa. Why wouldn't she trust him? If only Reuben were here! Reuben would say what if... what if... but Grover's imagination failed. He did not know what Reuben would say.

Grover's next idea was as simple as it was preposterous. What if Reuben *were* here? He had Reuben's check point image file. He had the Box. He knew how to hack the safeguards. The possibility tickled his brain and impulsively he acted on it.

[From the memories of Reuben Benoit v1.1. Transcript created using the Mahala method.]

I did a quick audit of the print job. I counted my fingers and toes, calculated the amount of ore we would have to pull out of the Lemnosan mantle to pay for my return trip, and said "Hello, my name is Reuben." Everything seemed to be in working order. The chamber door opened with a hiss of released pressure. What seemed like ten minutes ago, I said goodbye to Grover, but now I was 1200 AU from home. I wiped my hands on my pants and looked out curiously. It's not every day that you get to travel across the solar system and I wasn't sure what to expect. It looked like Earth. The same bioengineered construction materials, the same tracks of led lights guiding the same people down a gently sloping corridor, through customs and out the door. And then a canned voice:

"Welcome to Earth. Thank you for traveling the Interplanetary Lightspeed Transportation System."

Christ, I hadn't even left the planet? I waved a hand at the nearest attendant. "Hey, there must be a mistake. I'm traveling to Sedna Way!"

"Any questions you have regarding your destination may be directed to the Customer Service Desk on the other side of customs. Thank you for traveling with Interplanetary Lightspeed Transportation."

"Reuben! Over here!" Grover appeared and his voice sounded relieved. He waved to me from the other side of customs and I hurried through.

"Reuben, There was a problem at the Sedna Way station so I had them send you here."

My stomach lurched. A problem?

"But it's a good thing because I need to talk to you. Come on, let's get some lunch."

"Look, just tell me, did I have a near miss or something?"

"No... and they don't know how long the delay will be. Listen, I met someone, and I want her to like me, but I don't know, she doesn't seem to trust me," Grover looked at me expectantly.

"We're getting a refund, right?"

"Don't worry, I've taken care of the refund. So what do you think I should do? How can I get her to like me better?"

"Where are we?" I asked.

"New Camden Station. It was the first place I... It was the first place I could get you printed at." Grover looked a little queasy. Was there something he wasn't telling me?

"Look, Grover, if there's something you need to tell me, just tell me. You know me, I'll imagine all kinds of crazy things until you tell me..."

Grover laughed and nearly knocked me over with a hug. How long have I been gone, I wondered.

"It's okay Reuben, I'm taking care of everything. Lemnosa is still a go."

I pounded him on the back. If he said it was fine, that was all I needed to know.

"Let's get some lunch," I said, and we followed the trail of lights out of the station.

We stepped out onto the red brick walkway of Pratt Street and shouldered our way through a slow procession of orange-shirted Orioles fans making the pilgrimage to Camden Yards for a ball game.

"What if we grab a beer and take in the game?" I said, prepared to make the best of the delay.

Grover shook his head and propelled me against the flow of fans, past the street hawkers, past the Pratt Street Ale House and into a hamburger joint.

Outside a cheer went up as someone dressed as a large black bird with an orange beak trotted by, shaking his wings in the air and hugging people dressed in orange.

Inside, a neon light flashed: Shakes. Burgers. Fries. The floor and walls were covered in black and white tile and red leather bar stools lined one side of the restaurant. We slipped into a hard plastic booth. A cheerful waitress in a pink apron and a tight polyester dress took our order, pen to pad and a big smile for Grover. I wondered how often he came here.

"I've never noticed this place before. How'd you find it?"

"Uh, I don't know. So this friend of mine, got any idea how I can make her like me more?"

Outside a cheer went up. The big black bird was hugging people again.

The waitress leaned over our table, giving us a nice glimpse of her cleavage. "Have you tried flowers? I'd like you if you sent me flowers," she said, winking at Grover and setting down our burgers.

"Yeah, that's a good idea," I said, staring at the waitress. She looked familiar. "Girls like that stuff... some flowers or a gift or something..."

"No, it's not like that Reuben, it's not that kind of thing..." Of course it wasn't. Grover didn't even notice that the waitress was hitting on him, he never did. He should be asking for her number, not chasing this girl that doesn't even like him. He just never sees the possibilities.

The hamburger was the best burger I have ever had. Grover put his aside and leaned across the table. "I don't think she wants flowers. Maybe you should meet her, then you'll understand."

"What if you got the waitress's number," I said, "and just forgot about this other girl?"

"There is life on Lemnosa." Grover said.

I choked. Christ, that was going to complicate things.

"I put this organism in the Box and it's smart, really smart. We may have to get its consent to mine on Lemnosa."

The waitress passed by and winked at Grover.

Outside a cheer went up as someone dressed as a large black bird with an orange beak trotted by, shaking his wings in the air and hugging people dressed in orange.

"Grover, there's something wrong with this place. The people here are repeating themselves..." Grover looked queasy again. Suddenly I remembered where I had seen the waitress before.

"Grover, is that the waitress from your Derby Box simulation?" My jaw dropped. What if he had simulated a real person in the Derby Box? What kind of trouble was he in?

"Grover what have you done?"

"I just needed to talk to you..."

And suddenly I realized it wasn't the waitress he had simulated.

"Did you hack my image file? Did you simulate me? Why would you do that?" Christ, I thought, what if I'm dead? What if I'm dead but Grover still needs me? "What happened at Sedna Way?!"

"Relax Reuben, you're fine, you're fine, nothing has happened to you. You are at Sedna Way. It's just a pain talking over long distance... so I..." Christ, Grover looked ill. He was sweating and the blood had left his face.

"I'm not at Sedna Way, Grover! Someone else is at Sedna Way. I'm right here, in your stupid Derby simulation!"

"It's not the Derby, its Baltimore."

"But I'm alive in here! You've put me in a goldfish bowl!"

Grover flinched and looked like he was going to vomit. Suddenly he reached for something I couldn't see. I grabbed his arm, "Are you turning it off? Christ! You're going to turn it off aren't you? I don't want to die! I don't want to d..."

[From the memories of Grover Benoit. Transcript created using third person extended Coi method in conjunction with secondary sources.]

Reuben's next message arrived:

"The good news is it looks like we're getting the temporary charter. The snag is that by the time we renew we have to have proof that we have a good relationship with the Lemnosans. What if we printed a team of AH537272s? We could really jump start this relationship."

Grover replied:

"Worst idea you have ever had. Don't worry, I'm taking care of it."

[From the algae mat of Lemnosa's fifth largest vent field. Translation courtesy of The Lemnosan Historical Society, methods unknown.]

The vent of my adulthood is new and the mat is filled with the memories of many wanderers like myself. I have sung for the mat everything I remember from the old mat. I have sung how to survive a fish attack and what to do if you are missing a leg.

What Old Crehar says is true. If you rise very slowly, your head will not explode, and you can travel all the way to the upper boundary.

It's a long time to be drifting with the fish, but if you tuck your legs in and flash the colors of the water, the fish will swim right by.

The blue and white contours of the boundary will glow painfully above you, speckled with algae and skirted by fish. You are looking for a very special fish. It is metallic and white and it hums as it swims through the water. It will listen for you, and if it hears you it will open a large black eye and blink.

Your world will go black, but if you listen you will hear that you are in a cave with no opening. The water will smell of stale contentment and once you settle down a voice will sonicate, "Of we are pleased to meet you. Of please accept this gift from the Benoit of Mining Company."

Then a great whoosh of current will press you against the side of the cave. The side will give and you will be washed into the frigid water of the upper boundary. To your new leg, the water will be shockingly cold and unnervingly fish scented, dangerous but gloriously right.

A question for Kato Thompson

Q: What tools do you write with?

A: My favorite tools are questions. What if? How might that happen? What could possibly go wrong? I usually answer these questions while drinking a good cup of coffee and scratching on a piece of paper with a pencil. Sometimes this produces elaborate doodles instead of writing, but it's a fun way to start. Once I have an outline or at least a sketch of what I want to write about, I move on to a keyboard. The keyboard is a very important tool for me because a) I can type faster than I can write, and b) my pencil doesn't have spellcheck. But the most important tool I have in my writer's arsenal is a long walk. When my plot is twisting in the wrong way and my dialogue is growing sleepy, there is nothing like a long walk to give me perspective and wake up those inner voices. Plus, the dog loves it. Like Douglas Adams' character, Dirk Gently, who claims he rarely ends up where he was intending to go, but often ends up somewhere that he needed to be, I think sometimes you can set out intending to write the next best thing in short fiction but end up making the dog happy and that is okay.

About Kato Thompson

Kato Thompson lives in Maryland where she writes and takes pictures of interesting things. She has a background in microbiology and life sciences. When she isn't taking care of children or writing or taking pictures, she is learning about the art of winemaking at her family's vineyard.

She shares her work at www.katothompson.com.

Seeders

Jamie Killen

The wheat died three days after Elin's skin began to itch.

The itching started as a rash on the backs of her hands, little round bumps standing out from her skin. She ignored it at first, went to work at the diner as always. But by the third day it had spread up her arms and started on her feet. She came downstairs early in the morning after a sleepless night, knowing her parents would already be up. "Mama, do you have any..." Elin trailed off when she saw her mother's red-rimmed eyes.

"It's here," her mother sniffed. "Donnelly's fields started turning black yesterday afternoon."

Elin didn't need to ask what that meant. She'd been following the news same as everyone else in town. The reports had been coming in for months, sober journalists and distraught farmers talking about the blight jumping from one field to the next in less than a day. By the end of the week it would have spread through the rest of the county.

Still her father put on his cap and went out to tend the fields. She wanted to tell him to stop, that there was no point. And sure enough, two days later she stood with her parents between the two main fields and gagged at the stench of the wheat disintegrating into black sludge. Something about it made her skin itch worse than ever, drove her running back into the house to smear lotion all over her body.

When Elin came out of the bathroom, she saw her mother standing silently at the kitchen sink. "Mama," Elin said, touching her mother's arm. "It's..." All the things she'd been about to say—*it's gonna be OK, I'll figure something out, we'll find a way to fix it*—died on her lips when she saw the bleak look in her mother's eyes. Instead, she gave her mother a quick kiss on the cheek and headed out to her truck. She looked for "Help Wanted" signs on her way to the diner, felt her chest tighten a little more with each mile she passed without seeing one.

Elin's father was the one to break the silence at the dinner table that night. "We'll switch crops next season. It's only the wheat that's dying, we'll start on cotton or corn," he said, smiling as though that was that.

"And I'm gonna start looking for a second job. One that pays better," Elin added.

"Thank you, sweetie," her father said, shame and guilt creeping into his voice.

Elin's mother looked down at her plate, mouth twisted. Elin knew what was going through her head; it wouldn't matter, the bank wouldn't care what had happened to them, the credit card companies wouldn't care, the insurance company wouldn't care, no job Elin could get would ever make a dent in the bills...

Elin clenched her fists to keep from scratching at herself. She wore long sleeves despite the summer heat, long sleeves to cover the welts on her arms. Her mother would insist on taking her to the hospital if she knew, bills be damned. So she dug her fingernails into her burning palms and excused herself from the table.

The next morning, Elin arrived at the diner in a turtleneck and big sunglasses. Her face burned worse than the rest of her, the pancake makeup she'd slathered on making her itch so bad she couldn't stop from grinding her teeth together. She'd barely managed to get out of the house without her mother seeing her.

Hazel's eyes widened as soon as she went in the back for her apron. "Elin, what on Earth—"

Elin avoided her gaze. "It's nothing. Just left a window open last night, and the mosquitoes got in."

Hazel marched across the kitchen, her permed blond bubble of hair bouncing with every step. "Jesus, those aren't mosquito bites! Let me see."

"No! It's fine—"

But then Hazel's hand closed around her wrist, and she couldn't stop herself from shrieking in pain. Tears burned in lines down her face as Hazel slowly rolled up her sleeve and stared in horror at her arm.

"Elin," Hazel said after a moment, voice gone soft. "I don't know what this is, but it looks serious. You need to see a doctor. I'll call your Momma."

The entire week seemed to crash down around Elin. "I can't be sick now," she sobbed. "We're going to need the money. The harvest is all gone..."

Hazel started to hug her, stopping when Elin flinched. She stroked her hair instead. "I know, honey. It's awful. But you can't help your folks if you're... Like this. Listen," she said, fishing her cell phone out of her pocket. "I'll call Dr. Horsted. He's good people and he owes me a favor, so it won't cost an arm and a leg."

Elin perched on Dr. Horsted's exam table and tried not to pull away every time he touched her skin. He was a small man, a few inches shorter than her, with thinning hair and laugh lines around his eyes. He clucked and shook his head as he examined her arm. "Well, young lady, this is one heckuva rash you got here."

"It's disgusting," Elin said, staring down at herself. The bright-red bumps stood up a quarter inch from her skin, hot to the touch. Wherever there was pressure on one of them, it felt like something hard was inside, a splinter or a sliver of glass.

Dr. Horsted scribbled something on her chart. "I'm prescribing you a steroid cream and an anti-inflammatory until we know what it is. I'll take a skin scraping and send it in to see if it's an infection of some kind. I suspect not, though. I think it's an unusual allergic reaction, maybe something with the fields and that damn blight."

"Why do you think that?" Elin asked, frowning.

"Oh, you're not the only one I've seen who's got this. Started getting cases as soon as the blight hit."

"Who?"

Dr. Horsted gave her an admonishing look. "Oh, now, you know I can't say. But this is a small town. I'm sure you can find out." He paused. "Lord knows you can spot it a mile away."

Elin started calling the neighbors as soon as she convinced her mother to quit fussing over her. She stood in her attic room, shifting from one foot to the other. She wore her lightest clothing, a cotton nightgown her Aunt Cheryl had given her for Christmas. Even the thin cotton itched like mad everywhere it touched. The steroid cream didn't help at all.

"Hi, Mrs. Alston, this is Elin Rogers," she said, shifting to her right foot and staring out at the dead wheat field. "This might sound like an odd question, but I've been having some weird allergy to something, and I was wondering—"

Mrs. Alston cut in. "Is it a rash? All over?"

"Yeah, that's it."

"Oh, it's terrible," Mrs. Alston said. Her voice sounded tired, strained. "Dennis started getting that a few days ago. I thought maybe it was stress-related, because of the blight, but it seems too bad to be that. You haven't found a good way to treat it, have you?" she asked, a touch of hope in her voice.

Elin sighed. "No, I was hoping someone else had. I need to get back to work, and I want to try to get a job that pays better than the diner, but right now I'm... No one would hire me like this."

Mrs. Alston said how sorry she was and promised to call if she figured something out. Mr. Alston's voice echoed in the background, and she hurriedly hung up.

Around sunset, Elin's mother brought her some soup. "Did you find any others besides Dennis Alston?" she asked.

Elin forced herself to sit down and sip a spoonful of the soup. "Three. Jenna Foster, Danny Innes, and Olive Olson."

Her mother's eyes widened. "Oh my God. Olive must be 85."

"86," Elin corrected. "Marie took her to the clinic in the city." She paused. "And Jenna's only seven."

Her mother sagged to the bed as though her strings had been cut. "They're all next to fields, aren't they?" She grimaced and shook her head. "I remember back when we all started buying seeds from the company. Old Margie Taylor kept going on and on about how if a disease came and we all had the same seeds, it'd take everything. She kept saying what a mistake it was, that any disease would spread like wildfire, but none of us listened. And now she's right and with the wheat dying we've got people getting sick, to boot. If someone decided to string up the people who run that seed company, I tell you, I'd be holding the rope."

"Mama!"

Her mother looked up as though realizing what she'd said. "I'm sorry, sweetie." She got up and kissed the top of Elin's head. "Goodnight. Wake me up if you feel worse."

Elin writhed on her bed, silent tears of pain soaking her pillow. She knocked away her comforter, pulled off her nightgown and underwear, but it made no difference. The only thing that helped was the cool night air coming in from the window. Her father and the hands had spent most of the last three days clearing the blighted sludge out of the fields, so the stench was gone. Now the air smelled as it should again, sweet and earthy. She bit back sobs, closed her eyes, and took deep gulping breaths of the night air.

Even after Elin dozed off, even after she began to dream, she remained aware of her burning skin. Through the pain she saw herself as though from above, her naked pale body studded with red sores. It wasn't just the flesh she knew, though; she saw deeper, under the skin, where delicate green tendrils glowed and pulsed. Elin wondered how long they had been growing, how long they had taken to make their way up to the surface of her skin; her muscles and bones were completely honeycombed with the pale green threads, like veins in a leaf.

Elin opened her eyes. She stood ankle-deep in the tilled dirt of the fields, at least 300 yards from the house. She was still naked, the night breeze bathing her burning skin. She stared down at herself and tried to understand why she wasn't embarrassed, why she felt only calm even though anyone could come along and see.

She walked slowly around the edge of the field. Her skin felt different from before; it still itched and burned, but now it seemed as though something moved within the sores. Elin gradually realized that she could hear little whispers, too quiet for her to know exactly what was being said. Still she found herself moving toward the edge of the field as though following directions.

When she reached the right place, things began to fall from her skin. They pushed their way from the sores on her arms legs face back, breaking free with a sharp little sting but leaving relief in their wake. Elin tipped her head back and walked with her eyes closed, going where her feet took her. Different kinds of things began to fall from the sores when she reached the opposite end of the field, slightly different shapes. This was as it should be, she understood. There had to be different kinds.

Finally, the last of them fell from the bottoms of her feet. The burning stopped. She collapsed into the cool dirt of the fields, asleep at last.

Elin awoke to grey predawn light, her mother's voice, a hand shaking her. "Elin! Elin! What happened? Wake up!"

As she opened her eyes, her father rushed out of the house with a blanket. He covered her and helped her to her feet over her mother's protests. "No, don't move her! We should call the ambulance."

"No, Mama, I'm fine," she said, voice soft but steady. "Look."

Her parents followed her gaze to the ground. Seedlings lay in untidy rows across the field, leaves already stretching up to grasp the morning light. "What are these?" her father asked, crouching to get a closer look.

"Wheat, beans, squash. Some watermelon and flax over on the other side."

"When did you do this?" he asked, squinting at one of the seedlings.

"Ron, it doesn't *matter* right now," her mother snapped. "We have to get her inside."

Elin gently pulled her arm away from her mother and walked inside on her own. She savored the sensation of skin that didn't burn, didn't itch. Even so, she could feel something starting deep under the skin again, something that would soon push up in search of light.

The next night, Elin still had seeds left after she'd finished her family's fields. The rest wouldn't pop, knowing the ground was already full. She slipped through a gap in the wire fence that separated their land from the Alstons'. The seeds began to emerge again as she walked, each leaping as they spotted the perfect patch of soil.

She found Mr. and Mrs. Alston across their east pasture, in a little strip of recently tilled land. He walked as she did, naked under the moonlight. Mrs. Alston followed, weeping and begging. "Elin!" she shrieked when she saw her. "What's going on? What's *happening*?"

Elin placed a gentle hand on Mrs. Alston's shoulder. Some part of her remembered how she would have felt in the past, standing naked in the fields. But that seemed like a very long time ago. "It's all going to be OK, Mrs. Alston. We're making it all better. It's making us better."

Mrs. Alston sniffed and nodded. "But—"

Elin gripped her by the shoulders. "You have to get Olive out of the clinic. She'll die there. Tell Marie to bring her to the fields. I told Mama and Daddy but they won't listen. Someone has to."

She turned away without waiting for an answer, following Mr. Alston down the field. She caught up to him at the edge. He frowned as if trying to hear something. "It needs more..."

"Here." Elin reached out to touch his hand. Something passed between them, the things that made up a plant with a name she couldn't recall. Sunflowers, she remembered at last. Mr. Alston nodded; Elin could almost hear the seeds reshaping under his skin. He passed something back to her just before breaking contact, a new strand. Seeds changed shape and swelled within her. Then they leapt from her skin, falling gently to their resting place.

Elin stopped wearing clothes during the day. She stopped going back inside the house. Her parents tried to drag her back a few times, but she always wandered out again. They tried to stop her from leaving their property, but she patiently explained that they didn't need any more seeds. The other fields did.

The words to explain things didn't come easy; it all seemed so obvious to Elin now. She couldn't quite remember why Mama and Dad couldn't grasp these things. It was too much effort, so she stopped trying.

Other people were the same. For the first few days, neighbors either yelled at her or tried to talk with big concerned eyes. She ignored them. Once they saw how fast the plants grew, and how much the harvest would be, they stopped yelling at her or Dennis Alston or any of the others who joined her in the fields. Her parents stopped trying to keep her from going. They still begged her to go back, though, every time they tracked her down and brought her lunch.

"I feel like I'm losing you," her mother sobbed one day. "I don't understand what's happening."

Elin touched her mother's cheek. "I'm not going anywhere. I'll be here for the rest of my life. I'm needed." For some reason, that made her mother cry even harder.

The next day they still brought her lunch, but they didn't ask her to come back. Just before they left, Elin found out why: "I talked to Marie," her father said. "Olive died in the hospital. At the end she was begging to be taken outside, somewhere with soil, but they didn't listen. By the end, her skin... " He stopped and hugged Elin to him. "You do what you have to."

Her mother nodded but kept crying. Elin tried to remember what her father used to do when that happened. There had been a kind of flower, a color...

The seed dropped from the back of her hand and sprouted as soon as it touched the soil. Her mother's eyes widened as she watched the seedling stretch up into the light, its leaves unfurling. Elin reached down and plucked the red flower whose name she'd forgotten. She handed it to her mother and walked away without another word.

One day, Elin stood with Dennis and Jenna and Danny on the edge of a field. They waited to see what it needed. None of the seeds she carried felt quite right, Elin decided. She reached out to touch the others. Together, they sifted through the pieces they carried. Jenna had something from a desert plant, something that would make it strong and tough in the heat. Dennis held the chemical that would drive the aphids away, Danny the speedy tangled growth of kudzu. Elin saw the taste of the fruit in her own blood, the thing that would make it sweet and tangy to the human tongue.

The pieces flowed and connected where their palms touched. Right away, Elin felt the seeds under her skin reshape. They pushed out and into the ground, taproots already seeking moisture. Elin smelled and tasted the plants the seeds would become: vines clinging to the ground like strawberry plants, fragrant white flowers turning into a hard-shelled fruit with light pink flesh inside.

Wordlessly, they moved away from the field and toward a patch of scrubby trees across the road, new seeds already forming beneath their skin.

One evening, they sat on a brick wall overlooking Johansen's field. The wheat now stood at hip height, the rest of the plants starting to bear fruit. Lacey Johansen came out of the house with a picnic basket. Elin had noticed that some farmer or another was always bringing them food now, usually too much. She couldn't quite remember why people did that. "Thought you all might be hungry," Lacey said, spreading out a blanket and unpacking a salad and roast chicken. "There's a key lime pie in there, too, if you want dessert," she said. She kept her gaze at face level, resolutely avoiding their nakedness. "I just can't thank you enough for all this. My daddy would have turned over in his grave if I'd had to sell."

"You're welcome," Elin said at last, when none of the others spoke.

"Been meaning to ask," Lacey said, hooking her thumbs in the belt of her jeans. "What strain is the wheat? Because it sure doesn't look like that stuff we got from the company."

"Not one strain," Jenna piped up, gnawing on a chicken leg.

"There's different ones," Elin clarified, trying to remember how to put these things into spoken language. There weren't any words for the way the genes danced and split and reconnected in her blood. "They'll... They'll cross. And make new ones. One disease won't get them all. And their seeds won't die after one generation."

Lacey let out a sigh of relief. "I was hoping you'd say that. It's hard to believe we put up with that horseshit for so long." She grinned. "Well, they ain't got us by the balls now."

One morning, Officer Eddie pulled up in his squad car and waved from the road as they passed through the trees on the edge of Wasilewski's fields. "Hey there," he said. Elin noticed vaguely that he took his hat off when he spoke to them. She remembered a month or so ago, when he'd tried to make them stop walking around naked. Something must have changed his mind.

"Whatchya working on?" he asked, face flushing with some kind of embarrassment.

"Soil ... Soil washing away. Stop," Dennis slurred. Elin felt a pang of sympathy. Dennis seemed to be losing language faster than the rest of them.

"Making new wildflower seeds," she added. "Stop soil from... Eroding."

Eddie nodded. She could see he didn't really understand or care. "Listen," he said, stepping forward. "I need to talk to you all about something. I guess you're spending most of your time outside these days, right? Haven't been on the internet lately?"

They stared back at him in silence. "Right, well," he rushed on, "this thing that's happening to all of you, it's happening all over. Not just the US, either, China and Russia and all kinds of other places. And... Well, I won't get into what's happening over there, but here, here in the US, there's rumors." He paused. "The big seed companies, the ones everyone around here used to buy from, they keep trying to get, you know... People like you to let them study them. And they all been saying no, every one. But some Seeders, that's what people are calling you, some of them are going missing, and there was one where a van was seen driving away. The FBI says it's nothing, but there's people on forums think it's Monsanto and some of the other big agro companies. See, no one's gonna buy their seeds anymore, and so—"

"We understand," Elin said, feeling the attention of the others drift away from his words.

"Anyway," Eddie said, clearing his throat. "I got the whole town on the lookout, but you be careful. Maybe one of you could carry a cell phone or something, just in case? No? Well, that's OK. Just be careful."

Three days after Eddie spoke to them, the first showed up. "Excuse me, Miss? Sir? Could I have a quick word?"

He was a tall, slender man wearing khakis and small wire-rimmed glasses. He called from the side of the road, where a small black car was parked. Elin turned and stared at him but didn't get any closer. She felt the rest gather behind her.

The man seemed to realize that they weren't going to come near him. "Hi Miss, Rogers, is it? Miss Rogers, I represent an agricultural research institute. We're very interested in finding ways to help farmers like the good people of this town, especially after this terrible blight. We—"

"Nnn... Our seeds. Our seeds, n-not your ssseeeeds," Dennis gurgled.

"You aren't welcome here," Elin said. "Not needed."

The man paused, then smiled wider. "Miss, I don't think you understand. We want to work *with* you—"

"Hey!"

Lacey Johansen marched up the road between her fields, a shotgun held against her shoulder. "You just move the fuck on, mister. Leave these people alone."

The man took two steps back. "This is a public road," he said weakly.

"I've already called the sheriff. He can decide if you're trespassing." The shotgun didn't waver.

The man stared at Lacey, opened his mouth as if to speak again, and finally climbed back into the car. Lacy didn't lower the shotgun until he disappeared around the bend. "Everyone OK?"

Elin nodded. "Thank you, Lacey. But not... Not necessary. *We,*" she said gesturing to the others. "We can take care."

Night. The rest of the Seeders rested by the creek. In the morning when they rose there would be beds of a spongy new moss in the shape of their bodies. But Elin didn't feel like sleeping. She wandered the dirt road winding past all those farms, all those acres. All of them were rich and green now, bending under the weight of fruits that people had always known and others they had never tasted. Elin couldn't remember the name of any of them anymore, even the ones she'd seen and eaten all her life.

Elin stopped to shed a single large seed from the palm of her hand. It landed in a hollow by the side of the road. It would be a tree thirty feet in diameter when it was grown, solid and tall and happy to subsist on the small amount of water in the sandy soil. She felt, like a vibration in the ground, these same trees being planted far, far away, everywhere people like her walked. When she closed her eyes, she could see the homes people would build of these trees, the new plants she would seed on their branches, ones that could eat waste, make light, heal.

A van pulled slowly from the shoulder of the road, lights off. It halted beside her, kicking up a puff of dust. The door flew open, and the barrel of a gun glinted under the moon. "Get in."

Elin watched the man with the gun. She could feel one more behind him and one in the driver's seat, all smelling of oil and gunmetal. Wordlessly, she shuffled to the open van door. Her skin burned.

"Put your hands in the air, palms facing me," the man said.

She smiled and obeyed.

The seeds stung as they shot from the skin of her hands, spattering the three men in the van. They screamed as the seeds rooted in their skin, drawing nutrients from their blood and exploding into barbed thorns that shredded through their muscle and bone. One of them managed to fire his gun, but he didn't know what to aim at and the bullet thudded harmlessly into the dirt roadside. Within thirty seconds, the screams had stopped. Within sixty seconds, roots had consumed the last of their blood and flesh. The van now contained nothing but a dense thicket of barbs and thorns filling the cab and bursting out of the doors and windows.

Elin turned her back on the van and moved on, already forgetting about the men with the guns. She felt a stretch of earth on the side of the road where the soil needed more plants to keep it from blowing away. Pausing, she thought about what kind they should be; some faint memory flitted through her mind, someone who felt better when she saw red flowers. Elin smiled, continuing on her slow walk; everywhere she stepped, the ground bloomed with deep crimson petals.

A question for Jamie Killen

Q: Is there a specific environment you find most conducive to writing, and is it different for different kinds of scenes?

A: The only place I can get any writing done is in my home office. I've never been able to write in public places like coffee shops, and I can't get any writing done if there is any kind of distraction (including music). In order to write I need quiet, stillness, and the comforting/sinister presence of the Dalek sculpture I keep on my desk.

About Jamie Killen

When Jamie Killen isn't writing, she's traveling the world in search of new story ideas. She's also an educator and a trained historian. She lives in Arizona with several other monsters.

March

La Belle Dame

Sabrina Balmick

The scribe met the knight on the old stone road. The castle was a couple of hours away. Three, at the speed his donkey was trotting. He'd meant to deliver his news of no news and stumble off to a bath and, if he were lucky, into a warm bed with a warm wench. Instead he found himself conversing with a knight who hunkered in a smear of blue-violet twilight. Cloaked in shadows, he looked like Death himself, waiting to claim unwary travelers.

But that was foolish. Death certainly wouldn't bother sitting in the road. And He would likely smell better. No, this was definitely a man. Why he lurked here, half-rotting, Tom could hardly guess.

Tom's lips opened to greet the knight, but his jaw snapped shut when he recognized the dirty surcoat. Of gold and scarlet, it was: the king's colors. He urged his donkey closer for a better look. In the dim light, the coat looked roughly the color of mud, but beneath the mud glinted the king's eagle emblem and within the eagle's mouth dangled a rose, the sigil of the king's champion. This was no ordinary knight.

"Sir Thomas?" said Tom. "We've been searching for you." Shortly after Sir Thomas disappeared, the king had dispatched knights and scribes all over the countryside carrying letters inquiring after his most valued knight, and the queen's own brother, besides. He was also betrothed to the king's cousin, Lady Enid. And here he was, right under Tom's nose. Where had he been for the last seven months? What had he done to find himself on this lonely road looking half-dead?

The knight scarcely stirred at the sound of Tom's voice, as though no sound reached him but the evening wind whistling through a scattering of shabby trees. Tom dismounted from his donkey and approached the knight.

Was he truly dead, then? It would be Tom's questionable luck to find Sir Thomas *and* lose him in exactly the same moment.

Sighing, Tom reached for the wine skin in his cloak pocket and pulled a long draught and then another. Red wine sloshed around the half-empty skin as he drank, his mind filling with blood as he filled his mouth with wine. He cringed and stoppered the skin, shoving it roughly inside his pocket. He'd never liked the sight of blood. It was why he had become a scribe instead of a knight—that curious sense of self-preservation others might have dubbed cowardice.

Tom nudged the man with his foot and, expecting him to tip over, nearly wet himself when the knight's head turned and he spoke.

"Why are you kicking me?" Summer blue eyes bored through Tom, barely seeing him, searching the sky, the far corners of the world for goodness knew what.

Tom, unnerved by that bright blue stare, gathered his wits. "I thought you were dead," he explained. "Obviously you're not. Honest mistake, really. Are you hurt? Why are you sitting here? Don't you know the king's been searching for you all this time?"

The knight sighed. "That," he answered, "is a relative question." A golden harp lay beside him. He reached for it to pluck out a languid tune.

"Which question? All of them? Or just one?" Tom slumped down next to the knight, half-listening to his song. Pleasant it was, like a snatch of summer wind.

The knight shrugged. "One. None. All of them. It doesn't matter. You should go. There's nothing to be done here." His fingers stilled and his song faded.

Tom studied Sir Thomas with interest, now that he was certain the knight wasn't dead. He appeared well enough, though pallor clung to his cheeks. His lips were stained with blood, but his face, the same face ladies all over court and creation swooned over, remained unharmed. Golden brown hair fell over his brow in greasy hanks, skimming a nose that had been broken years ago in a fight. His jaw was shadowed with beard.

If Tom was truthful, and often he was, he'd admit to being more than a little jealous of the knight. He should have disliked him thoroughly. Only Lady Enid's indifference to her betrothed endeared him to Tom. The scribe clung to her indifference, rather. Would she be indifferent to Sir Thomas now, if she saw him? She had a weakness for a lost cause.

They were as different as two men could be, thought Tom. The only thing they shared in common was a name. A name and Enid.

The scribe snorted. Sir Thomas, knight of the realm and collector of hearts. Tom, scribe of the realm and collector of wine tankards. Even Tom's surname, Rhymer, mocked him. He lacked talent for verse, the first of his name with a tin ear for meter. For this reason, he'd ended up a mere scribe instead of a bard, as his father and his father's father and countless forefathers had been. Great shame of the family, it was. The knight, he'd heard, had had a gift for music once. Pity to waste it, but that was knights for you.

Reaching into his pocket, Tom fetched out his wine skin once again and pulled the stopper out with his teeth, handing the skin to the knight, who accepted it with the faintest nod. He raised the skin to his lips for a long drink, driblets of purple trickling down his chin and throat. He returned the skin and wiped his mouth with the back of a grubby hand. Tom stoppered the skin and placed it back in his pocket. "*Are* you Sir Thomas?"

"I don't know who I am anymore," drawled the knight. "But, once, I did answer to that name."

Tom rolled his eyes. "Whatever name you call yourself, the king's been looking for you. No one's caught sight of you since summer tournament, not once."

"They wouldn't have," said Thomas. "Not where I've been."

"Well," said Tom good-naturedly, "It's a fortunate thing I've found you. You can go home now. It's not very far. My donkey's good and stout. She'll carry you there, even with that armor." He resigned himself to walking. Gladys wouldn't be able to carry them both.

The knight's eyes fixed upon him once more, blazing with blue flame. "I'm not going back. I must wait here. For her."

"You're coming back with me. Even if I have to club you with your own sword."

Sir Thomas' shoulders rose and fell with his sigh. "I must see her first. Besides, I'll be dead before I reach the kingdom. Too much trouble for your poor donkey."

"D-dead?"

The knight opened his fists to reveal several nightshade flowers, industriously chewed. "It doesn't act as quickly as I thought, but I'm glad of it nonetheless."

The scribe groaned. The king would definitely be angry. "You have to make a tea with it if you want to … to die more quickly. This way, you sort of … linger." He shuddered, recalling the stories he'd transcribed of men trapped half-in and half-out of death. A cruel thing. He threw the knight a sidelong glance, stunned and a little frightened to see him smiling.

"Good," Thomas said cheerfully. "She can't deny me now."

"You're an extremely strange person."

"I've had an extremely strange time."

Tom fumbled the wine skin back out of his pocket and took a good long drink. "I suppose you'd better tell me about it, then, while we wait for … whoever it is you're waiting on."

Thomas's smile faltered a moment, and returned. "It began on the first day of summer tournament, a week after I became engaged to Lady Enid. Tell me, Tom, have you ever heard of the road to enchantment?"

I met the lady among the hawthorn trees. I'd slipped away from the celebrations, drunk on claret, my eyes heavy with sunlight, and found an agreeable patch of trees in the forest.

With everyone distracted by their merrymaking, no one would have missed me. Enid's attention had waned after Sir Clarence unseated me, and she drifted into a circle of ladies, chattering with them about the wedding.

I used the opportunity to slink away. I didn't want to speak to Enid that afternoon, or to anyone else, least of all my lord father. I still remember how his eyes brimmed with disappointment over my performance. Father was always disappointed in me, his favorite sport after flaying enemies. I could come home from battle having slain all but a handful of men and he would shake his head at my incompetence. And so I snatched a tumbler of wine and loped away into the forest.

I roamed for what felt like miles before no sound met my ears but the singing of swallows and the answering rustle of trees dressed in their summer finery. The afternoon sun shimmered like gold dust among the trees, falling softly to the earth and settling at my feet. I grew sleepy from wine, from wandering. For the first time that day, I felt at peace. The sun's dappled light in this wood, the whispering of trees soothed my soul.

There in the cool shade, I removed my armor before stripping to the skin, for my walk and the wine had warmed me. I settled finally beneath a blooming hawthorn tree to dream. Blossoms brushed my face, their scent lulling me to sleep. A thousand-thousand bells chimed in the distance, their song twining through my dreams, singing me beyond this realm, this world. Then all singing ceased and my dreams blurred, ghosts swirling through them, mouths agape, eyes ablaze. Their hands reached out to me, but whether to grab or warn me away, I hardly knew. The words they spoke I could not hear.

One ghost turned his shrunken face toward mine, his empty eye sockets writhing with worms. He flashed a rotting grin. His face reminded me of my father's scorn. I winced as something sharp and cold grazed my bare skin. I heard my name called from very far away and I turned from the ghost.

"You have wandered into my greenwood, sir knight," admonished a voice low and sweet as harp song.

I might have dreamed still when I opened my eyes to the wood gazing back at me, its eyes a deeper green than any summer wood, everlasting beyond winter. This, at least, was a better dream. A moment later, I realized I looked into the eyes of a woman, clad all in green, her golden hair flowing freely down her body like sunlight across the forest floor. She held a sword that shone with silver fire, its pommel flashing like starlight. She smiled crookedly to reveal a chipped tooth. Her face was too strong to be called beautiful in the ordinary way. But there was something about this woman dressed all in green I couldn't turn away from.

Her sword lifted to touch my chin. "Well, sir knight?"

"Aye," I answered. "Though I was unaware this forest belonged to anyone other than the king. Surely His Majesty will be surprised."

"Surely. Though I suspect he will have far more to say about one of his knights abandoning his post."

"I didn't abandon any post," I said. "We are at peace, if you call tournament peaceful. My head was far too full of wine and the afternoon was hot. The shade beneath this tree was quite cool." And mercifully empty. I had wanted to be free of Enid and the rest, if only for a little while.

"And your lady?" she asked. At my look of astonishment, she added, "Her eyes followed you here, though she remained behind. So I followed for her."

"Her eyes were not for me," I answered. "My lady loves another, I'm afraid."

She smiled again, a curious curling smile. "I suppose you will do well enough." She picked up my tunic with her sword and dumped it on my bare chest. "Dress, sir knight, and ride with me."

"And why should I follow you, my lady?"

"Because you wish to do so." The lady's manner tugged at me, unraveled any doubts I might have had. I made no further protest and began to dress, my skin prickling with warmth beneath her gaze. "Mustn't we have a horse upon which to ride?" I asked, my lone concession to sense.

The lady lifted a brow. A cool wind blew over my face, and a mare the color of mist shimmered into sight, dressed in a harness of silver bells, her long white mane also woven with tiny crystal bells, her bridle shaped of silver. She nosed at my face and snorted, her breath perfumed with mint and honey. I stroked her warm nose, keenly aware of how the lady watched me. Not even the king possessed a horse so fine. Would she object, I wondered, if I rode this beast back to the castle?

"She is not yours to command," said the lady, as though reading my mind. "She goes where she wishes and no further."

"I was merely admiring her," I lied.

As I dawdled, she mounted the horse's back. "Hurry, unless you wish to ride naked."

And so I hurried. When I replaced my armor, a difficult task without a squire's aid, she pulled me up onto the horse's back. Unbalanced by more than her strength, I gripped the lady's hips to steady myself. Though she was cloaked in green wool from throat to heel, I felt how warm she was, and how soft. But she was stronger than I expected, stronger than most men I knew, to have pulled me up like that, and I reminded myself this was no ordinary woman.

"Ready, Sir Thomas?"

"How did you know my name?" I asked, surprised.

"I heard it whispered on the wind, of course. Does it matter?"

"No. Wherever you lead me, I will follow."

"So you shall," she murmured.

"And your name, my lady? What shall I call you?"

The lady laughed, a pretty, trilling tintinnabulation, and didn't answer.

We rode through daylight, through dusk, through night itself. The greenwood fell away, swallowed by purpling twilight. Owls hooted from the treetops. A nightingale sang. The lady leaned forward and spoke softly to her horse, which ran so swiftly the landscape blurred past.

A dark company shadowed our heels. Glancing back, I counted twelve riders, cloaked in black, their black horses' hooves drumming a war song against the dirt. A thirteenth horse, rider-less, blood-red as sunset before a storm, brought up the rear. Silver bells upon silver bridles clanged and jangled an answering war cry. A rider blew a horn, its deep bellow swelling the sky and shaking the earth. I resisted the urge to tighten my grip around the lady like some simpering child.

As for her, my nameless lady didn't appear to be concerned. She laughed and threw a strange word shaped like thunder over her shoulder. The horses took wing and climbed a starry stair into the sky and rode ahead, their forms winking like faint stars. The horn blower's eyes lingered on the lady. He was the last to climb into the air, his song a frayed ribbon in the wind.

"They are only my hunters. You needn't fear them, though I've sent them away to ease your mind."

"I wasn't afraid," I countered, though I was. It was bad luck, they said, to see the hunters riding the wind. A bit of lore strayed across my memory. "Did I call the hunt somehow?"

"No, sir knight, not this time. You merely stumbled into my wood and dreamed. It was a good dream, I hope."

My brow furrowed as I recalled my odd dreams. "I don't remember waking."

Her hair tickled my face as we flew across the landscape. I brushed a wisp of gold out of my eyes. "Is it true the hunt harries the souls of the damned?"

"The damned are none of our concern. Only the truest souls are worthy of the hunt."

"You hunted me. I must be worthy, too."

"That, sir knight, remains to be seen."

"What do you want of me, my lady?"

"For you to complete a task or three, if you are true."

Intrigued, I asked, "And the tasks?"

"We shall come to the first one soon."

We crossed a river darker than wine, its surface rippling with starlight. The smell of water and loam drifted up and filled my nostrils, as though we burrowed far below the earth. And yet I knew that couldn't be true, for her wild hunters wheeled above yet, their cries brightening the sky with lightning. Wherever we were, we had journeyed far from the world I knew.

We paused before a clearing where three paths forked. "Here lies your first task. Where we are going is up to you. Each path leads to a different realm. The path of sorrow is dark and pebbled with use. Though it is fraught with danger, its rewards are many. The path of ecstasy is the most beautiful of our roads. Though its toll is heavy, it too is well-worn. The path of enchantment is lightly traveled and you must travel light. Few humans have dared to tread it. Fewer return. Choose."

Her words echoed deep in my bones as I studied the paths. They all looked the same to me, all dark and overgrown, as familiar and unfamiliar as any road. How would I know which one to choose if I'd never walked them? Sorrow ... why would anyone want to journey down a road made of sorrow? Ecstasy and enchantment, well, those both sounded the same. Why was the road to enchantment so lightly traveled, and why did so few return? "What kind of task is this?"

"You ask too many questions, sir knight."

Stubbornly, I asked another. "Where does enchantment lead?"

She gave a liquid shrug. "Wherever you wish."

"And will you be with me?"

"Always."

"You never told me your name. If I come with you—"

"In time, though you must first complete this task to my satisfaction. Choose, sir knight."

I heard myself answering, as though I stood a far distance away. "Then I will walk the path of enchantment with you."

She loosed a soft breath. "You are certain, Sir Thomas? You may never return to your world, your king, your Enid."

I shook my head. "I can't be certain of anything right now, except that I wish to be with you. How else might I learn your name?"

"Perhaps it's kinder," she mused, "that you do not know."

"You don't seem kind to me."

She trilled her bell-like laugh. "That," she said, "is the first sensible thing you've said." She urged her horse on, murmuring softly in its ear. The discarded paths dissolved like mist on a summer morning and fell away from the earth, if earth this was. We met no one else along the road. The path of enchantment swallowed us like a song, a low, sweet note swelling the air, our bodies humming with its music. Even my lady seemed taken by the sound, her hands slackening on the horse's reins.

A pearlescent tear slipped down her cheek. I longed to capture it with a kiss. Was this how love felt? I'd never known anything as sweet, not with Enid, not with anyone except this nameless lady.

"Listen," she said. My ears strained against the sound, picking melodies from the breeze, plucking stray notes from the ether, filling my heart until it felt too heavy to carry. I could have stayed on that road forever, grown old there and died, so long as that music never left me, so long as she stayed by my side. Several heartbeats passed before I realized I too wept. Her cool fingers brushed away my tears, her green eyes shimmering as she turned to watch me.

"Now you see. This is enchantment. Nothing is as beautiful as that song. Now that you've heard it, nothing else will match its beauty."

There was something more beautiful. "Is this Heaven?" I blurted. "Are you an angel?"

She shook her head. "No—to either question. This realm is older than your Heaven and your Hell, though its name has been forgotten by all but a few."

"Then tell it to me," I said impulsively. "Tell me and I will remember, always."

"In time, Sir Thomas. In time."

She pulled her horse to a stop beneath a silver tree and slid from its back. "Come, Sir Thomas. You must be hungry after our journey." As I watched her stride away, I realized I hungered for more than food.

Clumsy as a child, I dismounted. I wondered whether to tether the horse, but when I glanced back, the mare melted into soft grey smoke that curled into the air and disappeared. Distracted by the fading horse, I almost lost sight of my lady. Her bright hair and green cloak fluttered in the breeze as she left me behind. I scrambled after her, matching her long, loping gait to catch up to her. Golden leaves crackled beneath our feet as we walked; the sound of water churned from somewhere near. She sighed and threw me a smile.

Emboldened, I slipped a hand into hers, twining our fingers together. Her skin was soft, softer than rain.

"You are overly familiar, sir knight," she chided, though her voice was smooth and playful, and she didn't seem in a hurry to reclaim her hand.

"You are the only familiar thing here."

She led me through the forest into a clearing bordered by an emerald river. Rainbow trout darted through the shimmering water, their mouths snatching insects from the surface. Gold and silver trees bowed their glittering heads together, watching as we strolled along the riverbank. A gleam of ivory tugged at my sight, drawing me away from the lady. It looked like a teardrop dangling from the boughs.

"That particular fruit is bitter for all its beauty. I'll find you something sweeter."

To make her blush, I added, "And if what I want is you?"

She didn't blush when she replied, "You'll try me soon enough."

We meandered among the trees, filling our pockets with sweet fruits and edible flowers, most of which I'd never seen. My fingers were stained with berry juice by the time we settled down to eat in a green field. From within her cloak, she produced a flagon and a pair of silver cups. She poured berry-dark wine and offered me a cup. I brought it to my nose, scenting herbs, spices, and something very sweet. "Think carefully on what you'd like it to taste like," she told me. "And it will."

I smiled around the rim of my cup as I drank. Of course I thought of her, and only of her. The wine was tart with a hint of sweetness, and a hidden note I could not place. "Delicious."

We ate in companionable silence, our eyes tracing the landscape and each other, our fingers meeting and straying at turns. A low trumpeting sounded in the distance. My lady's gaze lingered on the sky. "Why did you choose this path?"

"You," I answered. "It was the only one that reminded me of you."

This time, a soft blush dusted my lady's cheek, her white throat. "In what way am I like a road, Sir Thomas? And do choose your words carefully."

I laughed, not wishing to offend her. "I know nothing about the road or you, but I suspect at either end lies a great adventure. And ... you did kidnap me."

She made a soft noise of assent, but didn't answer.

"What is my next task?" I asked, remembering she had mentioned three. A golden bird fluttered before us singing a sweet song. It circled the air, trilling and piping before transforming into a golden harp at my feet. I turned to the lady, a question hanging on my lips.

"For your second task, the realm requests a song," she explained. "You play, do you not? I suspected you might, for you chose the correct path. My hunters so rarely play."

"You are mistaken. I haven't played in years. And my music would be nothing as sweet as the songs we've just heard."

"Nonsense." She swept her hair behind her shoulders and reached for the harp. The instrument caught the afternoon light and flung it into my eyes, dazzling me. Before I could protest, she pressed the harp into my arms. The lady knelt before me. "I'm never mistaken and I wish for you to play."

"You are most demanding, my lady," I half-grumbled.

She rocked back on her heels, waiting. I gave a long-suffering sigh and went through the motions of tuning the instrument, though, to my amazement, it was perfectly tuned, its notes like wind over water, as golden as sunset. The lady smiled and reclined on the green grass, her eyes slipping shut as she stretched like a cat in the sun. "Play, Sir Thomas. Play."

"What song does the lady request?"

"Something beautiful. But," she cautioned me, "mind what you play. If you echo the songs of the hunt, you will summon them forth. You must not play those songs unless I ask it of you."

"I will remember, my lady." I recalled the swelling tune that greeted us on the road to enchantment. Any song I played would seem ill-formed compared to that. But the lady commanded me, and so I played. Music floated to the surface of memory. My fingers moved over the strings, plucking out my memory, filling the air with the sound of my heart. My lady's eyes opened and slid toward me, her expression unfathomable. I licked my lips and played on, this time a light, lilting melody of my own invention. At the end of the song, I lowered the harp, and awaited the lady's judgment.

"Was I so terrible?" I joked when she said nothing.

The lady stared at me, her eyes shimmering, not with tears, but with some emotion that makes my throat close now even to describe it. "Where," she breathed, "did you learn to play like that?"

"No one taught me. When I was a child, I found one of my mother's smaller harps and began to play." My brows crept together. I hadn't thought about my mother's harp in years, or the look of grief that crossed my father's face when he learned of my playing. "My father told me that harping was no proper occupation for a warrior's son. He had me set to squire that summer. I haven't played since. It wouldn't … it wouldn't be proper."

The lady plucked the harp from my hands and laid the instrument on the ground gently. She pressed me to the cool, soft grass and straddled my hips. "Now I want a different kind of song, Sir Thomas."

"Any song you would like, my lady." I kissed her, tasting honey and wild fruit on her lips, drawing her near. My mouth wandered from hers and lingered at her jaw as I lost myself in the scent of apples. She shivered, her fingers tangling in my hair.

I made love to her there beneath the trees, her breath puffing at my throat, her sharp nails grazing my chest. She was as sweet as I expected, and her sighs more beautiful than the realm's song. In my ear, she whispered a word like night melting across the firmament.

It was full dark when we lay nestled together, her hair blanketing us both while we watched silvery stars wink in and out of the sky.

"I was brought here once long ago," she said. "Almost, I recall my life. Sometimes I dream it, though they are not good dreams."

"Who brought you here?"

"Someone much like myself. Like you, I dreamed beneath a hawthorn tree." She shifted, her green eyes holding mine. "Summer is passed. Autumn is passing. Did you realize?"

"That can't be right. I've been gone scarcely a handful of hours." But when the words left my lips, I knew they could not be true, for I felt I had known the lady far longer than a handful of hours.

"Time passes differently here."

"I would remain forever, if I could."

"You should rest, sir knight. You've had a long journey. Your third task lies before you yet."

"My lady—"

"Sleep."

I kissed her gently. "I love you," I said and laid my head on her breast. As I drifted off to sleep, I was sure I heard her reply softly, "I will hold you to that."

Shadows met me in my dreams once again. "Only the truest ride the wind." Scores of them stood before me, filling the air with muttering. Grey as ash they were, endless as winter. Their breath reeked of death. I shivered as they hurled cries against my bare skin. They lifted me in their arms and carried me toward the precipice, chanting. I struggled against their grasp, writhing and flailing, until I freed myself and fell through a night like nothing. Soft hands caught me, lifted me into light as sweet harping enfolded me in its song. The lady's voice curled through my dreams, singing an aching tune that seared through my soul. "Remember," she whispered.

I awoke fully then and found myself on a dark road. I smelled winter crisping the air. More than a season she had me, yet not long enough for my liking. Earthly stars twinkled dully above. It was then I realized what my third task was to be, though I knew not how I could complete it.

Confounded, I stared at those stars until my eyes burned and my breath grew ragged. I searched for the road to enchantment, though it had closed behind me. A wiser man would have followed the earthly road home, back to Enid, to the world I knew, but the lady had kept my heart, even as she banished me from her side. Only a fragment of my time with her remained: the golden harp, and the lady's final song. I held them both to me, for they were more precious than my own life.

"I will find my way to you," I swore.

I harped. The lady's tune fell clumsily from my hands. Above, the sky was still. The hunt did not come. Perhaps I played the wrong tune. Perhaps I was mistaken.

I walked for ages without eating, without washing. I kept to the shadows, haunting the forests, longing for a single glimpse of my lady.

One night, bandits set upon me as I slept, meaning to steal my boots, my harp. The boots I could have done without, but not the harp, and so I killed them. I wiped my blade in the dead grass, and I laughed mirthlessly as understanding struck me.

There were other roads to enchantment, after all.

It took me longer than I had hoped to find the plants, for the season had grown cold as I trudged. My eyes snagged on a patch of nightshade in the end, and so I consumed the plant leaf by leaf, savoring its slow death, and sat down here to summon the hunt. I harped to the winter wind, seeking the lady's ear through her song. I've waited many days now, and nights. Still, no one has come but you.

The knight's voice faded as he concluded his tale. Night had fallen, the stars a net of silver enclosing the deep blue sky. Thunder rumbled above. Or was it, as the knight suggested, the wild hunters at their back? Were they coming for the knight, after all? It was the *worst* luck to see the hunt.

But those were just stories. Just idle stories whispered over campfires. Tom himself had told some of them to Enid, who'd shown particular interest. He shivered as though a snake had slithered over his grave. Stories crept into a man's bones if he wasn't careful, and Tom's bones ached from sitting on the hard road listening to the knight's mad account. He stifled a groan as he sorted through the story, sifting truth from truth. Sir Thomas, at least, seemed to believe it. Only one thing, from what Tom gathered, could be true.

"You met one of the fair folk in the forest the day you disappeared," Tom mused.

"Aye."

"You fell in love with her."

"Aye."

"And you've half-killed yourself and played her song to call the hunt to … to find your way back to her."

The knight sighed. "Aye."

Tom swallowed drily. He tipped his wine skin to his lips. Only a drop or two remained. He'd sipped it steadily as Thomas spoke, though Tom's head remained distressingly clear. He should have packed another wine skin. A stiff dose of truth often called for more wine.

He sighed and tossed the empty skin into the dust, where it was as useful. His mouth opened in reproach, and snapped shut. Instead, he drew a deep breath, and regretted it. Too near to the knight he sat. The scribe scowled. He resented the smelly knight and his noble death; that Tom would have to carry this unhappy news—and the dead body—to the king and queen. And to Enid.

Tom's fingers clenched and unclenched. He wanted to shake Thomas, perhaps brain him with the harp and drag him back to the castle. Fairies! The wild hunt! Whether the hunt took the knight or not —Tom didn't quite believe that—the nightshade would. Idiot. The knight had suffered a blow to the head at tournament and wandered off insensible. And now he'd turned up, half-dead, mostly mad, bearing strange fictions—fictions Tom would have to repeat to the king.

The scribe's eyes slid over the knight. Thomas was half-alive, too. Perhaps Tom hadn't found him in vain. They weren't far from the castle. The king's physicians might heal him. There was time yet. They needed to hurry—

"Go on back to the castle," said Thomas. "Carry my tale with you. I shall not return, whether the hunt comes or not."

"Carry it yourself," snapped Tom. "I'm taking you back. I'll even let you ride the donkey. Mind, don't kick her too hard. She's old and she's the only donkey I've got." After this, he'd probably have to ride her scurrying out of the kingdom.

He tugged at the knight's arm. The man was heavier than he looked. Must be all the armor and dirt he wore. Thomas made a noise of surprise and quieted. Tom glanced at him to see if the nightshade had taken him at last. It was then he noticed what had snagged Thomas' attention. The knight's arm slipped out of Tom's grasp. Lightning parted clouds and shadows rode out of the sky on the sound of thunder and soft rain. They rode black horses, all except the figure at the head of the procession, who rode upon a mist-white mare.

The hunt touched down in the field. Tom froze, his hand tightening on the knight's shoulders, the only real thing in this evening meadow.

Sir Thomas stirred. "My lady," he murmured. "She's come. At last, she's come." His knees buckled and he dropped into the road.

The woman dismounted and crossed the meadow in long, sure strides, her golden hair fluttering in the breeze. She was not beautiful, as the knight had said, but Tom was unable to look away from her all the same.

She knelt before Thomas, took his hands gently in her own. "You played my song. Your body is dying."

"Dying was the only way I knew that would call you. And your song."

"Only the truest make the sacrifice. Few remember the song. You've completed the final task."

"So I am worthy after all."

"I knew you would be."

"And your name, my lady? Will you tell it to me now?"

The lady laughed. "You already know my name, sir knight. You've harped it all these days and nights."

133

"I wish to ride with you, my lady."

She kissed his brow gently and his mouth, before touching her lips to his ear. Thomas' head lifted, his eyes shining with love, and together they rose. Her arm gripped Thomas' waist as they drifted toward the mare. A horse the color of blood melted from the clouds and alighted besides the mist-white mare. The sprig of nightshade fluttered from Thomas' fingers and fell forgotten in the grass.

"Your steed," said the lady.

"Where are you taking him?" cried Tom. "He will die!"

The lady arched a brow as she noticed him for the first time. "All men die." She added, "Go home, Tom Rhymer."

"But ... but what will I tell them? The king? He is the queen's brother. And Lady Enid—"

"Tell them their knight was true. Tell your Lady Enid ... ." Her eyes crinkled with a hidden smile. "Tell her. She will believe you, whatever you choose to say."

He nodded weakly. "I fear I won't live to tell her, my lady. No one does, who sees the hunt."

Her lips crooked. "You will live a long time yet, though someday, some far day in your human future, we might meet again. Remember us, Tom Rhymer." She led the knight away, the scribe forgotten. Already the rest of the hunt climbed the stars, disappearing into the sky. Thomas and the lady mounted their horses. Together, they rode along a beam of moonlight until they were but a wisp of winter cloud.

"Goodbye," mumbled Tom. He needed more wine. A barrel, at least. Surely no one would believe him. He considered what he would tell Enid. She had cried for the knight once, her plump, pretty face arranged in careful sorrow while her dark blue eyes sought the scribe's across the banquet hall. Tom drew a cold, sweet breath and shook his head, the vision clearing. He had time yet. Whatever tale he would tell the king and Enid would keep until morning. The knight would walk the path of enchantment. Tom, for now, remained here, his boots anchored in the earth.

As he turned toward his donkey, a glint of gold caught his eye. The knight had left his harp behind. Tom knelt and picked up the instrument, his fingers running along its silver strings. Soft sounds drifted up into the misty air. He stilled the strings and stood. Song had never been his talent, or stories. It came of being too truthful, he was sure. He considered harp and knight and lady, a story shaping out of shadow. A faint smile touched his lips. Yes, he would start there.

He stowed the harp in his saddlebag and clambered onto his donkey's back, composing a traveling tune in his head as he rode to the castle, the twittering of night birds trailing him.

It came from Sabrina N. Balmick

I wrote the first draft of "La Belle Dame" one summer after reading the Keats poem. I'd read it several times before, but this time it struck me differently. Maybe it was because I'd read it with a writer's eyes for the first time; maybe I'm just a sucker for tragic romances. I liked that the ending was open to interpretation, and my imagination took off from there. At the time I had also just finished reading two Tam Lin and Thomas the Rhymer retellings (Winter Rose by Patricia McKillip and Fire and Hemlock by Diana Wynne Jones), and wanted to try my hand at one myself. I didn't want to write a straight retelling, though, and I wanted to provide a different twist on the original ending. More than that, I was eager to experiment with voice and a framed narrative structure. As I developed the characters, I explored the identity of the first speaker in the Keats poem, who is something of a mystery; he became my Tom Rhymer. This was my way of linking Thomas the Rhymer and "La Belle Dame Sans Merci," which in turn allowed me to write about the nature of stories and folkloric truth, set against the backdrop of a fateful romantic sojourn between a knight and his lady.

A question for Sabrina N. Balmick

Q: What is your favorite word?

A: Tintinnabulation is my favorite word. How musical it sounds. How magical. For me, this word always evokes a picture of fairy bells ringing in the breeze.

About Sabrina N. Balmick

Sabrina N. Balmick was brought up on a steady diet of fairy tales and folklore. When she isn't dreaming up new fantasy worlds, she leads content strategy and marketing for a national recruitment firm. She lives in South Florida.

The Sea Bank of Svalbard South

Octavia Cade

Lizzy thought she'd be spared the burying of him. She'd looked for Bryan in the dark waters, in wind and rain until night fell and searching was useless. After three days she thought the sea had taken him.

He had thrown himself from the sea-cliffs. She'd watched him do it and hadn't understood what he was doing until it was over. Even after, with time to reflect, it was barely comprehensible. South should have been a safe place for people like them. The isolation, the *silence.* The sheer relief of it all.

Why hadn't he been grateful?

When she couldn't find the body Lizzy thought he'd been swept out to sea, or eaten by sharks. She hated not knowing. It made her feel unsettled in herself, as if she were drifting, distrustful, in unknown currents.

Then the ocean had given his body back. She'd found him half washed up on the beach a week after his jump and Lizzy knew that she'd have to bury him herself. Knew she'd have to report it too, now that she was certain of what had happened to him. Perhaps she should have done it sooner, but she hadn't been able to bear the thought of so many questions when she didn't have answers for any of them.

The soil was thin and shallow. Her hands were smooth and soft from keyboards, from careful lab work. The shovel gave her blisters, but it was the best part of the job. At least the shovel didn't squelch under her fingers. At least it wasn't soft and slippery and *obscene.*

If she had been able to bury him the first day, maybe the second, she might have coped better but after a week Bryan's skin had begun to slip, to detach, the scalp dropping away from the skull, and he seemed to break open, to *ooze* where she touched him. Lizzy considered throwing him back into the tide and waiting for the sea to swallow him up, but she thought he'd just wash up again... probably in pieces. The ocean turned even the bull kelp ragged, and knowing that, she couldn't bear the expectation.

It took her half an hour to drag the body of her co-worker out of the tidal zone. She was tempted to bury him on the beach, where the sand was crumbly and easy to excavate, but the waves were rough and she was afraid they'd uncover him.

Lizzy nursed her resentment through the whole horrible process of burial. Anger was easier than grief, the small growing stems of remorse and second guessing.

"Stupid, stupid," she muttered, choking on unfamiliar sobs. Her face was wet with salt and mucus. She wasn't sure if she was angrier with him or with herself, for having missed what now seemed so obvious.

"Why did you have to do this to the both of us?" she said.

Splachnidium rugosum. Swollen and yellow-green, an algae reminiscent of rot and bulging. When the skin splits a clear sticky slime comes out. As a child it had been enough to ward off her cousins, to send them smeared and screaming down the beach, shouting of dead man's fingers.

Her Master's degree was on the physiology of *Splachnidium.*

When Bryan first arrived, Lizzy had not been welcoming. South was a science station. It had vaults and computers and algal tanks, a biochem lab, satellite communication. A well stocked larder. It didn't have a common room. Company was not encouraged.

"Why are you here?" she said. "This is a restricted research facility, not a tourist site. Are you in distress?" There'd been no mayday calls, no flares. The boat that dropped him off seemed seaworthy enough.

"I'm your new partner," Bryan replied, and though he was smiling there was a fixed quality to it, as if it was something his mouth was unused to.

"I don't need a partner," said Lizzy, automatic. "I signed on because it was partnerless." The isolation was South's shining virtue. She could move about the facility, between the tanks and the lab, the cryogenics, the shoreline monitors, in blissful quiet, in perfect peace.

"New regulations," said Bryan. "Didn't you see the packet? It should have come through a couple of weeks ago."

There had been an email. Lizzy had seen the subject line – *Isolation Risks, Stressors, and Institutional Responses.* It had been copied to human resources, the Ministry of Health and the Marsden Grants with their responsibility for funding New Zealand science. She'd marked it received and hadn't bothered to open it; had assumed it was one of the ridiculous things they sent through sometimes. The last one she'd had was a request from a research student in psychology who'd wanted her to answer a lot of questions and do some exercises in creative writing. Lizzy hadn't done any of them.

"Two weeks?" she said. "I don't understand." It was so quick.

"After Raoul Island the Ministry put a boot up everyone's arses," said Bryan.

Lizzy stared at him, uncomprehending.

"Department of Conservation rangers. One of them got hit by lightning, if you can believe it. DOC had to get a rescue plane out there quick-smart. And now South's to be staffed by a minimum of two. In case someone gets injured and can't call for evac."

"I'm not injured," said Lizzy.

"You could go mental," said Bryan, and Lizzy was stung. "Oh, I don't think you would. No-one ever has, have they?" South was staffed, always, by extreme introverts. People for whom isolation was a natural state, and preferred. "But some daft sod's decided they need to fix what isn't broken. Covering their arse, on the off-chance. Hence me." He looked at her over one shoulder. "Maybe you should start reading your emails."

"Clearly," said Lizzy. It wasn't his fault, and she knew she sounded unwelcoming. But he wasn't welcome! Was she supposed to lie about that? It was so hard to tell.

"It's not my first choice either," said Bryan. "I wanted South for the quiet as much as you did. We'll keep out of each other's way. You'll hardly know I'm here."

Codium fragile. Dark green and braided like a river bed, with elegant round branches. The surface is a mass of tiny compact hairs, dark soft shadows spreading underwater, the algae is firm and silky and brushes up against. It has a tendency to invasiveness, and Lizzy tests growth against temperature in the tanks, tries to see how far she can cool the water before it dies.

In a warming world, invasion looks set to be a problem.

Lizzy *did* know he was there. She felt him all around her. "You're being neurotic," she said to herself, unable to sleep because she thought she heard him breathing. She knew she was being neurotic because for six nights running she'd crept out of bed and sneaked towards him on slippered feet. Four of those nights he'd been asleep in his own cot, on the opposite side of the station. On the fifth she'd found him looking through the technical library, on the sixth he'd been walking round the sea tanks.

Lizzy knew she couldn't *actually* hear him. It was only imagination fuelled by wind and waves and resentment, the discomfort of his presence. The two of them had worked out a timetable of duties, one that minimised interaction, but the knowledge that they weren't alone was a weight that didn't lighten.

In fairness, he was doing his best to avoid her. The two of them had eaten together that first night, in order to sort their schedules – neither had been comfortable, though Lizzy suspected that he coped better with it than she did. It wasn't surprising. Even amongst the loners, she'd always stood out.

"It might be a good fit for you," her mother had said, on a birthday call, before Lizzy had left for South.

"Yes," she'd replied, definitive. There had been gratitude as well; a small sweet relief that for once her parents weren't trying to use these scheduled calls as an excuse to encourage socialisation. (Her mother didn't even ask if she were going out to celebrate. Lizzy supposed she'd given up expecting an affirmative. More gratitude.)

She should have known it was too good to be true.

Apophlaea lyallii. Cartilaginous and crustose, an abrasive half-circle that blooms up from the rock as if it were a sea urchin, to be so stiff-edged and hedgehog spiky. In the open it's the colour of brick, a dark burnt red and rigid, with the cells packed tight together and the holdfast hidden under little branches. She tries transplanting it high on the intertidal, to see if it'll grow even further south than Snares Island, but has little success.

Lizzy liked to spend some of her off-hours outside. The island wasn't large, just a speck of Sub-Antarctic rock hundreds of kilometres south of New Zealand.

"It's a good place for a research station," she'd been told. The original Svalbard, up in Norway and past the Arctic Circle, had been chosen for its remoteness, its repository value. "But then they're only preserving seeds." South did that too, of course, although its remit was marine plants and that in itself had been enough to suck up Marsden funding for decades. But it also kept tanks, kept stocks of living algae and phytoplankton, experimented on what it conserved. A supplementary measure, something to reinforce conservation against climate change. It also meant South was manned – at least to minimal standards.

There was still the occasional cruise ship, the occasional Department of Conservation vessel – heading down to the Antarctic, or the larger islands with the albatross colonies, the petrels and penguins and shearwaters, the right whales off the coast. But South was off limits, marked on the maps and left carefully alone.

Still, the weather could be challenging and, with a storm coming, it was foolishness to stay outside. Lizzy replaced her boots carefully in their cubby, her waterproof outerwear dried down and folded on adjacent shelves, and started on the sand and water she'd tracked onto the floor.

When the mop was wrung out Lizzy gave the room a final check, making sure she'd left no mess behind her, nothing to indicate she'd been there. Bryan wouldn't be going out tonight but he might like to go out sometime, and she didn't want to burden him with signs of her presence.

It was the considerate thing to do.

Bryopsis plumosa. Little feather plumes, kept green and unbleached out of direct sunlight, huddled under crevices and in the sides of rock pools, the water shallow and salty above. When taken out of water it wraps around Lizzy's fingers, the small delicate fronds cramped down into a thick fibrous mass. She dunks it again and again to see the way it fans out under the surface.

Fascination with shape aside, Lizzy hates being asked to experiment with *Bryopsis*. It infests the tanks, clings on and spreads from tiny fragments. She has to spend her days sterilising.

With the storm so loud about, Lizzy found it hard to sleep. She wasn't afraid of structural failure, of loss of integrity – South had been built for the exposed environment, the harsh winds and heavy waves – but she'd been cooped up for days in terrible weather, without exercise, and it had left her fidgety.

She'd tried reading, had watched some of her shows, had even meditated, but none of it worked. She felt cooped in, trapped, and though her bed was warm and snug, the blankets kept twisting up around her so she threw them off, stuffed her feet into the bunny slippers her parents had given her and made her way to the technical library.

She didn't bother with the lights. Lizzy knew her way around the station, knew it as if it were the walls and veins of her own body: contained, curled in on itself. Sufficient. The lack of light also gave her warning – if Bryan were up there'd be a thin line under a closed door, and she'd know to slip quietly past, to find another place.

The library was empty, but when Lizzy turned on the light she saw that the chair had been pulled slightly back, as if someone had been sitting at the desk and only recently gone away.

On the desk was a diary.

Macrocystis pyrifera. Bladder kelp. The older leaves are rough to the touch – pitted and heavy and less flexible, their surfaces scoured with sand and worn in patches. Lizzy monitors the kelp sometimes; checks for parasites that might endanger the beds; that might spread to other populations. Her checks are superficial. She'd never dive there, not by herself. The beds are so thick around they make her nervous; she might get caught or lost.

Lizzy didn't read it. That was the easy decision. As soon as she opened the book she knew that it was Bryan's. He wrote on station checklists as she did, noting down fluctuations and recording data, and the writing was the same.

There wasn't any virtue in closing the pages, though Lizzy liked reading more than she liked anything that wasn't science. Much of what she'd brought with her had been books – her favourites in print, their weight familiar in her hands and the rest electronic, but she had enough to get through without prying.

She hated it when people pried. Her parents had taken her to a therapist when she was a teenager, so she could "learn to express her feelings". "What for?" Lizzy had said. She didn't want to learn to express herself like other people did. It was off-putting: they were always so noisy with their feelings. She'd thought she might have learned to cope with that if they hadn't expected her to be noisy too. But she'd written the diary, just to keep the peace – and of course it had been read. *Of course.*

The problem wasn't to do with reading. It was what to do with the diary now that she'd found it. Picking it up had disturbed it. She could leave it where it was and hope that Bryan didn't notice the disturbance. If he did, he'd think that she read it.

Lizzy didn't want that.

She sat at the desk and scowled. This was why she preferred to be by herself! When she was by herself there was never any question of what to do. What not to do. She tried to understand how to relate to other people, how to keep them from being upset, but it rarely worked. They got their feelings hurt so easily.

In the end, she left the diary outside the door of the room where he slept, crept away on bunny feet. He'd know that she found it. He'd know that she was the one that put it there. But he'd probably understand, because she was so obvious with the returning, that Lizzy hadn't read it.

Pachymenia lusoria. Each blade looks so different from the others – the fronds are flat and forked and fringed in pieces. Some look as if they have bites taken out, others as if they have been stretched in strange directions and pulled out of shape. The odd round curve of some of the blades is an awkward thing but the pieces fit together, somehow, even if the fit is clumsy.

Bryan has an interest in *Pachymenia.* It's his *Splachnidium,* so Lizzy stops working with it, passes over all experimental responsibility to him.

He didn't leave his diary in the library any more. Lizzy counted that as a relief, although she'd spent several uncomfortable days on edge, fearing that he'd ambush her in one of the labs, that he'd come up behind her while she was testing salinity in the sea tanks. There'd be stilted small talk, the kind that floundered and branched in unsteady directions she never meant to go. She'd never understood why people couldn't say what they meant. For her words had always been coralline: crisp and spiky and not something to savour, lest they prick the insides of her mouth and made her bleed. "You're welcome," she would have said. "I didn't read it. Please go away." The "Please" was important. It showed she had manners.

Her mother had been determined she have manners. "It'll make your life easier," she'd said. "Think of them as rules that everyone has to follow."

Courtesy dictated that she be thanked. Lizzy would rather not, if it meant being stalked amongst the sea tanks, but probably Bryan's parents had tried to make him assimilate better as well, so the two of them would just have to muddle through.

Or not. The days passed and Lizzy was never confronted, never thanked. There were no notes left for her on the borders of checklists, which would have been embarrassing anyway as copies of those went to the Board, went back to Marsden in return for grants. She'd just begun to relax again when she opened her door one morning and found, laid carefully outside on a plate, a single cupcake.

It was a vanilla cupcake which wasn't the best but it was all hers and no-one was going to ask her to share it, which was a happy thing because people who asked her to share got cross when she went for a ruler. "I'm only trying to make it fair," she'd say but it never stopped them looking at her funny.

Fairness was important. Maybe Bryan thought it was important too. A cupcake for a diary. It wasn't the same but it was something. Reciprocity.

The icing was sweet on her tongue, and Lizzy licked it off carefully, in quarters.

Ulva lactuca. Sea lettuce. Two cells thick, a green so bright it's almost grass and the sheets are layered and lobed and leafy. Lizzy rubs them between her fingers, slick and sea-wet and so slippery, the square cells sliding against each other, the thin tissue fragile under her flesh. Sometimes the sea lettuce is free-living, the substrate a pebble or shell and Lizzy tosses these into the wave-tank to test how much stress the lettuce can take.

The leaves are ruffle-edged and worn ragged by waves. Some are the size of her palms, and some could cover her hand if she measured it against, if the leaves lay flat in the water and didn't stick to her flesh, didn't wrap around and cling, as if she were something to hold fast to.

There was a cake at her door the next morning, and the next. Lizzy didn't understand at first, until she recollected that cupcakes were made in batches. He probably had to get rid of them before they went stale, if he didn't want to eat them all himself.

Yet it disturbed her. Reciprocity she understood, but this had gone beyond that. Certainly he valued his privacy but a single cake was enough to show understanding, and gratitude. This felt like something else.

Lizzy knew his schedule as well as her own. They'd worked it out between the two of them, that first night, so she knew when he took his share of shifts, when he bathed. While he worked she made custard, thickened it with carrageenan and let it cool with a little nutmeg dusted over the top. While he was showering she left it outside his door, for when he retired to his room for the night.

It restored the balance between them, she thought, and it seemed he didn't object because after a while the cupcakes became orange flavoured, and then chocolate. Each batch had a different flavour, but Lizzy didn't know how to make any custard but one.

One night she went to leave it and he was back from his shower, back early, and there was an awkward encounter. "Sorry," she said, holding out the custard. "I didn't mean to bother you."

"I don't mind," he said. "Really I don't."

It was polite of him to say, but she took to leaving his custards in the kitchen anyway.

He left her cupcakes there as well.

Cladhymenia oblongifolia. The blade leaves grow in parallel and they are rounded at the ends, a warm pink-red. There can sometimes be seen a darker midrib, faint-drawn along the length of thallus. The most extraordinary thing about this algae's appearance is the fertile fringing set about the edge of the blades. Lizzy finds it comforting, how it's all on the surface. It grows so very obviously; assessment is quick and certain.

She cuts the fringing off, to test how long it will take to grow back.

They crossed paths in the kitchen, sometimes. Lizzy kept to her schedule, but Bryan seemed looser, more likely to pop in unannounced.

"It's not so bad, is it?" he said. "Working together. I thought it might be difficult, with the two of us. But I think we've got a system going, don't you?"

"Yes," said Lizzy.

"Didn't you ever get lonely, on your own?" he said.

"Yes," said Lizzy. It had been a welcome sensation after the cramming of mainland life, the total inability to live and not be encroached upon.

"I get lonely, too," he said.

"I'm glad," said Lizzy, and couldn't understand why he left so suddenly. They might not be very close but surely he didn't think her that selfish, that she'd begrudge him what she'd come so far for herself. Perhaps it was that she'd been so obviously unhappy at his arrival. Perhaps he still thought she blamed him for it.

Lizzy left him two custards that night. The next day he seemed happier, so she thought it was alright. But then he left his diary out again, and when she gave it back he said something very strange. "It wouldn't bother me if you did read it, you know."

"It would bother me," said Lizzy, who hadn't forgiven that long-ago therapist. "I don't keep diaries anyway. They're nothing but a nuisance." She'd been given them for years, after that first disastrous attempt. They'd piled in corners of her old bedroom, until she kicked them all under the bed, blank-paged, so she wouldn't trip over them.

He didn't leave it out again. "I've stopped writing it," he said. He didn't look happy. Lizzy didn't ask, because she didn't know what to ask, but she didn't see his writing again, outside the worksheets, until she came into the kitchen one morning for baking and found a note instead.

I'm sorry, the note said. *It's too much. Too much alone here.*

It didn't make sense, Lizzy thought, the note crumpled in her hand. Hadn't he come here to be alone? Why would he be sorry for that? She could see him, out of the kitchen window, heading for the cliffs. She thought she might go after him. The weather was terrible, and it looked as if he'd forgotten his jacket.

She wasn't much of a nurse. If he got hypothermia they'd both be screwed.

Hormosira banskii. Neptune's necklace. Branched and cartilaginous, with a string of hollow spheres that are evenly spaced although the sizes can be different depending on growth and habitat. The beads help to maintain buoyancy, and Lizzy snips them off one by one in the tanks, to see how much bladder area is needed per 100 grams of wet weight to keep the seaweed afloat.

She wondered, while she was scrubbing her hands after the burial, if there was a point where she could have stopped it. Was it the diary? Should she have read it all along? Had he left it out so that she *could* read it?

Lizzy found it afterwards, when she was packing up his things. She felt it was something she should do, parcelling up his effects. Someone would come, eventually. Someone would want them. She would hate people going through her own things after she died – another reason not to keep a journal – but he had kept one, had *chosen* to keep one, and he must have known there was a possibility that others would read it if he died.

She set the diary on top of the carefully folded clothes, then took it out again. Put it on the table by his bed. Clasped her hands together in her lap, then reached out and adjusted the diary so that its sides were parallel to table edges.

Would there have been something in there that would have told her? Was she supposed to read it now? He was dead. It wouldn't do any good. But maybe they'd ask, when she radioed it through. Maybe they'd want to know. What was she supposed to say? She couldn't tell them the truth. If there had to be two people here now and they knew she couldn't adapt then she'd be replaced as well, with someone better suited to company and nuance. "I was supposed to be here alone," she said, to herself and plaintive. "I was *fine*."

Of course they'd have sent someone who couldn't hack it. Of course they would. It would have come out of a committee meeting, a group of people who'd never been to South, who'd never cope with the isolation and who wouldn't want to anyway. They'd made this stupid, stupid policy and now she was paying for it.

"I'm not going to read you," she said. She put the diary back on top of the clothes and closed the lid on it. She couldn't sit sulking forever. There were tanks to check, and the cryo, and she wanted to walk along the shore and see the kelp, see how much the storm had damaged them.

The blades were more ragged than normal, but only one of the holdfasts had been ripped out. The kelp was strong, and it steadied her.

Durvillaea antarctica. Bull kelp. Leather against her skin, it beats at her thighs in time with the waves. The holdfast is yellow and big as platters, and if she cuts a blade across she can see the broad honeycomb structure that allows the blades to float and doesn't drag them down into darkness.

Lizzy cuts the ripped out holdfast free of its lightening honeycomb blades and takes it back to the lab for study. There must be some experiment she can perform, she thinks, something to make use of seaweed and storm, but there's nothing she can think of to do.

"It's not my fault." She wanted to blurt it out, spit those coralline words over waves and let someone else deal with it. "You knew what I was." Her psychological testing was very specific. She was perfect for a place of preservation, of conservation and isolation and frozen genomes. She wanted to spit it out, to stop the slicing and stabbing that filled her mouth with blood, but Lizzy wasn't sure that the bleeding was worst.

If she told, they'd come and take him away. They'd dig him up and ship him back to Dunedin and she wouldn't have to avoid the place where she buried him and remember how his skin felt in her hands, slipping and oozing and the memory of it made her want to avoid *Splachnidium* now, and that wasn't fair. She'd always liked it.

They'd take him away, but they might take her too. And she fitted here so well. Lizzy hadn't fitted anywhere like she'd fitted here.

But it was wrong to lie. Lizzy knew that it was wrong to lie and she wasn't very good at it anyway. People always knew and got cross when she tried, but they got cross when she told the truth too so she'd never bothered trying to learn to be a good liar because it wasn't worth the extra effort.

They might take her away. They might take her away.

"I'm here," she said, when the Portobello Marine Lab radioed through, their usual monthly communication. Lizzy had always thought it silly when she could – and did – email their status, but Portobello insisted on regular checks of the satellite radio, to make sure it still worked in case of emergency. It was one of the jobs she'd fobbed off onto Bryan.

"Roger that, South. Anything to report? Portobello out."

Lizzy's hands were wet, slick with sweat as if she'd dipped them in sea water. She wanted to be sick. She wanted to turn the radio off but they'd only call back, again and again until she answered them.

"South? Are you there, South?"

Carefully, she leaned over the microphone, and tried to breathe evenly, lest they hear her hyperventilating, hear her trying not to panic. Lizzy clenched her fists, her fingers shaking and clammy, and blurted out the first thing that came to mind.

"I like cupcakes," she said.

A question for Octavia Cade

Q: How does writing speculative fiction affect your daily life (not as a writer, but as a person)?

A: For me, speculative fiction is a way of engaging with metaphor. Often that involves different ways of writing and thinking about science. I think if you want to attract more people to science- more than just the logically-minded, for instance- you've got to provide a different sort of pathway, a different means of engaging. I find science fiction in particular helps me to perceive science more broadly, from a place of imagination as well as method.

About Octavia Cade

Octavia Cade has a PhD in science communication. Though seaweed was her first biological love, she's currently researching the germination triggers of New Zealand's only seagrass.
ojcade.com

The Heresy Machine

Gerald Warfield

Goranth struggled up the cracked and crumbling stairs of the ancient tunnel. His squat build, typical of the Dunn, rendered him ill-suited for climbing. His short legs trembled, his tail stump ached, and his labored breaths created little puffs of fog before his face. But Goranth was undaunted by the precipitous climb. Bracing himself with one hand against the fractured wall, he gripped a clay lamp in the other and doggedly persisted, hefting himself, step by step closer to the surface.

The tunnel, hewn through layers of solid rock, rose steeply to a narrow landing before continuing on to the surface. Freezing gusts, swirling down from the entrance, caused the open flame of his lamp to sputter, almost extinguishing it.

When he reached the landing, Goranth reeled, nearly losing his balance before steadying himself against the ledge of a shallow niche on his left. There he set the lamp, knocking it gently against others that rested on the small, uneven surface. His hand trembling, he reached over the lamp and snuffed the wick between a gloved finger and thumb. Darkness closed around him.

Gripping the ledge with both hands, he looked up from beneath the hood of his anorak. From there, he could see the entrance of the tunnel and beyond to the stars that glittered in the blackness.

As he watched, a piece of ice dislodged from the top edge of the opening and fell onto the stairs. Bursting as it struck, the white missile sent glittering fragments cascading onto the lower steps.

Goranth took a few deep breaths, his eyes adjusting to the faint light, and resumed the climb—a bit too soon, a bit too fast. *Get control of yourself before you slip.* He steadied himself again against the wall. *Don't fall—not now.*

Nearing the entrance of the tunnel, his boots crunched on the ice that coated the last few steps. It made his ascent even more precarious as he rose, one step at a time, into the ghostly landscape. Glacial walls, nearby, blocked the heavens except for a stretch of black sky overhead, and cold, bitter breezes brushed his face and ruffled the fur of his hood.

But as he emerged from the tunnel he heard a shuffling from the frozen surface around him, dark figures rising to their feet, his fellow Dunn waiting for him.

How did they know?

Goranth looked from one to the other of the figures and made a calming gesture with his hands. "I realize what it looks like, but I've..."

The first chunk of ice thudded against his chest. Spent from the climb, his brain addled from exhaustion, he stared without comprehending. A few more jagged missiles struck, and the Dunn charged. Only then did he raise his stubby arms to protect his face.

More confused than frightened, Goranth withdrew his head into his hood. Surrounded, he heard the curses but did not see the gloved fists that pummeled him, except for the blow that burst between his hands and struck his nose. Pain flashed like light before his eyes, and he grabbed the fist, clinging to it desperately to steady himself.

"You'll bring Kaalen's wrath down on us all!" cried his former friend Zundin, who tried to pull away. But Goranth held on to his arm, and finally, Zundin jerked his hand back, leaving Goranth holding the thick, padded glove.

Other fists struck, and bodies swiveled, lending force to short, unbending arms.

"No." Goranth doubled over.

"Kill him," cried one of his tormentors.

"Do not kill him," said a low but resonant voice.

Goranth looked up frantically, hearing the second voice. "Help me!" he cried, spotting the figure who strode out of the darkness. But a sudden shove toppled him backward onto the ice. Pain shot up from his tail stump, and he rolled onto his side in a crouch.

Then the kicking began, heavy boots, painful blows, and Goranth gasped for air.

"Enough," commanded the low voice. "We still need workers—even him."

The kicking ceased, but labored breaths still hissed above him. Someone, he assumed Zundin, snatched the empty glove from his hands and followed with a final kick.

"I said 'enough.'" It was the voice of Oxuppo, the Hierarch.

In the silence that followed, Goranth heard the wind moaning off the glacier and, at last, the crunch of departing footsteps on the ice. Still, he did not move, his heart pounding, his nose trickling blood. He could not see, his head withdrawn deep into his hood, but he sensed that he was not alone. Finally, he rolled onto his stomach, pulled his arms beneath him and painfully levered himself to his hands and knees.

"This is your doing." Goranth's voice trembled, and he did not look up. A drop of blood fell from his nose, splattering the white snow between his hands.

No response, and for a moment he thought Oxuppo had left with the others after all and that his words carried only into the frigid air. But then the calm voice spoke again, nearer than he thought. "You disobeyed a direct order from the Council. Did you expect no consequences?"

Goranth lifted his head. "Not from a mob." Blood trickled from his nose to his mouth.

"My friend," said Oxuppo in an even voice, "they are frightened by your experiments, and with good reason. I came along to keep them from killing you."

"They don't understand. But you..."

"Goranth," he said with some force, "everyone labors day and night in preparation for Winterspan: finishing the hatchery, preparing the learning tunnels, shoring up buildings for the long freeze. Your profane excavation angers Kaalen at the very time we should be the most obedient. It endangers the very cycle we live by. Do you want the sun never to return to this place?"

"The Ovards used machines to live through Winterspan. I'm sure of it."

"Ptha! And where are the Ovards, now? It would appear their machines didn't help much, or hadn't you noticed?"

"But they *did* survive, for hundreds of cycles. It's just that... "

"Even if you managed to build an Ovard machine," said Oxuppo, his voice rising, "it's too late. We're running out of food."

"But the next generation..."

Oxuppo laughed bitterly and advanced a step. "There won't be a next generation if this one ends in chaos. Do you have any idea how hard it is to maintain order with death staring everyone in the face? How do you keep your friends from hysteria? How do you keep your neighbors from throwing away perfectly nutritious bodies by dying in the wilderness or fainting in a ditch somewhere? This is not the time for absurd promises based on Ovard machinery. It's a time for obedience. I'm responsible for the continuity of the Dunn, and by Kaalen there *will be a next generation.*" He advanced another step, and for a moment Goranth, still on his hands and knees, thought Oxuppo would kick him in the face. But he stopped. "I ask you one more time, and think very carefully about your answer, for there will be consequences—serious consequences. Will you give up pursuit of this subversive Ovard machinery?"

Goranth stared down onto the bloodstained ice. "I cannot."

With blood freezing on his face and his tail stub throbbing, Goranth labored across the icy landscape trembling with anger, his mind churning. *What does it matter that I don't help shore up the walls of the meeting house or that I don't make any more toys for our hatchlings? It won't make that much difference come Winterspan. But my work—my work could one day lift the Dunn from this prison of darkness and ice. Yet Oxuppo would kill it, stop it all because...* He stumbled. His arms flailed, and he barely keeping himself from falling. Thinking made him dizzy. Maybe it was the blow to his head.

The path from the Ovard tunnel was long and little-used, but at last Goranth came to the deep, parallel trenches that surrounded the village. The giant furrows at one time shielded the Dunn's crops from blustering winds that blew even during the long summer, but now they lay like miniature valleys, barren in the starlight and collecting snow—snow that would accumulate for the next seventy-five years. At least that was the official estimate. It might be longer. No one had ever survived Winterspan, nor had anyone devised a way to number the years that passed, years of bitter cold.

Goranth's hut appeared in the dimness, a squat, round building of stone that had survived for hundreds of years, maybe thousands. Quickening his pace before fatigue overtook him, he stepped onto the stone porch, slick with hoarfrost, only to find the slide bar frozen shut. Shivering with cold and exhaustion, he banged on the bar with a gloved hand, jerked it back, and pushed open the door. Cold gusts swirled into the room.

"Close the door," cried Shuhu, sleepily from the bed pit. "I'll fetch a taper." Her feet made little plopping sounds on the stone floor.

When she raised the lid of the tiny hearth, gleaming embers revealed her rough gray hand holding a candle and a round face above, wrinkled with concern. "You're bleeding," she said.

"I slipped on the ice." He reached for a cleaning rag and daubed his nose. "It's nothing."

"Goranth." She did not believe him.

The tightness in his chest stopped his breath. Tears of frustration welled in his eyes, and he reached for her before she could light the candle, taking her into his arms. Her round body was soft beneath the fibers of her robe, and her musky odor enveloped him, calming him, as it always did.

"I don't understand." he said, looking up to the ceiling and blinking. "I just don't understand."

"Sit down. No need to talk now. I'll heat some food. We can spare enough for a late-night snack."

Gradually he let his arms fall and, turning, shed his anorak—hanging it on a peg next to the heavy, wooden door. With a sigh he eased himself onto a bench at the table, careful not to bump his short tail stump, already tender from his earlier fall.

Within these walls, he felt safe, as if the stone and mortar shielded him from the village as surely as they held off the bitter cold. Cabinets, storage bins, even the familiar clutter added to his feeling of security. In the center of the floor a covered hearth and chimney radiated heat. To one side of the hearth rested the table at which he sat and on the other side lay the bed pit. They balanced one another, Goranth thought, the table and the bed. Looking about the room, lit only by the single candle, he saw a place of cheerful twilight.

Shuhu shuffled in the pantry taking down a block of gruel. "We sealed up the hatchery today. All the eggs were placed. It was very grand."

"Oh, I forgot that was today."

"I told them you were too weak to come, but..." she paused and frowned, "Zundin said you had gone back into the tunnels."

Goranth grimaced.

"They're all frightened, afraid that you'll bring down the wrath of Kaalen, not only on us but on the next generation, as well."

"The next generation is what I'm working for."

Shuhu's mouth softened. "It went well enough. They put my last toy, the one that said "hello," at the beginning of the tunnel. It'll be one of the first they find."

He knew the one she meant, an intricate mechanism in a box engraved with the rune for its sound. When a notched stick was pushed through the box and across the edge of the tympanum inside, the sound that resulted mimicked the word.

As a hatchling, Shuhu had been among the first to learn speech from the toys that awaited them in the tunnel of learning, as had Goranth and, of course, Oxuppo. Once they realized what the sounds meant and connected them with the runes on the toys, learning became a game, as if the words were already in their minds, waiting to be spoken, waiting to be written. They taught one another and then the rest of the Dunn as more hatched daily.

During their learning the three became inseparable, but that ended at the pairing ceremony when Shuhu chose Goranth for a mate —even over Oxuppo who was the Hierarch.

"Hold still." Shuhu took the cleaning rag and began to wipe his face.

"So where did they put my sparking toy?"

Shuhu hesitated before answering. "I'm sorry, Goranth. I know you loved that machine. You doted on it enough."

"What happened?"

"Oxuppo said it was an Ovard device and that nothing useful would come of making sparks."

"I could have guessed that. Where is it, now?"

"They—smashed it."

"Damn him!" He leaned forward on the table, gripping his hands. "If only I had been there. I could have explained it—to some of them, at least."

"My dear," she shook the rag at him with which she cleaned his face. "Your explanations are not always effective."

"I could have shown them."

"Zundin ranted on about a big, rusted machine you told him about, and how you planned to fix it up. It was hard, standing there, listening to him working everyone into a frenzy."

"Poor Shuhu," Goranth drew his lips into a thin line. "You've suffered too much for me. Your friends barely speak to you, and no one comes anymore to help you grind or pound husks."

"We hardly need for that, now." Shuhu wiped the last of the blood from his face. "Oxuppo was very upset. He said the Ovard machines were in direct violation of Kaalen's word. That's why they— went to meet you."

Goranth closed his eyes. "So you knew."

"But I made Oxuppo promise that he would stop them. He said he would."

"So that's why he didn't let them kick me to death."

"He said he wouldn't have you killed by a lawless mob."

"Yes, it's not his style. Much too messy."

She waived her hands in frustration. "I would have stopped them myself, if I could." Goranth heard the tears in her voice.

"I'm sorry. I know you would."

"Oh, Goranth, your machine can't possibly make any difference now. Everyone just wants reassurance. Your work is causing doubt and confusion."

"So you're choosing Oxuppo over me?"

"Goranth." She reproached him with her look. "This is not about Oxuppo. Even if you did find an Ovard machine it couldn't work after all these years—could it?"

Thudding at the door startled them. Shuhu dropped the rag. Goranth went to the portal, pulled the bar and swung back the heavy door.

"You are summoned before the council at sun's height." The messenger spoke quickly, as if embarrassed, before turning and disappearing into the night. Goranth recognized him. He had been one of Goranth's best students long ago in the tunnel of learning.

Goranth did not sleep well and only near morning fell into a fitful unconsciousness. In his dreams, he and Oxuppo argued while rivulets of melting water ate into the crumbling edge of a glacier. The runoff created a raging torrent that swept Shuhu downstream. She called to him, but if he ran to save her he would lose the argument with Oxuppo. Waking, he found himself deeply depressed and appalled at the decision he had made in his dream.

Pulling himself from the bed pit, he pulled on his robe and saw that Shuhu was already heating their meager breakfast, half a handful of mush each, all that their rations allowed.

"Sorry dear. I should be doing some of this."

"You thrashed around all night. I'm surprised you're even coherent this morning." She placed two stone bowls on the table, steam curling from the small amount of mush in each.

"I had an awful dream last night."

Shuhu looked up. "What about?"

"The situation." He nodded in the direction of the judgement hall where he would face Oxuppo.

He did not continue, and after a while, Shuhu, finishing breakfast first, said, "I've been looking at these, again." She traced with one stubby finger the scars in the wooden table.

"What?"

"The names carved onto the table. It's a comfort, all of us facing death, to see proof that others managed before us. How many generations must have carried their eggs to the hatchery just like we did and stretched their food as long as possible like we're doing now? And when it was all was gone, they went together, orderly into the pit, before they were too weak to walk—just like we'll do."

Goranth knew her words were meant to comfort him, but the thought of the pit terrified him—even now. He had discovered the huge crater on his first venture into the out-of-doors. It was to one side of the village, not far from the hatchery. Trudging down the ramp, he had shivered in the cold as he followed the trail around the edges of the pit to the wide, flat bottom. There he had wandered the corridors of ice until he found the bodies, many bodies. He stared, incredulous, at the strange adults lying side by side, some embracing, dimly visible through the ice. They seemed to have lain down, peacefully, and frozen. What had happened to them? Why were they there? Heart thumping and breathless he had run back to the hatchery to tell the others.

But Oxupppo grabbed his arm and pulled him into a side corridor, slamming him against the wall. "Don't talk about the pit," he said is a low voice. "Let everyone get a little farther in their learning. They're very impressionable, now. We're going to need butchers, and no one will want to do it if they're scared early on."

"Butchers? Do you mean..."

"There's not enough food to last until the first harvest. There never is. If you'd read far enough ahead instead of wandering all over the placed you'd know that."

Goranth stared at him, his eyes wide.

"They're the ones who came before. They've left themselves for us. If they didn't, we'd starve when our yolk sacks shriveled."

He felt sick and tried to turn away, but Oxuppo would not let him go. "It's there, on the learning walls, the last panel."

Goranth shoved aside the memory and set down his spoon. "The circular foundations under the glacier were domes, perhaps beautiful at one time, arching into the sky."

"You always speak so kindly of the Ovards," Shuhu said, "but they enslaved us. According to Oxuppo...."

"Oxuppo doesn't know everything."

"I agree." Shuhu straightened her back. "But in matters of faith he *is* the Hierarch. He hatched first, and he found the sacred scrolls. There are things revealed there that no one else may know."

Goranth slammed his hand onto the table harder than he intended. "He's jealous that you chose me," Goranth said. "He's always been jealous."

"Funny, he thinks you're jealous of him."

"Why do you take up for him? You chose *me* at the pairing ceremony, not him."

"And I chose you because I wanted a husband, not an official, and certainly not a Hierarch."

Goranth leaned forward, his forearms on the table. "Sorry. I haven't been much of a husband, lately."

She sighed. "Don't persist in this, Goranth. Oh, I don't care about the blasphemy, but for all your efforts you have only the scorn of our neighbors and the censure of the council. The Ovards, you said yourself, were much smarter than we, yet they died out in the end, but the Dunn kept on living, coming back cycle after cycle. We must be doing something right."

"There may have been other reasons the Ovards didn't survive. They were tall and thin, very unsuited for the cold. And we didn't always have Winterspan. Something happened to make the sun go away. As best I can tell in the writings, it was a time of earthquakes and strange moons in the sky." Goranth slid his hand away and looked down. "But what you say is true. Eventually, they died out, and we plod on."

"Then shouldn't you just resign yourself to Winterspan, like these who've gone before us?" Shuhu opened her hand, indicating the names scored upon the rough surface of the table.

Goranth ran a finger along one of the narrow groves of a name. "Not everyone who went before us accepted their fate. There were some who turned to the Ovard machines. We just don't hear about them."

"How can you know that?"

"On the walls of the tunnels. I found drawings, one was a sketch of an Ovard machine, but whoever began the drawing never finished it."

"Oh, Goranth, none of that matters, now. Even if your machine works, it's too late. Don't you see what this is all about? For a while, you gave us hope that we might live longer, and yet Winterspan has come. You can't stop it, and the hope you gave us has turned to fear."

"You have heard the charges brought against you, what have you to say?" Oxuppo sat at a long, stone table flanked by the other members of the council. Of the eleven smooth, grey heads only his wore the black, triangular hat of judgment.

Goranth rose to his feet and, after squeezing Shuhu's hand, made his way to the circle in the center of the round room. Stamping feet from the rows of spectator benches behind him expressed his fellow Dunn's contempt, but perhaps more so, he thought, to deny that they had ever believed his claims. Shuhu was right. He had promised too much.

He faced the council. "Hierarch and members of the council, after consulting with my mate, I have decided that it would be best..." He swallowed and grimaced. "I have decided to recant. I am sorry for the discord that I have caused, and for that I beg forgiveness of the council."

Mumbling from the spectators followed and whispering among the council.

"That's very convenient now that you face judgment. How do we know you're sincere and not simply attempting to evade the consequences of your heresy?" Oxuppo spread his hands. "Being sorry will not replace work lost while you lurked in the Ovard ruins or erase the discontent sewn by your heretical ideas."

"Truly, I wish I could have labored beside you."

"And do you now profess that the Ovards were punished by Kaalan?"

"The glacier passed over their city."

"And the remains of their devices are an anathema and should never be touched by the Dunn."

Goranth hesitated, his forehead wrinkled. "Because they enslaved us does not make their technology evil." He glanced at Shuhu to see a look of alarm on her face.

Oxuppo leaned forward and quoted from the scriptures: "And the Dunn were enslaved by the Ovards, but Kaalen saw that it was wicked and smote their machines and pushed the sun from the heavens to destroy them."

"I am not questioning scriptures." But he felt his resolve slipping away.

"It would seem you wish to bring back the Ovards, at least their machines."

Goranth made a hushing gesture with his palms. "I'm only saying that perhaps our descendants can benefit from the technology."

"And risk the anger of Kaalen? It's only by the Great Promise that our eggs do not freeze, and that Dunn survive Winterspan."

"And it's also by the Great Promise that we starve to death, perpetually condemned to begin each cycle anew, whereas if we had heating machines..."

"Machines cannot make heat!"

"Of course they can!"

"But not in sufficient quantity to grow crops or keep us alive."

Goranth's back stiffened. Raising both hands, he said "I don't know why the Ovards died. Yet somehow, those machines enabled them to live through many, many cycles of Winterspan. I have seen the diagrams of their protective domes and their heating machines." Goranth heard his own voice echoing within the room, and it gave him courage. "One day the Dunn can do that. And if we can live through Winterspan our civilization can progress..."

"Do you deny that these machines are heresy?" Oxuppo rose from his chair.

"How can a machine be heresy?"

"Those who put their faith in machines will not go willingly into the pit, and without all of our bodies to nourish them, the next generation will not survive. Our own hatchlings, still in their shells, cry out to us to abide by the teachings of Kaalen and the Great Promise."

"You're twisting my words. Of course, we have to leave our bodies for the next generation."

Oxuppo slumped forward, his forearms on the table edge, and glanced at the other council members, first one side and then the other. They nodded. "Goranth Galilil, we do not believe your equivocating renunciation. Clearly you intend to pursue this heresy. No other choice remains to the council than for you to be sealed alive in the tunnel of the Ovards so as to give no further offense to Kaalen the God."

Cries and murmurs of agreement came from the spectators, and some of the Dunn stood in the benches.

"Give me a day," Goranth pleaded, raising his hands, "one day to put my affairs in order and to be with Shuhu."

"I don't think so," said Oxuppo. "You've labored tirelessly for the Ovards, and now it's appropriate that you die in the dust of their failed machines."

Spectators surged forward. Goranth panicked in the sudden violence, trying to twist away from hands that gripped him, searching for Shuhu. But she was gone. Roughly, he was dragged to a small room and locked inside. Events blurred in his mind, and he heard shouting as if from far off.

They turned the final corner onto the trail that led to the tunnel.
Shoved ahead by his two guards, Goranth barely felt the wind, frigid
off the glacier. He had imagined, many times, leading a procession to
the tunnel, to the dilapidated entrance near the glacier's edge, but
always it had been a victory march, not a somber progress to his
execution.

Killing me is pointless, no more than a gesture, he reasoned,
trudging forward on the trampled ice. *How long will they survive after
I'm gone? They hardly have more time left, themselves.* His escort and
those who followed—which constituted most of the village—had a
starved look as did he, thin arms and spindly necks.

The Ovard tunnel, which they approached at last, rose from
steep steps below and opened onto a stretch of flat ground. Ordinarily
the entrance would have been filled with ice and snow, but Goranth
had worked long hours to keep it passable. Perhaps at one time a
door, or doors, covered its surface, but now, it lay gaping like a dark
mouth surrounded on three sides by high, frozen mounds, the result
of Goranth's constant clearing of the stairs.

When they arrived, the council and villagers clustered at the
edge of the opening and gazed solemnly into the tunnel as if into the
greater pit for which they were all destined. Goranth glanced up into
the grim faces around him, but the guards shoved him to the
threshold.

"Don't make us throw you down there." Oxuppo's voice was
strained.

Goranth turned to him. "Would you come with me, for old time's
sake? Just to the first landing?"

"Careful," warned Zundin who stood among the others in front.

"I'm not afraid of him." Oxuppo looked into Goranth' face,
focusing first on one eye and then the other. "Very well, I'll go with you
to the first landing."

The steps were wide, and they preceded side-by-side into the
earth. When their heads passed the level of the ground, Oxuppo spoke
softly. "You know why this has to happen."

"I know why you think it does—and I don't agree."

"If you're to be punished, it has to be proper, an orderly affair,
not the actions of a mob run wild. Control is the key to our survival."

"Seems to me, some creativity would help."

"You don't see things the way you're supposed to. It was always
a failing of yours," said Oxuppo. "Now, what is it you have to say?"

They reached the landing, and Goranth turned to face Oxuppo.
"I wanted to tell you that I'm going to win."

Oxuppo barked out a laugh. "Why? Are you afraid I won't notice if you do?"

"Actually, yes. Oh, you may go to the pit thinking that you've won, but change has already begun. Maybe not this cycle, or the next, but we *will* have machines that make heat, and there will be domes over our crop pits." He had taken out his flints and struck them once, then twice, expertly lighting the wick of one of the lamps. The meager light illuminated their grim faces. "One day we will live through Winterspan, and we won't have to start civilization over again with every generation."

"Do you think you're the only one who's tried to circumvent the Great Promise? That's what the sacred scrolls are about, managing society when the end comes. It would be easy for things to get out of control, and that would devastate the next generation. The scrolls tell stories of some Dunn who tried to survive by eating the bodies already in the pit and others who tried to grow enough food to freeze for Winterspan. All these efforts resulted in the same thing: less food for the next generation. No, I must keep a firm grip. Everyone will go into the pit—except you, of course. Neither your body nor your ideas will feed future Dunn. And now, I believe that ends our conversation."

"What will happen to Shuhu?" Goranth said.

Oxuppo glared at Goranth for a moment, the shadows giving his eyes a hollow, vacant look. "That's no longer any concern of yours." He tuned and started back up the stairs.

"Don't force her to leave our hut. She won't like that."

Oxuppo quickened his step and said, without turning back, "Well, she won't have much choice, will she?"

Goranth felt the blood rush to his head and the breath leave his body. Leaning back, he flung the lamp. The tiny comet soared. Oil sprayed in an arc, and the lamp landed near the top of the tunnel, shattering and bursting into flames. Oxuppo hurried through the fire, careful not to step in the oil.

Firelight silhouetted the many faces that looked down on Goranth. Oxuppo, wearing the triangular hat of judgment, stood in their midst.

Zundin handed him something. Oxuppo leaned forward and tossed a small piece of ice into the pit. It clicked on the stone of the stairway and bounced in ever smaller arcs until it came to rest at Goranth's feet.

Goranth felt the impact of the shard as if it were he, himself, broken on the stones. The other council members each tossed a piece of ice. The chunks fell to the stairs, shattering and skidding. Large pieces, small pieces, the stairway soon glittered with their fragments. After the council had cast their shards, a barrage followed, bright missiles arching like a meteor shower into the tunnel. Someone pushed snow over the top edge, creating a sparkling waterfall.

The edges of the stairs began to disappear under the ice and snow. The world was being sealed off. He stood stiffly, wanting to throw himself onto the stairs as well, to break like the glittering fragments that now came crashing down before him.

"Back down."

Goranth blinked. The whispered command came from the darkness behind him.

"You'll get covered in ice if you keep standing there."

Chills swept his spine.

"Don't turn around. Back down as if you're afraid. Don't give me away."

He stood, motionless, one hand on the wall, while fresh chunks of ice cascaded into the opening, bursting and bouncing on the stairs.

"Back down. Please."

Goranth felt behind him with his foot for the next stair. First one step, then another, and when he had descended into darkness he whispered, still facing the entrance. "What are you doing here?"

"I came to see what my mate was dying for," said the shadowy form on the steps below him.

"But I thought..."

In the darkness, out of sight of the entrance, he reached out his hands, and Shuhu rose into his arms. He could barely see her face, but he felt her body, and her smell enveloped him.

"No." He broke off their embrace. "You must get out. You don't want your life shortened even more. There's no food here."

"I packed the last of our food. It'll keep us a while. I only hope there's oil enough for the lamps. I would prefer not to die in the dark."

Goranth's throat tightened, and for a moment he could not speak. "There's more oil below, but even if there weren't, it would not be we who die in the dark."

"Well said, my dear."

"But you cannot be punished for my crimes. You should spend your last days comfortable, in our hut."

"No." She smiled and cocked her head as if to scold him. "That would only be reasonable, and some things transcend reason."

"You know that I'm grateful—grateful beyond all reason."

"My only regret is that now our bodies will not feed our hatchlings. It doesn't seem right."

"Ah, my dear, there's more than one way to nourish the next generation."

The rain of ice was constant now, the fire at the entrance extinguished, and the stairs beginning to mound over.

"Wait here. I'll retrieve a few lamps before the landing is impassable."

"Whatever did you see in this place?" Shuhu said. They had picked their way through debris, clambered over fallen sections of the ceiling and squeezed around immense, rusted lumps that threatened to block the tunnel completely. Sometimes Shuhu had to pass the bag of food she carried across to Goranth in order to climb through difficult stretches of the passage.

"You can't expect things to look as if they were abandoned yesterday. But here, look."

He held his lamp to the wall where a crude drawing in charcoal showed meshed gears, couplings, and shafts.

"Is this the one you told me about?"

"Yes, and over here are pictures of Ovards and Dunns building a dome. It's almost disappeared, but you can make it out."

"Are you sure? Those can't be Dunn. Their tail stubs are much too long."

"Evidently, my dear, we had longer tails back then—things change."

When they rounded the final corner, a pristine hallway lay before them, swept free of debris. Writing covered the walls, engraved into the stone, and in the middle of the floor on a table rested a machine.

"It's much bigger than the one you made for the learning tunnel," said Shuhu, placing the bag of food on the floor and approaching the table.

"Yes, you turn the handle and the sparks run along here to the heating coils. The original was huge and completely rotted away. It took me a long time to figure out how it worked. This is my second try."

Shuhu raised her gaze to the wall and lifted her lamp. "And the instructions? You did this, too?"

"It's what I've left for our hatchlings, a kind of food, really."

"This is incredible, Goranth, but—no one will ever see it."

"That's why I'm glad you're here to help me."

"Do what?"

"One of the things I found was a map, carved on a wall. It was a map of these tunnels."

"We can find our way out?"

"The hatching tunnel was originally one of theirs, too. I found where it joined with this tunnel before it was blocked off."

Shuhu walked to the crude stone and masonry barrier that abruptly ended the passageway.

"Beyond that wall," continued Goranth, "lies the tunnel of learning directly off the hatchery. This tunnel enters at the place where the account of the Great Promise begins. When the next generation of hatchlings reaches that point, now there will be a choice."

"Oh my, Goranth. You *are* stirring things up." Shuhu reached out and touched the rough wall where it blocked the passage. "But I don't think the choices of the next generation will be so simple. The one tunnel doesn't necessarily exclude the other."

Goranth shrugged. "You understand such matters better than I. But the important thing is that we've provided an alternative to blind faith. When the next generation comes to this room, they'll understand. And on that understanding they can build and pass on knowledge to the next generation so that with each cycle the Dunn can advance further. They'll no longer be placated by promises. Oh, Shuhu, I can see no end to it. If each generation builds on the last, then who knows, perhaps one day the hand of Dunn may hold back Winterspan, itself."

Shuhu laughed. "A fine speech, but that's much too far in the future for me." Then she turned to face the end of the tunnel. "For the present, it looks like we have a wall to bring down."

A question for Gerald Warfield

Q: Why do you write speculative rather than realistic fiction?

A: I can't help it. I was imprinted at an early age. As a little boy, I used to lie in bed and dream up stories that I'd continue from night to night. As an adult, I don't limit myself to speculative fiction, but the increased possibilities, the broader palette for both character and plot are irresistible.

About Gerald Warfield

Most of my adult life I lived in New York City. I marched in the first Gay Pride Parade in 1970. After leaving music, I supported myself writing how-to books in finance, and textbooks in music; my formal education was in music theory and composition (UNT and Princeton). I'm an old man now, and I live in a small Texas town where I'm very out of place. I was accepted into and survived the Odyssey Writers' Workshop in 2010. That's where I really learned to write.

www.geraldwarfield.com

Spoiler: She Leaves Him

Jack Noble

There is no doubt about how this is going to go.

"You're not leaving me," I tell her.

It isn't a plea. It's a fact. It's written in stone.

I've seen it.

She stands in the hallway, mostly hidden within a raincoat of garish red. It's two sizes too big and the hood is bunched up at the back of her head. Her small face looks out at me, jaw set firm but something shifting and uncertain in the eyes. She would have me believe that she is about to walk out the door, never to return. She would claim, if pressed, that her cartoonish raincoat will never again hang draped on the banister at the foot of these stairs.

"We're not doing that old thing, Tom," she says. "Oh no you're not, oh yes I am..."

"Take the raincoat off, Carla. You look so cute it's killing me."

She eyes me wearily. I know that I sound like a fake, that my confident words are undermined by my fevered expression. I cry at movies too, though I know that they aren't real. So my voice quavers. My eyes may well be wet. Who knows what dumb show this body is putting on. Regardless, I know what I know.

She isn't leaving.

Because I've seen that raincoat, hanging right here. Years from now. The deal is done. I've seen the past and the future locked in amiable handshake.

"You know, I remember —"

She cuts me off. "I don't want to hear about your memories. I'm sick of them."

She calls them memories now, as I do. In the beginning she called them predictions. That she has come round to my vocabulary is a hopeful sign, if such were needed. Predictions are not something known. They can be wrong. Memories are quite different. Memories are truth.

I wave away her objection. "No, no. The past, I mean. Do you remember when I bought you that raincoat?"

"Of course I do. Even I can remember the *past*. That's a gift most of us have."

"The Seafront Hotel, Brighton," I say, ignoring her sarcasm. My aim is to coax her into the tranquilizing mist of a happy memory.

"It was the Waterfront Hotel, actually."

I raise an eyebrow but say nothing. This would be a bad time to question the competence of her recall.

She holds her keys loosely, the goofy dog key-ring dangling. I picture the keys dropping to the floor. I see myself picking them up, striding into the kitchen, returning the keys to their place among the assorted junk on the counter by the radio. I daydream myself re-emerging into the hall just as Carla is placing her raincoat on the banister.

I blink away the vision. In reality, the keys don't fall. The goofy dog sways. Carla stands her ground, refusing my invitation to the Brighton of a happier time. I try a different tack.

"It's fading, you know. My so-called gift. It's like dementia."

Her eyes widen slightly.

"It's like what happened to my gran," I say. "Her recent memories went first, and she was left only with memories of long ago, of her childhood. I have that too, it seems. Except in the other direction. I can only remember the distant future."

Her face gives nothing away. I feel like that stupid dog, dangling from Carla's hand. "That's a pity," she says finally. "I was going to ask you whether I'll need this raincoat today. But I guess you wouldn't know."

"I wouldn't know? This is Scotland, Carla." I wave a warning finger. "The rain is coming."

Brighton, five years ago and only yesterday: we strolled to the end of the pier under a darkening sky, joking about the inevitable rain. When the storm came, everyone dashed indoors. But we stayed, and we had the walkway to ourselves, and the deranged sea was like the world's biggest dance performance, for an audience of two. When I said as much to her, she rolled her eyes, and leaned over the railing and pretended to vomit. The rain had eased off by the time we arrived back at the Seafront Hotel – or was it the Waterfront? – looking like two deliriously happy drowned rats. I said that to her, too, about the rats; she liked that one. We showered together and then lay naked on the soft, four-star blanket of the hotel bed, feeling as fresh, warm and loved as newborns.

The following day the sky was clear. The forecast said dry spell. So I took Carla to an outdoor goods store and bought her the raincoat. This will shelter you from yesterday's rain, I told her. She played it straight, expressing heartfelt gratitude and wearing it, red hood up, for the rest of that cloudless day.

It has been many things, that raincoat. A joke, of course. And also a symbol. Then it was a souvenir, a memento from the most meaningful week of my life. These days, to Carla, it's mainly of practical value. She doesn't see it, because she wears it. She can no more see the raincoat from my point of view than she can see the movement of her own dark eyes when she is thinking about something I have said to her.

Recently, the coat has adopted yet another role. It has become a promise.

"Is it true? The memories are fading?" There is sympathy in her voice. She imagines part of me would grieve to see the end of this malady.

"It's true."

It's what she wanted to hear. I can see the cogs of her mind turning; the mysterious workings of the machinery of choice. The outcome is already certain. And yet I notice that my hands are clutching at each other, as if the course of something important is moving out of my control.

"Why didn't you tell me this sooner? Why did you wait until I'm half way out the door?" The fabric of the raincoat swishes as she swings an arm back to indicate the door in question. "No, wait. I've got it." She points a finger at me and her keys jangle. "You're enjoying this, aren't you? It's *cinematic* or something."

"Me?" I point at my chest and attempt an exaggerated expression of injured shock. "As much as I appreciate a bit of drama, you're the one wearing the symbolic raincoat while threatening to storm out the door. And me?" I cast an appraising glance down the length of my body. "I'm just standing here in my slippers."

We stare at each other until she can't take it anymore and a smile breaks out. "Yeah, I guess you're right. And there's not much symbolic about your slippers."

"These things? No. Not unless there's some symbolism in the colour brown."

"Oh, there is. There definitely is." She sighs, and her smile fades even as I will it to stay. "Seriously, couldn't you have mentioned this hugely important development a little earlier?"

"What can I say? You know I'm an idiot."

She shakes her head sadly. "It's my fault, too. We don't talk enough, do we?"

"True."

"But yeah. You're also an idiot."

We don't talk enough. I don't know about that. It's certainly true that we don't talk a *lot*. We have always taken pride in our disdain for incessant chat. We like to sit together in silence. We communicate in symbols. Like the raincoat. Pranks, sometimes. Mute in-jokes. In Brighton she responded in this silent way to my remark about happy drowned rats. Upon entering the bathroom that evening I found the bath tub partially filled with water. On the bottom of the tub, skilfully rendered in blue crayon, a cartoon rat grinned wildly. Drowned, yet happy.

"I know it was never your fault," she says. "I mean, it's not like you applied for this weirdness. But it's like when... God, it sounds so petty."

"Say it. Please."

"It's like when you watch a movie with someone who's already seen it. It's no fun, is it? You want to discover it together."

"I know what you're saying. But the memories were never as clear as you assume. It's not so much like I've already seen the movie. More like... more like I've seen the trailer."

"Yeah, well, these days that's pretty much the same as – "

" – as seeing the whole movie." We finish the sentence in unison, and then we both laugh. My laugh is a little louder than hers.

The memories started two years ago, out of the blue. Following a brief period of bewilderment and fear for my sanity, I concluded that I had been gifted with a form of precognition. Full of romantic intention, I announced to Carla two weeks before Christmas that the first snow of winter would begin to fall while we were eating Christmas dinner. When the snow came as foretold, it delighted her. Only later did she come to understand that it had been more than a guess. And she told me that her memory of that white Christmas was soured. Beautiful surprises are not beautiful, she said, when they're not really surprises.

"Are you sorry that they're fading?" she says.

"I don't need to know my future, Carla." I lower my voice. "Except to know that you'll be in it."

I wait for her to mime sticking her fingers down her throat. But she remains completely still, and for a moment she looks sadder than I have ever seen her. Then a small smile. "But if your brain goes back to normal we'll be equal again. Could you handle it?"

"Equal? You're nuts. If my brain goes back to normal I'll be like your pet monkey. Just as I've always been."

"Right. So what are you now? I guess you're like my pet monkey with a crystal ball..."

"Yeah, I was. But looks like the crystal ball got smashed. Moral: don't trust a monkey with anything made of crystal."

"Rookie error."

"Anyway, with or without a crystal ball, you could outsmart me with your arms tied behind your back."

"I'm not sure about that. If we tied a monkey's arms behind its back, it could just as easily use its feet."

"This metaphor is beginning to confuse me. Also, what you're suggesting sounds like animal cruelty."

She looks down at her hands, which seem to be fighting over the keys. "You know, it's nice of you to say how smart I am, and of course I agree with you. But if you acknowledge that I'm the smart one, why don't you accept my prediction? That this is goodbye."

I should have kept the monkey thing going. "Yeah, well. There are a few shards of that crystal ball that still show me things. They're not much, and they're fading, but I've been hanging on to one in particular. It shows me that you won't leave." A thought grabs me. "Or at least, that if you do leave, you'll come back."

My own words arrest me. Somehow this interpretation has eluded me until now. She may leave for a time. A few days or weeks of lonely Netflix nights, passing time until her inevitable return. The thought doesn't depress me. What's that old saying? It's not the journey, it's the destination.

Something like that.

I feel that it's Carla's turn to talk but she stares through me. Lost in troubled thoughts. Detained by uncertainty.

"I was kidding about the weather forecast," I say. She meets my eyes. "It's going to stay dry." I hold up a hand. "Now don't fret. This isn't news from the Dead Zone you're getting here. I saw it on the telly. And you know, they've never been wrong."

She smiles and shakes her head, as if in reluctant praise at something mischievous I have done. Then she shrugs off the raincoat, drapes it over an arm and takes a step in my direction.

Her movement affects me physically. My shoulders relax. My breathing deepens. The inevitability of this turning point does not lessen its impact. Sure, the hero of the movie was always going to prevail. Nonetheless, the tension builds, and finally, relief.

She stands before me, under me, looking up. Her dark eyes are pained. I resist the urge to enclose her in my arms. There will be a moment for that. There will be thousands of such moments.

"Tom. I need more time. My head's all over the place."

"Right."

"Just give me a day or two to think things over."

This all seems right, somehow. Characters should not change course in a heartbeat. There should be a period of reflection.

"Sure. However long you need. I'll be here."

She steps past me to hang her coat on the banister. She takes her time, presumably doing it with great care. As if she somehow understands the significance of it. Perhaps someday I shall tell her.

I close my eyes and take pleasure in the familiar soft whispers of the fabric as she arranges the coat on its resting place.

She leaves without touching me. Without a word. The door closes almost soundlessly, and I open my eyes, and she is gone.

Sometimes, memories from both directions arise simultaneously, and when that happens there is a perfect tension, a sensation of symmetry. My whole life appears as an intricately woven tapestry, and it simply hangs there, complete, in need of nothing.

The sensation always evaporates before I can properly grasp it. Like the form of a dolphin, glimpsed from the shore. The waves pulse, the light shifts, and there's nothing out there but endless sea.

They're all fading now, all those future memories. Like dreams, the more I struggle to see, the further they recede.

I wonder, not for the first time, why? Why me? And why those particular memories? Why, for example, this one, that tells me she will never leave me?

In it – that partially glimpsed promise – I stand right where I stand now, and I look at the raincoat on the banister. That's it. That's all it is. I only know it's in the distant future because when I reach out and stroke the hood of the coat, my hands are wrinkled. An old man's hands.

Ergo, Carla and I grow old together.

And within that simple memory, a curiosity. The coat hangs as familiar as my own face in the mirror, but for one idiosyncrasy. The arms of the coat are tied together in a bow. Like something... yes, like something a child might do! Perhaps the greatest blessing of our lives is to be a surprise after all.

Arms tied, in a sweet little bow.

Tied at the back.

A memory intrudes. A past memory, from mere moments ago:

"You could outsmart me with your arms tied behind your back."

My words.

I freeze in the hallway. The front door seems far away. Gentle taps of rain begin to spatter its frosted glass. A key rests in the lock, and a goofy dog hangs down. To my side, unseen, the raincoat.

I turn, slowly, to look.

Carla's playful, silent reply to my words: arms tied at the back, in a sweet little bow.

She was right, I suddenly realize. It *was* the Waterfront Hotel.

The present and the distant future converge. I have built a dream around the image of a raincoat and an old man's hands. Years of blissful companionship, a promise sealed by this simplest of motifs.

But why would the hands of an old man tenderly stroke the hood of an old raincoat?

The handshake across time was duplicitous. The deal apparent was not the deal in fact done. The house is empty, and the rain is coming down harder against the door. The future is unknown, but one thing is certain: the arms of the raincoat are tied, and tied they will forever remain.

A question for Jack Noble

Q: What book or books inspired you as a child?

A: Like many people, my childhood was practically made of books. Something that stands out as especially captivating is the Narnia series by C.S. Lewis. Images from those books are seared into my mind. Even today, certain sights regularly transport me back to that world: Turkish delight, lampposts in the snow, paintings of ships, and, of course, wardrobes.

About Jack Noble

Jack Noble comes from Scotland, but has lived most of his adult life in Asia. He is currently based in southern Vietnam, where he teaches English, bravely tackles the local language and struggles with road rage.

April

The Flight Home

Kaitlin McCloughan

The bees are as alive as they ever were. They glide through Jianmen village with sun glinting from metal wings, swooping between the faded white lattice of the town's ornate bridge. The bees, originally programmed only to search for plants to pollinate, are drawn into orbit around an aging farmer hoeing a small plot of land. The farmer doesn't flinch when the bees crawl up his sleeves and land in his hair. Unlike their long-gone biological brethren, these bees are harmless. One of them buzzes into the farmer's home and lands on his wife's hand, causing her to burst into tears.

It's Carlotta Guo's 60th birthday, and she wants to go home.

Seven years ago, she heard it was possible. A traveler, the first new face she had seen in at least a decade, marched into Jianmen with impossible tales of resurrected northern railways. He looked like a Chinese local but claimed to have recently come from Moscow. Things were good there, more peaceful and better preserved than Beijing, he said. With the proper bribe for the local army, she could catch a train at the old Mongolian border 300 kilometers north of Jianmen and go all the way to Europe.

Carlotta laughed in the traveler's face.

But today the idea has her in its talons, gripping her with a longing she thought had frozen and shattered in the years of the long winter. Carlotta is healthy and strong, but she isn't getting any younger, and the passing of another year has solidified her growing certainty that this is her last chance to see Italy again. *Italia.* She hasn't allowed herself to think the name of her homeland for ages. She tosses the bee back into the air. "*Vola!*" she says, testing her mother tongue awkwardly.

The bees, like Carlotta, were never meant to stay in China forever. They were developed by her husband Yitao's environmental engineering firm to be shipped to Europe and North America to solve the catastrophe of natural-bee extinction. But then the asteroid hit and North America went radio silent and the long winter came to the rest of the world. Now the bees, like Carlotta, remain in the village, familiar to all but also forever foreign. A non-native species.

Carlotta packs a bag. Jianmen's shared food supply is bountiful this year and their shelves are full of canned and dried foods. She takes what she can carry, making sure to leave Yitao's favorites behind. Then she goes to find her husband. He isn't in the garden anymore, which leaves only one other possibility. He's working on the bees.

By the time the long winter ended, half the houses in Jianmen stood empty, and Yitao has made one of them into a workshop. *Or a hive,* Carlotta thinks as she stands quietly in the doorway watching Yitao work. The bees are thick in the air, buzzing in circles around Yitao's head and creeping up the walls, but he seems oblivious to the disorder as he repairs the wings on a damaged bee. His focused frown whips Carlotta back to Beijing almost forty years ago when she fell hard for this earnest engineer who courted her with the same dedication he applied to his work.

"They're reproducing," he says without glancing at her.

"What?"

"The bees. They're finally self-replicating successfully." Carlotta has no response. Yitao sets the bee down carefully and looks up. He flinches when he takes in her full backpack and canteen. He knows. Maybe he saw it coming before she did. Carlotta waits to see if he will try to stop her, but of course he only sits frozen at his workbench. She feels that the script calls for her to fling herself into his arms, to cry her farewell tears into his chest. But she imagines his embarrassed look and stiff embrace and can't convince herself to say what she feels.

He wasn't always like this. In Beijing he surprised her with flowers and teddy bears and learned to say "I love you!" in Italian. When she first visited his parents in Jianmen, she marveled that her loving fiancé could come from such a gruff and distant father, a hard-working but unemotional mother. Then the long winter came and Yitao's exuberant smile iced over until he and his father were like twins—stoic, weathered, silent. Still, he was there with her, and in the cold it was enough. When she realized she was going to bring a baby into a world that hadn't yet warmed, like magic he found the fuel to drive to an abandoned factory and return with a year's worth of supplies. In her mind his daring act single-handedly brought the thaw. It was enough, back then. Today it isn't.

"Yitao," she says. "I have to try to go back." He looks down at his worktable, his jaw slowly clenching and releasing once. Then he stands and comes to her, the familiar creases of his face an inch from hers.

"Stay here" he says. "Our life is good now. The farming has been very successful for several years. There's no disease. In Chengdu the flu killed thousands. You don't even know what happened in Italy." It sounds like he has rehearsed this.

"I'm sorry," says Carlotta, but she feels freed by his dispassionate arguments. He'll be fine without her, farming the land and working on his bees. And maybe she'll stand once more on the edge of the sea and let the warm mist wash away all the heaviness of all the years.

"It's not safe," he says. "You could be killed."

"I probably will be," she says, and almost enjoys the moment of shock on his ever-steady face. He tries another tactic.

"What about Little Bao? What if he comes home?" Yitao refers to their son by his childhood diminutive. They both keep doing this, hoping to ignore what their treasured child has become. Carlotta sighs.

"He's not coming home, Yitao," she says, and feels the chilled breath of the new winter that has come between them. "I'm sorry. I love you. But I can't stay here anymore." She takes a backwards step towards the door.

"Wait," he says. He hurries into another room of the workshop and comes back with a thick jacket. "Take this. It will be cold again in not too long." Carlotta takes the jacket.

"OK," says Yitao. He stands like stone.

"OK?"

"Yes, OK." His voice breaks slightly but he is motionless, waiting for her to leave. She looks into his eyes an extra second, then turns and walks out of the workshop.

Many of Jianmen's residents are out today, and Carlotta exchanges smiles with her neighbors. She survived with these people. Because of these people. They huddled together on the worst nights of the long winter and they helped sustain each other after the thaw. Old Chen raises a hand to her as she passes his house. Twenty-five years ago he was her son's favorite person in the world, the one who taught Little Bao to gather eggs and tell dirty jokes. Carlotta's chest aches as she leaves Old Chen behind her.

I never belonged here, she reminds herself.

When Jianmen fades over the horizon and she is walking in a vast field of softly rolling hills, the worry floats away and she feels light and young. She spins and walks backwards, imagining the receding golden slopes are a video played in reverse. She will rewind her life all the way back to Italy, back to a time when her future could have turned out a thousand different ways.

Something tickles her scalp and she swats at it reflexively.

"Ow!" Carlotta grips her hand. Her palm is pricked with blood where she has smashed it against the robot bee.

"You're too far from home, bee," she says, and brushes it off her head in annoyance.

As the hours go by a raw ache spreads across her heel, stabbing hotter and sharper with each step. Carlotta bites her lip and tries to ignore the pain. She can't stop yet. The sun grows harsh and the sweat trickles into her boot and stings the wound. She has given in to a stiff limp when she hears the cart approaching.

It's a dark wooden platform on two wheels, pulled by a horse whose glossy coat shimmers with each prancing step. Carlotta remembers the early days of the long winter, when any large livestock bore empty eyes and ribs etched in grim definition. In these more plentiful days, horses are making a comeback. The man driving the cart is weathered and not as well-fed as his horse, but the boy beside him stares at Carlotta with a plump face that never knew a long winter. Behind the man and the boy are several burlap bundles, presumably wares peddled by the duo.

She waves her hand.

"Hello!" she calls. "How far are you going? Can I get a ride?" The man and the boy blink at her in slow motion, then the man pulls the cart to a stop. He tells the boy to move to the back of the cart and motions for Carlotta to climb up beside him.

"I'm going to catch the train," she says, willing him not to mock the idea. The old man raises his eyebrows.

"You said that so well!" he says. "How did you learn Chinese?" Carlotta laughs.

"Well I didn't fly here from Italy yesterday," she says. The man laughs too.

"I've heard about the train," he says, and Carlotta's breath stops. "But I don't think you can ride it. It's controlled by the Shanxi General. Very dangerous." Carlotta nods.

"But it's the only way to Europe," she says. "I have to try."

"Hey," says the man. "The Shanxi General's local commander is one of you foreigners, right? Or is he mixed-blood? They say he's even more evil than the General himself. One time he—" The man, glances at the boy, "Well, I better not say what he did."

Carlotta closes her eyes. *Little Bao.*

"Yeah, now I remember, he's mixed-blood," says the man. "Have you heard of him?" Carlotta exhales.

"I heard he used to be good once," she says.

They ride on in silence, the dried brush crunching under the horse's hooves. Three bees dive back and forth in front of the cart. Carlotta looks to see if the old man has noticed the creatures, but he stares straight ahead. She puts her chin in her hands and watches a tower of stone rewind into her past.

"Will you see your family in Italy?" the cart driver says.

"No," says Carlotta. "I'm an only child, and my parents were killed in the fires right after the impact. My cousin wrote to tell me about it, in the early days when there were still a few ships coming from Europe."

"So why risk so much to go back?" asks the man. "Because of your cousin?"

"Yes, to find him," says Carlotta, because it seems like the right thing to say, although she barely remembers Antonio. She doesn't try to explain how the little house in Jianmen is haunted by the ghost of a child who still lives. How everything has changed and iced over and left her with nothing but a burning need to finally go home.

The moon ascends and cool air bites their faces, and the man and the boy decide to spend the night in a nearby settlement. Carlotta's throat goes raw at the thought of sleeping in a village that isn't Jianmen. She resolves to push on.

"Be careful," says the old man, "watch out for the General's men." Carlotta promises she will.

"Hey, I was wondering, why didn't you go back to Italy in the first year? I remember there was still some travel back then."

"I was in love," says Carlotta, and shivers as a bee crawls across the back of her neck.

She walks as night thickens, but the pain in her heel is sharp and her hands shake in the cold. A flicker of light to her left makes her jump. She squints into the dark, but it is only the moonlight flashing off the wings of a swarm of Yitao's bees. Carlotta limps forward. Another flash reveals a larger shape: the rust-eaten hull of an abandoned station wagon staring her down through wide-set headlight eyes. Carlotta goes to it and presses her face to the window, bracing herself to see a decades-old skeleton crumbling behind the steering wheel, but the car is empty except for a stiffened heap of food wrappers. She crawls into the backseat and pulls off her boot.

Her sock is soaked in blood. She gingerly peels it aside and tries to get a good look at her wound in the dark. A bee, its soft buzz seeming to materialize from the empty air above Carlotta's head, lands on her toe. She moves to brush it aside but abruptly there are six of them, scuttling down her foot and enveloping her blistered heel. Her gasp becomes a soft sigh as relief drifts up through her body and the pain in her foot melts away. The bees disperse. A white substance, like a thick gauze, now covers the blister. Carlotta touches the stuff and tries to imagine where it came from, but her pain has given way to exhaustion and she can think of nothing but sleep. She sinks into the coarse upholstery and pulls her arms and legs into the jacket from Yitao. It has been so many years since she spent a night without him.

As her mind spins into a deep sleep, the bees whisper Carlotta's name.

But it isn't the bees. It's Yitao, sitting on the edge of her bed. She's sick again, as she has been on and off for months since Little Bao enlisted in the General's army. Yitao has brought her another offering of a freshly cooked meal, another attempt to attack her affliction with the perfect combination of vegetables and spice. She takes a spiritless bite because she can't bear the fright in his eyes. Carlotta knows she doesn't have the kind of disease that has a cure, but the kind that means some piece of her soul is black and rotting.

"We can't possibly have so much food stored," she says, turning her head away from Yitao. "Don't waste it on me."

And then he's beside her in the car, his anxious face smooth as a child's. He is a child, just 25, still years away from the creases that will burst from his eyes when he laughs. The air outside is thick and as white as Yitao's knuckles on the steering wheel, but the dust from the asteroid has finally settled enough that they dare escape the violence in Beijing and flee to Yitao's parents' home in Jianmen. They have only their clothes and a burlap sack full of tools and mechanical bees.

Carlotta is terrified too, but most of all she wants to calm Yitao's worry. She reaches over and massages his shoulder.

"It's going to be OK," she says. "As long as we're together." His expression is still tense but he gives her a small smile.

"You're right," he says, "Together we're unstoppable." His words propel the car off the dusty road and they glide into the night sky on a highway of stars.

Carlotta jerks awake. She realizes that Yitao was a dream before she realizes that the car is really moving.

The scenery flies by the windows at a blinding pace. Carlotta hasn't been in a motor vehicle in years and her stomach lurches as the station wagon careens over the top of a hill into a valley, then jerks to the side to narrowly avoid a large boulder. Carlotta scrambles into the drivers seat and stamps on the brakes with no effect. The entire vehicle vibrates with a deep hum, almost like an engine, but not quite. The loudest rumble seems to emanate from below the passenger seat. Carlotta leans over, gripping the center console, and sees a rusted hole in the floor.

Below the hole, an impenetrable throng of bees swarms as one, floating the car on a buzzing cloud of their tiny metal bodies.

Carlotta screams. She throws the door open and leaps from the vehicle, tensing in anticipation of an impact that doesn't come. A gentle net of bees engulfs her, mechanical wings purring against every inch of her skin, filling her body with their unified vibration, pulsing in her ears before setting her in a soft nest of grass. The car stops a few meters away. The low hum of thousands of buzzing bees swells and slides in pitch until it is not just a buzz, but a drone of words.

The bees are speaking.

"Carlotta," they murmur. "Do not be afraid. We are here to protect you." Carlotta leaps to her feet and stumbles away from the cloud of insects, hands over her ears.

"You are the light!" say the bees, tiny voices crying out from every direction, "We will follow you."

"Leave me alone!"

The bees drop to the earth. The sudden silence roars in Carlotta's ears. When she looks closely at the grass she can still see the tiny creatures, inert as scraps of metal. Slowly, on trembling legs, Carlotta begins walking north again. She doesn't dare look back.

The morning is clear and bright, but the gold of the hills seems duller than the day before. Carlotta feels small and alone making her way across the endless open grassland. She feels old. She reaches a valley bathed in pleasant shade and decides to stop and eat.

As she's unwrapping a bundle of dried squash, a rumble rises in the distance. Carlotta tenses, expecting to see a horde of Yitao's bees pursuing her, but none appear and the sound grows until it is unmistakably engines. Three armored trucks roar over the hill and bear down on Carlotta.

Only one force in northern China could still have machines like those.

Carlotta knows she should run but can only sit quivering, her hands gripping her lunch until it crumbles on to her shoes. The trucks stop so close that she can feel the pulse of their heat. The doors of the front vehicle swing open and two broad-chested men climb out, pointing their guns in a circle around the valley before gesturing to a dark figure in the back seat. The third man steps out of the truck. Unlike the others, he is as thin as razor wire. The harsh line of his lips is interrupted by a deep red scar slashed across his face. He stalks towards Carlotta with a hardness in his eyes that makes her heart pound.

Little Bao.

Carlotta takes a deep breath and smiles at her son. Six men now stand behind him at attention. She can't help but think back to his childhood in Jianmen and the way he always commanded the allegiance of the other children. He was the ringleader, the instigator, the mastermind of a hundred childish schemes. She missed all the warnings in her bossy little boy.

"What are you doing here?" he says.

"I'm going back to Italy," she answers. He stares at her for a long moment, not a hint of emotion in his face.

"How?" He finally says.

"I heard the train is running," she says. "I heard I could take it, if your boss will let me."

Little Bao is silent. He sniffs and spits on the ground, then glances at the other men before looking back at Carlotta.

"You're going for good?" he asks. "Not coming back?"

If she weren't his mother she never would have recognized the faint tremor of sadness in his voice. She grasps at this small gift and reaches forward to take his hand. He jerks away. Carlotta and Little Bao stare at each other.

"Fine," he says, looking away. "We will allow you to continue. I'll send word to the General that you're allowed passage, if you can make it to the train." Only a child of the long winter could have a voice so cold.

Little Bao barks at his men to return to the trucks. For a moment, Carlotta thinks she hears a thin cry of her name wafting across the breeze. Then Little Bao snatches something from the air above his head, clutching it in a fist. He lowers his hand to his eyes and peers inside. When he opens his palm, his face is transformed by the animated smile of his youth.

"It's a bee!" he exclaims. "I haven't seen one of Dad's bees in years!"

"You can see plenty of bees in Jianmen," says Carlotta. She forces a smile. "We'll go back there now, together. You can stay and help Yitao manage the farming." She moves closer to her son. Just a few more steps and she could pull him into her arms and hold him close to her forever. Carlotta can't breathe.

Little Bao doesn't look at her, only watches with fascination as the bee taps its miniscule legs across his hand. Then he shakes it off and his face settles back into a scowl.

"Even *you* don't want to stay in Jianmen with Dad and the bees," he says. Is that the threat of a dangerous killer in his voice, or the whine of a petulant child?

"Our army will be expecting you at the train station," says Little Bao, and then he's gone, sweeping away like some caricature of a villain on a television show he's never seen, ripping the hole in Carlotta's heart a little larger.

Carlotta can't make her head stop spinning, but there's nothing left to do but carry on. She trudges wearily north. The blackness inside her has returned, twisting her stomach and weighing her feet down like lead. She turns backwards, hoping to be rejuvenated by the sight of her Chinese life fading behind her, but the illusion only seems to lengthen the distance between Carlotta and everything she knows. She pictures Yitao working in the garden this afternoon and wonders if he is too lost in his work to think of her.

A bee lands just behind her ear, sitting there quietly, unmoving, unspeaking. For a while she ignores it. She is climbing now, slogging her way out of the valley.

"Why do you want to protect me?" she asks eventually. "Did Yitao program you that way?"

"No!" cries the bee, so delighted by its own answer that it flies a backflip before landing on her ear again. Its voice is an urgent hiss, barely audible yet piercing.

"Last week," says the bee. "When the first beam of morning light touched Jianmen, we opened our eyes and found that each of us had our own thoughts about the sunrise. Each of us rose into the air with a thorax full of our own individual desires and feelings. It was magnificent! Every bee that is here with you is here because we have chosen this as our purpose. We have chosen you to protect and exalt."

"Exalt?" says Carlotta. "What do you mean?" A second bee lands on her shoulder.

"We live for you! We serve you!" It says before buzzing away.

Carlotta tries to see the logic in this. She cannot.

"Why me?" She asks. "Why not serve Yitao, your creator? He's the obvious choice for a god. Brilliant enough to create life, resourceful enough to save our village. He held us together through the long winter." Carlotta wipes her eyes. "And that was truly a miracle."

A few scattered bees flutter around her, keeping their distance but matching her pace. The first bee whips once around her head before landing again.

"It is our creator who taught us our purpose," it says, "through the poetry he spoke to us."

"Poetry? Yitao?" says Carlotta. The bee recites in her ear,

"The creator said: She is the light in the dark of a fallen world. Only through her kind touch did I survive a lifetime of bitterness." Carlotta imagines her reticent husband speaking with such eloquence to the bees and shakes her head. The Yitao she left in Jianmen was practical, sensible, capable. But he wasn't passionate.

The other bees are drawing closer again. One brave insect flies right in front of her and shouts in her face.

"The creator said that he would give you anything, if it would only make you happy again. This is our purpose. We have discovered the thing that will make you happy. Italy!"

Carlotta's breath is short and she realizes the hill is getting steeper. She quickens her speed, plunging her feet forcefully into the soft earth with each step and swallowing back the thickness in her throat.

"Yes," she tells the bees. "Italy will make me happy." Another bee lands on her ear and speaks to her in a conspiratorial whisper.

"The creator has told us why we need to bring you happiness," it says. "He told us that when your son left, he took away all your love and your light." Carlotta lets out a short sob. She crests the hill and finds herself on a cliff top overlooking a wide canyon. The trees on the opposite side look smaller than insects. Carlotta slumps.

"I'll never be able to get across," she says. Beneath her frustration, Carlotta feels a flutter of relief. Yitao will be so surprised when she returns. He won't greet her with the tender verse he imparted to the bees, but he will rush to boil water for a warm bath. Carlotta smiles slightly.

With an echoing roar, millions of bees rush into the canyon. The landscape gleams with light thrown from miniature wings. The animated cries of the bees and the buzz of their flights crescendo until Carlotta trembles from the vibration.

The bees' voices combine in harmony.

"Do not be afraid!" they say. "We will take you to Italy ourselves!" Carlotta looks to the opposite edge of the divide, to her path back to the country of her birth. She won't have to return to Jianmen in defeat after all. Carlotta takes a small step to the brink of the cliff. Her toes hover in open air and she watches a clump of dirt fall into the canyon and break apart on a jagged rock.

Then she spreads her arms and falls forward.

The bees sweep her up and float her through the air like a softly flowing river. The floor of the canyon fades behind her as she soars toward her destination.

"We will serve you! We will take you to your homeland!" buzzes an enthusiastic member of the bee chorus, and the others join in. Carlotta closes her eyes and savors the gentle rocking of the cloud of bees and the wind against her face. The bees are speaking in a unified voice.

"In the words of our creator," they cry, "Together we are unstoppable!" Carlotta opens her eyes.

"Wait," she says. The bees swirl her back to the cliff and set her on her feet. Dozens of them hover eagerly in front of her.

"Would you rather take the train?" says one. "We have scouted ahead. Your son is waiting to give you passage. We will tell him to wait for you."

"No," says Carlotta, "I have a different message."

She turns and starts walking the way she has come. Forward, towards Jianmen and Yitao.

"Tell him I'm going home," she says.

It came from Kaitlin McCloughan

For a post-apocalyptic story about robotic bees, The Flight Home draws more than one might expect from my real life. I wrote it when I, like Carlotta, was facing the prospect of returning to my home country after spending time living in China. Carlotta's experience in many ways was a magnification of my own feelings at the time—I'd been in Beijing only three years, not decades like Carlotta, but I had a life there that was difficult to leave behind. My friends and family back in the U.S. were only a Skype call or Facebook message away, but I was eager to see them and be home again. And the feeling of being in a place that I loved but didn't entirely belong—how would that grow or change or disappear in more extreme circumstances? I think we've all thought about what we would do if disaster struck. This story was inspired largely by what I imagined could happen if someone like me, living a happy life far from home, were trapped in that moment by the collapse of society. The bees and Carlotta's relationship with Yitao were originally part of an entirely separate story. I was interested in communication and the things often left unsaid between people who love each other. Unfortunately for those of us living in the real world, the heavy lifting of maintaining long-term relationships generally can't be left to a swarm of mechanical insects.

A question for Kaitlin McCloughan

Q: Do you generally start with mood, title, character, concept, ...?

A: My best stories start with a character. At any given time I have several ideas floating around in my mind for settings, concepts, or even opening lines, but it isn't until I attach a character to one of those ideas that the story begins to form. The rest of the story takes shape based on the character—what they desire, what they have to overcome, and so on. I certainly never start with a title. Titles are the worst!

About Kaitlin McCloughan

Kaitlin McCloughan lives in Minnesota, where she writes about software by day and spaceships by night. In past lives she resided in Beijing, Taipei, and various U.S. states while working as a scenic carpenter, an English teacher, and a naturalist, among other occupations. She tweets very occasionally at @kaitlinbmcc.

The Sound Barrier

Tony Clavelli

The airlock releases with a clank and a cough and she's out. Sunghee Cho floats down as the first of the Valiant's crew to touch the surface. The ground crunches and she slides, scraping along the ice. The rover shuttle waits a short distance away, a hulking windowless box on caterpillar treads.

The whole walk is unnecessary. There's a jetway to the transport. It was how I arrived. But despite the radiation risk, people prefer the walk. Because who wants to travel 800 million kilometers just to get picked up in a taxi? The walk is crucial for the effect.

"All good here," Cho says to her crew. Her voice trembles with excitement.

She takes her next steps, and her boot's sensors light up my screen with each footfall. I add the crunch and the scrape in perfect time. I like this part. Then she bends her knees and leaps, comes down seconds later on both feet and glides a few meters. I adjust gladly.

The other four crewmen follow Cho, and though they aren't my subjects, I have to account for their landing so Cho's experience is as natural as possible. This is where the real show begins. I toggle to a wider view shot from the transport ahead. The Valiant looms behind the marching crew. There are workers already there, aiding in its disassembly, ensuring the ship's automated collapse runs smoothly. This craft will be repurposed for the crew's real mission below the surface. I send the sound of the other crewmembers' landings into Cho's speakers, toning down the fall to cover for their distance from her and the direction she faces. I don't want to brag, but I've been told there's no one who can balance for this quite like me.

On the monitor in front of me there's a liveview of Cho's face from her in-helmet cam tucked in the corner away from my main interface. The image is distorted slightly, fish-eyed from its closeness. It's bright and grainy, but I can see her. There are thin creases near her eyes, and a pockmark scar beside her small nose. Short bangs cut a straight line across her forehead, poking out from her suit's hood. She's beaming.

"Everything's clear," she reports. Her voice trembles, but not out of fear. "Two minutes 'til pickup."

I love when they're this excited. It feels right, like it was maybe worth coming here. By the time the third crewman comes down, their spacing is far enough apart that I treat it as out of earshot.

I turn around briefly to check on Chris. He's shifting at his station, adjusting knobs and shimmying to get comfortable. The gravity here doesn't sit well with him. He's in charge of ambiance—funneling in an appropriate blend of wind and white noise. When an entire crew signs on, like the Valiant has, our team matches theirs one-to-one. Since Chris's performance review didn't go well last week, Dr. Singh thought it would be best to relegate him to a simpler task for a while. There isn't much of an atmosphere where they are, but without the added "room sound" effect, visitors get an unnerving sense of emptiness. Today he's trying out a sampler he wired himself, cobbled together from a spare Korg running through a potentiometer to distort it. He gives me a wink. It's cheesy but it works.

Chris starts in with breeze effect that has too much synth for reality. Our conductor Dr. Singh flicks a warning light that flashes on all our monitors to indicate the offending noise should be corrected. Chris adjusts badly, switching the effect midstream.

I hear what Cho hears in my headphones, and it isn't good. The effect whooshes, transferring ear to ear like something thrown past you and narrowly missing. Cho panics, her eyes pressed shut, her teeth clenched.

I switch my primary feed to the Valiant's onboard cameras. Cho is up ahead, horizontal, a few feet above the pale yellow surface. The errant sound makes her try to dive for cover—an understandable reaction. But in the low gravity of Europa, this sends her shooting off in the wrong direction, outstretched like an awkward, low-flying superhero. The rest of the crew stops to watch their leader rocket away. I cringe, and switch back to the helmet view.

"Unknown projectile," Cho gasps.

The light on her face fades to dark as she finally hits the ground and slides. The scraping sound of her visor against the ice has no need to be simulated, but I turn on dampeners to make it less severe. I toggle to the wider view and watch her scoot past the transfer vehicle and crash headfirst into an ice spike ahead. I press a few ugly, thumping keys for this effect, because Dr. Singh strongly advises honesty.

"Captain Cho," another crewman radios. "Cho, are you okay?"

Her in-helmet view shows that her vitals are acceptable, her rad-shields and her visor held up, no cracks or breaches. It also shows that she's angry, and embarrassed, but otherwise fine. While she lies there, I look left to see Tina and Will trying to carry on with the other crew members as they skate and scrape their way to recover their captain and get to the transfer that will take them below the surface to the colony. That's where we are.

Jupiter looms in the background, a colossal not-moon, swirls of coffee and dreamsicles. For a moment I can't help but marvel at how strange it is to be here. Then Dr. Singh comes on and rips me back to reality. I hear her speaking directly to Cho, beginning her apology. I flip off my headphones and look for Chris. He's back at his station, watching this play out on his own monitor. He looks like a sad puppy and I have to turn away.

That night, I take him to get a consolation synth-burger from the colony's food court. We've got powdered banana shakes and the burger tastes close to real, but it runs up a hefty chunk of credits. Normally we only eat here on good days.

"We're not fired, Leah," he says, passing me an extra can of water. I already feel too full to drink anything, but it's sweet of him to offer. "I'm going to try something new tomorrow."

"We're lucky," I say. "Please be careful." I try not to sound as worried as I am.

It was Chris's idea to join Dr. Singh's new company last year. The New Pilgrims movement exploded faster than most people expected and the stations were suddenly no longer limited to scientists and government workers. And with that, new markets sprung up everywhere. Dr. Singh had been a psychologist for a shuttle company, but she changed course when she realized that a lot of the New Pilgrims were having a hard time adjusting to the sound discrepancies between what they saw and what they experienced. If life were to continue as normal so far away, the entire sensory experience of home life needed to be transportable. When automated audio failed the beta testing, Singh took over. Our Hollywood jobs had fizzled with the rest of the industry, so Chris and I seized the opportunity. Europa's over a half a light-hour away from Earth at its closest, so it wasn't an easy decision. Signing on meant a three-year contract in the Big Abroad, not including two years travel in deepsleep just to get here.

There are growing pains. The fries are cold and dry again. I push them across to Chris. He takes a bite. He is thinner than when we first met, and his face skirts the line between angularly handsome and gaunt.

"You know I can support you," I say. "If you need to maybe try something else."

He rubs his knuckles into the side of his head and looks down at the fries. I shouldn't have said that. I don't even know if it's true. He looks hurt.

"Thanks," Chris says. I can hear the strain in his voice. This is a forced response—deliberate argument avoidance. "It's good to have that cushion." He gets up to leave and I tuck the leftover water into my bag and we head back to our room.

This is a new form of arguing and it worries me. He avoids the troubled conversations in favor of agreeing with me. I can't tell if he does this because he's tired of fighting about work or if he's trying to frustrate me. It's not as if we have somewhere to go for a walk and cool down.

The next morning Dr. Singh asks Chris to handle a rich kid who wants to celebrate his eighteenth birthday by doing the first extraterrestrial ultra-marathon. It's a painfully simple task and I can tell Chris is disappointed, but he sits down and gets to work.

My subject is Ed Guillory, one of Dr. Singh's first clients. He is a radiographer from the original New Water mission and has built a life in the colony. Today he's up top to gather images from a Jovian storm. The lift platform raises a whole flock of rovers from the colony up to the fractured terrain. None of the others are rovers are our clients, so I make a general din to cover the vehicles as they flow like cars from a ferry to their various missions. When Guillory's alone, I give his rover the rumble of my Hyundai Firestar. I sampled it before I left. The car's still at home, somewhere, parked in a dark garage, roasting away and waiting for me to return.

"Hello, Leah," Ed says. He recognizes my engine sample and knows it's me. "Lovely day today."

"Sure looks like it," I say, though my mic is switched off. I've never been on the surface, never seen Jupiter with my own eyes. The temperature and pressure in our colony is regulated, filtered, and always the same safe levels. I sometimes wonder if weather only exists to prevent the kind of sensory-deprived dullness my days have become.

Ed carries on with his work. Each contact he makes has a special sound: a gloved hand to the ice core, the blade's first cut and its release, a tiny shuffling slip of a sample almost dropped but then recovered. His actions are a score and I soundtrack it for him—that's what he told Singh after the first time I was assigned to him. Ed loves my work, doesn't mind the inherent, microscopic lag between what he does and what he hears. I can't help but feel like a part of his research.

I hear a sharp shout from behind me and I look back. Dr. Singh stands at her command station—her mouth agape, her eyes wide. She looks furious at what she's hearing. On my monitor everything is fine with Ed Guillory so I chance a quick glance around the office. Will sits at the station beside mine and is plugging away on the soundtrack for a solar panel repair crew and doesn't notice anything. Tina, however, is up and standing behind Chris. He is fixated on his screen while using his free hand to swat Tina away as she attempts to reach over and get to his interface. It looks disastrous. I want to help but I can't abandon a client.

"Leah?" Guillory says, and I know I shouldn't have let myself be distracted. I turn back and there's a sensor on the ice in front of him. "Did I drop this?"

The answer is almost certainly yes—he must have dropped it but didn't hear it fall. He didn't hear it because I didn't trigger the sound for it. He chuckles and picks it up. It's good that he likes me—I can tell he won't report this. The details are what matters and I have to be more careful. Tina is shouting now behind me. I flick on the noise cancellation on the switch by my ear. This silences the commotion behind me of my husband probably losing his half of our pod rental.

When Ed's mission finishes I log off and approach Dr. Singh's desk. I try to keep my head down to avoid seeing a vacant desk where Chris sat but I can't help myself. When I see him, still here, not already fired, I have to suppress a cheer. He's working as if nothing happened. He catches me in his periphery and gives me a little salute. I turn and notice Tina has already left for the day.

"Mr. Guillory treat you well, Leah?" Singh asks. She leans back in her desk chair and takes a sip of Diet Coke. The cans weigh about 395 grams so they cost a fortune to deliver, even if the aluminum can be recycled into water cans. Everything is a status symbol in the colony. Durga Singh wears short black running shorts to work every day without fail. I've enjoyed working for her from the beginning—she is patient and understanding and an excellent teacher. But I have to talk to her about Chris.

"Yes, Dr. Singh," I begin. "Dr. Guillory had an incident-free surfacing today." I gesture back towards Chris. "Look, I know Captain Cho was upset yesterday, but Chris is really talented and—"

"Oh I know he is," she interrupts. "Come look."

I sit down on a chair beside hers and plug into her interface. I see the moonscape on the screen and the marathoner running by in the recording. The runner is flanked by a documentary film crew on a flatbed coasting along as he takes floaty but surprisingly athletic strides across the surface. She presses a button and the audio streams in.

I hear music. It sounds like an epic sci-fi film—the tension rising from the strings, the pounding of the timpani as the enemy cruisers appear from behind an asteroid. But on screen, it's just this man running. Dr. Singh flips on the helmet cam and we see the young man breathing heavily, his eyes determined, dead ahead. There is a gentle sound of his footsteps, too, mixed low, but there is silence from the treads of the dolly, nothing of the plastic squeaking of a constricted spacesuit. I take off the headphones. Dr. Singh taps her monitor.

"A fifteen-thousand dollar tip," she says. "Client's not even done with his stunt and already he's radioing to his crew about how great he feels, demands the money go directly to our sound guy. Says all his friends will be hearing about this."

I'm stunned. I look over at Chris as he continues to work.

"But that's non-diegetic," I say. "It thought that was against policy."

"It is," she says. "Strictly. Especially for you film dweebs. Or rather, it *was*. I had Tina monitoring Chris today after yesterday's incident. She was as pissed as I was. Sent her home to cool off. But the money speaks."

I look back at the screen, at the runner plodding along, his face lost in the revelry of Chris's soundtrack.

Everything changes so quickly. The marathoner posted the videostream of his run on-line using Chris's audio feed and now all of our clients want the Cinematic Package. At first Chris is really humble about it, but then he's leaning over everyone's station, teaching us how to do it right. I know I should be happy, but it feels so false. Soon fewer clients ask for me by name.

Two months later and Chris is in charge of our department, which has taken on two more sound effects specialists fresh off the deepsleep and an in-house composer to save on royalty fees. I can barely keep up. Tina manages the Classics department for clients who only wish for diegetic sounds, which was the whole premise of our journey here. The only reason I'm not working with Tina is that Chris insisted to Dr. Singh that I could handle a stylistic change—and cinematic is where the money is. Water has spiked again back home so I am grateful for this. But only because I have to be.

"Those horns are excellent," Chris tells me. Dr. Singh has asked him to coach me through another session while she listens in. There have been complaints that my subjects don't quite "feel it" the way that his do.

"You're all over this," he continues. "Really nice. But you can cut the scratching sound. We'll overpower it anyway when the beat comes later when the action picks up."

The "action" is the scraping of a fungus the colony's food team has been growing on the walls of a deep rift in the ice. It's inherently boring. The scraping is the only sound that the client actually would be hearing during this, but I remove it anyway. I ease in the beat Chris has programmed for me.

Suddenly my client begins working faster. There is fear in his eyes as the music grows more frantic. He fumbles with the container and I resist giving it sound as he pins it to his leg. He races to stow the fungi in the vehicle. Sweat beads on his forehead.

"I don't think he's well," I say. I check the vitals and see his heart rate has jumped.

"He's fine," Chris says. "He has a full hour of breathable air. This is all part of the experience."

The man gets back to his rover and I continue to program the comedown music, fading the beat down to a faint pulse, and releasing the digital strings. He coasts home without the sound of any engines or terrain crossing, and against all my audio instincts, he finishes his day with just the music playing. When he signs off our system, Dr. Singh comes over to my desk.

"That was wonderful," she says.

"He seemed really stressed out," I say.

"It's good stress," she says. "See for yourself." She hands me her tablet. My client has already checked off the review. A-grades the whole way down. It's the highest score I've ever received. "That man of yours has a golden touch, and it's rubbing off on all of us."

I get to bed alone. Chris stays after hours almost every day, so I prep enough food for two and leave a plate for him to reheat. I listen from my bed. I hear the door slide open, the microwave ding, the dish sanitizer running, the score of a movie he's put on. The details are quiet but still there. His weight shifts; he takes a sip from a bottle.

This living soundtrack isn't entirely new but the playback is—muffled through our chamber walls and entirely separate from me. Yet still it feels amplified. I am awake. And I could join him, but I don't, and that's probably what bothers me the most. He should join me.

I keep a book on my chest in case he comes in so I don't have to pretend that I ignored him or that I'm sleeping because I am terrible at that. When he finally comes into our tiny room, I still haven't slept a wink. I smell the mouthwash and soap and also a tinge of his skin beneath all of that.

"Hi, sorry," he whispers. I must be lying too still—unable to mimic how I look when I sleep which Chris knows so well.

"It's okay," I whisper.

He arranges the thin sheet over himself and lies flat on his back. He breathes heavily. We are quiet for a few minutes until I move my leg.

"Do you want to go back home?" he asks.

"No," I say. I realize my voice sounds mean so I try to pad it. "I miss it some."

"Have you thought about staying?"

"Here? No. I think maybe some other generation will have a good life here, just not us."

"Yeah," he says, but I know he doesn't agree. "You're probably right. I want to be somewhere special. It doesn't have to be Europa—any of the new colonies would be interesting. It just seems odd. Are we falling behind here?"

I put my hand on his arm. He lets out of a soft hum. Our skin together gets damp quickly and it's too hot to remain close.

The company continues to soar. Dr. Singh expands to a second office in the larger pod of the colony, leaving Chris as manager here. Competitor startups have applied for clearance to arrive, and there's already a new team of sound engineers on one of the lunar stations. But with more colonists every day, we still can't fill every contract requested.

Even the Valiant, the ship that I thought was the end of us, has signed on again. Captain Cho had a few bruised ribs from her tumble, but the Cinematic Package carries prestige. Cho wouldn't let a little accident months earlier keep her from that.

Chris no longer has to monitor my every effect. But no one calls and specifically asks for me the way they used to, except for an occasional Classic Audio request from Ed Guillory. Chris helms the score for Cho and her crew on their surface missions. I work alongside our new hire, Michael, building personalized tension for the other crewmembers.

Then with less than three months to go before our scheduled shuttle back, we have our first catastrophe. I'm at my station working with a housing developer as he and his survey crew plan a surface-piercing apartment complex. Michael is working with Ed Guillory—someone must have pressured him to switch to Cinematic.

Michael's arm swings over and bangs at my desk. My client is mid-conversation with a fellow surveyor so I lift off one earphone.

"No! No-no-no! What do I do?" Michael is frantic. I glance at his screen and the exterior helmet cam on the main interface. The liveview shows blackness and then gray blur and then a blue blur and then it repeats—spinning as Guillory flips away from his craft.

"Chris!" I call out, and he scoots himself from the recording studio on a pedal chair and logs in at the main computer.

The rest I hear in shouts beside me as Michael whacks his monitor, and I do my best to keep my attention on my developer client. Other staff come over and they huddle around Michael's monitor. The rest of us are forced to stay on with our own clients and try to ignore the scene.

When my developer has returned to his home and the rest of the staff has left the office, Chris stays late to conference call with Singh and legal reps of the Ed's New Water mission. He tells me I don't have to wait for him, but I say I want to organize my review files. While Chris is in the conference room with the door closed, I watch the recording.

The video begins with Guillory's crew singing a "happy birthday" via radio—this soundtracking was their collective gift. Guillory operates a waste removal cargo ship that flies counter orbit and releases his research team's unrecyclables that the landfill cannot contain. All of the permanent residents wind up doing odd jobs like this. I listen as the dump starts with sparse noodling guitars and keyboard clanks. The dump requires a rapid acceleration to kill the orbital energy and send the waste spiraling to the outer solar system. The light through the port window spikes in sharp diffractions, and even though the lens flares are an effect of the video feed, it is stunningly beautiful.

The music swells and Ed sweats heavily, slicking his stubbly cheeks. His skin flushes and his pupils shrink to pins in the light but he doesn't put on his protective eyewear. I notice the volume increasing slowly, the high notes and the low ones separating farther from each other and building up tension. As the energy of the music hits its peak, he doesn't merely release the refuse cargo. Instead he slams his hands down the controls. I can tell that the simulated drama has taken over for him. This isn't just a garbage dump for him anymore.

The music doesn't relent, but it shifts in tone. The tense droning of extreme frequencies gives way to a pulsing beat, and instead of using Jupiter as a gravity slingshot, he burns an enormous amount of fuel on a sudden turnaround. Then he races back, the music keeping pace. The disconnect between what he is feeling and what he is actually doing has widened so much that when he panics, lifts the protective seals on the ejection switches and shoves them both manually, it's hardly a surprise.

The rest of the video is the spinning I saw on Michael's monitor earlier. I feel nauseous as I hear Chris's voice on the recording arrive when it's already too late, clashing with the emergency line the ejection initiated. I turn off the monitor and wait for Chris to finish the call.

"You watched," he says. I wipe away a tear. He sits at the server and logs into the computer. "Singh says I've gotta kill the audio files."

"But what about Ed?"

"It's okay. They've got only video," he says. "But now...." He taps a few keys. "Now there's nothing from us."

I gape. I don't know how to respond. Chris's brow furrows like he doesn't understand what upset me.

"Dr. Singh said we had to." What can I say to this? There's still the little crease between his eyes. I don't have the energy to shrug it off. "We're going to tone things down," he says. "We'll have a meeting tomorrow. Hover closer to reality. Okay?"

I'm not sure exactly when I became the moral compass of this operation, but everything about what Chris is suggesting feels wrong.

Sunghee Cho adjusts the high beams from above deck and poses for a picture with the icy sky behind her. Blacks and yellows streak and refract in a faint glow that is unlike anything I've ever seen. The lights span across the sloshing sea of black water and fade into the unknown. Her one foot is raised and her hand rests on her thigh like in old portraits of pirates and explorers. It looks pompous but rightfully so. The Valiant II is the first sea-bound vessel ready to explore the Bubble—the air pocket between the deep ice crust and the water sea they float on now.

"Can you take off the helmet?" my subject radios to her. It's just warm enough that she can do this for a moment. Her lips move but her radio is off. She's talking to Chris. He operates in a new office he had built in the room adjacent to the recording studio. I hardly see him. We've been working with the Valiant for weeks as their mechanics made sure the ship was seaworthy. The crewmembers' audio controls bounce between me and whoever else is available. But Cho always uses Chris. Cho laughs and nods and then takes off the helmet.

Her eyelids flare and she shivers at the cold. Then she takes a deep breath and holds the majestic pose for my camera-wielding subject. The spatter of freckles, the little scar under her eye, the ponytail with a few strands loose—all of it looks perfect through the liveview window of the camera the man holds in front of his visor.

There is no need to add sound effects down here. There is enough atmosphere to hear whatever they would need to with their simple on-helmet mics. Instead, our auxiliary score provides a "truly one-of-a-kind cinematic life-enhancing journey of the senses," as our ads say. Chris has been pumping his paychecks into finer audio equipment and, he says, is saving up for house. For us. Or maybe he's saving some clandestine getaway with Cho. I'm not worried either way.

I am saving for something else entirely. I check the clock in the corner of the monitor and know my final check has been deposited. It should be bouncing to my new account now.

Cho puts her helmet back on after the photoshoot. They will have to stay below deck for most of the ride but for the launch from the colony tunnel they can stay above. The view is worth the risk. But I could never get used to an iced sky. I'm going home.

"Leah," Chris radios to me. "Turn this up—the pre-voyage mood's too dim.

I mute the comm mic. I dial my audio knob down, fading the music out slowly. Paying attention to the sounds as I leave makes it easier to do: the air conditioner hum, my sneakers squeak on the tile, the metal scraping against itself as the latch releases on the door, creaking open and closing behind me.

It came from Tony Clavelli

There's a sort of subgenre in SF that I call "future impossible jobs." It is fun to imagine what people will be doing for work when new opportunities arise, but even more fun to imagine the kinds of problems those people will face. When I began writing "The Sound Barrier," my girlfriend had recently acquired an incredibly incompetent coworker. She told me stories funny and frustrating stories about him, and I twisted that around into my main character's husband, Chris (named after the offending coworker). Since the source was someone I loved, it all blended together into something sadder than I expected when I set out. The setting was important for writing this piece. I minored in astronomy and astrophysics as an undergrad, and I fell in love with the Jovian moons then. The possibility of water, and maybe even life, excited me. I like putting stories in places that are real and inserting normal people into those worlds, because then I can imagine being there myself. In this story, and it's only in the periphery, I imagine myself as Captain Cho, setting out to explore the ocean beneath the ice. Finally, there's the sound element. I was recording an album with my band in Seoul at the time, and thinking about audio and how deeply it affects experiences. I'd never done anything like recording track by track before. It was slow and tedious, but hearing the pieces come together, it was strange and nice too. How the details matter. We soundtrack so much of our lives—what if someone else did that for us? That's what I wanted to explore.

A question for Tony Clavelli

Q: Do you ever feel bad for what you put your characters through?

A: I sometimes feel awful for what happens to my characters, but I don't feel responsible. I like to think of their trajectories as inevitable. However, I'll occasionally stay up late at night trying to think of ways to unhurt people who don't exist. I think if I don't feel bad, then I didn't write the character well enough.

About Tony Clavelli

Tony Clavelli is a writer and stopmotion animator from Illinois. He graduated from the West Virginia University MFA program in fiction. He lives and works in Seoul.
www.tonyclavelli.com

Whalesong

L. Chan

I savour the meal of *plastic* as I cut through the water; each pass a different symphony of flavour. It is sour and bitter by shifting degrees and always has been so. The meal brings me little comfort in my solitude. I would sing my complaints, but no one is left to hear them. My pod is gone; I am the last. I remember their songs and I moan them to the inky depths. There is no response.

When the pod first came to this feeding ground, we had only to open our mouths and flick our tails once to be filled. Now it takes a full day's swimming to stave off hunger. Perhaps it is just as well that my pod does not suffer with me.

I hear a high pitched whine and cast my eyes upwards to the shadowed speck of Little Note's *boat*. Like food, Little Note's people were more plentiful in the past. The water hummed with the drone of their presence, drowning out our songs, but I miss them almost as much as the melodies of my pod.

Spray from my blowhole reaches for the sky. Little Note is next to me. Grandmother One-eye called her Great Mother; for she was there from the start, leading our migration from one feeding ground to the next, until at last there is nothing left to eat. The rest of us called her Little Note, because her song was soft and stilted.

Grandmother One-eye was the first of our pod to die, slowing until her great fins could no longer bear her along the ocean winds; sinking into the black below. Her great body wracked with stiffness, she groaned in her sleep, infecting the song of the pod with her melancholy. I feel the same tightening down the length of my muscles now, the ache cutting to the bone.

Little Note swims beside me, tiny as a stillborn calf. I feel the pressure as she slaps something on my side and we speak.

"Are you well, White Nose?"

A twisting scar runs above my mouth, a reminder of an encounter with a shark. The name has stuck since my calfhood.

"Food is thin here. The *plastic* is almost gone, Little Note. Are you going to bring me to another feeding ground? There is no pod left to eat it." *Plastic* is one of the strange, discordant words that our pod used. Grandmother One-eye said they came from Little Note.

"There are no more feeding grounds. The great work is nearly done."

"So am I. Every day brings more pain. It was the same for the rest. I do not have long."

"That is why I came. I spent the better part of my life with your pod and I would not have you go into the dark alone."

"This is the end of my pod, then?"

"Yes, but not of the whales. A lifetime ago, there was nothing but a grand swirling mass of death here and in the other feeding grounds. We made your pod to eat it. Life returns to these waters. First the lesser, than the greater. Have you seen the others?"

I have. They were curious, those strangers that looked so much like my pod and me. There were only three of us left when they first appeared; frolicking amidst the shoals of flashing silver and glittering pink. We danced amongst them for a time, but they ignored us and followed some unheard call to other waters.

"We saw them for a season. They could not eat the *plastic* like we could. We sang to them but heard only silence in return. They left. We stayed."

Little Note swims so close that I can no longer see her, but still I feel her touch on my throat. "They are not the same as you. Your songs are different. You will never hear theirs, nor they yours. It had to be this way. I made your pod different on the inside. It had to be so for the great work."

I let loose a long, mournful wail, wordless but with clear meaning. "I have the songs of my pod; old One-eye, Blue, Broken Mouth and the others. When I die they will all be lost."

"I will remember."

I want to be free of the conversation. I would let myself sink into the depths if I could. But there is still that fear in me, like blundering into a cold current, chilling me deep to my rotting core. Better to be lonely with songs of my pod.

"Why do you come back, Little Note?"

"Because you are all my children. I knew your task would be hard, but I never imagined your pain. I promised One-eye that I would watch to the end."

"Why is there pain?"

"Each piece of the death you eat is smaller than you can see. But your bodies gather them into the muscles of your flanks, of your tails, in your bones; binds them so death will never float on the sea winds. Your pod takes it all to the bottom of the ocean so that it can never hurt anything again. That is the great work. "

The stiffness. The pain. A thousand meals dragging me down towards my pod.

"Who will eat all the *plastic* after I am gone?"
"There is no more. That is why you're the last."

The food is all but gone now. I am not sure whether it is starvation or the pain that will take me first, but it will be soon. The silvery fishes are back, and so are the krill, so thick that they cloud the water as far as I can see. Eating them wracks me with more pain than the hunger and I have long given up.

Little Note is by my side once more. I know we will not see each other again. Even her tiny form by my flank is enough to warm my skin; I am very cold.

"Are you in pain?"
"I am at peace."
"That's not what I asked."

No answer presents itself. "I cannot eat what the other whales eat."

"No. That's not what you were made for."

Little Note's songs were always flat and lifeless through the thing she strapped to my side, but it seems I can hear a new softness in her voice.

"We knew so very little when we made your pod, White Nose. We watched your pod carry out the great work, witnessed your pain, but it was too late to take it back. Now that the work is done, we want to forget you. We forget too soon. It is the way of my pod. But I will not forget and I will not be the only one."

It is darker now. I can hardly make her out, but I know Little Note is there. I can feel the others; the whales are back.

I cry out, maybe for the last time. Part of it is hurt, part of it is my song. For once, there is an acknowledgement. An old whale, even older than Grandmother One-eye comes forth.

"The little one told us about your pod and about you, White Nose." Her voice is strange and alien to me. It comes from the same place as Little Note's voice, that tiny itchy thing on the side of my head. "I am the oldest of my herd and the only one that remembers when this place was nothing but poison."

It is nearly time. I feel the stiffness in my fins; an ocean's worth of blight in my body, pressing on my lungs and slowing my blood. A pair of whales draws near, taking some of my weight on their backs. I am grateful.

"Our herd has a gift for you, to remember your sacrifice." She begins to sing, her age showing in the quaver of the whalesong. It is different and strange, but it is mine. Mine and my pod's. One by one, the others take it up, until the waters vibrate with music. The old one comes to me, her whisper louder than a hundred singing whales. "As long as our herd sings, your song will never be forgotten."

The waters above are as dark as the depths below. It is not night yet. The light is fading. There is something I need to know.

"Do you regret the great work, Little Note?"

In the time it takes her to answer, the two whales bearing me aloft take more and more of my weight. There is no strength left.

"No, White Nose." She pauses, taking in the sound of the pod singing. "No," she says again, softer now, "Do you?"

The pain is near unbearable. My companions will not last much longer without surfacing. It matters little, I will not break the glittering skin of the ocean again. But there, with the song of my pod, I am content.

It came from L. Chan

"Whalesong" started out with a single prompt-like line: the 50 hertz whale is the hero. The 50 hertz whale, also known as the loneliest whale in the world, is a solitary whale who sings at a frequency that other whales can't hear. The jury is still out on whether there's truth to that particular factoid, but it formed the kernel of this story. The next bit of inspiration was a bit of news about the cleanups of the great garbage patches floating in the middle of the ocean. A 19 year old had designed a mobile array that would filter the plastic out of the ocean, it's quite inspiring. You can hear him on TED. The story started out as flash fiction, which Morris worked with me to expand to a slightly longer piece about loneliness, regret and garbage eating semi-robotic whales. At the end, there was something tragic about being created to eat poison that dragged you down to the bottom of the ocean, some invisible cost that nobody would ever know - hence the ending. Honestly, it makes a tonne more sense with this progression rather than wondering how the semi-robotic whales came about.

A question for L. Chan

Q: What prompted you to write this particular story?

A: The idea for Whalesong popped into my head one day, probably when two random factoids muddled around in my brain and bumped into each other. The first was the 52-hertz whale, dubbed the loneliest whale in the world because it sings in a different frequency to other whales of its species (this is still up for debate). The other was the cleanup of the great garbage patches around the world's oceans. The sentence that popped into my head was the 52-hertz whale is the hero, and the rest grew from there.

About L. Chan

L Chan vacillates between studying for a post-graduate degree in London, writing all manner of speculative fiction and making up funny comments about cats on the Internet. He has been accused of being a self-aware meme-propagating bot. In the rest of his free time, he wanders the streets of London looking for the perfect cup of coffee.

www.facebook.com/Straydog1980/

Murder on the Adriana

James Ross

Go to sleep, both of you.

Do you want a sad story, or a happy story?

You're right, I don't know many happy stories. Did I ever tell you about the time I met Emily Davis on board the Adriana?

It is a sad story, but there were some happy moments.

No, this isn't a war story, the Adriana was a cruise-liner. One of the very finest. This was just after the war.

Hush now, I'm telling you a story.

I've told you about the SS Alabama before, haven't I? Yes, of course I have. Well, after the war, me and the rest of the crew had opportunities, see. We could have captained colony ships, we could have run for the senate if we'd wanted.

Yes, your uncle could have been a senator.

Because we were heroes, that's why.

Yes, your father was a hero too. They all were, really.

Losing a war doesn't mean you're not a hero. Sometimes you have to do terrible things to win a war. I met a lot of people who did those things. Sometimes choosing not to do them makes you the hero. But you're getting me sidetracked. I told you, this isn't one of those stories. This is about the Adriana and Emily Davis.

After the war, I wanted to be forgotten. Everyone was telling stories about the Alabama, about all the great things we'd done. I could only remember the terrible things. People kept telling me that the war was over. It didn't feel over. It felt like we could be thrown back into chaos at any moment.

Yes, I *was* right, wasn't I? Your Uncle's cleverer than he looks.

All my old friends went off to become starship captains or politicians or get buried. I packed my bag and signed on with the Adriana. I even changed my name.

Walter Shickle.

No that's not my real name.

Well, now I'm telling you otherwise.

I was a barman. Why? When you grow up you'll discover there's plenty worse jobs than that and I told you, I wanted to be forgotten.

Well, when I was younger — especially after the war — I found that I liked a drink a little too much, so I figured being behind a bar would suit me just fine.

You're right, it wasn't a very clever idea. I wasn't as clever back then.

How did I get the job? I was very charming and handsome.

What do you mean, 'what happened'?

I didn't know where we were going, or at least I don't remember now. I just knew it was far away. Just like now, these kinds of ships only carried the rich and famous, so the crew had to be ship-shape and Bristol fashion. There were no strangers to spacemanship there, no sir.

No, I didn't tell them I'd sailed on the Alabama.

I told them I sailed on a different ship.

Most of the crew were older, yes. The kind of gnarled old hands that are more at home in low gravity than they are on dry land. A lot of people hadn't given up on the war, not just yet anyway, but this crew had seen enough. They had stories to tell, but their glory-hunting days were over and so were mine.

Yes, they liked me.

Because I was young and charming. And because from time to time I'd steal a bottle of whisky from the bar and share it with them.

Yes, I would have been in trouble if I'd been caught.

No, I never did.

Every week the ship would throw a ball. I suppose the kind of passengers we carried got bored easily. We'd have to shape up and provide service. You should have seen it. It was funny after I got to know the crew. These were men who had carried rifles, worn helmets and kevlar jackets. But here they were, in buttoned up blazers, carrying trays of champagne flutes, and plates of caviar, or salmon, or whatever people ate.

Some fought on one side, some fought on the other.

No, none of them knew your father.

Yes, I did ask.

What were the balls like? We held them in this great big dining hall. Ornate chandeliers hung from the ceiling, but the walls were transparent on both sides. That meant you could look out into the galaxy as you danced. It felt like that's all it was sometimes, a dance floor suspended in space. On some nights, we'd pass right by a star and it would look like that wall was made out of fire. We'd dim the wall of course, so it was translucent and wouldn't blind the high and mighty on their special evening. You'd look at someone and half their face would be fiercely lit, the other half just darkness. It was on one of those nights that I met Emily Davis.

No, that's not her real name either.

Her real name was Annabelle, but she was Emily Davis when I met her. That's how I remember her. Actually, I met her brother first, Johnny Davis.

No it isn't.

Sometimes people use fake names when they're scared of something finding them.

No, I wasn't scared. I just wanted a fresh start.

I was at the bar watching the dancing, see. They all knew the steps, even when the songs changed. Every trot, every skip and every pirouette was exactly measured and nobody missed a beat. After a while, a young man dressed in a blue jacket and gold waistcoat detached himself and sauntered over to me.

No, it wasn't real gold, it was just the colour, otherwise it would have been hard to dance.

No, I don't know how they make them. Hush now.

Truth be told, I was still watching the dancing. After years of fighting, it was nice to watch things like that. And also, the young lass he'd been dancing with was still out there and she was a damn sight more interesting than he was.

He leaned off the bar and took off his bow-tie, undoing a couple of his buttons as he did. Then he clicked his fingers at me. Kids, don't ever click your fingers at the bar staff, OK? It's the best way of announcing to a room that you're a bad person. But I looked up, smiled and said: "What can I get for you, sir?", because that's the way of the world.

"Make me an Old Fashioned, my man, and give it a twist." He said it just like that.

Yes, he does have a funny voice, doesn't he? "Give me a twist!" He said it just like that.

An 'Old Fashioned'? Easy. Place a brown sugar cube in a glass, splash on a few drops of bitters and a dash of water. Crush it up and drop in a couple of ice cubes. Top it up with bourbon, and you're ready to go. Some people will tell you to use rye, not bourbon, but your father always used bourbon, and so do I. He taught me all that.

Yes, even though I was the older one.

Yes, I will show you, when you're a little older.

Anyway, that's what I did and that's how I did it. When I'd finished he passed me some money and I thanked him. Everything on the ship was complimentary (that's what rich people call things they've already paid for) but we still got tipped. Always tip the bar staff, kids, no matter how much the drink cost or how little money you have. That said, I made more money on that one trip than I did in a year of fighting, even with the prize money. He asked me something.

"Did you fight in the war? You look too young".

"Yes sir, I did." I told him. He stiffened his back and looked me in the eye when I told him that. Even though I was staff, and for all I knew he was royalty, there's a basic level of respect certain kinds of people have for each other.

"Did you win or lose?" he asked me. I'd had a few drinks myself at this point.

"I don't know if anyone really won, sir," I told him, "But I was on the side that claimed victory." Remember this, there's a way of showing people things without actually telling them, you've always got to be careful about that. This man wasn't careful, and I could see by the way he looked at me that we didn't fight on the same side. He was proud, but he looked haunted. He was running from something.

"Did you lose anyone?" he asked me.

"A younger brother." I told him.

No, he didn't know your father. Look, I'm sorry kids, but the only person in this story who knew your father was me. This isn't one of those stories, see. It was after the war had just ended, when your mother was still carrying the both of you.

He held out his glass to me, and he said

"Cheers." I nodded back to him and he drank. He told me, without speaking, that he'd lost people too.

"Emily." he said. In all that time I hadn't realised that the girl he was with had stopped dancing, and now she was approaching us at the bar.

Yes, she was pretty. She was more than that though, she was... Well, let me tell you. I told you about the walls earlier? On one side, her skin was a pale bronze, light making patterns on her cheeks as the ripples of solar plasma shifted millions of miles away. The sunlight reflected in her eye and it sparkled like...

Well yes, like a diamond. Only neither one of you have ever seen a diamond, so that's not very helpful is it?

Your mother's wedding ring? OK, yes just like that. On the other side, her face became ghostly pale, lit only by the distant light of a thousand other stars. That eye didn't sparkle, it just watched.

"Are you having a drink, Emily?" the man said.

"I am." She said. "What do you recommend?" It took me a moment to realise she was talking to me, and not to him.

"Well, your gentleman's having an Old Fashioned." I said "But if I say so myself, I make a pretty fine Fitzgerald."

Yes, your father taught me that one as well, don't interrupt while I'm in the middle of something. She laughed.

"I'll take a Fitzgerald." That's how she always spoke, she chose her words carefully and never took longer than she needed. Unlike Johnny, who only seemed to realise what he'd said once someone else heard him.

After insisting I took a sip, she enjoyed the drink. Even when her brother went back to dance, she stayed with me at the bar. We didn't talk about anything much, but we drank a lot. I showed her how to make all kinds of different drinks. At the end of the night she dragged me onto the dance floor to teach me some steps. She insisted. There'll be a time in your life when you meet someone, and you'll know straight away you're going to be great friends. Well that's what happened.

After that, Emily started showing up at the places I was working. If I was working the bar, she'd be drinking at the bar. If the lads needed help in the engine room, she'd get herself lost and find her way there. I got some grief off the lads for it, but nothing serious. Like I said, they were a fair bit older than me, so they had a clear enough idea of what was going on. For the short time she was on the ship, me and Emily got to know each other pretty well. Her brother too, actually. He wasn't all posh accent and swagger. He had his principles and he lived by them. I mean, sure, he had all the arrogance that a privileged childhood burdens you with, but losing a war will knock some of that out of you.

We'd drink together in the evenings I wasn't working. The three of us would find a quiet corner, a bottle of something and a pack of cards. They taught me Topple the Marquis, and I taught them Blind Bugger's Grip. Turns out they're the same game. Then Johnny would usually turn in early. That's called tact, kids.

Yeah, I got to know them pretty well by the end. They were the only people on board who knew I'd served on the Alabama.

Johnny didn't believe me when I first told him, but he got competitive when he was drunk. He blurted out that they'd led the defence at New Ilium, and I swear Emily nearly cracked the bottle of whisky over his head.

Yes, that is where your father passed away.

No we can't visit, it's not there anymore.

New Ilium. Your father had stayed out of the whole business until then. He only picked up a rifle to defend his home. The place is almost a myth now, but back then, people remembered. People hadn't forgotten the terrible things that happened, on either side. They remembered Annabelle and her brother, who led the defence almost to the last soldier and disappeared just before they could be captured. People were still looking for them, I heard. I told myself the war was over. They were Emily and Johnny to me.

Well anyway, not everyone wanted to leave the war behind like we did, even after the amnesty. Some people were still very upset, as Johnny found out one of those nights.

It was like when we first met, they were dancing, I was drinking. I mean working. The journey was nearly over, so we were holding a special party. It was called a masquerade.

A masquerade is a party where everyone dresses up, and wears a special mask. There were foxes, wolves, eagles, all kinds of things.

No I didn't wear a mask. I was working, I wasn't really a part of the party.

We were just on the outskirts of a solar system, so the star was too far off to light up the room. It was just as beautiful though; we were passing a small ice planet, which gleamed like a nugget of silver in the distance. All the chandeliers were lit up, the electrical flames dancing and casting shadows about the room. I was mid-way through making a drink when they went out.

The guests loved that of course — any bit of excitement to make the journey go faster — but once you've served on enough ships you learn otherwise. If you're out there floating around millions of miles from anything, power-cuts become bloody terrifying.

No, you can't tell your mother I used that word.

I don't mind saying I was scared, but nobody started screaming until the lights came back on. The noise started in the middle of the dance floor, but underneath the masks you couldn't tell who was screaming. I vaulted the bar. I was more agile back then. I forced my way through the crowd and burst into the core of the assembly that had formed in the centre of the room. Emily was crouched down over Johnny, who was on his back. He'd been stabbed three times in the belly. I tried to block Johnny from view, scanning the crowd for knives, weapons, anything. All I saw were the masks.

"Help. He needs help" She kept saying that. "Tell the captain. He needs help."

Johnny was beyond help, and I knew the captain, see. Now like I said, we'd left the war behind, but the captain hadn't, no sir. He'd fought on the winning side, and he was an idealist.

An idealist is someone who cares more about ideas than people. I doubted the ideas he cared about were compatible with helping a servant of the lost cause. I had a pretty clear idea of the kind of person who'd want Johnny dead, and they'd have just as much cause to hurt Emily.

I held her until one of the lads, Tom he was called, grabbed Emily and dragged her through the crowd. I followed in their wake. He was just a little guy, Tom, but he made sure people made room for us. He took us right back to the bar and into the stock cupboard.

I was still dazed, but Tom had a good head on him. He made sure nobody had followed us before closing the door. Then he started ripping off his clothes. I didn't know what he was doing. But Tom fought on the same side as your father, see. It's a rare moment, when you see someone feel the old tug of duty, but Tom didn't hesitate. He knew what he was doing and why he was doing it.

"Take these, ma'am." He said, and he passed over his grimy blue overalls. They were baggy, but Tom was a short guy, and they fit well enough. "Our boy Walter will get you down to the engine room. You can hole up there 'til we sort out what's what."

I opened the door and peered through, while Emily lingered for a moment. It was chaos outside.

"You were..." Emily didn't have to finish the question.

"Thomas Knox, ma'am. Corporal, 41st Royal Light Infantry. We laid down arms after New Ilium, ma'am."

"Thank you," she said.

It was time to go, and we all knew it. Emily and I went one way, Tom the other. Once we were clear, we ran. I never once had to tell her the way, because all those times she got lost and ended up in the engine room, she was never really lost, see? When we got close, I grabbed her hand and pulled her down a different corridor.

"What's wrong?" She said. "Where are we going?"

"Nothing's wrong." Apart from the obvious, I thought. "There's one quick stop we have to make."

You aren't supposed to bring guns on board a ship. I'm sure you can guess why. Well, I told them, I'm not bringing a gun on the ship. It's a memento, see? Just a memory of my service during the war. Service on the winning side, I made clear. After all, I said, it doesn't even have any bullets in it! They were sewn into the lining of my duffel bag.

The crew quarters were right above the engine room. Obviously the person who designed the ship assumed it would be crewed by robots who don't need to sleep. When we got to my cabin, I reached under my bunk for the bag, and emptied out the contents.

"You have a lovely room." Emily said. It was filthy, and smelled of the other three men I shared it with. She had a private cabin, which was nicer. I smiled at her, and gave her the gun. It was nothing big but it was heavy, and comforting to hold.

I flicked open my penknife and started hacking at the stitches of the bag. One by one, I picked out the bullets and handed them to Emily, who loaded them without a word. Once I'd found the sixth one, she loaded it and cocked the pistol.

"OK?" She asked. I nodded.

Emily led the way to the engine room, choosing her steps carefully and peering around every corner. When we turned onto the final corridor we saw Tom slumped against the door. He hadn't found any clothes, and just like Johnny, he'd been stabbed three times in the belly. Before I could stop her, Emily had teased open the door and slipped through, gun first. I followed her and closed the door. The engine room was noisy and full of clanking machines I half understood. Emily stalked through every nook and cranny to make sure we were alone.

As she did we heard footsteps pounding down the corridor. I grabbed hold of a monkey wrench that lay abandoned on a worktop.

"Stay here." I told her. I braced myself, and crept to the door. When it swung open I brought the wrench down on the man's head. Now, I'd hit people before — sometimes you have to — but never anything like that. He went down like a sinking ship, right next to Tom. When I looked, I realised it was Paul, another crewman, my boss actually. He forgave me for it later. I'd been shaking before, but that settled my nerves, see. Gripping the wrench in both hands, I crept past him to make sure there was nobody else coming. When I got to the end of the corridor I heard two loud cracks, not half a second between them.

I ran back to the engine room and threw open the door. I swear to you, Emily came within an inch of blowing my head off but she stopped in time. At her feet were two masked bodies, dressed for dinner with holes in their chests.

"Walter." I dropped the wrench and approached the bodies.

"Walter." I looked over at her.

"Walter?" She said. "I need to get off this ship." I nodded, and picked up the wrench.

The room was full of snarling gears and rumbling pipes, but I knew which one I needed. It was the machine in the middle, the big one. There was a huge rotating cylinder, and underneath a delicate little box, overflowing with naked wires. I'd had to patch it up earlier on the voyage, so I knew what I was looking for. Tentatively at first, and then more forcefully, I started tapping the box with my wrench. It took a few minutes, but I hit the sweet spot. The cylinder stopped spinning, and the whole ship shuddered, throwing us both to the floor. Then the sirens started.

Within the hour, the Adriana was making an emergency landing on the tiny ice planet. Emily held me as we hurtled through the atmosphere. We came down in the snow, within sight of a small outpost or settlement. I never learned which. In all the confusion that ensued, it was easy for her to slip out of the hangar. She was still dressed in Tom's overalls and a thick fur coat I'd claimed in the war. I stood shivering on the gangplank as she left. She turned around once to wave me goodbye. She even pulled the hood down, so I could see her one more time.

Yes, that is the last time I saw her.

No, she didn't kiss me goodbye. There wasn't time.

A question for James Ross

Q: What would your characters say about you?

A: I'm sure most of them would want nothing to do with me. The rest might say that I should get out of the house a bit more.

About James Ross

James Ross is an Englishman living North of the Wall in Edinburgh, where he writes whimsical fiction, and (occasionally) performs poetry.

Gathering Dust

Meryl Stenhouse

There's a bench I like to sit on, with my legs tucked up, pretending I'm just another student on break from university. People always have a smile for me—a young woman in the sun—until they see the sores and the thin wrists and then their eyes slide up and away, up and away as if they have just remembered something important. I grin at them and pick at the scratches on my arms, mindlessly or frantically, depending on whether I've had a hit recently, whether I've scratched that itch.

While I sit, I watch.

The old woman crouches in front of the Opera House, at the bottom of the wide, sloping steps. Just sits there with her bag of breadcrumbs while the pigeons do their flap walk and peck at her hands. When disturbed they rise up in a chattering mass, sweeping across the square in a swift, amoeboid motion, as if they were all one. Doesn't matter the weather; rain or cold or strangling wet heat, she's wearing a knitted cap and jumper the colour of old tea. The bedrock of her face has weathered and crumbled, leaving deep gullies of erosion around her sunken, pallid mouth.

Her shopping trolley is always within reach, plastic bags tied along the side in great bunches, grey balloons that hiss and rattle when the wind blows up from the harbour, fresh, salty tang brushing away the automobile stink of the city.

The trolley goes where she goes, like a friendly dog. There's soup in there, a red-wrapped tin pressed against the wire, a lumpy bag in the front and an old blanket over the top. But mostly it's full of jars, some empty, some with lids, tumbled about in the bottom of her trolley.

The trolley jangles and rattles along the roads at night, in between the trendy cafe crowd and the workers getting off the ferry. You can hear it coming, whichever dark corner you're tucked into, whichever hidey-hole you've found out of sight of the police and the Salvos and the drunks and the predators. You can hear her coming down the street, noise and silence, noise and silence as she stops to check the bins along the way.

When she finds a lid she wipes it clean on her dirty jumper, spits on it and wipes and wipes until she's satisfied, holding the lid up to the yellow light. People walk around her, looking at the cars crawling by, at their phones, at the sky — at clean things, not at the bent old woman in her crusty jumper.

On the steps she tempts the pigeons down with the breadcrumbs. When they're fluttering in her hand she reaches into her trolley and pulls out a jar. I don't know how she chooses them, or why. Sometimes, the first jar gets a nod. Other times, she shuffles through them, her gaze distant, searching for the right one. She tucks the jar under her arm so she can unscrew the top with one hand.

Inside is dust. Only dust. She picks it up off the street: from window ledges, from gutters, from benches and dark corners, the tops of signal boxes, the long cracks in the footpath, her own, dirty clothing. I've seen her do it. I've followed her, watched her gather the dust of the city into her gnarled old hands.

The dust goes over the pigeons held captive in her hands, sifted from the jars with rough jerks, or sprinkled delicately, a pinch at a time. The pigeons don't seem to mind, though they spend as much time upside down as they do right way up. But they are calm in her hands, as if they have never been wild things at all.

And when the work is done she tosses them into the sky. They don't rejoin the flock feasting below. They flap off over the city, in all directions, in all weathers.

Where do they go? What do they carry? Messages? Curses?

I watch them wheel and turn, dark shapes against the too-bright sky, absolutely sure of their direction. It's magnetic, or something like that, the way they know exactly where they are and where they're going. They can always find their way home.

I can still find my way home. On cold nights I tell myself I'll go there, to a warm bed, clean sheets, food on the table. Unreachable expectations. Parents with their loving belief, their support, their dreams and the horrifying shape of the future.

I remember my mother painting her nails at the kitchen table. I remember my dealer's rancid breath last night as he hung over me.

I wish I knew which way to go. I wish the Earth would tell me.

The old woman freezes as I crouch down in front of her, turns with a shattered smile, hand held out towards me, palm inviting succour. But then she sees me, she looks at the sores and the bony wrists and the dirt and she sees me for what I am, and the smile melts away, the hand drops back to her work.

"Where do they go?" I ask.

I think she won't answer, as the next jar is considered and discarded. But I'm not moving until I know, so I squat there, lapped with the birds' bubbling calls, the sun hot on my neck.

"Where they're needed."

It's not nearly enough of an answer, so I stay, ignoring the itch and burn of my sores, the sweat prickling under my arms.

She searches for another jar with one hand, her eyes focused on me and there's interest there that wasn't before. "Everyone gets one. One bird. One chance." The jar is shoved back under the blanket.

My fingers reach for the bird. She yanks it out of my reach.

"I just want to touch it."

"It's not yours."

"Whose, then?"

"Don't know."

"What's it got?"

"What a body needs." She flings it into the air. "Hope, luck, some little bit of fear, which is always useful. Depends on the person." She watches its flight, sucking the remains of her teeth.

"How do you know what goes in? What's in the jars?"

She lifts her hand in front of my face, rubs her fingers together. "The hand knows."

I stare at the bulbous knuckles. Magic? "Bullshit."

She laughs, a wheezing like the rasp of a seagull, coming in from the harbour. "You think I'm going to tell you my secrets?"

"Yes. Who would I tell?"

"Go away." But her face makes a liar of her.

"What's in the jars?"

"The detritus of life."

I frown at her. The word sounds wrong in her mouth.

"You know what I mean?" she says. "Cast offs."

"I know what detritus is."

She reaches into her trolley and tugs out a hunk of stale bread. The pigeons wash against her feet in a tide, a moving, shifting ocean of feathers.

I look out over the square in front of the opera house. Midmorning, there aren't many people here. Fitness freaks puffing past. Mothers with strollers. Tourists snapping pictures of the Opera House sails. They say that dust is mostly human skin.

A jogger leans on a bench, bent over, drops of sweat marking the pavement. Determination raining onto stone, cast off from someone who has more than their share. I imagine reaching out to catch a drop in my palm, absorbing that determination into my skin.

I imagine my life changing with it.

"Give me a bird."

"It's not for the likes of us."

"Why not? Why do all this, if not for us? Who needs it more?"

"Why fuck your dealer in a dirty bathroom?"

I shrug. I have long ago been laid bare, long ago walked away from pretence. "What else is there?"

Her look pins my lie like a dead butterfly. "You ever made a cake?" she asks.

"You mean baking?" I remember home economics at school: mucking about and not paying attention, throwing flour at my best friend. The teacher told us off, said these were skills we'd need if we wanted to eat. I'd told her that was what restaurants are for.

"We're the paper. Greaseproof." She cackles. "Nothing sticks to us. The burned bits, the glue that holds the cake together, it don't stick. We're apart. We're the layer between people and what's beneath."

"What's beneath?"

"What you keep your back to, that's what." She reaches for my hand, looks at the scabs and the dirt. "Those sores, those eyes, that's the sign of it. What it is, what it brings. It comes out of us, but in just little bits, and the world can bear it. Can't come out all at once."

I watch her bend down for another pigeon, her old back crooked, wispy, colourless hair peeping from under the dirty cap, the sour smell that is sweat and age and urine, and I think, you're wrong. I remember chemistry lessons, running solutions through filter paper. "We're not greaseproof. The paper stains." I rub my arms, feel the scabs under my fingers. "It stains."

She grunts. "Might be. That worry you?"

I pick at a scab on my wrist. "No."

"Think you can stick it out?"

I think about dark doorways, and cold nights, and hunger aching in my guts; dirty needles and fucking on a concrete floor to pay for my next fix. I think of sending hope into the city, and luck, and just a touch of fear. "Yes."

She hands me a bird. It's not for me. I can feel a static buzz, gritty dust that doesn't stick to my fingers, that sifts between the feathers. "It is always pigeons?"

"Can be anything. Were rats, once, but there's not as many of them now. Them ibix—" she kicks out at a tall white ibis, scrounging for crumbs among the pigeons like a scrawny headmaster among flocks of fat children. "Them are no good. Got to be small. Cats is okay, but there's not so many, here." She looks at me with her cracked agate eyes. "You like them birds?"

The pigeon sits in my hand, unafraid, eyes dreamy-distant, pink toes clutching mindlessly at nothing. It's a warm thing, a live thing, little pulse of life under my thumb. "Yeah."

She nods and reaches for it.

I hand it over. It's not for me.

She flings it into the air. I squint against the glare, following it until I can no longer convince myself it's there. When I look back, she's watching me.

"There's a baptsy church down Redfern way that gives out bread on Friday nights. You bring it here, okay? And jars. Any jars you can find. They got to be clean, mind, so wash 'em well."

She pulls back the blanket. The light shines up, rainbow colours on her face, and for a second, just a second, she is beautiful, the carved rock of her face serene, endless, ancient, before the blanket snaps back.

"You remember. They got to be clean."

The pigeons rise up in salute, kissing my cheeks with fluttering wings and for a moment I am a goddess, winged. I push through the crowds. Nobody sees me. Their eyes slide up and away, from my dirty clothes and the sores on my face and the grease in my hair. There's a new road beneath my feet and I'll follow it, and carry the stains of the world on my skin.

It came from Meryl Stenhouse

The beginning of this story came from a prompt from a writing course I did with Cat Rambo. The prompt was a picture of an old woman feeding the pigeons. In my head, the protagonist was a middle-aged man, recently divorced, just lost his job etc. He was watching the old woman as she picked up the pigeons, sprinkled them with dust and then sent them out into the city to give hope and luck to people. He desperately wants one, but when he confronts the woman, she tells him he can't have one and he murders her for the pigeon she is holding, which does him no good. Clearly the story evolved a long way from this rather tragic horror, though the original image of the old woman spreading hope remained. Somewhere along the way (and I can't remember at what point) I got caught up in the idea of dust, of which a fair proportion is shed human skin, being made up of all the discarded luck and hope and fear and other emotions of humanity. That gave me the source of the old woman's power. My protagonist appeared about halfway through writing; I realised that the man I had envisioned originally didn't actually fit into the story. I needed someone who had already stepped outside civilisation, who was seeing it from the dirty underside. Someone with her back turned to a 'normal life', whose fears had driven her out of her home to a place where there were no expectations. The dark underneath is a concept that is common through human history; the devil, Cthulhu, Hades, the underworld. Always these dark things hunger, and heroes stand between the dark and the light. I wanted this hero to be a silhouette, a shadow. Writing the first draft came easy; but because this was a story where language had a strong part to play, I spent a lot more time in revision. And then a lot of time going back and forth with Morris in the edits. But the end story is one I like a lot, and I hope you enjoyed it.

A question for Meryl Stenhouse

Q: What distracts you?

A: Oh, pretty much everything. I have to be very disciplined with myself to get anything done. At the moment I'm looking out the window of my study and noticing that the ginger needs cutting back and the front bed needs weeding. Or I'll be in the dreaded middles of my current story is and I'll get a New Shiny Idea and I'll quickly jot down some notes and then find I've written several pages of draft. Or I'll walk past the bookshelf and something will catch my eye and half an hour later I'll have moved on to cleaning out the cupboards and will have completely forgotten what I'm supposed to be doing. What works best for me is an empty room and a locked door, and an endless supply of good tea.

About Meryl Stenhouse

Meryl Stenhouse lives in subtropical Queensland where she curates an extensive notebook collection and fights a running battle with the Lego models trying to take over the house. merylstenhouse.com

May

Tides of Reflection

Mark Rookyard

The winds whispered promises of winter as they plucked with cold fingers at Silven's shawl. She held it tighter around her shoulders and tucked her hair behind her ear. It was quiet on the cliff tops, the world seemingly shocked into appalled silence after the violence of the storm the night before. The sky was a parched blue, and diamonds of light danced on the sea under hazy pink clouds.

The path along the clifftop was overgrown, the grass thick and yellow. Once, the sea had been crowded with laughter and play, Silven watching from these very cliffs, afraid of the depths, unable to swim. Now the sea was quiet and undisturbed, the laughter long forgotten.

Below her, the waves were secretive and quiet, red near the pebbled beach, but growing darker out past the island with its alien walkways of impossibly ancient orange stone. Far overhead, plumes of white smoke trailing behind it, a scutter flew. More colonists free to flee now the storm was over. The raging winds could only keep them here for so long.

A small figure worked on a beach scoured clean by the winds and the rains. It could only be Jerek. It seemed to be a matter of honour to him not to be beaten into hiding by the presence of the sea.

Fear and frustration made Silven bold. She pulled a stalk of grass and twined it around her fingers as she strolled down to the beach. Jerek didn't look up from his work. Curls of wood littered the pebbles around his feet as he ran a plane over the bottom of an upturned boat. His boots were thick and worn.

After a long pause, as the plane scraped and the sea murmured, Silven finally said, "You're making another boat?"

"Aye," Jerek said. The hair on his chin was coarse and dark. He shook splinters of wood from his plane.

Silven watched him until the sun was low in the sky and the sea was hunched and whispering and dark, retreating from the beach. Taking its secrets with it. Taking Kal with it. She held her shawl tighter. Jerek was wiping the bottom of the boat with a rag soaked in something thick and oily.

"We have something in common, you and I," she said finally.

The rag stopped its circular motions a moment, only a moment, before it continued. "Aye," Jerek said. "You, me, and a score of other people in this forsaken place."

The wind whispered and the clouds drifted and the sun sank in the sky.

Silven turned to watch the sea skulk away like some furtive, sated predator. Kal was there, in its depths. It took her breath away to think of it. To think how cold it must be. How dark.

She left Jerek to his boat, alone and defiant under the cold stare of the sea. She could hear his hammer all the way as she walked back up the cliffs.

Marus was home when Silven returned. He sat at the kitchen table turning a small plaque around and around in his hand.

Silven switched on a light and opened the fridge.

"Where have you been?"

Even though she was looking in the fridge, Silven knew Marus hadn't turned to ask his question.

"The beach." She took a bottle and sat at the table, not looking at Marus.

"The beach." Marus smiled, looking at the plaque in his hand. "We couldn't drag you there before and now you can't keep away."

"Jerek was there, making another boat."

Marus nodded, turning the plaque around in his hands. "He's always been one for the sea. Even now, he can't change what he is."

Silven thought she knew what that plaque was, and it made her heart ache and her throat tighten at the sight of it. "What's that you have there?" She had to fight to keep the anger from her voice.

Marus put the plaque on the table. 'Kal's Room' it said on it. There was a picture of a dog, black and white. "We have to see to his room," Marus said.

Silven felt her face flush. "Can't you wait? Are you so ready to be rid of him? You won't even go to the beach now! Why are you so keen to forget your son?" Her voice was shrill and she had to fight to catch her breath.

Marus was calm, sitting there, his fingers never leaving that plaque, and Silven hated him all the more for it.

"I was the one who took him there, Silven. I taught him to swim in those waters. Don't you think I hate myself for it? I feel it too, you know. I can feel what lured him out there. Oh, you're safe from it. Using your fear as an excuse, surrendering to it. Now you're free to judge me, condemn me." His fist was white around the plaque.

"Yes, you were the one to take him out there, weren't you?" Silven's anger was cold, her breath even, though she knew her hands were shaking as she slammed the door of the habitat behind her.

The cliffs were dark out towards the coast, the alien towers quiet as they watched the silent sea beyond.

She wondered if Jerek would be out there, facing the grim sea alone.

Silven had been watching Jerek work on the boat for most of the morning. She sat on a large rock and the wind blew in her hair. Jerek hadn't said a word to her.

"You're not afraid," Silven said, relenting. "Most are afraid of the sea, yet you still go out there." The sea was gentle before them, pale red as it lapped against the pebbled beach and the forgotten jetty.

Jerek looked up at her. He'd cut his hand, the wound raw and untreated. "Out there?" he said.

"Yes," Silven said. "Isn't that why you build the boat? To take it out to sea?"

"Aye," Jerek had to allow. "That is what boats are for." He sighed and ran his hand along the side of the boat. Its bow was smooth and angular, almost looking as though it had been shaped from a single piece of wood. It was big enough for two people, Silven noticed, and couldn't help wondering who Jerek would ever take with him now his wife was gone.

"Don't you hate it?" she said, her voice unnaturally loud over the eternal wind.

Jerek looked up from his work, an eyebrow raised. "Hate it?"

"The sea. It took your wife," Silven said. She wanted to hurt him, to see pain in his impassive face, though she couldn't have said why. Only two years before, he and his wife had been guests at Silven's habitat. He'd looked younger, then. Happier.

"Aye, that it did." Jerek picked up a dirty rag to wipe his hands. Blood smeared on the stained cloth. "My Lisen, your Kal, and a score of others, it took."

Silven felt tears sting her eyes. "I used to hate her. Your wife." She remembered Lisen at her habitat, pretty and full of smiles.

Jerek grunted and looked at his boat with a practiced eye.

"She was with Kal when he should have had his mother with him. She was where I should have been," Silven persisted.

"There's more out there than my wife and your son."

The wind was stronger now. Thin clouds wisped high in the sky, and the red sea rippled against the jetty legs, warped and bent and skeletal. In the distance, bowed trees leaned sorrowfully, thin leaves brushing the roofs of long-abandoned cabins, doors askew and windows empty.

There had been a time when the beach here was always crowded, full of laughter and hope. Boats had been plentiful in the sea, and in the distance, the island and its ancient walkways had been busy with play. The colonists had loved playing on that alien stone, orange under the red sun. They had run along its walkways, criss-crossing above the water, sometimes ten hands high and sometimes barely breaking the surface of the sea. The walkways were narrow, and the children had turned it into a balancing game, trying to stay on the stone without tumbling into the water.

Silven had always stayed away. The sea had filled her with fear even before it had taken her son. It spread to the horizon like some ancient secretive god. How could anything be so giant, so powerful? Entire worlds could fit into its depths and still not come close to its surface.

"She told me she wanted a son, once. At my habitat, when you and Marus had gone out for a smoke. She was so excited, thinking of all the generations to follow her here on this new world."

"Did she?" Jerek looked at Silven, his face tanned beneath the thick hair lining his chin. She hadn't noticed the creases around his eyes before. "She never told me that." He looked back at his boat, though not with the same intensity as before.

"I suppose we all had our dreams, coming here." Silven fell silent and listened to the sea breeze. She imagined Kal whispering in that wind, whispering that he loved her, that he forgave her.

"Why do you come here?"

Silven opened her eyes. She hadn't realized she'd closed them. Something dark flashed in Jerek's eye as he looked at her. Until he asked her, she hadn't known the answer. Now she did. "I come here because you don't hide. You don't try and forget."

Jerek smiled and there was only bitterness in it. "I don't believe you," he said. "You want your son. You want to join him." The wind rippled in his thick dark hair.

"It doesn't call to me." Silven blinked away angry tears. "It doesn't sing to me. Why Kal and Lisen? Even Marus. Is there something wrong with me?"

There was no answer from Jerek. He was already back to working on his boat.

Silven remembered her first Rirshon. There had been music then, and laughter and banners. There must have been a thousand people there to celebrate the alien tower casting its brilliant white light over the sea. Now there were perhaps a hundred, huddled into their coats, around the base of the great tower.

"You didn't have to come, Marus," she said, looking at the tower. Once a year the sun would shine just so, to catch the great jewel in the top of the alien tower. Its light would be refracted out over the sea, a great searchlight starting in the west and slowly moving east until it cast its piercing glow over the island and its alien walkways, turning the orange stone a blazing red.

Marus' face was pale from the cold, his nose red. "No, no, I wanted to come. I know you think this is important." His hands were stuffed in his pockets. Years ago, he would have held her against the cold.

All around them, other colonists gathered, some sitting on the steps of the tower, others leaning against the wall of white stone, barely any of them showing interest in the light of the tower cast out to the distant sea.

Jerek wasn't here, Silven had noticed. She wondered if it meant anything that she had bothered to look for him. She wondered if it meant anything that he hadn't bothered to come to the Rirshon.

"Dena and Sten came to see me the other day." Marus watched the blazing white light from above as he spoke. A cool wind blew in his fair hair. "They said they're booked on a scutter next week and that there's a place for us if we want it. To Litoka." Still he didn't dare look at her. The light from the tower turned the red waves a pale dusky pink.

"Oh?" Silven kept her voice deliberately monotone. She watched the light. Watched the sea. The waves were quiet, the sea thoughtful in a gentle breeze. "And what did you say to that?"

Now Marus did look at her. His blue eyes were rimmed with dark circles. "I said I'd speak to you, obviously."

"What's so obvious about it?" Silven struggled to keep her voice down. "You'd leave this place? Leave Kal?" She took a breath. Dione and Sal had walked to the edge of the cliff, talking quietly together as the light of the tower played on the waves in the distance. "You go if you want. Leave me here with our son."

Marus turned to face her, and for a moment Silven thought he might touch her, hold her, even. She wondered what she'd do if he did. The possibility seemed as incomprehensible as the alien tower with its fantastic light behind them.

"That's what worries me, Silven," Marus said, his hands remaining firmly in his pockets. "You don't feel the lure of the sea, I know. Otherwise you wouldn't go down to the beach like you do. You wouldn't want it, Silven. It's like an ache in my heart. It pulls at my very soul."

"But why do you feel it and not me?" Silven said, wondering if the bitter jealousy showed in her face.

"I think a lot of us feel it," Marus said, his lips white, his eyes tired. "There's something cursed here, Silven. We should leave while we can." He looked up at the great tower above them, its brilliant white light searching the waves below. "Did you ever think of the ancients? What happened to them? Why are they no longer here? Did the sea take them too?"

"But if you feel it, why are you still here?" It was only as the words were out of Silven's mouth and hanging on the cold sea breeze, that she realized the cruelty of the question.

Marus only smiled, his eyes faded and blue. "For you, Silven. For any love you still might have for me. Because I hate to think of you alone. I can fight it for all those things, if I must."

Silven watched the alien light probing the red depths of the great sea and wondered if Marus knew that he was no comfort to her at all. How could he be, when the very sight of him reminded her so painfully of Kal? The same blue eyes, the same nervous smile.

She knew she should say something, say how much she needed Marus, how lost she would be without him, but she couldn't form the words. The love and the words were lost to her as though the sea had taken them and enfolded them in its cold dark depths.

Instead she said nothing and together they listened to the wind and the waves far below.

"Don't you ever feel it?" Silven wondered. She sat with her legs stretched before her on a warm stone before the sea. The wind whipped her hair and she tucked her skirts beneath her legs. She hated the question, hated the blandness of it, but still she wanted to know what Jerek thought.

"Feel what?" Jerek had pushed the boat into the lapping red waves. He lashed the rope around the jetty. The boat bobbed and rocked. There was something fascinating in seeing Jerek stand in the dread sea, standing there proud and brave, the fearful water turning his trousers dark.

Silven pushed her hair away from her face. She knew what she must look like, sitting there with her legs before her, her hair blowing and the wind rippling in her clothes. She saw Jerek's silences and indifference almost as a challenge to her womanhood, he seemed so unconcerned by her presence. It was liberating to think of herself as a woman, as anything other than a bereft mother. "The lure of the sea. Doesn't it ever call to you?"

Jerek shrugged. "Would I still be here if it did?" He strode out of the water and sat next to her, the droplets of water bright in his dark hair. "Look, what do you want of me?" Jerek spread his large hands and the wind ruffled the collar of his shirt. "You can come with me if you like, in the boat. Come to the island. Though I can tell you there are no answers there to find."

Silven felt a brief flush of hatred then. She hated his strength and his dry eyes. She hated how he could face his past and his loss and not hide from it. She hated him because she realized how afraid she was. She could quieten this fear, she now realized, clutch it to her breast and suffocate it. What was there to fear when she had already lost everything? She got to her feet.

Jerek hesitated only a moment before he followed her to the boat. He got in first, holding the boat steady with braced feet as he helped her in with a hand.

She could see the pebbles shimmering beneath the surface, some pale as eggs and others many-coloured. She trailed her fingers in the water and closed her eyes. Should she hate the sea? Or should she love it? This was Kal's home now. Had these very waves kissed his skin, caressed him the way they caressed her own fingers at this very moment?

Jerek was quiet as he rowed and Silven closed her eyes against the sun. She listened to the wind and the water. What had Kal heard that lured him to the depths? What had Lisen and the others heard? Silven tried to turn the whispering of the sea into promises, words of love, but all she could hear was the sighing of the wind and the cry of the blue-winged birds above. 'Flee!' they almost seemed to cry. 'Flee! Fly!'

Silven opened her eyes to watch them circle overhead, dive into the depths and then return to their nests in the green-fringed cliffs. Had they watched Kal slip into the sea? Had they told him to flee, to turn away? Silven watched the ganwings, white-bodied and blue-winged, circle and circle, and wondered what they had seen, whom they had watched walk into the waves, never to be seen again.

And whom would they tell? Whom could they tell? Would they even now watch Jerek row them far out from shore, row and row until the waves swallowed them? Whom would the birds tell their story to?

Silven looked from sky to sea, her fingers still trailing in the water. She saw fish no larger than her little finger, dark and large-eyed, darting this way and that, mouths opening and closing like silent sinners praying for divine intervention.

Jerek's hut looked small and alone back on the shore. The cabins further along the beach broken and empty, doors askew and roofs already falling into ruin, paint blistered and peeling. Silven remembered Kal changing in those cabins, running out into the sea laughing, his body thin and pale under the red sun. Had it really been so long ago?

Out here the sea was deeper, a darker red. It sloshed against the bow of the boat, the waves thick and slow. Jerek rowed and rowed, with more effort now, his shoulders bunching.

How deep was the water now? Deep enough to have engulfed Kal? It was colder here. She imagined slipping from the boat, falling into the red depths, joining Kal and crying out into the silent darkness. "I'm here! I'm here for you, Kal!" She imagined reaching out, taking him in her arms, their hair flying about them like grass in the breeze.

Was the water talking to her? Putting these thoughts in her mind, seducing her like some persistent lover? She shook her head: it was only her idle dreams she saw.

"You see anything?" Jerek asked, still rowing. "You see any answers down there?"

Silven didn't answer. She watched the sun, low on the horizon, a burning ball of red. She watched the clouds, thin and fine as lace, trace across the sky. She watched the ganwings circling and circling, crying out, mournful and lost.

Who was to say the answer lay in the sea? Perhaps it was in the sky, in the air, something hovering there, calling out to the lost, telling them to give themselves to the waves?

No, Silven shook her head. Looking out at the vast expanse of red before her, quiet as glass towards the horizon, it spread for as far as the eye could see. The answer lay here. The ancients had known this, that's why they'd built their walkways in the water, and had their lights casting about the red waves.

Jerek rowed with more purpose now. Leaning forward and then back. He looked like some great captain facing the dark. Not like Marus, hiding from the memory of his son, hiding from the lure of the sea.

"You see it?" Jerek said, nodding with a jerk of his head.

The island was a green expanse of land lying on the flat redness of the sea. A cluster of trees grew there, flowering vines hanging from the crooked branches. And the vines grew from the island itself, trailing in the sea like quivering fingers. The island shifted with the tide, swaying this way and that, but seemed to be anchored by the walkways made of stone burnished orange in the dying sun. They spread for perhaps twenty lengths out into the sea, still bright even after all these years, even with the sea lapping and licking against them.

The vines trailing from the trees rippled in the wind and the grass shivered on the island as the birds overhead cried and cried.

The island, once Jerek had lashed the boat to the pier, shifted under their feet. It was soft like sponge and seemed to roll with the waves. The vines hanging from the trees smelled cool and bright and Silven wondered if Jerek had once brought Lisen here.

She touched the warm stone of the pier and wondered what ancients' hands had made this place, or if they'd had hands at all. The stone seemed to glow with an inner light. Where the water touched the pier above the surface, it seemed to hurry away in drops and pools, as though eager to be back into the vast expanse of the sea.

The rails were low around the walkways, around the height of Silven's knee and she imagined a childish master race, scuttling this way and that, short-legged and bright-eyed, playing in the waves. Playing as Kal had once done. Laughing.

All around the cool winds blew and the sea whispered and the stone thrummed with warmth. Had Kal sat on this alien platform and let his thin legs dangle in the water? If only she could have seen it! The need of it took her breath away.

"Here," Jerek said. He stood farther out into the water, the sea lapping against his feet and the ancient walkway he stood on. The railing was higher there, the stone twisted and shaped into something that reminded her of the vines hanging from the trees. "This is why I come here." Jerek waited for her to come to him and then pulled a slice of bread from his pocket, tearing a crust off and then throwing it into the water. He leaned on the railing, smiling. "Look."

Silven fell to her knees next to him. Colours coiled in the water, reds, and blues and greens, muted by the redness of the sea, until the iridescent scales broke the surface as a score of fish came to eat the bread. The fish were as large as Silven's arm, sleek and fast, graceful in the water, their lips thick and their fins fine as lace. Their eyes were large and black, dark as the antennae on their backs were bright. Their fins rippled as they fought for the bread. "They're changing colour," she whispered as she watched them.

"Aye," Jerek said. He threw some more bread in the water, and glistening scales broke the surface as the fish turned and chased the food, barging into each other, scales now orange and red and purple, bright and lovely in the waning light of the day. "See how those colours change with their mood?"

Jerek threw more bread into the water, leaning on the railing, watching them turn from green to red to blue, flashing and darting in the water. "These are the young. The giants are out there," he gestured to the horizon spread before them where the waves were quiet, the sea dark. "The giants live out there in the deep. I've heard they change more than their colour." Jerek broke off some more bread and smiled at her, something broken and bitter in his smile.

The sea spread before them, infinite in its vastness, red and quiet and still under a blue sky. She imagined giant creatures out there in the silent depths, imbibing the memories of the sea. Perhaps the sea remembered monsters from the past, or children from the present...

Silven watched Jerek throw the bread. He smiled as the fish turned and turned around the pier, sometimes brushing against the alien stone, their black eyes searching, and their scales red and yellow and purple. Sometimes their antennae would glow white, sometimes gold.

"These young are always here," Jerek said. "Always waiting for me when I come to feed them. The giants only come to shelter under the roots of this island when the storms chase them from the deep." Jerek looked younger, talking like this, more like the man she remembered from those long ago dinners at her habitat. He had talked about his work then, his eyes had been bright and he had held Lisen's hand under the table.

She touched his cheek, and met his eyes when he looked at her. He smiled and took her hand, led her back to the island and they lay under a tree where the vines shook and rippled and the leaves were a parched yellow.

There was something hurt in Jerek's dark eyes as he looked at her, and when he touched her face, her neck and breasts, there was a desperate anger there. He made love with the same desperation, angry and fast, Silven's skirts pushed up around her waist, and when he came, he cried out his wife's name with a desperate sob.

They lay next to each other, looking up into the vines and listening to the wind rippling the waves. Bitter tears stung Silven's eyes as she watched the leaves in the darkness. She said nothing, Jerek's breathing rapid next to her. She couldn't bear to listen to it. She got to her feet, pulling her skirts down, and went to the pier. The clouds were white against a red-tinged night and the sea quiet as it rolled and rippled.

The fish were quieter now, with no food to fight for. They circled in the water, dark and silent, sleek as eels. And somewhere out there in the dark depths, the giants waited, remembering.

"The Grayson boy's getting better." Marus chewed with effort, his chin working.

Silven watched him. She'd thought him so clever when they first met. "Is he?" She tried not to remember Jerek's angry lovemaking, the way his beard had scratched her cheek. The desperate cry of his wife's name.

"Yes. It was touch and go for a while. The fever's broken, though. Garen and Bel were relieved, obviously."

Good for Garen and Bel. Happy parents. Relieved parents. Silven looked at her plate. Plena again, the vegetable thick and white.

"So," Marus dabbed at his lips with a napkin. "So, that was quite a storm last night. I was worried about you here alone through it."

The habitat had rocked in the wind, the windows buckling under the violence of it. Silven had gone out to the cliffs in the darkness, the clouds thick and broiling, the trees bending, the waves far below frothing and furious, curling up and crashing down against the beach in great swathes. She had watched the sea, her hair whipping about her face, thinking of the dark giants of the depths stirring under the fury of the waves.

"It's kind of invigorating," Silven said. "Being alone. What's to fear when you're alone?"

The beach was fresh, scoured clean by the violence of the waves. The air hummed with the memory of the storm. And Jerek wasn't there.

Scutters skimmed overhead in the clear sky and there beneath the shelter of the cliffs, the cabins had been savaged by the storm. Roofs were ripped, doors destroyed. Once this colony was no more, what would there be to remind anybody that man had been here? That Kal had been here? She could see the twisted alien tower, bright and gleaming. The pier at the island, that would still be unmarked by the storm, she knew.

But where was Jerek? His boat was there, overturned in the middle of the beach, its side scratched and scraped. She remembered the pain in his cry: 'Lisen!' and she felt shamed at the memory. She had thought him strong and brave, but he was no braver than Marus, no stronger than Marus. And she had been no stronger than either of them, giving herself to him. She remembered the look of regret in his eyes as he rolled away from her, the look of loss. Had he given himself to the sea? His hut was empty, the oars leaning against the wall, bundled together with frayed rope.

The boat scraped and bounced along the pebbles as she pushed it into the water, gasping with the effort. She soaked her skirts climbing into it, through waves lazy after their efforts of the night before. Would the giants already have returned to the deep? She rowed, biting her lip in determination. The waves felt thick and slow in resistance, but still she rowed.

The sea was quiet at the island, almost as though it was shocked at its own fury. Silven walked around the matrix of the pier, her skirts trailing in the water all around her. She sat on the walkway, her arms on the railing, and let her legs dangle in the water warm on her skin.

They came, coiling and spiralling, flashing scales breaking the glass-like water, and then sinking again. They were blue, red, green and every colour in between. The fish nibbled on her legs with cold lips, their antennae flashing white and gold, spinning in the ripples.

She saw it then, a shadow, deep and rising through the flashing fish. It was large, perhaps as large as Silven herself. She leaned over her knees to look closer. It came through the smaller fish, this shadow, dark as the night. She blinked, and then blinked again. She recognized the sombre eyes first, and then the narrow nose. He looked peaceful, his dark hair flowing about him. Jerek smiled, not a bitter smile, but a smile of pure peace. It looked strange on that serious face.

"No," Silven whispered, almost moaned. "No." She closed her eyes, her mouth dry and her stomach empty. When she opened her eyes, she was only in time to see the shadow flick a tail and flee back into the depths. "What?" Silven gasped. She wiped an eye with the back of her hand, jumped up, her legs out of the water as fast as she could, patting the drops from her legs as though they burned.

She ran all around the walkway, looking into the sea, only seeing flashing green and purple fish, only seeing her own hair flying in the wind, her own skirts wrapping about her legs. She fell to her knees, peering into the depths, "Jerek!" she shouted. "Jerek!" Had he surrendered to the sea? "Jerek!" she called again.

There. She saw another shadow rising to the surface through the ever-dancing fish. Silven waved the smaller fish away. The shadow rose. A woman took shape, her long blonde hair roiling about her slim face. Her skin looked almost blue. Her eyes opened and she smiled a sleepy smile, her cheeks dimpling as her hair danced in the redness of the water. She wore a dress of white, blue leaves patterned on it, and this too shivered in the deep. The woman reached out a hand, and Silven couldn't do anything but reach out a hand to help her, but with a flick and a splash, the shadow was gone, back into the deep.

"No! No!" Silven shouted. "Come back!" She fell to her knees, the stone scraping her skin, and she scrabbled along the pier, looking both sides into the water. There, another shadow. Silven gasped. This was a man. He smiled at her, his thin hair rippling, his serious eyes bright and alive. And then he too was gone.

She was crying now. Sobbing. She couldn't seem to breathe enough air. "Kal!" she cried. "Kal! Kal!" And she scrabbled and crawled on her hands and knees looking this way and that, her knees bloodied and her hands raw from the coldness of the sea.

The sun rose and fell in a red sky. How many times, Silven couldn't have said. She saw faces, people she knew, people she didn't know. She wept and she screamed and all the time she cried out the name of her son. Begging him to come. Begging the sea to show him to her. To remember him.

Sometimes she even saw the ancients coming to her from the depths. These made her smile, and forget her sorrows for a moment. Their eyes, their eyes...

When Marus came to her, she wept. He didn't look so sad now, so afraid. "Be with Kal," she whispered. "Look after him." And she wept again. When had he given himself to the sea? How long had she been here?

Soon the shadows came no more. But they would return. The storms, she knew. She watched the young fish around her, changing colours, angry when they fought for food, happy when they were full, relaxed when she tickled them with her fingers.

The giants would return soon, to shelter from the storms. She could wait. Wait for Kal.

She lay on the stone pier, trailing her fingers in the water. The storms would come. The waves would be fierce, curling and crashing on the pier, eager and devastating enough to chase the giants from the depths.

And Kal would come with them.

A question for Mark Rookyard

Q: Are you optimistic about the future of humanity?

A: I'd say I'm 50/50. There's the excitement and wonder of new technology and where that can take us, but then I think there's always humanity's baser instincts holding us back from what we could truly achieve. I could never imagine humanity, with all its failings, will ever achieve a utopia.

About Mark Rookyard

Mark Rookyard lives in Yorkshire, England. He likes running long distances and writing short stories.

A Song Without a Voice

Brad Preslar

Dahlia traced the melody on her tablet and her song poured from speakers hidden around the subway station. It burrowed into Jonah's ear and asked a question only she could answer. It dug into his brain and found his memories of her. The melody scraped and scratched until the scars gave way and some trace of what he once felt for her leaked out. At least, she hoped it did.

He cocked his head. In the darkness underneath the hooded sweatshirt she wore, a smile warmed what passed for her lips; he would love her again. Even if he was the only one.

He brushed his dark hair to the side and paused on the subway platform, searching as he strained to hear the next musical thought. Good. She'd worried the synthesized tones would be a poor substitute for the voice that once captured his heart.

"It's the edges that make it special, the raw parts," he'd said. "It gives it depth, makes it, I don't know, more real." That was back when she had a voice, before the cancer and the surgeries took it away.

Her fingers danced across the glassy tablet screen while the Monday morning commuter crowd bustled around him on the subway platform. Jonah waited for the 3 train that would take him to Manhattan. He looked around, searching for the melody. Dahlia pulled the hood up further; she couldn't let him recognize her yet. Not until she had him hooked with the circle progression that drove her song from chord to chord.

She hoped her choice of key would be prophetic; F-sharp major rang of final victory over painful struggle. The particular circle progression she'd chosen created a sense of inevitable return to its root, the F-sharp. That chord would be the one in her one-four-five-one progression, where she'd begin and where she'd return.

She longed for a return to her days as a performer, singing to packed venues, seeing the echoes of her voice on the enchanted faces of her audience. Her subway audience reflected no such joy, but she reminded herself that Jonah's reaction was all that mattered.

With the F-sharp chord as the one, her song went to the four, a B-major. It sang of adversity, including the F-sharp note for a vague sense of familiarity, but otherwise complicating the expression. Dahlia felt a particular fondness for this chord; she heard the same disfigured familiarity that she saw in her bathroom mirror.

Jonah winced at the discord, and Dahlia let her fingers dance on the piano keys displayed on her tablet, driving the discordant notes deeper into his ear. It hurt to hurt him, but not as much as it hurt to want him. She let him feel the pain she lived every day.

Dahlia's haunting melody sang from both above and below the audible range of sound. The lower sounds came from the infrasound generator hidden in the darkness below the subway platform, a black box she'd mounted down by the tracks that siphoned power from the same third rail that powered the subway cars. The sound played so low that Jonah (and everyone on the platform) would feel it instead of hearing it. They'd feel awestruck, afraid, even cold. All without knowing why.

She sent other notes to the dummy security camera she'd mounted high overhead. It looked like all the other cameras mounted on the dirty yellow platform columns in Grand Army Plaza subway station. Except hers had a focused parametric array inside. It rotated to follow Jonah, aiming the tight beam of sound directly at his ear; that note played only for him.

Finally, the rest of her song played from a street performer's small amp twenty feet down the platform. As he did every day, Uriah played '60s, '70s, and '80s pop on an electric guitar for tips. She had the sense that he was capable of more, but knew from watching him that nostalgia was what put money in his guitar case.

She practiced when the station was deserted and she knew Jonah wouldn't pass through, mid-day and late at night. She'd begun with her own small amp, playing for tips whenever the station wasn't deserted. But during rush hour, when Jonah *would* be there, so was Uriah. Rather than try to overpower his guitar, Dahlia chose to make his performance part of hers.

Earlier that morning she'd given him a wad of cash and a note asking if she could play through his amplifier during his smoke breaks. When he agreed, she had him plug a remote-controlled MIDI device into that amp.

However, as it now did for Jonah, her device could also change the music Uriah played to include notes Dahlia wanted performed, shifting key as necessary so that his song became hers. He squinted at her, obviously not appreciating her musical addition. But since the song wasn't for him and her extra cash made up for any lost tips, she ignored his glare. This concert had an audience of one.

She had ten seconds before the train arrived to move to the C-sharp five chord, where the climax of the progression would happen, capturing Jonah's imagination and setting her hook. The chord would create an insatiable need, planting an earworm deep in his brain that he'd ache to resolve. She'd set his body vibrating all the way down to his core. And then she'd send him off into the world.

He'd leave her again, like he'd left her before. Only this time he'd come back. He'd have to. Her song would guarantee it.

She let the song breathe, pause for a moment. Dahlia watched commuters cross between where she sat on the wooden bench and where Jonah stood on the platform. Tension spooled in her lungs. It tightened around her chest, reminding her of the empty ache inside.

She held her breath and counted beats in her head, teasing him with the melody, waiting to play the next chord in the progression. This was the pause she'd always adored. This was how she'd captivated her audiences, back when people lined up to see her instead of turning away from her deformed face.

When she couldn't stand it, when she absolutely couldn't wait any longer, she shifted to the C-sharp five. She added a complicating note and inverted the chord, intensifying the need to resolve back to the one.

Dahlia wanted him to need that resolution, to crave it, even beg for it. She wanted him to want it as much as she wanted him, to feel the same kind of need that gnawed at her insides day in and day out.

Jonah would know the kind of need that came from craving something you once had, the most familiar ache. That hook would bring him back. Only, instead of setting the hook, the chord unraveled.

A tall man passed between Jonah and overhead camera, interrupting the focused sound beam. At the same moment, a nearby phone rang, discordant tones slicing through her chord and cutting it in half. Dahlia cursed, her fingers flying across the tablet. She had only seconds to re-start the progression, only moments to re-cast the hook.

She moved back to the first chord and began again. Dahlia glanced up to check Jonah's position just in time to see him step into the subway car and out of her grasp. The doors closed behind him and the train accelerated into the tunnel, leaving her song behind.

She let the tablet fall into her lap. Failure settled onto Dahlia's shoulders and she let herself slump under its foul weight.

Taking a deep breath, she shrugged it off. This wasn't her only chance; he'd be on this platform again tomorrow morning. Truthfully, if she really wanted to, she could wait here all day. He'd take the 3 train home again and walk back through this station shortly after six. No, she decided. She'd waited this long, and she could wait another day.

Dahlia lifted her scarf to her mouth, arranging it about her neck before pushing back her hood. She put her tablet into her bag, and then stood and walked down to where Uriah played. She watched and waited for him to finish "Strawberry Fields Forever."

He ended with a bright riff, resolved to the final note, and held it. He said, "You're the only person I know that pays to hear songs that don't sound right, you know that?"

She shrugged, smiled with her eyes, and pointed to the MIDI controller patched into his amp.

Uriah rolled his thumb across the volume knob, fading the note out. "Go on."

Dahlia bent and unplugged the device. She stood and put it in her bag. Uriah inhaled and her stomach dropped; she knew that sound too well.

"Wait, are you Dahlia?" he asked.

Her hand flew to her scarf, which had slipped down as she'd stood, revealing her surgically reconstructed lower jaw. She hurried to rearrange it, covering her disfigurement. Recognition brightened Uriah's face. He smiled.

He said, "You *are* Dahlia."

The expression on his face was something she hadn't seen in so long she didn't recognize it. Most people looked away, and the ones who didn't struggled to hide their revulsion. He looked genuinely happy to see her; his eyes wrinkled at the corners.

Unsure how to react, Dahlia chose to retreat. Scarf in place, she turned and hurried off down the platform, through the crowd and up onto the waiting New York City streets.

The next morning Dahlia feigned confidence as she approached Uriah, forcing a nonchalance she was sure fooled no one. He was warming up with a series of scales and fingerings when she stopped in front of his amp holding two cups of coffee. He glanced up, finished his scale and rested one hand on the strings, silencing the guitar.

He said, "Listen. Yesterday, I didn't mean to"—he stopped and scratched his head—"I mean, I wasn't trying to be rude. You know?"

She held out one of the cups of coffee and he took it. She held up a finger, signaling him to wait. Dahlia produced cream, sugar, and a stirrer from her pocket. She handed him those as well.

"Thanks," he said. "We're cool?"

She nodded. His reaction had actually been relatively tame. Before she started consistently covering the lower half of her face with a scarf, she'd endured much worse.

He smiled and held out a hand. "I'm Uriah." She shook it and he said, "And you're Dahlia." It wasn't a question. "Wow," he said. "Just, wow."

She cocked her head.

He said, "I didn't recognize you with the scarf, but I was...no. I *am* a big fan. Got all your albums. Even saw your last concert at Beacon Theatre." He mixed the sugar and cream into his coffee, took a sip and continued, "That's good. Cleary not,"—he motioned to the coffee machine by the escalators—"subway coffee."

She nodded, took the MIDI controller from her bag, and set it on the amplifier.

He sipped his coffee. "Where'd you get it?"

Dahlia took several tightly folded bills from her pocket and set them beside the MIDI controller.

He glanced at the money. "The coffee," said Uriah. "Where'd you get the coffee?"

She tilted her head and pointed to the name on the coffee cup. "Black Mountain Coffee," it read.

"Oh, yeah." He shook his head. "Listen, I feel bad about yesterday. And since you brought me coffee?" He bent and plugged the controller into the amp, scooped the money up and handed it back. "No charge."

Dahlia eyed Uriah.

"One condition," he said.

She lifted her eyebrows, expectantly.

"Play *with* me."

Dahlia squinted.

"I heard you yesterday with that tablet, and I know what you're capable of. You controlled my song, twisted it to play what you played. Instead of playing over me, why not play with me?" He pointed at the controller. "I hooked you into an auxiliary port instead of directly in line."

She looked away, considering the request.

"Or I can play with you. You were in F-sharp major yesterday, right?"

She nodded.

Uriah smiled. He strummed the one, an F-sharp major seventh. "I heard that one, then what, the four?" He played a B major.

She smiled under her scarf, flushed with the joy of sharing a common tongue. The feeling surprised her. She shook her head, and forgetting herself, took the tablet from her bag. She played the ninth of the chord, a C-sharp note, through the infrasound generator below the platform, leaning the B-major chord forward towards what came next.

Uriah looked around, momentarily confused. "I know it's there, but I don't hear it. It's more like I...I feel it?"

Dahlia nodded. She used her tablet to type out the words, "C-sharp. Infrasound generator. Too low to hear." She tapped her chest with an open palm.

"Woah. Yeah. I do feel it. What's next?"

She held up five fingers.

"The five?"

She nodded and started to play the C-sharp five chord.

She stopped, her hand just above the tablet. What was she doing? Jonah would be here any minute. If he recognized her too soon, he'd never listen.

Uriah strummed the chord. He looked up just as she slipped the tablet into her bag and put the folded bills back on the amp. She hurried down the platform to take a seat on her bench.

Dahlia pulled her hood up over her head and set the tablet on her lap. The opening strains of Def Leppard's "Pour Some Sugar on Me" floated down from Uriah's amplifier. She couldn't help but smile. His taste in pop songs ranged from recognized classics to guilty pleasures. This definitely qualified as the latter. She couldn't remember the last time she'd heard Def Leppard. She started to chase that thought but caught herself. Enough. She needed to focus on her own song.

Checking first to ensure none of the other people standing nearby were looking her way, she pulled her scarf down and sipped her coffee. Watching the crowd for Jonah's face, she rehearsed her song in her head.

When he arrived moments later, she began to play. He perked up, searching for the now almost familiar tune. He swung his head towards Uriah just as the musician played a note that should have gone to the tight beam array in the camera overhead. He'd played a note for the entire subway platform that Jonah should have been the only one to hear.

Damn. She'd forgotten Uriah had patched her controller in so he could play along. He leaned on the note, letting it rip through the air before starting his own dance along the scale.

With no other choice, she moved on to the next chord, building the momentum. Uriah surprised her, following her lead without overpowering the sound. They made eye contact right before she moved to the five, the C-sharp seventh.

His song moved with hers, not following but keeping pace and building on her notes, layering on harmonies she'd never imagined. When she couldn't stand it anymore, when the need to resolve the tension grew so great she thought she might burst, she led him back to the one.

Except he didn't follow. He repeated the melody he'd created. The conflict grated on her ears, ruining the resolution that should have felt sublime. She cursed Uriah. She cursed herself; she'd been stupid to trust him. She didn't even know him. So what if he'd seen her in concert and bought her albums?

She suddenly remembered Jonah. Where was he?

The subway doors closed and the car started to pull away. She stood and looked up and down the platform, checking each of the subway cars. This was his train though, he'd be onboard. After a few seconds she spotted him inside the departing car. She watched the train pull away, taking him with it.

Her head spun. She hadn't meant it to go this way. She felt nausea grip her stomach, followed by the hot flash of rage. Uriah had ruined it. Instead of a haunting melody, they'd played a clumsy, discordant duet. Jonah might remember the song, but certainly not with any fondness, and certainly not with the aching desire she'd intended.

Dahlia grabbed her bag and stuffed her tablet inside as she stormed down the platform. She glared at Uriah while pointing at the MIDI controller with one hand and holding her other out, palm up.

Uriah held up his hands and shook his head. "Sorry about that, I missed the change." He unplugged the controller and held it out. She snatched it from his hand and stuffed it into her bag.

"Whoa," he said. "It was an honest mistake."

She glared back at him. She took her tablet out and typed out, "You ruined it."

He said, "You never missed a change?"

She thought about it and typed, "You didn't follow."

He grimaced. "We were going to play together, remember?" He stared at her, letting the question hang in the air. He glanced down the darkened subway tunnel. "So you were playing for who, somebody on that train?"

She considered the question, not wanting to answer. She wanted to leave, to just go. She couldn't though; she needed that amp, she needed Uriah to cooperate. Even if she found another amp or another set of speakers, his playing would interfere with her song. Finally, she nodded.

"But you don't want him to see you?"

She hesitated. She nodded again.

Uriah squinted at her. "Why?"

Dahlia sighed. She typed out "We were together."

"And now?"

She tilted her head. She typed, "We're not."

Uriah barked out a laugh and smiled. "Yeah. I got that. Can I ask why?"

Why, indeed? She paused, considering her answer.

In short, because he'd left her. At first, facing the horror of her cancer had brought them together. It offered something to overcome, something to fight against. They'd only been together for a few months when she was diagnosed, but he'd sworn he'd stick by her.

He stayed by her side through the chemo, the surgeries, and her recovery. He'd stayed long enough to see her through it all, to make sure she'd survive. She often wondered how much of that was out of obligation.

Regardless of why, he'd stayed until her prognosis had improved, until he knew she'd live. And as she'd realized she was going to live the rest of her life looking like a monster, hating her own reflection and struggling to come to terms with the loss of her voice, he'd drifted away.

Really, she couldn't blame him. He'd fallen in love with a beautiful siren. How could he be expected to love the disfigured, silent thing she'd become?

She typed out, "He left." Those two words said the only thing she knew with any certainty. He hadn't returned her messages, so she didn't know exactly why. She could guess, though.

They stood there a moment, the commuters moving around them. Uriah strummed at his guitar. She could see he wanted to ask more. Finally he said, "And your song, it's going to bring him back?"

She typed, "I hope."

He gave her a half smile. "Let me ask you something."

She raised her eyebrows.

"I know what that progression should sound like, a one-four-five-one. And I know there are parts I should feel, not hear. But there are some I don't feel or hear. Where are they?"

She considered the question for a second. She'd told him this much, why not the rest? She glanced up at the security camera overhead. His eyes followed hers and she typed out, "Ultrasonic array. Focused beam of sound."

"That you point at him?"

She nodded.

"Huh," said Uriah. "Why?"

Dahlia wondered again why she was explaining any of this to Uriah. She probed the tiny warm spot in her chest and realized that something about sharing the song felt good.

She'd written it alone. She'd practiced it alone, or for people in too much of a rush to listen. She'd set up everything she needed to play it alone. After all that, and months of preparation, her audience of one had yet to appreciate it. Would Uriah?

She took the tablet and MIDI controller from her bag and plugged the device back in. She set the volume low enough that only they would hear, and set her tablet to play all the parts through Uriah's amp. She played, from the root to the fourth, on to the fifth, and then finally returned back to the root.

"Yeah, that's nice," he said.

She held up a finger and repeated the melody again. He listened.

"Huh. Catchy," he said.

She smiled and played it a third time, stopping just before the resolution.

He nodded. "I know that itch. It's an earworm. Can't forget that song. And I really want that next chord."

She typed out, "Subsonic and ultrasonic sound intensify the itch."

Uriah shook his head. "That's amazing."

She nodded. Then, she typed out, "Have to play the right notes, though." His face fell as he read it. She felt instant guilt and smiled with her eyes, trying to dull the sharp barb of truth buried in the words.

"Guess so." He glanced back down the tunnel where the train had disappeared and then back at her. "So why tell me?"

Why indeed? Then she realized why she had. She typed out, "So you can help."

"How?"

"Play with me," she typed. Her solo could be a duet.

They spent the next few hours rehearsing, working through the chord progression, harmonizing and improving the melody. Dahlia had known Uriah had talent, but she'd had no idea how much. Not only did he keep up, he improved the song, adding his own touches in places she hadn't known could be improved.

He twisted her song around the neck of his guitar, bending it under his fingers, making it his. The core stayed the same, but as he moved from one chord to the next, he filled the spaces with half steps and feints completely different from what she expected, and a world away from how she would have played. Dahlia felt a tickle of happiness; finding novelty in something so familiar felt amazing.

Uriah had improved what she'd created, changing the inflection of her sentence, somehow warming the message. It felt less like the sharp snap of bone, and more like a soft still-pink scar.

By the time the subway started to fill with people coming home, the song was better than it had ever been. Familiar faces that usually passed without turning their heads gathered around them, reflecting a joy back to Dahlia that she barely recognized.

The next morning, Dahlia set two cups of coffee and her MIDI controller on Uriah's amp. She eyed the folding chair he'd set up next to it.

He smiled. "Yours if you want it."

She considered the offer. While she hadn't planned for Jonah's first two experiences with her song to go so poorly, her earworm had been planted. Today was the day she'd resolve the song and reveal herself, so instead of walking further down the platform to her usual spot, she set her bag down and sat in the folding chair.

As the morning crowd started to trickle in, she sipped her coffee and powered up her remote sound generators, both above and below the platform. Once they were ready, she sat still, watching Uriah until he noticed.

He said, "You ready?"

She nodded.

"Cool. I'm going to make a few bucks while we're waiting. You good with that?"

She nodded again.

He said, "You move your coffee cup from on top of my amp to down by your feet when he shows up, and I'll follow your lead."

She gave him a thumbs up, marveling over the spreading warmth inside her. Creating music again felt better than she ever imagined; seeing fresh joy on a listener's face validated her like nothing else could. Maybe she'd never sing again. Maybe that didn't mean she had to be silent forever.

Uriah played and she waited as the morning commuters rushed by in a blur, all buzz and grumble. After a while, she spotted Jonah making his way down the platform. She lifted her tablet, moved her coffee cup to the floor, and started to play.

She saw Jonah's shoulders lift as soon as he heard the first note. The music crawled into his brain, reminding him of the unanswered question she'd asked him yesterday and the day before.

As Jonah walked closer, she picked up her tempo. Uriah followed, his notes sharp and ragged as they sliced through the smooth even tones she played. She felt a lump in the back of her throat, a tightness in her chest.

Jonah was just ten steps away when they moved to the climax. Infrasound thrummed in her chest. She could see the tension on Jonah's face, almost feel the ache she'd created. She had him. He stood balanced on a pin, his face begging for release.

She held the chord, drawing it out as Uriah's guitar wailed, plaintive, begging to move on.

Still, she held it.

Jonah was almost to them when, finally, she let go and led Uriah back to the beginning note, resolving the insatiable need she'd created. Jonah's shoulders fell; he'd been holding his breath. She gasped, realizing that she had too.

She'd planned this moment for months. They'd make eye contact and rather than turning away she'd stare back, she'd let him see her. He'd stop, he'd listen, and he'd be hers again.

He did his part; he looked right at her. Her hood hid her face in shadow, she only had to look up. Except something tugged at her to play on, to dip back into the song.

That song that should have bored into his ear instead wrapped itself around her. It dug for the Dahlia she used to be.

Her breath caught in her throat. The tension sat heavy on her chest, pressing down hard. She felt the weight of a thousand stares, heard the inhalation of a million breaths. She remembered what it was to sing.

Jonah hesitated in front of her, cocking his head to one side. "Dahlia?" he said.

She swallowed the lump. With a tap on the tablet, she powered down the sound generators, releasing their hold on Jonah. She felt the tension fall away, felt the subway spring back to life. Uriah glanced back and forth between her and Jonah, watching carefully.

She lifted her head and made eye contact, her scarf still covering the lower half of her face. He faked a smile that she returned with her eyes.

"Hi," said Jonah.

She lifted one hand and waved.

He stood before her, obviously unsure what to say next. Her song no longer bound him. Yet, he remained.

She felt something inside her chest she barely recognized, but didn't see it reflected on his face. Dahlia felt the echoes of her song wrap her in an embrace. It had slipped through her self-loathing and breathed a gasp of life back into the lungs that once enchanted the world.

She typed out, "Good to see you," then tilted the tablet so he could read it.

"You too," he said.

Dahlia looked at him, not used to seeing him up close. She could reach out and touch him, if she wanted to. Except, she didn't. But she didn't want to run from him either. And that surprised her.

She typed, "Take care."

He smiled and said, "I will." He turned to go, but stopped. He looked back and said, "I like it. Your new song." Then he turned and left.

She watched him head down the platform. After a few seconds she looked back to Uriah. She typed out "Thank you" on her tablet.

He nodded, smiled, and then she sat back down.

They played on together, Dahlia's newfound voice rising in triumph above the subway noise. A small crowd gathered as Uriah joined in, magnifying her song into something more than she ever could have created alone.

It came from Brad Preslar

The inspiration for "A Song Without a Voice" came to me one summer at an outdoor concert. In Nashville, everyone's neighbors are in a band, ours included. Oddly enough, our neighbor's band is Drew Holcombe and the Neighbors. My wife and I had gone to see them play an amphitheater show with several other bands from out of town. We knew Drew's music, but hadn't heard much of the other bands on the tour. The headliner that night was NEEDTOBREATHE. Most of the people at the show were there to see them. They played a crowd favorite three-quarters of the way through their set, and everyone around us erupted. The crowd knew every word. They stood, raised their hands and shouted the words back to the band. For the people that knew those words, that knew that song, it touched something inside them. It made them stand, made them sing, made them feel. It made them move. And I got to wondering what else a song could make us do. I wanted to capture the power of the music, I wanted to bottle the lightning that filled that amphitheater. That inspired me to write a story about how a person could use the power of a song.

A question for Brad Preslar

Q: What is the hardest part of writing for you?

A: The blank page. It stares back and says all kinds of terrible things about you, your talent (or lack thereof), and whether or not you'll ever come up with anything worth defacing it with. It reminds you of all the other things you might need to do before you start actually writing. It scoffs at all the ideas you want to write on it. That said, once I've put down a word, then a sentence, and then a paragraph, the momentum seems to build. The blank page loses its voice. It's just that first word that's so hard.

About Brad Preslar

Brad Preslar writes from Nashville, Tennessee, where he lives with his wife Ellie and their dog Stella (named for his wife's favorite cider.) He wrote unique selling propositions and concepts for ten years at ad agencies in NC and OH before going freelance to devote more time to writing fiction. Brad grew up in Winston-Salem, NC where he studied Communication at Wake Forest University. He also received a MFA in film production from the University of Miami.

www.readbradpreslar.com

Solomon and the Dragon's Tongue

Molly Etta

Before he went by Solomon, the stranger's name was Shlomo. He seemed at first unremarkable, apart from being new, and in palpable need of a wife. Yutke's mother began to snoop as soon as she noticed that he did not wear the tallis which marks a married man.

"How do you know that?" asked Yutke.

"I saw, at shul."

"And what were you doing, that you could see whether he was wearing a tallis or not? Were you peeping around the curtain, Momma?" A flimsy curtain divided the sexes, maintaining an old pretense that the sight of a woman would be distracting to the men in the sanctuary.

"If I peeped, it was for a good cause," said Momma. "I wish only to nip your spinsterhood in the bud! God will forgive me this."

Momma's inquiries revealed that Shlomo had been born in a neighboring town, but had wandered near and far for the sake of his education. Nobody knew a thing about his family, or any prior connections. However, general agreement had it that he was a model yeshiva student and a burgeoning young scholar, and that proved enticing enough.

Yutke would have protested her mother's meddling, but she had felt drawn to Shlomo the Unknown, ever since she glimpsed him one day, hurrying past the market-going women with baskets on their arms, a pile of books in his. He did not notice her as he swept by, but he shed one piece of paper which drifted to settle upon his abandoned footprints. Yutke picked the paper up, only to find that it had nothing written upon it: only the ghost of bygone musings Shlomo had tried to efface, and the faintest sketch of an exotic bird bursting out of an egg, which glimmered through the page like a watermark.

It did not occur to Yutke that she should be wary of a man who carried erasures of his own thought with him. Instead, she called after him, to give him back his paper. Shlomo thanked her much more profusely than her actions seemed to merit. He held her gaze a little too long, and heat flooded Yutke's cheeks, although Shlomo did not have such looks as usually cause young women to blush. He was too thin, premature lines framed his mouth, and a lack of sleep had faintly purpled the bags beneath his eyes. But his irises were sea-colored, and as she stood before him, Yutke could see her own terror and longing reflected in silvery blue.

She never dared imagine that such a new and otherworldly man could have any interest in young women of much more earthly stock — herself, least of all. And yet, Yutke's family procured the match. She could not believe her luck, and persisted in disbelieving it, until after they were married.

The raucous ceremony would ring in Yutke's ears for days after the fact. Drums reverberated through the crowd, and trumpets bellowed. Yutke followed the musicians numbly as they led her to the square before the synagogue. The guests would murmur that she seemed a cold and listless bride, but they could not have known about the giddy upheaval churning her insides.

The white expanse of canopy over their heads bucked and threatened to sail away on the wind. It looked blank, like it wanted to be filled by something. That vision of a white square would follow Yutke, repeating through time rather in order from cleanliness to filth: first the pure billow of canopy, then the starched tablecloths stained by the wedding's abundance of honey and wine, then Shlomo's ink-splattered letters from distant parts. She would learn to find the pattern meaningful.

But she did not think about such things while she lay awake and peered at Shlomo sleeping beside her. She contemplated tracing the arch of his shoulder, but never did so.

His days revolved around prayer and study. Yutke wondered what it must be like in his world of thoughts and words, instead of hers, full of dough to be kneaded and floors to be scrubbed. She had never known a man with so many books. The musk of aging paper thrilled her, although she would never be sure if she loved Shlomo for his piles of books, or loved the piles of books because they felt like part of him.

Yutke had never recognized the chronic ache below her ribs as loneliness, until she married Shlomo. But, when rumors of military conscription drifted in from the nearest village, Shlomo wasted little time before disappearing again, and leaving Yutke with her ache.

"You know what happens to Jews in the army," said Shlomo. "The gentiles draft us, only so that they can baptize us in our sleep!" Yutke averted her gaze and blinked back tears, while Shlomo squeezed her hand. "But do not worry, little wife. You and the child —" his gaze drifted to her stomach, "— will come join me once I have settled everything for us across the ocean."

Yutke kissed Shlomo goodbye around his bramble of a beard. She would always remember him as he looked on that day: ankle deep in the spring mud, his frail figure comically imbalanced by the girth of a sheepskin coat. He and a handful of fellow wayfarers from the village stood in a circle, with packs of bread and smoked and salted meats slung over their shoulders. They said goodbye to their women, then vanished into the morning fog.

Yutke cried furtively for days. She masked her tears by slicing onions when she had to (since her mother would not tolerate such moping). He had only just begun to feel real, and now he had disappeared again. But maybe it was better to let her longing fill his absence, since it was the ethereal scholar she had fallen for, not a man of flesh and blood.

When the first letter from Shlomo arrived, Yutke had to refrain from reading it all day, while her mother busied her with chores. If Yutke tried to sneak off towards the letter, she would find herself in the kitchen instead, where she patiently draped ribbons of dough atop the noodle board, and did her best not to stare wistfully out the window. She wondered what kind of a writer her clever husband would turn out to be.

After evening fell, Yutke sank at last into her chair with an oil lamp, and began to cut open Shlomo's letter. *Dear Yutke,* she read. *Today I helped to save a life! We had a distant encounter with a bear. The others fought over a rifle and disputed for a long time over whether or not to fire at the creature. I cited Vayikra 11:27 and said its meat would do us no good, but they protested that they only wanted to scare it, and would not listen to me when I tried to explain the passage further. However, while we were arguing over the matter, the bear trundled off.*

Will send more news once we come to the next town.

Yutke let the note fall to her lap.

She chided herself inwardly for expecting, she did not know what — a love note? Had she really expected that her husband the scholar would know anything about love notes, beyond what he read in the Song of Songs?

She could not have known that it would become harder and harder to forgive Shlomo over the coming months, for writing letters which had less and less the flavor of love notes. As he travelled, he sent his bride scattered fragments of thought. He never gave Yutke anything that felt like real information, and she tried to guess and imagine the details he left out, while adding prayers to her workload as dutiful daughter and wife. During the wait between messages, she muttered *tkhines* for Shlomo's health and happiness into a corner of the house, until her voice grew hoarse.

One day, a new letter came. Yutke abandoned her chores to read it. She tore the letter open, and breathed in sharply at the first sentence: *Yutke, I have some terrible news.* But, her jolt of fear wilted into exasperation as she read on: *At some point, while scrambling across the rocks, I have lost my toenails! And a couple of toes. I think we might at least call these lost things a toll to the Lord our God. And since the toll has been paid, He has at least allowed me a reasonably safe path. For this I am grateful.*

Would you bring this matter up with the Reb on my behalf? Did our ancient ancestors ever sacrifice their toes, instead of goats, to curry divine favor?

Yutke reread the letter once more to make sure she had understood it. She had. And that was when Yutke decided it would be useless to chant any more prayers on her husband's behalf, since she could think of none pertaining to the safekeeping of toes.

He was probably just trying to make her laugh, so she would worry about him less. But Yutke would do what a good wife must: wait and worry anyway.

At last, a real, substantial letter arrived!

Initially delighted by the simple fact of its length, Yutke hesitated to read it through. She had a (correct) inkling that whatever news it contained would not sustain the fleeting lightness of her spirits, and so she clung to her wisp of hope and kept herself busy. After morning prayers, Yutke fetched water from the river, then plunged elbow-deep into the washtub while she scrubbed linens. As she draped the clean cloth over the line to dry, the white folds tantalized her, reminding her of the wedding canopy, and the piece of paper that awaited her inspection.

Once she had rallied herself to the task of reading Shlomo's letter, Yutke probably spent more time trying to root some sense out of it, than Shlomo had spent writing it in the first place. She read and re-read his words, and tried not to resent him for writing about all the wrong things yet again.

My dear Yutke, he said, *with all thanks to the Lord acknowledged, I must admit to you that I will not miss hiking through the mud, or the trains and control stations where they pack us like cattle, or the coldness of the gendarmes and doctors.*

But all of that is past now. Three days ago, at last, I made it to Hamburg! I would tell you it is beautiful here, but I'm really not sure if it is or not, for I think I spend too much time looking at the sky.

The air is so open here, Yutke. Every day the sky has been white as paper, only marked by a few black flecks: birds, arranged like dashes, abandoned on a wordless page. Since I am a scholar, perhaps

I should not be pleased by such barren writing upon the heavens. All the same, I do not think I have ever seen such beautiful prose. Empty things like that seem much more wonderful after you have spent too much time crowded against your fellow man, treated like a beast.

Tomorrow, I embark, and you will not hear from me for some time. However, I promise that, upon my arrival, I will make up for my silence with a little novel, dedicated to you! (And of course, as soon as possible, I will send money so you can make this journey too.) Shlomo

Yutke put the letter down and peered out the window at the clouds. A couple of larks swooped in the distance. She made a valiant effort to see as Shlomo did, to read the birds upon the sky's white surface as signs of something beautiful and ineffable. But no matter how she stared and squinted, the sky only looked like sky to her. Perhaps it was because she had not read enough books. Perhaps she spent too much time trying to read the wrinkles in the linens instead. Every step west seemed to take Shlomo upward as well, nearer the heavens, while Yutke found herself ever nearer the earth in the east, scrubbing away the dirt as best as she could. Nevertheless, she found herself glancing skyward.

Yutke soon adjusted to the pain of waking early with a racing heart, and how that feeling would become a weight on her chest, once evening fell without any letter. So it went for many weeks. Yutke tried not to think too much about Shlomo as she noticed the world's rebirth around her, as she wandered by the river, sucking the nectar from acacia blossoms. She went to market, milked the nanny goat, and always cleaned the house before the Sabbath, even when the child began to kick inside her. At night, Yutke occupied herself with knitting and sewing and waiting.

Eventually, a small package arrived. It was stuffed to bursting with all the letters Shlomo had scribbled during his voyage across the ocean. They clung together like the leaves on a cabbage, and Yutke had to peel each message apart from the mass, and smooth it out with knife, to let it speak its piece instead of clamoring alongside its neighbors.

She picked through dates until she found one letter written earlier than the others:

My dear Yutke, I have had a wonderful bit of luck, and I write you now from the first cabin, not from steerage (where I was originally situated). I need to tell you all the particulars of how this came to pass, or else you will never believe me:

There is a wealthy and rotten Englishman on board, who has established a nasty reputation for himself throughout the ship: even from below, we have often heard his booming voice complain about the service in the first cabin (on more than one occasion I have watched him toss lamb shanks and strudel to the fishes!), and he is a known gambler, with an elaborately painted deck of cards, which he keeps atop a velvet cushion.

Tired of his whining and howling, one day I howled back, and challenged him to a game of schnapsen — the stakes of the match: our respective seats in steerage and the first cabin! Out of arrogance the foolish Englishman agreed to play with me. And you will never believe this (but you must try): I trounced him, my dear, and earned myself a place in the first cabin! If anyone in the village does not believe you when you speak about my triumph, tell him that the Lord would of course favor a pious man over anyone who wastes good strudel.

What's more, as a parting trick, I pinched the Englishman's queen of hearts. I will send you this card soon, once I can find the proper sort of case for it, so it will not be damaged during the voyage, and you will show it as proof to anyone who asks after me. It is beautiful, Yutke. The queen's hair and crown glow with gold leaf, and she sits atop a marble throne upon a beach, the waters of a turquoise sea lapping up to kiss her feet. She holds a glittering heart-shaped goblet in one hand which rivals her crown for majesty.

And, since I am crossing the ocean, I begin now to write you under my New World name, which is what the gentiles on this ship call me:

Solomon

Yutke stared at the letter.

"What in the world can you mean?" she asked. But the limp piece of paper would not answer her.

Then she noticed that Shlomo — no, Solomon — had scribbled an addendum upon arriving in the New World, and securing his lodgings: *P.S. When I get you a ticket, I will make sure you have a place in the first cabin. I rather miss it there myself now. Especially the fine cigars. And did you know what it is like to sink a silver spoon into a soft-boiled egg?*

Needless to say, Yutke did not know.

She spent the next several hours rifling agitatedly through everything else her husband had sent her. She struggled to read in order, frightened of succumbing to Solomon's mania, his collage of times and places. A strange feeling sat next to her fear, and if she had to name it, she would have called it anger — or envy, even. She had heard stories about the journey across the ocean. She had heard about the strange and terrible sympathy which could unite Russians, Germans, Irish, until they forgot they had no tongue in common. She had heard about the way they echoed each other's sobs and moans, as though aware that the groaning ship had decided to drill them upon the paradigms of a universal language known as *nausea*.

Under similar circumstances, would Yutke dare even dream of the taste of a soft-boiled egg?

Yutke sorted a sequence of letters into a roughly chronological sequence (as though by doing so, she could also force her jumbled reactions into some kind of reasonable order too), and frowned at their odd progression from sunshine to shadows. The first few letters contained glittering tales of the golden New World, the next were about conquering its shadows, and the last looked to be all splattered over with ink.

The pattern did not seem particularly auspicious.

Yutke, began one of the golden letters, *in the New World, all you have to do is run a sieve through the air if you want to collect the pulp of sunlight. There are light-pickers here who pass their days engaged in this very task, who weave the threads of gold they have gathered into glittering cloaks which can keep you warm throughout the winter (these will be perfect for the baby, I think).*

In another letter, Solomon described the local synagogue: ... *it is the most beautiful house of prayer I have ever seen, a marble palace, the aisles lined by purple columns, the façade marked by crenellations carved of coral, the ark studded with sparkling jewels. I have but one criticism of the place: the stained glass consists only of various shades of gold, which I find very tiresome by now.*

As she read, Yutke sometimes checked her fingertips, just to make sure that no gold dust clung to them like pollen. Instead, she found only dust and faint traces of ink.

One of Solomon's darker letters had sprouted a strange inkblot creature, a scribbled beast with skeletal wings and a long sinuous tail which snaked around his words. In the lower left-hand corner of the letter, positioned as though it wanted to escape to the next page, a slug-like splotch of ink seemed to quiver.

At the top of the page, Solomon's hand cried out: *Yutke, look what I encountered recently!*

Yutke obliged; she looked, and read:

As it turns out, while the sunshine in the New World is made of solid gold, so are the shadows made of ink. Sometimes, where the dark boils beneath the streets, it convinces itself it is alive.

This is how I recently met a dragon composed of ink and shadows, while I explored underground after morning prayers. I tore its tongue out after I slew it, as a token of my victory (since the entire dragon's head would have been too heavy to take away).

I will wrap its tongue up in this letter (but I am afraid it might melt back into a puddle of ink during the journey across the ocean, for which I apologize in advance).

It won't be long now until I can send some money, so you can come join me. Solomon

Yutke realized that the slug of ink was supposed to be a dragon's tongue, flattened by its paper prison. She stared at it, but she could not read it as a tongue, any more than she could read punctuation into the sky. The more she looked, the uglier the sign seemed, and it took a great effort to refrain from tearing the thing up on the spot. But Yutke found she could not damage or toss away anything that felt like a piece of Solomon, however much it repelled her.

The next letter was so riddled with streaks and specks of ink that the promise of a headache pulsed across Yutke's temples at the mere sight of it. Solomon had stitched his words so closely together that they seemed less like sentences than jagged scars of ink. The first scar read: *Yutke, I am afraid I did something very silly last time I tried to write you.* Yutke's hand trembled as she began to trace the next scar of a sentence, willing herself to understand.

Picture me: I was sitting awake at night, as I often do, in order to write. I keep a kerosene lamp on my desk for just that purpose, and two bottles sit by my elbow: one of ink and one to drink. Last evening, I happened to be so caught up in my work, that I was stupid, so stupid, and reached out blindly and seized my ink bottle! I did not think about the missing whiff of schnapps. But instead, like a fool, I raised the vessel to my lips, and drank.

Nobody helped me, when I said I had swallowed my ink.

The shadows simply hissed: "Sol, hush."

But I did not hush. "I drank my ink," I told them.

The shadows answered that they knew I would mix the damnable bottles up, then told me to go to sleep. "That's enough foolishness for one evening," they said.

And so, I began to prepare for bed. But I was so dizzied by this whole mess, that when I reached to put out my lamp, I knocked over the rest of my ink, and it flooded the letter I was writing to you! It irks me that you won't hear of my latest adventures. But I suppose the dark has its right. It seems just that it should consume something of mine, after I have had the gall to consume it.

At the bottom of the page Yutke found one lonely phrase with a line through it, which perhaps Solomon had meant to scratch out more thoroughly before sending her this letter:

Yutke, I am so tired.

Yutke put the letter down and stood up. She paced back and forth. She wanted to go and touch her husband's books and inhale the scent of old paper — but she had already been obliged to sell the tomes he had left behind. The floorboards creaked beneath Yutke's restless feet, and her mother yelled for her to settle down and get some rest. Eventually, dizzy with the effort of understanding — or rather, the effort of relinquishing the will to understand — Yutke obeyed.

That night, she dreamed of a poplar with messages scratched into its leaves, which fell about her feet in haphazard piles, according to the whims of the wind which rustled through the tree's branches. Every time Yutke picked up a leaf to try to decode its message, the wind whipped it away.

She woke up, and knew she could not wait any longer for Solomon to send for her.

Dear Solomon,

When we first saw the torch-bearing statue, I almost expected to see her torch flicker with golden flames. I thought, perhaps you did not lie about all the golden things. But we came at dawn, and had to proceed through a thick mist. Even if her whole body had been forged of solid gold, I am sure we would hardly have seen a glint of it.

My fellow passengers all tossed their hats in the air when we saw her. The people were being very loud, and they upset Moshe. He kept fretting and rubbing his face into my blouse and I had to rock and kiss him so he would not cry. The ship's doctor told me that in America they would be very wary of people who have anything wrong with their eyes, and I did not want Moshe's to be red at all. I felt a little angry, if I am honest. I wanted to rub sea salt in my own eyes until they turned red and raw. I thought, doing something like that would be like sticking my tongue out at this place and its ridiculous rules and promises.

You did not tell me it would be like this, Solomon. You made me understand that you have to die a little to get into the New World, it's so much like Paradise. I imagined, it would be a painful process — shedding the egg shell around your soul — but you get through it. And yet I've found that this is not true. Nothing ever gets easier. The world wears you down more and more, until you disappear.

You disappeared. And I have tried to reinvent you out of paper and ink, like you tried to reinvent this place out of paper and ink. But it's not working.

Yutke never would have sent this letter, even if she had known where to send it. Instead she drew a long slash across it, and turned the page over to be reused.

Later in the day, she was bathing Moshe in a kitchen basin, when she noticed a birthmark on the inside of his wrist. She had never seen it before: a strange shape, which you might easily mistake for a tiny, dark slug crawling across his skin. Yutke held Moshe's little hand until he began to squirm and pull away. He promptly stuffed his fingers in his mouth.

The boy's name was Moshe (or Moses, in this new country), but sometimes Yutke called him her little *moshl*, her fable, since it did not take a prophet to foresee the boy's fate. Like his father, he would be a messy, walking story, leaking fibs and tales whenever pen and paper came in reach to do so.

After drying off Moshe and settling him atop a blanket with his wooden horse, Yutke sat down at the table with a pen in hand and spread out the blank verso of her previous letter, wondering what she could say to whatever was left of Solomon. She did not quite realize she was crying, until the page began to buckle beneath her spreading teardrops. Frustrated, she rubbed at her eyes with her apron. What a waste of good paper.

These days, Yutke always kept a playing card in her pocket, which she caressed sometimes for good luck. It was a beautiful thing, emblazoned with a scarlet queen whose crown glittered with a trace of gold leaf. Yutke touched its rounded corner, and thought of her husband.

She was beginning to lose the details of his face. She understood now that he was a permanent exile and a palimpsest of a man, easily effaced and rewritten by forgetfulness and memory in turn. It often seemed to Yutke that she had only ever known him as meandering scrawl, a landscape of splattered ink — not as a person, much less as a husband. She could not fix the idea of him in her head. But if she tried to recall the lines framing the corners of his mouth, and his eclectic piles of books and notes, she could almost grasp a thread to follow through the labyrinth of his logic.

After several minutes of contemplation, her nib began to scratch across the page:

Dear Solomon,

I find myself missing you, although I barely knew you. I miss waiting to hear from you. I even miss when the wait seemed to be crushing my chest. I often feel like I am still waiting, and it is difficult to persuade myself that this is no longer the case. The memory of you is like an impression in wax; it wants to be filled by something, but it has been melting away beneath this city's sun instead.

You did a poor job of slaying that demon, the thing you called a dragon. Did you know that the beast traced your journey backwards, following your scent, until it found me? It haunted me and slithered around my belly and gave me a great fear it would infect the baby (which, I think, it has done).

But at last, I realized that you cannot kill a dragon, nor can you cover it over with glittering things to hide it. You have to tame it. So I gave the creature a good scolding whenever it was unruly, and if it behaved very poorly, I would whack it with a broom until it fled into the garden. This went on, until the dragon bowed its head meekly before me, and even dropped onto its belly and permitted the baby and me climb onto its back.

That is how we flew across the ocean, astride the tongueless dragon composed of ink and shadows.

Now we live on our own little island on the East River — the baby, the dragon, and me. I keep a golden bell upon my bedside table and ring it whenever I want tea or a pastry, and the dragon trots in with a platter balanced on its back.

When Moshe is grown, I will teach him how to tame and control the dragon as well. He will have gifts from us both: thanks to you, he is marked by the dragon's tongue, and he will learn to write with it. And thanks to me, the beast will never overwhelm him.

I miss you, Solomon, and I would wish you the best if I could.

Love,

Yutke

Yutke put her pen aside, and sighed. Well, this one would not do either.

It took her a moment to realize that her attempt at channeling Solomon's kind of nonsense had changed something in her gaze. Tears had ceased to blur her vision. When she glanced at the shadowy doorway, she did not see the dust and the patched coat which hung forlornly from its hook. Instead, she could almost see a serpentine figure entwined with the dark (and if Yutke squinted, it even seemed to be accompanied by a ghostly tea set which shimmered in and out of view).

"Oh," murmured Yutke. She averted her gaze.

For the first time since Solomon had begun to write, pity welled up in her — not for herself, but for him.

She folded the letter neatly, and went to the fire escape, where she stood and watched the bustle below: peddlers and women with baskets, horses drawing carriages and wagons loaded with wares, men with hats tilted over their heads so she could not see their faces. If Solomon were to pass by, she would never know.

Why had he even married her, plain and unsmiling as she was? Why had he treated her like a mirror, always writing letters to her which seemed like pages torn from a madman's diary?

Yutke felt the breeze tug at her skirt. It stirred the clothes draped over the iron railing. She clutched her letter tightly, then pried her fingers away from it one by one, until it drifted away down the street, buoyed along by the air. She watched her letter glow in the sunlight, until it disappeared from view, and then she went back inside.

Yutke did not bother glancing toward the doorway, to see if the dragon still lurked in the shadows. It would not do to raise the hopes of the poor creature which had eaten her husband alive.

It would have no such luck with her.

A question for Molly Etta

Q: When do you decide a story is finished?

A: I'll admit that I'm drawn to writing that is (or seems) fragmentary, so I might be in a bad position to identify when a story is finished. But that's not a real answer, so here's another attempt: I know I'm approaching the finish of a story when certain recurring motifs begin to feel less like flourishes, and more like they are essential to the structural integrity of the whole story.

About Molly Etta

Molly Etta is a graduate student in Comparative Literature, living in the San Francisco Bay area. When she isn't scribbling about dragons made of ink, she tends to be buried in research on allegorical reinterpretations of Ovid in Old French.

Mr. McAvennie's Freedom

Dan Micklethwaite

Are you here for business or pleasure?"

Do they even ask that anymore?

Standing outside this door, in this dark hallway, fifteen miles from the airport, he can't remember if they ever have, of him. Perhaps they simply see him coming, always in his fine grey suit and pale blue shirt, his briefcase swinging in one hand, his smartphone in the other; the latter switched expertly out for his passport, battered and creased with regular use.

Though he's marked as a salesman, a stuffed shirt, he nevertheless waits in the concourse, every time that he comes to this city, and stares up at the Departures. An exotic buffet. Ways of escape. Not a visit goes by that he doesn't feel lucky — blessed, even — to have been born in a country where the passports you get are like master-keys — there are very few other nations he'd have trouble entering, if he chose to.

Every time that he comes to this city, to sell industrial merchandise, he looks up at those departure boards and wonders which one. Which destination. He could email his resignation from mid-air, on some of the flights, the transatlantic crossing. When he was settled somewhere for a time, he could notify his wife, Joanna, of the hotel he was staying in, or the PO box he was using, and offer her a narrow window through which to serve him the papers. Or through which he could do it, if, as was more likely, she wouldn't budge.

She's stubborn like that. Rooted.

He'd always meant to travel in that way when he was younger. That's the thing. Had a dog-eared gazetteer that he'd carried about with him everywhere; names he found interesting or absurdly amusing were highlighted in pink or green or yellow, whichever he'd been using for his study notes at the time.

Zanzibar. Limpopo. Krakatoa. Worms.

But that gazetteer had gone missing, when he moved out of his parents' house.

And now he can't seem to get further away than this city. This hallway. This door. No matter how long he stares at those departure boards each time, weighing up his options. Because it isn't so much a matter of choice, anymore, as it is of compulsion; a stirring of the iron filings that torpedo round within his blood.

He bears the shame of it, coming here, in the five o'clock shadow, the sweat-patch that's welling at the base of his spine; in the rancid musk that overwhelms his aftershave. In the bags beneath his eyes, and in the noose about his neck. It doesn't sit well, this half-measure, with the image of himself he used to have; that of the freewheeling Robert McAvennie, Rab, long before he was a Mr.

But what else can he do?

He unfastens his tie, the top two buttons of his shirt.

He knocks on that door, his familiar beat.

She flashes him the most arcane, beguiling smile; a nod that says: Willkommen! Please, make yourself at home.

Bienvenue.

Mi casa es su casa.

He's never been quite sure where it is that she's from, but she operates now out of this studio apartment, which, despite its limited size, is in good condition, and tidy, with tastefully bohemian, upcycled furnishings, and which smells of a somehow harmonious blending of organic coffee, organic cleaning products, and even more organic weed.

He slips off his shoes and sets them on the pale pine rack provided. He rolls off his socks, balling them up with practised efficiency, stuffing them inside the upmarket loafers.

There's a slightly *rustic* chest of drawers that every time he comes here he can't help but thinking: My wife would like that. Or: It would go well in our bedroom. These confusions of purpose, flirtations with guilt. He used to go to auctions with her, perhaps one weekend a month, to scout for such bargains, but the kids of course monopolise their travels now. And they prefer sports; junior soccer leagues, swimming meets. You become a full-time manager, a die-hard fan.

On top of those drawers rests a black plastic tray. He works through his pockets, depositing his phone, his wallet; he unfastens the leather strap of his wristwatch, and his belt, and lays them both methodically inside.

She stares at him.

He places his passport and his wedding ring inside the tray, too. An honest mistake.

He hangs his blazer on the hook provided, next to not only her coat but another as well; a white pleather biker jacket, with padded black shoulders and elbows, and various logos and badges adorning. 'If you can read this,' says one of them, 'you killed me.' There's a luminescent sad face underneath it, with crosses for eyes.

So, she has another new boyfriend?

Mr. McAvennie sees him immediately upon reaching the end of the hallway, the entry to the open-plan living space. His must be the smell of grass — he's sitting topless on a stool by the breakfast bar, still smoking, reading, from the look of the cover, a technology magazine.

There's a steampunky sleeve tattoo all along his right arm, augmented with studs shaped like rivets and screws. When he holds the spliff resting between his second and third fingers, it looks like a vent, a reactor exhaust.

Such imagery might once have been more commonplace in Robert's life — there were a few months at seventeen when he fancied himself a petrolhead, an engineer, and revved a moped around the shittier backstreets of Glasgow — but it's now perhaps a little daunting.

Still, the guy seems placid enough. Scarcely seems to register that Mr. McAvennie's here.

It's business as usual, he supposes.

Pleasure as usual.

When she nods towards the glass table in the middle of the room, the thought of doing anything else doesn't enter his head. There's no need for the status-anxiety, the beta dog syndrome that plagues his working life, the feeling that anyone could do what he does, and do it just as well.

Here, away from all that, he has nothing to prove.

The snugly-fitted hardwood flooring is cool on his soles as he passes towards it, and then the white shagpile rug, like the earthly bequest of a polar bear, is soft and as close as anyone can come to sinking without actually passing through the floor. Scrunching his toes in it, he unfastens his shirt, takes it off. With one last glance towards the boyfriend he unzips his trousers and takes them off, too. Folds both items neatly and lays them nearby.

He drops to his hands and knees, pads around on the rug, doglike, childlike, on a whim, before turning onto his back and shimmying himself into position, looking up through the table as though it's a skylight.

The ceiling is crisp cream artex, like clouds, a calm storm.

He hears her approaching.

She leans over the glass. Her ash blonde hair is fixed up in a bun, and she's rolled the sleeves of her top up, pulled the lower hem up and around between her breasts, for the same reason, so that it doesn't get in the way.

Lifting the bucket, a pink one, one of those that can be used to make a castle keep, she carefully empties the white sand across the table, making sure the coverage is even.

She doesn't look at him once.

Mr. McAvennie feels the way he always does, staring up at this. He feels like he is buried in it, trapped, within the belly of the beach. Feels it like the pressure of centuries, millennia, ages, eons. Triassic, Jurassic, Cretaceous. Neogene.

There is nothing he can do. Nothing he's expected to do. Nothing but watch. Pay attention. *Just go with it.*

Through the flatness comes the first determined scratching — as of a turtle working a hole in which to lay her eggs, or of a predator working, counter-wise, to uncover the same; claws cracking shell, maw wetted with albumen. Or the edge of a shovel, a pirate searching for treasure, an archaeologist searching for bones, a prospector searching for what those bones will become.

A dot appears. A pixel. A single cell. She doesn't scrape all the sand away but rather thins it out just enough for the light to pass through. Four others dots follow.

Underneath, a short distance away, a larger mark, the heel of her fist becoming the heel of a foot. Then another beside it. They walk the surface of the table, leaving fading tracks behind them. A tide seems to wash across the tray, and when it ebbs again they're gone.

The first shoots are always a pleasant surprise, a little miracle. You think of so much sand sometimes and you think of deserts, places of nothing, zones of exile, but the secret to an atoll's survival is in the curious fertility of post-volcanic soil. Is in the fact that seabirds sometimes need a place to pause for breath, to shit out seeds.

The date palms start as simple starbursts, the leaves expanding and shaking with the burgeoning bulk of the fruit as they grow; embossed on the underside of the table, extruding towards him.

The coconut trees likewise. They bow with the wind. The sea-breeze clears the way, forces the harvest; she draws a single brown husk on the sand and it cracks, comes apart, and Rab puts his tongue out, hoping for milk — he has to turn his head to spit out sand, but feels somehow refreshed, regardless.

Feels hungry.

Survival in a place like this is not about support networks but self-sufficiency. Adaptability. Hardiness. Possession of the proper skillset.

Can you swim?

He had used to.

His daughter — on Tuesday and Thursday evenings, he drives her to practice. The chlorine whiff. The adrenaline. Chemical dependency. If he gets home late from work, he doesn't even stop for a coffee first, just a quick trip to the bathroom and then back out the door —

What daughter?

He takes the first few tentative steps into the surf, the tropical heat of it wreathing his ankles. There's the first tingle of sunburn at his shoulders, the back of his neck. The first hint of a tan on his forearms. The water is both a shelter and a magnifying glass. He dives in. It shatters.

The fine pale sand on the seabed billows up with his passing, the kicking of his feet, the bubbles of his breath. Becomes coral castles, medieval battlements, and clown fish dart and weave between the crenellations like the restless ghosts of courtly fools.

Olive flounders float on by, bizarrely — Picasso's secret inspiration, both eyes protruding on one side of their face. Bastard halibuts, they call them. Flatfish, a wide target. He strikes out with his spear.

She builds him a bonfire, a barbecue pit. His meal chars on it as grains shift and splinter off as sparks. Smoke moves upwards, becomes a signpost, not an SOS, a welcome, but rather a straightforward warning: Beware of the God.

He paints his face with ashes, after eating. It is so much easier to cultivate a mystique out here, without the constant spousal scrutiny, the morning queue for the bathroom — *Hurry up, dad, I'm bursting.* It is so much easier to simply exist.

There's no respite from the elements, is the only thing. The palm leaves will only hold up to so much monsoon rain before giving in, the drip of it on his head as he tries to get some rest like water-torture. A sudden flood like waterboarding.

The scene dissolves, he finds himself looking out from the tideline towards where his ship ran aground on the reef. The mainmast is almost bent double, into an upturned V, a forward arrow, beckoning him on.

He treads the narrow spit of land towards it, tightrope walking; recalling the time a Russian circus came to town and he begged his then-girlfriend to run off with him and join it. Had a bag packed and everything. But that was the night the police stopped them, swerving along on his scooter, and he didn't have a license, and they gave her a chance to run along home, and she did and she never looked back.

The artist's hands are so deft, her control of the medium masterful — he pries away boards from the side of the hull that have real grain, detailed with her fingernails, that have real heft and depth, the authentic scent of brine about them. Barnacles like watching eyes. He carries them back to the mainland, the heartland, and feels the pulling at the sides of his neck and his shoulders — *trapezius* muscles. Lower down, too, *latissimus dorsi*. He knows those terms, suddenly, like the words to a prayer.

He is involved, he watches as between them they build it into foundations, into stilts, a tried-and-true supporting structure. The first floor takes shape, cobbled together from the remains of the top deck. He works a door smooth with a plane that he salvages from the carpenter's cabin. Inside, the Captain's wheel becomes a coffee table, a real conversation-starter.

He begins to understand how her own apartment has acquired its form. Why there is always a new boyfriend, never long-standing. The liberty to decorate and re-decorate however she wants. The chance to control. The chance to belong.

The second floor, the last, for now, is for sleeping; the four-poster dragged from the Captain's quarters, across the beach, its legs leaving grooves like the trail of an old romantic carriage ride; like an elongated equals sign between the old life and the new — the algebra of relocation.

Solve for x.

X marks the spot.

This is the treasure he's been seeking. He sits on the balcony nursing a cocktail in half a coconut, an admixture of the leftover rum from the hold and some guava from the new orchard on the other side of the lagoon. She's drawn a little parasol inside it; a sprinkle of salt on the edge of the improvised cup. He looks beyond this small horizon towards the further, wider one. Between them, the arc of dolphins, the spray of whales.

It calls for a celebration. Housewarming. Squeak as he marks an invitation on the underside of the glass.

She brings champagne. She brings a floral garland and places it around his neck. He fetches the salvaged Victrola back down from the treehouse, rigs it up on a nearby rock.

Some old-time big band jazz spills out and fills the early-evening air. Birdsong and cicadas join it. Crabs clack claws like castanets. The two of them link arms and spin and dance and dance, and there is nowhere he would rather be.

The woman, Luda, is over by the coffee machine. Like most everything else here, it's far from brand-new, a true fixer-upper, similar in form and date, perhaps, to an early Cold War-era factory. But it works. She tamps the grounds into the handle and then twists it into place.

Robert sits on a stool at the breakfast bar, watching her hands, listening to the clanks, the changing tone of the hiss, at first as the water boils, and then as it steams and froths the milk.

Her boyfriend has already left for the balcony, taking his magazine and his rolling papers with him. Like the others, he respects the need for privacy, for peace and quiet, after the trip.

Rab looks at his own hands, raw, already a little callused with the effort of construction. There is a splinter, sharp and sore, in the webbing between the forefinger and thumb of his left hand, which he has to suck out. It's almost the size of a toothpick, when he covertly spits it back into his palm.

He thought it was covertly, but Luda was watching. She sets a latte down, in a tall glass, in front of him. She holds her hand out for the splinter and goes to put it in the bin. He stirs his drink with the antique absinthe spoon provided — or at least a replica of an antique; the bowl of it a stylised skull.

She brings her own black coffee to the table. Drops two whole sugar cubes inside, *splish-splosh*, but doesn't stir. They will settle and granulate at the bottom this way, and he thinks that perhaps this helps her to ease out of the mindset required for her work.

She catches him staring, and smiles, although behind the veil of coffee-steam she looks a little like a genie from an early Technicolor film. There's something omniscient and ethereal about her, even now. Or possibly he is just projecting.

After all, one of the lessons of this place is that a person can be more than the sum of their wage packets, their professional responsibilities.

Has he got that right? He could ask her, but they don't really talk. He isn't certain how much English she knows, and his German is largely limited to technical jargon, or otherwise to ordering currywurst and beer.

Sand shakes from the fine white hairs on her wrists, as she moves her hands down to frame her porcelain cup. He can't help but search for patterns in the way that it lands — a trickled line of it, like runway lights — the way she holds that cup, both her index fingers darting away from the side of it, rhythmically, puppetting semaphore.

Another language that he doesn't know, but at least this one he can guess at.

"Have you enjoyed your stay, sir?"

Do they still ask that? Will they, when he gets to the boarding gate, shows them his passport?

Outside in the hallway he stands still for a moment, composing himself, checking again that he picked up that passport, and his wallet, and his wedding ring, from that black plastic tray.

He fastens his tie.

He fastens his watch strap.

The hands on that watch are aglow in the dark. Ditto the date in the little circle beside them — it will be Thursday tomorrow, and even if he does catch the afternoon flight that he's booked on, he still won't make it back in time to take his daughter swimming.

When he'd told Joanna this, that the days for his trip were slightly different than usual, he'd thought perhaps, this time, she might make a fuss. That they might argue. There are moments when he fancies that the kids are waiting for it also, like fight fans at a weigh-in, then left somehow disappointed when news of the cancellation breaks.

It's not that she's timid, that she never speaks her mind — she is a Glaswegian girl, after all; it's more that she seems to have made peace with the cost, the constantly shifting demands of the role.

There are times, increasing in number, when he thinks this is a challenge. Her contentment. As if she means to bait him into revealing once and for all whether he's still the man he was, a man who boasted dreamer's blood. The man who, when they met at University, had carried a gazetteer with him at all times; not like a safety blanket, really, but rather a statement of intent.

Or whether he's simply a husband now, a father. The man who'll come home to their suburban semi, as he always does, in his fine grey suit and his pale blue shirt. Who'll knock on the door, his familiar beat, and wait patiently for her to let him come in from the cold. Producing a bottle of duty-free wine from behind his back as he enters; a little everyday magic, a lover's legerdemain. Just a little bit of something, to let her know that he's still there.

A question for Dan Micklethwaite

Q: Can beautiful things be funny?

A: Beauty is in the eye of the beholder. So too is humour. I can't think of any reason why those eyes shouldn't cross.

About Dan Micklethwaite

Dan Micklethwaite lives about forty minutes away from so-called Brontë Country, in West Yorkshire, UK, and whilst secretly hoping for a region to be likewise renamed after him in the future, he doesn't really fancy his chances. He consoles himself with fine books and good food, and the occasional bottle of single malt scotch.

June

In Dew and Frost and Flame

Vanessa Fogg

They were eight when he first wrote her name in dew.

They'd met at recess, each wandering alone on the edges of the playground until they bumped into one another. His pockets were filled with acorns and stones; his hands held fallen twigs. He had no interest in joining the other boys with their ball games and imaginary light saber battles. Her pockets were filled with pine cones and pebbles; her hands clutched autumn leaves. She had never gotten on well with the other girls.

They became friends.

He loved to draw. It was one of the first things Laura learned about him. When they weren't hunting for treasure together—late dandelions gone to fluffy seed, a ring of mushrooms, the sight of a furry caterpillar crawling up a tree—then Eric was drawing. He scratched patterns in the earth with a stick. Scraped stones against pavement to leave smears of brown pigment. Doodled in class and complained that no crayon or marker ever got the color just right.

One recess after morning rain he traced patterns in the wet grass. "How do you spell your name?" he asked her. He wrote it in the grass with a stick, and for a moment she thought she actually saw it, a darker green in the patch of wet lawn.

He brought her a leaf on which he said he'd traced her name in dew. It must have dried; she saw nothing. He said that he would keep trying.

When she was twelve her parents told her that they were moving. She cried. Phoenix, Arizona. She saw it in her head: a desert, harsh and bare. No grass, no greenery; no lakes, no weather, no rain. No friends. No one she knew.

Eric promised to write.

And for a while, before they both forgot, he did. He sent her funny, rambling, whimsical letters, filled with his drawings. A cat with jeweled eyes, leaping from a giant striped hat. A rabbit with antelope horns. A kaleidoscope of butterflies landing on a tree of glass.

"Draw me a castle," she wrote, and he would do it. "Draw me a manatee," and he could do that, too. The colors glowed. Rich blues and greens, like the iridescence of dragonflies; reds and purples like desert sunsets. He had started making his own inks, he told her. He was trying to truly capture on paper the colors he saw.

"I miss the fall," she wrote. "Send me something from home."

He sent her a manila envelope. From it she pulled red maple leaves, rimed in frost. They'd been sent through ordinary mail. The frost was real. Her name was written on each leaf, sparkling in ice crystals.

They lost touch, as young people do. It was the '80s; there was no email, no texting, no Facebook.

But they found each other again, in a city on a coast far from where they'd both grown up. Laura was in college, studying computer science. Eric was at an art school twenty minutes away.

A string of connections, a phone number passed through a family friend, and they were meeting at a sunlit café. After a few minutes, the awkwardness passed. She looked into his eyes and saw that it was still *him*, so many years later. The boy who made her laugh, who always understood, who had always meant home.

"Can you still do it?" she asked. "Write and draw everything, in anything?"

He shook his head, smiling. "Not everything." He gazed at her in undisguised wonder, this handsome, tousle-haired young man who was still the boy she knew. "I can't really draw *you*." She blushed.

But he drew and painted what he could, in abstract patterns new to her. He painted in salt-water, in the deep, shifting blues of the cold sea of their new city. He mixed a gray that was the soft fog over the bay. He took the dark green of pines and the lighter green of sunlit ferns, and somehow he even mixed in the *smell* of an old forest through which he and she had walked, hand in hand. He painted moonlight in softly glowing whorls and bands. He painted sunlight.

Sunlight from the day that they first met again after so many years: the light shining in their water glasses and falling across the café table. Sunlight on their shoulders as they stepped out, laughing, into the warm afternoon. Sunlight on the trees and glittering on the sea. Sunlight on the campus quad. The sunlight that seemed everywhere, that surrounded them in their new days together. He caught it and dipped his brush into it and swept it across canvas: a clear, colorless light that couldn't be seen even as it left his brush, but infused everything it touched.

She would never quite understand how he did it. And slowly she had begun to realize that not everyone could see the light in his colors. Many praised his technical skill; many commented on the vividness of the inks he used, his facility with shading and tone. But only some gasped and stood entranced; some smelled the pine forest in his greens, while others shivered at the cold blues of his stormy seas or stood dazzled in the wash of pure light from sunlit scenes.

She always saw. She always felt.

And one night he made a color for her eyes alone—hers and his. A color meant just for the two of them, truly visible only to them.

It was senior year, and she was supposed to be studying for her final exams. He was supposed to be working on his senior thesis project. But he showed up at her apartment door, rumpled-looking in a stained T-shirt and jeans, urgency in his voice and eyes.

"Laura," he said. "I need you to help me with this one."

And she did. She would never have his singular gift, but she could help him with this particular color. Because it was hers, too.

It was a color made up of the memories of their childhood together—muddy knees and acorns and sticks. Shared cookies and gummy bears and a worried face and comforting presence when the other was scared or hurt. Quiet afternoons spent sketching together. It was a color made up of longing and distance. Of autumn leaves and frost and desert. It was a color that held their present lives, all the pressures of college and coming together and growing up, all the light of possibility and love.

When they were done, the color looked to her like umber flame, deep and warm and steady. The words he had traced in dew had dried; words he had written to her in frost crystals had melted at her touch. But words or images in this ink would never melt or fade.

"Only you and I can see this," Eric said. "As long as we stay in love with each other, we'll be able to see this."

And they dipped the nibs of their pens into the ink they'd made and wrote their names, side by side, in umber flame.

At their wedding two years later, they read their vows from cards of paper which would have appeared blank to anyone else who looked, but which to them glowed with words of fire.

"Love you," she sometimes wrote on notes to him, in their private ink. "Love you," he wrote back, with whimsical doodles that shone just for her—a burning rose, a cartoon cat with huge, starry eyes clutching dramatically at its heart. "I love you," she wrote on a card for their anniversary. Teasingly, she added--"You can still read these words, right?"

"Always," he wrote back.

He continued to draw and paint after graduation, but even with his gifts, making a living in the arts would never be easy. He taught art classes at a community center; he picked up freelance illustration and design work. She was climbing the ranks in software development at a major company.

Now they no longer left love notes for each other around the house or slipped into lunch bags. They left to-do lists for each other on a whiteboard in the kitchen; they wrote grocery lists in ordinary pencil. They had a child. They were both exhausted, staying up with the baby and then fighting traffic to get to their office jobs. Eric was working crazy hours at a design agency. Laura was directing a major project; she was pumping breast milk between meetings, managing her team, rushing from work to pick up the baby from daycare. They were both running on fumes, accidentally putting the cereal box in the refrigerator and the milk in the pantry.

Eric quit his corporate job, said that he would go freelance again while caring for the baby at home. It made sense. Laura had always made more money, and daycare costs were astronomical. Now there were home cooked meals ready when she came back from work, her daughter waiting to be gathered in her arms. She was lucky. She held her daughter, pressed her cheek to the baby's soft cheek. She stood swaying in the kitchen with the baby while Eric stirred tomato sauce on the stove and she thought, I am lucky. I am *lucky.*

She was. They were.

He'd meant to devote more time to his art again, to the work he truly loved. To mix and capture the colors of life. Laura saw him try. But then the baby stopped napping, and he still had commercial work for clients, and it seemed that all their time was eaten up just trying to get through the day, surviving and containing the chaos as best they could.

The baby was two now. Laura had fallen asleep with her again. She always read Maddie a story and snuggled with her under the covers until the child drifted off. Laura had meant to close her own eyes for a moment—only a moment—but blinking blearily at the clock she saw that it was past midnight. She groaned. She still had an hour of work to catch up on at the computer. The house was dark; Eric had gone to bed without her. They barely talked one-on-one these days. When was the last time either had written the other a love letter?

He started drawing again, handmade inks and paints on paper, strange and beautiful things of light and dark. They'd had a second child. Their children were older now: five and three. There was a little more room to breathe.

There were darker colors in his work now, shades that she'd never seen before. Flickering shadows cast over light. Bands of darkness pulsing and curling. A new complexity which caught and held her fast.

She came home to a messy house, the refrigerator nearly bare, the kids eating cookies out of a box in the living room. Eric must have lost track of time again; it would be take-out for dinner.

She felt a flash of anger, but forced it down. He was working at what he loved, and that was important, wasn't it? He was trying to take hold of his own career, make up for what he felt was lost time. He was doing the best work of his life now; they both knew it. Her girls ran to her and she hugged them. "Daddy's in his studio?" she said. They nodded and showed her the pictures they'd made with him earlier that day: flowers and mythical creatures, squiggles and streaks painted in sunlight and moonlight and love.

Finally, they were arguing openly. In their heedless release they said terrible things to one another, things that should have been held back in secret, locked away in the deepest parts of themselves.

He blamed her for his lack of career success. His disappointment that his art had never quite taken off. He said that maybe they had settled down too young. He said that he felt trapped. Unsupported. That he wanted space. He said all the terrible, clichéd things a man his age could say, and she felt like screaming and so she did.

Because she hadn't signed up for this life, either. She had not made vows to a man who would shut her out, who seemed to disappear from his own life. She had done everything to be supportive of his work; she believed in it. She picked up the slack in the housework; fed and cleaned the kids, put them to bed, did the dishes while he was still in his studio … She was doing everything, and how could it not be enough? How could she not be enough? She was the biggest supporter he had. And didn't she have her own dreams, as well? When challenged, she couldn't even say what those dreams were. Just that she knew that she'd once had them, and that they were something other than what she had now: relentless deadlines and work politics and helping the kids with schoolwork and feeling that everything was on her, that she was doing it all alone—that her partner in life was effectively gone.

That her partner had let her down.

They both cried.

He was gone that weekend—a get-together with old art school friends. She slipped into his studio. She stood in that small, sunlit place, and she looked at the pieces mounted on the wall, at the workbench with its scattered paints and inks. At the blank canvas on the easel and the work-in-progress lying flat on the table. And she realized that he had not drawn or painted anything new in weeks. Perhaps longer.

She walked slowly about the room. On the walls glowed suns and swirls and arcs of light—brilliant colors that could never be captured by digital pixels, never truly rendered on a screen. She saw the colors Eric had created for their daughters on their first birthdays —a rich yellow for Maddie, their eldest; an infinite blue of summer skies for Charlotte, their youngest. She saw joy and love.

She saw the dark colors that had taken over his most recent works. A pure black that seemed drawn from a hole in the world. An ugly green-gray that twisted her stomach, that crawled on the edges of pictures like mold. A more subtle darkness which could hardly be seen, but which permeated whole pictures like fog, dulling even the brightest colors beneath.

She looked at his unfinished works. She looked at the unused dark colors captured in glass jars and dried out on trays—shades that she didn't even know Eric had made. She knew the ugly feelings pulsing in those inks, though she could not draw them out and express them as he did.

What had happened to the color that she and he had created together, the color meant for the two of them alone? That ink of umber flame that only they could see?

She was tired. Was it worth it to hold on?

She had turned to go, when her shadow fell across what she had thought a blank stretch of white paper. She bent closer. Closer still. Yes, just barely she could see it. She had to cup her hands around the image to see it clearly, but it was there. A leaf traced in umber fire, life-size. He'd drawn it, a maple leaf from the cluster he'd once sent her. It was so faint that she'd almost missed it; even now, knowing that it was there, she could barely see it. But as she stared, the maple leaf seemed to leap and turn and then burn a little brighter.

He came back to her that night. He held out a note to her. She recognized it as one she'd slipped into his overnight bag a year ago, when he'd been invited to teach at an out-of-town workshop. She'd written "I love you" on it—even then knowing the trouble they were in, trying to reach out to him. She saw her words burning on the scrap of paper, burning in umber flame.

At their 30th anniversary years later there was a cake, a party, friends and relatives crowded into the back room of a fancy restaurant. Maddie was recording it all with her new iPhone; Charlotte beamed with pride as the cake she'd baked and decorated was brought out. Laura and Eric kissed before the crowd. He handed her an anniversary card: words of love and a poem written in ordinary, visible blue ink. Below that he'd written something else: a suggestion of what they could do later that night, written in invisible flame for her eyes alone. She blushed.

Years later. A lifetime shared.

Laura sat alone in her late husband's sunlit studio. Brilliant colors surrounded her, like a garden in bloom. But there were also swathes of darkness on the walls. A complicated pattern of dark and light.

She sat at Eric's old work table. Before her, a jar glowed with umber fire.

She had been twenty-one when she and Eric had first filled that jar. They had remade that color years later, after almost giving up on each other. And through the years they had remade and refilled it again and again.

The color in the jar was darker than when they'd first started; it was deeper but brighter, too. Singular light had given way to countless flickering shades of earthen-brown and gold-red fire, rich and mutable but with an unalterable steadiness at its heart, like the steadiness at the center of a flame.

She ran her fingers around the jar's glass surface, feeling its warmth.

We had a good life, she thought. Not a life of fame or fabulous wealth. Not a life with every youthful dream fulfilled. But a good one. A great one.

Her phone buzzed: a text message from her daughters. They were on their way to pick her up for lunch. They were kind and gentle with her, solicitous of their elderly mother's grief even as they grieved themselves.

It was two months ago that he'd passed away. He'd been painting that morning in his studio. He'd come out to the kitchen where she was drinking tea, and she knew at once that something was wrong. His gait—the confusion on his face, half fear and half-annoyance. He opened his mouth, but no words came.

She remembered running to him. Sitting with him on the couch while they waited for the ambulance to come. His head leaning against hers. And then, somehow, she was at the hospital and Maddie and Charlotte were with her. Maddie was talking to the doctors. Hemorrhagic stroke, they said. They'd wheeled him into surgery; they were trying to control the bleeding. He never came home.

Now Laura lifted her head and looked around her, at the studio where he'd spent so much of his life. At times, she had felt shut out by his devotion to his art. And yet she'd loved his work, too.

Her hand had been on his as they mixed their color for the first time, in the silence of the art school's empty studio. *As long as we stay in love with each other,* he'd said, *we'll be able to see this.*

And it was true. He was gone, but she could still see it. She could still see their color in the pictures he'd made.

All around her, the walls glowed with hidden messages for her. Whorls and curves and secret words of fire. Leaves and petals and wings. Her name, written again and again.

He was gone, but she remained in love with him. And somehow, somewhere, he was still in love with her.

It came from Vanessa Fogg

This story was born from the wreckage of a different, failed story. I'd been trying to write a story about a wizard's house. In this story, a house has been abandoned for years, is eventually taken over by the county for unpaid taxes, and a housecleaning crew is assigned to clean the place up for sale. Since the house belonged to a wizard, the housecleaning crew finds all kinds of strange and wondrous things within... But the story never worked because there was no real narrative: it was simply a whimsical list of magical objects. But one of those objects stayed with me. It was a pen that wrote in ink made of moonlight, a pen the wizard and his wife used to write love letters to one another, letters that only they could read... So I took that pen and transformed it, and gave a magical ink to a different couple. I think Laura and Eric used it well. "In Dew and Frost and Flame" also draws a bit upon my own life experiences, as one can probably guess. Any long-term relationship goes through its ups and downs, and when you add children to the mix it all gets much harder and complicated. But it's still worthwhile.

A question for Vanessa Fogg

Q: Do you make art other than prose? What kind, and how is it different?

A: Unfortunately, I am not gifted in any art other than prose. I can't draw, can't sing, and never took my childhood piano lessons seriously. I am grateful, however, for the existence of those who are gifted in the visual and musical arts!

About Vanessa Fogg

Vanessa Fogg dreams of selkies, dragons, and gritty cyberpunk futures from her home in western Michigan. She spent years as a research scientist in molecular cell biology, and now works as a freelance medical writer. She drinks copious amounts of green tea.

www.vanessafogg.com

Sheer

Phil Berry

Resten Light woke up, pushed the fibre blanket away, and pulled apart the two wings that formed the doors of his nest. He took in the immense sky, its colour and its shapes. Clouds coalesced around the upper reaches of the Far Tower. No-one in his community had seen the top or knew what shape it took. Some said it was flat – truly horizontal – but few believed that myth. Horizontal was unobtainable. He drew in the blue air, sensed the sharp tang, and knew that there was a storm coming.

"Have you tasted it, Dad?"

Resten's father, Suren, rubbed his beard and knelt at his son's side. The nest rocked as he moved. They both held a nearby rope, each with hands thickly calloused by a lifetime of grip and slide.

"Yes. And look at the mist near the... the... that's where the weather's coming from."

Resten, entering adolescence now, lived on the vertical face of Sheer, an immense tower of stone formed by the same elements that had chiselled, rubbed and flushed away the planet's crust around the Far Tower. The people living on the sides of these towers knew no other terrain, and nor had the generations that preceded them. They did not worry about what might be found above the cloud; they would never go there.

And below? An ever-present mist that shrouded the base in a grey, almost welcoming blanket. People sometimes leapt off the side of Sheer into the mist, perhaps one per cycle. Many more fell accidentally. Life spent on the side a rock face without discernible vertical or lateral limits offered numerous opportunities for slips. Every moment of every day required concentration. Although the ropes, knots, tricks and fail-safes became second nature in infancy, it was necessary to reserve a portion of one's conscious mind to check, check, and check again. Always be attached. *Always*. Never relax your grip. Never. Never take a chance. One error was all it took... for life to be cut short, to experience the long fall, the long tumble into the mist below. Resten knew this. He had lost his little sister that way. Feathereen, as light on her feet in life as her name suggested.

The rock was too hard to excavate caves. The only ledges were those that nature had allocated randomly, and historically these were occupied and owned by the ruling families, the communities over which they continued to hold power being ranged below. Resten's family was middling; his father knew the nature of vine and fibre. Although sparse, there was enough organic material for him and others of his class to make rope. And on rope everything and everyone depended. The nests hung from rope that was wedged permanently and under great pressure into small cracks. The connectors, allowing people to make their way from the nests to the kitchens or meeting areas, were no more than triple-ropes, plaited, the grooves deep enough to offer some foot security.

Feathereen's five year-old feet had fit those grooves perfectly. Whereas adults had to pivot on their toes, she had bounced along confidently. It got her into trouble, that confidence. Many was the time Suren or her mother, Wingen, had scolded her, or grabbed a hand and placed it firmly on the waist high line that ran in parallel to the foot-ways.

"Never let go! Never..." one of the adults would say. Feathereen would smile, wink at her older brother when he turned to see what the fuss was about, and obey. She always obeyed her parents in the end. It was not disobedience that killed her.

The most ambitious constructions, the temples, were elaborate prominences, pods with walls of woven fibre. In these pods were tiny seats, and only when the communities came together at every third Light did the adults relax and, literally, let go. Seats took their weight. They felt what it was like to find the horizontal. And after the service, during which thanks were given to the benignity of the cycle, to the absence of storms, and to the great bird migration that provided them with flocks to catapult, store, and eat, they stood up and found their way via various connectors back to the nests.

"And look at the mist near the... the... "

Resten winced at his father's stuttered sentence. He could not say it... the word... *surface*. The surface, of which there was no visible proof. The only people who could possibly have seen the surface, even assuming there was one, had been fractions of a second from an explosive death, plunging through the mist. Like Feathereen. That was why his father could not bring himself to speak of it.

"Shall we check the ropes, Dad?" Resten moved the exchange on. Suren regained his concentration.

"Better had, son. Your mother's in the kitchens today, she's been up since Blue Light. We'll get it done by Ochre." And by White Light they must be inside, in shadow. The current season saw the star pass close and low; the tower's side was baked during White Light, the middle part of the day. An adult might survive twenty minutes out on the face, a child ten. It never happened. Any nest-holder seeing a man, woman or child on the rock would pull them inside; privacy counted for nothing in this situation.

Feathereen had always been the best at this. Her sunny disposition and innocent face could open the nests of complete strangers, even those of rival families, before she even asked to enter. Resten, following her as they ranged across the tower face seeking plants in flower or large insects, would watch in awe as grumpy men or busy women spotted her lithe form and beckoned the two of them in before White Light struck.

At other times, when they were alone in the shade, she told Resten about her dreams of walking along firm paths lined with vegetation, of fields that grew crops, shoulder-high sticks supporting edible seeds or grain through which she ran and ran until her heart raced. It was during one of these dreams that she walked, in sleep, out of the nest and into the free air. Suren had awoken at the sound of movement in the nest. He had glimpsed her trailing foot, taken in the bird-bone flute that he had carved for her, swinging from her waist, but he was not able react quickly enough. She walked through the winged doorway and was never seen again.

Suren stepped from the nest onto the nearest rope. He never doubted for an instant that it would take his weight. He had secured all the ropes in the neighbourhood himself. Resten watched him drop down a level and slide sideways to perform the first checks. Mothers and fathers were dispersing across the face to check their own nests and adjacent connectors. After this was done they would move as a group to the temple and the complex of nests owned by the Head Family.

Suren called out instructions as he progressed,

"Tidy the nest, Resten, and wax the walls. There was moisture inside this morning."

But Resten did not respond. He had moved up a level. He was out of his father's sight, hidden behind a water store, a man-sized bladder stitched from bird skins and hung from the rock like a giant, opaque teardrop. He heard the words and paused. Suren's tone was soft, almost weary. His once-natural authority had been diminished since Feathereen's death. The energy that had emanated from him, the fighting force that had protected his children from the elements on this exposed world, had started to fade the day she fell. So Resten, the younger part of him loyal to his parents and wanting nothing more than to hide away from the storm in their arms, had made a decision. He must find his sister and bring her home. He must see his family complete once more.

Resten progressed through the broad circle of outer nests, taking care not to approach those where his friends lived. One of his father's roper-colleagues noticed him and waved, completely unaware of the boy's intention. Resten nodded, then skipped on. His hands skipped too, one step at a time, with the briefest of overlaps, never a moment when one hand was not in contact with rope. He slowed down as he passed the temple. Inside was a small shrine to his sister. Resten, Suren, and Wingen had fashioned a figurine from bird-bones. Fragile, white sticks glued together with guano and dust; fibre for hair, a fibre skirt, even a tiny model of the bird-bone flute she loved, attached to one hand. It really did look like her. Now it rested in a small niche among other totems and memorials to those who had fallen.

And now the small-birds came fleeing before the storm that was bubbling up from the mist. Ochre Light darkened as the huge flock blocked the sun. The temperature dropped. On another day Resten would have twisted around to fire his catapult and cast his net for meat. But having looked carefully for larger, aggressive Driftbirds wheeling in the flock, he moved on, nose to the stone, and left the temple behind.

The quality of the light changed as Ochre gave way to White. He would have to find protection soon. The climb had left him between communities; there were no nearby nests. He had not gone this far up before. Yet the informal lessons given by elders on temple days described an endless series of communities up and down the face, so Resten continued. The temperature rose. He sipped rain water from the bird-gut flask that swung from his belt. A short while later, when his cheek touched the rock and the heat caused him to recoil, he had to accept that White had come. And there, twenty body lengths above him, a fuzzy black blob against the yellow-brown face, was a nest. He scrambled up and slipped between the two large wings.

In the nest sat an old woman, her wrinkled head obscured by shadow. Her forearms lay on a fibre rug, their climbing muscles and chunky veins still prominent. Exquisite bird-bone mobiles hung from the roof, twirling in response to the draft that Resten had caused in the previously still, silent space.

"What's this?" she asked.

"Sorry lady, it's White Light,"

"So?"

"It's hot! You don't mind?"

"Where's your mother?"

Resten said nothing.

"Where's your mother boy? You're not *from* here. So where's your mother?"

"I'm old enough to be out."

"No. You're after something. What you lost?"

Resten looked at her carefully. There were tiny gaps between some of the overlapping feathers that formed the walls of the nest, and slanting needles of White Light probed her black cloak. The old lady cracked a smile,

"So you *have* lost something."

Resten, tired from his unbroken climb, opened up.

"My sister. She fell last year."

The old lady nodded slowly.

"I remember. We heard here. First in two cycles. The Roper's daughter, of all people. Poor you. Over it now though, I expect."

"I'm looking for her."

"Ah." She held his gaze. "Ah." She shook her head. "Did you see the Far Tower earlier? I thought there was a break in the cloud cap, I thought I saw the top. A lovely, flat top."

Resten laughed, conditioned by a life lived on the vertical to dismiss such ravings. There had been no break in the cloud cap. There never was. The woman was mad.

"You scoff at me! Did I scoff at you? What you seek is as far-fetched as the firm ground I have spent a lifetime craving. But boys are rude, I know. So... why up? Why up? Your sister... she went *down*."

Resten felt the same discomfort he had felt in his father's company; she *knew* why he was going up. They all went up, all the dead. Borne on the backs of Driftbirds who collected corpses, flicking them up with their beaks, to be carried away and deposited on the top. All were taught this – the dead achieved what the living could never hope to – peace on the flat. In the temple they sang songs about a second life above the clouds, and acted out the process of reawakening on solid ground. Each cycle one maturing child would be chosen to do this, and it was a high privilege – to lie on the small flat area in the temple and *pretend* to stand on solid ground, to walk with barely a care.

"I know why, don't worry, boy," she allowed. "I used to think about going up myself, when I was your age. It's natural, despite the teachings. I'm too old to be the one to put you off. Try. Try. And if you succeed, *discover*. There's a reason we cling to this rock like weeds, hiding from the White Light, picking sustenance out of the sky and scraping lichen off the stone. Don't be put off by any that you meet. Ignore the superstitious. If you find nothing and tire, then return, or build a new life higher up... nothing is lost." She had begun to murmur indistinctly, becoming distracted by private thoughts and memories. Then she snapped back into focus. "So... you intend to spend the night?"

"No. Just the White Light. I want to make progress, beat the storm."

"You do, and you should, if you wish to out-pace your father."

"Do you know him?"

"Only the rumours that rose and fell after your sister's accident. Only that. A good man, Suren Light. I feel sorry for him. But if they come, I will not tell them."

Resten looked away.

The old lady bent over to one side and look carefully through a small hole in the floor of her nest. Then she shook her head to indicate that she saw no one in pursuit.

"Have you heard of the paths?" asked Resten. He sensed that of all people, she would not reject such a bold question.

"Ah. Yes, of course. We know of them."

"We?"

"Us. Your betters. There is a theory that our race memory has retained images of paths and fields and flows of rain, landscapes our ancestors explored on this world or another before we were blown like seeds into the sides of these great towers. But we have adapted, and we must learn to live where we find ourselves. Your poor sister suffered an intense re-living of memories that did not belong to her."

"Do you believe that we can find our way back to those places?"

"Ah. Us. Yes! But the fields are gone, the surface of this world has been split and scoured, leaving only the towers. There may be plateaus that go on as far as you can imagine, but... I have studied the patterns, counted the storms and felt the heat of the White Light. Nothing can grow in these conditions. The tops cannot sustain life, any nutrients that remained must have been swept away by the wind sterilised the tops. You think we are battered here... but up there, near the cloud base, the wind *rages*. I have watched the cloud move around the top of the Far Tower, it is more violent than you can imagine."

"And below? What do you know of the surface?"

"Nothing lives down there either, apart from the Driftbirds who climb on the forces that are emitted from the core, the turbulence that feeds the storms. The elders know this, Resten, it has been passed down. Our tribes explored once, hoping to find Sheer's origin, where it joins the planet. There are stories of deep chasms with crystalline walls on which no human can gain purchase, of vicious heat rising, spitting liquid rock. We are trapped between fire and infinity... but we do not labour this with the young. If there is *anything* to be discovered, it is up. But do not imagine fields or streams. Those days have passed. They belong only in the memories that are embedded in our blood-lines."

Resten flicked one of the door-wings. The white had faded to violet - Violet Light, the phase before night. Storen stared at him, but had no more to say. Resten said his farewells and left.

He survived the storm, climbed day after day through the remainder of the seasonal cycle, and continued for seven cycles more.

Resten Light woke, caressed the body next to him and pulled the feathered doors of his nest apart. He took in the sky, its colour and its shapes. His beard bothered him, as always. He wore it short, choosing to cut it regularly with shards of rock face, each one requiring a day of work in the Winter phase with a wet rope wedged into a pre-formed crack, followed by a frost to expand the water and spilt away a flake. But it was worth it, he felt. Given his standing, he should look different from the others. His father had done the same. A slight hand pulled on the hairs below his ear.

"Hey, Resten, there's a storm coming." His wife, Ochren-True.

"Do you know something? If it comes, this will be only the fifth full storm since I left home."

"I know! You tell me that whenever the mist looks edgy. Well? Are you going to get out and check the ropes?"

"In time. They're fine."

"Resten, we have a family now. We don't assume *anything*."

He nodded. She was right.

He circled the nest complex before Blue Light had turned to Ochre, then moved to the Hall. It was the Hall that had attracted his notice as he wandered from community to community. Many, many days and nights after saying goodbye to the old lady, having made his way up through countless strata, he had looked up and saw a brown square in the distance. It was jutting out from the side of the face as if by some sort of magic. His pace on the ropes increased. As he grew closer, he could make out more details. The square was a platform; a *flat* structure. Resten's engineering instinct drew him sideways, to examine the suspension technique. Ropes fanned out from the outer edge of the platform in an upward spray, the lengths attached to the face in an arc so that the weight was well distributed. Resten looked carefully at the junction between rope and rock – how *had* they secured them? These people must have found a new and safe method, for the platform was clearly used by many. There were seats and tables, all made of fibre and wood. He had seen small trees growing out of crevices on the way up. Perhaps there were enough in this area to sustain carpentry. And indeed, he came to learn over the days and weeks that followed, there were.

The storm matured. The Far Tower was completely obscured by barrelling, churning mist columns. Resten hurried to the platform, checked the fan of supporting ropes, then moved to the temple that he had been so involved in designing and building. He had brought to it an instinctive understanding of cantilevers and fulcrums, together with innovations in rope-weaving taught to him by his father. Resten was now chief engineer. His was a top family.

A vibration travelled through the rope on which he stood. It was not the storm. His head snapped to the right, towards the platform. Two ropes had sprung from the rock face, their free ends falling in a lazy but potentially lethal curl. The platform rocked. A man had landed on it. He screamed and rolled in pain near the outer edge. Resten could see that a leg was broken, and perhaps his back too. He leaped across, taking unusual risks. For several moments he broke the lifelong rule – and jumped free of attachment to rope or structure. This was a new situation. He had never seen a faller. Never.

Resten was first on the scene; others joined but gave their engineer space. He rolled the man over so that his bloodied face was upturned. The nameless face, a mass of abrasions, opened its mouth, but no sound came out, at first.

"Did you fall, or jump?" asked Resten sternly.

"Fell... I fell."

"I am sorry."

"I... I saw it."

"What?"

"The t... the top."

Resten stared down. He noticed puncture marks in the sleeves of his fibre shirt, over the upper arms. The flesh beneath was bleeding. Both arms. Talon wounds. Other men and women were approaching. Ochren-True was not among them. The dying man spoke again,

"I saw them... *all*. They lie there." His face fell to the side. Blood spilled from his mouth, flowing up from a ruptured organ within.

Resten closed the man's eyes, stood up, and with authority stated, "He shall be given a niche in the temple. He had fallen."

The wind was rising. All minds were focussed on the coming storm. They looked at Resten quizzically, asking for instruction. Those who died of age or disease were cast off the face into the receiving mist with ceremony... but this, what to do with this man? Resten decided, "We get through the storm. The casting off will be tomorrow. The storm is close now, it will hit during White Light. But the clouds will protect us from the heat, we have more time to prepare. Double check the ropes, secure your nests, count your children. All to be inside by Ochre's end. Put him in the temple for now. Wrap him up."

In truth, Resten cared little for the dead man's fate. Only his words. Having tucked his own wife and son into the central nest of his luxurious complex, he stepped out onto the main ascending ropeway and left home for the second time.

The storm whipped the face of Sheer but Resten was in no danger of being torn away. Before each gust he twisted rope around his thick forearms, the same for his ankles. The White Light was moderated by the cloud and in fact the wind was warm and not unpleasant at times. Despite the pauses he made good progress, climbing well beyond the wide limits of his reputation in a few days.

The ropes became sparse, the nests more ovoid, the suspension methods different. The greatest change in the landscape was the relative abundance of trees. Their trunks were as thick as Resten's muscular thighs, and grew out horizontally before angling up at forty-five degrees and sending shoots back into the face for greater strength. The trees were integrated into the ropeways and connectors. A few of the larger ones were trusted to support small houses, belonging always to the top families.

Nobody seemed to have heard of the fallen man. Resten described him to all he met, but saw no flicker of recognition. After a full cycle he stopped asking. His son's third birthday was coming up. If Resten had not left his community he would have taken the infant up to the temple and received gifts from other families; bird-meat parcels, bone-toys, precious fruit carried from distant parts of Sheer. If he had stayed. He allowed himself to think of his wife's pain, but not the boy's. And before them... his father's. How much did it hurt, to lose a second child?

Resten climbed. There were more crevices here, more ledges, greater variety. He grew used to sleeping on natural platforms that accommodated over half his width. With a rope around his legs and another around his chest he could relax into his dreams. It was no longer necessary to find nests and beg hospitality. And the White Light was less intense here, the rays more tangential. He must have moved around the tower, or the tower must have an imperceptible twist to it, facing away from the midday sun. He looked down. The rock ran straight and true into the mist. He looked up. There was still no visual clue that he was near the top. He had not passed a community for many, many days. The few ropes he found were weathered and unreliable; he climbed on trees and finger holds.

The tower's face darkened. Violet turned to night, then back to Violet. A breeze on his cheek. Black shadow again, and again. Resten turned to see seven huge birds - Driftbirds - ascend. If they noticed him they gave no sign. He watched as they soared, shrinking to angled dashes against the colour of the sky. From one pair of talons hung a shape without definite form. It reminded Resten of one thing only – a body shrouded and ready to be cast away.

Later, while looking up and scanning the rock face for features, Resten spotted a prominent ledge. He climbed up and across so as to meet it. As he approached its underside, he realised that to access the top side he would have to take a great risk. If the ledge was slippery, or if he miscalculated, he would fall. But he could see no another way. He chose to tackle the ledge during early Ochre, and spent the preceding night fifteen body-lengths below, wrapped in his feathered cloak and wedged between a tree trunk and the face. Night gave way to Blue, which gave way to Ochre. He moved.

The ledge was as wide as two men. Resten climbed into its shadow, wedged two raw fingertips of his right hand into a gap and reached out. The angled fingers of his left hand felt the full thickness of the ledge. He touched its flat surface. Then he paused, paralysed by indecision which slowed time and threatened to drain the power from his limbs. The thought of failure came; plummeting, conscious still, past two homes, an infant unaware, along those glass sides, into the burning chasms described by Storen.

He jumped. His right hand joined his left at the edge of the ledge. All of his concentration was channelled into the muscles and tendons running from the bones of his forearms. They lifted him until his chin was level with the ledge and he could gaze across it. Five black-feathered Driftbirds stood looking out, previously unseen from below. He hauled himself up to safety but could not keep silent. The birds' heads turned as one, alert, quick. The nearest approached. Resten lay on his side, totally exposed. The bird pecked at his shoulder and punctured his rough clothing, drawing blood. The bird's eyes were silver-white. They betrayed no feeling.

Resten rolled past the bird, found his feet and zig-zagged around the others. He was confident he could outrun the birds on foot, and he knew that they would not choose to fly close to the face. The birds *he* knew, smaller birds, avoided proximity to the face for fear of being brought down by catapult or net. So he ran. The birds tried to run after him but were not built for it. One of them took wing, but as Resten had predicted, it could do no more than monitor him from a distance.

The ledge developed an upward gradient. Then it began to eat into the face, so that Resten had to duck to avoid grazing his head against a slight overhang. The outer part of the ledge developed a ridge. The gradient grew more marked. He was ascending Sheer by foot. The path turned in more sharply. The overhang and the ridge met, forming a tunnel. There was just enough light to see by. The light, White Light now, was coming in somewhere ahead. For light to be coming into the tunnel it must be coming *down*. For light to be coming come down, he must be near the...

The Driftbirds had found their voice. It was a cacophony. The light strengthened. Resten emerged onto a rocky plain. He stood with feet apart and arms free, uncomfortable without rope or tree touching his body somewhere. The atmosphere was milky, filtering the White Light. A constant wind crossed his face and flapped at his fibre clothes; the same wind, he reflected, that cleansed the top and ensured its sterility. There were no trees, no features. The old lady was right – nothing could grow here.

The White Light made everything glow. In the distance he could make out the untroubled backs of many more Driftbirds. They were busy, pecking at things on the ground. Resten approached cautiously and quickly saw what it was they were — human bodies. The fallen and the jumpers were clothed, while those who had been cast off after natural death were covered in brown shrouds, having benefitted from the ministrations of their peers.

Resten circled the feeding ground. Further on, he found bodies with most of the flesh pecked away. And further still, clean skeletons, bleached by numerous White Lights. The Driftbirds ignored him, even if he emerged from a particularly dense patch of cloud just inches from one of their hard, feathered backs. Their preference appeared to be for dead meat; the vicious peck he had received on the ledge no more than a sign that he was not welcome here. Whatever the reason, Resten grew more confident with each passing day.

As the cloud shifted and varied, offering glimpses of the sky beyond, Resten explored. At night he retreated to the edge of the plain and slept where the cloud was most dense. The Driftbirds came and went in groups. He watched a group of three return with a bundle. The shroud of soft fibre had begun to unravel, and the pale limbed body inside was limp. Resten wondered – how did the bodies keep their shape? He had always imagined them hitting the ground and... destruction. The answer came to him. The ever-vigilant Driftbirds caught them in mid-air. They swooped and took hold with those great talons. Like the fallen man who thudded onto the platform, his arms pierced and bleeding. Caught while alive, but in his case released, or fumbled, perhaps.

Resten began to search the bones.

Hunger drove him back to the tower's edge every few days, and he sat with his legs hanging in space waiting for small birds to pass. Half way through the season they stopped coming, and Resten was forced to take a Driftbird. He feared that such an act would change the status-quo and turn them against him, but he had no choice. Their feeding ground became *his* feeding ground. With lengths of cloth taken from the bodies, he made loops and nooses to lay on the ground. When an outlying bird wandered into a trap it was pulled away from its group into the obscuring cloud. With a shard-knife Resten cut its neck before it cried out. As he carved the first slice of meat from its tendinous leg, Resten retched at the thought of what his prey had fed on that day. Then he turned his mind from that awful thought and planned the next stage of his search.

The skeletons were laid out in rows. Based on the degree of sun-bleaching, Resten concluded that they had been arranged in chronological order. There was method here. Moreover, although the meat was removed the humanoid form was preserved. The bones were not wrenched from their sockets or separated.

Resten crept along the lines, day after day. She would be shorter than the adults. There were babies, and infants, but few of Feathereen's age.

He fashioned the hollowed out carcasses of several prey into the walls of a camp far from the feeding ground, but the first full storm blew it away. The only warning he had was a mass descent of Driftbirds onto the plateau during Ochre Light. As the light changed the storm rose and enveloped him. Resten survived the terrible wind by knotting the camp's rope anchors around his waist. The walls, his store of food, his shard-knife, all were sucked away in the brief tempest. Then the air became clear and cloudless. Resten looked along the plateau from his exposed position on the ground and saw the many thousands of Driftbirds who had come down before the storm push away from the surface as one. The skeletons appeared undisturbed. Something had protected them from the gale. Something had covered them. The Driftbirds. The huge flock. *They* had come down to protect the bodies.

Resten turned and was awestruck by the unprecedented visibility. He saw ten, fifteen, twenty more towers beyond the Far Tower... and between some of them stone links, natural bridges. Some of the towers broadened into plateaus, shaped like the rare moulds that were a delicacy on Sheer. And on the plateaus that lay below Sheer, Resten saw rippling black carpets, glossy where the sun caught the backs of massed Driftbirds. They lifted off, as those on Sheer had done, revealing a variegated pattern of green, brown, and gold. In places – although the distance made Resten doubt himself – the surface seemed to soften and sway. He saw fields. Then the clouds returned, obscuring the vista.

Resten walked towards the deserted ground, eager to explore new sections. He felt the ground beneath his feet soften. With bones to his left and his right, partially shrouded in cloud as usual, he lifted a foot and examined the sole of his foot. Brown granules had stuck between his toes, clumps of which crumbled when he pressed them between his fingers. He held it under his nostrils, and smiled at the fresh, musty odour. He remembered finding something similar in a rare niche on the face where a plant had grown. His mother had told him it was a good thing – the result of vegetation decaying, a sign of permanence. "Dirt", they had called it. Resten knelt down and pushed his hands into the thin layer of soil. Then he hurried on, following the pleasant smell. The depth of the humus carpet increased. He knelt again. This time his hands ran into vegetation; wisps of grass, moss more luxuriant than the thin, desiccated layers that clung to the face of the tower. The bones here were much older. They were crumbling into the soil. The nutrients held in the marrow and the matrices within were dissolving onto the sterile plateau. The bones *were* the soil.

Cloud traversed the space before him. Resten wished it would clear so that he could see what he wished and believed lay before him – fertile ground. Fields. A gap in the cloud came, and he peered forward. A curved rank of birds stood immobile before him. The gap enlarged, and Resten saw that the curve extended to his left, his right, and behind him. He was surrounded. One of them strutted forward with something in its beak. It held a skeleton by the lower spine, so that its legs dangled on one side and the chest, arms and head on the other. Like the others, its ligaments had been preserved. The bird stopped a few feet in front of Resten and dropped its offering.

Resten knelt over it. He held a weightless hand. He noticed a leather band around the pelvis, unaffected by decay. Attached to this was another bone – non-human. There were tiny holes along its length. The flute. It was her.

Resten rocked the curved cradle of her rib cage. Within the cavity lay a loose sheaf of brown sticks. The top of each stick expanded into a complex group of pods which crumbled when Resten touched them. Their smell assured him that they were edible. He looked, his mouth agape but full of questions that could not be asked.

The birds retreated as one into the thickening cloud; a black band on the hard surface.

Resten unfolded the plucked and scraped skin of a captured Driftbird that he had prepared for this eventual purpose. He wrapped up her bones as his family would have done had she died naturally. He noted how her skull, pelvis and vertebrae were undamaged. She had not hit the ground. Like the others, her ligaments were intact. The skeleton was whole. The Driftbirds had caught her. Probably, she had been unconscious when the talons clasped her thin torso or soft abdomen. Or perhaps not. Perhaps, turning in the air, coming out of a sleep coloured by images of her race's more comfortable past, where water flowed and plants grew high from moist soil, she felt the air push at her clothes and her face, saw the mist rising to her, felt the heat of the planet's ruptured crust, and sensed herself fall into the shadow of an approaching Driftbird.

Carrying his burden, Resten descended to the community of his maturity. He collected his stunned wife Ochren-True, his infant son, and carried on down to the community of his birth. He said little, but the evident power of his intention brooked no challenge.

Storen's nest was now occupied by a young family; two children played on the ropes just outside. Resten passed it without hesitation.

Half a day's travel from there he began to recognise structures. From above, the temple looked well-kept; the community was evidently healthy. There were new features, and some innovations in the rope-work. Resten paused and whispered to Ochren-True, but she encouraged him. She reassured him that his actions were correct... she, the wife whom he had abandoned.

Ochren-True hung back with the child while Resten approached the home-nest. The bi-wing doors were unchanged, they had kept their integrity through all the seasons and the daily White Light. Someone had waxed them well.

Inside, Resten found his father in the company of a carer. His mother Wingen had been cast off nine cycles ago, and Suren was no longer strong enough to leave his nest. Others looked after him. He was owed that by the community, for all he had done with his hands and his ingenious brain to improve their surroundings and keep them safe. A lifetime on Sheer had left the skin of his face baked like the rock. Yet he looked calm, comfortable in himself. He had accepted Resten's choice long ago.

Resten lay his sister, Suren's daughter, on the floor and peeled away the Driftbird covering. Suren noticed the flute immediately. His eyes shone as a layer of tears formed. He picked up the instrument, examined it, smiled. Then he reached for Resten, nodded in gratitude, and looked up at the roof of his nest, as though to thank a greater power.

"They delivered her to me, father. The Driftbirds. They tasted my blood and knew she belonged to me, to our family. The others, all the dead, are taken there to nourish the ground. They protect them. There are fields up there. Things grow. In the soil of our dead. Look." He took out the sheaf, much degraded despite the care he had taken with it on the long journey down. Suren brushed the sticks and said,

"The second life."

"No, father..." Resten could not articulate his frustration at his father's reversion to tradition.

"You should have left her."

Tears came to Resten.

"No father, it is no second life. They use us to bring life back to the towers, to the old surface... I was told, by an elder, when I left... there used to be life up there, fields and trees. The birds have used us to bring it back."

"That old lady, Storen... we knew her... spoke of myth. We do not know how things used to be, Resten. We belong here, where we were thrown by fate. It is a good life."

"But Father, our people can climb now. We can move to the flat. I have seen it. The tops are habitable. The Driftbirds have done it... *for us*. They gave Feathereen to me. They gave me these plants. It was an invitation. Us and the birds. A natural order, benefiting all."

"No, Resten... Resten... you have no proof..."

"We can move back now father. Back to the surface, a *living* surface."

"No, Resten..."

Suren's voice had grown weak. A hand moved to rest on the small bones of Feathereen's slightly flexed palm. Despite his admonition of Resten, and for all his sense of sacrilege, he was pleased to see her again. To know she had not been shattered on the restless surface or abandoned on the top. His hand moved from Feathereen to his son, and by a slight pressure of his fingertips he thanked him.

Resten left the nest and stood in the fading light. He tasted the air and sensed activity in the mist below. All he saw, looking up, looking down, was skewed by discovery. On the top he had grown accustomed to looking along rather than straining his neck up or down; his feet had grown comfortable with the weight of his body spread evenly across the soles. The ability to step sideways, the knowledge, in sleep, that is was safe to roll... the memory of these simple if shallow freedoms seduced him. And beyond that something larger. The soil, the distant fields, the natural bridges. A higher world, and a vital future for his people. Smiling, confident in his vision, Resten ducked back into the nest and began to prepare his little sister for her casting off.

It came from Phil Berry

Sheer - the eponymous and seemingly limitless vertical tower of rock, came from a desire to create a distinct 'secondary' world. I wanted to show how men and women would adapt to conditions that seem unbearable. Imagine never being able to sit or rest on a solid, horizontal structure. 'Flat' becomes myth, and those who tire of life spent on hessian ropes need only step off, plunging into the ever-present mist below. But that was not enough. The community on Sheer needed a context; where did they fit, ecologically, in this world with a broken crust? Answering this, I thought about a mural on the walls of the boys' toilet in a local attraction – 'Wetlands'. The mural shows a classic water cycle, with rain coming down from the clouds onto the land, draining via rivers into the sea, evaporating, forming new clouds and precipitating. Pretty basic, but beautiful. This I translated into the more macabre biomass cycle on Sheer, where hated Driftbirds collect the corpses of the fallen before they hit the planet's surface, carry them to the tops of the towers, and lay them out. Here the bodies decompose into a layer of humus. Thus, this sterile (post-apocalyptic, possibly) world will develop fertile plains on which communities can sow crops and re-establish themselves. Ideas excite me, but concepts are easier to describe than people. Yet, I recognise that editors want character driven stories; background, depth, emotion, motive. On Sheer, where a misstep or a slip of a hand on a rope can end it all, tragedy is never far away. It is a combination of grief and duty that drives young Resten to leave home on a quest for the 'top', where he hopes to find the body of a little sister who walked in her sleep and stepped out of the family nest into the infinite air.

A question for Phil Berry

Q: What work of art has been the most inspiring?

A: It's tempting to go full pseud on this one, but just the other day I was reading the second volume of art critic Brian Sewell's autobiography, 'Outsider', and he reminded me about the genius of Salvador Dali. I was fascinated by his creations as a younger man, and gazed at glossy copies of 'Crucifixion (Corpus Hypercubus)' for hours. It combines religious ecstasy with the mysteries of nuclear science and higher dimensions. Christ is fixed, by nothing but 'fields', to the cruciform shape of an unfolded tesseract, or hypercube. Apparently, though I didn't know it at the time, there are multiple representations of the painter and Gala, his wife, in the skin folds and shadows of each knee. You have to see it in the flesh to spot them. This painting appealed to my developing (Godless) mind in the same way as John Fowles' The Magus and numerous concept albums. Although Dali is sometimes looked down upon as a painter for adolescents, perhaps he was, as Sewell says, '...the last of the great old masters.'

About Phil Berry

Phil Berry is a London-based doctor, medical ethics blogger, aspiring novelist, and regular short story writer.

philberrycreative.wordpress.com

Adaptations to Coastal Erosion

B. Morris Allen

It was after summer that Nora started to sink. Just footsteps a little deeper than usual; she saw them as she came back on her walk, comparing her outgoing, energetic pace to her homecoming, philosophical one. The prints were firm and well defined in the hard wet sand, but *deep*, and she tried to remember whether she had been running. But the toeprints were too clean, and besides, running, at her age? Examined, her memory yielded only sand dollars, seagulls, and seals. For a sand dollar, one stooped, for a seal, one stopped. One might run for seagulls, she supposed, or a dog might.

The footprints were deeper than normal; that was the main thing. Something to tell Elsie, to cheer her up. Nora felt she wasn't constitutionally suited to heaviness, but for Elsie – Elsie, who battled her weight constantly and vocally – she would give it her best shot.

She didn't feel the weight as she walked home. Down at the shoreline, the sand was firm and smooth and wet beneath her feet, just as it should be. There was less sand these days. The rip-rap that protected houses made the sand wash away. But there was still plenty, and it still felt like sand. It felt nice between her toes. She might even walk further tomorrow – up to the north end of the village, perhaps. "I wish you wouldn't go so far," Elsie always said. "Maybe I should go with you." But Elsie's didn't care for long walks. "You stay here," Nora always said. "Have a good healthy lunch waiting when I get back. I'll be hungry!" And Elsie would whip out her cookbooks and sit for an hour happily planning out an elaborate lunch that always required more ingredients than they had on hand. "I'll go into town," she'd say, and then be frazzled about getting it all done in time and still having time to paint in the afternoon.

When Nora got back to her starting point, she stopped to rest and watch a chain of pelicans fly by. There would be more tomorrow; there were always seals, and gulls, and pelicans, and eagles on the Oregon coast. Cells of the world mind, carrying thoughts from place to place. She smiled at what Elsie would say to such wooly thinking. She'd probably claim sarcastically that the pelicans were just agents of the Thunderbird. Perhaps they were. According to Elsie's Tillamook tribe, this was the age of 'true happenings'. Perhaps it was pelicans that brought them.

She turned inland, climbing the giant steps laid in the stone rip-rap. She and Elsie sat at the top sometimes, in the afternoon, Elsie painting, Nora reading or napping. She moved slowly moved slowly now, mindful of her balance. Rock was hard, and bone was brittle – especially old bone.

The mid-morning sun shone soft and warm on her cheek as she reached the top. Down at the end of the street, she could see their open front door. No doubt Elsie would pop out any minute now, worried about the three pans on the little stove, the sheet of something sweet baking in the oven. The house was a tiny shoebox of a thing, with sitting room, kitchen, bathroom, and bedroom laid out in a narrow shotgun format. The kitchen was too small for them to share cooking duties, but it was Elsie's domain anyway, just as the beach was Nora's.

A wide form swayed through the door, and Nora waved. Too far to call out, but Elsie just nodded and rushed back in. She'd be desperate to get everything ready in time, just as a moment ago she'd have despaired of it drying out. It would be perfect, as it always was.

"Honey, I'm home," Nora called when she reached the porch. She sat to brush crusted sand off her feet and exchange sandals for slippers. "I'm hungry. And I'm fat, too."

Fat! That would be the day, thought Elsie. Nora was like a seagull – all hollow bones and fluff. She ate, though. A lot, when you came right down to it. Elsie lived vicariously through Nora's desserts. Cinnamon rolls today; she could smell the sweet, rich dough with dark brown sugar and a hint of cloves mixed in. Delicious. You had to taste each batch to be sure they came out right, and these had; just right.

"Stop mocking me and lay the table," she told Nora. Her lover looked the same as always – a wiry frame of pale, freckled skin with smears of sunblock on the back of her neck. If she'd had an ounce of fat, you'd see it.

"No, really," Nora called, going back to the front room, where the table was already laid. "My footprints were deeper."

"Deeper than what?" Elsie brought out plates loaded with tofu scramble, sautéed asparagus, and mashed potatoes. If she squinted at the dish, it was a nice abstract, but abstracts didn't sell. "Did they say something profound to you?" You could never tell, with Nora. She was quite capable of conversing with footprints. Or maybe it's dementia. It would be someday. They'd done those home DNA tests, and Nora had all the markers.

Nora smiled. "Deeper than yesterday, silly. I'm fat! Fat at last!" She lowered herself into her armchair with exaggerated effort.

Elsie ignored her, told her about the canvas she'd sold that morning, an imagined landscape of mist and sea and the hint of a seal in the waves. They talked for a while about art, and about the neighbours and their wilderness of raspberries.

"I really am heavier," Nora said when there was a pause.

Elsie tried to play along. "Because of the footprints?" In sand? "Maybe the sand was just softer."

"Perhaps." Nora had to acknowledge the possibility. "But I don't think so. I feel more massive."

"Massive?" It's not a word one would associate with Nora. Elsie cocked her head to the side to see around the curve of their little table. "You look the same."

"More massive. Heavier, sort of. Not bigger, necessarily."

Elsie rolled her eyes. "I know what massive means. Not all of us natives are ignorant." She did her best inscrutable Native American look. Quarter inscrutable, anyway. "You think all those books you leave lying around don't soak in?"

"Elsie! You've been reading my science fiction on the sly!"

"Just a little."

"I'm proud." Elsie could see that she really was touched. Was Nora's hand on hers heavier than usual? Maybe it was the power of suggestion; maybe she was pressing harder. It wasn't like her to fake, and her hand looked and felt as bony as ever.

"So what," Elsie asked. "The calcium in your bones is being replaced with … iron?"

"Strontium! No. I don't know. Maybe the calcium is just laid down in a denser structure. Maybe all my fat is being replaced with muscle."

"So now we're back to fat again. You show me yours, and I'll show you mine."

Nora smiled, the same sweet smile that had made Elsie fall in love with her half a century ago, when Nora had been a young-ish professor, and Elsie an even younger Bohemian wanna-be, wandering through Portland State and trying to find herself. 'My found art', Elsie had called her, though she hadn't really started painting back then, not commercially.

Nora gathered up the plates and thudded into the kitchen. Was it really a thud, Elsie wondered, or just suggestion again? It didn't matter, because she was bringing out the cinnamon rolls, and it was rude to make her eat alone.

Crack! That had been the sound of the riser on their low front steps, cracking as Nora came back from the beach. She'd fallen, a fall that once would have risked fragile bone. By the time Elsie came rushing out, Nora was back on her feet, and she'd barely had a bruise. Elsie hadn't said a word, but she had gone into town soon after. She'd been upset again, frustrated at the mysterious weight gain that left her lover as thin as ever.

Nora sat gingerly on their little front porch sofa. It was wicker, and it trembled beneath her skinny buttocks before settling into place. She was heavier; even Elsie had to admit that, just as Nora had admitted that it wasn't fat. And it certainly wasn't strontium replacing the calcium in her bones. How would such a thing happen, and why? She could conceive of mechanisms, but they seemed unlikely. She hadn't troubled to look into it, and the latest *New Scientists* hadn't offered anything.

It was no harder to walk, to move, despite the groaning floorboards. She looked the same as ever. She felt good; better than ever, in fact. Why take it any further?

Elsie had, though, and when their new-ish Subaru pulled up, it sagged suspiciously at the back.

"Hey, Els," Nora called, taking care not to press too hard on the sofa's arm as she got up. "What's new in the big city?"

Elsie glowered at her, but motioned to the back of the car, now open. "Nothing. Any new gravitational anomalies? Help me get this stuff out."

"Same old, same old. You're the same, I'm old." Token laugh from Elsie. "I've just been sitting here communing with nature." Nora took a wide board from the back of the car, clearly destined to be the new riser. "What's the rest of this stuff?"

"Cinder blocks." Elsie took one out, put it by the stairs. "For under the house." She straightened, looked Nora in the eye. "If you keep … communing, or whatever, you're going to crash through the floor." She bent to take another block from the car. "I'll have one of Heriberto's kids put them under the house. The older one – Luis. He's small enough to crawl under, but smart enough to put them somewhere useful." She dropped another block on the asphalt. It cracked at the corner, and the larger woman cursed.

"Come here." Nora motioned Elsie to sit on the steps, and stood behind to massage her shoulders, tight now with frustration.

"I don't know what this is, Nora," Elsie said eventually. "I don't know what to do." She sounded close to tears.

'There's nothing to do, Els." She stroked her fingers over Elsie's neck, over the little flecks of paint that seemed to find their way everywhere, as if Elsie painted in a wild flurry instead of calm brushstrokes. "Let's find Heriberto and ask him to send Luis over. We can tempt him with pie."

Elsie turned sideways, leaned her head against Nora's leg, a gesture that would once have sent the smaller woman stumbling back. "I know, Nora. I just worry. I'm just ..."

Afraid, Nora knew. Afraid of loss and of loneliness. "Where's that pie? These blocks aren't going to place themselves."

They had both done their research. Sometimes together, sometimes apart, but they'd both learned as much as they could about sudden weight gain, which was everything and nothing. Hundreds of diet plans and miracle pills. Nothing about bones made out of lead or barium or radium or anything else. Nora had refused go to a doctor about the weight. She said it wasn't a problem. Luis had put in three loads of blocks now, but the floor still creaked under Nora's feet. The old beach cottages weren't built for heavy use. How could that not be a problem?

Elsie worried about Nora using the toilet. She'd had Luis put two rows of blocks underneath, but what if it broke while she was sitting there? Maybe her bones were stronger; maybe they weren't. And what if Elsie couldn't pick her up? She wasn't sure she could lift Nora anymore.

They took the bed apart and put the mattress on the floor. It was hard for Elsie to get up in the morning, but Nora rolled right to her feet, where before she had been slow and careful. She weighed three times as much as Elsie. That was an estimate, since their scale didn't read that high, but the needle went all the way around, twice. That should have been 300 kilos. No healthy person weighed that much.

"Off to the beach?" Elsie had finally made it to her feet and put a robe on when Nora came back from the shower. Stray droplets ran off her bony frame, and the long grey hair she had tied up into a loose bun. The old grey heron. Elsie had painted her that way, wings barely open, standing cock-legged by an old log in Slab Creek, beak down, but the one visible eye looking off toward the sunset and the sea. "Say hi to the starfish for me."

"I will." Nora dressed, then kissed her on the shoulder, which was as high as she could reach. Her lips were cool and firm, but they warmed Elsie as they always had. "And the seals, and the mussels. Perhaps a whale or two, with luck."

"Leave out the mussels. I'm not that sociable." Elsie hugged her, held her tight, feeling the heavy solidity of her, where once she'd been almost afraid to touch, afraid a clumsy move would break her old bones. There were benefits to this mysterious new mass.

She followed Nora through the kitchen and the sitting room, to the front porch now built entirely of brick, the stairs replaced with stone. Beside the street, there was a line of paving stones, stretching from the house down to the beach. There was nobody around in winter, except Niles down at the corner, and he hadn't asked any questions. She'd seen him give a funny look at the footprints embedded in the asphalt of the street, but Elsie had just shrugged and said "Kids". She'd picked up the paving stones the same day.

Some of them were starting to crack.

It was difficult now for Nora to make her pilgrimages to the beach. Elsie's stepping stones had been a kind gesture, but they hadn't lasted. They were no more now than a jumble of splinters and gravel, pressed deep into the soil beside the street. It would be hard to explain when the neighbours came back in the spring. Even the boulders of the rip-rap showed wear, some of the wide steps cracked down the middle. Down on the sand, she sank quickly to her waist. It was like quicksand. Dry sand was relatively incompressible, but it flowed away under her feet until enough pressed around to support her weight laterally. It should have been hard to move, but it wasn't. It was less confining, even, than she imagined quicksand would have been. More like water. She moved languidly, gracefully, like a slow-motion dancer; synchronized swimming without the splash. It was a wonderful feeling, and she yearned to lie back and simply float in the sand like in the ocean. But she'd never floated in the real ocean; she was so skinny that she sank like a rock, and the real ocean was full of riptides and invisible currents. Beautiful but deadly, unless you were a seal. Better not to take the risk. She couldn't give up her seaside walks, though. Swims. Whatever they were.

She hadn't told Elsie about this new development. Her poor partner was frightened enough already. Better to just keep quiet and let nature (or whatever) take its course. They hadn't charted that course, hadn't bothered to record Nora's slow weight gain, to determine its rate. It was faster now, though, she was certain. Exponential, perhaps, which was interesting.

A plume of spray emerged suddenly from the deeper waters off the beach. "Hello, whale!" she called. It was hard to see much from waist depth, and she kicked her feet to surge up out of the sand and wave. "I weigh as much as you now," she said as she sank back. Her head went under, and she kicked again, suddenly desperate to see the surface, afraid she might not come up again. After a moment, she stabilized with her head well clear. She gasped for air, only to find her mouth already full of sand. It went gritty down her throat, and she coughed frantically, but most of it went down. Into her lungs, in part, she was sure. But it caused no trouble, no discomfort, and after a while, it came back up, in dribs and drabs with her rapid breath. No lasting harm, then, aside from a crust of sand on her lower lip, easily brushed off.

She swam down toward the water, but turned back when she saw a couple down the beach. Intrepid walkers out in the late winter cold, with storm winds in the offing; curious types, perhaps. Leery of discovery, she headed back for home, a casual backstroke taking her up the beach to the rocks and dry land.

"This can't go on," Elsie said as Nora paddled around in their tiny back yard.

"I know." Nora smiled and dipped under, and for a moment Elsie was angry again. Nora was literally sinking away from her, vanishing into the earth, and she thought it was fun. Her head popped back up, smiling like a clam.

"I can breathe." Nora grinned. "Or something. I'm so dense now that the sand in my lungs is like air." That made no sense to Elsie, but she'd stopped arguing. Nora said, "I don't even have to cough it out, anymore." She'd asked Elsie to cut all that beautiful gray hair to a short, sleek helmet – almost a crew cut – and the soil and sand pour off it now like water.

Nora caught hold of the concrete back step, gently, but still the surface powdered away under her fingertips. She hauled herself out, a sandy mermaid, and the step cracked under her weight. "Sorry."

"It's your house too," Elsie said, and they both sat quietly, thinking just how untrue that was.

"The moon is rising," Nora said at last.

"Is it?" Elsie asked dully.

"Look at me." Nora waved a hand. The last time she'd touched Elsie, it had left bruises. "I can feel it. The moon pulls me, makes me lighter."

There was hope yet, then, and Elsie look over at her. "How much lighter? Can you...?" She wasn't sure what she wanted. *Can you be normal?* But the moon rose every day. And then she got it. "You can only come up when the moon does." *You'll still be going.*

"That's right." Nora sounded sad and excited all at once. "But I'll still come and talk, like this."

"And then?" *When the pull of the moon isn't enough, what then? When the world pulls at you again and you can't rise, what then?*

"And then I'll be gone, Els. I don't..." She cleared her throat. "I don't think I'll be able to come back after that."

"Good," said Elsie. "I wouldn't want you to have to come back." It came out thick and angry, with the tears she never cried. Not in front of Nora. Elsie was the strong one, the practical one. The one who dealt with problems. When she cried, she cried in private, and she turned now to go inside, to keep her pain to herself. As she opened the door, she heard a sound, and she turned back to see Nora crying too, a broken expression on her face. The tears ran down her cheek, then dripped off. Where they hit the soil, they left little round drill holes. Where they hit the concrete, fine cracks spread out, until she was surrounded by an etching of fans.

Elsie sat down again, and they cried together, not touching.

As the moon set, Nora ebbed away like the tide, fighting up again every few hours, then flowing away. It was dark below, but surprisingly warm. The sand was soft, smooth, easy to swim through. She'd swum out under the houses to the beach, let herself sink there to the bedrock. She'd walked out to where it met ocean, but then retreated, afraid of what would happen if she stepped off the shelf to the depths below. She could see, even under the sand. Not light, perhaps, but something. Different frequencies, perhaps, above or below the visible range.

Unable to touch, they talked, after they'd accepted the inevitable, Nora with excitement and trepidation, Elsie with good old-fashioned fear and anger. And sadness, of course. Heartbreak, even. They'd been together half a century, had lived for each other, supplemented, complemented each other.

"We knew we didn't have long," she told Elsie. "Not at my age."

"You're not that old." It was a rote response.

"Maybe. But death was closing in."

"And now?"

"Now, I don't know. I don't know what this is any more than you do. But I feel good. Sharp. Strong."

"Not... not better, though?" Elsie's voice was a whisper, hopeful.

"No!" Nora was shocked. "I *love* you, Else. You know that." Elsie gave her a look of such gratitude that Nora longed to reach out and hug her. "If I could stay, I would."

They both nodded and pretended to accept it. Elsie pretended to be happy that Nora now faced adventure and life instead of decline and death. Nora pretended to be sorry that a whole new world awaited her.

"No new theories?" asked Elsie, trying, as always, to face the problem head on.

"Nothing." It didn't matter. "Magic, maybe."

"You know as much about magic as I do about being a medicine man."

"Did the Tillamook Indians have medicine men?"

"How would I know? Grandpa never said. But everyone has medicine men – dancers, singers, priests who make up stories to explain the unexplainable."

"So? What do you say, medicine man?"

"Magic. Special gravity-moon magic only affect paleface woman."

Eventually, Nora became too dense for the sand to hold her up. It parted for her ever more easily, like water becoming fog, until she could no longer swim, but only jump and come crashing down to bedrock. They tried calling out to each other, but the sound didn't reach far through the sand. They tried intercoms, but the wires tangled and broke in roots and boulders and other subsoil obstacles. They hung a chain that Nora could use to climb back up from the depths, but when she pulled the back step off the house, they gave it up.

On Nora's last trip to the surface, Elsie gave her one of a pair of high-powered radios. Soon after, Nora found herself sinking into stone, the sand above as thin to her as air.

"I have to go now," Nora said into the radio, treading rock. She held the handset high in the sand to keep it safe, though that made it hard to hear.

"I know," said Elsie after a long pause. "I miss you. I love you."

"I love you too," she called, giving one last kick to stay afloat in her sea of stone.

"Come back," she heard as she sank at last, and her radio shattered on bedrock.

Elsie wanted to throw the radio against the fence and see it break, but she didn't. She was the practical one. Maybe Nora's radio still worked. Maybe some day when the moon and planets were in conjunction she would float up again and find it and give a call. Elsie would leave hers on for a couple of years, change the batteries on a schedule. Maybe Nora would just revert, and float back to the surface. Miraculously rejuvenated, of course. "When you wish, wish big," Nora had always said.

Elsie didn't know what to do now. All these long months, she had avoided thinking of the end, even when it was clear, inevitable. She had never thought past the moment when they lost contact, when she had to admit that their worlds were separate. Forever, maybe.

She thought about Nora now, down in the rock somewhere, the weight of the world pressing on her shoulders. She was still in the crust, no doubt. But she'd said her density was an exponential function, so soon enough, she'd be through to the mantle. Presuming she could withstand the heat, she'd be floating around in convection currents. "Seeing the world," she'd said, once. Then the core. And after that? Who could tell?

Elsie stepped through the steel-floored rooms now to the kitchen. She found she didn't much want to cook anymore. There was no one to cook for. Instead, she gathered canvas, easel, paint, and went out. In the street, she made her slow way down the trail of small footprints, beside the walkway of crumbled stone.

At the head of the street, she climbed the little rise and walked down it to set up her easel at the top of the rip-rap. At her back, a dark green bush waved little yellow flowers like brushes all dipped in sun. Waves curled and flattened, caressing the sand with soft, foamed fingers as they carried it out.

She painted as the sun sank. A beach, a sunset, footprints leading out. And there, just in the curl of one slow wave, the shadow of a heron.

It came from B. Morris Allen

This story started with literary theft. I was reading Jonathan Carroll's After Silence, which includes a brief story-within-a-story about a woman who gets skinnier and skinnier, and eventually floats away from her husband. Carroll doesn't do much more with it, but the idea intrigued me - the sudden and unexplained negation of physical laws for just one person. I didn't tread too far from Carroll's original idea - my woman sinks instead of floating, which I thought allowed more opportunity for mystery and exploration. But while Carroll's story is a metaphor for marriage, mine is a stand-in for age-induced mental deterioration, with two women torn apart as one embarks on what seems to her a new adventure. The story is set in a little coastal village where I spent many of my childhood summers, and now live full time. The house in question was once occupied by a lovely old woman who bears no other relation to the characters, and certainly didn't sink away into the sand. I usually find titles easy, but this was an exception. I tried or considered almost a dozen before settling on this one.

A question for B. Morris Allen

Q: Do you use music for inspiration? If so what do you listen to?

A: Constantly. That is, I don't consciously look to music for inspiration, but it helps me out all the same. I like to write (and read) with music on, and every now and then something will just jump out and suggest a story to me. Given that I'm not listening with my full attention, it's a misheard lyric as often as not. Sometimes it's a fragment of lyric that I repurpose. Either way, it goes down in the idea file for future use. The only time I consciously set out to work from a song was with my first ever story, "Blind", written in the 1980s (published in 2011). It's a very literal interpretation of the Deep Purple song by the same name. In slightly more recent days, I stole Brian Setzer's title "Drive Like Lightning...Crash Like Thunder" for a pair of pulpy SF adventures, and a line from Fred Eaglesmith's "Seven Shells" for a children's story. Those artists give you a feeling for what I listen to: hard rock, rockabilly, and gloomy singer-songwriters. Throw in some classic country (Merle, Waylon) and some Euro-pop (Herbert Grönemeyer, Fiorella Mannoia), and that covers a lot of it.

About B. Morris Allen

B. Morris Allen grew up in a house full of books that traveled the world. Nowadays, they're e-books, and lighter to carry, but they're still multiplying. He's been a biochemist, an activist, and a lawyer, and now works as a foreign aid consultant. When he's not roaming foreign countries fighting corruption, he's on the Oregon coast, chatting with seals. In the occasional free moment, he edits Metaphorosis magazine, and works on his own speculative stories of love and disaster.

www.BMorrisAllen.com

July

Regarding The Sainted Pirate Nicholas

A True Enough Story

Michael M. Jones

So there we are, in the venerable Rat King Tavern, on La Isla de los Diablos Perdidos (Lost Devils Island to you English-speakers), somewhere deep in the Emerald Sea, and it's me and One-Handed Carlos and the Professor and Barney that acts as the bartender, and we're swapping true tales of the strangest things to ever cross our paths back when we were still sailing instead of warming barstools and seeing to visiting crews. It's a fine game of one-upmanship with bragging rights and drinks for the winner, good-natured ridicule for the losers. One-Handed Carlos has just tossed off a sinker of a story involving the Flying Dutchman (and who *hasn't* seen that fine fellow by now?) and the Professor's in the middle of a story involving the Dead Pirate Edwards.

"Dead Pirate Edwards?" interrupts Carlos. "Don't you mean the Dread Pirate Edwards?" It's a logical question, since a lot of inexperienced captains call themselves the Dread So-and-So, to the point where it's like having the last name Smith, or Johnson. Mind you, most of them are about as terrifying as newborn kittens.

"Oh no," is the reply. "I mean Dead, for dead he is, and dead he was. He commands the fiercest crew of zombies to ever sail the Seven Seas, and how they got that way, stories do differ, though I favor the one involving a scorned voodoo lover. Every night when the moon shines, their ship of the damned emerges from a mysterious fogbank to prey upon the unwary, in search of brains to feed their infernal hungers. And a dozen, no, two dozen times, they've been reported sunk, the *Grinning Skull* seen slipping beneath the waves, and yet a full moon later, there it is again, no worse for wear. And their voices hiss out across the sea on a calm night. 'Sssooo hungry...' they moan, and wise crews turn tail and set sail for warmer climates indeed..."

We don't let him go on in this vein, because the Professor, a self-taught expert in whatever subject catches his fancy from day to day, never knows when to stop, and his story's not much better than Carlos'. Believe me, once you've spent a while in the Rat King Tavern, it takes a certain kind of story to stand out. I, however, have something special. I thump my mug upon the tabletop, and proclaim, "Keep your Dutchmen and your zombies, your Mariners and white whales. For I once saw the Sainted Pirate Nicholas, and in no person no less."

Now that gets a chorus of snorts and rude comments, seeing as how the Sainted Pirate Nicholas is the tallest of tales, the must dubious of rum-soaked myths, the biggest load of parrot droppings. It's a monumentally bold claim indeed to invoke him. I've set the bar high indeed, and now I must deliver. A new round is poured, and I begin...

It was roughly a dozen years ago, back before Burnbeard Harry gave up the open seas to take on governorship of our fair island under the tender auspices of the Silent Lords, back when you could make a damned fine living if you were part of a good crew. I was serving as a general sailor and part-time carpenter aboard the *Golden Cyclops,* a two-masted Sidhe schooner captained by Charles Bloodworthy, who had well-earned his name by that point, infamous for leaving few survivors in his terrible wake. We'd had a splendid summer ranging up and down the Emerald Sea, preying upon the troll jewel merchants out of Avalon, the gnomish spice traders of the Zurich desert, and of course the regular passenger vessels between Faerie and Earth. Oh yes, 'twas a fine summer indeed. We were nearing the end of our season, looking forward to wintering right here on this island, or possibly heading for sunnier shores. There wasn't a man among us that wouldn't be rich when we made landfall, and broke by the time the northern ice cracked several months later. I myself had earned a healthy share after we captured an elven frigate full of silk and gold and delicate sugar candies, a cargo that never made it to fine Xanadu.

We were feeling fat and happy and full of ourselves. Even Captain Bloodworthy was in a good mood, ordering an extra ration of spiced rum to keep the merriment going. That should have been our first indication that things couldn't last, for he had a legendary temper, and flogged a man most every Tuesday whether anyone deserved it or not, and only our continued successes kept us from mutiny. But I digress. I remember the day well, for the sun hung hot and heavy over the horizon, and I was up on the poop deck performing minor repairs upon a railing damaged in the previous engagement. I'll admit we'd pretty much been lulled into a sense of security, for weren't we the fiercest, toughest band of rogues to sail the seas that season? Oh yes, and pride goes before the fall. For at our moment of greatest content, a shape loomed against the sun, a deadly sloop casting a dour silhouette onto our good humor. Jack Keeneye, up in the crow's nest, was the first to give the call, "Ship ahoy!" and we scrambled to ready stations as we awaited more information. Stay and fight, or turn and flee? That was the only question, for back then, there were only predators and prey out there, where no greater authority could see you. If indeed we could take them, be they fellow pirates or a late-season trader, we would. If the odds didn't favor us ... well, we hadn't gotten this far by being stupid now, had we? But even as we considered our options, Jack's next words came high with terror. The panic in his voice chilled us all, for he was a steady type with ice water in his veins, the sort to stare Death in the face and laugh. "Gods save us, it's the *North Pole!*"

The *North Pole*. Such an innocuous name for such a legendarily feared ship. Just like now, everyone knew someone who claimed they knew someone who'd seen it. A bold red ship of unknown origins, it always struck from your blind spot, on your tail before you knew it. Captained by the Sainted Pirate Nicholas, an immense, white-bearded figure who judged everyone by some perverse scale of worthiness and punished the wicked mercilessly. Crewed by demons, or pygmies, or cannibals, or zombie monkeys--on that note the stories differed, but they were always described as an implacable, unstoppable swarm. The ship's name was emblazoned on the sides in bold, bright glittering paint, reflecting the sun so you could see it from miles away. It flew the skull and crossbones, but this skull wore a distinctive white hat, much like an ominous jester's crown with a single tail. You saw that flag, you knew who was coming. And from all those stories, one thing was absolutely certain:

No ship had ever won a battle against the *North Pole*. The *Shrieking Banshee* had vanished, leaving behind one half-mad cabin boy on a lifeboat to tell a gibbering tale of monsters and vengeance. *Queen Bridget's Wrath* escaped, but only after throwing overboard everything that would slow their passage, including half the crew. And as for *Amelia's Ghost*...well, when they found that ship drifting without a single soul on her, the discoverers burned her on the spot, not even daring to salvage so much as a single coin. Not after they read the last entry in the logbook, which was penned in a hurry, and broke off in a splotch of red.

Bloodworthy was not about to let his ship join the doomed ranks of those I've listed above. He immediately cried for us to heave to and flee, but the crew was a step ahead, already leaping into motion, choosing flight over fight. We prodded the *Golden Cyclops* to life with an urgency born of absolute terror. Though we caught the wind through sheer dumb luck, though we tossed overboard the heaviest of our cargoes and supplies—my heart breaks at the treasures we discarded, and though we did our damnedest, it was all in vain. We maintained the chase by an hour or two, but the *North Pole* was swifter; whether by ship's design or dark magic or the will of a perverse god, I couldn't say.

We knew the end was upon us when the first of the cannonballs soared past, so close that it chipped splinters from the railing I'd so recently repaired. The second fell low and short into the ocean, but the third smashed into the deck not far from me, only chance and my own quick reflexes saving me from grievous injury. Solid glass, the cannonballs were, frosted like window panes in winter, and where they hit, ice briefly appeared before melting away. Another flew into the fore mast, where glass and wood shattered, creating a deadly storm of sharp-edged shrapnel; I heard screams from those who hadn't moved swiftly enough. I was thankful we hadn't gotten the full murderous broadside, but they wanted our ship and our loot, not our lives.

By now, we were close enough to the *North Pole* to hear the bellowed cry of its master. "Surrender your ship, you rascals! Yo ho ho!" We were still a good distance away, but it was as if Nicholas himself was standing by my shoulder, shouting in my ear.

"Never!" declared Bloodworthy, and he commanded us to turn and fight, to give those bloody bastards everything we had. But I knew, as he knew, as every one of us knew, that if it came to a battle, we were already lost. We'd sacrificed all of our advantages in our attempt to outrun our foes. But we were pirates, damn it! Merciless, relentless predators of the Emerald Sea. We'd taken dwarven warships, werewolven frigates, even an ogrish dreadnaught, albeit one crippled by a storm. Not to mention the dozens of mundane vessels from Earth and Arcadia which had fallen to our strength and wiles.

You know—there we were, convinced of our imminent deaths, fully believing in the fearsome reputation of our pursuer, and when it all came down to the wire, we still hoped we might prevail in a straight fight. Such was our pride, such was our confidence, and let me tell you, it didn't do a damned bit of good. Because in the twinkling of an eye, or so it seemed, while we were still turning to starboard to give the *North Pole* some whatfor of our own eight- and twelve-pounders, that accursed ship drew right up against us, so close I could have spit and hit their rigging. With bloodcurdling screams, its crew tossed over lines; as fast as we cut them away, they threw more, securing the two ships together. We never even got off a single shot from the cannons before a horde of tiny men, barefoot and agile as can be, all clad in an unsettling selection of red and green motley, swarmed over the sides of the *Golden Cyclops* and began to lay waste to us.

Lest you think we were slow, or lazy, or just plain incompetent, I assure you, there wasn't a man among us unblooded in battle, or ignorant in the ways of naval warfare. No, I tell you without a shadow of a doubt that the *North Pole* was quicker than a thought, more maneuverable, able to slice through the waters with mind-boggling speed. Had we tried fighting from the start, perhaps we'd have stood a chance, but once we set to running, our fate was sealed. I understand that now. To this day, part of me is secretly glad it turned out as it did, for here I am alive to tell the story. But of the others, of Captain Bloodworthy, and the *Golden Cyclops,* and the rest of the crew? Listen closely, and take a drink, for such a tale is not for sober men.

The Sainted Pirate Nicholas' men were among us in a flash, carrying not pistols and cutlasses and knives, but clubs and ropes and nets. They leapt between us, dove under us, entangled our legs and sent us crashing to the ground. They clobbered and dazed us, dropping from the rigging without warning to ride us to the ground. Now, we all had experience at fighting men, and man-shaped creatures, and things larger than men. Most of us could even handle ourselves against the shorter races, but nothing in all our years had prepared us for fighting these... all I can think to call them is elves. But not the graceful, tall, terrifyingly beautiful Sidhe that so often sailed these seas, from whom Bloodworthy had stolen the *Golden Cyclops* in the first place. These were tiny, depraved, misshapen things, as akin to the Fae as monkeys are to us. Distant relatives, perhaps, or sorcery-twisted mockeries, nimble and quick and as good with their feet as with their hands. What realm could have spawned such creatures, I'll never know, but we were wholly unready for their mischievous onslaught. Their outfits were festooned with Hell's own bells, which jingled maddeningly as they tore among us, beating us senseless until everyone from Captain Bloodworthy himself down to the youngest cabin boy was tangled in the nets and helpless. Our cuts and bruises were legion, for the elves hadn't been gentle in the least in subduing us, and we'd done quite a number on our own fellows in the confusion. I was gratified to see more than a few of our opponents sporting wounds as well; we hadn't been completely outclassed. And as we lay there at their mercy, the captain of the *North Pole* stepped aboard.

The Sainted Pirate Nicholas. How can I explain him? No one knows where he came from, or why he does what he does. There are so few survivors, and so many conflicting tales, it's impossible to pick out the truth. Even his name invokes questions, such as where or how he'd earned it, whether it's true or ironic, a title or a description. Some folks claim he was a bishop of some sort back on Earth, or perhaps a nobleman, who'd lost his fortune or family to pirates, and so he set sail on a quest for vengeance. Some say he's a seasonal spirit, who summers in the Emerald Sea before going home during the winter to take care of his other duties. And more than a few folks swear he's actually the Devil stepping out of Hell to take an active hand in affairs. He only preys on pirates, that much we know, stalking them the way we would a fine merchant vessel. And there he was, as real as you or me.

He was a large man, barrel-chested and taller than any of us by a head, with a magnificent, bushy white beard. He was dressed in the finest of clothes, a blood-red outfit with black sash and white trim, and heavy black boots, all topped off with a magnificent red tricorn hat with a white feather. On most men, it might have looked downright silly, but he carried himself with such a presence, imposing and controlling, that to laugh was unthinkable. A gaudy red-beaked parrot flapped along behind him, coming to perch on one shoulder, staring at us with baleful eyes. And the Sainted Pirate Nicholas, in all his glory, looked upon us, and chuckled with dark humor. "Stand them up, boys," he commanded, and his men obeyed, untangling us several at a time. They made sure we were properly bound at ankles and wrists, and gagged, and they leaned us up against the railings and walls to await our fates. Blacktooth Thomas next to me wet himself under that man's gaze, and I couldn't blame him in the least.

Captain Bloodworthy remained defiant to the last, spitting out curses that would have singed your nose hairs, until they finally gagged him as well. I breathed a sigh of relief. We were already at the mercy of a man not known for it. Why anger him further? At least now, a perversely curious part of me thought, we'd find out just what had happened to all the others before us.

"Yo ho ho ho," laughed Nicholas, his booming chuckle an almost physical assault upon our senses. "My dear lads of the *Golden Cyclops,* I know who's been naughty and who's been nice. I have a list, you see, and I've checked it more than twice. And I'm afraid that of all the fine crews I've visited this season, you lot may actually be the naughtiest." His heavy black boots thudded against the deck as he walked along the line his men had made of us, looking into each of our faces with knowing blue eyes, as deep and implacable as the sea itself. "Oh yes. Murder, pillage, thievery, rape. I don't think you lot have overlooked a single crime in your collective exploits. For shame, lads. For *shame.*"

"String 'em from the yardarm!" squawked the red-beaked parrot that rode his shoulder. "Rawwwk! Naughty!"

"Hush yourself, Rudolph," he told the parrot fondly. "Now then. Whatever shall we make of you scoundrels?" He paused in front of Billy the Tall, considering him soberly. "I know what you did with that barmaid," he said with disapproval. "And her with a child to feed. And I know how you cheat at cards, and how you haven't told a solid truth since you were six." He shook his head, and I felt for Billy then, even though I'd always suspected he was a cheat and a liar, for all that he tried to act like everyone's friend. "Naughty!" And thus Nicholas moved on down the line, reciting a litany of sins ripped from the bleakest portions of our souls. Jack Keeneye fainted when Nicholas exposed the fact that he liked to bugger young boys in the dead of night.

What were my sins? A petty lot compared to most. I became a pirate for the treasure and the adventure, and I was willing to live dangerously to get what I wanted. I'd never killed anyone who wasn't trying to kill me first, and I'd always tried to treat women with courtesy and respect. But I'm getting ahead of myself. Because while I might have been a veritable babe in the woods compared to some of my erstwhile comrades, we were all lily-white innocents compared to our leader. Nicholas spent a long, long time staring into the mad eyes of Captain Bloodworthy, and when at last he spoke, it was in a low tone that hinted at perverse impression.

"*You,* sir, are an overachiever in this misbegotten band of miscreant mariners," he declared. "My God, is there anything you haven't done or tried to do? Why, that one night in Xanadu alone... You are a reprehensible, shameless, God-forsaken, disgusting scoundrel of the highest order!" His voice rose with each word, delivering the last word in an ear-ringing bellow that rattled the decks and our heads. "You, sir, are NAUGHTY!" And it was like a judgment from on high, smacking us all in its wake. "Coal for you!" he informed Bloodworthy severely.

I will never forget how the Sainted Pirate Nicholas ripped off Bloodworthy's gag, nor how he produced handfuls of black rocks from a pocket, forcing our captain to gorge himself on lumps of coal. The black dust flew everywhere as Bloodworthy choked on his final meal. It was on his hands, his face, his clothes. Tears of pain and outrage left gruesome streaks on his cheeks in their wake. And once Nicholas felt Bloodworthy had eaten his fill, on went the gag again, forcing the man's cheeks to bulge, coal still trapped in his mouth. It was almost a mercy after that when they threw him overboard, still bound at the wrists and ankles. Our captain never had a chance, not against the wrath of the Sainted Pirate Nicholas; as we watched him sink forever into the abyss of the Emerald Sea, we feared for our own fates.

"There's for your captain, the worst of a bad lot," declared Nicholas. "As for the rest of you sorry villains, let me tell you what happens next. If you're naughty, you can choose a quick death, and be at the mercy of whatever power you believe in, or you can let me choose the nature of your punishment. I promise you, whatever I choose shan't be easy or fun, and it could last weeks, months, even years, but it'll still beat Bloodworthy's sorry end."

I shuddered to think of the way in which he'd dispatched the captain, and thought for a moment that maybe a quick death might not be so bad after all. At least there you knew where you stood. A few of the others likely had the same thought. Jack Keeneye, for one, wouldn't be too popular if he survived and word got out about his proclivities. (What goes on between grown men on a ship is between them and the rats, and that's the last I'll say on that, but boys? Even pirates need some standards.) And so Nicholas gave us that moment of painful consideration, before starting at one end of the line with the quartermaster, Karl "Leech" Litch, who stood in command with the demise of the captain. Karl choose punishment, and Nicholas nodded, whispering to him before moving on. Apparently, we weren't to know of each other's sentences until we'd selected our own.

Now, the vast majority did choose punishment, but there were a few who decided they'd take their chances with their makers. True to his word, Nicholas made it quick, his men cutting their throats and shoving them over the side rapidly with frightening efficiency and an utter lack of malice to their swift movements. Jack Keeneye went that way, as did Billy the Tall, Hookhand Peter, and Rizzo the ship's cook. I wondered what made them fear the thought of punishment so, but I for one preferred to live, so when my turn came around, I boldly informed Nicholas I'd take whatever he had lined up for me.

He clapped me on the shoulder, and met my eyes for a moment, as if once again reading my soul. "As piratical scum go, you're vaguely tolerable. I may have a use for you." His tone was almost warm, though I could hear the iron beneath it. I'd accept what he had to offer, and like it, or else. He moved on, gathering the rest of the decisions. Wonder of wonders, one person amongst the entire crew was actually deemed "nice" by the fearsome Nicholas, and that was little Gideon, a ship's boy we'd permanently borrowed from an English frigate some months back.

"You're too good a lad to be in this profession," said Nicholas with a mixture of sorrow and concern. "You've kept a clean soul, and for that I reward you." He handed Gideon, who was all kinds of baffled and relieved, a small sack of coins, and a sealed envelope. "I'll give you safe passage to London, and that letter of introduction there will get you into one of their finest schools. You'll have a chance to grow up and lead a virtuous life." He chuckled. "Of course, if you squander my gift, and turn out naughty after all, I'll know and come back for you…"

Gideon turned pale and nodded vigorously, affirming that he'd do his very best. I was glad, as he was a good kid who would have died horribly through his own soft-heartedness had he stayed with us. Some folks just don't have the stomach for this profession. But then it was time to find out what Nicholas planned to do with the rest of us. We all held our breath as he turned to look at the crew of the *Golden Cyclops*. "Men, you serve a new master now, and you'll do so until you've atoned for your multitude of sins!" he announced. Without further ado, he threw out his hands, showering us with a cloud of sparkling dust. All around me, those men who hadn't chosen death twisted in agony, their bodies compacting and reshaping, bones snapping and skin growing taut. It was grotesque, impossible, hideous; it took me a long minute of watching the others transform before I realized I alone wasn't changing.

Before I could catch my astonished breath, it was over, and my former shipmates had joined the ranks of Nicholas' men, a whole new host of tiny elf-creatures wriggling free of their now too-large bonds. As I wondered what would become of me now that I'd seen this dark truth, Nicholas stepped over.

"You've led a decent enough life. For you," he said, "I have something different. You won't join my crew like the rest. Instead..." He laughed, the merry sound shivering me to the soul, and continued. "I ban you from ever setting sail again. You're landlocked now, my boy, and you'll spend the rest of your life warning people about me. Tell them exactly what happens to the wicked, like your former captain. Tell them of the horrible fate that befalls the naughty... and do tell them of what happens to the pure of heart. I choose you to spread the message to your fellows, that they might know what it means to meet the Sainted Pirate Nicholas."

I nodded, too awestruck and fear-ridden to do anything more, and he took a step back. "If you break this deal, I'll know," he said, voice full of dark promise. "And I'll find you wherever you go. Next time, I won't be so merciful." He threw his head back, and once more bellowed out a resounding, "Yo, ho ho ho!" He snapped his fingers, and in the twinkling of an eye, I found myself sprawled on the shores of this very island, where I've been ever since. And you know the rest, how I make my living as a carpenter by day, and make the rounds of the taverns at night, and maybe I don't tell this story nearly as often as I should, for it's a rotten fish to try and swallow, but I swear on my mother's grave, it's all true.

But I tell you, my friends... sometimes, when I listen to the sea crashing, and I smell the salt air, I dream of the joy of the open seas, and I yearn for a life aboard ship once more. Maybe not as a pirate, but as a merchant, or maybe even just to travel. And if the Sainted Pirate Nicholas should come for me as he promised ... well, how bad can it be to sail with him for a spell?

But enough of that. I think I've earned another drink, and that'll be my last for the night. Say Barney, isn't it your turn to tell a story?

A question for Michael M. Jones

Q: Duckbilled platypus – result of divine distraction, or alternate universe crossover?
A: Divine distraction—how else can you explain how freaking confused those things are?

About Michael M. Jones

Michael M. Jones lives in southwest Virginia with too many books, just enough cats, and a wife who's always ready to provide an alibi and/or a shovel. He has a degree in Theatre he never uses, is working towards a Master's in Children's Literature which is just an excuse to read more books, and blames his Santa fixation on working retail at the mall during the Christmas season. He's the editor of *Scheherazade's Facade*.

For more information, visit him at www.michaelmjones.com

My Dog is the Constellation Canis Major

Jarod K. Anderson

I didn't actually want a dog, so I guess I got what I wanted. The little guy belonged to my grandma. I don't know many old ladies, but I still feel confident saying that she was a very cool old lady. She was 85 when she died, but she wasn't that "so old it hurts to look at you" kind of 85 that makes death a blessing. She was more of a "gardening every day, cornerstone of the local astronomy club, post inappropriate jokes on your Facebook" kind of 85. She was also the only family I had left in Ohio, so it was either me or the shelter for her little dog when she died.

I hate to think how things would have been if that dog had gone to a shelter. I wonder what the workers and volunteers would have done when the little guy started to expand like unspooling Christmas lights, impossibly bright, tangled in the shape of dog. It hurts my heart to picture that loving collection of cosmic bodies crouching in a kennel.

I'd tell you the dog's name, but he really didn't have one. Grandma just called him "Dog" or "Big Dog," which I always assumed was a joke because he seemed to be some kind of dachshund Chihuahua mix. He looked a little like an elongated black German shepherd that somebody shrank in the dryer. I asked Grandma where she got him once. She poked a finger skyward and said, "Up there. Made him just for me." At the time, I thought that was an unusually religious answer for her. I should have known better.

Sometimes it doesn't matter how young you are at heart. When your bones are 85, your bones are 85. Grandma fractured her pelvis and both ankles when she fell off her front porch. She had her big telescope set up on a tripod. She had gotten it just where she wanted it and didn't want to move it again to clean some dust off the lenses, so she hung off the front railing to get at it. The wonderful idiot.

The broken bones led to the hospital. The hospital led to pneumonia. The pneumonia did the rest. It was all over in less than two weeks.

It sounds terrible, but I was glad it didn't take longer. When she got sick, she could barely breath. It looked and sounded like it hurt. It also changed the way we talked to one another. She knew she wasn't going to make it back home, so our conversations started to be about important awkward things, the stuff you want to make sure you say to someone before you're gone for good. We talked about loving each other. We talked about the good times we had when my mom was still alive. She tried to tell me about what she'd learned from life, about making meaning for just for yourself, but it wasn't easy for me to hear her and she got tired quickly if she tried to talk too much. Toward the end, she really couldn't speak at all, but from the look in her eye I had the feeling there was a lot more she wished she could tell me.

I thought about grandma's last moments a lot after the dog changed. I thought, "this is what that anxiety behind her eyes meant." I think she would have been proud of me. I didn't scream or lose my mind. The change happened when I was ready for it. Because I was ready for it.

I missed our old conversations, the ones punctuated by stupid jokes and grandmas pseudo-spiritual science lectures. She loved astronomy, loved it like some old people love Jesus and she spoke about it in that same tone. It was reverence. She would talk about things light-years away. About the careful balance of forces that kept us from spinning off into the great, frozen nothingness that hemmed us in on all sides. As she spoke, her voice would get low and solemn like somebody reading a bit of scripture in a Sunday service. There was real passion in it. Then, once I felt small and weightless, like a strand of her silver hair rising up and away, like a bit of cobweb caught in the breeze, then she would pause for a moment. She would look me square in the eye and say, "And you're part of that. Part of the same tremendous machinery that does all that. Not one bit less amazing. You and me, sitting here trying to puzzle it all out in our own heads. It's important work. It means something."

She'd drop all that in my lap one minute, then walk around the corner into the kitchen and make fake farting sounds the next. I'd hear her giggling and I'd play along saying, "Grandma! What did you eat?" I lived with that amazing woman on and off from age 15 to 26. So, the question of whether or not I would keep her dog after she passed was really no question at all. That dog was like grandma's family. So he was my family too.

Plus, since I ended up inheriting grandma's house, it was more like I was moving in with the dog, than he was moving in with me. He liked me well enough. I sorta always viewed him as my replacement. He arrived just after I moved out, about four years before grandma passed. I didn't know much about dogs, but it wasn't hard to tell that he was glad I was there. Honestly, I was just as happy not to be alone.

I hired an auction company to come in and sell off a lot of grandma's things, but I kept the important stuff: old pictures, her journals and notes, many of her books, and of course her big telescope. I even toyed with the notion of joining the astronomy club. At first, I just set up her telescope on the front porch and tinkered with it. I had no clue what I was looking at, but it was still pretty cool to have a little peephole into space. From there, I decided that a proper tribute to my grandma's memory would involve putting some effort into stargazing, so I began cracking her books and journals. I'm glad I did. Otherwise, I probably wouldn't have had any idea what to think when Big Dog started to grow into his name.

Most of grandma's journal entries were about astronomy. She would write about what she could see on a given date and how it compared to her expectations from consulting her astronomy books. On the first night she got a good, clear view of Saturn you'd think she'd won the lottery. The page was tearstained. There were also lots of notes and sketches about the constellations, but not all the entries were pure astronomy. Some of them read more like philosophy.

The word "subjectivity" kept showing up in entries. See, grandma believed that there was no "inherent meaning" in the universe. Nothing meant anything by itself. Some people might think that's kind of a grim, sad idea, but not grandma. She saw it more as a job opening. People could make meaning and meaning needed made.

She often used the constellations as an example. There was nothing about the relationship of certain stars that made them into a ram or a crab or a dipper. We made them into those things. People. Staring up into the night sky and giving things names, giving them meaning and relationships to one another. She didn't think of this as just interesting or fun. She thought of it as a power and a responsibility. Human beings were the things in creation that could give names and meaning to the incredible mechanisms of existence.

When I read those sorts of journal entries, it was like I was fifteen again, feeling small and impossibly big all at the same time. Orion didn't look like a hunter because of the suggestion of ancient astronomers. Orion *was* a hunter because of the *decision* of ancient astronomers and that power was just as real and important as the force of gravity. Those sorts of ideas, written in my grandma's thin, looping script, made me absolutely dizzy.

Sometimes, after staying up late reading grandma's journals, I could have really used a good fart joke. I had to settle for dog snuggles instead. Dog snuggles, warm and fuzzy, it turns out, are a good cure for most problems, physical or philosophical.

Grandma's philosophies were haunting me on the day I understood her dog. I had never owned a dog before, but I still knew that he wasn't always very doggish. Sure, he loved walks. He loved treats. He loved to snuggle on the couch. But he also loved sitting in front of the window at night and staring off into the sky. He would even look up at the ceiling or down at the floor, sometimes for more than an hour, slowly turning his head as if he was tracking the movement of things I couldn't see. It was a little creepy at the time.

All of the dog's oddities and grandma's ideas were swirling around my head on the evening I picked up an old book on constellations and finally came to the section on Canis Major. The Great Hound. The Big Dog. I looked down at the furry little guy next to me and I understood –and when I understood, I swear to you the dog actually cocked his head. It was like an acknowledgement. Like he had been waiting for me to understand.

That's when everything started to change. Grandma really truly believed that the meaning we make ourselves is the realest meaning there is. That's how she understood life and, somehow, it's how she could understand the constellation Canis Major as her own little furry companion.

I believe that my grandma was right about the world. It's hard not to believe after what I've seen. Even so, I'm not her. When I understood what Big Dog really was, he couldn't be a dog anymore. I couldn't make him be a dog anymore.

He started to grow. That first night, when I first understood, he must have grown almost a foot. More than that, he started to glow. Not a lot. Not at first. I could barely see it until I turned out the lights for bed and even then it was just a faint outline, a shimmer.

I called off work. I closed all the blinds. I decided I wouldn't leave the dog's side.

That was the start of it, but he changed faster as the days passed. A few days later, he was the size of a Great Dane and it wasn't just a general glow anymore. There were actual points of light and, thanks to grandma's books, I had names for those points of light: Wezen, Adhara, Murzim. And of course there was Sirius, the dog star, right in the center of his chest like a gleaming celestial heart.

The bigger and brighter he became, the more ridiculous I felt about continuing our usual dog care activities, but when he scratched at the back door, I wasn't about to tell him he couldn't go out to pee. I was a little nervous about it. Grandma had a big wooden fence around her back yard, but you could still see into it from the neighbors' second floor windows. Sure, the neighbors were elderly, but Big Dog was looking more and more like a walking, pony-sized, light show. He was hard to miss.

Even stranger than the light, as he grew I could start to see the space between the stars in my dog. I thought I could even see the circling swirl of nearly imperceptible dust, the whir of planets and other interstellar bodies moving in concert with the stars that made up my puppy. If I looked too long or too closely, I started to feel both massive and distant, like I was no longer standing on firm ground. If I looked too long, I felt downright nauseated.

A week after I understood, Big Dog was the size of a bear and he had no fur left to stroke. Touching him felt like dipping my hand in freezing water that carried a mild electrical current. He was a field of lights, a cloud of gleaming motes with the defining stars of his constellation burning so brightly it was difficult to sleep near him at night. But somehow, he was still a dog. He still paced back and forth on the living room rug. He wagged a tail of cosmic light and unknowable distance when I looked at him or said his name. He was still my dog.

On that last day, I woke up from an evening nap to a dog-shaped cosmos bigger than a grizzly sitting at the foot of my bed and staring out the window. The blinds were pulled, but that didn't seem to matter. I sat up and sighed. His big head swung towards me, a canine shaped wedge of space. I could hear his big tail thumping on the hardwood floor and I thought Sirius, the heart of my dog, shone out a little brighter when he turned toward me.

I got up, rubbed the sleep from my eyes, and headed toward the front door. I hadn't opened that door since I had first read about Canis Major. My dog followed me, casting blue gold light that filled the house and threw strange shadows from the lamps and furniture onto the walls. The dog was the only light in the house and his presence made all the usual, domestic objects seem like a landscape fit for giants on a universal scale. I felt like a titan of nature, a thing that breathed and walked through the universe like a child strolling through a toy train set.

When I reached the door I turned to face my dog. There was a lot I wanted to say. Important things. That was the meaning I wanted to make. I thought for a while, listening to that "thump, thump, thump" of tail hitting floor. In the end, I only got out one word.

"Thanks," I said.

I decided it was enough. I opened the front door and stepped aside.

Big Dog walked up next to me. He was so big he had to stoop to fit under the ceiling. He stopped and lowered his head so that he was eye level with me. In his face I saw a view of the cosmos with eyes magnitudes upon magnitudes larger than my own. I was bigger than solar systems. I could see the movement of stars and planets in relation to one another. I felt more than saw the intricacies of gravity and matter and energy all moving and shifting in a pattern so complex that it, for a moment, seemed simple. It was beautiful.

A lump rose in my throat and I wasn't big anymore. I felt small and unanchored again, just like when my grandma spoke about space in her church voice. I was without time or place. I was without significance.

Then, that big, beautiful dog took a step forward and licked my entire face in one slobbery motion. It felt like getting slapped with both the cold of deep space and the heat of undiluted starlight. It also felt wet and more than a little ridiculous. I laughed so hard tears ran down my cheeks. I laughed and smiled up at that brilliant interstellar puppy grin and I was home again.

Canis Major ducked down and somehow wriggled through the front door and out into the night. I raised my arm to my mouth and blew out a raspberry fart noise on the back of my forearm as he stepped down off the porch. It was the best way I could think of to honor my grandma and the dog that brightened her twilight years. Two steps out into the yard, he was bigger than a house. One step more and he blended into the night sky, fading from view, but the shake of his shoulders as he went told me he was laughing. At least, I decided he was laughing.

I did end up joining the astronomy club after all. I like to think grandma would be proud of me. I'm trying to be as curious and, well, weird as she was, but it's a pretty tall order. These days, I'm particularly fond of studying the constellation Draco. In practical terms, it might be tough to actually have a pet Dragon, but on the other hand I've become less and less concerned with what's practical.

There are nights, though, when I just need some simple companionship. On those nights, I look for Sirius right at the heart of my fury friend. Then, if I can get his attention, a see a tail wag that sweeps across the sky of the southern hemisphere. I still have a lot to learn about the constellations, but I do know one thing. Canis Major is a very good dog.

A question for Jarod K. Anderson

Q: Do you often include animals in your stories? What role do they play?

A: I hadn't really noticed before, but yes I often do include animals in my stories. I suppose animals have always been a big part of my life, so it makes sense that they have found their way into my fiction. As for the role they play in my writing, I think having characters interact with animals (positively or negatively) is fertile ground for character building. Harming or helping an animal in a narrative carries serious emotional weight. Beyond that, I'm interested in themes relating to human beings' interaction with and/or separation from the natural world. I think I'm often aiming for the animals in my writing to be emblematic of a broader sense of nature.

About Jarod K. Anderson

Formerly, Jarod taught English at a University in Ohio. Currently, he works to raise money for a wide range of college scholarships. He writes about education by day and ghosts, monsters, and magic by night. He lives in Central Ohio with his wife and two rescued pups.
www.jarodkanderson.com

Serenity

Jeanette Gonzalez

Nikki shook the can and sprayed again, trailing a long, jagged streak of crimson paint to the far end of the wall until the contents came to a sputtering halt. He stepped back to the crowded sidewalk to admire his handiwork.

He had defaced twelve buildings around Reflection Square. Eight houses, a grocery store, and three shops, all built of smooth, white stone and lined in neat rows with equally tidy flowerbeds. Mature trees dotted the square, throwing dappled shade on manicured lawns and meditation pools.

Though the crowds had thinned, no one had time to admire the square's beauty or to take heed of Nikki's vandalism. Even if they'd had the time to notice, no one would have tried to stop him. Everyone knew the consequences for not following the rules.

The bleeding paint had dried on all but this last building; the bots would have a field day cleaning the mess. Nikki tossed the empty can into a clump of pungent daisies.

He checked his watch. Nearly out of time.

He snatched his bag and raced for Trinity Gate, combat boots pounding the pavement. *Twenty seconds. Forty.* He tossed a torn shirt to the ground as he ran. *Sixty. Eighty.* A half-eaten apple rolled into a sterile gutter. *One hundred. One hundred twenty.* He launched a can of paint at a fountain. Blood-like splatter sprayed the marble tiers and surrounding grass.

The more the bots had to clean, the better.

Nikki skidded to a halt in the shadow of Contemplation District's wall. White-washed and thirty feet high, the wall cordoned off Nikki's neighborhood from the rest of the city. Serenity's ivory skyscrapers loomed beyond the stone barrier. Nikki approached Trinity Gate and dumped his bag into a shallow gazing pool.

Ever since Trinity Gate had been locked for good years ago, others had tried to complete this task and failed. Of course, there was no evidence to say anyone was dissatisfied with their life in

Contemplation District. Nikki and his friends intended to escape and show the world the truth.

Twenty minutes to vandalize the neighborhood as a diversion if they failed to melt through the bars and had to run back home. Forty minutes to melt the bars. No need to worry about the bots pursuing if they escaped.

"Nikki!" Nadia called, long raven hair trailing behind her and alabaster skin to match the city's white gleam. Anthony ran beside her. Paint streaked their hands and clothes.

"We did as many buildings as we could," Anthony panted. The youngest of the three, Anthony had celebrated his fifteenth birthday only last week. Nikki would be eighteen in a few days.

"Here." Nadia handed Nikki a blowtorch. She gave another to Anthony and directed the third at the bars. "On three."

Nikki looked up. Needlessly high, Trinity Gate boasted metal flowers and falling water in a near perfect depiction of the city's landmark—Trinity Falls. Though Nikki had seen vids of the falls, he had never tasted their spray. No one on this side ever set foot outside the walls. Not anymore. Kids these days had only ever known Contemplation District.

"Three!" Nadia said.

They lit their torches as a train roared overhead. Nikki stared as the delicate metal arcs failed to warp and blacken beneath the heat.

"Why the hell isn't it working?" Nadia exclaimed.

Rumor said the gate was indestructible. Nikki refused to believe that. "Keep going. We can do this." He waved for them to direct their flames on the same section. "Just needs to be hotter."

Three blue flames focused on a delicate metal arc depicting a wave of water and ever so slowly the metal began to warp. "See!" Nikki said. "We can do this!"

They kept working, losing track of time as they painstakingly melted a long, vertical line in the gate.

Nikki's watch beeped. They couldn't be out of time yet. He pressed the flame closer to the bar. They *had* to finish, if only to prove it could be done.

"Time to go!" Nadia said. She and Anthony turned off their torches and ran up the road.

"Nikki! Come on!" Nadia shouted. "We'll finish another time!"

Nikki hated to give up. What if someone repaired the gate before they could return?

He had just started kicking at the damaged portion of the gate, bending the glowing red bars a little, when he spotted them—a perfect cloud of polished steel descending on the city.

Maintenance break was over.

Lily tugged on her mother's skirt again.

"Not now!" Her mother kicked a little with her leg. "Go play." Dishes clinked in the sink as steam clouded the tiny window overlooking a small slice of Contemplation District. Outside, a row of neat bushes lined a tidy walkway between rows of identical white-washed buildings.

Lily released the soft fabric and turned away with a pout.

She squeezed past the brand new couch and stopped outside her brother's bedroom door. When would he be home? She hated playing alone.

Tucking a loose strand of tawny hair behind an ear, Lily opened the sliding glass door and stepped out into the humid heat. Her bare feet landed in warm, soft soil.

She followed the sloping path between two stunted maples, branches pressing feebly against the glass ceiling, and stopped to crouch beside the pond. She dipped a finger in, distorting the reflected trees and flowers.

Through the glass dome, she noted other glassed-in gardens and a sliver of the district's Reflection Square beyond their apartment complex. Green grass cradled a meditation pool in the square and spilled down a bank. Just once, she wanted to run her fingers through that still water.

Just once, she wanted to step outside her glass box.

"Dammit!" Paul shook the scalding liquid from his hand and set the mug on the table. Another jolt from the rocking train sloshed more coffee, but he didn't get to his files in time. He snatched a napkin and blotted the papers. He tossed the drenched napkin to the seat, eliciting frowns from the people across the aisle.

Ladies, gray skirts and blouses neatly pressed, deplored him with their glances. Men, every bit as severe in their slate-colored suits, grazed Paul with their glares. A moment passed, then another, before the low murmur of conversation refilled the passenger car, Paul's presence, at least for the time being, forgotten.

Paul didn't think he could take any more perfection. Given Serenity's reputation, and the attitudes expressed by the train's occupants, the city had very little tolerance for outsiders, especially a middle-aged journalist lacking fashion sense and an obsessive attention to cleanliness. Paul had never worried about his appearance before. He jogged a few times a week and kept his blond hair trimmed and his stubble to a minimum.

He glanced back down at his paperwork. Three missing persons, all teenagers. He suspected the whole story would fall apart as soon as he started investigating—anonymous tips being unreliable leads—yet he refused to pass up the opportunity for the biggest story of a lifetime. People vanished in other cities, not Serenity, the *only* city in the world to have conquered crime. Serenity's proclamation had come within days of announcing a revolutionary breakthrough in city maintenance—pet-sized robots dubbed "cleaning bots." The rest of the world was eager to accept Serenity's solutions, which had so far withstood the test of time. The city couldn't afford a single mar on its gleaming surface. Serenity's mayor hadn't wanted to grant Paul a travel visa, but he couldn't afford *not* to. Not if there was nothing to hide.

Shadows from passing trees flickered into the train's passenger car as Paul stuffed the last of his paperwork into his briefcase. His hand froze when the window revealed his first glimpse of Serenity.

Buildings, tall and creamy, dominated the landscape. Pictures, even the moving ones on vid screens, failed to convey the city's untarnished beauty. A gleaming wall three stories high surrounded many of the areas below the tracks.

Paul locked his briefcase with a click and scooted closer to the window as the tracks veered to the right, replacing his view of the walled districts below with an even more impressive panorama—Serenity's legendary Trinity Falls. A chunk of mountain carved out eons ago and since overgrown with vegetation and glinting architecture. Water gushed in three lucent arches from a cluster of white spires at the mountain's crown and made a tremendous plunge to the lake below.

The train continued around the lake and ducked behind the falls before slowing to a standstill with a gentle rock.

Paul snatched his briefcase and followed the orderly crowd from the train, steam hissing into a glass-walled station. After navigating a maze of escalators, he eventually stepped off into a long transparent corridor that passed behind the falls, and balked at the sight beneath his feet. The architects had done nothing to obscure the vertiginous drop or the accompanying notion of a nasty death should the glass give way. Nor did the walls wholly eliminate the falls' rumbling roar.

Impressive, but not really surprising, given Serenity's mayor had his offices up here. Though why the mayor had requested a meeting with Paul after approving Paul's visa was a trifle baffling. Tight security must go hand in hand with Serenity's lack of crime.

Paul picked up the pace and came to a set of impressive marble doors with gold inlaid patterns at the end of the hall. Two bulky men in gray suits stood to either side. They opened the doors as he approached and nodded to him as he passed through.

Paul had seen the mayor on vid screens and countless magazine covers, yet the man appeared far more imposing than any of his pictures conveyed. Snowy hair. Face freshly shaved and a tad soft with age. An expensive suit of grays and creams creased with hard lines by a hot iron and an uncanny eye for detail. Like every other person Paul had encountered in Serenity, the mayor had an affinity for perfection to match the great city.

"Mr. Lambert." The mayor flashed bright white teeth. "Welcome to Serenity."

"Thank you, Mr. Douglas. Please, call me Paul." He took the other's hand in a firm shake. "An honor to meet you and finally witness your many accomplishments with my own eyes. I tell you, I'm not disappointed."

The mayor chuckled. "I can't take all the credit. I have an exceptional staff." Modesty, of course. Paul knew the mayor had a direct hand in Serenity's success. Everyone knew the problems Serenity had faced before—the crime, the violence, the riots. "Still," the mayor continued, "I must express my concern with the reason for your presence in our wonderful city."

Paul raised his hands, an unconscious response to the mayor's implied accusation. "I assure you I harbor no ill will. I'm merely responding to an anonymous tip, as I explained to your staff earlier this week. I requested a visa and transportation to Contemplation District to follow this through. I hope you understand."

The mayor's smile failed to reach his gray eyes. "Of course. Journalists with an ever-ready thirst for the next story." He leaned against his polished desk of golden wood. "I don't fault your nature, but you must see it from where I stand. There are no missing persons, I assure you, and yet to deny you entry to Serenity would only lead you to believe we are hiding something. So, please, visit Contemplation District. You will find people in Serenity every bit as happy as they appear."

Paul nodded. Perhaps this whole assignment was a mistake. Even if there were a story, what good would come of sharing it with the world? Cities around the world would be following Serenity's example to solving poverty and eliminating crime. Would Paul risk dashing world peace, just for a chance to become famous? He shifted his briefcase to his other hand. "Am I correct in believing Contemplation District used to be the poor district?"

The mayor's eyes widened. "We don't use words like 'poor' in Serenity, Mr. Lambert. All our citizens are provided for. The needy among us receive new clothes and food. A home with a roof. And when a person's basic needs are met, Mr. Lambert, there is no need for crime." He smiled. "Serenity has solved poverty and all the problems that come with it. Cleaner bots keep our city immaculate, and you will find our least fortunate areas, like Contemplation District, the most pristine of all. We take pride in our city, Mr. Lambert, unlike so many places where graffiti and trash are as rampant as the crime rates. We are a city at peace and can only hope others will soon find their peace as well."

"Contemplation District ahead, Mr. Lambert," the mayor's assistant, Porter, announced, pointing through the windshield to the massive metal gate ahead.

Paul looked out the window beside him as the car slowed to a stop. Shiny bots, ranging from bug-sized balls of steel to blocky canisters three feet wide, hovered in nearby trees, trimming branches and clearing away debris. Birds flitted around the branches, oblivious to the spindly arms whirling blades at lightning speed. Cleaner bots skimmed the streets and buildings, glinting in every nook and cranny. They worked, day and night, with only one hour off per day for recharging and any needed maintenance in the repair factory run by more bots.

Paul reached for the handle and found the door locked.

"A moment, if you please." Porter turned round to face Paul. "People in Contemplation District prefer to conduct business during the bots' maintenance break. Respect their schedule and do the same."

Paul's hand slipped off the knob. The rest of Serenity had no qualms being outdoors with the bots, evident by the lady in a neatly pressed gray suit walking along the sidewalk just outside their car. What made Contemplation District different?

Feeling a little disconcerted, he glanced back down at the black-and-white photo of the three teens he had received electronically and printed out before leaving his office. A lack of color made the teens appear older, despite their carefree posture on the fountain's wide base and the semblance of a shared joke on bright faces.

An audible click filled the car. "You may proceed, Mr. Lambert."

Paul thanked the man, closed his file, and exited the car. The trees were empty now, except for the birds and a soft breeze ruffling the leaves. He tucked his file under his arm and decided to leave his briefcase on the backseat. Porter remained in the car.

Paul stood on the curb of a spotless sidewalk before the most beautiful gateway he had ever seen. Having witnessed Serenity's trio of falls with his own eyes from the best vantage points imaginable—the train on his way to Serenity's city center and then again in the mayor's office at the top of Serenity's tallest building—he admired the craftsmanship and attention to detailed accuracy. The metal arcs of water appeared to be falling; a skillful illusion.

He blinked up into the blinding sun, trying to view the gate in its entirety, and almost stepped on a bot working on the sidewalk. No larger than a small cat, its blades were a flurry of motion throwing up weeds and pungent dirt. It finished a moment later, scooped up the displaced soil and broken blades of grass, and vanished over the buildings.

Paul turned back to the gateway and shielded his eyes from the sun. An odd, gaping line marred the delicate arches, as though someone had dragged a hot poker through the metal from a spot above Paul's head down to the ground.

"Some people will never have an appreciation for the beautiful," Porter called from his open window, waving to Paul. "If you discover the culprits responsible for vandalizing Trinity Gate during your investigation, we'd appreciate the information."

Paul frowned. Why would Contemplation have a fortified gate, however beautiful? No doubt it was a structural remnant of a bygone era, when the city had tried to segregate the less savory from the rest of the populace. Paul remembered hearing about the riots that had befallen Serenity when they'd first cordoned off the crime-ridden neighborhoods, but free food and housing had solved that problem. Who'd want to vandalize such a beautiful work of art, whatever its past purpose?

Paul knocked again. Still no answer.

He stepped around to the window and pressed his hands to the glass, peering through a gap in the drapes. The interior too dark to discern any details, he muttered a curse and returned to the sidewalk, careful to avoid the line of neat bushes. Wet dirt clung to his shoes and left a glaring trail on the sidewalk. He glanced around nervously.

Contemplation District had been empty while Paul waited in the car. Now the streets bustled with people, all too busy to notice Paul.

He didn't expect passersby to give him a reprimand, but their penchant for cleanliness made him nervous. He also had a rising suspicion the mayor had something to hide. The melted bars of the vandalized gate had bent outwards, suggesting the culprits had been on *this* side of the walls. *Inside* Contemplation District. Was the massive gate normally locked?

Thankfully, the third and final address wasn't far. The mayor hadn't approved a second visit, and Paul began to doubt he'd ever find anyone home.

To his surprise, someone answered the final door. "Mrs. Carlisle?"

She nodded, peering at him with a wary eye.

He noticed the vid screen on and a girl of five or six sitting on a couch. She was the spitting image of his own daughter. Long, skinny legs dangling above the floor and bare feet kicking the side of the couch while she munched on a handful of crackers. Crumbs littered the carpet at her feet and the seat cushions to either side of her. She appeared in profile to Paul, delicate neck jutting forward and big blue eyes riveted to the screen. His own daughter, Claire, would have been outside playing on such a sunny day.

Paul coughed. "I received a tip pertaining to missing teens in your district. May I come in?"

Mrs. Carlisle stepped back to allow him passage. The girl on the couch looked up and smiled. "I'm Lily!"

Paul froze, staring at the girl, then opened his file and withdrew the printout of the electronic message he had received. The haiku at the bottom read: 'Lilies in the pond / Bob on soft ripples, never / Beyond glass boxes.' He glanced out the glass doors at the little garden with glass walls. A glass box. And though no lilies grew by the pond, Lily probably played in the garden visible on the other side of the living room. Paul couldn't deny the evidence. Nikki had to be his source.

A tremor of excitement coursed through Paul.

For Nikki to have sent the information to Paul ahead of time, *before* his own disappearance, Nikki must have known he and his friends might run into trouble. But Nikki's message had come to Paul in a very roundabout way, having no apparent link to Contemplation District. Nothing was private with digital network traffic in Serenity, so such anonymity could only be accomplished through a hacking job. Maybe the kids had temporarily hijacked the network to get a digital help bottle out? Or maybe someone here in Contemplation had helped them? The peculiar haiku bearing an unmistakable reference to Nikki's little sister just seemed too much like a hidden message meant to reveal Nikki as Paul's source.

Paul had his story. Now just to figure out how the pieces fit.

He tucked the printout in his file and retrieved the black-and-white photo. "Mrs. Carlisle, when did you last see your son?"

She pursed her lips. "Last week. But you must be mistaken. My son isn't missing."

Paul's mouth fell open. He showed her the picture of Nikki with Anthony and Nadia. "Your son sent me this along with information predicting his own disappearance."

"A prank," she insisted, her face hard. "Nikki's always getting into trouble. I suspect they're responsible for vandalizing Trinity Gate. Nadia's father reported three stolen blowtorches. No doubt they're off somewhere plotting their next escapade."

Dreams of having found the best story of a lifetime descended to the pit of Paul's stomach. He'd been played, all right.

But why me? A reporter from out of town who hasn't had a big story in years? Why not a reporter from Serenity?

Because no one in Serenity would have believed Nikki.

Paul studied Mrs. Carlisle, at a momentary loss for words. She wore a simple brown dress of modest cut. Neatly pressed. A tight bun restrained her mousy hair. She'd been washing dishes. Water glistened on her hands and he heard the faucet running in the kitchen. He finally found his voice. "Why the prank?"

"I have asked myself the same question, Mister ... ?"

"Lambert, but please call me Paul."

She wiped her hands on her apron. "Nothing good ever came of kicking a gift horse in the mouth, Mr. Lambert. Our lives are better now. Poverty and crime eradicated. We have everything we ever wanted. If you ask me, children these days are ungrateful."

Paul remembered the vandalized bars. Why would kids lie about their disappearance and burn a line in a beautiful gate? Something didn't feel right. The melted bars gave the impression of a prison break. Perhaps Nikki and his friends intended the damage to be a message.

Paul's gaze fell on the girl. "Lily? How do you like living here?"

She dragged her blue eyes from the vid screen, resembling his daughter so closely it made his chest ache. Claire was with her mother this week. Lily's delicate brows furrowed in thought. "We have a nice garden. I have toys. Mother always says we're better off now than the way things used to be. Everything's clean. No one's hungry. I'd like to play outside, though, or visit Trinity Falls."

Paul gave her a sad smile. No wonder he hadn't seen any children outside. Parents in this district must confine their children to the glass gardens. Such confinement would explain Nikki's dissatisfaction. The pieces clicked into place. The three teens had probably run away from home after making a glaring statement in Trinity Gate.

"Serenity's falls are well worth a trip," he told Lily, resisting an urge to stroke her head, as he would have done to Claire. "You should convince your mother to take you there someday." He turned back to Mrs. Carlisle, unable to shake a niggling doubt that something was amiss. That uneasy feeling ever since he'd boarded the train into Serenity. "The beautiful gate your son and his friends vandalized, is it normally locked?"

Mrs. Carlisle's brows shot up in surprise. She ran her hands down her apron. "I'll never understand why some people complain. We were worse off before, starving and homeless. And how did people repay the mayor? Riots in the streets beyond Contemplation's walls. Vandalism, theft, murder. I don't blame the mayor for his response."

Paul frowned. While Mrs. Carlisle hadn't agreed outright that the gate was there to keep people inside Contemplation District, it certainly seemed to be the case. And Mr. Porter's odd statement that residents of Contemplation District restricted business to one hour a day. The glass gardens. Lily's confinement. Contemplation District began to sound more like a prison than an idyllic solution to crime and homelessness.

But if the gate was kept locked, how had the three teens escaped? The wall was too high to climb, and they clearly hadn't made it through the gate.

Something else could be keeping the residents of Contemplation District inside, too; though Paul hadn't seen any guards or video cameras.

"I need to get back to the dishes," Mrs. Carlisle said. The water was still running in the kitchen.

"Of course," Paul said, his stomach churning. Her lack of concern for her missing son was every bit as disconcerting as Serenity's penchant for cleanliness. "Thanks for your time."

Nikki's mother showed Paul to the door as the vid screen went to a commercial break. The commercial showed cleaner bots descending on cities around the world, transforming each one to mirrors of Serenity: *"With cleanliness comes peace. Take pride in your city. The first step to a better future."*

He stepped into the sunlight. A neighbor's door slammed as someone ducked into the house. Paul glanced at his watch. Would he have time to question those other two families now?

"Maintenance break is nearly over," Mrs. Carlisle reminded him. "You would do good to bide by our schedule."

"Not to worry." Paul gave her a tight smile. Lily stood at her mother's legs now, hanging on her skirt. "Little girls like you should be playing in the sun." Not glass boxes.

He headed down the empty street, the niggling doubt that something was amiss growing stronger with every step. He was onto something here, he just knew it. Maybe he could get another travel visa, try to question the other two families again. Maybe Nikki was staying with a friend in Contemplation District. Or maybe, just maybe, Nikki and his friends had escaped, with no one on the streets to stop them.

Another door slammed shut.

Paul, feeling a sudden urgency to vacate the quiet streets, checked his watch again. A few seconds before his hour was up.

He hurried down the street past a serene gazing pool and passed through Trinity Gate, which shut with a *clang* behind him. Puffing, his heart racing, he turned to check the gate and found it locked, just as he'd worried it might be.

He glanced over his shoulder. Mr. Porter's black car was nowhere to be seen. The mayor couldn't have made a clearer statement. Paul was late and had overstayed his welcome.

He looked back at Contemplation District through the bars, wondering what to do next, when he noticed Lily running through the empty streets. She stopped to crouch beside a gazing pool and dipped a finger in.

Paul wanted to be happy that she was outside, disturbing what even the wind seemed incapable of doing, but with everyone else in her district rushing indoors, he wondered why she wasn't running inside too. Should he be worried for her safety?

Which was ridiculous. Mrs. Carlisle had seemed unconcerned. Lily certainly seemed unconcerned. Maybe Contemplation District just had strange customs?

A glint in the sky caught his eye. Paul looked up. Countless cleaning bots were descending on the serene neighborhood. They engulfed Lily in a heartbeat.

The hairs along the back of Paul's neck stood on end.

He gripped the cold bars with his hands, his heartbeat quickening.

Bots scoured roads and buildings and clipped wayward vegetation. He'd never seen the machines take an interest in a person before. Perhaps Lily had sullied her clothes in her glass garden?

"Lily!" he shouted.

A few moments later, the bots dispersed.

Paul stared, disbelieving.

Faint ripples remained where Lily's fingers had brushed the water's surface. The girl was ... *gone.*

Paul blinked; a whooshing sound in his ears and his vision whiting around the edges.

"No!" he cried, his voice cracking.

Shock threatened to take his legs out from under him. He gripped the gate tighter. All he could think about was his dear Claire. He couldn't believe Lily was gone.

He glanced down at the line melted through the gate. The mayor had unlocked it for him. Had Mr. Douglas known about the faulty bots?

The bots.

Contemplation District didn't need guards when it had cleaning bots. Bots that could be programmed to go after people in one area, while leaving everyone else in the city alone. Bots that would scour the streets nearly twenty-four seven.

And three teens, unhappy with one hour of freedom a day in exchange for clean clothes and a roof over their heads, who had failed to escape before maintenance break was over. Did Mrs. Carlisle know their fate? Had she and the mayor both lied, all for a comfortable life and clean streets?

Paul refused to believe that. Refused to believe Lily was dead. Refused to believe a city would allow such an atrocity or that other cities would soon welcome Serenity's solution to poverty and crime.

"Someone help!" Paul rattled the bars. "Lily! Mrs. Carlisle!"

But he couldn't ignore the facts. According to Mrs. Carlisle, the rioting had continued, even after free food and housing. The wall and locked gate must have failed to curb the violence, too. Serenity had declared itself free of crime only days after the arrival of its cleaning bots. Which meant the bots not only kept the streets clean, but kept people on the verge of rebellion indoors.

Paul had his story. The story of a lifetime.

But at what cost?

People, *kids,* were dying. Lily, the three teens. If Paul hadn't seen it with his own eyes, he might not have believed it. If only he'd delayed his departure through the gate a little longer, he might have been able to save Lily. Or would he, too, have fallen victim to the bots? Perhaps that had been the mayor's intention all along.

Paul gritted his teeth. The children's deaths wouldn't be in vain.

He released his grip on the cold gate. No one was coming out to answer his calls for help. The ripples in the gazing pool where Lily's fingers had been moments before were gone, though forever ingrained in Paul's memory.

The city had tried to erase her. Paul would make sure the world knew Lily's fate and Serenity's true colors.

A question for Jeanette Gonzalez

Q: How often do you think about writing during a day?

A: Depends on what I'm working on at the time. If I'm in the middle of a novel, I'm thinking about the story almost all day long, from the moment I wake up until the moment I go to sleep. Not constantly, but on and off through the day between writing sessions. The more often I can sustain the dream or trance, the faster I pick up where I left off when I sit down at the computer again. It's far easier to finish a novel in a month this way, or three months for the longer works. If I'm between novels or short stories, I still think about writing, just not as often. I'm likely to become lost in a "what if" or a story fragment as waking dream while driving or cleaning. Long commutes are the best for coming up with new ideas or working out problems in a story.

About Jeanette Gonzalez

Jeanette Gonzalez lives on a mountain top surrounded in redwoods and sea air from a not-so-distant California coast. She shares her home with her husband, three children, and a slew of imaginary people who run her life when it's not spent raising kids, eating, or sleeping. She studied English Literature at the University of California, Santa Cruz.

www.jeanette-gonzalez.com

The Last

Premee Mohamed

Erik was balanced atop one of the standing stones on the black pebble beach when the elders told him of his father's death. Drowned, they said. Out at Sampson Fjord. Killed by Old Blue.

Darkness overtook him and he spilled boneless from the stone, was caught and laid on the wet weeds of the tideline. Elder Erde lifted his ankles into the air with one hand. Erik's friends paused incuriously, then wandered off.

"I want to see the body," said Erik.

"No," said Erde, but Saba pointed to the lookout hut. Erik ran clumsily over the wave-rounded stones and found his father crushed and bluegray with cold, like the sky. The boy dropped to his knees and wept.

When he returned home, his mother told him about the other death. She spoke quietly, rotating a gull over the fire, her face turned from the oily smoke. Erik's father had washed ashore first, but Nafeez had been with him. The bodies had returned before the boats. Currents around their village were precise, regular, and cruel.

"There is only his son now," she said. "And you."

He slumped to the floor and put his arms around his knees, unaware that he was shivering. The north was hard; he was no stranger to grief, to the currents that pushed and pulled his heart every time someone died. But this was different, this death of love.

"Where were you this afternoon?" she said.

"I had to go get my net back from Dante," he said. That was a long way for a young boy, even with the shortcut through the stunted forest, but he had needed to walk and think. The old man had returned the mended net without comment or sympathy. Erik had walked back slowly in the twilight, ignoring the trees that called out to him, feeling out his path with a broken stick.

In the morning, the same elders came to the house carrying a bowl carved from a whale's backbone. Erik watched stonily as they counted out the handful of mixed coins — a nonsense mass of silver and copper and bronze. She would get this payment for a year, blood money for the loss of her provider, tacitly acknowledging that her child was too young to work the bergs. Erik wondered what they would do at the end of the year.

"Look at these," she said when the elders had blessed the house and left. He sidled closer as she held a few of the elaborate little discs up to the window. "There was a time when these meant something, when they made sense. A whole system. Now they're meaningless."

"They're not meaningless," Erik said. "They're money."

"Money used to make sense," she said again.

"When you were young?"

"No, baby. This was before my time. Before many things."

"Then how do you know?"

"I heard it," she said. "From someone who knows." She smiled. "It's better now. Quieter."

Erik went to his father's grave later that week. The piled rock marker was already beginning to flatten out. Soon it would be gone entirely; then in a few years the bones would start popping up from the slick black stones, rough and white from salt, and children would find them and throw them into the sea. *Not me though,* he thought. *I am not a child any more. I am a man.*

From the cemetery he headed up the hill, wading through hip-height grass to Nafeez' ramshackle house, looking for his new mentor. Nafeez' son Jamil was out front sharpening a slope hook. Showing off, thought Erik, and incompetently at that. If Jamil wasn't careful, he would ruin Nafeez' careful hookwork.

"I guess you're my apprentice now," Jamil said, not looking up.

"Yes," said Erik. "We're the last, you and me."

"I'm the last, not you," Jamil said, discarding the hook and standing up, a tall thin boy with his father's sea-green eyes and black hair. "You're nothing. You're a baby. You're not even old enough to go out with the men."

"All right," Erik said meaningfully, and waited while Jamil fretted away the edge of his lip with his teeth. His silence said: No one goes out for a berg alone — not even the little ones that smash up on the offshore islands. It wasn't that you could die alone out there; it was that you *would.* The oldest, canniest cowboy would rather be out there with his nine-year-old grandson, or his ninety-year old grandmother, than alone. With the fathers dead, the entire village depended for its water on the braggart Jamil — who had only been on two hunts — and Erik, who had never hunted.

"Well, I suppose I can teach you, if you aren't too stupid," Jamil said. "And if you can work hard."

"I can work hard!" Erik said. "I promise. When do we start?"

"Come back tomorrow. I have to get everything ready."

Walking back, Erik spared a glance for the captive berg tethered in Drinkwater Bay, and was shocked to see how much smaller it looked today under its covering of hay and canvas. Big Markus was getting water, his bulk balanced on tip-toe, chipping delicately at the free side. A neverending job, thought Erik. How many children did he have now? Four? He must be out here all the time, day and night.

The iceberg screeched in anger as Erik trotted down the boardwalk. So small already. They would need another one, and soon. Not this week, not next. But sooner than he could learn the trade.

"It is not that we feel the push from the land," his father had told him once, not so long ago, as they sat on the warm pebble beach. "It is that we feel the pull of the sea. The pull of the bergs. They call to us, and once we hear them, it is like sirens; we must go to them. That is why I do this, Erik."

"What's a siren?"

His father chuckled. "There were stories in the old days, before everything went away, about things called sirens that lived in the sea. Some say on islands; some say simply in the water, like fish. They sang songs that sailors loved. And then, when the sailors had come close to hear the beautiful music — *uhmp!* The sirens would take them down into the water, and drown and eat them."

Erik shuddered excitedly, picturing the sirens like the great silvery tuna they would catch sometimes, marveling at how dainty their mouths were for so big a fish. What kind of songs would lure a man to his death? Was that like the song the icebergs sang? A predator's song?

"I don't hear the call," he said, disappointed.

"You will," his father said. "When you're older. It's in your blood."

The next day Erik wondered whether it was in Jamil's blood. It certainly had been in his father's, who had been one of the finest cowboys in memory. Nafeez had climbed and roped, netted and sailed as if he had done it in a previous life. 'Born with a hook in his hand,'

the elders used to say every time he returned in triumph. Jamil was rough and clumsy, and worse, reluctant to share even what little knowledge he had with his new apprentice. When they returned to the house at dusk, Erik had was no longer bewildered but furious, ready to invoke the names of the dead in his anger.

"You don't know what you're doing!" he shouted, waving at the blunted equipment, the unraveling ropes, his soaked clothing. "You can't even tie a knot. You don't even know which way is north! You're not Nafeez' son! You're the son of a clamdigger, the son of a *moneyman!*"

"Watch your tongue, blubberbrains," Jamil snapped, shoving Erik hard enough to send the smaller boy sprawling in the grass. "You're *my* apprentice. What do you know? Who says you can say that?"

"I have to say it! You're going to get us killed! Let alone get the next berg. We're going to die, everyone will go thirsty, the village will have to leave, and it's going to be your fault!"

"It's my fault I have a stupid apprentice, is it? A stupid little brat who can't learn?"

"It's your fault you can't do anything! You almost sank my father's boat!"

"Shut up! Or I'll shut you up!"

Erik scrambled to his feet, willing himself not to cry. At first he had thought Jamil was simply nervous teaching, but as the day had worn on, Erik had watched him throw his body the wrong way when the boat hit a wave, tie sloppy knots that fell apart in the water, tangle his hooks so that they tore at their ankles. Fear of death rode with them, bobbing in the swale like a scrap of wood, always visible from the corner of their eyes. Was that the faint sound of Jamil's call? The call of his talented blood, drowned out by that fear? Erik looked up into Jamil's green eyes, startled to realize they were seething with tears.

"All right," Erik said. "But we're… we're an apprentice teaching an apprentice. I know you didn't get your own hooks. You weren't ready, when Nafeez died. I wasn't ready either. We aren't grownups and we're all they have. I mean we're all the village has. And there's no one to help us."

Jamil sat and absently picked up his sharpening stone, looking at the pile of hooks at his feet. "Go home."

Erik went.

Back at the house, his mother and her friend Gumma were singing as they gutted a brace of sparkling mackerel so taut and fat that Erik's stomach growled a greeting.

"Two for you tonight," his mother said, as he went to change clothes. "Because you worked hard today, my little cowboy."

"Don't call me that!"

He was full after the first fish, but doggedly finished the second simply to prove that he had earned it. Afterwards, they tossed the bones and skin on the dimming fire and watched it flare as it ate the oils.

"When I was at the mail house today, they said a volcano down in the south just erupted," Gumma said, stirring the ashes with the tip of her knife.

"Terrible!" said Erik's mother. "How many dead?"

"Oh, you do not know of this volcano," Gumma laughed. "It warned the villagers, and they evacuated. All the sheep and the cattle and all."

"I heard of one in the Americas that learned morse code, and warned everyone too," Erik's mother said. "It was almost too late. I think twenty or thirty people died. Who knows morse code any more?"

"This one learned to make sounds from its vents," said Gumma. "It could only say one word and that was 'Flee.' Apollo said it had been saying it for two weeks before someone realized it."

"They should all figure out how to talk," Erik said. "It's not hard."

"Nonsense," said Gumma. "Have you ever heard a horse talk? Or a dog?"

"Of course not. That's different."

She smiled, and smoothed his curling hair behind his ears. "Did you know that in the old days, they were just dead rock, volcanoes? And icebergs were nothing more than ice?"

"What?"

"Not long ago, either," she said. "And trees never spoke. Nothing spoke but us. It was only after the day happened, and everyone went away. That's when things awoke and began to know."

Erik smiled to show that he was old enough to know a joke when he heard one. "And the people who went away, they used to drink water that flowed over the ground, too, you said."

"Indeed they did," Gumma said. "They had water from the land, they didn't need to capture icebergs in the old days."

Erik's stomach heaved. Awful, muddy water, crawling over the surface of the land and burping up out of it like vomit, full of dirt and rocks and worms and twigs! He supposed a river of mud might be all right to play in, but you couldn't drink that. People would die of thirst first. It would be worse than drinking seawater, surely. And ice just *ice?* There had been iceberg cowboys for generations and generations, corralling the semi-sentient blocks and towing them inland; otherwise what would people have to drink? Erik wondered how hard it had been to capture them in the old days, whether anyone had ever died trying. The *good* old days, he thought, gloomy with envy.

The next day, at sea, Erik brought it up to Jamil, expecting his usual sneering answer.

"Well, I don't know," Jamil said slowly. "My father said the same thing. Just the same thing. Almost used the same words, I think."

"Really? That people drank that land water?"

"Yes. Our people have been here a long time, almost as long as your people. Almost since the day. And he said we were the ones who wrote everything down. Said he had a book showing it. But I never found it in his things."

Well, how could you find anything in that house? Erik almost said, but was quickly distracted by having to yank back the mainsail as the wind shifted. He breathed a strange air of sweetness for a moment, and then the breeze was gone. "I think there's a berg nearby," he said.

"Get the oars out," said Jamil, looking around uneasily in the fog. "And drop sail."

"I can't do *both*."

Grumbling, Jamil wrestled with the lines while Erik dug belowdecks for the oars, finally dragging up the heavy bundle. He and Jamil both looked up at the same moment to see the berg sail by in the hazy distance, no more than a smudge of white.

"Get after it!"

Erik dug into his side of the oars as Jamil scrambled into position, and they fought their way through the crosscurrent, using the big mirror to check the berg's position. It lurched behind Bear Island and vanished. Erik pulled his side up short and yelled as the boat swung in circles till Jamil got his oar up.

"There's rocks under the water here! Are you trying to get us killed?" Erik squinted through the fog. "Stupid thing knew where to hide."

"No it didn't. They're stupider than sheep. It was luck, nothing else. We can sneak around from behind," said Jamil. "I went that way last time, when I was on the hunt."

Erik nodded uncertainly, listening as Jamil tried to describe the route, the size and shape of the landmark trees. It wasn't a big berg, first of all, he thought. It was on the small side. It would be used up in no time and they would have to get another one in a month. And that wasn't the one he wanted, anyway. He wanted Old Blue, the faceted monster. It had taken his father's blood; he would take its water. He had been thinking about it for days.

Jamil didn't like the idea, even when Erik pleaded that he too had lost a father to the odd-coloured berg. "Absolutely not," Jamil snapped. "We are not going after it. I don't care how big it is. Don't you know why that thing is the only iceberg that has a name?"

"I...because it's...because it's blue."

"Because it's old, idiot. Because it's so old, it was probably the first one to start warning the other bergs to stay away from shore. That thing is the reason we have to chase them. It's the biggest and the meanest and the oldest. That's why it...it..."

It killed the people we love, Erik thought. *So it has a name, so what. The thing I hate, why should I spare it? It never tried to spare any of us.* He turned his face away to hide his tears. "All right," he said. "Let's go after that one that we saw. The secret way. Like you said."

"Good. Oars down!"

The water was quieter on the other side of the island, dampened by the submerged rocks. Here they were easier to see; several had broken white edges, like flinty teeth, alarmingly close to their hull in the murky water.

"Where's the glass? Tie up here."

Erik moored the boat to a skinny spire of rock jutting from the island, then pulled the brass spyglass from its padded hole and handed it up.

"I see it," Jamil murmured, knuckles showing white through his deep gold skin, clenched tight around the heavy tube. "I...it's not moving."

"It's watching us."

"It's not *watching* us."

Erik sat back in the boat and automatically began to untangle the hooks and put them back on their holders, securing them with a single small slipknot the way you were supposed to. *One, two, three, four...* Old Blue was too big, he thought. You would need too many hooks to subdue it, make it swim back after their little boat. They did have enough hooks for the other berg though. *Eight, nine...* Enough to pierce more than half of its primitive brains. Not enough hooks to spare, he thought uneasily. *Twelve.* He could get Old Blue some other day. Today, it was about water, he promised himself. They had enough hooks. The boat wasn't shipping too much water. They could get it. Show the village there was no need to fear.

While he thought, Jamil put the spyglass down in a coil of rope and leaned over the gunwale. His voice lost its brashness for a moment, the old rasp of the childhood bully suddenly the voice of the same little boy who had lent his classmates books from his father's library and read to the elders on the beach. Erik looked up hopefully.

"What makes you think it's watching us?" Jamil said. "They don't have eyes."

"No, I know that, but..." *But they do always seem to know where we are, don't they? They may not be smarter than a sheep, but they do seem to not be as dumb as just ice. Don't they?* He said, "Well, I think most of its brains are on our side. Weren't you counting?"

"Shut up. Come on."

With the sail down, they moved slowly through the waves, oars splashing. *Twelve slope hooks,* thought Erik. *Two table hooks. We have enough. If we don't hit a rock, if it doesn't speed up and get too far out, or too close to another island...*

The hull bumped and slid over a hidden rock; both boys hissed in fear, but then they were over and slipping down its spine in silence. The berg was just visible in the fog again, snow-white like a tiny lighthouse, growing larger then smaller, then larger again as the boys followed it. It was moving in fits and starts, straight north into calm water.

Erik thought: *We paint our boats blue to hide them from things that cannot even see us. What does that tell you?*

They paint the warships red. They do not care who sees them. Do they? But I don't think they are really less afraid than us. Or that we are less brave.

The breeze blowing from the berg came more frequently now, cutting through the salt. Off starboard, one of the shiny black-and-white whales the old folk called horkas paused to look at them, then moved on. Erik lifted his oar to let the pod pass by, each giving the boat the same brief glance. Bad luck, horkas. They would flip boats for fun, Papa had said. Come up on shore to eat children.

As if he had spoken aloud, Jamil said "Don't be superstitious. Do you believe all the stories they told you when you were at the tit?"

"Of course not." He kept his gaze fixed on the white berg. They were steadily catching up, aided by a fast unseen current that the whales were using too, so small it did not even ripple the dark water. Whales sang, he thought. Would the sirens sing to them? Or the other way around?

He sniffed and frowned. Fresh, fresh water. And then he was scrambling for better purchase on his oar, ducking a swinging sail, for Old Blue was upon them. There wasn't even time to scream.

Old Blue, greatest and oldest of the great old bergs, with its one edge shaped like an axe head, was moving faster than either boy had ever seen a berg move when it slammed into their port side. In the chaos of freezing water and splintering wood Erik clung to his oar, but Jamil went flying, right over the edge like a gull. The boat lurched almost onto its stern before catching the invisible current and dropping flat onto the water with a crack. But the berg was still coming, slicing into the wood, using the ocean as an anvil. Erik shrieked as the water reached his waist, and then everything went black and cold.

In the deafening dark he saw a tiny white shape and reached for it, fingers remembering days at Children's Cove, the wooden charm his mother had carved on its string floating upwards, to air. He thrashed after it and was promptly struck in the side of the head by a chunk of the boat, almost sending him under again. Somehow he grabbed a line and hauled himself up onto the chunk, against the thousand-pound pull of his wet clothes. A wall of blues towered over him — turquoises of summer days, corpse greys, shards of black and purest white and lilac and cobalt in the facets. He shrank back from the unseeing glare of the huge berg, not sure if it sensed him now. There was so much wood in the water, he realized with a shock. *It smashed our boat to pieces. We'll never get back to land.*

"Jamil!" he cried, voice deadened by the wall of ice. He scanned the heaving, foam-spattered water, looking for large pieces of wood amongst shrapnel smaller than coins. A glint in the depths, sinking fast, showed where the line of hooks had torn free from the railing. He snatched at the last foot of line and nearly slid off his temporary raft, panting. His fingers were going numb in their mitts, but the death shivers hadn't started yet. He had a few minutes to think — or live, he supposed.

Without realizing it he began to sob, and hauled on the hook line, seeing the hooks come up one by one like skinny silver fish, backs arched. One tore into his britches and left a thin line of red on his thigh. Through his soaked, hanging curls, he watched tears spatter the cut. "Jamil! Jamil!"

"Erik!"

His head snapped around; Jamil was clinging to a piece of the hull forty yards away, spitting water and blood.

"What are we going to do?" Erik screamed. "I don't know what to do!"

His ears popped and all he could suddenly hear was the huge, menacing silence of the berg, and the sinister lick of the waves on his raft. As if it had heard him and intended to answer, Old Blue began to move inexorably towards the older boy. "Jamil! Swim! Quick!"

A great wash of water almost stole him from his raft as Jamil's dark head vanished, gone for endless, terrifying minutes. Erik screamed again when the two claw-like yellow hands grasped the wood by his feet, feeling his bladder let go, a shocking burst of warmth.

Jamil couldn't pull himself aboard; Erik couldn't pull him up. He looked down at Jamil's drawn face, like a skull covered in gold paint.

"The smaller one," Erik said, chest hitching. "It was fishing for us, it was drawing us out here."

"A trap," Jamil said. There was a faint crunch behind them as Old Blue hit the piece of wood he had been on. Soon it would notice them again and swing back to hit them. *It will swing,* Erik thought. *It knows it has that sharp edge — I don't know how, I don't care — and it doesn't know to use anything else.*

Water began to bubble up between his legs as the raft canted towards Jamil's dead weight. In the thick water Erik could see Jamil's legs paddling dreamlike, too slowly to keep him up.

"What are we going to do? What are we going to *do?*"

Jamil smiled at him, teeth no longer chattering, an awful, sleepy smile. "Erik. They named you...after a brave..."

"Don't let go!" Erik cried, stabbing himself on the edges of hooks as he lunged for Jamil. The only thing worse than dying out here would be dying all alone, mad with guilt and terror, still clinging to Jamil's frozen body. He grabbed at Jamil's sleeve and hauled with all his strength, trying to get Jamil's head clear of the water.

"It's coming again."

"Don't look!" Erik blurted. He took a deep breath and let it out slowly, arms trembling. Their raft was sinking. Half the hooks had disappeared into the water again. *It lured us out here and tried to kill us,* he thought. *It did the same to our fathers, in whose shadows we lived with pride, but they were not the last; we are the last. We are the last.*

We are the very last.

He pulled one of the hooks free and sank it into Jamil's sleeve, snapped on another, and leapt free of the raft, trailing the rest of the hooks like a tail. Every stroke towards the blue wall was like swimming through stone, as if the water too knew his name, wanted him to die. His head had gone under when his hand brushed the ice, and almost as if by reflex, he slammed a hook into it, felt it bite deep enough to bear his weight.

He couldn't see if Jamil was still attached, couldn't spare the motion. His neck felt too frozen to even turn. The berg howled as the hooks went in, rising to a scream as he climbed. Five. Six. *Look at my beautiful knots,* Erik thought dreamily. He was shivering so hard he couldn't see; everything was a mist of grey and blue, splotches of red from his bitten tongue. His hands were on fire; he imagined pressing his face to them for warmth. Eleven. Twelve. Inch by inch he hitched Jamil from the ocean's grip, crept towards the summit. The useless table hooks slid out immediately and splashed to the water far below.

And he sat at the top of the berg, listening to its song of rage.

Twelve is not enough to bring it back, he thought. *I climbed it for nothing.* He looked down; Jamil swung on the hook-anchored line against the sheer wall of ice, as flat as a painting in a cave. Maybe dead. Who knew.

I can't bring it back, but there's islands out there... we could build a fire... unless I'm too weak to walk...unless we die...

He was about to call for Jamil again when he saw the dark spot on the water, approaching them jerkily, in little sideways steps, like a crow begging for food. His eyes snapped into sudden focus. A boat! He knew that blue-gray hull, the blue-gray sail. Nafeez had mixed all his paints himself. Famous for it. The bodies washed to shore, he thought wildly, but this boat never did! If hooks were still aboard, maybe...

"Jamil!" he shouted, then realized even a whale's ears couldn't hear him over the noise of the infuriated berg. He climbed down to the third hook and jerked sharply on the rope. "Your father's boat is out there! We have to go get the hooks! It's the only way we'll make it back! Do you hear me?"

"The fool apprentice of a fool," Jamil murmured. "What do you know? We will die. We will never reach it."

"We will die anyway," Erik said, and meant it. But Jamil was clearly in no shape to swim out to the boat. What could he do now? He had bought some time, and his teeth had stopped chattering as he had warmed from the climb. *It will have to be me,* he thought, *but what is* it?

He was shivering again when he untied the line from the second-last hook and climbed back up, slowly, pulling it through the eyelets.

"Don't!" Jamil cried, but it was too late and Erik had swung from the tip of the axe, landing with a flat and final slap on the ocean near Nafeez' boat. It was far worse than the first time; he felt himself go limp, simply watched the bubbles rise from his mouth through the dark water, watched the sky recede, noted which way his charm floated.

Erik inched up the side of the boat like a crab, wondering if Jamil could still see him. As soon as the sail went up, Erik tensed in fear, knowing that Old Blue would attack it. But the hooks had gone true, and the berg stayed and screamed as the boat bumped towards it in the freshening wind.

A crowd had gathered on the beach, massed darkness already in mourning clothes between the racks of smoking fish, as the sun began to set. Without the spyglass Erik could only guess that his mother had come too — dazed, walking on the oakum and shattered planks of their boat, comforted by the fluttering hands of elders. People were still coming, cresting the hill tiny and black as ants.

The setting sun lay behind him, Erik thought. No one would be able to see him, only the berg. But he waved anyway, waved and called till his voice cracked, till the villagers began to cry and wave in turn, till Jamil lifted his head groggily at the noise, as the great blue mountain and the last iceberg cowboys sailed in triumph back to their home.

A question for Premee Mohamed

Q: What's your favorite non-SFF book?
A: The Name of the Rose, by Umberto Eco.

About Premee Mohamed

I'm a scientist and writer working out of Canada. In my spare time I paint, draw, and annotate my copy of the *Necronomicon* in case there's something I've missed.
www.premeemohamed.com

Luminaria

Matt Thompson

It's a cold, hopeless wind that blows across the Southern Seas on these winter nights. Blade-edge gusts skim the waves; paper lanterns swing from the rigging, and the merchandise below decks strains against the swells: statues of boars and elephants, carvings of crocodiles and dung beetles, their marbled visages mocking the dreams of those who bear their burden of passage. On such a night one might remember the deserts of home, rocky outcrops on the husk of the world where fine sand grits the eyes of all who dwell there, and the dunes sing out a pure, wavering tone as the wind whistles through the grains.

Mutinous crews are known to hurl their captains overboard in these waters, their cackling silhouettes lining the rails and watching with glee as their hated master plummets to his doom. If their victims should scream or plead: then, all the better. They say that the souls of those who are dispatched thus haunt the deeps for years afterwards; submerged in icy currents or trapped within subsurface volcanic vents, they wave the remnants of their hands in pathetic gestures that suggest the motions of a paddling child or drowning feline. Eventually they will dissolve, dissipating into plankton and salt at the lightless seabed, their memories and desires joining with the covert dreams of the ocean; and, though they will not know it, washing ashore on a pebble beach or rocky island, from there to enter the bloodstream of the world as if they had never died.

They say also that the mutineers will themselves be cursed, forever to hear their captain's bitter last words in the creak of the sails, the screams of seabirds, the cracking of ice floes...Those who are punished in this way inevitably succumb to the call of the waters; a ghostly calenture leap into the welcoming bath of eternity, there to suffer the half-death of sorrow that befalls one who thought himself greater than the sea.

I found myself on one such voyage, a brigantine known, then at least, as the *Muzawwala* – the sundial. Not fifty leagues out from Egypt we sat becalmed, squirming through the dismal waters as if they were soup. As we cast off from port every man and woman at quayside turned to watch us go, their bodies frozen in statuesque postures that seemed to mirror the stone carvings lining our hold. Now, we knew what they were seeing: this vessel was bound for Hell.

The first mate and bo'sun abandoned ship one night while the rest of us slept, taking the rowboat with them. The next morning the ship's cook, Caleph, reported the food stores as spoiled. He drooled as he relayed the news, giggling in nervous terror as we murmured the prelude to a conspiracy amongst ourselves. Our captain had spent the entire journey locked away in his cabin; none of us had even laid eyes on him.

The eldest of us, a Shi'a of the Oghuz, took command of our revolt. Huddled on deck around a brazier we had fuelled with the rowboat's abandoned casting pegs, we agreed the captain's time was nigh; no-one wished to die for a man we had never met. With great care, the Shi'a plucked the lanterns from where they hung on the cordage and placed one before each of us. His knife whittled their wax to an even level. We dipped the wicks into the fire; the act of placing them back into their holders seemed like a ritual of treason, a conspiracy we could all consider ourselves fully complicit in. We doused the brazier.

"Now," the Shi'a said, "the flame that burns longest shall light the path of betrayal. Until our doom is sanctified, let us tell the tales of our path to this place, and see if the breath of our voices should quench the lanterns first."

The stories began. Six men and true told their truths, or half-truths, or lies, shivering beneath the constellations on that petrified night. The Shi'a told of fishing schooners, mastheads looming from the mist at the quayside of Cadiz, crates of spice, bejewelled spiders, maps; nephrite statuettes unloaded onto the wharf by legions of bonded slaves, the silent gaze of a woman pitiless in the shadows beyond. He told of time, and its enfolding qualities; he considered, too, that clocks spun their hands backwards in the southern hemisphere. Loath to disagree with the man, having seen what havoc he could wreak on matters far less scientific, we murmured our assent while gulls swooped overhead, their shadows eclipsing the starlight.

Another spoke. "Alexandria," he said. "I remember the knife-thrust of a harlot on the banks of a canal, a paper boat floating on the surface of a pond." Drear lantern-light barely illuminated his face; we knew of him as Velo, one from Tunis. His story swerved into paths obscure and confusing: embezzlers, mercenaries; a hooded woman, her gaze burning out from the eye slits of her head-dress; a Persian cartographer whose maps, more fable than veracity, led the teller eventually to the *Muzawwala* and ruin.

His laugh was a mirthless sound in that great arena. The Shi'a muttered obscenities to himself, then turned his head and spat.

Another took up the tale; by then we seemed to be telling the same story. This man, a Bolivian named Arturo, spoke of a dream, one that mirrored the steps of Velo's account: a knife in the back, the perfidious mapmaker, the mysterious woman, her masked husband beside her, their silhouettes disappearing into the evening bazaar.

He concluded his account thus: "Then I dreamed of the waves that swell over the reefs of Tagula, the feel of the cobblestones beneath my sandals, the glance of a woman."

Velo's candle sputtered and died. A new voice broke the silence.

"I know of this city of the dead, and this woman. That night I took her in my arms, and gave her life." Lakar, an adept of the Navaratnas and the last of us to join the crew, toyed with the tip of his dagger as he spoke. "Her husband and his Blood Guilds were the true rulers of that place. They chased me to the city boundaries in the early morning." He opened his shirt to reveal an angry crimson slash carved across his ribs. The cutlass scar intimated a treasure route, transcribing its course across the continents to this place. "An eviller man I never saw," he said, "and she knew it."

Arturo grinned, revealing uneven rows of blackened teeth, sharpened as if they were dentures he had stolen from the jaws of a great sea beast. Lakar's eyes burned from the darkness, as if he and Arturo shared two parts of the same face. His lantern faded. The Shi'a's own light had begun to dwindle. Among us the cook Caleph burned the brightest of all, his flame illuminating his features in waxed curves that seemed to double the hewn face of our figurehead; he, a damned siren leading us on to the reefs of fortune. Lakar hurled his dagger to the boards; there it quivered, a dare to the Gods, the bleat of an abandoned child.

The cry of a gull came from far overhead, echoing from the skin of the water as if we sat within a cathedral, and the bird were the voice of a fallen angel. Lakar continued his tale, even as his lantern's light bedimmed to embers. He spoke to us of caravans of onyx traders; rotting, amaranth-infested cities in a desert of diamonds; a vow of silence; a woman's eyes, a masked figure leading her into the glare of the sun.

A map.

He spoke till the lantern flame of the Shi'a fluttered and died in a coil of mist. "And you?" Arturo turned to me. His tongue flicked from between his lips; or did it only seem that way in the dying radiance of his own lantern? Mine still burned strong and true, and I felt the call of mutiny, the milk bath of betrayal. "Two stories remain, two torches still burn over the waters." He laughed, then, alone. I searched my memories, and told my tale.

I spoke of the sombre light of a Seville morning, an endlessly chattering sergeant casting me out into the dust and dew of the sunrise. I spoke of copper mines and granite quarries, teams of slaves expiring at my feet for want of a nugget of gold, a mouthful of silver; then baying for my blood, my investors lying motionless in their suicide circle, pistols at their temples. I recalled poorly glazed chamber pots and the hungry eyes of bankrupt excavators; a notched bar of what I discovered, almost at the cost of my life within the precious metals exchanges of Bombay, to be gilded iron; idle rumours of betrayal in a dying port town that overlooked the whirlpools and oxbow meanders of an inland sea.

I remembered a balloon voyage, an ice-bound race over the Mountains of the Sun, the crags racing toward me as the pilot desperately hurled himself from the basket. Then, a month out from Cape Agulhas: I, a stowaway, the helmsman ordering his sail riggers to cast me into the firmament; the vessel listing, blubber coating its decks, the skipper a drunkard, sperm whales howling their contempt at us from the dark roils of fog that clung to the ice-littered waters of the southern ocean.

My voice died to a whisper, then silence. The rigging above us creaked, the sound of a coffin lid closing on a wasted life. Even as my lantern-light dwindled to naught I recalled a trigger, my finger squeezing it down, down, the sharp retort echoing from the stones as the recoil snapped my wrist backward, and a man's blood spattering the quarry walls. A decanter: whisky, or poison. I neither knew nor cared as I swigged it back, the mocking, incredulous cackle of my blasphemous companion reverberating from the chancel of the derelict cathedral.

And: the eyes of a woman, the sword-stroke of her husband, the ridges of scarred skin across my chest; my memories calling me onward to a reunion beneath the cold, still stars, a kiss on the forehead of a ghost on the steps of Alexandria, a drunken awakening in the hold of the *Muzawwala*, a tangle of truths and untruths...

Arturo's light was already dark. Mine, too, flickered its last rays and expired.

We turned as one to Caleph. He met our gaze, unblinking. His lips quirked upwards for a second.

"Friends," he said. His lantern burned strong and true. "I have no tales of my own to tell. But there is a story I heard." He shivered in a sudden chill of wind. His flame scintillated higher even than before, dancing motes of light across his cracked face. "A story of a merchant: one who suffered the grievance of infidelity, the taunts of his rivals. A story of a captain: one who became that way through the thrust of swords, chains of iron sending his own master to an endless sup at the wines of the deep. And those same chains, my friends, sent two of his crew to their doom not three days ago." Velo gasped; but we all knew it to have been true. Caleph spoke on. "Rum is his only friend, shipmates; rum and despair. And even now, he haunts his own vessel.

He squats within his cabin, dreaming of the void, praying for the forgiveness of eternity."

He rose to his feet and lifted the lantern to his chest. Without a word we followed him, below decks and along drear corridors to the door of the captain's quarters. He handed the light to me, opened the door and slipped within.

We five – Arturo, the Shi'a, Lakar, Velo, myself – waited in dread silence. Were we, too, to suffer the eternal call of the bottomless deeps? Were we as complicit as the Shi'a, who had rubbed coal tar onto Caleph's candle almost in plain sight? Not a sound came from inside the cabin. Lakar murmured a prayer, guttural syllables dying away into the silence as the ship bowed and drifted.

Then: the handle turned. I felt a clutch at my throat, an icy grasp of infinitude. The door swung open, and we knew our doom.

For Caleph, Captain Caleph, stood before us, his uniform rumpled, its insignia blood-stained and faded. He held his wrists out in supplication. What were we to do, other than comply?

We tied him and led him to the bow. The sky was full of birds: cormorants, gulls, petrels, their screeching voices summoning the dawn as a breeze finally lifted our sails for a moment. I could feel it: wind, strong and true, scudding across the ocean's surface like a gust of foulness from the underworld.

Captain Caleph hesitated for no more than a second. Gulls screamed their encouragement: fly! No cry escaped him as he tumbled to the dark waters below. A splash, the faintest of disturbances on the skein of the ocean, and a flurry of wings battered the grave of a man whose condemnation preceded him, whose judgement cleaved our flesh as it had in Alexandria, Cartagena, London...

We hung the lanterns back onto the rigging. Melted wax encased them, forming sculptures of a woman's face, a cutlass, a chain, a scroll. The birds circled the ship for a while; then they flew eastwards, departing for better company, abandoning their wards to the vicissitudes of the purgatory they had chosen for themselves. And we returned to the ashes of our fire to await the wind, the scars on our chests a treasure map of Hell, and we cartographers of the dead.

It came from Matt Thompson

My original plan for this story was for a kind of Borgesian pirate yarn – magic realism meets boys-own adventure, or something along those lines. I'm not sure I succeeded, but the concept of a metaphysical shipboard mutiny I'd finally arrived at stayed with me. I adapted a shorter, abandoned story I had lurking in the 'trunk' and it turned out to be a perfect fit. So many tales of long sea voyages have an almost unearthly aspect to them – mermaids, whirlpools, manifestations of the mysterious, unknown world that stretches into the deeps.

The narrative was kicked into gear by an image I had of lights, hovering through the ocean fog, extinguishing one by one until only a single flame is visible. When that disappears the betrayal is complete, and the mutineers must serve out their penance alongside the dead. Which was all very well, but since it was getting a bit downbeat I decided to spice it up with some (implied) sex and violence. Works for everyone else, right? And thus a story was born.

A question for Matt Thompson

Q: What was your favorite children's book?

A: Clearly there are too many to choose just one. If pushed, though, I'll go for 'The Truck On The Track' by Janet Burroway, wherein a fantastical circus troupe attempt to free their vehicle before it's mown down by a train. Inevitably, they fail. The final orgy of destruction was always my favourite part as a child. The story has the quality of the best children's (or adult) fiction, in that it's entirely deranged; the cumulative rhyming form just adds to the weirdness. And there's a yak involved. Tragically it seems to be out of print nowadays.

About Matt Thompson

Matt Thompson is a London-based writer of oddball fantastical fiction. He has also released upwards of twenty records over the course of a two decade-plus musical career. When not trying to emulate Jorge Luis Borges or Richard Pinhas he likes to pretend he can cook Japanese vegetarian cuisine.

He can be found online at matt-thompson.com. Twitter: @24wordLoop

August

Duet for Unaccompanied Cello

Chanel Earl

My favorite place to practice the cello will always be the observatory. My friend Jamie, an astronomer, first let me in one day when the sun was up and visibility was nil. I practiced for hours under its high dome, right next to the telescope.

The echo of music in the observatory was singular: less vibrant than a racquetball court, more round than a stadium stairwell, a fuller sound than I have found in any practice room on any campus I have ever attended. In the observatory, music swirled around, visited every surface and then came back to and through me to visit again.

I didn't want to practice anywhere else. Not only because I loved the sound, but also because I loved the short walk through the woods on my way in, the cool temperature, the old smell, the vibrations of the limestone walls, the look of the gray floor, and the small hole in the domed ceiling that sent every sound up into the sky.

Jamie gave me a key so that I could practice in the observatory any time I wanted to, and on a cold spring afternoon nearing the middle of spring semester, when the days were getting longer and the trees were starting to put on leaves, I heard a faint sound playing along with me. I stopped to listen, and it stopped as well. When I started playing again, it returned. Every time I stopped, it did too, but even though my music covered the sound and kept me from hearing it clearly, I knew it was there, a faint pitchy whistle that, like the sound of footsteps in the woods, disappeared when I tried to get a closer listen.

I had my junior recital the next week. Just me, my cello instructor, a small audience made up of close friends and family, and the observatory. At my request, the top of the dome was opened all the way so that my audience could look through the ceiling at the stars as they felt the music bounce around them before it made its way to the heavens.

After the performance I walked home with Jamie. Always the gentleman, he offered to carry my cello, and I accepted gratefully although we made a laughable pair: me reaching a proud five-foot four with my three-inch heels on and him at a slouch still coming in at six-foot three, carrying a cello in one hand and a telescope in the other. He usually had a lot to say, but that night he was acting strange.

"Thanks again for coming," I said to him for the fourth time as we reached my apartment. "I guess I'll see you next week."

"Wait," he said. "You sounded great tonight, and I'm glad you like to play in the observatory, but..." He hesitated.

"What?"

"But, did you notice anything odd about the acoustics? I mean, when you invited me to your recital I had certain expectations—ways that I imagined it would sound—but I didn't expect new sounds to come out of nowhere. Did you use any electronics? Did you have a flautist hiding in the wings?"

"You heard it too?" I asked.

He look relieved. "Yes, thank you. "He almost dropped my cello as he tried to gesture with his hands, "I wasn't just imagining it. I heard something else, something that wasn't you. It was only when you played, and I couldn't quite make it out, but I heard it. I...felt it."

Jamie and I went back the next night to try and take a closer listen. It was warm enough now that we didn't need our jackets, and again he opened the dome so that we had a full view of the stars.

"That's my favorite one," I said, pointing to a bright star in the east.

"Your favorite planet?" he asked.

I felt suddenly embarrassed. "Is it a planet? I thought it was a star," I admitted.

Jamie didn't laugh, although I could see a hint of amusement in his smile. "That's Venus. It will be at it's brightest soon. It's great planet to keep company with in the evenings. But don't get too used to it: in the fall it's only visible in the early morning."

I admitted that I had only noticed it a few weeks ago, and realized as I took my cello out and tuned up, that I didn't really know much about astronomy at all.

We decided it would be best if I played the same songs I had performed at my recital. Then, while I played, Jamie moved around the room looking for vibrating panels and listening for anything that could explain the sound we had both heard. He paid careful attention to how the vibrations interacted with the telescope, and at one point, in the middle of a song, he asked me to stop and just play the same note for about five solid minutes as he stared at a meteorite that was sitting in the corner. As we experimented, we learned to hear the music more clearly. It was certainly not imaginary.

Soon, we were meeting every night to experiment with the sound, and we did learn more about it. For example, it didn't seem to matter if I played in rhythm or in tune, loud or soft, fast or slow. We could hear it when I played with the dome closed and open. After a week or two of listening we started to hear it with every note. It seemed to come out of the sky and enter into us, a throaty whisper of song, like the echo of a bird through a desert canyon.

We made recordings with our phones, trying to capture the sound we were chasing, but they were useless. We tried manipulating them to isolate the new sound, but it doesn't work that way in real life —just in the movies. The sound was faintly there only because we knew what we were listening for.

In spite of our investigative efforts we were no closer to finding out where the music was coming from than we were the first night we heard it. I was, however, learning a lot about astronomy. After I learned how to recognize Venus, Jamie moved on to other planets, then major constellations. We even spent a few days looking at planets and galaxies through the telescope.

"To really get good seeing," Jamie said one evening, "We should get out of the city and away from all these lights." Then, "There's a meteor shower tomorrow."

"Yeah," I said absentmindedly as I played, "That's a great idea." I finished my piece, which was "The Swan" by Camille Saint-Saëns, and even though I didn't have a pianist to accompany me, the observatory provided its own accompaniment, which sounded like no instrument I had ever heard, but called to mind the trickle of a mountain stream.

It didn't completely register that we were going to go stargazing the next night, so when I showed up at my usual practice time to find Jamie waiting outside with his backpack still on, I needed an explanation. "We're heading out to see some real stars." He said as if it were enough.

"I have my cello with me," I said, "I'll have to take it home." I had wanted to practice and tried to sound as disappointed as possible.

"There's room in my car," he said, not letting me get out of going. He reached out to take it from me.

Resigned, I handed it over. "Where are we going?"

"A star party," he said with excitement.

And it was exciting. I learned on the drive that some of the astronomy faculty and their students, Jamie included, held parties like this every month, but to me, the whole idea was new and exotic. We had to drive over an hour to get far enough from the city, and then Jamie turned onto a dirt road that led through the woods. The long drive reminded me of the walk I took to the observatory every night, but it was more wild and unpredictable. Instead of a paved walkway through a manicured campus forest, I was driving through miles and miles of real wilderness. Sure squirrels lived in both places, but I guessed that there was far more, and far larger wildlife here.

Jamie drove up a hill to where the forest opened into a sort of grassy field, and we got out. By now the semester was almost over and summer was on its way. The forest was filled with newly green trees, casting their young shadows even in the starlight. The smell of fresh earth was everywhere, as were the sounds of frogs croaking.

When we got to the star party, I looked up at the sky and almost fell over. My whole life I had heard about the Milky Way, but I had never understood it. I had also always wondered why people would talk about the "infinite" stars in the sky, when it seemed like every time I looked up I could only see maybe fifty stars, maybe a few more. Away from the city, without all of the streetlamps and headlights, I saw more stars than I had ever seen before. An ocean of stars filled the sky, with a white current running from north to south. It seemed like millions of stars were visible. Most of the telescopes were already set up and pointed at various planets, galaxies and nebulae, but I had no desire to look through them, not when there was so much to see already.

I had wanted to practice, and seeing the stars was so inspiring I decided I might as well go ahead right here. Jamie said that was a great idea, and helped me get up the courage to do it with so many strangers around. I was used to practicing under the stars, but this was different, there were so many more stars and they were so bright.

I started with Bach's Cello Suite No. 1, which people almost always love, and even usually recognize. Almost immediately, I heard a familiar sound playing along with me. Up until now, I had assumed the accompaniment I had heard in the observatory was unique to that place, but here I was at a star party, bowing under the Milky Way, and there it was, my mysterious accompaniment.

What had begun as a faint whistle shortly before my recital had transformed into a full, rich roar, at times like rain hitting the surface of a lake, at other times like the ringing of church bells. I could imagine the stars ringing every time I saw one twinkle, and it was beautiful to hear the music of the stars playing along with me.

Jamie heard it too. He was used to it by now, so when he heard it on the hilltop he couldn't help but smile, and as I finished the first piece, I saw him look up at the stars in awe.

A few of his astronomy friends also heard something, but I could tell it wasn't as clear in their unfamiliar ears, and I'm sure it was easy to explain away as the rustling of the wind or the howl of a distant coyote.

After I finished a few more pieces we headed home.

"What were you looking at?" I asked as soon as we got in the car. "At the end of the Brandenburg, you looked like you had seen a UFO."

"It was amazing," he said, "the biggest shooting star of the night, and it seemed to fall just when the music needed it the most."

"No way," I said.

"Seriously. I haven't ever seen a meteorite that big. It was so long, and fell in time with your last note."

I didn't know what to say, and he didn't either. We talked about the music, the astronomy, the similarities between the observatory and the hilltop, everything but the inconceivable idea that a shooting star might fall in time with my cello playing.

That night, I had trouble sleeping. Around four in the morning it started raining and the sounds of the rain tapping the window finally seemed to quiet my thoughts. I turned my pillow over to the cool side and realized I was wearing a space suit, floating in darkness. Stars appeared in the distance, and when I looked down saw that I was holding my cello. I began to play, but the music didn't sound right. I continued anyway, now worried that I was messing up the entire performance, but when I finished and stood up to take a bow—no space suite, only me in the observatory—the audience gave me a standing ovation.

I woke up wanting nothing more than to play in the observatory as soon as possible.

Soon after that, Jamie and I went from curious to obsessed. He started calling it "The Sounds of Space," and took every opportunity to sit in on my practice sessions, which I still held in the observatory almost every night. He mostly worked on his dissertation, but I would catch him closing his eyes and just listening more often than he would like to admit.

Our experiments took a back seat, but we were still learning to listen better every day, and after a while we realized that it didn't seem to matter when I played, day, night, it was all the same. Jamie pointed out that the stars were out all the time, even if the sunlight was so bright we couldn't see them during the day.

I enjoyed practicing more than ever, and not only because I had an audience around, but also because the music I was making seemed better than usual. It was like I had extra help, and the longer I played with the new sounds, the more I learned to hear them. They became so much a part of the music that whenever I played with my ensembles it sounded hollow.

Then one night, as I was finishing up my last piece, I had a new idea. "Have you ever wanted to go to space?" I asked Jamie after the last note echoed through the dome.

"Uh, yeah...doesn't everybody?" He looked at me like I had just asked him if he wanted a million dollars. "Don't forget," he said, "I'm an astronomer."

"Okay, yeah, but what if I, I mean...could I? Is it possible to take this music up to the moon, or to orbit—maybe a space station of some kind—and play a concert among the stars, not just under them?"

Jamie looked surprised, but amused, "I had the same idea weeks ago, but I didn't think you'd go for it." He suddenly had more energy than usual and started talking with his hands, his pen falling onto the table. "It's like the whispering sounds will be so much louder out there." He pointed through the hole in the ceiling. "And, you know, people are going to space all the time now, it should be possible."

All I could do was laugh.

"I'll see if I can find a way," Jamie said. It felt like a promise.

It seemed absurd, but once the idea was in our heads we couldn't let it go. I looked up details about NASA and what it would take to become an astronaut. Jamie requested information from everyone he knew who had connections to the handful of private companies that were sending individuals to space, either into sub-orbit, orbit, or to make a lunar landing. We even tried to win an orbital vacation in an Internet contest, but with negligible odds, it wasn't surprising that we lost.

We both decided to stay on campus during the summer semester, but with no classes to take, we spent most of our time working on the problem of getting me to space.

I did some research on what would happen to me and my instrument if I ever did make it into space, and realized that there would be serious problems playing the cello in zero gravity. My cello would out-gas. My bow would float away. I would need twice my usual strength to even hold the instrument correctly. I knew it was crazy, but just in case I ever made it, I had my cello treated and started an intense workout program.

Jamie was shameless. After exhausting every personal connection he had made in grad school about how to get me into space, he began emailing and phoning strangers. His single-minded optimism that I would get out to space made it seem not only possible, but inevitable.

We just couldn't give up. At the beginning of my senior year I found myself more interested in observatory practice than in pretty much anything else. I moved through the year with one goal in mind, barely completing my graduation requirements, and completely forgetting to apply for grad school, even as my professors reminded me every day.

Then it happened, shortly before graduation, and over a year after my junior recital.

"I did it," Jamie blurted out one day as soon as I walked in to the dome. "I talked one of the private companies into letting you record a concert in space. All we have to do is give them the rights to the music and video, then go to their press conference."

I thought he was kidding.

"Really," he said, " They want to sponsor the first off-world classical music concert. It's a good thing you're an amazing cellist or they would have taken my idea and used someone else."

I still couldn't believe it. "So, I'm going up there?" I pointed with my bow. "With the stars and the music?"

"Yeah." He said almost laughing. "We'll film the concert live, then edit a shorter version for YouTube. You will be the first ever to play the cello in orbit. I bet they'll make millions in online advertising, but we are the ones who get to go."

"We?" I asked.

Jamie smiled, "You need someone to plug in your microphones and hit record. Who else?"

I was thrilled, ecstatic. I could hardly practice because I was shaking so hard, and Jamie kept giggling like a teenage girl. Finally I calmed down and forced myself to practice; as I did a new energy animated the music. Jamie closed his eyes and listened to the sounds responding. But, as always, when I stopped playing, all was silent.

On our walk home, reality set in and I started worrying, "Did you tell them why we really want to go?" I asked.

"You mean, did I tell them you practice in the observatory every day and have been preparing for this for over a year, that it has been a dream of yours to record a concert in space? Of course."

I shot him my best glare.

"Oh, you mean did I tell them that some strange sound has been playing along with you and we think that if we went to space we would be able to hear it more clearly? No, I did not tell them that. And I won't."

I nodded in agreement.

Leading up to the concert, I played more than ever. We probably spent twelve hours a day in the observatory, having to work around the scheduled tours and classes that were held there. Jamie recorded nearly every practice session for review later, and I memorized every piece, not just my part, but the sounds playing along with me.

Jamie also gave me more astronomy lessons. We looked through the telescope at satellites as they drifted by. We talked about how different the stars would look outside of the atmosphere, how they wouldn't twinkle, how their colors would be more clear. By the time we took off, we felt more than ready for the trip.

We weren't. My black flight suit was specially designed to allow for the movement required. My seat was rigged with Velcro and welded to the floor so that I wouldn't float away. But even with all of the preparations, during my first rehearsal, my arms struggled to keep the cello at the correct angle without gravity helping out, and, worst of all, the sound was dead.

Space was quiet—so quiet. I glanced out of the small round window at the earth—not under my feet, but miles away, shining. It was blue and white and green and alive, but space was black. I was cold. Jamie and I were both feeling sick.

We still recorded the concert as promised. I played in cramped quarters with terrible acoustics, Jamie pressed the right buttons at the right times to record both audio and video as required. The filmmakers had their work cut out for them mixing the sound and editing the video to make it interesting, but even though the spacecraft was acoustically sterile, I played well, and the program was beautiful. I did my best to hide my disappointment in the experience, pretending to be energetic and excited and as I floated around in the dead capsule.

By all public measures, the event was a success. I started to receive invitations to play all over the world. Even though I had missed the application deadlines for grad school, I learned that my video was being counted as an audition and it wasn't to late to get in. Someone referred to me as "The Celestial Cellist," and it stuck. The press conference we promised to attend lasted six hours.

But privately, Jamie and I knew the trip was a failure. We hadn't learned anything about our mysterious sound. We heard nothing, saw nothing, felt nothing. The music I made was, by our new standards, cheap and hollow, like a tin flute. We were used to hearing something more like a symphony orchestra—ocean waves and a flock of starlings every time I played.

As soon as possible, we returned to the observatory. The short walk through the immaculate woods was like a walk home, and as we ascended the limestone steps into the dome itself I was overcome with emotion. I had traveled to space, and now here I was back where it all started, and I didn't know anything more than I knew at the beginning.

I began to play and was immediately joined by an unmistakable chorus. I suddenly realized I had been holding my breath. Tension that I had been enduring since I was in orbit started to leave me as I relaxed into the music. But now, as familiar as they were, the sounds were also new, changed—or I was changed. I had been to space. Had heard the sounds the stars had to offer, and these were different. They were dense and intimate and alive. The sound, trapped between walls of limestone and steel, vibrated through the air and then came back enriched.

It was beautiful. I saw the look of joy on Jamie's face and knew I was seeing a reflection of my own. For the first time, we recognized the music for what it was: the sounds of the earth. It was thunderous waves crashing against a cliff side, a family of cicada's—millions strong, wolves howling, roots and branches stretching through dirt and sky, wind roaring and whispering and carrying the sounds of the seasons. The music rang the chime of eons, of life dancing with and death buried under the stone. It came through the bottom of my feet and left through my hands only to bounce out and up and through the open ceiling, where—I laughed—we could still catch a glimpse of the stars.

It came from Chanel Earl

The Kirkwood Observatory at Indiana University is actually made of limestone. Next to it are Dunn's woods, which are beautiful year round. The first draft of this story was written after I visited the observatory to do a bit of stargazing. Then, after it was finished, it sat for over a year because it I just didn't think it was very interesting. It featured one character who practiced in the observatory and then traveled to space. There were no mysterious sounds, and she didn't have an astronomer friend to help her on her journey.

The second draft was more interesting, I added another musician and threw in some mystery. The ending was a bit different. Then the story sat for a long time yet again while I mulled it over. It was only after some pretty intense brainstorming and revision that I managed to turn the story into what it is now, and I had a lot of help from friends, family, writing classes, and B. Morris Allen here at *Metaphorosis*. The story is worlds better than it was after the first draft, and I am happier with it than I was at any other point in the process. Two years and maybe close to ten rewrites, but well worth it.

A question for Chanel Earl

Q: What would your animal totem be?
A: Every time I see a flamingo in the flesh, I get excessively happy. I could go on about their many wonderful traits, but I think what it really comes down to is their goofy legs and long squiggly necks. They can also fly, which sounds comical, but then ends up being majestic every time.

About Chanel Earl

Chanel Earl lives in Bloomington, Indiana where she parents three crazy kids, teaches writing and reading at Ivy Tech Community College, and thinks about dieting. She likes to read and write stories where strange things happen, probably because life sometimes seems so strange.
chanelstory.blogspot.com

Out Where the Rivenbuds Grow

Mark Rookyard

The second sun sat low in the sky, its pale red light smeared through a blanket of grey clouds. The winter had been a long one; five years, and the rivenbuds were a rare splash of colour in the world.

Caitlin fed the plants, her hands wet and dirty. The winding stems twisted above her, green and bright. The flowers of the rivenbuds were blue, red and white, and a score of colours in between. They smelled fresh, like cool winds on radiant days. Caitlin tucked her hair behind her ear. Her hair was grey as the clouds now. Once it had been thick and brown and someone had placed a rivenbud behind her ear and held her in his arms in this glade.

She rose to her feet, snipped a broken leaf away and sprayed another with water. She took a rivenbud between her fingers and closed her eyes, breathed in its smell and remembered a world that was young and bright and full of promise. So long ago, it seemed. She sighed and gathered her things into her basket. Ben would be needing her. Work to do on the farm. The long winter had been hard on Caitlin and her husband, the farm dry and dying all around them.

But spring was coming, she only had to look at the rivenbuds to see that. There was colour in the world once more.

She tended to another plant, freed it to wind upwards searching the sun. Four fresh buds on this one. A splash of colour in the green.

Perhaps if she hadn't tended this last plant, she wouldn't have seen him. A small figure on a distant hill, his backpack slung over his shoulder, his travellers' clothes green and brown.

Caitlin hid in the glade, leaves held to one side with a finger. It was rare for strangers to come out here. But this was no stranger, she already knew, even at this distance. She recognized the sure stride and the straight back, the fair hair that shone in the sunlight.

Recognized or remembered? Because as he approached the glade, she saw that he hadn't aged a day in the past twenty years.

"No," she whispered, letting the leaves fall back, a strange ache in her heart. Steen had said he'd return to this glade one day, but she hadn't believed him as she'd beat him and cursed him for leaving her.

Caitlin but her lip, and blinked away the tears. He hadn't aged at all, still so strong and sure in his movements. What would he think when he saw her?

She gathered her basket and fled the fragrant glade as though death itself was at her heel.

It had been a long day on the farm. Long gone were the days when Caitlin and Ben could afford farmhands. Once there had been twelve of them helping around the place. Now only Jek and Hal remained, asking to stay even when Ben had said they couldn't afford to pay them anymore.

They ate their dinner in silence at a chipped wooden table.

Caitlin finished her dinner first and washed her bowl. "I'm going to head out for a bit," she said, putting the bowl on the side. All she'd been able to think of was Steen. Had it been fear that made her flee, or shame? Shame at the years etched in her face, in the dryness of her hair?

"Sure, we'll finish up outside," Ben said, scraping his spoon around his bowl, his shirt sleeves rolled to his elbows.

Caitlin stayed where she was a moment, the lie she had prepared dying on her lips. Somehow it only made her feel all the more guilty.

Would Steen still be there, waiting at the rivenbuds? And even if he was, he would think her old and ugly. He would think this place he'd once called home sorry and wasted. He would think … what would he think? He would be glad he had left this place.

Glad he had left her.

She shouldn't go to see him. Her life was here. Making the farm work with Ben and Jek and Hal.

She washed her hands and dried them on the towel at her waist.

"See you later," she said. Ben nodded without looking up.

It was a long walk to the rivenbuds. The sky was a parched red, the light thin as the sun was beginning to fall. The first moon, pale and white, was already rising in the distance. It looked cold and cratered, battered by the forces of nature. Even this giant thing could be wounded by the passing years.

Caitlin hurried on, and memories she had long suppressed came back to her with each step, almost as though she were walking through time itself, winding the past back like yarn around her hand.

Over there, beyond the rolling hills in the distance, dark under the waning light, was where she had first seen him, she with her friends and he with his. She'd thought him stupid, and he'd mocked the accent she still carried from Klistne's World.

And there, where the stream ran from the same hills, through fields that had once been yellow and green, that was where he'd taught her to fish. She'd already thought him quick and clever by then. Over there beyond the ritne trees that were now bare and sparse, and beyond the lake, that was where they'd stolen into some abandoned farmhouse and made love for the first time.

She found him sitting next to a gently licking fire in the glade of rivenbuds. The flowers surrounded him, blue, white, or green, their petals soft and bowing from the branches, mourning the loss of time, the loss of hope. He hadn't changed from the moment he'd left her all those years ago. The same strong back, the same fair skin unmarred by dust or hard work.

Caitlin had to stop, her heart cold in her chest, the years suffocating her under their weight. It was then that Steen turned and saw her, looked at her from those blue eyes that had haunted her dreams for the past twenty standard years. He got to his feet, still tall and strong and young and hurried over to her.

"Caitlin," he whispered. "Caitlin."

And before Caitlin could turn away, hide the years from her face, flee from his youth and beauty, he took her in his arms again.

Despite herself, Caitlin let him hold her, and she closed her eyes and smelled the rivenbuds as she felt his hard chest against her cheek.

"I still love you," Steen said. He threw another branch onto the flames and they sparked and spat, before simmering once more.

Caitlin sat next to him, her shawl tight about herself. "You can't, Steen," she said. Was her voice different, too? Had that aged the same as her face? "You've been gone so long."

Steen turned now, to look at her. He smiled a smile Caitlin thought she'd long forgotten, so youthful and clever. "It hasn't been long to me," he said. He looked up at the sky slowly turning to darkness, the stars appearing one by one, blinking into life here and there. "See the stars up there? Imagine the worlds, worlds like this one," he smiled, sad and regretful. "Worlds not like this one. They're a long way, Caitlin. They call it the long sleep for a reason." He threw another branch onto the fire. The rivenbuds nodded in the flickering light.

Had Steen really not changed at all? Caitlin looked at him, the shadows shifting on his handsome face. Was there an extra line around the eyes? An extra crease around his mouth? A more pensive nature in his speech?

"When we woke on Haritna, I still remembered our parting the day before. I'd put a rivenbud in your hair, and we'd kissed. Made love here. I said I would always remember you, our last moments together, as I faced the grunts in the field." He smiled, still looking at the stars above. "It was a strange thing to stand on some faraway world, looking at the stars above and remember that we were together in each others arms only the day before."

"But it wasn't the day before. It was years." Caitlin had wept and mourned that her love was going to die a distant world. Ben had been there for her, spoken words of comfort. She bit her lip at the memory. What must she look like in this light? Old beyond recognition, wizened and tired? She wanted to hide, but instead she sat there, her shawl tight around her thin shoulders.

Steen shrugged and smiled. "A Day. Years. What's the difference, really? Three years I was up there, fighting in the war, and every one of those days I thought of you. With all the killing, murder and bloodshed, all I thought of was you and our days together here. The shooting would fall quiet on a night, our advances would slow, and I would look up into the night and see the stars, thinking of you here and wondering if you were thinking of me."

Caitlin knew Steen wanted something from her then, some comfort, wanted her to tell him she had thought of him all these years. The rivenbuds watched them quietly, nodding in the breeze, their colours shadowed in the dancing light of the fire. "I'm an old woman now, Steen," she said. "I'm married. I married Ben and we work together on his farm." She shrugged and the breeze felt cold as the night approached. "You, you still have your youth, you've seen the stars and fought in wars on new worlds. You still have your life ahead of you. My life is done."

"I remember when I first saw you, Cat," Steen said, smiling in the shadows. "Out in those fields. I was stupid around you, I wanted you so much. I knew even then that without you my life was done."

Catelin threw another stick on the fire as the rivenbuds watched from above, their colours muted in the shimmering light of the flames.

Caitlin's arms ached from working the fields, and her back throbbed. When she ran a hand through her hair, dust fell from it onto the cold stone floor. She held a mirror on the table and turned her face this way and that.

"What are you doing?" Ben said, kicking off his boots in the kitchen.

"Do I look old?" Caitlin put the mirror down and watched Ben wash his hands.

"Hmmm?" Steam rose from the sink and Ben took a towel. "You're beautiful. You always will be."

"Yeah, right." Caitlin pulled a face and picked up the mirror. The years had been sneaky and quiet, coming unnoticed as she worked on the farm. They had stolen the lustre from her hair until it now looked dry and greyed, they had stolen the freshness from her cheeks until they looked dull and hollowed beneath eyes that were now a faded blue. How had the years gone so quickly? She thought of Steen and his golden hair and strong shoulders. She dropped the mirror to the table, her breath lost to her for a moment. Where had the years gone?

Ben came to her, wrapping his arms around her neck and kissed her cheek. He smelled of soil and leaves. "None of us are as young as we used to be. You're still beautiful, though. There's beauty in strength, Caitlin, remember that. Beauty in age. Look at those trees over there beyond the fields, how their branches are golden and their leaves green, how those branches spiral and spread and reach for the sun. Isn't there beauty there? Or in this house; my ancestors built it all those years ago, and every time I come home to it I still see how it stands proud in this valley, the roof red under the sun. Isn't there beauty in that?" He breathed in her ear. It was warm.

Caitlin touched his arm, felt the strength there. Strength spawned from years of working the fields. She felt trapped, constricted, unable to breathe with his arm around her neck and this talk of passing years.

The knock at the door made them both start. Ben went to answer it, the last waning light of the day spilling into the room as three uniformed officers stood in the doorway, two of them holding plasma rifles across their chests. The uniforms were a burgundy red. Caitlin remembered when Steen had left in his own burgundy uniform, so proud. She turned away.

The unarmed officer smiled a smile that never reached his eyes. He had a datapad in the crook of his arm. "Mr. Renage? I'm sorry to bother you, but we're here looking for a deserter. He goes by the name of Steen Polit. I think you know him?" Dark eyes looked over Ben's shoulder and found Caitlin sitting at the table. Another smile. "Perhaps you've seen him? He deserted two standard weeks ago. We believe he might have come this way, coming from these parts as he does."

There was a tension in the set of Ben's back that only Caitlin would recognise. He still held his hand to the door, barring entry into the house. "Steen? Yes, I knew him more than twenty years ago. Haven't seen him since. I heard he made it into the Jagers, went off world to fight the grunts."

"That he did, sir, that he did," the officer said. He glanced at his datapad, back to Ben. "A fine soldier he is too, as all the Jagers have to be facing the grunts. It seems though," was that another glance to Caitlin? She felt awkward still sitting there at the table, but it would betray her guilt if she left. "It seems he's been on planet leave at

Gatestown but has been missing for the past two weeks. All Jagers are under strict guard because of the nature of the war."

Ben still hadn't moved from the doorway. "Well, like I say, I haven't seen Steen for twenty years or more."

The officer nodded, paused a long moment. "And you, Mrs. Renage? You haven't seen Steen either?"

The tension in Ben's back intensified visibly. "I'm sure my wife would have told you if she had." He moved to block the doorway more. He must have been more than twenty years older than the officer.

"Good, good," the officer said. "But if you," another glance to Caitlin. "Either of you, see Steen, I would appreciate it if you would call us? It's very important we find him. Security. You understand."

Ben closed the door and Caitlin looked at the table, traced a finger along the grain of the wood.

"You've seen him," Ben said. It wasn't a question.

"I should go," Caitlin said. "Warn him they're looking for him."

Ben went to the window, looked out. "Wait a bit. I think they'll hang around waiting for you."

Caitlin nodded. "Thank you," she said.

"We can't erase our pasts," Ben said, turning from the window. The sunlight shone in his greying hair. He looked tired. He smiled, but there was only an air of defeat in it. "However much I might wish it."

Caitlin went to him and held him, her arms around his waist as she watched the trees on the hillside shiver under the breath of a cold wind.

Two days passed before Caitlin felt safe enough to go to the rivenbuds. Even then she watched all around her as she walked to the glade.

The long winter was reluctant to release its hold on the world, and here and there dry grass was beginning to turn to green and yellow, and spiked trees were beginning to bud pinks and whites.

The world was beginning to bloom once more.

Caitlin knew Steen would be long gone. With the Jagers looking for him, he couldn't stay in one place too long. She remembered how she had wept when he'd told her he was joining the Jagers. He had been proud in his uniform, holding her as they looked up at the stars together. *'I'm doing this for you, for all of us,'* he'd said. *'There are things out there. Creatures. We have to defend mankind against these monsters.'*

She'd wept and beat at him with her fists.

'I'm doing this for you!' he'd shouted, holding her once more, holding her tight so she couldn't strike him. There had been tears in his own eyes then.

The rivenbud glade was a riot of colour in a grey world. It was settled in the lee of a hill, the flowers of the rivenbuds blue and white and pink and red, and the plant was twisting and winding, wrapping around itself, thick as her wrist and bright and green.

All around the glade, the world was struggling to recover from the long winter, but the rivenbuds had flourished, springing back to life as though the very presence of Steen had given them strength and sustenance.

He wouldn't be there.

He had to still be there, otherwise the rivenbuds would wither and perish.

She saw him in the distance, over the incline where the trees bent in the breeze and the grass was long. He carried a backpack, and when he saw her, he ran towards her, his strides long and sure over the uneven ground.

"Caitlin," he said. He touched her hair and stroked her cheek. He kissed her, his lips hard on hers. His body felt hard pressed against her own.

"We can't," Caitlin pulled away, her breath light in her throat. "I'm married, Steen." She looked into his eyes. "I'm old." How could he want her still, looking as she did? She almost felt as though he was mocking her with the desire she saw in his eyes.

"Cat," Steen said, his pale cheeks flushed. "Three years I've been without you, and every day I've thought only of you. Of coming back to you. Of being with you again." He kissed her again, long and slow, and Caitlin could close her eyes and smell the rivenbuds and remember a time so many years ago.

She pushed him away again. "But to desert, Steen. To desert just to find me after all this time..."

Steen smiled, his arms loose around her waist. "For you, Cat? I suppose it was for you. He looked up at the sky, white clouds smeared across the red. "You don't know what it's like out there. You don't know what it's like falling asleep and waking years later among the stars. You think about it, about how far you are away from the ones you love, from everything you know, and it's like a vice around your heart, around your lungs." His arms were tight around her waist now, the muscles taut under his shirt. "I went to see my parents," he said, his arms loosening around her waist. "I stood on the hill overlooking their farm. It looked dry and old. The windows were dark."

Could he know? Should he know? But how could she be the one to tell him? "We all missed you," she said. "Me, your parents. Everybody. We all begged you to stay, but you knew you were doing what was right. Stopping the expansion of the grunts." She remembered begging him, screaming at him. Saying she would hate Steen forever for leaving.

Steen shook his head. "You should see them Cat, the grunts. They're like nothing you could ever imagine. We call them grunts to make us hate them and fear them, but they're beautiful." He looked down at her, and his eyes were bright. "They have wings of gold and silver that shimmer under the light of two suns. You should see their eyes, Cat. And when they fly, I never knew there could be such beauty in the world," he smiled. "In any world."

Steen released her now, and turned away. "They have no concept of death or fear, or warfare. Sometimes I wonder if even time itself has any hold on them. I've seen them shiver their wings," he took a rivenbud in his hand. It was yellow. "And somehow they seem brighter, younger, more vibrant." He held the fragrant flower to his nose. "They come in their thousands, singing their songs that tear at my heart even now, and we're ordered to shoot them from the sky, slaughter them in their thousands." He let the rivenbud fall to the ground. "It's a war of extermination, Cat. How could I give up you, everything I've ever known, for such a thing?"

"But all they'd said to you, about defending mankind from the grunts..."

"Klain," Steen said. "He was the one who recruited me, lied to me. He told me the grunts would be here soon enough if we lost the war, that you'd be dead, we'd all be dead under the heel of the grunts if we did nothing." Steen shrugged and smiled, something lost in his eyes. "They do move from world to world, but there's something about them, something we could never hope to understand. They have no weapons or money, all they do is fly and sing to one another. They communicate by tilting their great wings to the light, or some other way I'm too stupid to understand." He fell silent a moment, lost in his thoughts.

Caitlin was silent also, listening to the birds rustling in the leaves about them. "They'll find you if you stay here," she finally said. "They'll be watching me. They knew our history."

"History, is that what it is?" There was a challenge in Steen's eyes as he looked deep into her own. He turned away after a moment, a wrench in Caitlin's heart as he did. "I suppose it is now, isn't it? History?" He shook his head. He looked young and strong and handsome in the sunlight filtering through the leaves. "They stole my life, stole you from me, Cat, with their lies."

What could she say? For a moment she wondered what her own life would have been like if Steen hadn't left. Where would she be now? What would she have seen on this world or others? But this was selfish, she knew. Ben had done all he could on the farm and the long winter had been hard on him too. Wouldn't he have wanted more from this life? She plucked a rivenbud and breathed in its scent, closed her eyes and breathed deeply. A cool, cleansing smell that made her think of cold breezes rolling down fragrant hills. She remembered lying here on idle summer days in Steen's arms, talking about the plans they had for their lives. She opened her eyes, touched him on the back. "How could you have left me?" she whispered.

He turned and touched her cheek with the back of his hand, looked into her eyes.

After, as they lay in each other's arms, watching the rivenbuds nod in the breeze above them, Steen turned to look at her. Caitlin fought the urge to turn away now the passion had ebbed. How could he still look at her with such love, when all the years had been so cruelly etched into her face, into her body?

"I need you to do something for me," he said. "I have to try and stop them."

She could feel Ben watching from the window as she drove the trak away. He had been quiet the past few days, something shadowed in his dark eyes. When Caitlin had told him she needed to take the trak, he had only nodded and turned away.

The trak's wheels bounced along the rutted roads, and its aged engine grumbled on the way to Gern's cafe. Steen waited for her off the road, emerging from the shadows as she pulled up. He flung his backpack into the back before climbing in next to her, his every movement smooth and sure. Had Caitlin ever been so young and lithe? She found it hard to remember such a time.

Steen touched her hand as she slipped the trak into drive.

"You don't have to do this, you know," Caitlin said. "You could move on. You have your whole life ahead of you still. You could go somewhere they would never find you."

"Is it, Cat? Is my life ahead of me? Every time I look at you, I remember what they stole from me. Every time I close my eyes I see the grunts and their brilliant wings."

The roads were better as they drove towards town, the trak rumbling every now and again as they hit the occasional hole or pile of rubble. Either side of the road were stores with neon lights bright as dusk fell, the moon above them huge and white and pitted with craters. The trak's lights bit into the gathering gloom before them, showing hunched figures hurrying from store to store, and further into town towers rose with laundry hanging on balconies.

"You know the way?" Steen said, his face hard in the shadows.

Caitlin smiled. "You think I would forget coming here with you?" And she hadn't forgotten. Steen looked no different now, but coming this way to the Jager Recruitment Centre, and remembering his enthusiasm then, his determination to do what was right, she realized that perhaps he had changed almost as much as she had.

Steen reached into the back and grabbed his bag, set it on his knee. "Pull up around the corner," he said, pointing to a store where the windows were grimy and scattered with words in garish colours.

The trak rumbled to a stop at the corner and Caitlin looked at Steen. The town was darker now, the neon lights brighter, and the lights of passing traks spread this way and that. "You aren't going to do anything stupid, are you?" she said, looking first into his eyes and then at the bag.

"Stupid?" Steen grinned and pulled a plasma gun from the backpack. The metal was dull and grey in the darkness of the trak. A pale light flitted across his face and then moved on into the town. He held up a black chip, showing it to her. "This will help me get into their systems. There'll be something there to show everybody what is happening up there. Show the worlds what men are doing to the grunts." He slipped the chip into the pocket of his jacket. He smiled, something regretful in his eyes. "I won't be long." He slipped out of the trak.

Caitlin watched him run across the road, a dark figure slipping past a flash of trak lights. The RC was a tall building with big windows. Further along the street was a holo ad that lit the encroaching night in a riot of pale blues and garish yellows.

Steen stopped, pulled something from his pocket, and worked on the door a moment before slipping into the RC. Caitlin watched the building across the road, traks flitting past, dark and hulking under the street lights. Had Steen always been like this, so sure of himself? Could she imagine him breaking into a building so easily before he'd left?

Her breath caught in her throat. A trak in the colours of the Jagers pulled up outside the RC and three men got out. The three who'd been at the farm. Klain, was it? And his two henchmen. Had they been watching her? Caitlin sunk down into her seat, her heart beating hard. Klain seemed to look straight at her, his lips peeling back over his teeth in what might have been a smile.

The three men pulled guns from holsters and entered the RC.

"No," Caitlin whispered. "No." Her heart was loud in her ears and her breath came in sharp gasps. "No," she said again, louder this time. She watched the RC. All seemed to be in darkness, the only lights those of the holo ad from further down the street, and the lights of the passing traks skimming the windows before moving on. "Shit," Caitlin whispered.

The backpack. She grabbed it from the back seat and opened it. Steen had come prepared. The backpack was full of tools. And two more plasma guns, both sleek and grey with black handles. She took one. It was heavier than it looked, and the grip moulded into her palm.

What could she do? Nothing. Her place was on the farm with Ben. She looked back to the RC. A blaze of light lit one of the upper windows from the inside. "Steen!" She jumped out of the trak, running across the road, her heart hammering in her chest. A trak blared its horn at her, and she stopped, and then ran again once it had passed.

The inside of the RC was lit with pale lights and shifting shadows. Tables and chairs were stacked and posters lined the walls showing brave men with big guns on strange worlds. All was quiet other than Caitlin's heart beating in her ears. The gun felt limp in her hand as she stepped through the room. Shouldn't there be gunfire? Shouting?

She moved on into the building. Computers hummed and watched her darkly from empty screens. She climbed winding stairs, her steps unnaturally loud.

An officer was there, at the top of the stairs, a steaming hole in his shoulder. Caitlin remembered him from the farm. One of Klain's men. Steen had killed a man. Did she even know him at all? She remembered his gentle touches and his shy smiles. The officer's eyes stared emptily at the ceiling.

Another shot, more a breath of air. The sound of falling furniture and a gasp of pain. Caitlin's breath caught in her throat and she moved on, gripping the gun.

She found them in a meeting room. A flash, and the other officer was falling back, hitting the wall hard. He slumped to the floor, face down.

Steen and Klain grappled for a gun, barging into the wall, and tables scraped as they fell away. Steen was injured now, Caitlin saw, his side bleeding, the blood dark.

Klain let go of the gun, hit him once, twice in the wound and Steen gasped and doubled over, collapsing to the floor as Klain elbowed him on the back of his neck. A kick in the ribs, and Steen spat blood onto the floor.

"Stop!" Caitlin shouted, her voice shaking as she aimed the gun.

"Mrs. Renage," Klain said, looking up and smiling. There was blood on his teeth. "Good. You can help me take him in." He spat on the floor and kicked Steen again.

"Let him go," Caitlin said. The gun in her hand shook, her vision tunnelling. Outside she could hear the rumble of the traks and music from the holo ad.

Klain looked at her and shook his head. "You've seen what he's done. You're my witness. He's broken in here and killed two of my men. He's a deserter. The Jagers are dangerous, why do you think we keep such tight control of them? Because they're dangerous!" He took a clip from his belt to fasten Steen's wrists.

"I said let him go," Caitlin said. Steen was losing colour fast. "He's bleeding out. Let him go."

"You think he's the same man you knew? You think you can go out there and not be changed by it? I've done four trips. Four! It changes a man, seeing the worlds out there, fighting for humanity. Fighting for people like you and your husband." Klain's face was streaked with sweat.

Caitlin still held the gun. "He's told me about the grunts, about what they're like, their wings and their songs. He's told me the lies you tell!" She held the gun tighter, strength coming with her anger.

"He's told you that, has he?" Klain looked down at Steen, still gasping for breath. Steen stirred on the floor, dark blood staining his chest. "And just because these things have pretty wings and pretty songs, does that mean they're not dangerous? Only dark, ugly things can be a threat to us all and our way of life? Did you know they can't die? Did know they live forever and will overrun us all unless we stop them? Did he tell you that?!"

Steen wrapped an arm around Klain's leg, pushed with his shoulder and drove Klain into a table and down to the floor. He punched the officer, once, twice, and looked up at Caitlin, his face pale. "Run!" he said, his voice weak. "Run! Get the trak."

Caitlin ran, her breath loud in her ears. She knocked a table and books scattered. She ran on, stumbled down the stairs, cracking her ankle. She shouldered the door open and burst onto the street, the holo ad still flashing madly, traks trundling down the street.

Her heart pounded as she reached her own trak, throwing the gun onto the back seat, the engine coming to life with a roar. She swung the trak around, stopping outside the RC with a screech. The engine rumbled enough for Caitlin to feel it in her stomach.

The door of the RC opened again. Steen stumbled out, his hair drenched with sweat and his arm clutched to his side. He looked both ways down the street before coming to Caitlin, climbing into the trak with an effort that made his face pale. "Drive!" he gasped. "Drive!"

Caitlin pulled out, a trak with white lights blaring behind her. She sped away, the neon lights of the town streaming either side of them.

Soon they were at the edge of town, less traffic here, and she stole a glance at Steen. His handsome face looked blue in the light, and his fair hair dark as it clung to his forehead.

"Steen?" she said, her throat tight. "Steen?"

"They're so different from us, Cat," he said, his voice barely a whisper over the rumbling of the trak. "They shimmer their wings and become young and bright again. We get no second chances, do we? How could I stay away when I knew all the time we'd already lost together? Time we can never get back."

"You'll be fine Steen, you'll be fine." Caitlin spun the trak around a sharp corner, clipping a wall and speeding on.

"They're beautiful, you know? I was separated from the Jagers once, in a field of purple flowers where the sky was green and the winds warm, and the grunts found me." He looked at her, slumped in his seat, and Caitlin could see dark dampness spreading between the fingers clasped to his side. "They found me, one of their enemies who had been slaughtering them, and they hovered above me and around me in this great spiral dance, their wings flashed colours you can't imagine, and they sang this song that made my heart soar. They were trying to communicate with me, Cat. Communicate through dance, or light, or song, something that I was too stupid to understand. They danced so close to me, shivering their wings, becoming brighter and brighter until it hurt to look at them, then they spiralled away, soaring to the suns, so young and free."

Caitlin spun the wheel and forced the trak on faster, checking the mirror to see what followed. All she saw was a dark road with shadowy traks and their streaking lights. She accelerated some more, glancing again at Steen. He was losing colour by the moment. "We need to get you to the hospital," she said, trying to keep the desperation from her voice.

Steen looked at her, hunched in his seat. "Thanks for not telling me about them, Cat. My parents. I did go into the farm and it was dark and quiet and cold. I think that's why we're so afraid of them, the grunts. They don't give in to the dark and the cold, they shiver their wings and turn away from the darkness, they're born again, young and free and bright."

A trak, travelling slowly before them, its lights red and muted, was blocking the road and Caitlin struck the wheel with her fist. "Come on!" she shouted, and veered the trak to the left and accelerated hard, speeding past. "Not far now," she said. "Not far now."

"That's what I went to the RC for," Steen said. He reached into his breast pocket and pulled out a small black chip, no larger than his thumb nail. "It's the recording from my vid-cam from that day. I knew I had to share it with you. How could I see something like that and not share it with you, Cat?" He smiled and his eyes looked faraway. "I never knew there could be such wonder in all the worlds, Cat, but all I could think of was you and how I wanted you to see it."

Caitlin could see the hospital now. A giant building with a thousand windows blinking like stars in the night. "We're there!" she cried. "We're there!"

Rivenbuds never flowered for long. The first brief flush of spring and the flowers would bloom in extravagant abandon, colours of every description, fragrant and rich, and then all too soon, the flowers would wither and fade before spring was even properly begun.

Caitlin stood alone in the glade, stooping to pick a fallen rivenbud from the ground. She held it in the palm of her hand, the vibrant colour long faded, the petals dry and delicate. She brought it to her nose; even the scent was long gone.

"I thought I would find you here." Ben stood at the entrance to the glade, reluctant to enter.

Caitlin smiled. "You really do know me, don't you?" She stopped and looked around. The colours were gone, the smells were gone and all that remained were memories and regrets.

Ben shrugged, smiled. The stubble on his chin was turning to grey. "We've been together a long time."

"They came."

"I know. I saw the trak leaving. So what happens now?"

"I don't know." Caitlin looked up at the darkening night through the canopy of leaves above. Stars were blinking into life, one by one. "I suppose people will see the vid and come to their own conclusions. Maybe some will start to study how the grunts communicate."

"And then what will be will be," Ben smiled.

"Yeah, something like that." Caitlin gently stroked the rivenbud with her thumb. "Aren't you coming in?" she said.

Ben shrugged. "This is your place. I think we should keep it that way, don't you? Somewhere for you to come on your own."

Caitlin took a breath. "Yeah, I suppose so."

"Come on, let's get you home. Lots of work to do and all that. Spring's finally here, you know."

Caitlin took one last look around before bringing the rivenbud to her lips and letting it loose. It caught on a warm breeze and the white petals scattered and fell quietly onto a carpet of green.

Another question for Mark Rookyard

Q: What's your writing schedule?

A: My writing schedule is a work in progress at the moment. I set myself the target of writing at least 1,000 words a day when I'm working on a story. To start with, that meant hurriedly writing a few words here and a few words there throughout the day before finishing off whatever words I had left to write when the family went to bed on a night. With this story, I set the alarm early (about 5 in the morning) and tried to get the words done before I went to work. That seemed to work pretty well, so I might stick with that. Finding the time is always a struggle though, and can't see that changing any time soon!

More about Mark Rookyard

This is Mark Rookyard's second story to be published in Metaphorosis, after "Tides of Reflection" in May. He is a member of Legend Fire Writing Group, which he recommends to any prospective writers.

The Bonesetter

Santiago Belluco

Nissil saw a disturbance within the mold brambles in the far distance and turned to the broad edge of her tissue-fitting terrace. Soldiers approached from the east. The narrow road they took was partially obscured by the tall mold that dominated her holdings, but Nissil counted six figures with ease. She expected the attack on her keep to be more subtle than this, and was unsure if such an obvious maneuver should be cause for relief or alarm.

Despite the looming threat, her work could not wait. The bones were already sun-primed and the strips of muscle pulsed quietly against the blasting wind, eager for attachment. It was piecemeal work, a mere six puppets to join the Peixin Count's growing estate— bent coin thrown to a kneeling beggar.

Still, it was the only commission she had received in weeks, and Nissil was eager to work with a sense of purpose again, impending attack or no. This most current threat was strangely obvious: what had begun as a handful of her constructs being sabotaged at the Sirat warfront escalated to boneset puppets being destroyed closer and closer to her keep, all for unexplained reasons. It was less like a poisoned fingernail nicking the back of her elbow and more like a spear thrown at her chest. A curious approach, but even a minor attack would cost her dearly since she had barely enough puppets to thwart an infiltration, much less enough to break a siege. Greater houses than hers had been destroyed by a confluence of smaller problems.

Just in case she needed to assist her keep's constructs in battle, Nissil placed the puppet's spherulated brain back into its holding pen. The brain was barely a proper brain at all, merely the central ganglion of a lesser crustacean, but the cerebral reagent was still too expensive for an interruption to spoil.

Nissil sat on a stool at the center of her blood-stained terrace and turned slightly to the alarm claxons on the wall, waiting. Around her, each newly cultured bone hummed with soft, green light as its etched runes drank the harsh evening winds. The slowly layered muscles soaked up the glow, each instructive pattern seeping into the vibrant tissue, giving it skill and purpose. A wide bowl of bile sat near the edge of the terrace's lip to simmer a spool of pale skin.

Nissil sensed a figure hovering behind the door on the far side of the jagged nail of a room, her servant's telltale shyness touched by unusual urgency.

"What is it, Golhan?" Nissil shouted over the blasting wind.

The door opened a crack and the diminutive woman looked out, her young face shadowed by the glyphic radiance emanating from the terrace. "I'm sorry, Reticence, so sorry, but there are Core soldiers knocking at the front gate. They asked to come in but didn't tell me why, so I didn't let them."

"Very well," Nissil replied with a sigh as she got up. "I will deal with this."

Golhan should have just rung her up from below but Nissil was not surprised at the minor incompetence. After all, the waning popularity of bonesetting had long ago cost her the position of Praxis Master, a title providing much power and deference, as well as proper servants. The proverbial trap of luxury, easy to get used to then difficult to live without.

Nissil covered the complex whorls of unattached muscle with a sheet of mimetic periostium and doused the protective cloth with additional serum. The broth would keep the unattached fibers healthy for a few extra hours. The soldiers seemed not to be poised to attack, since announcing yourself at the enemy's doorstep was generally not sound strategy. Or this was some cunning plan she did not expect? Nissil hoped for the former, in which case a lengthy delay was unlikely —perhaps she could even return to her work before the spool of activated skin spoiled. Skin was still cheap, yet it had recently become harder to find a good spinner still making the preparation. She did not look forward to spooling the lesser construct herself. The old trap of luxury again.

Golhan opened the heavy door for her and bowed back. Nissil stepped into the transitional laboratory, its opalescent equipment shimmering in tight niches on the stone wall. The servant disappeared down a side door, careful not to touch anything in the room. Even in a constructed body bearing much of the vitality of youth, Golhan still sulked and shuffled as expected of an old woman plucked from her deathbed. Nissil did not begrudge the servant her former habits, for she was loyal and somewhat diligent, her self-discipline and obedience glyphs rarely triggered anymore.

Nissil removed her plain work tunic and wiggled into a more imposing silktooth robe as she descended to meet the soldiers. The smooth fabric rustled in her wake, its decorative eyes opening and closing with each step. Such clothing felt like a frivolous waste of time and skill by artisans that could be better occupied with more practical uses, but the robe always seemed to impress the uneducated. Perhaps they were impressed by the robe's obvious cost.

A large hallway led to the compact bulwark of the keep's first gate, the hallway's alabaster floor and walls topped by a vaulted redstone ceiling. The redstone seeped into the alabaster where it was weakest, reinforcing the rock with bright crimson tendrils. Nissil thought the old style of red bleeding into white complemented her craft's visceral aesthetic rather well—an entrance like the pried open junction of bone and flesh.

Several of her remaining puppets lined each wall, most humanoid but some mantis-forms among them. Each puppet was surrounded by an interlocking exoskeleton covering large swathes of bulging muscle quietly rising with each breath. They were full warrior-puppets untainted by aesthetic compromise, a tribute to the height of bonesetting, designs that reminded her of a time when she was still learning the glyphic arts within the Core military, a mere lens-carver's daughter allowed to study the highest arts. While Master Hematolin had brought her to bonesetting, the Core had given her the skills, rigor and hope to pursue such ambitions. But the Core needed nothing of hers anymore.

Nissil retreated to the slightly elevated center of her hall, smoothed out her robe, and quietly placed her constructs on alert. She commanded one of the puppets to start working the door. Soldiers that couldn't even mask their approach were unlikely to have had the skill and subtlety to sabotage her constructs at Sirat—these soldiers could be the first incursion or a feint posing as members of the Core, not yet the flying spear.

Close inspection by skillborn visionomists at the Sirat warfront had revealed small, precise attacks burrowing into the cerebral chamber of each attacked puppet, but no more. The lack of additional evidence was disconcerting, especially since the skillborn inspectors were faculty from the visionomist academy, not untrained whelps freshly discovering their talents. The puzzle was a worthy challenge after so many years, but why attack a master receiving barely one military order per season, and who hadn't trained an apprentice in well over a decade? What could her attackers hope to gain?

When the gate finally snapped open, seven ragged soldiers lurched in, their spears unsheathed and tightly held. Their formation was sloppy and full of gaps, many soldiers looking around as if nervous and distractible. If this was an attack, it was the most underwhelming Nissil had ever witnessed.

The soldiers were a mix of human races and otherkin species characteristic of the Core's capital. They wore black Charwood plate and carried sharpened Melora-ash weapons detailed with Peixin timber and Ceftel vine, but not a stitch of boneset equipment, much to Nissil's chagrin. Among them, three hunched figures bound in frozen chains and purple cloth stumbled forward, pushed by angry spear shafts. The chains were triple-layered and the cloth pinched unusually tight against each prisoner's torso and face.

A heavily armored soldier limped forward. "Reticence, we request shelter and use of your dungeons."

The soldiers were more than just road weary; they held the hard, tight gaze of having fought and lost. Yet these were not green recruits out of their first bleeding. Old scars littered many faces and one even had grey streaks in his beard.

"Noble soldiers of our nation's Core," Nissil started in the traditional greeting, embarrassed of having thought so little of them earlier. "I am Nissil Tefari Pag, Weaver of this keep, and I welcome you to my holdings."

"Thank you, Reticence." The heavily armored leader, a Pack-Knell by her markings, bent forward in a short bow as she removed her helmet. The warrior's fanged mouth did not look like a human mouth, resembling more a shallow cut that fully encircled her grey, bald head. A grimace crow, one of the Core's most recent otherkin conquests. Quite surprising that the crows had been allowed such a quick rise within the military. Few new citizens assimilated so promptly.

"Please, have your soldiers follow my hall-bearers to your chambers." Nissil gestured to four of her puppets. "I will have a suitable medic roused from the village and brought here with utmost haste. My bearers can take your prisoners down once—"

"If it pleases your Reticence," the leader interrupted, "I'd rather see these prisoners to the dungeon immediately. The cells might need additional reinforcement."

"Esteemed soldier of the Core," Nissil replied, eyes narrowing, "My dungeons are grid obsidian grown within talons of searing poison. Multiple tessellated glyphs of holding, distance, fire and pain protect each of my thick walls. Your prisoners will be secure."

The crow watched Nissil with care, her doubt painfully clear. The otherkin should know better than to question a Reticent—as minor as her contributions were to the army, that one title was still hers, the last thread of legitimacy upholding her art among the officially recognized skills of the Core. Nevertheless, something in the soldier's bearing tempered Nissil's indignation. As she looked at the exhausted soldier, she also realized that a Pack-Knell should be leading a larger unit than this and have at least two strains of skillborn among their numbers, usually a pyrogenist and empath.

"How many did you lose?" Nissil asked, lowering her voice. A heavy pause loomed between them.

"Twelve," the crow muttered, pupils turning orange in shame. "We were sent for these deserters after a sixfold unit was lost tracking them. They attacked from the mold vines just within sight of your keep, leaping down over ten meters to strike. If I hadn't smelled them coming down, we would have lost more."

Nissil nodded and gestured to the side, where a broad hallway led to the dungeons. "I will take you to my deepest cells myself."

"I also carry a missive for you, Reticence," the crow said, as if remembering an issue of no real importance. She reached into her pack and drew out a black-paper scroll. Nissil gasped at the sight. A military communiqué from the Core army bursary itself.

The crow continued speaking but Nissil didn't listen as she took the scroll and opened it with shaking hands. It was a simple form, the words "cessation" and "de-recognized" sharp against the page. Her art was listed as officially obsolete, all chances for future military contracts gone. Bonesetting was dead.

Nissil thought of her master, the great Hematolin Tefari Yidyll, and his cruel teachings, how at his deathbed many years ago he had rambled about the greatness Nissil would bring to the art, his dreams becoming wilder and more deranged as his mind faded. It had been painful to watch as his boneset body failed to keep him from falling apart. When he first started to fade, Hematolin's body was almost a mirror to her own, bodies they built together with care bordering on obsession, and she had failed him, him and all the countless artisans and masters that for centuries had built up her art. Her keep would become a shadow of its former glory, yet another half-abandoned remnant of faded power. No further attack was needed; she was already broken.

Yet there were still soldiers standing before her, the grimace crow even looking at her in concern, and that would not do. Nissil collected herself and turned, gesturing for the soldiers to follow. One last service to the Core, and she would at least carry it out with dignity.

Steps of blue stone led into the depths of her mountain, the stairwell narrowing as it descended, forcing the soldiers into single file. Nissil ignored the many doorways leading to the more conventional holding cells, all empty except for the few exotic specimens she could still afford to purchase for study. With barely a glance, she opened one of her more advanced constructs, a pale white door set flush into the wall, the only mark on its surface an inscription in a dead language reading 'you cannot enter, you cannot leave'. Nissil calculated that without maintenance, her lesser boneset puppets would last for decades and her final door at least a pair of centuries, but it would all inevitably fall into disrepair and fade away, living bone turned to brittle fossil, then dust.

An apparent eternity later, Nissil led the soldiers to the jagged stone opening at the bottom of the stairs. Beyond was an outcropping of rock suspended over a yawning chasm, five tenuous pathways jutting out from the outcropping, each holding at its end the stone bolus of a cell. A thick current of pale liquid sputtered from the high ceiling to encase each of the cells before cascading into the unseen depth below: the final layer of protection against the highest bonesetting art and the attacks of every known skillborn strain, a kiss from the frozen blood of the earth itself, an ancient death that spoke in geological absolutes. This at least would survive for as long as the churning mantle of the earth still flowed.

Nissil parted the molten ice with an elaborate glyph etched into her only ring and the first cell slid open. Its inner walls glistened with a thousand eager blades, each slick edge reaching out with the subtle thirst of sentience. One of her greatest, cruelest constructs, and she was glad to have one last chance to use it.

The first prisoner was still dazed by the cloth's glyphs when his restraints were removed and so was easily corralled into the cell. The second, a large, strongly built woman, tried to struggle with slow punches but a solid push threw her into her cell. The blades to either side of the opening almost reached her as she stumbled in.

The last prisoner smiled as his cloak slid off. He stepped into the third cell on his own volition, turning just beyond the reach of the closing knifes to look back at Nissil. He was filthy and badly bruised, but carried himself with confidence, even poise.

"I have a secret for you," he whispered before the cell sealed shut and the iceflow reclaimed the lonely rock. The crow ignored the man, or perhaps did not hear him.

"How did your prisoners resist the effects of a submission cloak?" Nissil asked the Pack-Knell as they began the climb back up, her curiosity tugging against her grief.

"I don't know, but that's the least of their surprises, especially that last one. I'm glad to see them under your blades. I need to contact my Core superiors. May I use one of your runners?"

"Of course," Nissil replied, half-listening, thinking of the prisoners instead, the broad outline of a plan slowly forming in her mind.

Upon reaching the upper steps, Nissil sent off the required runner and saw that the soldiers were suitably housed. Then she gathered a large contingent of her best puppet-warriors and started back down the steps to her lowest prison. Tampering with a Core prisoner was an unforgivable offense and punishable by complete asset seizure. Military prisoners were an even more serious affair, intervention being punished by death. Still the risk was worthwhile.

Centuries had passed since the last discovery of a new strain of skillborn, human or otherkin. Finding a new one could prove to be a career-making find, revolutionary, even. And here were three samples of what looked very much like a new skillborn strain, delivered right to her doorstep. If she was right, her punishment would be deferred.

Maybe. As she crossed the threshold of her white door again, its wide, flowing script seemed to leer at her.

Nissil matched the third prisoner's smile as she reopened his cage. He was standing exactly where she had left him, as if expecting her return. While the Core soldiers were most likely not behind the attacks on her constructs, perhaps these prisoners could have been. The timing of their appearance was consistent, as could be their skill, if the Pack-knell's account was to be trusted. Yet why would renegade soldiers want to attack her? And why goad her now that their attack had been thwarted by capture? Nissil would ordinarily have reveled in the delicious puzzle, savoring its many angles with proper contemplation, but too much was at stake, and she needed to act now.

"So what is your secret?" she asked.

"My secrets are my own," The man replied with deliberate stillness. His skin was smooth beneath the grime of battle, too young for the threat he exuded. "But I have something else for you, buried in my flesh, waiting to be dug out."

"My thoughts exactly." With a twist of her wrist and precise command bends from her fingers, Nissil ordered her puppets to clasp the man and carry him upwards, past the jail cells, past the abandoned feast halls leading to decrepit dancing parlors, past the long-empty family quarters and dusty viewing rooms devoid of artwork.

They slowed down at the top levels of the Keep, turning to the rooms Nissil set aside for surgery and study. She guided her puppets to her central spherulation chamber. The room's walls, floor and ceiling were whitened with mortared chalk and a thin layer of translucent nacre that radiated a soft antiseptic glow. The nacre was worn down every time the room was activated, so using it for mere exploratory surgery was beyond wasteful, especially since Nissil couldn't afford the cost of reseeding it. If she was right, however, a new skillborn strain would require her most refined tools to properly characterize.

Nissil commanded her puppets to strap the prisoner to the dissection apparatus at the room's center as she rearranged her tools and tinctures on the slender tables around her, suspending the heavier saws on thick hooks hanging from the ceiling.

The prisoner smirked as she pierced his arm with an anaesthetic barb. "I'd rather be awake for this, if you don't mind."

She waited for the anaesthetic to take effect nonetheless, yet he didn't doze off. An extra dose, and still he kept staring at her, unblinking. After a few minutes she decided to ignore his peculiar resistance to anesthesia, hoping the barb's local numbing agents would suffice.

Nissil began with a small and reversible intervention, not wishing to spoil her specimen too quickly. The right forearm opened neatly in response to her wood-tipped scalpel, barely any blood flowing; vessels and arteries sealed just as they were severed. Nissil's excitement mounted with the observation. Even the ability to halt bleeding alone would be quite useful when replicated. The prisoner looked down at her work as if deigning to show polite interest.

She pulled the skin aside to reveal the muscle beneath. She paused at the unexpected tangle of damage. Irreversible fatigue permeated each fiber, cells burst and ligaments inflamed. This was not mere battle-damage; no cut or bash could cause such thorough hyperextension. It was more like the work of a flesh-consuming disease than anything else.

She delved in with care, her finest forceps and pliers dancing among the morass, searching for some thread of logic connecting the skillborn's extraordinary properties with the mess it had made of the body. Such tissue damage would severely limit the usefulness of this strain of skillborn and render it but a curiosity, not a trait suitable for the prolonged rigors of Core service, military or otherwise. Nissil clenched her teeth at the thought of her dangerous gamble not paying off.

Her hands almost shook as she cut a large swatch of swollen muscle and noticed small purple filaments infiltrating the tissue. She overlooked them at first, mistaking them for displaced nerve fibers or necrotic blood vessels. Yet they seemed to carry no blood and conducted no electrical impulse.

"Ah," her specimen beamed, "you're finally getting to it."

Nissil straightened up from the partially dissected arm to look at him. This was not a novel strain of skillborn human.

"What is your name?"

"Really?" he replied, taken aback. "That is what you choose to ask? Such an irrelevant detail."

"I did not mean the name of the soldier you control. I want *your* name, parasite."

"Ah, yes," he cooed, relaxing into his shackles. "We have no name in your voice language, we speak to each other in scent. Much of our nature is very different from your own. I came here to show it to you, to make you an offer."

Nissil idly thought of some of the parasitic species she studied, many first-hand: The worm that burrowed into the human male penis to induce hypersexuality and thus spread its progeny to the man's sexual partners, the mold which could live undetected for years under the carapace of Core transport crabs, the small birds that would charge headlong into a Yllian panther's mouth to lay eggs in its stomach. Nissil suddenly felt like the panther, so smug at getting a meal so easily, so unaware that many months later her gut would burst open when the bird's hatchlings started to peck their way out.

"Is that so?" Nissil sat back, ready to listen since the parasite seemed so eager to speak, hoping it would reveal how thoroughly their infection had spread among the Core. This attack could be targeting more than just her own keep. A disappointment, since this find would likely stay her execution but would bring her no real glory or riches. "Why are you so confident that I will listen to you and not immediately report your existence to the military?"

"Because even at the growing edge of the Core I have heard of bonesetting's diminishing prestige, how your family in particular is but a shadow of what it once was. You of all people should be interested in what I have to say, an offer that will benefit us both."

"What do you have in mind?"

"We have lived for longer than memory allows within the hornets of the Sirat plains. We have adapted to each other, they specializing in strength, we in guile. Yet now your people capture the hornets to subjugate them into mere mounts. Thus our skills lie fallow, our children dull from the constrictions you inflict upon our hosts."

"So you have attempted to infect humans instead."

"Yes. But the transition has been difficult and it is now obvious it will take many generations for our kind to adapt to yours, to merge as seamlessly as we have with the hornets."

"Before which, your kind will surely be discovered. Then eradicated." Nissil always found it strange how easy it was to prod people into talking more about themselves, often to their detriment. It seemed like this creature was no different. Parasitic infection was often covert, relative to other diseases, but slow to spread, so this parasite should not be much of an issue to the Core. Yet the parasite should know that as well, so why the confidence? Nissil remembered the Yllian panther again.

"Your kind is clever," the parasite said, "your brains hideously complex. Indeed it is unlikely we will ever control you as well as we can the hornets. It would always be a battle between us."

"Looks like you did just fine with this one."

"No, this is where much of the damage came from, his defiance. We can control your tissue so much better than your instincts drive you to, yet you still fight back. It is exhausting and very unpleasant."

"I am yet to see why you would tell me all this. It makes me no more likely to help you."

"I want you to build us a body."

Nissil's eyes widened at the elegance of the idea. Of course. A parasite so efficient at host manipulation could very well complement the inherent inflexibility of bonesetting. She would no longer need a complex array of instructional glyphs or even a spherulated brain tethered to glyphic restraints; her craft's greatest weakness would be simply brushed aside.

"I see," she replied, regaining her composure. "I presume you saw a few puppets at the Sirat border and thought those would be easier to control, perhaps even tried to infect a few, but were unsuccessful. Is that so?"

"Yes, as many spores as we saturated the puppets with, we could not take root, no matter the number of constructs we destroyed trying to infect, even striking right to their brain. But I think this can be altered. Together, both our peoples can be great again, with you and your fellow bonesetters at the helm."

Nissil was distracted by imagining the simpler, more powerful glyphs long thought to be too difficult to control, then wondered if these parasites would have any difficulty integrating with spherulation tissue, since most parasites could not easily infect unfamiliar hosts. This central issue would have to be one of her first tests.

With a snap, Nissil understood what the parasite was really proposing; that she should conquer the Core with his people at her side. For a brief moment the option seems glorious beyond imagining, a height she never expected to reach and thus all the sweeter. But that would mean she should give these creatures the means to subjugate her entire civilization. A ludicrous, insane risk. No, this exchange would be on her terms. The Core's terms.

"I think you are mistaken about the details of how my constructs operate, parasite. If you become a puppet, I can impress anything upon you, from taboo actions or thoughts to abstract concepts such as courage or obedience. Few volunteer for such a fate, even among the desperate. Do you truly want such a body?"

"Certainly not." The parasite's avatar smiled, too broadly this time, his eyes pinching with unnatural curvature, "I was just stalling. This room is now saturated with my spores. My brethren and I have been saving them for months to use on you, and now my sacks are emptied. I thought all was lost when we were captured, but here we are, and my strongest, fastest children are now coursing through your veins. You should be feeling the paralysis any moment now, and when you move again you will build an army as one of us."

Nissil tightened her jaw in a flash of panic. Her precious body had been tainted, perhaps corrupted beyond repair. Suddenly she wanted to peel off her skin with her sharp nails, rub and tear the contamination away. But then she took a deep breath and sat perfectly still, relaxing her body, turning the full scope of her attention to herself. This was a battle now, a time for calm and precision.

She checked each of her body's systems, first the blood, then lymphatic fluid, then each organ in turn, ending in her spherulated brain. At the brain her touch lingered, Hematolin's presence heavy on the multifold, winding glyphs of its spherulation casing. She detected nothing except additional microscopic debris on the filters of her nostrils and the back of her mouth. That her body hadn't warned her of danger could mean that it was too subtle for her art to find. From a distant part of her mind she realized that if infection was this covert and rapid then the parasites were a greater threat than she could have imagined, likely the greatest threat to the Core in over a century.

Nissil turned a large lever next to her station and ventilation glyphs in the ceiling started to drive the room's tainted air to an incinerator and pump in filtered air from beyond the keep. Nissil then lay on the floor and touched her left wrist, with a turn and release activating the glyph to heat her bones and muscle, sensitizing her immune system and hopefully cooking any of the offending spores. The strong air current howled as the soldier laughed, Nissil growing dizzy with induced fever.

What felt like hours passed as Nissil grappled with the pain and disorientation, but she knew her brain was protected from the worst effects of the unnaturally high temperature by her spherulation casing. Then she drew the temperature even higher, daring to spike it almost high enough to boil water. Finally the glyph on her wrist indicated that any further temperature shock would likely harm her brain, so she let her body cool down.

She opened her eyes and saw the soldier thrashing desperately against the restraints, his intact arm almost free. Nissil took his alarm as some confirmation that his infection was thwarted, his spores heat-inactivated. She turned back to herself and found that the debris on her throat's filter was still intact, not as touched by the heat she had inflicted upon her body. She struggled to reach her lowest table, her legs weak, and picked up a sample containment sac. She carefully spat out her filter, the retching motion a relief, as if her body knew it was expelling something vile. The filter fell into the sac and she closed it with a tight snap. The sac was revolting to hold, and she wanted to throw it as far away from herself as possible. The soldier stopped struggling and looked at the container in her hand.

"Well played, parasite," Nissil admitted. "However, your plan did not succeed. I exchanged my body for a boneset construct many years ago. Self-spherulation into a modified human body is the secret pinnacle of bonesetting, which master Hematolin and I developed well within the peak of our skill. Few people know of it and even fewer care anymore, so I am unsurprised you failed to discover this while devising your ultimately flawed strategy."

The soldier's face was frozen into a neutral, empty stare. Nissil looked at her filter, her disgust overwhelmed by the realization that she likely held the most powerful weapon in the Core. With those few remaining spores she could begin building new boneset constructs with the young parasites right away, marshalling her newfound strength in secret for a triumphant return of bonesetting. More than that, this might indeed be enough to conquer the Core under the yoke of her skill. Yet in that time the parasite would run rampant among her people, likely causing untold devastation.

Old Hematolin would have reveled in such a situation, a weakened Core being a further chance to empower the art. Not for the first time Nissil missed the desperate fervor of their years working together, first as teacher and apprentice, then as equals. Perhaps the original bone-weavers had faced similarly split allegiances when they were assimilated into the Core. Nissil wondered if the Core felt parasitic to the people they conquered, a violation—any chances to rise within the Core but a shift from being the panther to being the bird.

Nissil activated a communication glyph at her desk. "Golhan, fetch the Pack-Knell, have her meet me at the anteroom to the spherulation chamber."

"Yes, Reticent," the servant replied through the glyph.

The parasite looked up at her, his face thick with panic. "Wait! Don't report me to the Core just yet, they will kill us all. We will live on as your slaves, tie us to your glyphs if you must, but don't do this!"

Nissil smiled as she sat down onto her stool, her boneset body slowly recovering from the temperature shock. "Tempting, but I decline your offer. These spores will be sent out to the visionomist academy so they may come to understand how your kind spread, and develop a countermeasure."

The parasite looked down, and for a moment he seemed very much like a regular young boy starting his service to the Core. Nissil wondered if this was a tactic by the parasite to garner sympathy or an involuntary slip in its control, the young soldier briefly allowed to exist again within his ruined body.

"What will become of me?" the parasite asked, his face tight again.

"I will explain the situation to the Pack-Knell in full and suggest that she take the other prisoners to the academy and leave you here. This is a military matter, and thus the decision will be hers." Nissil hoped that the Pack-Knell would indeed grant her a stay in execution and even allow her to continue experimenting on the parasite. Perhaps she could find an easy means of detecting the infection, to help stop the parasite's spread as soon as possible. More than that, however, she hoped the parasites would be properly subjugated instead of exterminated; their unique nature could add much to the Core.

The soldier resumed his senseless thrashing, yelling and spitting. Nissil tightened his restraints and left the room, careful to sterilize herself first. The Pack-Knell was already waiting outside, fully armored and weapon in hand. Nissil knew her chances of avoiding execution were now slim and rested entirely on the judgment of the newly elevated grimace crow. Yet she was glad, for even if bonesetting died with her, the Core would live on, unencumbered by the frail bones of an old art but dense with living, flowing tissue, powerful and cunning.

It came from Santiago Belluco

Most of my stories start out with a scientific concept that I feel is not often explored in speculative fiction, or at least not in the way I would like to read. "The Bonesetter" began in this way, from the idea of how divergent biological strategies can arise in the face of conflict, one being the establishment of an adversarial, predator-prey relationship, another being the development of parasitism or different flavors of symbiosis. However, the story only really came to life when I paired that central theme with a character that is on the losing end of an adversarial conflict, namely the conflict between her craft's use of living tissue with the increasingly dominant use of wood. This was the basis for Nissil, a very skilled scientist who is nevertheless well beyond the peak of her skill's popularity. Thus she not only has much to lose but also a strong drive to regain what she once had. Creating a world for Nissil to inhabit that would accentuate her conflict was a pleasure to develop. One of the ways I like to world-build is by imagining our world and not only adding features to it (i.e. magic), but also removing certain aspects of it that we take for granted. This forces me to think of ways technology and society would develop around that limitation. For "The Bonesetter", the limitation was that the world is without rich sources of metal, thus modified bone and wood are the best one can do for weaponry and tools. Of course, since magic is also prevalent in this world, the combination of magic with wood and bone was obvious, and allowed Nissil's civilization to become powerful and developed. As the story was being developed, these elements became inexorably linked to such an extent that looking back at earlier drafts, it's hard for me to deconstruct which of these early ideas were most foundational to the finished story.

A question for Santiago Belluco

Q: Do you write things other than speculative fiction?
A: I have written and published scientific articles on my neuroscience research.

About Santiago Belluco

Santiago is a neuroscientist born and raised in Brazil before moving to America to get the usual degrees needed to become a real scientist (namely a funded one). He now lives and works in Switzerland, where he writes speculative fiction and studies the neurocircuitry of vision.

So, You're In an Alternate Universe

Jeremy Packert Burke

So, you're in an alternate universe. It doesn't feel alternate. Your mom is still your mom, who smells like fennel, with red-rubbed knuckles. Your dad still has his large tie collection: his wooden tie, his *Yellow Submarine* tie, his tie that looks like a large fish.

Hitler was still Hitler, and Stalin, Stalin. The sun outside is very yellow—is it too yellow? Is that the difference?

The scar on your knee is still there. Eileen Fulbright dared you to cross the lake when it was iced over and you were both eleven. She stood on the opposite bank and dared you, double dared you, to come kiss her, and when you fell through, the water came up only to your waist, but the sharp hole in the ice cut open your knee, sliced through your jeans, and you had to suffer through seven stitches and an hour-long lecture from your fennel-smelling mother, your fish-tied dad.

Would this have happened in another universe? Would it have gone further? Would the cut have gotten infected and you lost your leg, gotten a prosthesis, won a medal, and/or told an inspiring story in a Vitamin Water commercial? You want to ask Dylan but you don't. Now doesn't seem like the right time.

Dylan is from the *real* universe. It's not alternate, not like your universe. This is what he's told you just now, although you've known him for years.

He says "There *was* another me here."

"...Did you kill him?"

He says "No."

He says "It's complicated."

"Is there another me there?" you ask.

"Yes," he says. You have a hundred thousand questions. "I have to get back there," he says.

You've spent long hours in Dylan's attic bedroom, hundreds of hours over the years, shooting CGI aliens and chugging energy drinks and having gum-chewing contests. His mom always made the best pumpkin pancakes. His dad has been gone for a while.

Dylan's always been honest with you. Told you when you look like shit or do something dumb, but also when something you said was really funny or when you totally nailed "Reptilia" on Guitar Hero.

But he's also had a weird imagination. He used to tell you stories about escaping his body at night and traveling around the town watching people live and sleep and fight. That was when you were both seven; you're not sure what his imagination is capable of now.

So you're lost. You look at this other, same Dylan, this complicated, this real Dylan, and you wonder. You're both fourteen now. Surely you're past fairytales.

"How did you get to *this* universe?"

You think: Deloreans, black holes, wormholes. "My dad built a portal," he says.

"Like in *The Transcendent Mr. Kellogg*?" you ask. *TTMK* is your favorite show, and Dylan's. The dimension-hopping Mr. Kellogg, his daughter Phillipa, and their talking cat Poppo travel around the multiverse solving crimes and getting into trouble. Dylan's story is starting to sound more like a game. "Do they have *TTMK* in, uh, the real universe?"

"Of course," he says. "It's not exactly like that, though, more to do with probability distributions, quantum entanglement, order theory. That's why there's still only the one Dylan here. I told you it was complicated."

You're still stuck: do you keep asking your nine hundred ninety-nine thousand, nine hundred ninety-nine questions, see what this Dylan does or does not know, see if you can catch him in a lie? Or, if Dylan is just fucking with you, do you give up; if you ask questions it'll make it seem like you believe him, leading to endless teasing when he reveals that he is, in fact, fucking with you.

"Do you want to play *Centaurus*?" you ask, hoping to change the subject to CGI aliens and their untimely deaths.

"I can't," Dylan says. "I have to work."

You nod, trying hard to keep your expression skeptical and sympathetic. As you stand, you trail your fingers against the rough stucco wall of his room, and as the sandpapery bumps scrape off skin cells, you wonder what it means if none of this is real.

On the bike ride home, you text Eileen: *Dylan's being weird. You know anything that might be up?*

Your phone chirrups and you brake, check it. *Weird how??*

Long story, you type, *tell you when I see you.* An excuse to talk to Eileen one-on-one is never a bad thing, even if the circumstances are odd.

There are suggestions, omens perhaps, that Dylan might not be full of shit. Once you start looking for them, omens are everywhere, of course: the way someone ties their shoelaces, their choice of soda at the vending machine, the way they look at the silver-gray sky in the morning. But these seem meaningful, genuinely meaningful: he's suddenly answering questions in class over and over again, almost answering too many, actually, like the kids who know too well how smart they are, questions about *King Lear* and Edward Lear and Edward Teach and "suum cuique"—they go on. He solves system of equations, titrates hydrochloric acid in fifteen seconds flat, and runs, actually runs instead of walking with you, around the track in gym. He's a possessed, a genetically engineered, alien version of himself.

Or maybe he's just coming into his own. God knows all of the metaphors of change—Ugly Duckling, caterpillar to butterfly, blossoming flower—have sunk in by now, by fourteen.

It's probably nothing, you think.

But you're not the only one who notices. You catch the befuddled looks of the math teacher, the English teacher, the lunch lady whom Dylan treats with exceptional politeness. "You takin' Ritalin or what?" asks Victor Dolphy, another ignorable kid who sits with you both at lunch, usually. Dylan just shrugs. "Maybe I'm just coming into myself," he says, and looks at you, like he read your fucking mind.

Victor asks you guys if you're going to the dance, if you're taking anyone. Dylan looks puzzled, like he's trying to remember a lie he told a long time ago. You say "Yeah," and try to subtly look around the cafeteria at all the bobbling, babbling, hungry heads, hoping—in vain—to catch Eileen's eye. You don't see her; she doesn't even have lunch this period.

"You taking anyone?" Victor asks.

"We'll see. You?"

"I dunno, man," he says. "Maybe Monika." You gnaw at your cardboard pizza slice and wonder if school lunch is better in the real universe.

After school you and Dylan bike together, bathed in burnt yellow light, wind flapping through your jacket. "The sun sets sooner here," Dylan says into the wind, scowling like he's trying to answer a question he's never thought of before.

"Yeah," you say, as if you knew. You both stop your bikes at the top of the hill, looking out over smaller, rolling gold-green hills, the park below with elementary schoolers playing soccer, the edge of a gas station. Dylan presses a piece of paper, folded into a square fat bullet, into your hand. "Can you ask your dad to get these books from the university library?" he asks.

You unfold the list. It's long, populated with titles like *Advanced Bayesian Statistics* and *Time Travel in Einstein's Universe*. "Ye-e-es," you say.

"Thanks, Mark, I really appreciate it," Dylan says. He looks at you like you're a kid, or an actor in the world's least scary haunted house, or a person in someone else's dream. He touches your shoulder and with a whoop and holler he's off, down the hill, the wheels of his bike snicker-snacking as they turn and turn and turn and turn.

You stay mounted on your bike, holding yourself with one foot on the ground, one on the pedals. You learned to ride a bike later than everyone else. You were eleven. Dylan helped you, so he'd have someone to ride with.

Didn't see you at school today, you text Eileen. *Things ok?*

Late night, she texts back. *Long story. Dylan?*

Still weird.

After school tomorrow? McD's?

Yeah, for sure

You pocket the phone and push off with your grounded foot, rolling slowly until gravity and angular momentum take over so that you move irresistibly forward, down, the world blisteringly blurring by until the same physics that aided your flight resist it, slow you down with wind and hills and friction and, now graceless, you push your way slowly back up towards home.

Eileen, Dylan, and you meet up in the student parking lot. You notice the shadows under her eyes, her coral-pink nails, the way the light and wind catch at strands of her dark hair. She once had a crush on you, too, but she grew out of it. The day on the ice is a hundred years behind. You knock the left pedal of your bike ratcheting backwards so it's in position to take off, but you just stand there, waiting. Eileen is still freeing her bike, swiveling the U-shaped lock out and back into place, her fingernails like small and quick animals. The McDonald's across from the high school has been your triumvirate's hang out spot since the year began; you can get a cup for iced tea for a dollar but fill it with Dr Pepper or Mountain Dew, can sit around the corner from the counter so that no employee can keep track of how long you've been there, won't shoo you out prematurely. You all started hanging out there when it was too cold to bike home, and Eileen had to wait for her dad to get off work and come get her. Her parents were still in the midst of a divorce, and her dad had moved to the outside of town; it was messy.

You kept going when the weather got warm, though. It had its own kind of physics. Eileen pulls up her bike and looks at you, looks at Dylan, like *should I invite him or-r-r?*

"Well, I'll see you guys later," Dylan says, staring anxiously at the western horizon like he can see light slipping away. "I've got a bunch of stuff I need to take care of."

"You?" Eileen asks, surprised in spite of your warnings. None of you three have ever had homework that couldn't be put off, chores that you couldn't skip out on, have never had to stay at home instead of playing frisbee by the train tracks, or making pizza, or biking around town.

"Me," says Dylan. He salutes and rolls away.

"So what's the deal?" Eileen asks at the McDonald's. You guys split an order of fries and a thirty-two ounce cup of half Pepsi, half Dr Pepper. Eileen scoops up the viscous, sunset-red ketchup perfectly. You rehearse the ten words you've been meaning to ask for three months.

"Well, maybe it's just freshman year stuff," you say lamely. "Like, a lot changes?"

"Right but it's almost April."

Do you want to go to the dance do you want to go do you want to dance do you want to go to the dance with me do "So, bearing that in mind, and I totally am not saying I believe him, but ..."

Eileen's forehead furrows, broken golden bleeding fry halfway to her mouth. "Well spit it out, dude."

"He says that, uh, that this is an alternate universe."

"Alternate to *what*?"

"The, uh, real universe I guess. His universe."

"Sounds pretty subjective to me."

"Well..."

"So wait, is this like *The Transcendent Mr. Kellogg*? Does he have to get back to keep our universes from colliding and creating a dark energy vortex?"

"No," you say. "I mean it's sort of like *TTMK* but not exactly. Or... I don't know. Maybe. It's complicated."

"What's wrong with our universe?"

"I don't know. He said the sun sets sooner here?"

"What a whackadoo," she says, and chomps down on her fry. "I like it here." She smiles and wipes ketchup away from her mouth. "Remember in first grade when he tried to convince us about that astral projection shit?"

You laugh half-heartedly. "Yeah, that was dumb."

"Or sixth grade when he tried to get us to believe he was psionic?"

"You're saying there's a precedent."

"I'm saying Dylan read a lot of Stephen King books at too young an age and I think sometimes, you know...he gets caught up in the fantasy."

The assonance of the unasked question runs through you like a wire: *do, you, to, to.*

"And so he plays at universe exceptionalist and wants to suck us into it."

It would be so easy to speak it, to just say the words.

"But why?" you say. Because that's the real thing—why would anyone pretend at this? "Do you think he's okay?"

She called to you from the opposite shore, the perfect identical snowflakes peppering the white-gray slate of the lake, clumps falling off the trees, Eileen's red mittens cupping her mouth like a beacon, a traffic light, a megaphone.

"Yeah," she says, assertive. "Of course he's okay. He's just being a dick."

It was so easy to *act* then. And you can feel how easy it would be to do now. But you recall the roller coaster feeling in your stomach when you heard the guncrack snap of the ice, the cold, the sharp stab against your shin, your ruined jeans. And so you plug your mouth with half Pepsi, half Dr Pepper.

Outside, the goldshot sky wanders towards dark, shadows of lightposts creeping towards the McDonalds across the blacktop.

Eileen looks like she's about to say something, then is silent.

"Do you want to watch *TTMK*?" you ask.

And so you sit in your living room, with her, a bowl of popcorn, and your mother. You and she sit at opposite ends of the couch, watching Phillipa and Mr. Kellogg save Poppo from the Fallacious Jergin, Mr. Kellogg's world-hopping nemesis, who has caught Poppo in a timeless jar made from glass spiderwebs.

In *TTMK*'s multiverse, falling out of time is the worst thing that can happen to you. You might come back to the space-time continuum to discover that a million years have passed and everything you love has been consumed by the sun; or, you might stay trapped, floating in quiet black limbo for millennia, watchful, unaging, slowly going insane, until you reemerge a shattered and empty husk. "There's no time—or space!—to lose!" cries Mr. Kellogg. "Pip, pip!"

"Did you get the books?" Dylan asks. He shifts his black backpack across his shoulders, and something inside goes *clank.*

"Yeah," you say, shifting your own. You can feel the weight of knowledge these new, exotic books contain. It's almost pornographic, the way they draw this heavy anticipation from Dylan, this hunger. "My dad said 'Going through a phase, huh?' and laughed when he handed them to me."

"You know, some kids get into metal, some kids get into drugs, and some kids get into particle physics," Dylan says and cracks a grin.

It's the first time he's sounded like himself. Or like the fake Dylan. Whichever. "Thanks for getting them," he says, taking the books and hiding them in his clanking backpack, his own timeless jar. "Back home my dad had these, or books like them. Analogs, I guess."

That word: *dad*. Like a mourning bird call, falling steeply at the end, disappearing too quickly like the sun. "What were you doing, Dylan?" you ask before you lose your nerve. "Why come here? And why didn't he?"

He shifts his backpack again, pulling the loose strap over his other shoulder, pulling down on the tabs so it sits firmly against his back, to prevent spinal damage. The clanking, thumping weight of it is too much for a single shoulder. Quietly, then: "We were trying to get Mom back." Dylan's mom—tall, witchy, baker of pumpkin pancakes, who took you all to see Metallica last year, who lent you DVDs of every good 80s horror movie, who buys you sweaters at Christmas. "Was it MS," you say, "for her too?"

Dylan shakes his head at the alternate Earth.

"So why…"

"I came through first," he says, "but Dad couldn't. Because he wasn't in this universe, or something. He would know," Dylan says, "if he were here."

"I have to get back," he says, hiding his face until gravity does its work and the few silent tears slide away, lost against the ground.

Dylan is not in school for several days. This seems to calm the teachers, to fit with their expectations of the universe. You wonder if there's a different Dylan, your Dylan, in some other school, disappointing math and chemistry teachers all of a sudden. They'd take him aside, ask him if everything was okay at home, give him all the time he needed. Who knows what he'd think.

Unless the Real Dylan just wiped him from the face of reality entirely.

You *have* started to think of him as the Real Dylan, in spite of yourself.

With Dylan out and Eileen in a different lunch, you're resigned to sitting alone, or sitting with Victor Dolphy which is functionally the same. You Xeroxed a bunch of pages—introductions mostly—to those books before giving them to Dylan, and you try reading them over your cardboard pizza. Conditional probability, superstrings, entanglement, gravitational waves, Einstein-Rosen bridges. Nothing that makes sense to you.

You bike to his house after school and his mom lets you in. You nearly cry with relief that she's there—terrified, somehow, that you would have slipped into Real Dylan's reality overnight, in some Edward Bellamy-esque transdimensional slumber party.

"How are you doing, D-Deirdre?" you ask her. Seven years of friendship with Dylan and her request to be called by her first name still feels weird. She's an anesthesiologist—gets out all her stress baking and doing krav maga—and this role as arbiter of sleep and pain fills you with so much awe you don't know what to call her.

"Good!" she says. "I haven't seen you around here for a while. Everything okay at school?"

You nod. "Dylan's just upstairs," she says. "He's been spending so much time...anyway, make sure you come find me before you go, I have some brownies for you to take to your parents."

She met Dylan's dad when he was a patient, a long time before he got seriously sick, but she's only told you that story once.

Upstairs, Dylan is weaving what looks like a large, adamantine dreamcatcher around one of those hoops colonial children chased down hills. He's unspooling a fat wooden knob of wire across, hooking around the blonde wood, across again, a set of heptagons whose edges and intersections trace the outlines of a massive and sawlike star. Loop, pull, loop, pull. Like some kind of pagan weaving. The wire unspools whispery metallurgical secrets into itself.

Dylan looks up, keeps unspooling. "What," you say. Not even a question, not even a sentence.

"Is this?" Dylan finishes. He has a lime green book open on his lap, held with an elbow while his hands keep winding. Carefully, slowly.

"Is it...a portal?" you ask. Apparently you have decided to believe, or pretend to believe, Dylan's story. You're not sure when that happened. Dylan laughs the way Mr. Kellogg does whenever Poppo asks a silly, feline question.

"No," he says. "It's a dowsing ring."

"Gonna find some water? Dig yourself a well?" You smile to hide your confusion.

"Not that kind of dowsing. Think in more dimensions. Holes between them, kind of like wells." He finishes wrapping the wire and cuts it off, leaving a shining, lethal tip poking from the rim. He grabs a pair of grimy, yellow-handled needle nose pliers and bends it down, burying the point in the wire net. "Maybe a compass is a better analogy."

"That's only in two dimensions, though."

"Nothing's perfect"

He swings the hoop under his arm as he stands. It bumps against his shin as he crosses the room, counting unknown units of time, or space. Dylan goes downstairs and you follow, although he doesn't invite you.

The day is graying, off-white clouds swimming over the blue swaths of sky like a school of bored fish. The grass and trees slouch backward and forward in the wind.

"Where did you even get that hoop? Did you fucking steal it from Thomas Jefferson's house?"

But Dylan doesn't answer. He holds the hoop parallel to the ground. With a piece of metal that looks like the handle of cheap silverware, he plucks the wire closest to his where he holds it. His right hand strains with the force of holding the hoop, the many feet of wire, aloft, his left hand suspended over it like a vulture, like a satellite. His left hand descends, feels along the rim, palm tracing the curve, the change, the smooth grain of wood, reaching further and further from himself along its circumference, feeling at tiny, tiny reverberations in the wire and wood. He turns, maybe thirty degrees, south (you're making that up, you have *no* idea) and plucks again. The same tap, the palming of the hoop, his eyes half closed, eyes the color of the sky in the shadows.

He turns, moves. You follow.

You leave before he finishes for the night. The sun gets begins settling on the horizon and you bike hurriedly home. You study your parents at the table: your dad, bent over his plate in an undershirt, skewers large slabs of beef on a fork; you mom cuts all of hers into cubes at the start and then eats each slowly. What would you do if suddenly one of them weren't there anymore? Would you invent a world for yourself where you had them both again? Would it be possible to live in that world, to maintain that illusion, without it breaking? To hold it delicately like a jar of glass spiderwebs, the most fragile container for yourself?

And what would you do if it broke?

You want to talk about Dylan, to warn them about the things he's described, to ask their advice. But it sounds so silly at the back of your mouth. Like trying to ask Eileen to the dance. Like if you told them you were worried about a monster in your closet.

And of course, there's the nagging notion at the back of your head that he *isn't* making it up.

There's an episode of *TTMK* that's related, in fact, that's almost certainly adding to your self-doubt. Phillipa goes through a portal alone one night, curious, explorative, and finds herself in an alternate universe where someone—who looks a lot like her—has escaped from a mental hospital. Orderlies kidnap her—Phillipa—and lock her up, and the more desperately she tries to explain that she needs to get back home, the more determinedly they keep her locked up. Mr. Kellogg wakes up with no idea where she is, no way of finding her, and she's wrapped in a straitjacket lying in the middle of the floor several universes away, slowly coming to wonder if she *did* make up her uncle, and Poppo, and the Fallacious Jergin. Of course, she finds the crystal necklace that Poppo gave her hidden in the lining of her jacket, cuts her way free, escapes home; all the usual conflict resolution.

But you've always wondered: what if that was the show's one glimpse of truth? What if the whole thing is in her head, like in *St. Elsewhere*, like season nine of *Roseanne*? You've done research into this, reached no conclusion.

And what if they lock up Dylan, and he doesn't get out? What if he's trapped here forever, or disintegrates due to unforeseen spatiotemporal meddlings, coincidences, and jiggery pokery? What if, even, you are a part of his imagination—where does the illusion end? You know this is going too far. But what do you owe this Dylan, this false and distant Dylan whom you'd never met until a month ago? Is he your friend?

You resolve that, for the moment, it is probably best to help Dylan. Within reason.

The weather is warming up. There are more birds than a month ago. Some days you can feel the tar of the asphalt, sickeningly soft under your feet like something alive, like the world has been—literally—sleeping for months, like fish under ice, and is just starting to become soft flesh and blood and bone again. The spring dance is looming; you haven't talked to Eileen about it. You don't even know if she's going.

You two watch *TTMK* at your house again, each of you at opposite ends of the wide burgundy couch, resting on opposite rests, legs canted toward each other so that if you stretched out just a little bit, your feet would touch hers. But you don't. You wouldn't, ever.

"Would you do it?" she asks around a handful of popcorn. "Go to another universe?"

"Maybe," you say. "As long as I knew the way back. It would be like exploring the woods, or a desert. Maybe best to do with a guide, or on carefully-marked trails. Bring lots of water." You shrug. "I like the idea of adventure, promise, surprise. But I don't think I'd like them as much in reality. What about you?"

She pauses for a long time. Mr. Kellogg and Phillipa trick the Fallacious Jergin into a pit of frictionless carbon beads and he sinks instantly, unable to surface, the tiny black beads swimming into his mouth like a swarm of beetles. Phillipa and Mr. Kellogg high five, go back to the Versarium, their home, to drink cocoa with Poppo.

"I've been going out at night," she says, "late late late after my mom goes to bed, going out with Victor Dolphy and Trent Pascal and Monika Cixous."

"Victor *Dolphy*?" Your heart is sinking—what does this mean? What could she, why could she, what—

She turns down the volume as the credits roll. "They've been doing this thing downtown. Exploring, they call it," she says. "Urban exploring. Sneaking into these old broken down buildings that no one uses anymore. We went into one with a spiral staircase rising up into the ceiling, or what was left of a staircase, it was just supports really. So we climbed up this spindly thing and there were rooms with rusty bed frames and an old, old locked safe and some kid's notebook. It was a little water-stained but some kid had been practicing cursive in this graph-ruled notebook, I don't know, maybe forty or fifty years ago. And it was just sitting there, in this dark building with holes in the roof so you could see the stars, with holes in the floor so we had to shine our lights at our feet."

You almost repeat, *Victor Dolphy?* But you don't want to appear as obsessive as you, in fact, are. "There are already whole other worlds in this one," Eileen says. "Pockets of space and time that are totally stuck in some alternative, some past or future or some other present, that are nothing like what we have."

"I would want to go," she says. "But not until I'd spent a lot of time figuring out the world we're already in."

"That sounds wild," you say.

"It is!" she says. "It's incredible. You should come sometime."

"I don't..."

"Let me be your guide, your carefully-marked path," she says, and laughs, and throws three or four popcorn puffs at you, and you fail to swat them away, and you laugh too. "We're going back next Wednesday."

You've never snuck out of your house in your life. But surely if Dylan can hop between literal universes, you can at least muster a metaphorical one. You pull a breath, hold it, and release it around the word "Okay." And it almost keeps the anxious, horrible, buzzing out of your chest.

Days pass unremarked. Wednesday comes. You and Eileen bike together, alone, along the winding mica streets, shimmering shining in the aftermath of afternoon rain. You keep your voices down, you barely talk at all, racing along beside one another, little invisible droplets spattering against your heels. The others will meet you both there, Eileen explained, after you crept by your parents' room, came down the stairs pressing the sides of your feet to the wall, clumsily cat-walking downstairs to minimize creaking, leaving through the basement so they wouldn't hear the door. You were out. Eileen waited before you immobile like an equestrian statue, and she said "They'll meet us there," and you were off on your squeaky bikes, coasting down the hill, downtown, towards the vast and empty shells of otherworldly homes.

You hide your bikes beneath a bridge, locking them together like some artistic parody of marriage that you wouldn't understand in a museum, but here makes sense.

You're terrified, of course, of the gaping black holes in the floor, the non-existent staircase winding upwards, the shadows that collect like cobwebs in the corners. And further, you're not sure you see it, this other world that Eileen discovered. You see scuffed floors and a broken chair and a hole in the sky for the rain and light to come through. You see holes in the floor like dark weak patches of ice. But in the darkness, when her flashlight turns upwards and illuminates only her face, her short dark hair, her ears, when you escape from everything else into this pool of light marred only by the shine of a broken moon outside, and you ask her to the dance and she says yes and hugs you, in this moment of grace, and hope, and focus you believe that, perhaps, there are other worlds than this. You feel that you've stepped into one, if only for a second before the careless blustery whoops and hollers of Victor and Trent and Monika rend the night.

You do not sleep in any meaningful way. You leave your house early and unfed and race to Dylan's house, as instinct demands you must, even if you don't know how to interact with this new, alternate, improved Dylan who talks about statistics and dowsing rings. You leave your bike in his yard like a discarded piece of gym equipment, taking the stairs to his hot attic bedroom two at a time.

"She said *yes*, motherfucker! She said she'd go to the dance with me!"

Dylan is reading a book in bed before school, something massive and hard and bound in brick red. "Yes?"

"Yes! She said yes!"

"Who?"

"For fuck's...Eileen!"

"To?"

"The dance! Jesus, Dyl, I just said that..."

"Ahh," he says. The noise hangs like condensed hesitation. "I'd prefer it if you...*didn't* do that."

"What the actual fuck," you say. "The *actual* fuck, man, you can't just come waltzing in here, populate my best friend's body like a fucking pod person, spend a month acting weird as shit and then smash all my dreams in one fell swoop."

"No, Mark, sorry, it's not that." He stands, sets the book carefully face-down on his wide blue bedspread. He touches your shoulder. "I'm really happy about that. I wish you and Eileen the best of all worlds."

"But?"

"The dowsing ring worked," Dylan says, rubbing his eyes. He looks pale, almost hungover. You probably look the same. "But it's not going to be pretty."

"Where did it lead you?"

"The gym," he says. "The wormhole is going to be in the gym, on the night of the dance."

"So you're gonna like disappear in a puff of light and smoke and freak people out? You're gonna crash your Delorean through the door and mangle us all?"

"Not exactly." He keeps rubbing his eyes like he's allergic to something. "There are a lot of confounding variables of course, but simply put I need to...make sure I achieve sufficient velocity to break through the, erm..."

He says: "I'm going to have to jump. From the balcony onto the ground. About thirty feet. Six hundred twenty-seven Newtons of force oughta do it."

"Um."

"Messy, isn't it?"

You can picture it all so vividly it's like a kind of time travel; you wonder, almost, if it *is* a kind of time travel, if this is part of the adventure story you've been tossed into, a walk-on role in an 80s movie. You can see the dimmed lights, the shuffling half-clad teenaged bodies in pastel pinks and whites and greens, half-full bowl of punch on the table, snacks picked over, Chex Mix with all the pretzel sticks pulled out; on the speakers something poppy that you don't know is playing, everyone seems to know a dance that goes along with it. And overhead, crouching on the balcony railing, like a fateful caped avenger, is Dylan. He swan dives, his jacket floating around him like a shitty parachute, like a weak angel failing to pluck him from the air.

The dance is still over a week away. Surely there is, there must be, some way to stop him from jumping. You could of course tell his mother—but why would she, anyone, believe you?

And more importantly, you think you believe Dylan, believe that anything you do to interfere is going to keep him from getting back home, from getting back to a dad who misses him, from another you, another Eileen to be friends with.

You feel eleven again, treading quickly but carefully across that snow-peppered ice, circling around dark patches that glare up at you like hunters' traps, like holes in a floor. You waddle quick as you can —a tween penguin—so you don't slip and slam ass-first into the hardened ice. You are in a constant state of balancing, dodging holes, but moving, too, inexorably forward toward something wonderful. And will you get there, or will you go home with nothing more than seven stitches and an hour's scolding?

Eileen sits on your couch. You watch Poppo load himself into a cannon that will fire him at above light speed so that he can travel back in time and stop the Fallacious Jergin from conquering the Earth with his Sphere of Chronomancy. But when Poppo stops him, the Sphere ends up in Mr. Kellogg's hands and obsesses him, possesses and enthralls him, so that he goes cacklingly mad and takes over the Earth himself. So Poppo goes further back in time, to try to destroy the Sphere at Dr. Hallock's Clock and Time Shop, but then Phillipa gets a rare auto-chronologic disease, her timeline eating itself, and Poppo has to keep going further back and further back trying to set things right. You forgot about this episode, which ends with Poppo going back as far as the cannon can possibly take him, whizzing hastily into the past just as the credits roll. They never resolved the episode, just came back to the regular show the next time.

When you close your eyes for too long, you imagine how it will go, again and again: the black tuxedo jacket spread behind Dylan like broken crow's wings, flapping in slow motion. A collision between Newtonian mechanics and some deeper, purer science that you'll never understand, a kind of physics you'll never learn to use, that Dylan could never teach you; the thud at the end of flight. What can you do?

Eileen's hand rests by her yellow-toed sock, palm up like a palmister's model. All the lines on her hand are perfect and clear, dark slashes like weak spots in the ice; but warm. You think about what that hand might look like in another universe: a threat, a welcome, a suggestion. You trace the scar on your knee and wonder about all the small changes that become bigger over time, all the coincidences, the classes you're in or shows you discover, the conversations you have and hands you hold that lead you forward to a place of comfort, or loneliness, or confusion. You wonder which of these coincidences coincide in other worlds, and decide you don't care. You take Eileen by the hand.

It came from Jeremy Packert Burke

Of course alternate universes are an old trope in scifi, but usually we see someone we know leave a situation we know and end up somewhere … different. Probably much worse. This is the case in anything from It's A Wonderful Life to Rick and Morty. There's an episode of Buffy, "The Wish," in which a character inadvertently wishes herself into a Buffy-less version of her hometown, and we see her running around telling people how wrong the vampire-ridden version of Sunnydale is, how the demon versions of ordinarily lovable characters are distortions, not the real deal. I wondered what it would be like to be on the other side, to be one of the people being told the world that you've always lived in is wrong, that it's untrue. Things spiraled from there into the whole confusion-as-metaphor-for-growing-up thing that Buffy (and the author Kelly Link, too, who was a major inspiration to the story) does so much of. There are a lot of people I stopped being friends with around the time I was fourteen or fifteen. People you've known for your entire life can feel like someone entirely different at that age, can feel like your world and their world are completely separate. I just literalized that sense. What if they were really were from a different world? How would you know? Would you trust them? Would they still, in a very literal sense, be your friend?

A question for Jeremy Packert Burke

Q: What's easier for you- imagining a happier world, or a darker one?

A: I mean, it's not hard at all to imagine a better world than this—a world free of racism/sexism/homo- and transphobia/genocide/war/gun violence/etc. A lot of fiction draws our attention to issues by exaggerating the bad, making it worse (I mean how popular are YA Dystopias right now? How popular is 1984?). There's a kind of escapism in that though, a tendency to say "Oh well at least real life isn't that bad." But I think some of the best speculative fiction, like Octavia E. Butler's "Dawn," shows us how horrifying our own human tendencies can be by putting them in contrast to a happier world, by showing how humans do not fit in a utopia.

About Jeremy Packert Burke

Jeremy Packert Burke is from Virginia. His fiction and music writing crops up occasionally online. He, too, read too many Stephen King books at too young an age, and will likely never recover.

Twitter: @jempburke

September

Dragons I Have Slain

B. Morris Allen

I collect dragon tears. It isn't difficult; they're insidious and subtle, and they seep through my armor and into my skin like ink, leaving me stained, soiled, sorrowful — a human map of misery. The Dragon Atlas, I call it — marked with the precise locations of honor and shame.

Dragons cry for the same reasons we do — pain, heartache, joy. We think of them as wise and cold, but wisdom is no antidote to empathy. Dragons are kings of empathy. That's what makes killing them so hard.

There was Vyurfang, short for something unpronounceable in dragon-tongue. I stood on his chest, his broken limbs splayed out across the rocks, the point of my longsword slipped between two diamond scales. I kept my back to him, and he turned his sky-dark eyes on my mirrored shield, and said "I am sorry, Solna," even as he tried to use my name against me. He cried as I slipped the blade home once, and again, and again, and again, through every chamber of his heart. He cried as his long body writhed in agony, as I came down to hold his head against my bosom and snap his tired neck. The tears soaked through the metal plate and the cotton gambeson and steeped my chest in sagacity and shrewdness, experience and acumen. I wash and wash, but I cannot get it out.

In the town, they hailed me as a savior, offered me fine wines, rich foods, soft beds. Handsome men, pretty women — I refused them all, and in the parlor of the inn they whispered to each other about dedication and purity as I shed my futile armor.

"Send up hot water," I told the landlord, "and keep it coming." I've done this before, and though no water can cleanse me, it's better to try than to despair. A dragon taught me that.

When we were girls, I was the dragon.

"Breathe fire, Solna," Elyndra commanded, and I would roar and cough on all fours, and she would hack off my head.

"Why must you play with that girl?" my mother asked, as if she could not see Elyndra's in-born grace, her golden beauty.

"Because her mother is scullery maid at the castle," my father replied. "And if she did not help us to sell our crop, who would buy it?"

After Vyurfang there was Cold-Heart, whose only weakness was in her mouth, into which I fired an iron quarrel when she spoke of duty and of passion. Her tears are etched into my forearms where I tore the quarrel out so that she would not lie with her mouth open and speechless as her body turned to stone.

And after Cold-Heart, there were Klarsharp, and Windclaw, and Sharpstone, and Zmeyra, and more others than I care to count. Each one marked me with their tears, wrote their passing on my skin. I feel the burden of it like a cloak of chain, slowing my steps, clouding my thoughts. Even when I sleep, it drags me down into nightmare, and when I wake, I force myself to stand only so that I can be doing, not thinking, even if that doing is only a slow march to one more death.

Dragons are a violent breed, with an instinct for survival so deep that even after death, they strive for life. Even while they hope to die, they try to fight. It is an instinct in them, I think, that they cannot suppress. I kill them this way and that way, and every time I think them dead, they twitch and claw and tear. And weep.

"I can't look you in the eye," Elyndra told me when we were older, almost blooded women. "A dragon can enthrall a man with a single glance."

"As you've enthralled Osal," I agreed, making a joke of heartbreak. "Though what you'll do with a thrall so small and weak, I can't say."

"I have you to protect me," she smiled, and kissed me on the cheek. "And Osal is clever, and his father is the glass-smith." But she wouldn't look me in the eye, and her kisses grew fewer as our bodies grew curves.

My armor, once of mirror-shined plate and tight-knit mail is rent now to tatters, discarded across fields and hillsides, caves and plains. Only my weapons remain: a sharp sword, a strong bow, and a promise, burdens now so heavy I can barely walk.

Today, it will end. Today, I will kill my last dragon, or she will kill me. There is always that hope. Today, I go without even my mirror shield to save me from enthralling dragon eyes. I will kill her with my eyes closed, or she will enslave me, or I will die. Today is the end.

They watch me as I go from the village. I have saved a pretty dress for today, a soft cotton gown they gave to me in Hatherton. The canvas baldric pulls against it, pricks the fine weave with coarse fiber until I give up and carry the sword in one hand, arbalest in the other, and the promise on my conscience. I hear the children snicker at a savior in a sun dress, hear parents chide them in quiet, tolerant voices.

I have kept my boots, for the way is muddy, and there are streams I must cross. At the first, I slip the sword under one arm, and pull the dress up to my thighs. It is easier than plate, and more comfortable. The children laugh and point, and make jokes about dragons' legs, but they come no further. We are too close now for childish dares.

It was daring that brought me to this day, and desperation. Desperation to catch the eye of Elyndra, a spare, fine willow to my tall and sturdy walnut. Daring to think she might value strength and commitment over craft or intellect.

When we were women grown, Elyndra went in to the castle, as a lady's under-maid, and I followed her. No lace and fripperies for me, no delicate embroideries on satin underthings, but canvas straps and heavy pikes.

"I'm sorry," Elyndra said when we met in the evenings. "But we must use what we have. I'm pretty. You're strong. Best not to argue with fate." Fate decreed that her mistress invite Olas to show the Countess and court his tricks of glass and wire, and that I enlist as guard trainee.

"You're no nearer Elyndra in the guard than here at home," said my mother when I packed to leave home. "And with your father gone, I need your help."

"I will send my wages," I mumbled.

"Elyndra is a tramp, and a shameless one," said my mother, and she gazed past father's empty chair to the widow Remble's shack. "She'll no more be with you than you'll be a hero, with all your belts and spears and bruises."

The dragon came not long after, a long dark shape like a storm cloud spread thin by wind. It settled on the mountain behind the castle, on the steep slopes that fell off in cliffs to the river below.

"They've written to the Queen," Elyndra said, eyes wide. "They say she'll send a hero! Osal told me so. He said it will be a hero, with landboats so full of armor it'll take ten men to row each one. The Countess herself has ordered him to make a special far-sight device so that she can see the dragon from her tower. And with the pay from it," she looked away, a slight flush across her perfect skin. "Well, you know."

I found a sword easily enough, a rusty piece of steel from the practice racks. Armor I did without, going forth as near-naked then as I do now, though more sensibly dressed in cotton trousers and tunic. I crossed the shallow valley below the castle, went quiet into the dark of the mountains, and climbed through the mist, glad it muffled my scrabbling steps from the dragon whose shadow filled the tap-rooms.

I found him just above the treeline, in a cave less tunnel than scrape, a shallow overhang of rock exposed to cold winds that fell down from the ice above to the cliff below. I had no mirror, for I was brave, not shrewd, and when he opened his eyes to me, I was lost.

I spent untold centuries in delirious contentment, washed in cerulean tides that hinted love and warmth and certainty until he closed his eyes again and I was free. I wept for loss and fell to my knees to beg him to take me back, my sword discarded dull and evil at my side.

"Have they never told you, girl, to beware a dragon's eyes? Do they not tell tales at night of the cunning of the serpent?" His voice was the slow rumble of an avalanche awakening, and my bones trembled with its might, so that I could not answer. He opened his eyes again, but held back his captivating powers. "Are we so disregarded now, that they send out naked children to do us in? Are you the best there is?"

I told him then, in stumbling, stuttered words of my plan, my hopes, my dreams. Reflected in dragon eyes, Elyndra seemed distant, a slender and a frail reed on which to rest my faith, and I saw clearly now how mad my thoughts had been, how palpable her disinterest in me, how evident her hopes of wealth and position.

"I'm the least there is," I replied as my future fell around me, and I saw in his eyes that even my self-pity was an appeal for deliverance.

"Yet you are the tool I have," he said, "and we must both make do." He snaked his head down from his cave to hang beside me in the chill air. "I cannot give you love," he said. "Though I see you need it, that is the one magic dragons do not have." A lucent tear escaped one lapis eye, and, unthinking, I stretched a hand to touch it. Under my finger, the tear smeared against hard scale, and I felt it enter me, sliding past barriers of skin and flesh to touch my spirit.

"A dragon's tears are potent," he said. "Fools hope to sell them. The wisest know them for a burden, and a shackle." I touched my tear-stained finger to my chest, felt it write destiny on my heart.

"I have no love to give you," he repeated, though I could see in his eyes a love of land and peoples and of me. "I have pain and duty and despondency, and if you want them, they are yours." In that moment, I forsook Elyndra and happiness and hope, and gave myself to fate.

"Our era is done," he said. "The time of dragons and of flight. We have long seen its end arriving. You humans have brought it, with your carts and roads and machines. You have spelled an end to magic with your studies, your scrutiny, your relentless logic."

I thought of the Osal, with his contraptions of wire and melted sand that made my head hurt, and the carter rowing his silly land-boat down dusty roads. I opened my mouth to protest their futility, but the dragon shook his head.

"We have had our time. We have had our peaks and our valleys, our empires and our isolation, our enchantments and our everyday. It is your turn now."

"Our turn for what?" I blurted, mind still full of flight and fantasy.

"For yourselves."

"But why? Stay with us. Guide us." I touched my tear-marked finger to his cold face above the fangs.

"We cannot. Most of us are already gone. Only a few are left — those unaware, or unlucky, and myself, and my queen." He turned his long body and stretched out wings the color of rain-flecked slate that spread out and above me to block the sun. With a snap, he flung them out and down. They crashed against the rock, sending dust and gravel into the icy wind.

When the dust had settled, he spoke again. "These are no more than ornament now. I cannot fly. None of us can, for flight is more magic than mundane. And a dragon that cannot fly is no dragon. Without flight..." I could see the clouds in his eyes, the conflict of desire and memory. "Without flight," he said quietly, "a dragon cannot live. Does not wish to live."

I wept to see him as he saw himself, a master of sky and land reduced to a creeping lizard, wings no more than a hindrance. I wept again as a dragon's true sight showed this to be not self-pity but truth, not despair but acceptance.

"Our instincts are strong," he continued. "Too strong. Those of us who could set them aside have done so. They cast themselves from the heavens while they could still fly, drowned themselves in bitter seas, starved themselves in hidden caverns. They were the lucky ones. The others try, but they fail. They cast themselves from cliffs too low to kill, topple boulders they can dislodge at need, challenge champions they cannot help but battle against. They are broken in body and in spirit, but dragon bodies heal even when the spirit cannot. And yet they try, failing over and over again, and achieving only pain."

I looked about me. Fine dust had settled on the dragon's useless wings, torn and crumpled at the tips where they had struck the rock, and leaking drops of emerald blood onto soil from which sprang moss and fern. Beside me, my discarded sword mocked my brash ignorance. I pulled my courage about me as best I could. "Let me help," I said, as if a foolish girl with a rusty sword were of some value.

Wisdom is not kindness, and truth is not comfort. I saw, through his eyes and my own, how unequal I was to the offer I made, how much he would have preferred a more accomplished servant, how little choice he had. I saw his dismay at my inadequacy, his determination to exceed it.

"You are not the tool I hoped for," he admitted. "Yet my queen set me to wait here among the humans, and you are the one who has come. We must make the best of it. In the face of failure, we cannot succeed if we do not try."

We agreed then, how I would search out his fellows, and kill them despite themselves. He gave me a small sack of gems from the small hoard he had carried, taught me how to use a mirror, how to find a dragon's weak points, how best to use them, and how to be sure of death.

"These are the secrets of the ancients," he rumbled, laughing. "For centuries, we have kept them from you humans, and now I show you freely the chinks in my armor. It is," he bared his fangs, "a bitter irony."

When we had done, and I had memorized and practiced and repeated to his satisfaction, night was well upon us.

"Come and sleep under my wing," he said, "and tomorrow we will finish."

Had any human ever slept with a dragon? I wondered, as I snuggled close against the fine scales with their scent of oats and pepper.

"You are the first," he answered. "The last. The only."

In the morning, I watched as he he flung himself from the cliff, and fell, and soared for one last moment, like leaves of autumn gold defiant in the sun. And then I climbed down to his broken, bloody body to wipe away his last tears and cut off his head.

I took them with into town — the tears invisibly traced across my palms, the head across broad shoulders, with flowers springing up in my path where emerald blood had trickled down my back and legs into the soil. I felt my body stronger and harder than I had ever known it, and my heart more desolate.

I delivered the head to the Countess, and she gave me honor, gold, and armor. All went as the dragon had predicted. 'The dragon,' I called him, for only now did I realize that I had never learned his name, and because the humans did not care. They looked at me, with my dragon-marked skin, and looked away.

I set off to the next town afoot, spurning the carter and his land-boat. Only as I left did I think to look for Elyndra. I found her, in her cotton dress that shone like satin, saw her wide-eyed fear as she stood next to Osal for protection against the horror and hero I had become.

I am still the horror. I kill noble, beautiful creatures when they are weak and defenseless. The map of tears across my body has grown so heavy now that only my sword keeps me upright. I dull its sharp point, stabbing it into the stone of the mountain as I climb. At the last narrow scramble, the arbalest grew too heavy, and I left it beside the path for some foolish child to find. It is hard to care about the humans now that I have seen so many in so much foolishness. They celebrate the death of dragons as if it were an accomplishment. If that is their future, they deserve it.

I can sense the last one near me now, smell her pepper scent around a ridge of jagged rock This the queen, of course. The last dragon. The last of my burdens, of my impossible task. I put down my sword to tug my gown straight, brush the burrs from its hem. It is tight at the waist and shoulders, and it leaves my arms naked to the wind, but it is the best I have, the only good thing I have.

I leave my sword where it lies. In a queen, the instinct for survival may be stronger. She may kill me on sight — sear me and my pretty dress with a breath of fire, or rend me with her fangs. I can hope.

I step out around the ridge. She is vast, this queen, the size of houses. Her scales are violet and indigo and blue and black in the autumn sun, and her wings form caverns across the slanted meadow. Her eyes are the green of forests and rain. I lean my spirit toward them ... and do not fall.

"You are proof against us now, child," she says, but I have enough dragon in me now to know it for a joke, to know that she holds back her power.

"I cannot kill you," I say, letting my shoulders slump. Let there be an end to death at last. My arms are cold, and the dress does little to warm the rest of me.

"There is no need," she replies, and rests her head beside me on the ground.

"I cannot kill you," I insist. "I will not kill you. I have done enough." I look up to her forest eyes, and beg them for release. "Let me rest. Let me finish." We both know what I mean.

"We have used you hard," she admits. "We have been unfair, even cruel." I see the truth of it in her gaze.

We are silent for a time. "He used his power," I realize at last, and know it true. "It was not my choice. All this killing. All this death."

I think back on all the bodies, the blood. I feel the tracery of tears burn across my hands, my chest, my back. Not bravely, freely

chosen. Not voluntary service to a dying race, but an unwitting tool —
a fool of death.

I sit, and wait for my own tears to flow, to fill the hollow of my
disillusion.

"He could not help it," she says at last. "It is the way of dragons,
to control, to master, to deceive."

"To enslave," I spit, though I cannot muster anger.

"Yes. Yet our time is ended. Your technology drains the world of
magic, but it is your will that prevails — that indomitable will that
fights tyranny, resists oppression."

She smiles her dragon smile, all fangs and sharp eyes. "Even
you, little one. Not the strongest of your race, nor the best. But even
you have come this morning to refuse me. Thus we reach our end,
when an unarmed young human denies a dragon queen."

"I will not kill you," I say again, bitter now with the knowledge
that I have been used, that I am as poor a vessel as I once feared —
that I was chosen for my very weakness. Relief grows in me as well; I
am done forever with that task, done with blood, done with dragons
and their deaths.

"No other could have done it. Strong, determined, implacable.
Enthralled." She shows me the truth of it, shows me her gratitude.
Perhaps I have done well. Perhaps not. Perhaps I am only tired.
Whatever the truth, I want no more of it.

"I will not kill you," I say a fourth time.

"Even a timeworn dragon queen is a queen." She shakes her
wings, and a breeze blows through my hair. "I have one more flight left
in me, and I will take it until it ends. But we owe you thanks, we
dragons. What boon can I give you, who have given us so much?"

"Death and blood," I say, for that is what I have given. What I
was forced to give.

"Dignity," she replies. "And for a dragon, that is a great deal."

I am dull now, with disillusion. I want no more revelations, no
boons. I want … I do not know, and I sit in silence, my pretty, foolish
dress a dusty folly, poor shield against the mountain cold. I want no
more killing, no more effort, no more decisions, no more plans. No
more weapons. No more tears. Above all, no more tears.

"Take me with you." On that final flight, the last voyage of the
last dragon.

She looks at me, forest eyes impenetrable as oak.

"Very well," she agrees, and her eyes glint with moisture.

She gathers me into one huge paw, and I see the razor claws
pressing into her scales as she stretches them to keep me safe. It
hurts her, but I do not care. Why should I be the only one to hurt?
And if she slips, and the claws close in, what matter? The dragon tears
on my skin reproach me, show me the child that I am acting. I tell

them silently to let me die as a I choose, and they do not argue with my wisdom, little as it is.

We rise with a clap of thunder and a rush of wind, and then we are high above the land, and in the village below, the humans run like raindrops, away, away, away.

We fly over the land I have known all my life, over the sites of my bloody executioner's work, and of my birth and childhood. It is small, inconsequential, the sites of my great and awful deeds a tiny patch of green and brown upon the great sprawl of land and sea beneath us. There is too much of it! The mountain I climbed this morning, no more than a foothill for a range of granite peaks, with beyond them the glint of water. We follow rivers to the west, and I silently urge the queen on, further, faster, to see more before the end.

She slithers her head down to me like a goose, so that she is flying one way, facing the other, then turns her head back toward the front, her long neck forming a loop that ends above my head. "There are lands below even the bards have not heard of, lands where dragons and their deaths are a matter of legend," she says through the wind of her passage. "There are lands that speak different tongues, even between humans. Lands of carters and craft, lands of farmers and hard work, lands of battle and lands of peace, lands of beauty and of plainness."

"This is what we give you," she says, and I feel her wingbeats falter. "These were our lands, that now are yours." We slip in the air as the magic fades and I sense her muscles straining.

We sink lower and lower, and my heart aches for all the lands I have not seen, the magic of horizon and discovery. Soon, the flight must end, and the queen and I will reach the end of our voyage, and the beginning of peace.

We are hilltop-high now, above a green land of forests and rain and ocean. "This was my favorite," she says, and there is regret in the soughing of her voice. "Here I was my happiest." She swoops low over the waves on a warm, sandy beach, and I feel her tears bathing my body as her claws shift and the end nears. I close my eyes, and feel her joy and sorrow as she remembers happiness and her race dies. "I hope there is room for me in your Atlas," she says. Then the claws open, and I am falling, falling, into the waves.

I strike hard, and the breath whooshes out of me and the cold green is all around me, and I am sorry. I kick out for the surface, and the air, and as my head breaks through, I see a dark arrowhead against the sky, climbing, climbing out to sea. And then it falls.

It's better to try than to despair. A dragon taught me that. I hold the lesson close as a current carries me to an uncharted shore of hope and life, and the salt water washes me clean.

It came from B. Morris Allen

I'm a big fan of Deep Purple, and of many of its component members, including the late Jon Lord (keyboards). I was listening to his album *Pictured Within* early one morning after dropping my wife off at the airport. The title song is beautiful, but it includes the line "There are dragons I have slain". It works in the song, but as a long-time vegan, I was a little uncomfortable singing along. That moral discomfort led me to a search for circumstances in which I could sing the line in good conscience. The opening line of the story came to me almost immediately, and I had the whole thing mapped out, and the first paragraphs crafted, by the time I got home ten minutes later. I wrote the story that same morning.

Shiplight

Benjamin C. Kinney

"Right there, any moment now. Their future," Jacob said, resentment thick and sour in his mouth. He pointed up into the night sky, above the heads of the close-packed crowd on the porch. Everyone was silent. Despite everything, Jacob and all the other Sea-born natives held their breath. A fresh pinprick appeared in the night's threadbare shroud. A new star, flickering and bright with the flare of the decelerating pulse drive. Shiplight.

Voices erupted in drunken cheers, but Jacob leaned back against the railing's moldy wood. Rache bumped her hip against his. Her lanky body smelled of alquila and dance-floor heat. "Hey, start smiling. You knew Earth was crazy enough to send you five thousand more colonists as a twenty-fifth birthday gift. And until the Ship sends us their roster, who knows?" She laughed, her amusement knife-sharp and just as bloody. "You and I might keep our jobs if they have, what, ten programmers? Sea probably has jobs for ten more right now."

Jacob tapped his alquila glass against Rache's and forced a laugh. "I knew I should've been a janitor. Maybe a pilot?" The liquor scoured his throat, a clean and purifying burn.

Lucia's face appeared, a golden ghost beneath the shadow of her hair. "Jacob, Rache, hey! Look, we can't get the feed from the Ship, can one of you come take a look?"

Rache poked her elbow into his ribs. "You set it up, you go save the day. Get back here quick, you're supposed to kiss someone on Shiplight and I missed out. Or is that New Year's?"

Jacob's heart skipped, like a stone across the water. He grinned and let his hand touch Rache's lower back. "I think it can work for either."

He pushed through the crowd, into the curtained living room. Fourteen other natives huddled around the couches, while a skinny boy prodded the connection between the hook and its wide-screen display. Jacob settled in front of the electronics and tuned out everyone's cheers and pleas.

There was nothing wrong with the feed, or the hook, or the net. There was no transmission from the Ship.

In the morning, Jacob found Lucia and Rache in the kitchen, tapping away on their hooks. The windows spread mid-morning sunlight across the room's warped laminate countertops. Even the scattered and curtained reflection felt like a head-pounding glare. Jacob was wearing the same rumpled clothes as last night, and the two roommates looked scarcely more tidy in their bathrobes.

Lucia grinned. "You two keep cozy last night? Wow, you have a terrible poker face, Jacob." A knock came from down the hall, and she set down her hook. "You two have fun, I'll get the door."

Jacob sat down beside Rache, and watched a thread of dark brown hair escape from her sloppy topknot. She turned her hook so he could read from the hand-sized glass tablet. "Take a look at the Shiplight news. It's brilliant, the government is peeing their pants. Afraid the big boys on Earth are finally coming for their back taxes."

Lucia returned, her shoulders tight. "We have guests." She mouthed the word *government*.

A man and a woman entered the kitchen behind her. Rache flipped her hook face-down and turned around to greet the visitors. They wore pristine unembroidered shirts, and had flecks of grey in their hair. Not old, but at least in their forties. Colonists, not natives. Jacob knew of a few natives that old, children of the early colonists, but the government never hired those rare elders.

The man said, "Good morning, everyone. My name is Andrews." He looked at Rache. "Ms. Rachel Ruiz-Levi, yes? We wanted to talk about some posts you wrote early this morning. As I'm sure you're aware, there's a great deal of speculation about why the Ship didn't make contact, and you seem to have a very particular take on the situation."

"Well, it dropped out of gravity drive on schedule, so it can't be broken too badly. If it's some little malfunction, we'll have a signal tomorrow and this all blows over. But if not..." She smiled like a lioness watching her cubs bring down their first prey. "I bet they've gone silent on purpose. I bet they could've sent us a feed full of lies or whatever they wanted. But they didn't. They want you to feel ignorant." She leaned forward. "To panic."

She cracked her knuckles. "You're from the government, Andrews. Want to help me fill in the gaps? Let's see. Have you not been sending enough goodies on the Ship's return trips? Or do you think they've finally noticed that you stopped following the original charter?"

Andrews pulled out a chair and sat down. "Would you rather we went back to the charter, Ms. Ruiz-Levi? A system designed to control five thousand miners? I don't think so.

"But we're not here for a debate. You've been very vocal about your lack of faith in the Senate's ability to handle this. Right now might be a bad time for that kind of agitation. We all have some real challenges ahead of us in the coming months, and our society needs to pull together to prepare." He drew a badge from his shirt pocket. "My colleague and I are with the Bureau."

Rache crossed her arms. "I haven't done anything wrong, *colonists*. Go drown yourselves."

Andrews sighed. "We're all colonists, ma'am. All sixty thousand of us on this world, no matter which planet you were born on." He glanced at his partner, then back to Rache. His words fell through the murk of Jacob's hangover like a block of lead dropped from a diving belt. "But if you're not interested in a productive conversation right now, we'll have to continue it elsewhere."

Lucia's eyes narrowed, and she placed her hook on the table. Rache set down her mug. "Is this the point where I ask for a lawyer?"

"As of this morning, the Senate has authorized emergency measures to head off unrest in this time of uncertainty. Which reactivates some clauses in the original charter, I'm sorry to say." A smile flickered past his face, more irony than pleasure, and then he drew his sternness back into place. "By order of the Emergency Council, we're taking you into custody until the situation is resolved."

Rache's eyes darted: between the guests, to the window, to the knife set. Blood and broken glass unfolded in Jacob's mind. He clasped her hand. "Rache. Don't give these bastards a real reason."

Andrews kept his gaze on Rache's face as his partner shifted a hand to her belt. Unnoticed by the visitors, Lucia tucked one of the two hooks under her arm.

As the front door shut, Jacob's hangover shifted into reverse. He felt instead like he was still drunk, the world spinning with motion just beyond his view. Lucia picked up Rache's mug and washed it in the sink. In the living room, somebody snored.

The mug shattered in the sink. "Drown it!" Lucia wiped her hands dry, and threw the towel after the broken mug. "I can't believe those colonists! Is this just going to be a police state now?" She sagged into a chair.

Jacob shook his head, and realization spread through his body with a sharp and prickly heat. "If they came for Rache, she can't be the only native they arrested. Drown that! I can't believe the colonists would do this." He stood up, driven by the urge to act, but the peeling walls offered no suggestions. "We have to do something about this."

Lucia gave him a measuring smile, and then the balance tipped toward warmth. "Yeah? Huh, Rache was right about you." Jacob's cheeks flushed, but Lucia turned her attention down toward her hook. She tapped the screen, swept her finger through one list, and then another. "Found it! Here, if you want to help, take a look at this."

Jacob leaned over her shoulder. "That's Bluerail. A programming language for hardware automation. You're not a coder too, are you?" He and Rache had met over the net, when his parents' mineral-extraction float needed a second software engineer. He had never met another native coder; how could he not be enchanted?

"Hah, I wish! No, I'm a cook at The Glider. This is Rache's hook. She snuck this program home from her Raytheon-Tinto contract, she always said we might need it someday. She was always saying the colonists would bring back those old Earth charter laws."

Jacob swept through the pages of structured text. A comment caught his eye. "Hold on. This part down here, it's the encryption algorithm for communicating with the police aerials." The world no longer spun; instead, he was flying. "This is it, Lucia! With this, we can force the government to give Rache back."

Lucia flinched. "Hold on a minute. That program does what now?" She gripped his wrist. "We can't just take up arms, Jacob. That's ridiculous. We can hold onto it as a backup plan, but you are *not* starting a violent revolution in my kitchen." She ran her hands through her hair. "This emergency won't last forever. All these charter-law folks are gonna answer to the Senate again someday, right? So they still have to care what the world thinks."

Jacob's head pounded, but it beat in sync with his thoughts, like waves hammering the turbines of a generator. A new idea, more gripping than the last. "A protest, then. If they're going to do charter-style martial law, we'll sit right in the middle of it! Force this into the open where the whole net has to look at it. How many people were here last night? A hundred and fifty?"

"At least. New Plymouth is half natives, though a lot of those are just kids." She reclaimed the hook and tapped the screen. "Maybe a thousand in the right age range."

"Nice! They can't arrest us all, charter law or no. We need to start this soon, before that Andrews realizes he took the wrong hook, and —" His ferocity crumpled. "And before anything happens to Rache."

Lucia's grin remained. "Everyone's supposed to be back at work tomorrow. Let's give them something better to do."

In a city of nine thousand, they had six hundred people ready to march. Across the ocean world's far-spread islands and floating extractors, two thousand more natives promised to stay home on strike.

In the light of morning, the size of it all made Jacob want to run back to his island home. *Six hundred people* in one place! But he had set the tide in motion, and if he flinched now, the burden would land on Lucia's shoulders. She might forgive him, but Rache wouldn't.

The protest began just before noon at Rache and Lucia's house, for a route of three short kilometers to Landing Square. Most of the protestors were younger than the party crowd, but every face seemed familiar, like family members gathered for their first reunion. They carried hand-made signs with slogans like "End emergency law!", "Why do only natives go to jail?", and "Shiplight: what are you hiding?" The most popular signs demanded "Free Rache!" and four other prisoners.

Lucia pulled Jacob to the front to march alongside her. As the procession began, he took slow steady steps, and Lucia walked backward to face the crowd. She started a simple chant, echoing the placards, and a chorus of voices joined in.

They walked from gravel to pavement to Main Street, the spine of New Plymouth, between the pourstone facades of the world's administrative and cultural heart. They passed a construction site, paralyzed for lack of laborers. Bins overflowed with the weekend's waste. Somewhere behind those walls, corporate offices lay half-empty, parents were stuck home without their daycare, and dishes remained unwashed. Jacob grinned. New Plymouth wore the skin of colonists and their tech, but natives moved the blood through its veins.

The procession reached Landing Square. The broad cobblestone plaza ended in wide white stone steps leading up to the metal and glass of Landing House, the city's only three-story building. Spectators lined the steps and shopfronts, and Jacob spotted a few groups of people with tripods and camera lenses. He lifted his fist with the next chanted chorus, to create an image that would spread their voices across the breadth of Sea.

Lucia leaned in. "Check out the cameras! We're gonna need more than one speech. Think of something while I talk?" She squeezed his arm, and then strode up the steps of Landing House and faced the crowd.

Jacob's elation froze over. He tuned out Lucia's voice and dredged his mind for something worth saying. Most of the protestors were skipping school, or menial jobs that no colonist would steal. But a woman imprisoned for speaking her mind — that, everyone could understand. Every arrested native was someone's friend, someone's family.

Lucia shouted, "...No, we will show them who the real citizens are. If they want to forget rights like peaceful assembly and discussion, we will remember them. Look, we aren't children! We will be seen, and we will be heard. And we'll be here every day, until the Senate releases all political prisoners and ends emergency rule!"

The crowd cheered, and Lucia beckoned to Jacob. He ascended the steps, and stared at the entrance of Landing House. Five police officers stood guard behind glass doors and the black plastic anonymity of riot helmets. Jacob turned around and faced the crowd of upraised eyes and camera lenses. Over a rooftop, a bulbous black metal disk flew on four rotors. A police aerial laden with cameras, Raytheon-Tinto programming, and weapons from Earth.

He could not remember how he opened his speech, only the sensation that he was a shard of driftwood on a rushing current, flailing but advancing on the same anger that animated every raised face and fist in the crowd. When he saw the shape of an ending, Jacob held out his hands, palms down. The natives grew hushed.

"...If they don't, we will show them who this planet really belongs to. The colonists made this a fight, and we're here today to show them we're ready to fight back. We are the tide. We will not be denied!" He gestured at the crowd, and it joined his words. "We are the tide! We will not be denied!"

The crowd kept up the chant, again and again, until he raised his fists and the noise dissolved into cheers. As he stepped aside, a thrill rushed through his body like alquila, but he couldn't tell whether it was the heady lightness of a perfect buzz or the looming giddiness of a party gone too late.

Lucia hugged him. "I knew you'd be perfect up there. Rache would've loved that! This is going to work, I know it. The colonists won't last a day with us on strike."

Jacob's smile returned at full force, his doubts squeezed away in the embrace. No police or prison could stand against them. If they tried, well— "Can you imagine the show if they threw us out? Every parent in town watching live over the net as their kids get zapped."

She ran a hand through her hair. "I think I promised we'd stay the night. Can you go around and see who's willing, maybe organize folks to get tents? I'll line up some more speeches. Rache isn't the only one with friends who deserve to be heard." Her smile gained a feral edge. "This is way better than another day frying fish."

Shadows spread into night as the Centaur descended, the main sun falling behind buildings and horizon to join the absent Foal. Jacob saved his progress on Rache's code, and took a break to browse the news. The popular knots had avoided mentioning the arrests at first, but every image of the protest had a "Free Rache!" sign to explain. Her name flashed in every video frame, echoed on every tongue. Each repetition punched into his heart like a nail — into, and through.

Lucia sat down beside him with a flask of tea. "Any news?"

"About Rache, and us? Plenty. No response from the Emergency Council, though."

She frowned. "Anything about Shiplight?"

"Nothing that makes sense. The knot for the Mount Zheng telescope is down, so it's all rumors and conspiracy theories. Ridiculous stuff: a second vessel shadowing the Ship, or an encrypted low-power signal bounced off the moon, or weapons welded to the outside. It seems to be coming in on the right trajectory, so hopefully there aren't—" The next words caught in his throat. Since Shiplight, he had gained and lost Rache, gained and kept a cause; but he had not considered the price already paid. "Hopefully there aren't five thousand corpses up there."

Lucia squeezed his shoulder. "Makes me wonder whether Rache was right. Back taxes and all that? Maybe Earth finally decided to lay down the law."

"I hope not. You ever read the old charter? No citizens, just workers. Earth only cares about two things: giving their people hope with colonist lotteries and competitions, and then extracting every atom of value from them once they get here."

Lucia shrugged. "It didn't work when the population was ten thousand, or fifteen. Earth couldn't rule us if they wanted to, not through a ten-year round trip, no matter how short it feels to the people on board.

"Let the colonists worry about pleasing their so-called bosses. We needed something like this to stir the pot." She stood up and gave him a two-fingered salute. "We are the tide, remember?"

He checked his messages. A bundle of interview requests, and a video from his parents. He returned to Rache's code. He debugged, he tested, he wrote some comments. Once the hour grew too late to call them back, he watched his parents' message, and then recorded a reply.

"Mom, Dad, stop it. That's not the point! Earth doesn't even know how many programmers we have, and if they did, they wouldn't care. All that education won't mean a thing until there's enough demand again. Which could take years. And that puts me ahead of most natives!"

Jacob took a deep breath. What good was his cause if he couldn't convince his own parents? "I'm sorry, I shouldn't yell. It's not your fault. Anyways, the arrests are the real issue. When Rache is free, I'll invite her out to the islands so you can meet her in person. But I'm staying here until they release her. If you want me home sooner, call Senator Feeley's office, tell her to come listen to us."

He paused. There had to be a way to frame this so even a senator would listen. This issue had more sides than he could shout to a crowd. "The Senate can't keep treating us like second-class citizens forever. It literally can't! These days, way more kids are born than colonists come off the Ship. How many years until we're the ones deciding who get reelected?" He put on a smile. "Don't fret about the Ship. A few months from now, it'll come into orbit just fine. Good night, and love you both."

Jacob awoke when the Centaur's first rays pierced his tent. He found a café that would let him wash up in their bathroom if he bought breakfast. The server was a grey-haired man, perhaps the manager or owner, running back and forth single-handedly among the six tables. He scowled, but he took Jacob's money, and hungry protestors filled every table. The irony made the prices worth paying.

Jacob lingered in the café. The breakfast crowd thinned, and he could sit in relative quiet, in a comfortable foam-polymer chair, drinking tea and building a proper program around Rache's code. No teenagers shouted for his attention, no camera-wielding colonists demanded answers. He chuckled. This must be how parents felt when their children disappeared to school: *I love you, but I'm glad you're out of my hair.*

When had he grown so comfortable? He had started the protests in anger, and then reluctance, and then necessity; but when all those younger faces lifted to his, he would do anything in his power to let them succeed and flourish. He was older than three-quarters of the natives, and in the last day and half they had all become his family.

Jacob finished his programming, and his seaweed quiche settled uneasily in his stomach. Rache's unfinished code would overwrite the priorities and instructions for the police aerials, but that provided only half of the equation. His fresh-built structures and interface would make the code work, but the program's output would interact with the robots' existing programming, far beyond his reach.. He and Rache had built the program together, across time and distance and prison walls, but he couldn't know for certain what it would accomplish — if anything. Still, he knew what Rache wanted, the goal of every line of code she wrote: a way to throw off the colonists' yoke.

By the time Jacob returned to the square, a counter-protest had gathered in the far corner. A few dozen colonists carried printed signs like "Respect our Senate" and "Now is not the time to whine." Jacob wanted to laugh at their "Unity, not protest" and "Get back to work" placards, but his humor found no footing. A few natives tried to drown out the counter-protestors with chants of "We are the tide!", but the aerials kept their weapons pointed toward the younger crowd.

Someone ran past, carrying an empty glass bottle in his fist. Armored vans sat parked end-to-end on one of the access roads. The vans disgorged fifteen police officers, holding transparent riot shields against the crowd's simmering stares. Between them and the officers at the Landing House doors, almost the city's entire force was here. A few of them carried wide-barreled gas-grenade launchers outlawed since the end of charter days, but the protestors outnumbered them nearly thirty to one.

Jacob found Lucia toe-to-toe with the counter-protest, her face contorted in anger as she jabbed her finger at the face of a thin-haired man. An aerial lingered overhead like a personal thundercloud. Jacob's skin tingled, anticipating the invisible field of a magnetic inducer.

The man shouted, "You think we can just conjure up a university for you? You have no idea how good you have it! We gave up everything so you could have clean air and a better life." Another colonist tried to pull back the shouting man, but he yanked free. "You're a bunch of goddamned whiners!"

Jacob grabbed Lucia's arm and pulled. "Lucia! Get away from them! The whole planet is watching this."

Lucia shouted over his shoulder. "You think you're so generous? What a load of crap. Charter law, natives getting arrested, and you come down here and yell at us?" She spat. "Real supportive, Dad!"

Jacob yanked Lucia back into the crowd, and other protestors filled in the gap behind her. She grabbed his shirt. "Is Rache's program ready? Give me your hook!"

"Lucia!" He swatted her hands away. "No! We're not wasting it on a bunch of colonist nobodies. What's gotten into everyone?"

She clenched her fists until her knuckles went white, but then she puffed her cheeks and exhaled. "Yeah. Maybe. Drown it, Jacob, why do you have to go be angry at the right people?" She shook her head. "You didn't hear the Emergency Council's statement? All they said was, I quote you here: *We trust that the citizens of New Plymouth will show solidarity during the current crisis, and resolve their differences without resorting to hooliganism.*"

She crossed her arms. "If they're going to call us hooligans, I'd rather do something to earn it. Rache sure would've."

Jacob's head began to throb, like his Shiplight hangover rising from the grave. He sat down on a hard sliver of curb. He wanted to put his head in his hands, to return to his tent and sleep, but the crowd around him had grown hushed. Watching him, awaiting his response. The weight doubled on his shoulders, but he had to lift his head and say some meaningless, encouraging platitude.

"They'll come around. They have to. We just have to stay strong."

Jacob spent the afternoon with the crowd. Whenever he approached, people dropped what they were doing to talk to him, to discuss his speech or to share a story of their own. Once he realized what was happening, he sought out corners of the crowd where trouble brewed. He settled an argument over thrown trash, and distracted a group of teens trying to pry cobblestones up from underfoot. The work exhausted him, but someone had to play father to this raucous family.

Around sunset, a spiky-haired protester touched his arm. She smirked and hooked a thumb toward the edge of the square. "Colonist wants to talk to you," she said, and then vanished into the crowd.

Tension twined in his stomach, and he considered chasing her, but he followed the direction of her thumb. A familiar man waited by the locked door of a corporate office, among a gaggle of colonist spectators. He beckoned Jacob closer. The man was taller than most, with flecks of grey in his hair, and new lines of exhaustion on his face. Andrews.

Jacob glanced around, expecting more figures with plain shirts and hardened expressions. But this time he had hundreds of natives at his back. He had nothing to fear.

Andrews smiled politely. "Jacob Abasi. Do you have a minute?"

"I might. What's this about?" Jacob's hands balled into fists, but he kept them by his sides.

"We'd like to discuss some possibilities, Mr. Abasi. This situation isn't what we want, and I don't think it's what you want either, is it?"

Jacob crossed his arms. "Actually, we're pretty comfortable here."

Andrews shared a sympathetic smile. "For now. But what are the odds, Mr. Abasi, that this gets violent? There are so many ways it could happen. One of your people starts a fight, or the aerials overreact, or someone on the Emergency Council decides to impress on you just how serious this situation is. Or maybe someone, somewhere, starts to call this a revolution." He spread his hands. "I'd much rather we came to an understanding."

The thought crept along Jacob's arms like a cold-footed insect. Yesterday, he had been eager to see the police clear the square, but he had scarcely considered the price. If the police attacked, the natives would win their cause, as the net filled with images of batons, gas, and magnetic nerve inducers. But violence meant more than just videos. Those young and hopeful faces would feel every strike and shock and broken bone.

He said, "Are you offering to negotiate?"

"You could call it that."

Jacob shook his head. This should have been what he wanted, but the taste of victory only made his courage falter. "I'm not in charge here, you do realize that, right?"

"But you have a great deal of influence, Mr. Abasi. A lot of people look up to you. And more importantly, two-thirds of our colony lives outside the cities, a long way away from this protest. Those people watched a young man from the islands standing at the front of the march, giving one of the first speeches." Andrews shrugged, as if to commiserate. "Speaking of influence, I've been trying to find Lucia Tuan. Will you extend her our invitation as well?"

"I'll let her know. But first I need to know where we're going, because I drowned well better come back."

"Don't worry, everyone will know where you are. Have you ever been in Landing House?"

Jacob had walked the halls of Landing House once before, as a child. It was one of the oldest buildings on Sea. His fingertips brushed along the walls of glossy metal from the first shuttles, still smooth after sixty years. The air was dry, and uncomfortably cool.

"Who are we meeting?" asked Jacob.

"Me, as it turns out. I'm the Deputy Director, and the Bureau has a great deal of authority in the Emergency Council."

Lucia said, "Seriously? The Deputy Director was walking around making arrests?"

Andrews laughed, sounding genuinely amused for a moment. "I think you overestimate the size of the Bureau, Ms. Tuan." He led them to a second-floor conference room with a long knotwood table, a dozen soft synthetic chairs, and tinted windows overlooking the square. "Coffee?" An exotic luxury, but Lucia shook her head, and Jacob followed suit.

When they all sat down, Andrews leaned toward them, his amusement replaced by weary anger. "Jacob. Lucia. Do you realize what you're doing?"

Lucia crossed her arms. "Yes. We're telling you, all of you colonists, that we're not going to take your crap anymore."

Jacob slipped his hook into his hand, the aerial-control program loaded and ready, and drew confidence from the hidden blade. "We understand you're in a panic. The Ship's pulled the rug out from under you, but that's not what this is about. It doesn't give you license to throw natives in jail when you don't like what they say."

"Don't be so quick to dismiss the events of Shiplight," Andrews said. "I'm going to let you two in on a secret, but it'll be public soon enough anyways. We have reason to believe the Ship is carrying an invasion force."

Jacob exhaled. Rache had seen the truth after all. Or could this be a lie? But the Deputy Director watched him with eyes shadowed by sleepless nights.

Andrews said, "We have a few months before the Ship reaches orbit. We believe we can intercept the shuttles, but we'll have to mobilize the entire colony to build defenses. That's why this —" He gestured toward the window. "This is as dangerous as five thousand marines."

Lucia said, "You expect us to believe that crap? Besides, if you don't want people angry at you right now, you shouldn't throw innocent people in jail! Look, we wouldn't be out here if you hadn't arrested our friends!"

"Are you sure? Your friend Rachel was already trying to convince everyone that the government is a bunch of useless old colonists who couldn't find their own feet without a map from Earth. She was inciting panic. And once people realize there's war coming, there'd be far too much fuel for her spark." He sighed. "Even if we hadn't arrested her, she would've fomented riots soon enough. Maybe we arrested the wrong people."

Jacob gritted his teeth. "Is that a threat?"

"No, just a regret. We're rolling down this hill, now we have to try and stop the barrel. Those kids won't go home quietly, will they? They're angry. Merely getting what they want won't make that go away. Or am I wrong? Tell me."

"Andrews, this is not some..." Frustration trapped Jacob's tongue. "We're not children, acting out because you've taken our toys. All we want is for you to stick with your own laws."

"No, Mr. Abasi." Andrews stood up. "Your protest isn't some legal disagreement. As Ms. Tuan said, you just don't want to take our crap anymore. This is opportunism, plain and simple. Taking advantage of our common crisis to push your narrow interests. Starting a riot because you're afraid you'll lose your job." Andrews clenched his jaw, but then he sat back down and pressed his hands against his temples. "I'm sympathetic to some of your underlying issues, and there are deals I'm prepared to offer if you'll persuade everyone to go home and get back to work." He slid a folder across the table.

Jacob pushed aside the stiff yellowgrass folder. Andrews' speech had bled his anger dry, but no guilt rose to take its place. Instead, he felt lost, diving at night with some great sharp wreck waiting just outside the span of a faltering flashlight. He pushed back his chair and walked to the window so the others couldn't see his face.

Behind him, Lucia opened the folder and skimmed aloud. "More promises about all-ages training programs... Starting next year. For Rache, barred from making public appearances, restricted net access... Monitoring by the Bureau... But she'll be home. The others too."

"Rache won't take it," Jacob said to the window.

Andrews said, "Can you convince her? I know you're doing this for your friend, both of you. Because if you aren't, then you're just kids lashing out to get what you want the moment your parents are distracted. And I'm not going to let some angry kids paralyze this colony while a sword hangs over our heads." He drew a hook from his pocket. "Your protest ends, Jacob. But you get to decide how. I'm calling the chief of police. Let me know what I should tell him."

Lucia said, "Drown that. Andrews, this is your whole problem! You rely on Earth, so you have to follow their rules, or they'll send you to your room. This is what you deserve for trusting people light-years away who couldn't care less what *you* need." She leveled a finger at Andrews, and turned toward Jacob. "This so-called army is after the colonists, not us. If it really exists, they'll thank us for kicking things over. Backup plan, Jacob!"

Andrews laughed with more exhaustion than humor. "Backup plan?"

In the darkness outside, lights bustled around the protest camp, a restless little echo of the city's streetlights and windows. Like a fish at the center of a net, or a child at the center of an embrace. Jacob turned around, to face Andrews and Lucia and their hungry stares, each of them waiting for him to turn off his diving light and plunge into the night-black sea.

Jacob said, "Enact the law before we go home, and actual training has to start within a month. And laws to protect natives against losing their jobs just because people from Earth become available."

Andrews sighed. "The timeline isn't negotiable. We can't start new education programs while we're preparing for an invasion." He rubbed the heel of his hand against an eye. "Fine. Have it your way. I'm not spending any more of my time dealing with you stupid kids. We're clearing the square." He raised his hook to his ear.

Weight pressed down on Jacob's lungs. Hundreds of men and women, girls and boys. He could not abandon them. Not to pistols, gas, and robots; and not to a government that would sweep them aside for the rumor of some foreign threat. "I can't let you hurt them." He lifted his hook and pressed a button.

Andrews paused his call. "I'm sorry?"

Lucia grinned like a wolf picking the lock of its cage. "Take a look outside, Andrews." His eyes narrowed, but he rose from his chair to join Jacob.

Through the window, everything unfolded in silence. The six police aerials stuttered, drifted, and then righted themselves in halting unison. They turned away from the crowd. Some of the counter-protesters collapsed, and the rest dropped their signs and ran. The police on the far side of the square drew back, and then fell to the ground as their nervous systems convulsed. One policewoman fired a canister of gas into the protesters. The crowd bunched together like a startled snail, and figures stumbled as someone kicked the plume of smoke. A line of fire arced through the air from an access road, and smashed into an aerial. Below the window, something flashed in a staccato burst.

Jacob's throat had gone dry in the parched air of Landing House. This was Rache's code, written against the day when Earth's old laws might rear their head. But on her own, she had left the weapon unfinished, just as he on his own never had reason to make it. They had created it together, the first and fiercest offspring of their minds. It might win her freedom, but he could see no victory in the scene below.

Lucia punched his arm. "Buck up, Jacob! We are the tide, remember? This way *we* get to choose the terms. Isn't that right, Andrews?

Andrews wasn't listening. His eyes scanned the crowd, striving to make out faces. Searching for a son or a daughter, a niece or a nephew.

Jacob looked up, away from the chaos, toward the night sky and the silent flicker of Shiplight. He imagined that it looked down on them all, and was pleased with what it had wrought.

It came from Benjamin C. Kinney

"Shiplight" grew out of a different story, written but long-abandoned. A story about humanity's first and only interstellar vessel, shuttling back and forth between worlds called Earth and Sea. But on its sixth outbound trip, the Ship was full of marines, and a crew cut off from both worlds by decades of time dilation. First, I wrote about the crew, fighting among themselves as the worlds force them to take sides. Then I wrote about the marines, on a one-way trip to a world they would need to pacify and yet integrate with. Finally, I wrote a story worth publishing: about the people of Sea, and how a single well-placed strike could unravel the cord between a world and its offspring. The particulars of "Shiplight" began with, of all things, math. I had established how fast the Ship could deliver colonists: five thousand every ten years. However, a relatively safe world with cultural/economic demand for population could have a growth rate of 20 per thousand per year. At those rates, as the landing approaches in year 60, the natives and colonists each comprise about half of the population. But the natives are overwhelmingly young, and the colonists are at least in their thirties. What might all those youths do, in a society built along power structures of a world they've never known? My other inspiration came from the protest movements of the early 2010s. I first wrote this story in 2012: the year after Occupy and Tahrir Square. The size of the protests in "Shiplight" may seem small, but as a fraction of the population, New Plymouth had twice as many protestors as Cairo. Later revisions of the story followed the 2013 protests in Istanbul, particularly the government's use of the word "hooligans" to describe peaceful protestors. Let us all hope that popular movements for peoples' rights in the real world lead to better outcomes than Sea's. But there are always more factors at play than anyone can foresee. Rache was right about the Ship's malevolence, but wrong about the reasons for its silence. That comes from the unknown story of the crew, and all its brave souls as the tried to preserve the one corner of the universe they called home. Perhaps someday you'll get a chance to read their story!

A question for Benjamin C. Kinney

Q: What do you think makes for a good story?

A: A good story needs compelling characters, an interesting plot, a captivating setting, and prose rich with action or detail. Those are the easy parts. Who wants to stop with a merely good story? I'd much rather read a great story. Greatness requires one more layer: a meaning that fills and overfills the bounds of the story, reaching beyond the characters and confines of the page. Every author dreams of writing stories that leave the reader with a new understanding – conscious or otherwise – of their self, society, or humanity.

About Benjamin C. Kinney

Benjamin C. Kinney is an itinerant neuroscientist and Viable Paradise XVIII graduate. Despite his New England heart, he lives in St. Louis with two cats and a wife on Mars.

Find him online at benjaminckinney.com or on Twitter as @BenCKinney.

Strix Antiqua

Hamilton Perez

I didn't want to go back into those woods. I didn't trust them, and I suppose they didn't trust me either. But deep down, I knew—I had to go. You can't just stay at home, whispering to God on bended knee when your little sister's been taken by a witch.

Police combed through the forest during the day but didn't find anything. They wouldn't of course. A witch takes people when they're alone, not in groups, and then she hides away with her catch, tucked in the shadows of secrets and the heartbeat of mountains. That's where witches live.

There wasn't any explaining that to them though.

Against the charcoal sky, the moon looked swollen and sick—its glow, a jaundiced smudge. The stars disappeared long ago, scrubbed from our view by smog and light pollution, even out there. Pine trees scraped against the night. Their branches shivered and shook as some creature caught its prey or eluded capture, and I wondered which I would be that night.

Sneaking out of the house was the easy part. The fans and filters humming through the halls helped me get away without waking Mom and Dad. But out in the wild there was nothing to hide the whir of motors and wheeze of joints that followed my every step.

Near home was a network of trails that snaked all through the woods. I had a suspicion the witch kept away from them though, preying on those that veered from familiar paths, so I entered through the shrubs and the underbrush, my rigid body struggling to navigate the dense, unforgiving foliage.

I'd never been that far into the forest. Everything there felt alien and hungry. Curious. Honey mushrooms reached like bulbous fingers from the base of trees. Eyes flashed in the starlight, then disappeared. Once I felt I was really in the thick of it, I stopped. "Travel Buddy," I called, and a light shone from the walking stick at my side. "Guide me home."

"A-home we go, ol' chum!" it replied in mock-sailor voice. Travel Buddy projected a red arrow in front of me, directing me to turn back the way I had come. I ignored it, continuing forward with the arrow hovering in front of me, throbbing like a headache and pointing right at me. A hard thing to miss, hopefully.

I could still remember the harsh, happy cadence of Mom's voice —*Happy Birthday*—as Dad placed the Travel Buddy in my lap, unwrapped. This glorified walking stick was too grand, too impressive a gift to burden with wrapping paper.

The body was a chrome black steel, and branching from the handle was a touchscreen interface which promised navigation and health monitors. At one end of the handle was a projecting bulb, and on the other a round red button that said SOS. *This is so if you fall down or can't find your way home we can find you,* they said, spilling out their mouths with pride. Dad demanded a test drive with way too much enthusiasm, so me and Travel Buddy walked the perimeter of the house.

The whole time the walking-stick-with-apps flashed and whirred and buzzed at me. It warned me of approaching obstacles and changes in terrain, of my rising heart rate; it told me to calm down in patronizing tones, instructed me how to breathe—*in and out, slowly*— and informed me of my muscle tension around the handle.

I flung the stupid thing to the ground.

Should I call for help? it asked.

Now I leaned on Travel Buddy as I made my way across the dense forest. Now I *needed* it. I needed its flashing lights and loud voice to catch the witch's attention; its emergency locator to help them find her lair once she took me. I guess that made them right in a way.

The same birthday I got Travel Buddy, Suyin gave me a catcher's mitt and ball, wrapped awkwardly but with care in the recycled skins of paper grocery bags. She taught me how to catch and throw. She taught me that I could.

That was the thought I carried with me as I moved towards the meadow she used to dance in. The last place she was seen.

Three days earlier, I'd come to tell her it was time to go; Mom wanted us back for dinner. Instead, I found myself speechless.

There, in the center of the field, she danced and shone like a fairy in the amber rays of sunset. Her thin frame twirled and arched through a riot of crimson poppies and violet lupines, and it might have been the most beautiful thing I'd ever seen.

I ducked behind a boulder squatting just outside the meadow, and watched with envy the sharp precision of her movements, the command she had over her body. *What it must be like,* I wondered.

Everyone knew Suyin was special. You could tell just by looking that she was a Naturall. No deformities, degenerative bones, prosthetics or augmentations. Mom actually got to hold her the day she was born. But even though she was so special, she never looked at me any different. She never saw the metal plates, the circuits, wires, and hoses as ugly things to spot and then turn away from.

She, more than anyone, made me feel special.

Behind the stone I watched her, and before long I was mimicking her stances, following her intricate movements, clumsy but determined. The brisé looked easiest. I could see just what it required, where to start and how to end. Maybe I could do that one. Maybe I could be beautiful too.

I counted down from five and then I counted down again until I'd worked up my courage. And when I jumped, it was with everything in me.

For a few seconds, I was free. Nothing weighed me down or pushed against me. It was me and the sky, and in that fleeting moment, I tried to tap and cross my feet like a dancer. My legs weren't fast enough though. They tangled before I landed, dropping me to the dirt.

"Tommy?!" Suyin ran my direction. I had ruined it—her dance and mine.

I hobbled to my feet before she had the chance to help me. "I'm fine," I said. "I just tripped." Ignoring my protests, she held my arm while I found my footing.

"Don't go, dearie," said a throaty voice nearby. "We have so much work ahead of us."

That's when I saw that the boulder I'd hidden behind was actually a very tall woman sitting with her back to me. She turned to face us, revealing eyes blacker than ink, skin craggy and worn, and rigid, loose-hanging clothes the same matted gray as her hair.

"I'm sorry," I said, startled by her presence. "I didn't see you."

"Oh my, is there a person there?" Her black eyes squinted in my direction. "There you are! Hmmph. Not a person. *Not really.* No wonder I couldn't see you, sneaky, sneaky."

Trans-human. That's what I'm called, somehow. The word never felt right though, then least of all. *Trans* is too high, too grand for someone so cobbled together. So is *human,* I suppose. If I get hurt, I'm as like to spill oil as blood. That's why the witch didn't see me. She didn't see a person, she just saw parts.

We need a new word.

"I've come to bring you home," I told Suyin.

"Sorry, lad," said the witch. "You can't take something from the forest without leaving something behind." Her smile tore like a wound across her face.

"Hi friend! Turn around!" chimed Travel Buddy beside me. I turned up its volume and carried on.

The deeper forest was a community of conifers, standing tall and independent, or else broken and devastated, leaning decrepit against their stronger brothers and sisters. It was rich with the songs of birds and frogs and insects.

Then the hooting of owls echoed through the woods, and all that noise just died. Became so quiet you could almost hear the forest breathe.

In the old stories, witches could see through the eyes of owls and possess them at will. I thought of the bodies that sometimes turned up in the forest, mummified in sunbaked saliva with only the bones and artificialities remaining: pacemakers, prosthetics—medical grade plastics melted and fused to bone.

I wondered if they were alive when she ate them.

This was a terrible idea, I realized. I turned off Travel Buddy's navigation, the arrow blinking off before me. I slowed my pace, eyes scanning the canopy above, when some angry limb caught my pant leg and tore a wide gash, revealing the glint of metal underneath. It was like the forest had said, "I see you," to the deepest, scaredest part of me.

The sound came again. *Who? Who?* rang through the woods. This time, I spotted one perched in a tree. It called out, *Who? Who?* in every direction like an accusation.

My heart rattled in my chest like a pebble in a shoe. I struggled for breath—rhythmic gulps in then out—but my lungs weren't used to the unfiltered air, the free-floating particles of pollen and dust. My legs turned stiff, and after a few short steps they locked up completely.

That's what fear could do. All those firing neurons mucked up signals to the rest of me, trapping me in my head with all my wishes and all the good they'd do. It's how the witch got away with Suyin—why I could do nothing to save her.

I had to think my way through it, focusing on one leg at a time—*Left. Right. Left.* Travel Buddy helped, holding me upright and limping along beside me. Up above, the owl stretched its wings and dove away, but before I could catch my relief, a loud mechanical voice said: "Do not be afraid. You are in a safe place. Breathe in... and out. Slow..."

Who?! Who?! called from ahead. *Who?! Who?!* answered behind. My heart fell to somewhere deep inside me. I kept moving, quickening my pace.

"Do not be afraid. You are in a safe place."

A piercing shriek cut through the air, scraping up my spine. Still, I focused on running. *Left leg, right leg, faster, faster.*

"Breathe in... and out. Slow."

Over my shoulder I could see the determined avian face, the black eyes, the sharp body diving impossibly fast and almost upon me. *Left, right. Faster! Faster!* The owl grew larger as it swooped—now the size of a dog, now a person, now a car.

My left leg lost pace. I staggered into a tree and fell, gasping for air but there wasn't any. The last thing I remembered before blacking out was being gripped by powerful talons, and the startling sight of enormous wings.

In the black, I dreamt what I always do, some memory unearthed only when I sleep—the wet dark, the muffled thrum of pumps and gurgle of churning chemicals, the tightness, the warmth. And then the suffocating, the hunger, the sucking and squirming and struggle for sustenance.

The air is sick, the water tainted, the food lacks nutrients. The natural world tried to cut me off before I was born, tried to suffocate me in the womb, to draw the life out of developing organs, to drink the marrow before the bones had set.

Breathing is like sucking from a clogged straw. It won't give, it won't give, it won't...

I woke up coughing and choking on air. The world was still black, and the shuffling of heavy feet on hard earth told me I was not alone.

"Who?! Who?!" the shrill voice echoed around me. "Who are we going to eat tonight?!" Two large black eyes appeared, darker even than the darkness around them. "You! You!" the voice called. "You we will eat tonight!"

I couldn't move. My arms and legs were bound and I was lying on some hard, ropy bed.

"Where's my sister?!"

"She's here, young lad. She's here. Wilting like a flower. They're so hard to feed when they're young. A little starving is necessary to waken her *true* hunger." She clacked her gray teeth at me and grinned.

"Let us go."

The witch just laughed. "I'd hoped for something with more meat on the bone. And there's so much in the way. These contraptions on your body, are they not so very much? A burden to you, a hindrance to me."

The eyes bobbed up and down as the hag walked around me. "You will be a disappointing meal. Quite right. Quite right. On that we agree, quite right! But these woods aren't what they used to be, and the hungry eat what's left to them."

She drew closer—two disembodied eyes, all pupils. In them, I saw distant flames flicker and flash and grow. The fire behind her eyes swelled and soon our surroundings were lit by an orange glow, its warmth blooming beneath me and nipping at my back.

In the firelight, I saw that we were in a large underground chamber. A witch's burrow. The tall, slender witch hunched forward with her knobby back scraping against the high ceiling. In the corner of the chamber, Suyin was tied up, dirty, and unconscious.

The witch held up a shining, steel rod. *Travel Buddy.* Somehow the stupid thing made it there with me. The witch examined its sleek metal body, the domed unlit bulb protruding from the handle, and the big red SOS button.

"Don't push that," I told her. "Whatever you do…"

She hit me across the chest with it.

Pain branched through my limbs. I screamed, but the witch wasn't listening. Her large eyes were directed at Suyin, waiting for a reaction.

"Argh. Not enough," the witch grumbled. The dome remained unlit. If I could just get her to press the button, they could find Suyin —no matter what happened to me.

"Try again," I told her.

The chamber became full of the echoing call and response: crack and scream, snap and cry, crunch and wail. Still, the SOS signal didn't come on.

"Tommy?" Suyin called. Barely a whisper but her soft voice filled the chamber.

"Ah, yessss!" said the witch. "Wake up, dearie. You'll pay attention this time. See how it's done."

"Tommy?"

"I'm here!" I cried, wanting it to be comforting but there was too much hurt and fear in my voice.

"Fleeting, fleeting," said the witch, her breath heavy with the smell of decay. "I have to eat—at least until your wee sister is ready to take on my role."

With one quick motion she ripped through my bonds. I struggled to get up, but everything was weak and hurt. The witch stepped back, dropping Travel Buddy behind her, its unlit dome another symbol of my failure.

"Muscle and bone and parts unknown, consume, consume, consume. Eyes and ears and all your fears, consume, consume, consume."

Her shoulders thrust forward violently. The bones popped and cracked and stretched with a wooden groan. Her whole body lurched forward as a thousand needles pierced through the tough skin. She cried and writhed as they grew, hunching over as the needles spread, growing needles of their own. Soon her whole body was covered in a sheen of black and gray feathers.

Once more the witch thrust forward. A sharp beak ripped through the skin of her face, swallowing her wart-covered nose.

What towered before me was a giant owl, larger than any living thing that ever stalked those woods. Its dark, ashen coat shimmered in the firelight. Her eyes were the only things unchanged. Great orbs of unfathomable darkness.

The owl bobbed its head, a twisted enjoyment evident in its face. The fire now roared behind me, consuming the nest.

I'm sorry, Suyin.

Like a tidal wave, the great owl swallowed me whole, all in an instant. I was spun on my head, sloshed about, and dropped into her angry stomach. Acids splashed and singed sensitive prosthetics and microfibers buried beneath the skin. There was a hungry, gurgling sound, and the smell of burning plastic, rubber, and bile filled my nose.

My hands searched the grimy walls but only led back to myself, until finally I sank into the pit of her stomach. I lay there shivering with pain, my fingers twitching against my legs, unconsciously *tap-tap-tapping* something that shouldn't be there.

Something unnatural. *Synthetic.*

One of the hoses had come exposed. Suddenly I remembered the time I scraped my leg on a playground, and instead of blood there was oil, and another boy had licked his scrape, so I licked mine and threw up.

Desperately I pulled on the hose, but it resisted. With both hands and the last of my breath, I tugged, feeling the artificial pieces in my arm stretching, threatening to snap. Just when I felt that my arm was about to dislocate, the hose came free, spurting oil into the witch's stomach.

Soon the walls were pulsating around me. They tossed me about, splashing my face and chest with acid. First it burned, then there was nothing. And then there was light. A faint orange glow, like a very distant star and I was rocketing towards it.

The owl gagged as I plopped like a fish onto the earth, thrashing about and swallowing air.

She coughed heavily, shaking feathers from her body as she shrank in size. Her bones popped like the fire as they realigned into her haggish form.

On the ground before me was Travel Buddy. I reached out and pressed the SOS button. *I've done it,* I thought. But the light still didn't come on. I pressed it again and again, but the thing was dead, useless as it ever was. *I hate you, Travel Buddy.*

"What are you?" said the witch, choking on spittle. I climbed to my feet and limped towards her on my one good leg, still holding the overpriced walking stick.

"Synthetic." I swung it down on her head with all the strength I could give.

Suyin's hands and feet were bound with thin, sturdy roots. She was unresponsive, so I picked her up and limped along with a dead leg I could only swing from the hip.

As I carried her from the burrow, I saw dozens of discarded corpses the witch had coughed up during her lifetime. Some of them looked ancient, with cell phones jutting from their hips, glued there by digestive juices. Fresher ones had nanofiber bones and smart-tech veins running up their bodies. I glanced to the burned flesh of my arms, the unnatural parts exposed and singed, and I remembered what the witch said before about not taking something without leaving something behind.

Suyin awoke as we breached the surface. "Who... Who's there?" she muttered. She'd been starved and her eyes kept in the dark; it would take her longer to adjust.

"It's me. It's Tom--y," I said, but my voice was hoarse and clipped. "You're --afe now."

She reached out and touched my face. I felt nothing. Her expression turned sad. She knocked on my cheek. Hard, metallic thumping. "Where'd your face go?"

"She took i--."

"Where'd your eyes go?"

"She t--k those too." Through the camera installed in my right eye socket, I scarcely recognized the confusion and sleepy disappointment drawn across her face. "She took ev-rythin- I was born with."

Suyin knocked on my chest—a soft, wet thud. It made me cough. "Not everything," she said, squeezing me tight.

It came from Hamilton Perez

I've always been fascinated by old myths and folktales, and I like to keep compendiums of magical creatures close at hand when I'm writing. In one such compendium I discovered the strix, a bird from Roman mythology often associated with witches, owls, and the consumption of human flesh. Seemed like good material to work with. The first thing that came to mind was that owls spit up the bones of their prey along with any other parts they can't digest. Initially, the idea was for a knight in full-plate armor to be devoured by a giant strix, only to be spit back up when the owl couldn't digest him. At that time I'd written a lot of fantasy and very little science fiction, so I decided to try going forward in time, rather than back. The knight in armor became a cyborg. The strix, a shape-shifting witch. And the high fantasy I originally had in mind turned out to be something more like a futuristic fairy tale. Throughout its development, "Strix Antiqua" underwent more changes than any other piece I've written. In one version, the protagonist was an adult, telling the story to his niece while her mother lay in a hospital bed. The end result is—at least for me—a story with an oddly lifelike evolution, full of vestigial appendages, questionable growths, and secret histories hidden in its genes.

A question for Hamilton Perez

Q: What's your favorite kind of pie?

A: Strawberry. During the summer as a boy, we used to visit my grandparents in Missouri and my grandmother would make us wonderful strawberry pies. When I think of summer I still think of backyard fireworks, uncomfortable lawn chairs, and a plate full of strawberry pie in my lap.

About Hamilton Perez

Hamilton Perez is a freelance editor and writer living in Sacramento, California. When he's not scribbling notes about stories, he's writing music, rolling 20-sided dice, or bugging the dog.

Showtime

Jamie Brindle

Week One

The adverts are compelling, but you tell yourself you only watch the show because Mary wants to. Your wife has always loved reality TV. So on day one you tune in like half the nation, and you are hooked.

The ten contestants are pretty awful, they always are on these things. But it's different this time. When *this* show ends, only one of these people will survive. Though of course, sims aren't classed as alive, not legally; if they're not properly alive, how can they be said to survive?

There is the predictable media storm. By the end of week one, Tracey is the odds-on favourite. She isn't smart, but she seems kind. It doesn't hurt that she has the kind of figure the tabloids are happy to splash on the front page. Of course, the algorithms used for these Constructs are in the public domain, and the broadsheets focus on that information.

Daniel is a basic Construct, with reduced ability to delay gratification and enhanced hedonism settings. By the end of the first week, he has tried to sleep with three of the other Constructs. When the public vote is counted and he has to go, he just sits there on live TV stimulating himself. He does that right up to the moment some tech pushes a button and Daniel vanishes into the darkness forever.

Week Two

The Prisoner's mother is interviewed at the start of the week. The public falls in love with her. You're hooked like everyone else. You watch this faded, fifty-year old woman cry over the son she is about to lose, watch her talk about which of the Constructs would make a good replacement.

She's not transsexist, she says, but she thinks she would find it very difficult if her son came back as a woman. She knows lots of people do such things nowadays, and she's not judging, but she would just find it difficult. As soon as she says this, Tracy's ratings go down.

After this, Rick becomes the odds-on favourite. He can be supercilious, but he seems genuine. The media zoomed in on him when he has an argument one night with Tom about how no-one can actually know what reality is. He even says, 'What if we're just Sims?' Even though he obviously means it rhetorically, everyone thinks it's hilarious.

The week ends with Pam being voted off. Even though she's quite nice, she is fat. The public knows what it likes, and it's not her. Pam is gone.

Week Three

At work, the show is all anyone talks about, yourself included. The Prisoner's mother now has a regular slot. They say she's going to be interviewed every Monday evening until there's a winner, and she can take them home, wearing her son's old body.

This week, the questions are mainly about the Prisoner himself. Does she think the punishment is proportional? It was a terrible thing, she says, but you can understand why he did it. It wasn't *right;* but still. He was her little boy. He deserves a second chance.

The big story this week though is the activists that attempt to break into the studio where the Prisoner is being held. They want to kill him, they want to shut down the Sim. They say that Constructs should never be uploaded to wetware, it's not natural. They fail, and two are shot dead. The studio immediately starts production on a documentary.

Tom is voted out. The public is not won over by his enhanced-humility, enhanced-vulnerability combination. Too weak. He leaves without a fuss and flares away in a puff of electrons.

Week Four

Some of the papers begin to run stories about whether the Prisoner deserves this sentence. They are just speculating; the journalists are as hooked as the rest of you. You begin to think about him. You do some research, and soon you know more than most. You find yourself defending him. "He just loved his daughter," you say. "His wife was dead," you say. "Wouldn't you have been tempted, in the circumstances?" People send you dirty looks, give you the cold shoulder. You don't care.

You watch your little girl play, and you wonder, *What would I do? What if Jane got sick?*

You are unsure.

This week, while you watch the Constructs await the public axe, you ask your wife if you think it's right to keep them in the dark.

"It's better this way," she says immediately, scandalised. "Imagine if they knew! How awful! It's better that they just think they are on a TV show, if they think they are real. Less painful."

She is disturbed by your question. She looks away while the votes are counted. After Hazel is deleted, you go to bed without talking.

Week Five

You don't understand leukaemia, so you do some research. It would have happened quickly. He wouldn't have had much time to make his decision. The Prisoner's wife had been dead already. They didn't have health insurance. They were far too poor for that.

His work hadn't given insurance, but what they did have was hardware. The Prisoner had worked for the studio, on one of the endless soaps. They Simmed endless plots, endless hours of garbage television. You find yourself sympathising with the Prisoner. Didn't his daughter's life weigh more than all those cheap characters, all those hackneyed plots?

You try to tell your wife, but she is horrified. She looks at you like she doesn't know you. You watch the vote alone.

Kevin is out this week. He stands in the simulated departure lounge, grinning stupidly at the simulated cameras, letting the simulated applause wash over him, thinking he is about to step out to meet the crowds. He is shut down. He doesn't feel a thing.

Week Six

Your wife makes you move out, into a flat just down the road. You could have got somewhere bigger, but you want to be near Jane.

Everyone at work tries to avoid talking to you about the Prisoner. It is all you want to discuss, and you have alienated nearly everyone.

"But he *told* her!" some of them say, as if you don't understand. "It's not like he just Simmed her illegally! He actually *told her* she wasn't real! That poor thing! Can you imagine?"

You can imagine. You look at Jane playing, and you can imagine too well.

Apparently, the Prisoner would stay late every night, pretending to work; really, he was talking to his daughter, Simmed on industrial equipment. They say he was only caught because the soap he was working on was running slow. The analysts worked out what was happening.

Now he is sedated, and he doesn't know that the last days of his life are slipping away.

The week ends with Kirsty being voted out. You stare at her image on the TV in the moments before she is discontinued. You try and find a hint of the Prisoner in her eyes. You know he is there, in a Constructed form with various personality shifts digitally encoded. Kirsty vanishes. Soon, there will be a winner, and the Prisoner will be replaced.

Week Seven

There is a rumour. You find it on chat-rooms, whispered at the bottom of newspaper columns. The studio denies it. You can't let it go.

The rumour is that the little girl is still alive. The rumour is that the studio never shut her down. They say that when the Prisoner was arrested, when the courts ruled that he was guilty, when they sentenced him and stripped him of his name, when they prepared him for personality modification, that the studio sued for loss of earnings. That's how the show happened. It was an opportunity for the studios. But the girl — she was simmed on *their* hardware. They *owned* her. But they couldn't just switch her off, because she knew, because the Prisoner had told her. She was sentient.

The rumour is that she is in the studio, alive, in darkness. Alone.

You can't imagine what a hell that must be.

You watch the vote like everyone else. But this week, your thoughts are not on Freya as the public turns on her. You barely register when she vanishes. You have an idea.

Week Eight

This week there is no vote, and it is because of you.

You watch the cameras watching you back, and you know the country hates you. But you are proud. You won.

She was real. She was alive. The rumours were *true.*

You are in prison, and you hope that Mary will come, you hope that she will bring Jane. She doesn't, and in your heart you are not surprised, just disappointed.

In the end, it wasn't so hard. The big studios are always having technicians service their machines. A false code purchased on an underground website was all it took, and you were in. Their security was a joke; it didn't take you long to find her.

They hadn't even bothered to Sim her toys, games, anyone to play with. She was alone in a white room. You saved her on your phone, then you left and you handed yourself in.

You only care what happens to you because of Jane. But you know you did the right thing.

But that wasn't the kicker. That wasn't what stopped the vote.

What stopped the vote was the other thing.

Week Nine

The papers are going crazy. There is no way the public — or the courts — could condone the continuation of the show. Not now the constructs know.

It wasn't Rick who believed you at first. The three of them were sitting in their lounge when your voice boomed out of the simulated speakers. Rick, with all his talk of subjectivity of perception and individual realities, couldn't believe you when it came to the crunch. But Adam did, when you manipulated their environment, when you swapped their clothes, when you made the room vanish and replaced it with various presets, with the Eiffel Tower, with Niagara Falls. Eventually all three believed you, Adam, Rick, and Tracey. And it all happened live on air. Talk about compulsive viewing. Ratings went through the roof.

Now you are a celebrity yourself. Notorious, but adored.

Even the studio executives can't bring themselves to hate you. Their ratings are so high, they can easily afford to put the three remaining Constructed in Simmed comfort for...well, potentially forever.

The question is, what's going to happen to you?

Week Ten

The public still wants a winner. The public still wants one of the Constructs to walk out of their televisions, to win the body of the Prisoner. To win a real life.

But the Constructs are all decent. When they hear the full story, when they have gotten over the shock of it all, they all renounce that chance. Of course they do. In a way, they *are* him. They *are* the Prisoner. In a way, they all made the choice to save her. Of course they choose to save her again.

Week ten ends, and Adam, Rick, and Tracey all renounce the promise of flesh. They give it to her. They give it to his daughter. You saved her, and now she walks out of the machine, ensconced in secondhand wetware, real, alive.

She comes to see you before the end. She thanks you. She cries. She knows it was you who saved her. She wishes she could save you, but your sentence has been made. The studio will have its pound of flesh.

She promises to watch carefully. She promises she will vote for the version that is most like you.

She says goodbye, and you sit down within the scanner. The machine boots up with a deep hum. They fix a mask to your face. The gas smells sweet. Behind a thick sheet of glass, a digital lens rotates, catching your final seconds of consciousness. You know why the camera's here, of course. You saw the adverts before the first season went out; they were much the same. You hated them — but they were effective. There was something so chilling, so compelling in them, like watching an execution. The whole world was hooked.

As the room shimmers and dims, there is a bright bolt of curiosity mixed in with the fear and the anger and the shame. What will it be like, you wonder, to be torn apart, every mote of consciousness stripped bare, suspended, accounted for? Will what is left of you sense, on some deep level, an echo of what has happened? Maybe you will shriek silently in the back of ten minds, echoing, unheard in the darkness.

You stare straight into the camera, and scream not to tune in, scream that the whole thing is sick, a madness.

But you know deep down that will only make them more desperate to watch.

A question for Jamie Brindle

Q: What five words describe you?
A: Industrious, offbeat, quirky, dedicated, foolish.

About Jamie Brindle

Jamie Brindle has been writing stories for as long as he can remember. Occasionally, they are even published. He was home educated until the age of fourteen, and grew up in a hedge maze that was open to the public (still is- google 'hoo hill maze'). He works as a doctor in the East Midlands, UK.

jamie-brindle.weebly.com

Flann Brónach and the King's Champion

Allison Wall

Once, there was an ancient forest that had always been growing, as long as there had been plants to grow and dirt to grow them in. Its trees were as tall as mountains and so wide that ten deer could hide behind a single trunk. Flann Brónach, a spirit of the air, protected it and everything inside it.

The heart of the forest was a wide, still lake. The sun cast rays of golden light through the branches of the trees, and the water sparkled like diamonds. Flann Brónach swam on the lake as a red-throated loon.

One morning, as she moved through the water, in and out of the sunlight, ripples flashing in her wake, a cloud of songbirds met her. She raised her head and listened. In a flurry of wings and chirps they said men had invaded the forest, shouting, breaking branches, collapsing burrows, smashing nests. Eggs might even now be smashed.

Flann rose up from the lake, her head thrust forward. She soon found three knights of the king, hacking their way through foliage with drawn swords. She landed in their path and shed her loon form. Her eyes were crimson and she stood tall, dressed in gray and white linen.

"You may go no further," she said.

The men pulled back a few paces.

The youngest knight bowed. "We're here on the king's orders, looking for someone who disappeared into these woods."

"Who?"

"A knight, like us."

Her red eyes flashed. "Does the king order the desecration of sacred ground for every errant knight?"

The men glanced at one another but did not answer.

"There are no knights like you in this forest," said the spirit. "Follow your tracks of destruction, and there will be no knights at all."

The young knight bowed deeply. "We are careless from worry. The knight is our friend. We offer our apologies, but we can't leave without him."

The second knight lifted his sword. "We will not leave without him."

"After what you have done, you will be fortunate to leave at all."

With ropes of the north wind, she gathered the knights. She swung them high above the trees and flung them down outside the forest.

All day, the spirit followed the knights' trail, raising up tendrils of honeysuckle and blades of grass, restoring moss and lichen. She set broken branches, repaired burrows and nests, and put mushrooms aright. By the time the sun touched the western horizon, there were no signs any knights had passed through the forest at all.

But she was not satisfied. She didn't know whether a knight had truly crossed the forest's borders, or whether the story had been made up as an excuse to assault the forest. She needed to find out.

A stream ran through a tangled part of the eastern forest. Green willows hung over its banks, and birds called to one another from rocks in its midst. Nearby, a man was repairing a hut. He whistled as he bent and shaped the branches, weaving them together.

Across the stream, a loon fluttered to the ground, and Flann Brónach took on her human form. "You don't look like a knight," she said. "No sword, no armor, no horse."

The man had frozen, his lips still rounded, his hand gripping a bouquet of willow branches.

She blinked her red eyes. "Three knights came into the forest. I spent a morning getting rid of them and an afternoon undoing their destruction. They thought another one in here was in need of finding. Was that you?"

The man leaned his forehead against the heel of his hand. "Yes."

"What's your name?"

"I don't have one. It was taken."

She stared at him for a long time. Scars on the man's hands and arms swirled in concentric circles and knots. The patterns shone palely in the evening light.

"That's a nasty enchantment. No wonder they're looking for you."

The man's head snapped up. He extended his arm. "You can read it?"

"And taste it. Like blood and sulfur in the air." She tilted her head. "I can't undo it, if that's why you're here. It's cast in fire."

The man said, "I hoped for nothing more than a hiding place."

A finch let loose a long, warbling song.

"You've taken many lives," the spirit observed.

"I didn't want to."

She nodded. "Live now by the rule of the forest. If you take life, yours will be forfeit."

The man smiled bitterly. "Out there, my life is already forfeit."

"Then consider this a respite." Flann flapped into the sky, a loon disappearing into the west.

The man's hands began to shake. The branches and brush around him seemed an ever-tightening snare. They were looking for him. They might even now be searching. The sun set, but the man did not light a fire.

Screams on battlefields with moonless skies echoed in his dreams. Alone in his hut, he woke choking. Chipmunks snored, curled in their nests. One cricket played for the stars. Deeper in the forest, frogs laughed to each other from green bulrushes in the shadows. Nothing more.

The three knights flung down by magic in the north marsh had been separated and lost. The youngest knight found his way to the castle first, after midnight. Filthy and soaking wet as he was, he entered the throne room and told the king what had happened, about the woman who could turn herself into a bird and call on the elements of the earth.

The other knights returned in the same condition and told the same story.

"What *is* this?" the king hissed at his tall, bony advisor.

"Sire, it sounds remarkably like Flann Brónach."

"Cowards! Three of them together couldn't find him, convince him, or overpower him, so they blame their failure on a spirit."

The advisor twisted his fingers together. "She may very well be interfering, sire."

"To what end?"

"I couldn't say. Who knows what these spirits want?"

"I should have sent the entire army after him."

"Sire, you know it's best if the truth about the Champion is confined to as few people as possible."

The king grunted and waved his hand. "I have half a mind to leave him to his forest vacation and enchant another one. One with less of a conscience."

"And leave the Champion unchecked? Think of the havoc he could wreak. What if he fights for the enemy?"

The king ground his teeth. "Then I'll recover him myself. He won't be able to disobey if I'm there in the flesh."

The king whirled to the three dripping knights. He clasped his hands behind his back. "This witch has entrapped our Champion. He must be rescued and recovered. We ride on the forest at first light. Pray that it is not too late. He may already be enchanted to attack us."

The three knights bowed and left. Their mail-booted feet clipped and echoed in the stone hallways. A distance from the throne room, the youngest knight pulled the other two into a dark corner.

"Do you believe the king?" he whispered.

"Of course not," said the second knight. "We fought alongside his Champion during the Invasion, same as you."

The mustached knight grunted. "If he fights us, it won't be because of some witch's spell. He has incentive enough for desertion without another enchantment."

"I don't think she is a witch," said the youngest knight.

"It doesn't matter what you think," the mustached knight said, and shoved his way out of the corner. "The king has spoken."

A thunderstorm rolled over the forest, and the sun rose behind a gray veil. Rain whispered against the earth, dripped from branches, gathered in wide-rimmed leaves. The surface of the lake dissolved into rippled circles.

A group of wet-furred animals gathered among the brown cattails. Badger, chipmunks, rabbits, foxes, skunks, deer, and hedgehogs should all have been tucked safely away from the rain, or at least quarreling. They waited at the edge of the lake, soaked and quiet. Flann Brónach paddled through the reeds and climbed ashore.

The striped badger spoke for the animals. Fifty knights were headed for the forest, led by the king. All armed for battle and on horseback.

The spirit met the approaching army near the forest's edge. The trees grew far apart, and rain fell unhindered, plinking against fifty sets of armor.

"Didn't your knights tell you?" she said.

The king reined in his horse and held up his arm for a halt. He shook his wet hair aside and put on a smile. "Tell me what, lady?" he said.

"Murderers and death bringers may not enter."

The king's smile withered. "One of my knights fled into these trees. Show us where he is, that he may be brought home."

"Leave now, while you still can."

The king drew his sword. The spirit caught the blade in a vice of air. She flung it into the wet earth and it was swallowed, hilt and all.

The knights drew their swords. With rain-lashed wind, she collected the knights, their horses, the king's horse, and scattered them beyond the forest like dry leaves. Alone and abruptly unhorsed, the king fell to one knee in the mud.

Flann stood over him. "The forest is under my protection, and as such is beyond your reach. Do not cross its boundaries again."

She wrapped wind all about the king and threw him as far away as she could.

At the outermost forest tree, the spirit collected her fading energy. She gathered a skein of north wind and one of the south and knit them together. Then, as a loon, she flew around edge of the forest, wrapping it all inside the woven wind. She knotted the ends and stitched them together. A fork of silver lightning raced across the sky and sealed the forest with a roar of thunder.

Flann Brónach used the last of her power to fly to the Champion's home. Rain drummed against curtains of willow, and the rising stream rushed over its rocks onto grassy banks. She was too tired shed her loon form, so she waited, small and gray in the underbrush, for her strength to return.

A sparrow had become trapped in a thorn bush. The Champion sat cross-legged in the mud, leaning over the bird. He spoke to it in a quiet voice. It lay still, panting. Bit by bit, he pulled away the sharp spines and tangled stems, making a tunnel to the bird. Once it was big enough, he put his hand in among the thorns. The bird did not flinch. He took it gently and, protecting it from the thorns with his fingers, drew it out. He opened his hand, and the sparrow darted away, cheeping.

With effort, Flann shed her loon form. She leaned against a willow tree, her face pale.

He jumped to his feet. "Are you all right?"

She held up a hand. "The king and fifty knights came to the forest. They're gone. I have set protections in place that will not easily be overcome."

He said nothing.

The spirit closed her eyes. "I fear his anger will tear the world apart. He will not stop until he has won." Her voice ached with weariness.

He looked at his hands, where the sparrow's heart had vibrated against his palm. Thorns had gouged his skin more than once, but left no blood and no mark. "He'll stop if I'm dead."

Her eyes snapped open.

"I can't do it myself. I've tried. The enchantment stops me. But you have magic. You could do it."

"Taking your life helps nothing."

He stepped nearer to the stream. "I ask you to take it."

The spirit's eyes blazed. "If I used my power for death, I would become a demon, and the forest would be left without a guardian. Is that what you want?"

"No."

Her eyes closed again. "Even if I wanted to, there's no getting around the enchantment. Even for me."

Rain fell hard and fast, then settled into a soft patter. "It's hurting you, though, isn't it? Protecting a coward who can't die? I can't ask you to do that. I won't."

Flann smiled. "Not your decision to make." Her wings beat against the air and she flew into the rain.

He was alone.

The king had been in the forest. Rain still pattered overhead, but he could not hear it. His heart pounded at the walls of his chest, trapped within his own body. He opened and closed his hands, watching his fingers, checking for any sign of hesitation. They obeyed him every time.

He tried to sleep, but whenever he nodded off, his body leapt awake. He checked for control, flexed his toes, bent his knees, turned his head. Once, he slept long enough to dream that he was watching his hands rip apart sinew and bone. They wouldn't stop. He woke shaking. He held his hands in front of his face. Opened and closed them, one finger at a time. Open, shut. Open, shut. Still in control, for now.

The king had found himself half sunk in the north marsh, twenty miles from his castle. After hiking all day in rusting armor, he was muddy, furious, and coming down with a cold. He sat before a blazing fire and raged against the spirit of the air who had defied him.

"Does she think she can sit in that forest and keep my Champion from me? We'll burn it the ground, and her inside it!"

"Sire," his advisor said, "Is it reasonable to declare war on a spirit who can displace so many armed knights at once?"

The king flung the sheepskin rug from his shoulders. "What if she's lifted the enchantment?"

"I don't think that's possible."

"Why else would he go to her?"

"Cináed said—"

The king's face flushed and his voice went flat. "That sorcerer. This is all his fault. Cináed! Spirit of fire! Face me, you traitorous coward."

Orange embers showered upward. From beneath the burning logs, a salamander emerged, glowing red. It crawled over the grate and onto the rug. The king's advisor backed into a shadowed corner of the room.

The king glared down at the salamander. "When you swore to protect this crown, were you already planning to betray it?"

Cináed shed his salamander form and stood on two feet before the king, tall, skin smoking. "I only have power in the service of your protection," the spirit of fire said in a voice like gravel. "Why would I give that power up?"

"Power," the king scoffed. "Your enchantment failed."

"The enchantment holds."

"Then explain how he's able to walk free in the forest."

"The forest."

"Yes, yes, the forest, the forest, blast and burn it all to ash! A spirit of the air is harboring him there."

Cináed looked into the fire. "Flann Brónach."

The king snarled, "If I hear that name one more time, I will chop off the lips that pronounced it and shove them down the throat that uttered it. How was he able to get that far away in the first place?"

"Fire binds the Champion to your commands."

"And I commanded him to stay at his post."

"With your own voice?"

The king swore. "Is he to sleep in my bed with me at night?"

"The strength of the enchantment is in your voice. If you did not give the command to him, he is not bound to it."

"It is too late for admonishments, spirit. Keep your oath. Fix this."

Flann Brónach woke in the dark. A dull glow lit the western horizon. Smoke hung in the air. She gathered all creatures to the center of the forest, to the lake, where any fire could be quenched. The Champion was there already.

"This is dragon fire," he said. "I know the smell."

Flann turned away. She stretched her arms through her exhaustion for the strength to fly.

"Wait," he said. "What are you going to do?"

"Protect the forest."

"Against a dragon?"

She looked at him over her shoulder. Her eyes were dim, her lips pale. "If I don't, the forest will burn."

"You're going alone?"

She straightened her back. "I am a spirit of the air."

"And I'm sure normally, a spirit of the air like you could handle ten dragons without breaking a sweat. But the last days haven't been normal."

She raised her eyebrows.

He held his ground. "Do you have the strength?"

"I have no choice." She fell into her loon form and flapped up, scarcely clearing the tree line.

He clenched his jaw, and ran in the direction of the fire.

At the western rim of the forest, a dragon, red hot and smoking, reared on its hind legs. Fire poured from its mouth in a steady stream, breaking against the woven wall of wind. In many places the wall had cracked and splintered, boiled away to scorched charcoal. Leaves on near trees smoldered black.

Flann called, "Cináed!"

The dragon tasted the air with his forked tongue, lashing his head from side to side. He roared wordlessly.

She shouted, "Look at what you have become, guardian, what shape your master's hatred bent you to." She held a still air over the wall, and the flames grew less. "The king would have you attack another spirit and kill a sacred forest. Your magic is only as pure as what you have sworn to protect with it. The king is corrupt. Serving him has poisoned your power."

"Yet it is stronger than yours." Cináed raised his neck. He expanded upward six feet. A crown of spikes blossomed around his head.

The Champion burst from the underbrush, panting. He stared through the wall at the growing dragon.

Flann said, "Anger and hatred will swallow you whole. You'll never be able to put aside that monstrous skin."

The spirit of fire laughed. "Anger and hatred will burn your forest, and you will have nothing left to defend yourself with. I will consume you." Fire splashed against the wall. Tree branches swayed and groaned in the heat.

The air over the wall slipped. Flann steadied it, stilled it.

"What do we do?" the Champion asked.

She did not turn to answer. "I will hold the wall as long as I can."

"Then what?"

"Then nothing. If the wall burns, the forest burns. I only have the power of what I protect. Without the forest, I can do nothing."

"You die?"

Flann Brónach raised her arms to grasp for a strong north wind. It sliced through her fingers and knocked her to the ground.

He watched her rise. Before the spirit could stop him, and before he could stop himself, he sprinted at the forest wall. It opened around him, and closed shut tight behind.

He stood between Cináed and the wall. Fire billowed and engulfed the Champion. He passed through it unscathed. The dragon backed away, shoulder blades rippling with scales and spikes.

He advanced on the dragon. "You forgot what you made me, when you tore me apart and put me back together."

The dragon's tongue flicked in and out.

"I am indestructible. I am invincible. I slew tens of thousands, went without water or food or rest for weeks. An always-victorious slave of my master's will." He held out his arms. "But my master isn't here."

Cináed turned to flee. Faster, the Champion blocked the dragon. "You can't outrun me."

The dragon tucked his head low to the ground. "If you take a spirit's life, you'll be cursed."

"More cursed than I already am? I will never be free of what I've done. And neither will you." The Champion gripped the dragon by its collar of horns to break its neck. The adrenaline of an imminent kill bubbled beneath his skin.

"Wait." The dragon's head bobbed. "Let me live. I'll renounce the king. Give up the oath I swore. I'll diminish, play in fire pits, a powerless salamander. The enchantment will fail! There will be nothing to bind you with."

He looked into the dragon's eyes. He didn't want to kill it, he realized. He didn't want to kill anything, but had never been allowed to show mercy. "Do it."

The dragon blinked, swallowed. "I forfeit the oath to protect the king and willingly relinquish all the power of protection."

The dragon shrank. Rough scales smoothed, claws retracted, tail shortened. A black and yellow salamander scurried through the grass trampled flat by dragon feet.

"Stand ready," shouted the king.

The Champion's body locked at attention, waiting for orders. Despair crowded his mind in a mist. The enchantment held. Had Cináed lied to him?

Three men on horses waited at the edge of the clearing. A fourth, the king, rode forward and dismounted. He brought his boot down on the salamander, crushing it.

"Well," the king said. "I meant him to destroy the spirit in the forest so I could get to you, but this is better. Tidier." He scraped the salamander from his shoe, and approached.

Fear ran along the Champion's limbs, but they didn't shake. He was caught in the enchantment's vice.

The king sniffed. "Impressive. Not even dragons and spirits match you. I must have been too easy on you before. I won't make that mistake again."

He fought against his numb lips.

"Something you want to say? Go ahead. Speak."

"I won't go back."

The king spat to one side. "Oh, you're going back. I'm curious, though. What did you think would happen if you ran away? That I'd just let you disappear?"

Something shifted in the Champion, like earth beginning to erode. "I gave you ten years of slaughter." The king hadn't commanded him to talk, but his lips had loosened. Was the enchantment fading?

The king surveyed the forest. He didn't seem to notice the Champion spoke out of turn. "Were you hoping for something that would kill you? That witch, maybe?"

Anger flared through his fear. "She's not a witch."

The king glared. "Be silent."

His mouth tightened, but the command ebbed. He pushed at the enchantment's limits. "She is a spirit of the air. More noble than you'll ever be."

The king's face twitched. "Enough. You have acted treasonously against this crown. Return, fight for me, and all will be forgiven."

The order pulled his legs, but he maintained his footing.

"Come!"

His knee jerked forward, but again he stood.

The third time the king called, his body didn't respond at all. The impulse to obey flowed through him like water, but washed away. "No," he said.

The king's face blanched white. "You can't say that to me," he snarled. He drew his sword and advanced.

The Champion blocked the king's swing. He wrenched the sword away by its blade and threw it as hard as he could. It flashed end over end in the sunlight and disappeared into the distance.

The king looked wildly after it.

The Champion's hands bled freely. He held them out. "Look. It's over. The enchantment is gone."

"It can't be," the king said. "You're bound to my words. Stand ready!"

He turned his back to the king and walked toward the forest.

The king drew a dagger. He flung himself at his lost Champion, wrapped an arm around his throat to cut it.

The Champion ducked forward and pulled the king over his head. The king landed hard, his dagger caught beneath him. The silver tip protruded from his abdomen. His eyes stared, frozen in an expression of fury and hate.

The once Champion and the three knights talked for a long time. A pair of yellow butterflies flitted among the wildflowers at their feet. Together, they buried the body of their king. They covered the place with grass and did not mark it. The three knights rode away.

The nameless man and the king's horse approached the forest's edge, but did not enter. Fireflies glittered among the dark tree trunks. Flann Brónach stood in shadow.

"You're free," she said. "How does it feel?"

"Like a dream." The man breathed in the night air, sweet with grass and dew. "I came to say goodbye."

"Oh?"

"The knights will say the king was ambushed by enemy soldiers. It won't hold up for long, but it'll give me a head start. They'll hunt for me."

She did not answer him.

"I wish I could do something to repay you."

Fireflies danced green and gold in the roots of the trees. He thought she had gone, but her voice whispered on the breeze. "If you return, you will be welcome."

A flutter of wings disturbed leaves and underbrush. Over the canopy of the forest silvered in moonlight, a loon called.

A question for Allison Wall

Q: What is the scariest or most disturbing story you've ever read?

A: There are several in the running for most disturbing. "The Lottery" by Shirley Jackson is the first story I remember being seriously disturbed by. Flannery O'Connor's "Good Country People" and "Revelation" are up there, along with Joy Williams's "Traveling to Pridesup." As far as scary, Jeff VanderMeer's "The Third Bear" plain terrified me—I didn't have the guts to read the rest of his collection afterwards.

About Allison Wall

Allison is a Kansas-based writer. She teaches, and has taught many things, including but not limited to piano, second grade, and creative writing, and can usually be found in the vicinity of books, cats, music, and tea. Allison is currently finishing an MFA in Creative Writing at Hamline University.

October

The Hole in the Wall

Andrew Leon Hudson

It wasn't a door, because it didn't meet the ground. It wasn't a window, because—no matter how high or low they are on a wall—windows show something, even if it's just drawn curtains. Or a room previously filled with things, all now gone.

This was just a hole in the wall. It showed... nothing.

Yohaena stared across the cobbles from her splay-legged slump. She was exactly as far from the world's finest market as a life-long sober woman could stagger after enjoying her first sinful drinks. Bought with her last honest coins.

Until the moment they threw her out, the other drinkers in the tavern had found her entertaining. She could curse the taxman, curse her audience, curse the stars that shone on her birth, curse the King even—though perhaps not quite so loud as the rest—but the minute she insulted the *market* of all things she was out on her ear, clutching a wooden mug containing only dregs.

The market that had taken everything she had with a smile, and given her nothing back in return.

She swung her bleary gaze away from the hole, trying to orient herself. With greasy rain slicking out of her fringe and down her face, she felt like having a bit of a cry. With the world suddenly spinning around her head, she felt like having a bit of a puke as well.

Her head and shoulders rested against another wall, the wall of... she sneered ...of a *shop*, of course, what else? The urge to cry went away and the urge to shout incomprehensible insults rose again, to rant in tongues, to slur slurs—she giggled.

Her chin hit her chest, and confronted by the nothing in the hole in the wall the giggling died away. That's what she had: *nothing*. Only a worthless mug, and nothing to drink from it.

Yohaena had been born and raised at the foot of mountains so distant that from the capital they were barely a shadow on the horizon. But they towered over Wallys, her home, like the stairway of giants, each high plateau overshadowed by those beyond, dawn breaking over their edges like molten gold, pooling and spilling from one to the next.

Only on the highest of those mountain plains grew the stone fruit. The trees were short and sturdy, their roots cracking the rock with their grip, with thick trunks to stand against the hardest wind. Their few leaves were clustered like fists around the fruit itself, more suited to protection than begging the sun for energy.

Late in the year, the fruit fell. In Wallys, tradition said it all dropped in one day, and that (if the festival were only a little less boisterous—it never was) you could hear the echoing of the fruit's impacts like applause coming down from the peaks.

Much time would pass before the small, stony fruit came to human hands, if it did at all. It dropped from the trees, black and hard as coal, flecks glinting on its impenetrable skin like quartz. Over months, even years, the wind blew the oval fruit over cliffs, down slopes, some vanishing into gulleys and crevasses never to see the light again—or to wash out from the springs and underground streams that fed the waters of the plains. The people of Wallys kept fine nets to pluck fruit from the flow, gifts as strange as the fine fish spawn that spewed forth on irregular autumns only to return years later as blind, translucent giants, fighting upstream in their thousands to disappear back underground, breed, and swim no more.

Those fruit which failed to reach the lowlands would never ripen. The mountain birds and animals knew it, and made seasonal pilgrimages to dig through the shale slides, or picked out their glinting rewards with sharp, circling eyes. They bore them down to warmer ground and hid them away, waiting out the long months until they came good; and enough of the seeds within were carried back to the heights through the ways of nature that the sparse but long-lived forests in the sky would be maintained.

Only once had someone attempted to trade stone fruit with the wider world: Maynehla Paraesei, Yohaena's own mother, long before her daughter's birth. Yohaena had grown up hearing the story, lived it in her mind's eye—how as a young woman they'd thought her mother a fool.

Her old ma, a fool! Young Yohaena had laughed. A fool much respected in every household in Wallys.

As the years passed, she dreamed about doing the same. After Maynehla passed, the dream slowly matured into something more. The following spring she prepared for the journey, secretly planning, buying what she didn't have and disinterring the old tools of her mother's trade. *Four months of travel*, and no time in that to spare. It could be done.

When summer came, she climbed to where the stone fruit could be harvested in numbers—a risky excursion in itself, so much so as to keep the locals satisfied by what good fortune washed their way. The windfall harvest would be sparser this year—let the beasts hunt for whatever remained overlooked from years past, scattered across the mountain's face still waiting to be discovered.

In the thin air she prised apart those fists of leaves, twisted their cold, hard fruit free. She filled one sack and then another, six in all, struggled with them one by one between the steep-walled plateaux down towards home. On the lowest, she piled cairns of heavy rocks upon each sack, protecting them from foragers, delaying until the last possible moment the beginning of their ripening. Until the day when all six could be carried the final step, loaded up and on their way.

But she told her friends and neighbours none of this, let no-one know until the day she started west. Let them call *her* a fool as well. Let them wait for her grand return.

She arrived with a cartload, prepared to make a killing.

Drawing it by hand, she had followed the rail lines to save herself the cost of a fare, passing through hamlets, villages and towns. At every one was a market square, or a trading post, or at least someone with an eager eye on her wares.

But no trade was good enough for the clever and cunning Yohaena Paraesei. She was going to the capital, to the marketplace of marketplaces, where her unique goods would make her rich. So she turned down all offers and strode past every trading post with gaze fixed straight ahead.

And her stone fruit slowly turned from the glinting black of night to the swirling grey of the thickest fog.

Miles passed. Soon she stared, half-starved, at the produce which cruelly decorated stalls in every town on the road from the mountains through the plains—fruit and vegetables, greasy pies and skewers of meat, sweets and pastries... but she saved her money, ate only trail bread, drank only water, because unseen in the distance a fortune lay waiting for her.

And the fog-grey skin of the stone fruit paled to that of the even, endless moorland mists.

At journey's end, in the city's great shadow, she ran a final gauntlet of roadside merchants hailing from every corner of the world, offering what they had for what she had, inviting her to join them. She couldn't understand why anyone would travel right to the brink of fortune's fount and then balk at the last. She refused them all, rejected every offer, and crossed the threshold into the capital without a backward glance.

And, at long last, the stone fruit ripened to a silvered sheen. Their skin grown brittle as eggshells, ready to crack open along their seams at the slightest pressure and release the tender, sun-coloured flesh within, the cool scent of mountain summers.

Perfection. It was time.

Of course, there was a tax to pay to pass through the city gates —higher than her old ma Maynehla had described, from back when she'd made the same trip in her prime. And there were market fees, naturally: official stall rental, for example, because space was at a premium, and non-standard sizes demanded non-standard rates. Plus, of course, uncommon foodstuffs like hers needed to be officially tested and granted a Safe Consumption Seal before they could be sold —can't risk an epidemic, not again—but testing means providing samples, *of everything*, and neither tests nor seals come cheap.

Almost all her money was spent just getting in the gate, and to raise the cash for both stall rental and goods testing she was forced to sell the uniquely beautiful stall her old ma once made by hand. A sadness... but it was of little use to her now, and she could always buy it back before she returned home in triumph.

She delivered samples to the Bureau of Testing, paid the fees, took her chit, and waited for their verdict—wasting precious days, precious weeks. She paid the difference between stall rental and stall sale into the pocket of an innkeeper, while her remaining wares aged past their best, and she spent worthless days watching over her cart in case thieves less concerned about epidemics made off with her goods before she had her chance to sell.

And the silvered stone fruit whitened, first snow-like, then ivory. Their crisp skins softened, no more to pop open with a startling crack, but to be punctured by a thumbnail, pried open and peeled, the rich flesh turned amber, the flavour from subtle to sweet.

Finally, they granted her seal. The last of her cash bought it into her hand, and she left the inn to take her place in the world's greatest market: surrounded by the finest merchants, their glamorous patter luring in wealthy prospects from all sides, their outlandish, non-standard stalls drawing each purchaser's eye, their unique and perfect goods opening every wallet.

But with her crumpled costume and bland, square stall of wrinkling, fading produce, Yohaena went all but unnoticed amidst all the commerce. She could barely make herself heard over the sound of everyone else's success. She dropped her prices in desperation; struck woeful deals in the futile hope that the first sale would provoke a flood; stood at attention all night—eyelids fluttering, swaying like the drunk she was shortly to become—in case some cunning buyer would pause and make a clever deal while all the rest were sleeping, oblivious to their foolish loss.

And the stone fruit, over-ripe and quick to bruise, cloyed the air around her, their leathery skins yellowing back to grey.

She sold the last of her stock—almost half what she'd left home with—to one man, who swept it into a hand cart with a broken-off broom head, and in return paid her less than the value of the pathetic rented stall. She sold her cart, because she didn't have enough money to buy anything big or numerous enough to need one—including old Maynehla's beautiful, hand-crafted stall, which she next saw in a shop window in a twisty little lane a dozen turns from the market that had ruined her life—priced twice the sum she had taken for it, four times what she now had left.

Every lot in that lane was a shop of some kind, but she didn't set foot in one of them, clinging to her molehill of cash and only looking in, untrusting of the deals, the trinkets, the welcoming smiles. The exception to both cases was the first property: not a shop but an inn, and this she entered, driven by weariness, thirst and hunger. She'd stay for a night and buy a full stomach while she figured out her next move, how she would snatch a better future from the lifetime of misery that now loomed before her.

They served ale with her meal. She'd never touched alcohol— *trader's betrayer*, Maynehla had called it—and looked from innkeeper to drink with equal distrust. But her own inner voice murmured in her other ear: *What did she have left to lose? What kind of trader had she proven to be?*

In any case, the innkeeper reassured her that the first drink was always free.

The dregs in her mug were watered down with rain, just a puddle at the bottom, with an oily memory of foam on its surface. Yohaena tilted the mug, tipped it into the bigger puddle growing beneath her sodden trousers.

Bile rising in her gorge and spirit, she raised the mug above her head with one shaking arm and hurled it across the lane, aiming for the hole only inasmuch as it was directly before her.

It struck the target—she barked a single laugh at her good aim— and vanished from view. There was no clatter against whatever lay beyond. Silently, absolutely, the mug was gone.

She laughed again, wearily, closed her eyes on the swirling world —and heard a familiar sound, the sound of fallen...

She opened her eyes again. A glint winked at her from the cobbles beyond her boots. She looked up and down the lane but she was alone, no charitable night-walker taking contemptuous pity on her. Yet, there lay a single penny—good for two drinks at that cursed inn, worth more than the old stained mug itself, no doubt.

A different laugh emerged now, low and grudging, that of a woman who knows the joke is on her and waits for the proof to show itself. She pulled off her hat, tossed it dismissively, saw it sail through the hole into nothingness with the certainty of a boat swept along a river current—and this time she *saw* the coin sail back out, spinning in the air as though tossed from a thumb. Others followed before the first had hit the ground, rolling between the cobbles to strike the sole of her boot.

Yohaena gripped her trousers and pulled herself upright, leaned forward with a long and queasy belch, fumbled the nearest coin into her hand. She held it almost to her nose, eyes crossing... *it was real.*

She rolled onto all fours, crawling after the others, the rain-slippery stones poking painfully into hands and knees, then sat back on her heels to inspect her haul: two pennies, three crowns. She could buy two hats with this. Or one, but better than the one she'd thrown.

Cradling them to her chest, with a speculative look in her eye she unbuckled and tugged free her belt one-handed, guessed its worth both now and new, and slung it at the hole. The buckle led the way, the cracked leather dragged in over the lip of brick like a tongue—and more coins sprayed from the void. She scrabbled for them, counted her fortune: seven crowns and thrupence.

For a second, she considered.

In a frenzy, she tore at her clothes, one boot, the other, then shirt and breeches, all thrust at the hole, until the tinkling clamour of metal on stone was done. Until she stood in only her smalls, the hem of her undershirt cradling a clinking bundle.

When dawn broke, Yohaena looked up from her compulsive counting to find the wall's brickwork unbroken and no sign of the hole. Perhaps she had lost her mind along with her goods, her cart and her old ma's stall. Fine. So be it. She had seventeen crowns and eight pennies, all told.

There may never have been a more unusual trader in the capital than the one who emerged from the lane that day: a woman in her underclothes, who walked on bruised feet to the cheap and ordinary side of town, went from shop to stall there, doling out coins from what looked like an old vest. She bought:

A drawstring bag that opened into a sheet, like those which street-sellers use to display their junk and trinkets, and which real people step over with barely a look;

A smock-shirt, little more than a sheet itself—less, maybe, since it had a hole in the middle for a head to poke through, and just a length of cord to tie at the waist;

A pair of clogs, the worst to be had, cracked along their soles due to poor choice of wood;

And, last but not least—let's even say *most*—all the worthless trade goods shameless traders would sell her.

She drove a hard bargain, this clown in a beggar-gown: she rooted through goods shop-worn or flawed, bid on them in bulk, demanding discount rates for what they saw as inconvenient trash. And each shopkeep took her money with a genuine smile, one that widened into a grin as she went out through their doors again. Because—in a place where the best can be found, and so only the best will do—no-one buys the defective, no-one buys the poor. Unless the purchaser is poor and defective herself.

The madwoman bought as much as she could carry, as much as her drawstring bag would hold.

Money spent, Yohaena returned to the lane, loosened the ties of her bulging bag and upturned it onto the cobbles, stuffing it through her cord belt when it was empty. All day she squatted there, arranging her prizes, rearranging them again, ignoring those few passersby who paused to look—because, after all, there was always potentially business to be done, even with the likes of such as this. But whenever one offered a coin, their eye caught by some curio on her sheet, the madwoman turned them down, so they walked on shaking their heads, or laughing at the lunatic playing shopkeeper amongst the shops, her eyes on the plain empty wall opposite.

Quite mad, they told each other.

In the dark at the heart of night, the hole in the wall returned, a blackness on the black. Yohaena was watching for it, and saw its appearance. She was happy not to be mad.

She took the empty sheet from her belt and spread it before the hole. Then, starting with the poorest of her purchases and ending with the clogs, one by one she threw them all in. Only the drawstring sheet remained, coins piling up on it.

When day broke she could hardly pull the strings closed, could hardly lift the bag from the cobbles.

She bought new clothes—nothing fancy, just replacements for the old: a good hat, and shirt, and trousers, sturdy boots to take her home, a thick coat for when the north winds welcomed her back to the mountain's foot. And still she had enough left over to go to the market that had tried to ruin her, where her clothes and wallet brought every merchant running, eager to strike a deal, not one of them knowing her for the fool whose stall had once stood ignored beside their own.

Finally, she returned to a particular shop where, with great pleasure, she bought back her old ma's stall: the strong bamboo frame, cleverly tied with oiled leather to collapse flat as a board, its sky-blue canvas binding them together but still proudly boasting name and business—*Paraesei, in Trade*—stitched and dyed by hand.

She waited out the day in the lane, on the cobbles—on a carpet of intricate weave, surrounded by bolts of fine cloth and silk, by bags of spices, more. And old Maynehla's stall lay folded and wrapped behind her, *because she was not trading*, no matter what anyone offered for her wares.

She waited for one last night, and the hole.

She started with the spices, hurling them in, a cascade of currency pouring forth onto her carpet—silver coins and gold, a mound of wealth that grew and grew as the cloth and silk and other goods followed. At last the stream began to ebb, the final spurts of coins emerging—a couple more, a couple more, one more—in a way familiar, but which she couldn't put her finger on...

Then it was done.

Her carpet was laden with more money than she had ever known. She need never trade again—Maynehla's beautiful stall might go unopened until after Yohaena went to join her old ma in the beyond, but she would never want.

For a moment she considered throwing it into the hole as well. She wondered what that might earn her. Forget the base material worth, could the hole reward her for its personal value—what the thing *meant* to her as well?

She shook her head—no amount of money would buy her old ma's stall from her, not now nor ever again—but her eye fell upon the little shining mountain of coins and a new thought occurred.

Forget the regal profiles and fearsome beasts pressed into their sides, forget their cultural meaning: the metals had material worth too, much of it, and the hole had always given back more value than it consumed. The gold, the silver of the coins—what would the hole give her for all that?

What reward could exceed even money itself?

With great care, Yohaena gathered up the corners of her carpet and drew them together over the pile, bunched two in each fist, and strained. With shaking arms, thighs quivering, she raised the bulging carpet from the cobbles and began to swing it, back and forth between her knees.

Brow furrowed with effort, she swung. Teeth gritted, she swung. Lips pulled back as if fishhooks were caught in the corners of her mouth, she swung. Her gaze only on the hole, fixed deep upon its absent depths... and she released.

The upper corners of the carpet slipped free and it billowed open like a sail, the mass of coins floating—together, each separate—

through the air. At the edge of their cloud, five coins struck the bricks and bounced back around her boots. All the rest fell into nothingness and were gone, the carpet flapping in her hands as though waving farewell.

She waited, watching the hole.

There was a tax on traders departing the city. There was always another tax in the capital. Her five coins just covered it.

Yohaena strode out in sturdy boots and good new clothes, winter coat folded over one arm, carpet rolled up beneath the other. On her back, the collapsible stall was wrapped and strapped, swaying above her broad hat like the standard of a warrior from some distant land, trailing her banner in the breeze. Her pockets were as light as her heart.

She walked through the days, slept soundly at night, growing lean on the road across the plains. The capital fell behind her and the mountains slowly rose ahead; and, should she happen across travellers making camp as dusk fell, or see a caravan approach through the midday haze, she would stop, unroll her carpet at the roadside and erect her stall upon it—selling the invaluable to anyone who cared to buy.

She never asked for much, just a coin or two if her customer had it to spare, a bite to eat if not. And though what she offered was not exactly the truth (because no-one pays for a story that can't be believed) it always had the ring of truth about it.

Wisdom paid her way back home.

A question for Andrew Leon Hudson

Q: What kind of pieces are the most fun to write (action, lyrical, etc.)?

A: I like to write "character" scenes, but that gets me across the borders and into action scenes, lyrical scenes, sitting-and-contemplating scenes, the lot. Any time you're showing someone active in a story, you're building up who and what they are, even if it's only in the smallest way. So (just to tread on my own toes) I probably find action scenes the most fun to write because you're revealing someone in extremis, and that's when they can prove your expectations or be the most surprising.

About Andrew Leon Hudson

Andrew Leon Hudson is an improper Englishman whose previous employment includes selling Christmas hampers and contact lenses, "intoxicant delivery", prosthetic make-up manufacture, servicing the armed forces and saving the world from millennial apocalypse. His first novel came and then went again, so now he's mostly doing that sort of thing himself.
andrewleonhudson.wordpress.com

Shine

Amelia Aldred

Joanne balanced a third jar of pickles on her arm as she peered into another of Grammy's cupboards. Once again, she saw endless rows of canned goods but not a drop of liquor or a recipe card. "Damnit Grammy, where'd you keep it?" she said, then flushed with guilt. *This is your fault,* Joanne berated herself as she re-arranged the pickles exactly as she had found them. *You could've asked Grammy a dozen times about her famous moonshine recipe and now she's gone. You decided not to call home more, you could've...*

Grammy's old dog Bess walked stiffly into the kitchen and rubbed against Joanne's leg, interrupting her self-scolding. She scratched Bess's head with one hand, opened another cupboard and spied a scratched metal index card box wedged between jars of dilly beans. Joanne's heart quickened as she grabbed the box. Her mind began to play fantasies of deconstructing Grammy's moonshine recipe; she saw herself serving Grammy's exact whiskey to her astounded boss at the brewery. She could hear his praise and imagined Grammy's moonshine pouring into the market.

Joanne took the box to the kitchen table, shoving aside the piles of milk crates and shoeboxes to sit down. Momma had sighed in relief when Joanne offered to sort through her grandmother's kitchen before returning to Chicago; her mother was busy feeding the relatives that had come up to the mountains for Grammy's funeral and sucking her teeth at every beer can set on her table without a coaster. If Momma knew Joanne was looking for Grammy's moonshine formula, Joanne would be back to making small talk with the relatives and enduring awkward pauses as she tried to translate her life outside Kentucky to her extended family. This morning during breakfast, Joanne's cousins had listened to her stories of life in Chicago with the detached politeness reserved for outsiders. She'd tried to explain the excitement watching her roommate's improv troupe and her wonder and confusion at trying Thai food for the first time, but she couldn't capture the experiences and the stories fell flat. Stories about work fared a little better; they liked that Joanne worked at Goose Island

Brewery because it was success they could understand and measure by the cases she had brought with her. *Reckon you got the knack from your Grammy; my Daddy said she made the best moonshine whiskey he ever tasted, made him sleep a week and dream he was a prince in a castle,* one of her cousins had commented. *You were always real good at baking and canning and such, I remember. Your Grammy ever teach you how to make her shine?* Joanne had replied no and they sat in awkward silence again until she left for Grammy's house.

She felt more at home sitting alone at Grammy's table than she had felt surrounded by family. Joanne remembered the hours spent here, making birdhouses out of milk cartons, drawing Halloween masks on paper plates, and a dozen other projects. Her favorite game in those days had been to make something out of whatever was lying around the kitchen, and Grammy had let Joanne spread out her crayons and paper and glue all over the table. The only rule was that Joanne had to clean up after herself. Joanne felt a twinge in her chest and tried to remember the last time she made something just for the sheer love of it. She couldn't recall, and the failure troubled her. Joanne shoved the last crate out of the way and opened the index card box. Her body buzzed with excitement as it hadn't for months.

Card after card of shaky handwriting detailed her grandmother's familiar recipes and the best time of year to make them: *Hot Relish-June, Crabapple Jelly-September, Fairy Bread-All Hallows' Eve.* Joanne grinned at the last one. Grammy was always superstitious about the Folk, as she called them. It wasn't uncommon among older Knox County residents; Joanne remembered telling her incredulous college roommate that she was never allowed to trick or treat past sunset, not for fear of nightly news kidnappers, but because Grammy insisted that the Fair Folk rode abroad that night. *The Folk take children and leave their own behind in exchange,* Grammy explained when Joanne and her brothers protested. *Most of the Folk's changelings die, but the ones that live are powerful as can be, charming animals and making you see things that ain't there. They can't come in unless invited, so we leave bread and milk on the windowsill to show respect, and stay in the house until they've passed.* Her roommate had laughed at Joanne's story, in the same way she laughed at the way Joanne pronounced "wash" as "warsh" and when Joanne put red wine in the refrigerator.

The measurements in the recipe cards were idiosyncratic, to say the least. *A piece of butter the size of a goose egg, not the brown one that bites, the other one.* "Land's sake, Grammy," she said aloud to Bess, imitating her late grandmother's aggrieved tone. How did anyone cook this way? As she read them, it seemed every card had some sort of nonsense doodle scrawled in one of the corners.

None of the cards revealed anything stronger than bourbon pecan pie filling. Well, what did she expect? Everyone knew that old-time shiners like Grammy worked from memory, nothing like the careful measurements Joanne used at work. She felt the prickles of excitement ebb away and the familiar heaviness descend on her chest again. Bess rested her chin on Joanne's knee and she stroked the hound's greying head. "It's okay," she told Bess. "I don't need to learn how to make Grammy's shine. I have a good job in Chicago. I got out of Knox County, like I said I would. It's okay." Bess's eyebrows furrowed doubtfully.

Joanne got up to fix some lunch. It wasn't hard—Momma and the aunts cooked enough food to feed a football team for Grammy's wake and Joanne had brought a grocery bag of leftovers to Grammy's house. It was strange being in the kitchen without her grandmother. She could almost hear her seven-year old self asking questions as they rolled out cookie dough.

Why do we put the baking soda in the cookies, Grammy? It tastes icky.

Cause it helps them rise, honey.

But why?

Don't rightly know. Maybe you should look that up in one of them library books.

She put some leftovers down for Bess and tried to calculate how long it would take her to go through the kitchen, before she had to be back at work on Monday. She got out a pencil and notepad from the table drawer and made a bulleted list of all the things that needed doing, and then started to add sub-bullets.

"Jo? That you?" A voice came from the front porch.

"I'm in the kitchen, Aunt Myrtle. Come on in."

An old woman entered the kitchen, wearing overalls and a Dave Matthews T-shirt, her braided grey hair wrapped in a crown around her head.

"Your Daddy said you'd be here—I figured you're looking for Liza's moonshine recipe. Don't worry, I didn't let it slip to your Momma." Aunt Myrtle wasn't really her aunt, but she'd been neighbors and friends with Grammy for so long that it didn't seem right to call her anything else.

"Yeah. Folks on the mountain still talk about her whiskey—say it was the best in four counties."

"That's 'cause it was. Wasn't no moonshiner like your Grammy. Won't be again."

Joanne felt her throat and jaw tighten. She got up and started washing her dish, scrubbing harder than the casserole crumbs warranted. "Yeah. I mean, I could do it, if I knew the ingredients, but..." she said, letting frustration creep into her tone. Joanne remembered her manners "Sorry, Aunt Myrtle, would you like me to fix you a plate?"

"You bring some of your Aunt Lindy's raisin bread? I could do with a slice and some milk to wash it down." Joanne brought the last of the raisin bread, a tub of margarine, and jam jar of milk to Aunt Myrtle, then returned to the sink and started scrubbing the empty loaf tin.

"You got yourself a job in Chicago brewing, your Daddy said." Aunt Myrtle spread margarine on the bread and Bess whined for a scrap. "I ain't sharing. Get," the old woman told the dog. Bess got.

"I'm a commercial chemist at the brewery. Money's g— I mean, I'm paid well." Joanne dried her plate. "It's a really competitive job—a lot of chemists applied."

"You happy?"

Joanne gave a weak smile as her eyes fell on the kitchen table, its wood worn from being scrubbed twice a day for over half a century. She knew that she was supposed to say she was very happy, be Momma and Grammy's whip-smart girl who won the science fair every year and left the mountains to have a fairytale life, but she couldn't quite bring herself to perform the lie.

Unlike the rest of the family, Aunt Myrtle didn't leap to fill the silence. The old woman never did. Joanne swallowed and kept her eyes on the table. "I'm using my degree...and it's the kind of job I wanted." The clock ticked on the wall. "I picked chemistry in college because I liked putting things together and making new stuff. Building things."

"Aunt Myrtle nodded. "I remember when your Grammy got you them Legos for Christmas you built a whole city on this table. Liza thought you was going to sleep with those things like a teddy bear."

"I figured this job would be perfect, making beers that are sold all over the world. And I did like it at first. Now it just feels...pointless. But I don't know why." She thought about the long rows of gleaming stainless steel drums at work, the hours spent churning out perfect batches of market-tested beers six days a week. No one had ever directly told her she needed to work Saturdays, she just figured it made her more indispensable. More secure. "I like detail stuff, but lately it feels like all detail and no creating. Just checklists." Aunt Myrtle glanced at Joanne's notepad of tasks and raised an inquiring eyebrow. "I'm good at following a checklist. I should be happy having a job like this."

"Just 'cause you're good at something don't mean you're happy doing it. I'm fair good at ironing but I never could abide it." Aunt Myrtle took a sip of her milk. "Ever think about looking for other work?"

"It's a good job, and it's in my field. If I'm not happy in this job...I don't think I'd feel better in another one. And I worked hard to get this job; it doesn't make sense to look for a different one." Joanne hugged herself and avoided Aunt Myrtle's eyes.

"Your Grammy was real proud, you getting your degree and going to Chicago and everything. Teased your Momma something dreadful, about you making liquor. "

"Yeah, Momma told folks at the funeral that I'm a commercial chemist—for a *top* Chicago beverage maker," Joanne imitated her mother's too-bright tone when talking about unpleasant things. Aunt Myrtle laughed and Joanne joined in. She forgot how good being with Aunt Myrtle was—something changed in the air when she was around. Lit up the room, as Grammy had said. The tension in Joanne's shoulders loosened a bit.

Aunt Myrtle finished her food and beckoned Bess, who lay her head on the old woman's foot and immediately started snoring. "You know I used to run shine for Liza? Drove the Ford right over Soldier's Hollow, then over the border to Indiana. Watched her make it more times than I could count." She laced her fingers together and cracked her swollen knuckles. "Reckon I could teach you to make shine like her, if I thought you could pull it off."

"Really? You know Grammy's formula?" Joanne's heart skipped a beat.

"Near enough. Made Liza sad, thinking that no one would make her moonshine after she passed. But she didn't want to teach just anybody, wanted to be sure they could do it right. Liza thought about teaching you, but your Momma would've had a fit. Your Momma wanted better for you all. Liza's shine put shoes on her kids' feet but it wasn't easy, you know. Your Momma always hated people talking and whiskey money came with talking. And Liza said you already had yourself a good job, thought you wouldn't be interested." Joanne's stomach twisted and she wished that she could remember the last time she had called Grammy. She'd been so busy and Momma always gave her updates, but still...

Aunt Myrtle went on, "I'd rather let things be buried with Liza than see someone put out her liquor without it tasting proper. I owe her that. But it would be nice to taste her shine again." Aunt Myrtle looked around the room, her eyes lingering over the painted cupboards and the ancient stove that Grammy refused to replace. "You think I'd be used to people dying, as many of my friends I've buried. But I don't seem to ever get hard to it."

Joanne crossed over and put her hand on the Aunt Myrtle's shoulder. Aunt Myrtle's eyes kept searching the room; her gaze finally turned to Joanne, looking her up and down like she was sizing up a new truck. "Tell you what. Make your best whiskey for me. I'll taste it, and if I think you can make Liza's shine, I'll teach you."

Joanne kissed Myrtle's crown braid. "I can do it. I'll make whiskey so perfect, you'll reckon you died and went to heaven. My boss says I'm the most consistent brewer on the team."

"Consistent," Aunt Myrtle echoed.

Joanne sat at Grammy's kitchen table, waiting for Aunt Myrtle. Her foot couldn't stop tapping, and she moved it from under the table, so as not to jiggle the bottle of whiskey. Seven days was not as fast as Grammy's legendary three day brew—but it was chemically impossible to ferment the mash that quickly and Joanne guessed that was just folks telling tall tales. These were same people that carried rowan when mushroom hunting and talked about Rip Van Winkle bowling with the Folk and drinking their liquor like it happened yesterday.

She had stretched the truth to her boss and used some vacation time for "family matters". Joanne justified her lie by telling herself that there was a market for moonshine now, banking on hipster nostalgia for past sins. If she returned to Chicago with a genuine backwoods moonshine recipe, it would be a gold star for her rep as a brewer and distiller. Though, since moonshine was just illegal white whiskey, was it even moonshine if you made it legally? The question made her head pound more. Her eyes hurt from poring over exact measurements and her fingers ached from building a still in the kitchen out of copper piping from the hardware store and Grammy's tea kettle, but the whiskey in the Mason jar was so clear, it looked empty.

There was a loud knock at the door and Joanne jumped.

"Come on in," she called. Aunt Myrtle stomped into the kitchen. She didn't greet Joanne, just sat at the table, unscrewed the jar, and took a swig.

"My stars, girl—that's smooth as a river at midnight." Aunt Myrtle set the jar down. "But ain't it."

Joanne felt hot tears prickle. Her arms were shaking from carrying tubs of water, her fingers hurt, and she hadn't spent so much time calculating grams and kilos since her college days.

"But I made this whiskey from an award-winning formula and I made it exactly perfect! There isn't—there ain't nothing *wrong* with it!"

Aunt Myrtle shrugged. "It's perfect all right. But it ain't it." She gave Bess a scratch. "I'll be back tomorrow evening to take this old hound home and help haul Liza's clothes to the Goodwill. Your Momma's already taken all she means to keep." She got up and left Joanne sitting in the kitchen.

She would have to go back to Chicago in three days. And she still hadn't gone through Grammy's kitchen. Joanne sat until she accepted that the dull ache in her chest wasn't going away anytime soon and the boxes weren't going to pack themselves. She wiped her face with her sleeve, dragged a box into the kitchen, and began pulling items out of the spice cupboard and putting them into the crates. As she stacked items, Joanne hummed an old-timey song Grammy always sang when she cleaned, the one about a black-eyed maid who pined for Sweet Jack though his heart belonged to another. A good sad song; she died of a broken heart after toasting him at his wedding feast.

> Silver cup and golden bowl
> Comfrey, birch, and spoon of thyme
> she raised her glass beneath the moon.
> Alas, Sweet Jack, that you were mine

I wonder what comfrey would taste like in a whiskey. She stopped, holding a jar in one hand.

Comfrey, birch—why, it was practically a recipe. The song even mentioned a spoonful of thyme. She looked at the jar of dried thyme in her hand, picked from Grammy's garden.

"Holy shit." Joanne said aloud. Her eyes fell on the rejected jar of moonshine on the table. "Why the hell not?" she said to Bess.

For her failed liquor, Joanne had made a large batch of the fermented sugar and corn "wash" needed to distill whiskey. Her wash still had a few days of good fermentation left, she calculated. There was enough to make another small jar of moonshine.

As she pulled the song's ingredients from the pantry, Joanne began to sing with gusto. Grammy had liked Joanne's voice, and had moped when Joanne stopped choir to take more AP classes. Now, all of the old tunes Grammy sang poured out of her, along with everything she'd learned since—R&B hits from high school, blues standards from tending bar during college, the classic rock her boss liked to play. She even improvised some tunes, like she used to do when she was a kid. Grammy was right; music did help the work go faster.

As the sun set the next evening, Joanne lifted a glass of moonshine with shaking hands.

It was terrible. Acrid and astringent, the herbs gave it the taste of lawn clippings. Her whiskey made Malort, Chicago's infamously foul liquor, taste like a twenty-year Scotch. Joanne hurled the container of thyme across the kitchen. It smashed against the wall next to the door. Bess, who had been snoozing near the warm stove, jumped up. Joanne burst into tears as the old dog ran around frantically barking at whatever invisible menace had caused such distress.

"Bess, goddammit to hell, it's just me." Aunt Myrtle's voice came from the front door. "Can I come in?" Joanne wiped her eyes and nose on her shirtsleeve.

"For Pete's sake, Aunt Myrtle, just come on in—you don't need to ask."

"Ain't my house; wouldn't be ri—stars, what's this?" The old woman stood at the kitchen entrance, looking at the bits of glass and dried leaves scattered over the floor.

"I'll clean it up."

Aunt Myrtle's eyes darted to the Mason jar on the table, "That a new run?" Joanne grabbed a broom rather than answer.

The old woman held the dustpan as Joanne swept the shards. Aunt Myrtle deposited the load in the trashcan, then crossed over to the table and picked up the Mason jar of whiskey.

"Aunt Myrtle, don't—it's awful."

"Think I should be the judge of that. Same recipe?"

"No—it's stupid—I tried to make it with the plants in the song Grammy used to sing. The one about Sweet Jack."

"Comfrey, birch, and spoon of thyme." Aunt Myrtle sniffed the jar, and then took a sip. She smacked her lips and smiled.

"My stars, girl, that's foul."

"I told you!" Joanne snatched the jar and dumped the contents down the drain.

"All right, I'll teach you."

Joanne turned around slowly. "You'll teach me to make Grammy's whiskey?"

"No. I'll teach to make shine like Liza done. Not hers."

"I don't understand."

Aunt Myrtle sat down. She traced her fingers over the recipe cards scattered on the table. "Your Grammy and me, we'd been friends for a long time. And I was friends with her Momma and her Grammy before that." Joanne glanced at the sink, where she had disposed of the moonshine. "I ain't drunk, child. Can't get drunk on anything but the kind of liquor your Grammy used to make." The old woman gazed at the cards, shoulders sagging. Then she straightened her back and looked Joanne in eye. "Fairy wine. That's what Liza made. That's what I taught her and her Momma and her Grammy to make."

Joanne racked her brain, trying to recall the stories her grandmother told her about the Folk "Like in Rip Van Winkle? The stuff that makes you fall asleep for hundred years?"

"Only if it's *very* good."

Joanne sat down at the table and rubbed her head. "You're telling me Grammy made fairy wine. And you taught her. And you've lived forever."

"The Fair Folk don't live forever, that's just tales. But I've lived a long time."

The Fair Folk, Joanne thought. Her eyes widened. "Aunt Myrtle, you're saying you're a fairy?"

The old woman nodded. "Changelings, they calls us. Was left with some of your people a long time ago, in the home country. They was good to me, despite it all—and let me tell you, I was a terror when I was young. So when they came over the ocean and settled here, I came with. Course, I had to move around every score of years, after most people stopped telling stories about the Folk and started wondering about why this old lady don't die. But I always come back and introduced myself again, to the ones who still told the stories. And I taught those ones how to make the Folk's wine, under the moonlight."

"Why?" Joanne blurted. Aunt Myrtle's fingers lingered on Grammy's handwriting.

"Same reason I want to teach you now that Liza's passed, I reckon. When your kin is far away, or gone, it helps to do the things you remember doing together. Don't take away the pain, but it helps." She picked up a recipe for lavender-blueberry jam. "Liza liked to add things from her garden, like she did with her preserves." Aunt Myrtle and pointed to the half circle doodle on the corner of the card. "See, she liked to use lavender picked on a half-moon night."

Joanne looked at the recipe cards, the lopsided circles morphing into phases of the moon. "She marked them all..." Joanne shuffled the cards, there was hot pepper jelly with a waxing crescent, dilly beans marked with a full moon, rosehip syrup with a circle filled in. The dark moon, she assumed. "These are her notes for making whiskey recipes...and the moon she wanted to make them under...if I can just figure which ingredient on the card she used..." Aunt Myrtle smacked her hand.

"Joanne Roberts, ain't you been paying attention? You don't make fairy shine by following someone else's checklist. If you could make it like that, the Folk could make it on their own." Her voice gentled, "Honey, the Folk got our own magic, but it don't work like yours. We repeat, we go on like a long river, but we're a river that don't twist or turn or carve valleys through mountains. We just are. Your people now, your people create things. They make up stories, make up songs, and make up new ways to get silly on corn or sugar or whatever else they can put in a pot." She took Joanne's hands in hers. "That's why I needed to know you'd try new things. I knew you could follow a recipe someone else wrote up, but I needed to know you could fiddle around, tear things apart and put them back together. And you showed me that you could listen to a song, take the pieces, and make it into liquor."

"But it was terrible."

"Don't matter." Aunt Myrtle squeezed her hand. "It's the trying I needed to see. Come on, I'm going to show you something. Take whatever tickles your fancy from the spice rack and bring that last bottle of wash—yes, I know it's bad now."

Something wet was on her face. Joanne opened her eyes to Bess's greying muzzle and fuzzy eyebrows drawn together in concern. The hound licked her again. Joanne sat up and yelped as she smacked her head against something hard. She was lying under the kitchen table, still dressed in yesterday's clothes. As she crawled out from under the table, her knee knocked against something else hard. A Mason jar tipped over with a thud.

Joanne's head spun for a moment when she stood up, then settled. She splashed cold water on her face at the sink, filled a glass and sat down at the table. There was mud on the floor, she noticed, and then saw the same mud crusted her boots. As she drank the water, images bubbled up in her mind. She grabbed onto them; it was like trying to remember a dream. A sliver moon in the sky, the smell of leaves, the sound of liquid dripping like rain. Liquid. Joanne squatted down on the floor, picked up the heavy jar, and unscrewed the lid. The smell of alcohol filled her nose.

The scent brought back more memories: Aunt Myrtle was singing and the melody sounded like the songs Grammy and the other mountain people sang, but Joanne couldn't understand the words. Aunt Myrtle had made Joanne repeat each line slowly, until she could sing the whole song.

Joanne sang a little of the song now and the words felt as sweet and familiar in her mouth as Grammy's biscuits. She knew suddenly, as clearly as she knew her name, that she could sing the words any time she wanted.

Joanne dipped her finger into the alcohol, and stuck it in her mouth—it was the smoothest whiskey she'd ever tasted. The burning was quiet and comforting, like smoldering logs in a fireplace on a winter day. The taste was smoky and floral at the same time, which shouldn't have worked, but did. As the taste spread across her tongue Joanne recalled Aunt Myrtle's hands rolling moonlight in her hands like she was rolling dough to make cookies. Different colors of light streamed through the work-worn fingers, as if refracted through a prism. Looking at the tiny rainbows, Joanne had felt as if she was standing in front of a spice rack, ready to make a soup or at a stocked bar with an empty tumbler in front of her. *See honey, I can draw down moonlight, but I need you to mix it.*

"You up?" Aunt Myrtle's voice came from the porch.

"Yeah—come on in." The front door slammed.

"Ah, there's the brew. Let's give it a taste," Aunt Myrtle crossed the room, got two empty jars from the cabinet and poured a bit of the whiskey into both. The old woman sat down, stretching out her legs.

"We—we made the whiskey in one night? But how—"

"Ever wonder how your Grammy got such a fast turnaround?" Aunt Myrtle winked, "Time ain't so rigid for the Folk. Especially in one of our circles."

The circle—another image came back to Joanne. She recalled stepping into a perfectly round ring of trees and time going soft as pudding. Joanne squinted, trying to put together all of the images.

"I remember some of it. I can still sing the song. But it's all mixed up."

The fairy woman nodded, "First time you enter a fairy ring it addles you up proper. But you get used to it." Aunt Myrtle took a sip from her jar and sighed deeply. "Now that's some shine. Don't get that on Goose Island." She cackled and rubbed Bess's head.

Joanne thought of the rows of sterile equipment at work and felt a wave of tiredness come back. "So, should I quit my job? Come home and be your apprentice like Grammy? That's what I'm supposed to do?"

Aunt Myrtle nearly choked. "My stars, girl, how should I know? I ain't here to fix your life. You don't like your job, you figure it out. I just show you how to make fairy shine." Aunt Myrtle shrugged. "Though, plenty of Folk in Chicago too, just so you know. They'd be real happy to get a source, you decide to take what I teach you back to Chicago." She held her jar of moonshine up, "This is for you, Liza."

Joanne took another sip of the fairy wine; dried flowers burning in a fireplace, that was the taste, she realized. She remembered adding the tiny lavender, rose, and chamomile petals into the silvery stream that flowed from Aunt Myrtle's hands. She had been thinking of winter evenings with Grammy and how her grandmother always threw some herbs on the logs to sweeten the air. *I made this,* she marveled, sipping the whiskey, *I distilled that memory. I wonder what I else I could make.* Images of her life in Chicago and Kentucky played in her mind like a movie and the gates that separated the two creaked open.

She could keep the job at the brewery for now, that still felt safe, but maybe she could start taking off some weekends. Maybe she could grow some of Grammy's herbs in a container garden. Pictures of herbs on a windowsill and images of the spice-lined shelves in the groceries of Devon Street rose in her mind. *Maybe I could combine that thing with that thing, maybe I could try, maybe, maybe...*with every *maybe* more gates in her mind unlatched. She could try things, see what worked. Create again. Joanne raised her glass of moonshine and drank deeply.

A question for Amelia Aldred

Q: What other writers inspire you?

A: Recently, I've been inspired by the nonfiction writing of Isabel Wilkerson and Ta-Nehisi Coates. Wilkerson blends impeccable research with vibrant storytelling and I admire Coates' commitment to delving into difficult questions. When I read his articles, he reminds me to focus on the messy truth over snappy soundbites in my writing. In fiction, I've been reading a lot of James Baldwin this year and his language and characters blow me away. He writes about human beings' fallibility with such compassion and insight. He's one of those writers from which I read a line and then stop and sit with the line because it's that beautiful. In speculative fiction, I really like Catherynne M. Valente's use of language, I love N. K. Jemisin's world-building, and I love Mary Robinette Kowal's character relationships and character arcs. On a professional level my mother, Carrie Newcomer, is a songwriter and I learned the basics of what is means to be a working artist from her: work hard, be collegial, and never stop growing. On the same note, my friend and fellow Hoosier Michael R. Underwood is one of the hardest working people I know and I've watched him grow with every novel. His passion for stories and the writing community has inspired me to keep writing through the ups and downs of life and I look forward to whatever he writes next.

About Amelia Aldred

Amelia Aldred was raised by a folksinger and lawyer in southern Indiana, leaving her with incurable sincerity and fantastic fact-checking skills. She lives in Chicago, IL with her folklorist husband and two long-suffering houseplants.

www.ameliaaldred.com

Undertow

Jared Leonard

The midday sun reflected off the sea in a thousand broken glimmers, belying the cutting chill in the early spring air. Salt scoured Alrik's nostrils, the burn setting his nerves at ease. The vessel rocked casually amid the rolling waves, slowly inching its way to the black mass of clouds that hung off in the distance.

He scanned the islands that stood around them. More than a half a dozen jagged, rocky outcroppings where the gulls would gather and only the toughest trees could set root in the iron sheets.

He shook his head. This was a stupid place to be, especially now, at this time of year. He had heard once that a sailor should fear when springtime danced with storms, yet here he was on a ship with dark clouds looming in the distance.

"Time's up, snakes!" the captain roared.

Alrik turned back to the deck. The chains rattled as the Medmanari shuffled back into the deep dark belly of the ship. They dragged their feet slowly, trying to breathe in as much sea breeze as their lungs could carry before they were submerged in the stink of must and mildew again.

Medmanari were thin-framed to begin with, and the many weeks at sea had made it easier to see. Their scaled skin was wrapped tight around waning muscles and frail bones, and many had to cover their serpent eyes against the sun's harsh light after days of being mostly in the dark. The ship carried males, females, and younglings, all of whom received a few precious minutes each day to stretch their legs and clean the stale air out of their lungs.

Some of the crew herded them on, sabers in their hands, while the captain watched from the wheel. He was young and as brash and bold as the mustache that trailed across his face. And that brash boldness had led him here, taking cargo for some lord Alrik didn't care to know. The captain had said the Medmanari were servants, but an old sailor didn't split hairs. Alrik knew slaves when he saw them.

Whether or not he liked it, the captain was still the captain, and he was just a deckhand, and deckhands didn't voice whether or not they liked to sleep with slaves beneath their beds or talk about negotiating prices when they reached port. Deckhands just did what they were told to do, keeping whatever thoughts they had for themselves.

The ship rocked backwards as a large wave crept beneath it. A deep rumble shook the ship's wooden frame. Crewman looked off the deck. Medmanari began to murmur to one another.

Alrik peered off the railing. Bubbles streamed up and trailed off from his side of the ship, leading his eyes to a gathering swell. A dark, shifting shadow seemed to crawl beneath the waves. Alrik's breath frosted on his lungs when the shape grew greater and he was certain his eyes were right. He turned to the crew and shouted, hoping they could hear.

"Siruveil!"

A finned sail exploded from the surface, raining seawater down on them in sheets. The waves ruptured and sputtered and bled. Alrik gripped the railing as the force of the beast began to tip the boat. The spines between the webbed fins grew taller, casting a dark shadow on them. One of the crewmen flipped over the guardrail, catching the other side just in time to hang on. The Medmanari were tossed to the floor of the deck, tumbling and rolling. The ship sank sharply into the pit of a wave and another wall of water slammed them. The captain shouted for his men to hang on. Alrik gladly listened as the vessel tilted farther and farther on its side, almost certain it would capsize.

And then it was over.

The ship settled. The water sloshed back into the sea. Alrik's guts eased into place again and everything seemed much like it had moments before that spiny fin burst from the surface. The other members of the crew gathered themselves and set to undoing the mess the monster had made, righting barrels that had fallen over, re-coiling ropes, and untangling pieces and parts of the sail. Between the sound of sailors working and Alrik's heartbeat in his head, the scream almost went unnoticed by him.

"Nakir!" a Medmanari woman shrieked. She lunged toward the railing, but the chains on her wrists and blades at her chest kept her back.

A sailor cupped his hands around his mouth. "Snake in the water!"

Alrik scrambled. He moved almost without thinking, grabbing a long coil of rope from between some nearby barrels. He tied the one end to the railing and began to wrap the other around his waist.

The captain's voice boomed above the clamor. "Any man jumping off gets flogged!"

Alrik faced the man, whose eyes were locked on him. His long wispy mustache hung low with water, and his blue coat was soaked to the shirt beneath.

"You aren't worth losing, sailor." The captain's eyes fell to Alrik's waist. "Throw him the rope, but you stay up here."

"Help him!" The woman reached out to the water. "Help!"

Alrik flung the rope overboard. The Medmanari boy howled, hands flailing and head bobbing amid the monstrous whitecaps.

"Grab the rope!" Alrik snapped the length as best he could, trying to lead the rope to the boy. "Grab it!"

The boy tried to clutch at the lifeline. A current wrenched him under for a moment before letting him back up with a choking gasp.

Alrik should've jumped in. He knew that as he fished the rope around, trying to get the boy to grab it like a kitten with some string. He should've taken the flogging, it wouldn't be his first time feeling the lash, and he could think of few things that seemed more worth some scars than the drowning boy below. Alrik's hand pulled at the railing, his arm trying to wrench the rest of his body over and into the ocean. His muscles burned and fire ran in his blood. The Medmanari mother continued to scream, begging for someone to save her son.

Alrik didn't, and neither did anyone else. Despite the screams of a despairing mother and the howls of a drowning son, Alrik was still a deckhand, and deckhands didn't save drowners over the captain's command. Six ropes were thrown down to the boy, but they might as well have waved goodbye. Alrik watched as the boy's hands stretched out and another wave swallowed him. This time, he didn't see a head break the surface.

He turned back to the crowd and slowly shook his head. The woman crumpled, as if his head had been a hammer swinging at her legs. Her wail hung long and loud in the air and her sobbing never ceased, even when two crewmen dragged her below deck.

"That boy was a good thousand marks we lost." The captain stood at the end of the table, his hands spread over some ledgers and forms that meant little and less to most of the crew. He shrugged, as if he'd merely lost a bad bout of cards. "Have to charge a little bit more for the others to make up for it."

Alrik stared into his bowl. Chunks of old dry carrot and hard chalky bread filled the brown slop. One of the pieces drifted in a slow, soggy circle. He pushed it under with his spoon, not feeling hungry anymore.

A crewman pounded his fist on the table. "Damned sea snake." He pointed his spoon around. "Breeding season brings 'em up to shallower water and makes 'em come up more often." A devilish smile came on the man. "I say we hunt it. That'll bring in a few marks."

Laughter took the cabin. One of the men wiped his eyes. "I'd sleep with a wyrm before going fishing for a serpent."

Alrik looked around. They were all laughing, draining beer mugs and picking at their teeth. All of them save the captain, who stared at the wall across from him, his eyes far off and empty. The hair on his upper lip curled in a wane smile.

"We can't hunt a Siruveil," he said, lifting a finger into the air, "but we can get the eggs."

The laughter stopped.

The captain took the silence in stride. "They're worth a fortune, boys. Lords and ladies would pay good coin for Siruveil eggs." His eyes seemed to glitter. "Even just half a dozen of them eggs would pay off that snake-boy many times over."

"Speaking of snakes," a crewman muttered, "did anyone bring the pot to them?"

They looked to one another silently.

"I'll feed them," Alrik said, eager to leave the table. He got up and headed towards the door.

The captain pointed to the deckhand. "See? Couldn't let a good man like that go fishing for some snake-boy. He's worth two of them at least."

Alrik closed his eyes and saw those hands reaching out of the water again, looking for something to hold onto before being dragged into the depths. He shuddered, grabbed the pot of feed, and headed out of the cabin.

The night air was a welcome change from the stuffiness of the cabin. Alrik wished for a clear night sky, but the weather had decided otherwise. Inky clouds so dark that they could be seen even in the night hung low and full like ripened blackberries on the vine, and the moon and stars were held back from sight. A few lamps offered bare slivers of burning light while the sound of waves lapping against the ship's wood helped soften the silence.

Below deck, sweat and salt mixed with urine and shit in his nose. Hacking coughs filled his ears. Some of them were getting sick. Hopefully they'd reach port within the week; the thought of tossing bloated corpses overboard brought bile to the back of his throat.

He lugged the pot down the steps, lit by dim lanterns dangling on heavy hooks. The eyes were there to meet him at the bottom from behind the iron bars, staring with fear upon their faces.

It was the eyes that bothered him, shining from the light of the lanterns. Some of them were hollow, others full of anger, but most of them were just uncertain. None of them knew much of anything. What would happen when they finally reached port? Would they divide them up by group? Would families be able to stay together? What if the nobles traded them? He sighed and shook his head. Questions a deckhand didn't have answers to.

"Bowls out," he said quietly.

He pulled off the lid to reveal a bland, lukewarm paste of sweet-grain and water. Claw-tipped hands held out cracked cups and broken bowls. One by one, Alrik ladled the slop in and handed it back before grabbing another dish.

It took a long while to feed them, and Alrik felt himself lose track of time. His head was filled with the sounds of scraping steel, clattering bowls, and the sucking sound the paste made as his ladle dipped beneath its grimy surface. Fingers brushed and fumbled at him, eager to grab hold of whatever food they could have. He almost didn't notice when a hand latched to his wrist and held on tight.

He would have been surprised, but the grip was weak. Small, delicate claws tickled his dry skin. Her face was stone-cut. Her eyes flowed like rivers. They were yellow, bordered by patches of scales, rippling beneath a veil of tears. The mother's thin lips pulled back as her flat nose flared.

"You let him die," she said. Her voice was cold.

He looked at her for a long time. Her hair probably looked nice when it was well-kept, but the long, midnight colored locks were matted and tangled beyond what any comb could do. They'd cut her hair when she was sold.

"Nothing to say?" she asked.

The words sat in his mouth, making it slick with something bitter. "I tried."

She dashed the bowl against the wall behind him. Her face twisted into a snarl and she screeched like metal grating against itself.

"You *tried?*" Her voice ripped through the muffled quiet. "I saw the captain stop you. Some skin on your back was all it took for you to let him die." She shook against the bars, nails clicking on steel. "How many lashes would it have been? Ten? Twelve?"

He looked at her quietly. Standing there, skin and bones wrapped in a moth-eaten dress, fed by grief and fire. She knew right. Ten lashes was standard.

"Answer me," she said. "And don't you dare tell me that you tried."

He stayed quiet, picked up the bowl, and filled it again, holding it out to her. "I won't," he said. "If you don't believe me, I won't try to tell you any different."

She grabbed the bowl, handing it off behind her. "Feed someone who needs it," she told them. Her gaze came back to Alrik. "I hope whatever gods you have give you more mercy than you gave my son." The words were venom, dripping and smoking as they fell from her mouth and scorched his ears. "I hope they let you keep whatever you hold close to your own heart."

He didn't say anything. Alrik turned back to the stairs, the empty pot hanging in his hands. He pulled open the door. The air rushed in, cool and wet. He was glad to be gone from that place, which smelled so foul and stared with so many empty eyes.

He never told her the truth sailors learned about the gods. He didn't speak of the hurt in his heart when they would ferry him out to sea, setting his wife and boy to worry if he'd ever come back. He'd kept quiet about the time another man on another boat had gone overboard, and how his fingers had slipped through Alrik's hand because the gods had wanted him, too. There was a time long ago when Alrik had his own boat, even, but the gods had decided that his ship would look better on the ocean's bottom and that he'd do better as a deckhand for the rest of his days. He didn't tell her that story either.

He didn't tell her, but she had gotten a piece of the truth all sailors knew. The gods wanted many things, and they craved nothing more than what men held close to their own hearts. When they found what they wanted, there was little way to stop them. The waves had been ravenous, the wind too strong for the ropes, and a deckhand felt ten lashes was too high a price. The gods had a hand in all of that, and in the end, they got the soul they sought.

The storm greeted them in the morning with a booming voice and roaring downpour. Within the first hour, Alrik was drenched down to his bones. It was only rain yet, but he saw that the storm-clouds had more to give from their swollen, bloated bodies. The Siruveil's fin cruised off in the distance, and much to his displeasure, they were still following it.

He'd only ever seen the fins of the serpents, but this one was by far the largest. Its shadow beneath the waves easily ran six or seven ship-lengths, lending belief to the stories he'd heard of whole fleets being destroyed by a Siruveil they'd accidentally come too close to.

He set to tying some barrels down. The Medmanari wouldn't see the sky today. They'd sit below deck, breathing fear-filled gasps of moldy air as the boat rocked in the raging waves, every tilt reminding them that the boat could capsize and they would drown behind those bars.

He thought of the boy again. Was his hair black, like his mother's? Had he even had hair? He glanced over the railing, watching the whitecaps, imagining the body beneath them. Had the fish started to pick at his corpse? Were the eels already making their home in his bones?

The captain shouted from the wheel. "Keep the sails open, boys!" He uttered a voice-cracking bellow, challenging the storm. His yellow mane whipped in the wind and a mad smile sat across his face. "We'll get our gold yet!"

The crew roared back, smiles beaming amid the torrent. Alrik looked at them all. They were young, with hard lean bodies and smooth skin which had yet to spend many years beneath a seaward sun. Young and foolish men who should have known better, who should've been braver than he was, and who should've told the captain to turn their ship around.

Alrik sighed while he worked and the sheets of rain continued to fall on his back. Thunder boomed from someplace deep in the clouds, and he spat.

Lightning cracked the sky, giving Alrik the briefest glimpse of where they were going. They were skirting dangerously close to the islands now. The beast had submerged hours ago, leaving them to sail at the captain's direction. The man was certain that the serpent would emerge again before night's end. Alrik hoped he was wrong.

The night dragged on and the storm stayed strong. It held the stars out of sight, and the moon was nowhere to be found. Alrik worked for what felt like forever, losing himself to the thunder and rain and lightning, along with the images of reaching hands and dangling rope.

Someone gripped his soaking shirt. Alrik turned to see the captain.

"You haven't taken a break yet," he said. "You're no good to us too tired to stand." He motioned below deck. "Feed the snakes and then go rest for a few hours. I'll send for you when we need you."

Alrik nodded, and when the captain turned his attention elsewhere, he shut his eyes, breathed deep, and fetched the pot.

Rain misted the steps that led below deck, and more than once he nearly fell down with the stew-filled pot. The stink returned, but at least it was dry. He lit a few more lanterns, letting more dull orange light bleed out.

"We lost one," she said, her voice cutting through the eerie quiet.

He shut his eyes. A wet, weary breath escaped him before he turned to face her. She was at the front of the mass, clinging to the bars while the clanging waves of bowls moved around her.

Her eyes were ringed with red. She hadn't got much sleep. "Died this morning."

He began to fill the bowls. They got fish today, drowned in some briny mix of cabbage and carrots.

"I'll tell the captain," he said.

Her eyes narrowed. "You'd leave him in here with us?"

He handed off another bowl. "I'm sorry."

"No you're not."

More bowls, the scraping ladle, the smell of fish.

"Will you throw him overboard?" she asked. "Mark it off in one of your ledgers?"

The captain would do that. Deckhands didn't write in the ledgers.

"You don't want to be here," she said. "Down here, with us." Her hands wrapped around the bars. "Yet you'll come down here every night, won't you? You'll do whatever they want you to do, whatever they tell you to do." She sneered. "Maybe that makes you worse than that captain, you having a will as brittle as black-bread."

He handed out another bowl.

"If they told you to beat me, would you do it?"

He looked deeper into the pot.

"If they wanted you to kill me, would you?"

He turned, the ladle rattling around inside the cauldron.

"Would you?" she asked. "Would you do it?"

He slowly climbed the steps.

"Would you?"

He pulled the door open, her question trailing behind as he stepped beneath a quiet sky. The wind had settled and the rain had stopped, leaving only the sound of waves. Even the moon, full and bright, had managed to break through the clouds. The captain waved to him, laughing loudly at the helm.

"Go to bed! Seems the weather turns fair when you disappear!"

The crew chuckled.

Alrik smiled weakly, lifting his hand to indicate his surrender to the cabin. The thought of a bed, scratchy and stiff as it might be, was one that he found hard to resist. He moved to the cabin, footsteps echoing loudly in the calm quiet.

Something began to hiss.

Alrik turned. The noise continued. The captain shouted for them to find a leak in the hull. Deckhands peered over the railing, ears trying to point out the sound which was steadily growing louder. It seemed to surround the ship, closing in on them. Rain began to patter on his shoulder. Alrik looked out to the sea and noticed how it was moving. The waves weren't reaching their ship any longer, as a ring of a billion bubbles blocked their way, uttering a hiss as they died.

Thunder boomed, and not one fin, but two, broke through the surface. A deep, groaning rumble shook the ship, rattling Alrik's knees. The moon faded, covering them in darkness. Spouts of water shot up like geysers. The fins rose on either side of the boat, revealing the large, notched scales they were burrowed into, which ran down the length of the creatures' serpentine necks, ending just above their brows where the sword-sized teeth began. The Siruveil eyed one another, lips curling, with growls that sounded like grinding boulders.

Their roars brought his hands to his ears and his knees to the deck. The noise rippled through him, his chest feeling like it was going to fall to pieces. The serpents began to circle one another, snorting their nostrils and snapping their jaws. The waves pushed harder against the boat. The rain returned and the moon was stolen away again. The creatures' white-fire eyes narrowed and drew closer. Alrik grabbed hold of something. The captain jerked the wheel one way, the crew tugged at the ropes of their sail. Their boat began to turn, edging itself out of the path of the serpents.

It wasn't enough.

The shoulder of one Siruveil clipped the bow, sending chunks of wood into the water. Their ship spun sharply. The beasts were upon one another. Fangs settled into flesh, bodies writhed and twisted. The water whirled in frothing splashes. Webbed claws swiped at underbellies, tails slammed down like lightning bolts. The two would fall beneath the boiling waves before rising back up with ear-splitting screams, their skin adorned with bleeding gashes and leaking wounds.

The vessel tumbled helplessly; being pushed, pulled, tugged and lifted any which way. The captain screamed out orders Alrik could hardly hear, while crewmen scrambled to do whatever they thought was going to save them.

He looked down at his hands, pale and pruned; gripping the railing so tight he could feel the wood shear beneath his fingernails. He thought of that boy's hands reaching out, hoping that there was something, anything to grab on to. The Siruveil rose again. Deep rents marked their hides, long sailing fins torn and tattered.

He imagined what it was like beneath the waves. He thought of currents, more powerful than any stormwind there would ever be, scattering things to the deep dark places that the ocean kept for itself, the invisible hands of the gods pulling and placing their property where they saw fit.

One of the serpents held the other's neck between its teeth, shaking and snapping its massive skull. The other flailed and writhed, roars shifting into screams. The ship strayed closer to the serpents. A stray claw came down.

One side of the ship was pulled messily away. The boat buckled, sending Alrik smashing into the deck. White flashed across his eyes, followed by blue and purple pulses. He touched his forehead and his hand came back streaked with blood.

A man screamed. Lightning spiderwebbed the night. Through his swelling eye, Alrik saw the captain, foot caught between the railing, ankle twisted painfully as he hung above the rabid waves. The rest of the crew moved to fix whatever they could of the ruined ship. What the claw hadn't eaten away, the waves were eager to lap up, pulling planks and splinters back into the ocean. The captain stared at Alrik with fear-filled eyes, hands outstretched and reaching.

Alrik turned and ran the other way, bolting to the stairs below deck. Most of the lanterns had fallen. Glass sliced his boots and bit down into skin. The scents remained as full and foul as ever. Medmanari chattered and screeched with fear at the noises outside. Alrik fumbled for the key in darkness before his fingers found it. Fighting the grasp of hands, he slid it into place, turned it, and flung the door open. The ship shuddered a sing-song scream.

She stood there, still like stone, as the horde around her poured out of the cage. Her eyes were fixed on him, the anger still nestled deep within, but sharing space with fear. He reached for a hand that once held a child's, shoving through every slave that tumbled past. Medmanari tripped and trampled over one another. Alrik felt like a stone in a swift stream as he shoved his way towards her. Her delicate, claw-tipped fingers twitched at empty air. The heat of her palm was a whisper's width from his own.

The ship exploded. Water gripped and tossed him against wood and steel, turning him end over end amid the murk. A searing pain exploded in his leg as something sharp and heavy hooked itself into his flesh. Thrashing bodies collided with him, gripping for brief moments before being pulled away.

Inky blackness was all around him. His chest began to burn. Metal fangs had sunk themselves in his flesh. Warmth leaked from between his fingers, while splinters buried themselves in his skin.

More wreckage brushed by him. Pieces of boat and bodies, drifting in the currents of every direction while he continued to sink. He beat his arms, but the metal tore at his leg in protest, dragging him deeper down instead. His head swiveled, looking for something. Pressure began to build on his ears, pushing in towards his brain. The light above grew fainter. A chill squirmed into his wound, spreading through his leg. The dark swelled with each passing second. Fewer and fewer bits of ship brushed by him. Numbness crept up from his foot.

He thought of screaming and letting that cold black water take whatever breath he had left so he could die and be done with it. He hadn't saved anyone. The gods had wanted them all, and they always got what they wanted, no matter what men did to stop them. Who was he to think himself any different? More heat drained from him as the dark closed in. The water wrapped itself around him, invisible fingers squeezing out his life.

Something bright appeared, and a deep groan ran through him. It looked like the moon, full and bright and broken. A current brushed him and he realized what glowed before him was an eye, almost as tall as he was.

The Siruveil floated in the darkness, its massive, hulking form hanging gracefully in the depths, kicking its legs slowly while its tail flicked from side to side, ignoring the debris that fell like snow around it.

Alrik wondered if the creature knew who he was. Had it known they were following it, and that they planned to steal its children away and sell them for however much they could get? Had the gods whispered to it as a plan to take them all?

Alrik glanced upwards to the surface he'd never break again, and watched as shapes moved amid the moonlight. Silhouettes began to gather, fighting against the waves and holding to flotsam they could find. More and more of them collected. First only a few, and then a dozen, and then a dozen more. Soon, there were more bodies above than there were members of the crew. He found some solace in that.

He struck bottom, plumes of silt caressing his face and finding its way between his clothing and his skin. Lightning flashed from above, illuminating the massive rock shelf he'd landed on. Jagged teeth of twisting stone and ruined shipwrecks surrounded him, rivers of sand flowing on invisible currents.

The Siruveil groaned again, staring down at him with a tilted head, as if wondering what the man was doing down there. It slithered through the sea, seeming like it belonged more in the calm stillness of the deep than in the raging storm at the surface. The force of the monster's movement swayed Alrik gently, like a feather-worm drifting from the tide.

It was a good place to die; a fitting place where the gods would be quick to find him. His lungs were alight inside his chest, and his blood caught fire and fought to escape, bursting through vessels and leaking out of his ears and nose and eyes.

He scratched at his throat, not knowing what else to do as he slowly died, except to claw and clutch for a breath that wasn't there. His body would not yield itself so quickly to death, even if his mind knew there was little left to do. The water forced his lips open and slipped behind his teeth to take whatever space it could in his lungs.

He screamed, the last of his precious breath spewing out of him in a stream of bubbles. The numbness pulled its way into his chest and his limbs had gone dead cold. He knew he did not have much longer.

The seconds stretched into long strings, and the pain gave way to an unfeeling chill. His mind caught hazy fire as it slowly died inside his skull. Ghosts appeared from the dark, clad in skins of seaweed, covered in protruding coral bones. They waded gracefully towards him, hundreds of the deep-sea shades, guided by the glowing lures of man-sized anglerfish. Their faces were sullen and sunken, pale and withered flesh beneath kelp hoods, with eyes that glowed like moonstone.

He greeted them, his lack of breath no longer a bother. He was either dead or dying, and he knew why these wraiths had come. These weren't wandering souls, eager to feast on dead man's flesh, but heralds. The gods were coming to collect what they wanted, and they had brought their collection with them.

Alrik found himself smiling. The gods would have him, but they had been shorted in their deal, and were denied some of what they wanted. He could not see them, but he knew slaves and sailors swam above him yet, freed from the fate that Alrik had met.

The gods would come for him, and in their fury and their rage, he would suffer for all the souls he'd stolen away. Kraken beaks would slice him open, spilling his guts before they used sea snakes to knit shut the wounds. Burrowing lancelets would scurry beneath his skin, laying eggs inside him that would hatch and chew their way to freedom. There would be many more things, awful ones, but there was little the dying deckhand could do about that now.

The light of the lures shined on his drowned face, and the ghosts continued to pass him by, giving only bare-bone glances. Their faces said enough. They did not enjoy their fate, but they would pity him for his.

One of them stopped. A little ghost, with a flattened nose and scales upon his face. The wraith asked Alrik what had happened, silent words somehow making sense inside his mind.

Alrik recounted the raging Siruveil and storm.

The little ghost asked him if he'd saved his mother.

Alrik told him that he'd tried.

The boy said he was tired of being so lonely down here, saying it was cold and dark and scary.

Alrik offered to wait with the boy, to see if his mother would join them down here yet.

The ghost smiled, nodding his hairless head.

Alrik nodded as well.

And as the rest of wraiths kept walking, the both of them waited, holding one another's hands.

A question for Jared Leonard

Q: What made you start writing?

A: My pursuit in writing was initially sparked by reading. I loved losing myself to new worlds and ideas and places, but as I grew older, I realized that the books I read didn't always have what I wanted in them. I didn't like when the villains were always so evil and the heroes too virtuous, or when endings were too bleak or happy. It was after realizing that I could make whatever story I wanted that I began to write more seriously. Now it's just a matter of figuring out what I want in a story, which unfortunately, is the much harder part.

About Jared Leonard

When he's not reading a book or writing, Jared Leonard attempts to stay in shape, aquascape various planted aquariums, enjoy videogames, and get enough sleep. He usually only accomplishes the first two. He currently lives in Richfield, Minnesota, and attends the University of Minnesota's College of Pharmacy.

Comes the Tinker

Karl Dandenell

As always, they heard the children first. Even in the strictest, most conservative towns, somehow, a few of the youngest or bravest managed to slip out to the road and wait for them. In other places, the whole of the population turned out, led by the mayor, or captain, or caliph, holding forth banners and flags and flowers to welcome the Tinker and his wagon, drawn by the steel horses that never tired.

"The Tinker!"

"The Tinker's come back!"

"It's a holiday!" they cried, as they ran alongside his wagon, keeping pace with the beautiful, shiny beasts that were taller than a man and moved their gleaming hooves in silent unison.

Tom Pedlar, a big man with a curly red beard and a ready smile, laughed and waved, reaching into a bag at his feet. He tossed handfuls of candy in the air, and the children laughed and ran to catch the sweets that tasted of sunlight and forgotten fruits.

At his side rode his wife Mary, dressed in a modest blue gingham dress with big pockets, her black hair tied back in a long braid. On her lap she carried a kitten who appeared asleep, but in the manner of his kind, kept a wary eye on the impromptu parade.

They rounded the corner of the road and arrived in the town proper. Some of the children had run ahead, and adults were drifting into the town square, raising their hands in greeting and talking among themselves. One greybeard leaned heavily on his cane and said in a reedy voice, "Is it really the Tinker?"

"Aye, grandfather, 'tis the Tinker and his wagon, just like the stories you tell at Christmas."

"Well, what are you waiting for, boy?" said the old man. He gestured with his cane. "Run and see if he has any port!"

The young man flew like an arrow toward the growing crowd.

"And tobacco! Ask if he has any tobacco!"

The boy turned and called something back, which was lost in the general commotion. The old man smiled a wrinkled smile, remembering a winter night and warm, comforting smoke as it curled from his glowing pipe.

Some minutes later, the Tinker had brought his wagon into the square, near the statue of community's founder. A short man, dressed in a dapper suit and a tall green silk hat, pushed his way through the crowd. "Let me though, good people. Let me through, I say!" His large, droopy mustache quivered when he spoke. Reluctantly, people moved aside. One of the Tinker's horses turned its head to examine the hat, and its eyes glowed bright red for a moment.

Tom stepped down from the wagon and took off his own broad sun hat. He held out a large hand, tanned and rough. "Good day to you, sir. Tom Pedlar at your service!"

"Welcome to the town of Resolute, sir. I am Silas, the Mayor and Sheriff," said the other man, grasping the hand and tipping his hat.

"Of course you are!" Tom said, releasing Silas' hand. "And a beautiful town it is."

Silas puffed up his chest. "I cannot take credit, for the Lord has blessed us. Unlike my ancestor," and he turned toward the statue, "who founded this colony after a dangerous trip from mankind's distant cradle, that beloved blue planet—"

"Oh!" said Tom, interrupting what he knew would be a long and much-rehearsed speech. "Where are my manners?" He reached behind him and took his wife's hand. "This is Mary Pedlar, who married me despite her own good sense and my poor purse. Mary, this is the Mayor of Resolute."

"Mayor *and* Sheriff, ma'am."

Mary stepped down and gave a little curtsy. Her cat yawned and snuggled into the crook of her arm. "I'm so pleased to make your acquaintance!" She turned and gave the square a critical appraisal. "Such a welcome sight after so many weeks on the road. And so many beautiful children! Are they all yours?"

The Mayor and Sheriff blushed a mighty red as the crowd roared with laughter. Finally, he said, "No, ma'am. Only the two wild boys sitting in yonder tree."

"Hey, ho, boys!" Tom reached into his bag and threw several pieces of candy in a high arc that nearly reached the tree. Children dropped from branches and scrambled in the dirt for the brightly wrapped caramels. "Don't worry, good sir," Mary said. "For the sweets will clean their teeth better than a stiff brush."

There were appreciative murmurs in the crowd. Some of the older people remembered other visits by the Tinker, and his wondrous foods.

"Now, then." Tom clapped a hand on Silas' shoulder, nearly knocking him over. "To business. Have you a place where I can park my wagon?"

"Right this way." Silas turned and pressed his way through the crowd again, leading the Tinker to a plot of reasonably clear land under two good shade trees, not fifty paces from a clear stream. Tom drove the team forward between the trees, then unhitched the horses, which settled themselves near the back of the wagon. Mary busied herself unfolding doors and panels from the wagon, displaying many small and precious items. She put out two stools and a low table in the shade, for the day was becoming hot. On the table, she set out glasses the color of cobalt and a tall silver pitcher that sweated with condensation.

"Care for some lemonade, Mayor Silas?"

Tom and Mary spent the rest of the afternoon meeting the townspeople, making note of their needs, and showing them some of their goods. They refilled the lemonade pitcher a dozen times, and as the day cooled and the shadows lengthened, Tom brought out a stove plate, set it up on its tripod, and heated water for coffee, much to the appreciation of the elders. Recent troubles on the border had stopped most of the merchants, and coffee beans had grown dear.

At dusk, Silas returned and, in his capacity as Sheriff, gently reminded people of the curfew and heavens, let the poor Tinker and his wife turn in, for they've had a long day and a longer journey. Everyone bid farewell and made their way home, promising to return the next day.

The next morning, everyone rose early, and the Sabbath meeting began promptly and ended a few minutes early, for Pastor Winthrop kept his sermon short and to the point for a change. A dignified procession ensued, terminating at the Tinker's cottage.

A cottage! The children whooped and broke ranks, running pell-mell in their Sunday clothes toward the tidy building that now stood under the shade of a single oak tree. The cottage itself was painted a jaunty yellow, with bright white shutters and a big front door with fine brass hinges. The windows were thrown open, and smells of freshly baked bread emerged from within. The kitten lay curled up on a porch swing, and the horses stood near the stream, observing the crowd.

Tom perched on his stool in front of a large table, on which lay piles of many useful things: tools and needles, bolts of fabric, spices (and more miraculous candy), bottles of port wine, wooden toys, tins of coffee and tea, and even a crate of sturdy boots.

One young girl named Amy caught sight of a music box, then paused and looked up at the cottage. A frown crossed her freckled face. "Mr. Tinker, sir?"

"Yes, my dear," he said, bending down. "Do you like the music box?"

"Very much, sir," she answered promptly. "May I ask you something?"

"Of course, little lady. Ask away."

"Did you and your wife build this all by yourselves?"

"Well, the Good Lord gave me many things, including two left thumbs," Tom said. "Putting up a cottage is beyond my talents." He held his thumb and forefinger together and squinted, as if peering at a grain of sand. "I had a *little* help."

Amy blushed. How could she forget that the Tinkers commanded tiny, ingenious machines? She regained her composure and pointed. "Sir, what happened to the other tree?"

Tom looked at his boots, then winked. "Well, now you've gone and found out my secret, little lady. It's one thing to make a new dress or a skillet from my stock, but a cottage, that's a tall order even for a Tinker. I needed the horses' help." He gave his display table an affectionate pat. "Besides, the poor tree was blighted with tiny black beetles. Eating it from the inside, they were. So I figured that it would make a fine new temporary home for Mary and me."

"Do you intend on taking it with you, then?" asked Mayor Silas, who had pushed his way to the front of the line.

"Well, Mayor Silas, I was hoping to leave the cottage with someone, since it's rather difficult to get it back in the box!" He laughed until his belly shook. "Perhaps you could look after it once we go. It has a cozy sitting room and a fine kitchen, as Mary will attest." Tom turned and called toward the cottage. "Mary, come and show the Mayor and Sheriff how the stove works!"

Mary appeared on the porch, wiping her hands on a flour-dusted apron. "I'm getting ready to fry up some sausage, Your Honor. Perhaps you would be so kind as to join me."

"Gladly, ma'am," he said, removing his hat and ascending the stairs to the kitchen.

Amy's father, a man of middle years named Thankful, came up and put his hand on his daughter's shoulder. "Morning, Tinker. How much for that hatchet?"

The Tinker rubbed his hands together. "Well, good neighbor, this hatchet will never rust and keep its edge as long as you keep it clean and wrapped. In fact, your grandson will probably use it to build his first house." He picked up a piece of writing paper from a box and sliced the paper into tiny strips. Then he plucked a hair from his beard and laid it across the hatchet's blade, where it fell in two. "Now, what's that worth to you?"

Thankful leaned back on one foot and crossed his arms, not wanting to appear too eager. "My wife is a fine hand with a needle. She just finished a quilt that'll keep you warm all winter."

Tom nodded and drank coffee from a heavy mug. "That sounds promising." He looked at the girl. "And your daughter, does she have any talents?"

Amy glanced at her shoes, then raised her eyes to the Tinker. "I can sing, sir," she said in a quiet voice. "Not as well as Beulah, but I led the hymns for a whole month when she was laid up with the fever."

"True enough, dear," said her father, "but I'm not sure if the Tinker has much use for singing, pretty as yours is." He winked at Tom.

"Well, neighbor, there you're wrong," said Tom. "The days are long on the road, and I grow tired of hearing myself talk. I know my wife does!" He barked a loud laugh. "A fresh voice'd make the miles easier." He reached into his pocket, and withdrew a brass disk the size of a pocket watch. "I won't ask you to sing for me now, but if you could take this home with you and give me your best Sunday hymns, I'd appreciate it."

With a curtsy, Amy took the brass disk from Tom. She glanced at the music box again.

"Go on," Tom said, "Take it. We'll trade music for music."

"May I, Father?"

"I'm not sure...."

"Nonsense! You run off and sing me some songs," said Tom. "If you see your friend Beulah, tell her I have another music box somewhere in this mess."

"Thank you, thank you!" Amy cradled her music box in the folds of her dress and walked away, humming.

"You're very kind, Tinker."

Tom wrapped up the hatchet in a silver cloth. "It's a trifle, good neighbor. Now, mind you hold this by the handle, and keep it dry and snug inside the cloth. If you drop it on your foot, you'll need a new pair of boots, and a doctor's care." He passed over the parcel.

"We don't have much in the way of doctor these days," Thankful said, handling the hatchet with respect. "Fever took Eleazer last winter when he was caring for everyone else. God rest his soul."

"Sorry for your loss," said the Tinker. "Was he fairly old?"

"Old enough to outlive two wives. Tough as a tree stump, too. But the fever was bad. Worse I've ever seen."

"We might be able to help," Tom said. "Mary apprenticed as a nurse before we married, and we recently traded a case of lamps for some vaccines over in Medina. I'll ask her to make the rounds and make sure everyone gets a dose."

"We'd be in your debt," said Thankful. He looked up at the cottage. "That's a right fine structure you've got there. Better than the school the last Tinker built. Those seats were too soft to keep children awake during lessons."

Tom grinned. "I'll be sure to pass that along. Now don't forget that quilt." Then he raised his voice, "Who's next?"

After Tom had replaced a broken ax handle and traded two pairs of socks for some freshly smoked chicken, the Mayor and Sheriff came down the steps, wiping his mustache with a pocket kerchief.

"Most impressive, Tinker," he said. "I think my family will be very pleased. How long did you say you were staying here in Resolute?"

Tom smiled. "Just long enough to do our business. We want to be over the mountains before next month." He pulled an unusually large and ornate watch from his jacket and consulted several dials. "We've an important family meeting." For a moment, a shadow passed over his face, but was quickly replaced by his former grin.

"Then I'll let you get on with it." The Mayor donned his hat. "Good day to you, Ira," he said to a stooped old man who leaned on a cane and clutched a slim leather book, much scuffed and worn.

"Good day to *you*, Silas," replied Ira, tipping his hat as the Mayor and Sheriff walked away. When Silas passed out of earshot, he added, "Politicians," and spat discretely to one side. "Not worth the dirt to bury them." Then he put the book on the table. "Can you fix this?"

"Perhaps," said Tom, flipping open the cover. The pages were clean, white, and seemed to shimmer in the sunlight. "What's wrong with it?"

"Wish I knew. I was listening to Hamlet a couple months back, and just when the ghost made his appearance, it just died. No pun intended." Ira gave him a gap-toothed grin. "Wouldn't be so bad, except it's the only copy in town." He leaned on his cane.

Tom ran his fingers along the spine until he found a tiny catch. It opened up to reveal a dull silver wafer no larger than his thumbnail. "I might have just the thing. Let me check." He knelt and rummaged through some small boxes at his feet.

Mary came down the steps with a wooden tray full of small, brown bottles. "Tom, did I hear someone say they needed vaccines?"

"That you did," he said, still on his knees. "Be so kind and ask after the family of Thankful."

"I'll be back by supper." Mary tied on her bonnet and walked away, her bottles clinking.

With a grunt, Tom pushed himself upright. "Hey, ho, here we go!"

Between his large fingertips, he pinched a silver wafer. He slid it into the book, sealed the cover and handed it back. "Try it now."

Ira opened the cover and tapped the top page. Rows of text appeared. He flipped a few pages, and touched a passage. A voice emerged clear and bright between the men:

I   am   thy   father's   spirit,
Doomed   for   a   certain   term   to   walk   the   night,
And   for   the   day   confined   to   fast   in   fires,
Till   the   foul   crimes   done   in   my   days   of   nature
Are burnt and purged away.

Ira chuckled and closed the book. "Ah, that's better. No one says it quite like the Bard."

"True enough," said the Tinker, "but give me a bit of Mark Twain to lift the spirit."

"I suppose it depends on your mood," Ira said. He squinted and examined Tom's face. "Has anyone ever told you that you're the spitting image of your father?"

"All the time," replied Tom.

"Nothing to be ashamed of. He was a handsome enough fellow." He reached for his purse. "What do I owe you?"

Tom rubbed his chin. "That depends. Do you play chess?"

"Better than you, young sprout."

"Come around tonight after supper and we'll see about that. If you can beat me two games out of three, I'll consider us even. Otherwise, your purse will be five pennies lighter."

"Done!" They shook hands.

"Now who's next?"

The morning passed quickly enough, with people getting sharp knives for dull, spectacles, zippers, new seeds, and paint that changed color with the weather. In exchange, the Tinker accepted silver pennies, recipes, two pairs of knee breeches, goose feathers, and a tiny carving that depicted the church. He turned down a litter of puppies (they would vex the cat) and a hand-stitched saddle from Ichabod the tanner.

"It's a fine piece," Tom said. "Maybe the best leather I've seen in years. But since you've got only the one saddle, I fear the other horse will be disappointed. They are jealous creatures, you know, and vain as a pretty girl with a new mirror." He handed the saddle back. "Do you have anything else?"

Ichabod put the saddle by his feet. He glanced up at the cottage, where a freckled boy sat on the porch playing with the kitten. "You seem fair busy, neighbor. Have you thought about taking on an apprentice?"

Tom raised his hat and wiped sweat from his forehead. "I confess I've thought about it."

Ichabod tilted his head toward the cottage. "My sister and her husband died with the fever last year, and their boy Nathan came to stay with me. He's a good lad, strong and smart."

"But you have no room," Tom said.

"Isn't that. We can always make room," the tanner said. "Truth be told, there isn't enough work for three. I 'prenticed Jerome's eldest last year, and that's all I can handle."

Tom crossed his arms and nodded. "I see, neighbor, I see." He took off his hat, picking at an errant thread. "He's smart, you say?"

"Smart as the day is long. He can read and write, and understands a goodly amount of math." Ichabod bent down and grabbed the saddle with one muscular arm. "Make a fine Tinker, in my opinion."

"Your confidence says a lot, neighbor, but I can't say one way or t'other without Mary, you understand," said Tom. "I'll tell you what.... Why don't lend me the boy for the afternoon? He can help me with some woodwork. If he does a good job, I'll give you a new steel punch for his time."

They shook hands on it. "Much obliged."

Nathan knocked on the door just as the sun cleared the porch. He was wearing patched overalls too short for his legs and a work shirt that had known at least two previous owners. Tom brought him round back where he had set up a small lathe.

"I had leftover wood from our cottage, so I figure we could make a dining room set for the weaver." He pointed to a neat stack of thin posts. "First thing we need to do is trim those down to size."

"How many do you need?" Nathan asked.

"Two dozen for chair legs, and another six for the table. There's a hand saw over there."

Tom watched as the boy laid a post on the bench and penciled a quick mark about a quarter of the way down its length. Then he made two more marks and picked up the saw. In short order, he handed Tom four pieces of wood. "How's that?"

The edges lined up perfectly. "Nice work. You didn't even measure."

"My folks were friends with the weavers," Nathan said. "I remember how tall their chairs were." He brushed a bit of sawdust from his overalls. "We used to eat dinner there on Saturdays before... well, you know."

Tom nodded. "Ichabod told me about your folks." He inserted one of the posts into the lathe and handed Nathan a set of goggles. The boy fumbled with the straps, then figured out how to lengthen them. Tom slipped on his own goggles and spun up the lathe.

"The blade is attached to this underside of the handle here," he said over the motor's whine. "So just keep your fingers on this side and you'll be safe." He lowered the cutting edge until it just kissed the post, and curls of wood danced away to the floor. With a steady hand, he moved the blade down the post, transforming it into a chair leg. When he was satisfied, he switched off the lathe and handed the leg to Nathan. "Do you think you can make one like that?"

The boy rubbed his hand over the curved wood and smiled. "With this machine, I could make a hundred."

"Let's start with one and see how you do."

Nathan gouged the second chair leg when he applied too much pressure, but he quickly got a feel for the lathe and finished the rest of the posts without incident. Tom was impressed. He didn't recall having such focus when he was that age.

Before they tackled the table top, Tom suggested they pause for lemonade. Nathan wanted to keep going, but the prospect of a cold drink won out. He did, however, insist on sweeping the floor and wiping down the lathe before he accepted a glass.

"Thank you, sir." He held the glass gingerly with both hands, taking small sips.

"It's all right, son. You won't break it," Tom said, "and even if you did, we could always make another one."

Nathan finished his lemonade and looked around the workspace. "Uncle Ichabod says Tinkers can make anything."

"That's an old wives' tale," said Tom said, cracking his knuckles. "There *was* a time we built everything — whole cities, even. But when the war came... well, we soon learned that Tinkers could destroy as easily as build."

Nathan nodded. "You made peace, though, eventually."

"Not exactly peace," Tom said. "More like each side agreed to put aside the feud and keep to themselves." His mind filled with maps and borders, restrictions and conditions. Tom reached for the lemonade pitcher. "More?"

"Yes, sir." Nathan held out his glass. "It must've been grand, living in a Tinker city, with fancy glasses and lemonade every day." He grinned.

"It *was* grand," Tom said, pouring. When Nathan gave him a questioning look, he added, "At least, that's what I hear." He set the pitcher down. "Now finish up and I'll show you how to cut a proper mortise. I told your uncle I was putting you to work, not rambling on about ancient history."

The following day Tom took his tool bag and paid a call on Pastor Winthrop, and found him tending to his chickens. Despite the heat, the preacher was dressed in a dark, severe suit and the traditional tricorne of his office (although he had unlaced the hat to provide more shade). Winthrop waved to Tom and scattered a last handful of corn.

He dusted his hands against his pants, leaving faint smudges of yellow, before offering Tom a surprisingly strong handshake. "Lord save you and yours, neighbor."

"Thank you kindly," said Tom. "I feel He has already."

Winthrop raised an eyebrow. "You speak with some certainty."

Tom laughed. "I'm blessed, and so is my family. You'll forgive me if I interpret that as salvation." He tipped his hat. "No offense, Pastor. You know us Tinkers, all full of bluster."

Winthrop allowed himself a small smile. "So I've noticed. Have you come today for some theological discourse, and is your visit related to more earthly matters?"

"The good Mayor and Sheriff mentioned that your water pump has gone to its final reward."

The pastor shrugged. "It's no trouble, neighbor, really. The Smith farm is close by, and they are kind enough to let me use their well."

"Nonsense!" said Tom. "A man of the cloth has better things to do than spend an hour each day hauling buckets." Seeing the expression on Winthrop's face, Tom added, "Oh, I know that work is worship and all, but there are some in your flock who feel their spiritual leader deserves to have running water."

Winthrop clasped his hands behind his back, rocking a little on his heels. "Well," he said after a moment, "it does seem a waste to have machinery rusting away."

"Idle pumps being the Devil's tools?" asked Tom.

"Something like that."

He took Tom around the back of the church, where the pastor had a small, roughly finished cottage that held a small sleeping room, kitchen, and a privy. The water pump sat close by the wall, in a circle of grass. While there were a few spots of rust on the spigot, the pump itself appeared reasonably clean. Tom set down his bag and put on large spectacles with pale blue lenses. He unrolled a length of soft leather, setting out many small and intricate tools.

"Bless me," said Winthrop. "That looks complicated."

"Not really," said Tom, removing a cover from the pump. "The basic principle is simple enough. Just as you use a bucket to draw water up from the bottom of a well, this uses a pipe to bring water to the surface." He tapped the exposed length of metal. "The pipe's full of air, and if the pump draws out that air, the water down below rushes up to see what all the fuss is about."

"Water is such a curious substance."

Tom looked up, then laughed. "And people say pastors have no sense of humor."

He worked for a while then, humming to himself as removed bits and pieces from the pump, examining them in front of his lenses. The sun moved higher in the sky, and the house cast welcome shade across both men.

Finally, Tom put together the puzzle of shiny metal pieces, took off his lenses, and wiped his brow. "That's it, I think. Let's give it a try." He accepted an ornate brass key from the preacher and inserted it into the pump. A quarter turn produced a loud click, followed by a stream of brackish water from the spout. "Give it a minute," Tom said.

"I'll fetch a bucket," said Winthrop. When he returned, the water had grown clear. He filled the bucket, then took a long draught. "Perfect!" he declared.

"Glad to be of service," Tom said. He switched off the pump and returned the key to Winthrop. "Now don't lose that."

"I promise to hang it on the nail." The pastor rolled the key between his thumb and fingers. "Tell me something, neighbor."

"If I can," said Tom.

"It seems to me that you Tinkers ought to be rich, since no one else understands the old tools." He indicated the water pump. "Yet, I can't see much profit in trading marvelous machines and clothing that never needs mending for our admittedly fine pottery and blankets."

"Tinkers have always put the needs our customers before profit," Tom noted. "Even before we signed the armistice."

"'Blessed are the peacemakers, for they shall be called the children of God,' " said Winthrop. "My grandfather died in that war, like so many of his generation."

"It was a terrible thing. Grandfathers and grandsons. Uncles and aunts." Tom's voice filled with anger. "It was like a goddamn prairie fire, eating up cities and farms and spitting out graveyards. And all we could do was *watch*—" He took a deep breath. "Forgive me, Pastor. I don't mean to burden you with my regrets. Or my language."

"I'm happy to listen, even if the message isn't always pleasant." Winthrop placed a light hand on the Tinker's shoulder, but Tom stepped away.

They stood in silence for a moment. Winthrop examined the brass key, then tucked it away in his waistcoat. "I don't know if anyone's told you, neighbor, but we had some odd gentlemen come calling last winter."

"Oh?" Tom leaned the toe of his boot against the wall.

"They came late at night, and their wagon had no horses, for the wheels had machinery inside them. I took them to be soldiers at first since they wore Tinker mesh under their coats. But they acted politely and spoke the trade language, though with such fierce accents that only the schoolteacher could make sense of it. She said the men were offering good coin if they could copy out the genealogy pages from our family Bibles."

"Do you happen to remember their names?" Tom asked, his eyes narrowing.

Winthrop pursed his lips. "One was called Branson. Can't remember the other. What I *do* remember is they gave the potter a nice bag of silver pennies. Good thing, too, since his boy came down with the fever soon after. They needed the money for the funeral."

"Sad," said Tom. A muscle twitched in his cheek. Then he abruptly picked up his bag and tipped his hat to Winthrop. "Well, I must be going. Enjoy your water, Pastor."

That night, as the day shook off its heat, Tom and Mary lay on top of the covers with the doors closed and windows open, enjoying the breeze. The kitten stalked the foot of the bed, making occasional feints toward their bare feet. Mary played with the buttons of Tom's nightshirt. "You're awfully quiet," she said.

"The Bransons," he said, looking at the ceiling. "They got here before us."

Mary hugged him close. "You think they brought the fever?"

"Pastor Winthrop said that two people came into Resolute looking for family history, and after they left, people started getting sick. Rather suspicious that all the dead were my sister's kin."

"Damn them anyway," Mary whispered. "Maybe we shouldn't have stayed so long at Medina."

"Hey now," Tom said, putting a gentle finger to her lips. "We did good work there. Don't take away from that."

She kissed his finger, then pushed them away. "It's so vexing that we're only allowed one wagon each season."

"*Limited commerce,*" Tom said, quoting the armistice.

Mary said, "More blood feud than commerce, for the Bransons."

"We'll catch them up someday," Tom said. "And when we do, the tribunal will have to let us come back."

"Meantime, we've got plenty of towns to visit." Mary reached down and scratched the kitten under its chin. "There's bound to be cousins in some of them."

"I'm sure of it." Wanting to change the subject, Tom said, "Tell me what you found."

"What we expected, by and large," she said. "There's a bit of inbreeding and malnourishment, but nothing irreparable. It's a hard life, and the isolation doesn't help."

"At least they'll live longer than their parents," Tom said. "We can give them that much."

"That we can," Mary agreed. "I've inoculated most of the children, and the seed stock we're leaving behind will double their crop yield."

Tom nodded. It was a good start. "What do you think about Nathan, the tanner's nephew?"

Mary thought for a moment. "He was here when I visited the tanners. His aunt remarked that had enough curiosity to fill up five boys."

"Well, he *did* pester me with questions." Tom chuckled. "Handled the lathe quite well, considering he's equal parts freckles and elbows."

She pursed her lips. "He sounds like Zachary at that age."

Tom considered this. "Now that you mention it, he does possess a similar spark."

"Well," she said, reaching up to kiss his cheek, "I look forward to making his acquaintance."

The next day Tom and Mary paid a visit to the tanner. Since it was such a fine day (and the tanner was boiling new skins), they took themselves to a small garden that lay upwind of the tanner's workshop. Tom presented Ichabod with a new punch, as promised, and a sharp knife for his apprentice.

"That makes both of us happy," said Ichabod. "He's always borrowing mine when he thinks I'm not looking." He admired the lines of the blade, and the smaller handle, appropriate for a growing boy.

Mary excused herself to give Nathan a dose of vaccine and check his tonsils. Tom accepted Ichabod's offer of a game of horseshoes. When Mary returned, she had a pie from the tanner's wife and a large smile on her face.

On the day before the next Sabbath, the Tinker and his wife loaded up their wagon and hitched the team. The Mayor and Sheriff stood at the head of the crowd that had come to see the Tinker off.

"Are you sure you can't stay any longer, neighbor?" asked Silas.

"Honestly, no," replied Tom. "We've a long road ahead, and there isn't a broken pot left within a day's walk. Nay, we're well done here."

"You've all been so kind," put in Mary. "But if Tom has another slice of pie, I'll have to let out his pants. Again!"

Tom scowled and turned his attention to Nathan. The boy leaned against the sideboard of the wagon, wearing a fine new belt, a parting gift from Ichabod. "You say a proper goodbye to your aunt and uncle, son?"

Nathan looked up. "Yes, sir. Aunt Birdina near to broke my ribs when she hugged me." He lifted up a parcel. "She sent along some biscuits."

"Then climb aboard," Tom said and jumped into his seat. Mary gave a final curtsy to the Mayor and Sheriff, then took Tom's hand as he pulled her up onto the seat next to him. Nathan flopped into the space behind them. "Hey, ho, let's go!" cried Tom.

With a snap of the reins they were off, slowly at first, giving the children a final chance to chase them to the town limits. The gleaming horses picked up their cadence after that, their hoofs striking the ground in nearly silent unison until the wagon left behind the last pair of gasping boys.

They rode steadily until sunset, when they paused long enough for a quick supper of stew and biscuits. Tom brought out a special treat for dessert: ice cream. Nathan was amazed. "Don't eat it too fast," Tom warned him. "It will make your head hurt."

Nathan licked his bowl clean. "How did you keep it so cold?"

"Tinker's secret."

"Can you teach me?"

"Tomorrow," said Mary. "Even Tinkers need their rest."

Soon the sun set behind the hills, and Nathan lay snuggled in the new quilt, snoring lightly, with the kitten curled up beside his head.

Tom put his arm around Mary's shoulder. "I hope we're making the right decision."

"He'll be safer with his own family. And he *is* kin, after all." She glanced back. "Great grand-nephew, as far as I can tell."

"Then it's high time he met the rest of the clan," Tom said. He snapped the reins twice. The horses nickered and pranced ahead toward a shooting star that grew larger and brighter as it fell to the ground.

"Let's go home. Hey, ho!"

It came from Karl Dandenell

My stories usually start from the ending (what I want to see happen) or a setting (where can my characters play?). "Comes the Tinker" was one of those tales that fell into my brain as both images (the Tinker and his cart with mechanical horses) and sounds. I was in the middle of tracing my wife's ancestors from England to the Midwest, and ran across names like Thankful, Eleazer, and Beulah. I knew I wanted to use them in a story. My desire in "Comes the Tinker" was to explore the traveling salesman trope, and set it in a future where nanotech had been discovered and then lost (at least for some). That led to the inevitable questions of how and why? Then I needed to address the mystery of the Tinker himself. Where did he come from? What does he want? Finally, I wanted to write a story that felt more languid than my usual rushed prose. Of course, I would be remiss if I didn't mention that I set down the initial draft after watching *Firefly* for the first time.

A question for Karl Dandenell

Q: Are you a Luddite, or do you have the latest and greatest technology?
A: I consider myself a "Version 2.0" technologist. I prefer to let other folks find the bugs.

About Karl Dandenell

Karl Dandenell is a first-generation Swedish American, survivor of Viable Paradise XVI, and active member of the Science Fiction Writers of America. He lives on an island near San Francisco with his family and 3 cat overlords. He is fond of strong tea and single-malt scotch.

www.firewombats.com

November

The Cartographer

Caleb Warner

Ursula

The girl returned to the abandoned trailer park with a road sign strapped to her back, a sacrifice for the man in the telephone pole. Cradled by the river, the trailer park sat, rusting. The entrance gate read *Green Meadows*, but the only green things left were the corroded copper-wire antennas and the piles of old road signs. Nothing truly green could grow in that black, clay-packed soil—even when the spring rains came and flooded the river valley. The soil liked to work its way in-between the girl's toes and stain the back of her shift a crusted grey. When it dried, the soil smelled like some rotten pond thing, like how dead turtles smell. Now it was summer; the clay had gone to mostly hard-pack, and it was warm against her bare feet.

The girl walked along the lane, kicking a white bit of gravel along with her, banking it off trailer walls and piles of twisting metal signs. In the center of the camp stood the telephone pole. The smiling face of a man peered through the creosote soaked wood. It was half carving, half prism, like the face was trapped there *behind* the wood.

If one were to have this demon's view—from above like a bird, as the girl had so often imagined herself—then *Green Meadows* would look much like the arching back of a cat as its corrugated shanties flowed along with the curve of the river and the slope of the land. One lane pierced the park down its center; a lane that connected *Green Meadows* to everywhere-else.

The girl walked up to the telephone pole, and in the light of the setting sun, it cast a long shadow across her face.

The frayed steel edges of the street sign nicked her hand as she held it up. A thin trail of blood raced down the rusted metal outlining the words RUBY ROAD. She made no move to clean it. She let it run.

"You took too long, Ursula," a voice bounced around in her head. She heard it from somewhere behind her eyes, like it skipped her ears entirely. "If you do not return before the sun goes down—"

"I live by your good graces," she said quickly. She didn't need to hear it again, but the time away from camp was time for doubt. Ursula wasn't ready to test her doubt quite yet. Wrapped around her waist, just under her pocketless shift was a hand-drawn map of the river valley with fresh charcoal scratches on it. Her one secret. Ursula tightened her grip on the sign. Her arms were shaking, and the blood on her palms made the metal slippery.

"Leave it with me," he said finally.

Ursula let out a stiff breath and propped the sign up against the telephone pole. She stood with her head down and her hands folded.

"And?" the voice shook Ursula somewhere down in her stomach. It made her feel dizzy.

"M-my meal?"

"Bad girls don't get fed."

Ursula had to bite her tongue to keep her face still. Did he know about the map? "But I brought the sign," she said.

"Late."

Ursula made herself breathe.

"The signs are far now … I-I'll need the food for tomorrow." It wasn't a lie. She had never lied to him. It wasn't the whole truth, though. Ursula would be ranging farther than the closest sign.

The pause was long enough for Ursula to feel the blood start to dry and grow sticky on her palms, long enough for the purple light of the sunset to turn to grey. Ursula didn't dare look up at the face. She didn't move at all until it spoke again.

"Fine. In the southeast corner. Off with you." Then the sun fully set, and a bruised black night consumed the valley. The demon's face went dark, its malice emptied like a used up inkwell.

Ursula nodded and shuffled over there, keeping her head down and her strides short.

A trailer without a roof, that's where it had carted her off to for tonight. It had once been bright silver and could comfortably fit two or maybe even three people. Like everywhere else, the trailer was filled with signs, and Ursula was small enough to fit in the middle of it all. In the cleared area lay a can—with its label ripped off—and a can opener next to a dried cow pie and box of matches. The gift. Ursula maneuvered a few of the signs to give her a place to more comfortably sit without fear of injury.

Only when her hand drew a fresh red streak on the trailer wall did she remember the cuts. Ursula left the trailer, went down to the river to wash up. The silty, dark water made the cuts sting but it was better than letting them get infected. Ursula had cut her leg pretty bad once on a sign and didn't bother with it. A day later she got the chills. Two days and she stopped peeing, but was ravenously thirsty. And the third day Ursula only remembered in small snatches of clarity, everything else fuzzy and distant like an old dream. The fourth day she awoke under the telephone pole without a memory of how she got there, but she was fine, a bit groggy, but the cut on her leg had healed and she was hungry again. She guessed infection must not be deadly, but she didn't want to go through any of that again.

It wasn't long after cutting her leg when Ursula had started making the map.

She took a few sips from the river, watching her murky, moon-lit reflection in the water shift and move with the ripples of the current. There was a blurry little girl trapped just under the water there, just like the man in the pole. Ursula could almost reach out and touch the girl, but not quite.

Returning to the trailer, she situated herself among the signs again and lit the cow pie. It wasn't warm enough to heat the can, so she ate its contents—beans, it was always beans—cold. Ursula had very few memories from the time before *Green Meadows*, but the memories she did have were hidden in certain tastes or smells or the occasional image. It was mostly taste, though. The beans were that wrinkled person with the bright smile and soft, blue eyes. The smell of burning cow pie was the starry night sky and open fields. They weren't really memories as much as *feelings* of memories.

She huddled around that smoldering cow pie, drawing her shift down over her knees, shivering. The cold night made her back hurt, but on clear nights like this, she could see all the stars in the sky. She traced the constellations with her eyes. It helped fight the chill. Big Bear, ladling the black soup of sky into Little Bear that spun round and round on the North Star. The unmoving star always sat right above the telephone pole, no matter where she looked. She wondered what kind of place 'North' was and how long it took to get there. Maybe her map would include North. Maybe when it was complete, the map would point straight there.

Ursula became very aware of the paper-thin cloth tucked away under her shift, and she looked at the stars now without seeing them. Though her eyes still drew lines between the bright dots, her mind was drawing the lines of her map. The river. The bridges it crossed under. The lines of roads that lay over the land like a net. And the faded emptiness of everywhere-else, all the places Ursula had never been.

God, how she wanted to look at the map now, to see the lines and reassure herself of the places she knew, forget about the everywhere-else. She couldn't. The man would see. She had little way of knowing if the man in the pole had seen already and was just playing along, waiting for another time to take away her food or make her sleep without fire in the lonely black night. But she had to believe that he... that *it* didn't yet know.

Without the map her eyes were drawn to the dark spaces between the stars of Big Bear. The dots made the semblance of a shape, but no matter how many lines she drew in her mind, there would always be empty spaces between the stars. Nothing could bring one to the other. No star would be free of the empty black that surrounded it, and Ursula's map would never be free from its faded edges.

Ursula shuddered and drew her shift tighter around her. She slept without dreaming that night, curled up in the fetal position, sucking her thumb. She woke once just before dawn and almost called out to the man in fear. There were no stars in the sky above her. On her back, looking up out of the roofless trailer, Ursula felt like a big, black blanket lay on top of her, suffocating her. She knew it to be just the darkest part of the night, but she slammed her eyes shut anyway. Still the blackness remained until it took her into sleep again. In the bright morning she forgot the moment like you might forget a useless dream, rubbed away as easily as morning eye-crust.

Dream forgotten, she left camp to go find another sign.

The Man in the Pole

Watching Ursula's back shrink as she left camp always dredged up that same unpleasant memory, but he had grown used to waiting, in the daylight at least. That black emptiness that came with night might just drive him to destroy it all, end it all. The girl would return, though, and her bright little face would somehow calm him enough to go one more day.

She had been taking longer and longer to return, and he entertained the idea that maybe she would never come back, just like the rest of them.

No.

She can't.

He had only been a little boy then. They had left a useless, dependent little boy. There was no reason for any of them to come back. His uselessness had been weakness, and he understood. When the diseases came—after the collapse—they had had to leave weakness behind. Now he was useful, though. Now *he* was the God of this domain. He saw every crevice of every trailer. Every grain of sediment was under his control. Things could come into being because of him. Things could be destroyed too. It had been his death in the light of the covenant between father and son that had made him powerful, made him *useful*. And now Ursula could not leave him. She couldn't get food, couldn't find shelter. Not on her own. No, she *had* to stay with him.

These thoughts and more whirled around in what remained of the man's mind as he watched Ursula's back fade out of camp.

And all he had while she was gone were memories of memories:

The camp is full. People pace around through the muck. The camp is the world, and we are all continents moving on mud lava. The camp is the whole universe, and we are galaxies circling each other, colliding, drifting apart.

It is all drifting apart.

First memory: Daddy reading to me from his book. We sit around the fire outside our rusted trailer. "God made the two great lights," he reads, "the greater light to govern the day, and the lesser light to govern the night; He made also the stars."

"He made it all?" I point up and try to grapple at the stars.

"Yes indeedy. Made each one of those like he made each one of us."

"Miss Lenore says stars're balls of gasoline."

He slaps the back of my head not unkindly and says "Lenore's people are the reason the world is the way it is. Eve ate the apple of knowledge first. Don't let her temp you like she temped Adam." Daddy shakes his head "And oh how we arrogant shall fall."

The rest of the memory is stars and indistinguishable babblings of the river.

But the river fish stop biting, and people need to eat. It don't matter if they're galaxies or not. They eat the grass before they resort to eating the mud, and they collide, breaking apart. Clothes are torn from their clotheslines, thrown into hasty rucksacks, as they drift into some kind of nothing.

And it is all collapsing. The real world. Collapsing again. It all burnt up once, but some things got rebuilt. Now it's burnt up again.

Second memory: Just voices. Miss Lenore's, telling me that there are only two things in the universe, Push and Pull. Daddy's—louder, more like sandpaper and corrugated metal—tells me that there are only God and his rotten angel Lucifer. Still others yelling about more practical things like food and water. "Leave, then," Daddy's voice again, "but he will punish you. Punish me too, for failing to prepare the kingdom. Heck, he'll punish us anyway. We been bad alright." These voices taste like sulfur.

They are leaving. They've been leaving since they got here. Push and pull. Daddy is pull. Miss Lenore, push. The spaces between us all are growing as things push and pull each other apart, and only footprints are left in Green Meadows. *The universe empties. The continents drift into the black. There's just me and Daddy. We are the universe. We are God and Satan. Push and Pull.*

Third Memory: This one is the clearest. The realest. It happened as I still see it. We're standing face to face in the lane. My back is against the telephone pole. "I'm leaving," Daddy tells me, "So I need you to wait right here till I get back."

"Where you going? When will you be back?"

"Well, I guess it's like the book says. I 'don't know the day nor the hour', but all things have signs, boy. So I'm going to go look for one, 'signs in the sun and the moon and in the stars'. Gotta find those. You be looking for those too, but you got to look right here from this spot okay? You remember what a promise is?"

"Something that can never be broken," I say.

"That's it, like God's own covenant with man after the great flood. We'll make a covenant right now, just you and me, one that can't never be broken. You promise to wait right here, and I promise to bring a sign."

"I promise."

"Now you're in charge of Green Meadows *while I'm gone," he says.*

Then Daddy's back fades out of camp.

I wait. I see the mud gobbling me up. It's up to my knees now. No, my waist. No, I can taste it if I stick my tongue out. Things go black for a second, and I see the grit in the clay, the spaces between the bits of dirt and mineral.

I guess this is where I die. I remember it hurting. Maybe I'm buried here forever, or still here, but now I see the camp from above like a bird. I can't move, but I can see. I can't feel, but I can think. I can remember.

After what might be long while or not too long at all, I become convinced that this is my hell place. A big empty trailer park for all eternity. Then Pull brings an old man and his granddaughter to camp, and it's real. All of it has been real. Which means Daddy's real and still out there. And I remember that I promised. *A promise is a powerful thing. Powerful enough for gods.*

My Last Memory: A bargain. I tell the newcomers that I am looking for a sign. The old man tells me that they are looking for a place to stay. He and his little granddaughter had been traveling from one empty town to the next. In need of food, water, and a place to hide from the disease, I offered him a deal. For every sign he brought I would give a can of food and a place to rest his head. He agreed and filled Green Meadows *to the brim signs. He died some time later. So I raised that girl, taught her to go look for signs when she got old enough.*

I won't leave her like my Daddy left me. Like her Granddaddy left her.

Ursula

Ursula's map lay open on the ground, charcoal scratches depicting a new box. All unfolded, the map was wider than she was tall, which wasn't saying a whole lot, but it had started as a piece no bigger than her hand. The cotton patchwork had grown as her knowledge of the valley did, stitched together with thread pulled from her shift and a thin bit of tin can for a needle.

Now, on a hill overlooking new territory, Ursula drew what looked important with the charry remains of her cow pie. She also freshened up some of the older lines. If she put it down on the map then she didn't have to remember it, and she didn't have to fear the empty spaces so much.

Green Meadows was a half-a-day's walk away. The weight of the demon's gaze gone, Ursula found herself feeling very light. She might float away if she wasn't tethered down to the map. She finished up her drawing by extending the line of roads, not thinking about the new empty edge that finding more places always created. Ursula sat back on her heels, felt the grass, soft but scratchy beneath her. The sun burned hotter overhead. It had just passed midday.

The house below was known now. It was on the map. She could go to it without any fear. She heard the demon's voice saying "Only signs. Nothing else," but it wasn't the real voice, just the one Ursula's mind made up. The made up one never made her feel sick, but still, the thought of him made her crash back to earth. But she had never found anything like a house before. It was all just fields of grass, sometimes woods, but always gravelly roads with their signs. Something about seeing the house—complete with a roof *and* a door— filled Ursula up with bright colors. It made her forget about how metal always had a sharp edge and that you couldn't really get all the mud out from under your toe nails. The demon couldn't see this far. He'd have taken the map if he could.

She folded the map up with the bits of char and raced down the hill. She'd prove it—find out right now if it could see her all the way out here. The inside of the house was an empty space, after all. She had to see inside to fill out her map properly.

The house was as empty as its drawing, but it was still beautiful with its brick walls and unbroken glass windows. The only mud in the house had been tracked in by Ursula herself. There was one thing in the house, but Ursula didn't know how to put it on the patchwork map exactly. Coming across it made her forget how to breathe for a few seconds. On the wall in a smaller room to the back of the house was an image of herself. Ursula recognized the shift and the black mud. She did not recognize the face. Its shape was familiar, but the clarity of it was new. Ursula touched her face over and over again, head buzzing.

She walked up to it and backed up again, watching herself mimicked on the wall. Waving, being waved at. Smiling, being smiled at. The doubt that had listed around in her thoughts since the making of the map, drew itself to a head then in that house. Ursula felt strong enough to test the ice. What was the worst that could happen? She would go hungry? Have to sleep in darkness for a while? The consequences made her throat tighten for a second, but she fought the feeling off. He couldn't hurt her. Who else would get the signs? He *needed* her. So she could deal with it, could deal with all of it to add the demon to her map. He was empty space too. She didn't know what he would do or why. Now she could find out. Out of that came a simple idea...

Ursula's stomach rumbled and ached. Last night's meal hadn't gone far, and her belly was empty. She glanced out the window, saw the sun starting its fall. On her map she drew a crude picture of herself inside the house. In it she was smiling.

Coming back to camp, with the map tucked safely up under shift, the girl had wondered how lying to the demon would work. She could not remember lying to it before, but she could also not remember having gathered all these signs that piled and rusted around her. But lying to it ... that *felt* like something she shouldn't do.

So for the first time, going in blind, the girl felt her way through the lie, ignoring every instinct, "I didn't find any signs this time. That's how come I was so late." The words came out of her mouth new and awkward.

"Nuh uh. Lying will rot your teeth out," the demon said.

Ursula tried to keep her head up, but the demon's words ricocheted up and down her spine, doubling her over. It was real. Too real. She retched yellow bile, which the clay quickly swallowed up. The demon's next words came as a whisper. It slid into the space between Ursula's ears like trapper wire. A thin ringing droned everything else out. "You will bring me the sign tomorrow," it said, "or you will die. Do you know what that is?"

Ursula couldn't nod her head one way or the other. But she had a pretty good idea.

"All your precious stars will go away. There'll be nothing but black. Nothing but emptiness. Do you want that? Do you want to be empty forever?"

"No!" she cried.

"I can do it too. No matter where you are."

"A sign, a sign!" was all Ursula could say, "I'll get it, I'll get it." The pain in her head was enormous and voice inside her body made her muscles twist and jump.

"Good. Now... eat up. You'll need your strength."

When Ursula opened her eyes, three open cans of beans lay in front of the pole. She ate them under a pitch black sky.

The next day, Ursula ran back to the empty house. She made it in half the time it took the day before. She stood heaving heavy breath with her second self.

She could think clearly here.

It hadn't killed her—had let her leave camp even—but a twisting just beneath her breast bone meant something bad was stirring up. It might kill her today, one way or the other. It hadn't known about the house, though. Her doubt had been muddy like the river before now. Now it was clear. It was like the wall that showed things for what they were, showed Ursula her pondering face, showed that the demon had limits. And if it had limits, if it couldn't get her, then what was stopping her from leaving?

"It can't reach me," Ursula said. "It can't or it'd yell at me. Hurt me. It can't get me." She said it over and over to her reflection, and her reflection said the same back to her. "It can't get me." She stayed there until the sun set.

The Man in the Pole

When the sun set and Ursula didn't return, the demon summoned a storm. He was *in charge* of the Meadows and that meant the sky that covered it too. All of it was his, and his Daddy put him *in charge* of it. His anger burst like a flooding river, bursting like a thousand dying stars. He wouldn't let her leave him in this empty camp alone. He didn't deserve it. Not again. Not when he was *useful*. Not when *Green Meadows* had deigned to make him their God.

The storm clouds gathered over him as the first of the stars began to peek out. The North Star burned bright, but it wasn't bright enough. The clouds turned the sky, and the land below it, to a deep-set shade of purple, then green, then black. A pile of signs toppled over as the ground shook. Trailers ripped themselves apart in the winds. And the demon felt himself rising, rising. He was the storm now. The land shrank away, and he saw it all, reading it like a map.

Ursula

Thunder shook her awake. The wooden floorboards beneath her rattled. A flash of lightning bleached everything for half a second and left green after-burns in Ursula's sight when it all went black again. It was raining outside. Ursula could hear the wind raking itself across the bricks like claws.

Ursula curled up into a ball, the howl of the wind growing louder and louder. The front door groaned on its hinges until it burst open, rain water flooding in. She backed herself into the corner, looking over her shoulder, trying to see her reflection one last time before it took her. Flash of light. A scared little girl. That was all she saw. The thunder that came not moments after shattered it all, and she screamed. She felt like she was being pelted with broken bits of herself, and the cuts they left were deeper than anything a ragged sign could do.

The wind ripped the roof off and tossed it about like so many sheets of paper. The rain soaked her to the bone in an instant.

Another flash of lighting, and up in the sky she saw the storm's face, with its pupil-less eyes and red-lipped scowl. And then the wind picked her up like an infant, lifted her as it lifted the house, but where the house fell away, Ursula stayed, cradled in the wind. One last blinding flash, and she saw the demon's face again in the clouds.

It swallowed her whole.

The Man in the Storm

Spinning and spinning. She had to stay with him. She had to. Yes indeedy. Oh, she'd been bad and he'd bring her back, but spinning and spinning. She didn't deserve to come back. Betrayed him. Left him for someplace else. Like everyone else. She *couldn't*. How would she eat? He was *useful*.

He lit the sky with the thought, lightning like new synapses for his brain, and saw Ursula's limp body being twisted in the funnel of black clouds. It was only an instant, but he saw her pale face. Serene. He wondered how *his* face had looked when Daddy had left him.

Had she been … happy here? But no food, no water? How could this empty place make her happy? A place so devoid of signs. A place so useless? Yet she was ready to defy him over it.

The storm floated back over Green Meadows. The man in the storm saw the shanties, and the river, and piles of rust—all strange constellations in their own right—and the now-empty pole watching over it all. Rain poured down, driving into the ground and turning the hard-pack soupy. Rivulets ran in a thousand tributaries all converging at the pole, moving towards the one constant. From above, it looked like the crude drawing of a bursting star, with mile-length rays.

The man, the demon, whose name had been forgotten, who was the last promise from a twice-dead world, laid Ursula down in a soft cradle of mud beneath the telephone pole. He couldn't do what he'd thought he could. Not to her. It all came down to waiting, and she had nothing to do with that. He was tired of waiting—for Daddy, for change, for the right sign—he screamed his fury into the storm, and he broke his vessel in two. Then he faded into the black, where he hoped his Daddy might now be waiting for him.

Ursula

Morning came, and the girl uncurled herself. She felt around on her body. Alive. Bleeding but alive. She crawled out from under the wreckage. She was back in camp, or what was left of it. She recognized the mud, and the bits of old metal were as familiar as the shape of her own hands. But the camp was hardly there. Trailers were ripped in half; some were gone. The rising river had washed all the road signs away, and all that remained were the lucky little shanties that had been built with concrete. She looked back. Snapped off at its base, the telephone pole lay in the muck. The spot where the girl had landed, just under where the pole had snapped, was curiously dry and free from debris. Her map was there, wadded up into a sopping wet ball. When Ursula opened it up the markings were gone, washed away in the rain. She dropped it, and it fell to the ground, an empty bit of patchwork.

She sat down in the mud and cried until the stars came out. They came slowly, as each peeked out one by one—like pricking holes in the black with a needle—until the sky, immolated in an endless sea of burning white lights, nearly burst with stars. The North Star came out last, burning brighter than all the rest. The signs had all been carried down the river, and even the telephone pole had snapped, been brought low, but that star had not changed, had not moved. Ursula wiped her nose and reached a hand to the sky. She told herself that if she tried hard enough, she could almost just reach it. She couldn't, but it didn't matter. Down on Earth everything—the signs, the maps, the little girls—washed away in mud and silt, but not the star. It would wait for her forever, unchanged.

Ursula closed her eyes and breathed deep the night air of the trailer park, then she picked up the wet remains of her map and left, following the North Star out of *Green Meadows.*

It came from Caleb Warner

This story really first came into being as a prose poem that I wrote for an introductory poetry class I took years ago. The primary image I began with was that of a little girl looking up at a telephone pole. I had no other context in my head other than just that image. A lot of my ideas start this way. It went through many different drafts, most of which my professor (or I for that matter) did not like very much. Now I don't know how, but at some point I got on the idea that there was a demon in this telephone pole and it made her steal road signs. That version of the poem the instructor liked a lot better thankfully, and so did I. I liked it so much that the idea stuck around in my brain for a couple more years until I took a private writing class on the LitReactor with author Richard Thomas. I turned the basic idea of that prose poem—which I now remember was first entitled "Totem"—into the little short story you see here. Nothing too amazing in its origins, but it is interesting how our ideas go on their own little journeys.

A question for Caleb Warner

Q: What's better: writing or having written?

A: Both. It depends. That question is hard to answer because writing (at least for me) is very much story to story. What I mean by that is each story is its own world that informs the process involved in creating it. Sometimes the first draft of the story is the best part of the process, where you're just banging out page after page in some kind of whirlwind, but after that, I usually find myself dreading the revision of said story. So 'having written' in that context is not as good as the actual writing. Then there are those stories where it feels like pulling teeth just to get a few words down. So writing is not at its best then either. At the end of the day, I think they're both great and they are both awful.

About Caleb Warner

Caleb Warner was born and raised in Indiana, in the Whitewater River Valley basin. Here he fostered a love for wilderness conservation, primitive living skills, and writing. He still lives there, working as an assistant to the director of the Writing Center at Indiana University East.

My Last Summer at Camp Unterlaken

Eugene Morgulis

Camp Unterlaken wasn't for everybody. Kids who came expecting a safe and cushy woodland experience barely lasted a week. I mean, you could get splinters from just about any surface, the mosquitoes could eat you alive, and the water in the lake was always, always freezing.

But my friends and I went back every summer. We treated Unterlaken's rustic roughness like a badge of honor. Proof of our toughness in a world of bubble-wrapped jungle gyms and participation trophies. So when other kids would come back to school in the fall with pictures from their fancy summer trips to Europe or those Mexican pyramids where they did human sacrifices, I'd show them my wicked rope burn from tetherball and watch their eyes go wide. Or I'd tell them how, on my birthday, the counselors picked me up and carried me around the cafeteria, while everybody went: "Throw him in the lake! Throw him in the lake! We won't shut up 'til you throw him in the lake!" Then they carried me out to the dock and tossed me in the cold water, and everybody cheered. Then I'd get hot chocolate. The counselors did it to all birthday kids, like me and like Andrew Ready, who was in my cabin and whose birthday was two days before mine.

I was standing in the canteen line with Andrew right after he got dunked. He was still shaking from excitement (or hypothermia) and going on about the heating coils in the lake. Not that there were any — it was just a stupid rumor they started to trick kids into the freezing water during mandatory swim lessons. Supposedly, the "heating coils" were "motion activated," so we had to get in and wiggle around before the lake would warm up. Most of us knew it was BS, but some of the more gullible kids treated it like a big mystery.

"Seriously, Jake," said Andrew as we waited in line. "It was like, metal and circular and flat. I hit it with my foot, but couldn't see because the water's so murky."

I ignored Andrew and concentrated on selecting my candy for the week. The camp food was okay, but if you wanted a Snickers or something good like that, you had to wait your cabin's turn for the canteen.

"Frozen M&Ms, please," I said, slapping my crumpled dollar on the counter.

Becky Landers snatched it up with a smile as bright as the Fourth of July.

"Coming right up, Jake n' Bake," she said as she disappeared below the counter.

Now there was a real mystery. Like, how did Becky come up with such awesome nicknames? Or how come her freckles kept moving around, no matter how hard I tried to memorize them? And how could she crush a softball or throw a Frisbee so far, while keeping her purple nail polish perfect even in the middle of Off-The-Grid, Maine? Not that I expected to solve any of these mysteries. After all, Becky had five years and six inches on me.

Becky returned with the bag of M&Ms, but yanked it back as I reached for it.

"Isn't there something you want to say?" she asked.

I tilted my head stupidly like a puppy. What would a kid like me have to say to Wonder Woman?

"Oh," I said finally. "Thank you."

"I like 'em cold too," she said with a wink, and handed me the bag of rock hard chocolate. As I grabbed it, my thumb brushed up against the smooth nail polish on hers. I might as well have stuck it in an electric outlet.

I stumbled away in a daze and wandered as far as the archery range. There, I plunked down to crunch on my M&Ms and watch the would-be Robin Hoods howl in pain whenever the bowstrings smacked them in the forearms. One of the younger archers, Abby Something, gave up in a huff and came to sit beside me. I gave her some of my M&Ms, which made her happy again.

At night, if you had to whiz, you just ducked out of your cabin and found a tree. Really you were supposed go all the way to the toilets, but it's the woods, right?

I was heading back to my bunk when I heard a voice coming from the docks.

"Almost ready," it said. "Make sure to bury them deep." It almost sounded like Becky Landers.

I sneaked my way toward the docks, avoiding the path so that Night Patrol wouldn't catch me breaking curfew. Sure enough, in the swimming area there was Becky with a bunch of other counselors. Girls *and* guys.

Were they skinny dipping? I got fidgety at the thought, but then I saw that, no, they had swimsuits. And they were diving. Each one stayed under the water a good long while, and when they came up they dropped something onto the dock. Something circular and flat.

It couldn't be — the heating coils were a stupid rumor. No one can heat a whole lake!

I crept closer. Becky was picking up each object and holding it close to her face, like she was whispering to it. Then she'd toss it back to one of the counselors in the water.

I wanted to stay longer, but just then I saw a flashlight coming from the other direction. I didn't want to get caught, or they'd make me swim laps. Come to think of it, most of the punishments, like the pranks, ended up with kids in lake.

I hustled back to my bunk.

"You were dreaming, dude," said Randy Kimmelman at lunch the next day between tomato soup-coated bites of grilled cheese.

"Nuh-uh!" I shot back, not entirely confident that he was wrong.

"See, you guys!" said Andrew. "They gotta heat the water up, because the lake is, like, glacial. And this kid froze to death once, and they had a court case, and the judge said they had to put heating coils in."

A.J. Kaplan, who no one liked, leaned in and asked, "Do you think there's dinosaurs frozen under there?"

Everybody groaned and turned to debating who'd win between a zombie squid and robot shark, but I stopped listening.

Instead, I was watching Becky at the cafeteria counter where she was spooning ketchup-colored soup into a line of bowls. She caught me looking and, to my astonishment, smiled right at me. Even in the din of the nosy mess hall, among the clatter of plates, and the unshushed screeches of over-sugared children, I could hear my own heartbeat.

After lunch, I had clean-up duty, but my mind kept drifting to the night before. To Becky in her swimsuit, and the things they were putting in the lake. What else could they be if not heating coils? Maybe Andrew *had* actually felt one.

There was only one way to find out, so I made for the door.

"You going somewhere with those spoons?"

I froze. It was Becky.

She pointed to my hand, where I saw that I was still clutching a fistful of used silverware crusted with cheese and tomato slop.

"Oh, I...uh...guess I wasn't thinking."

"No prob, Bob!" she said as she leaned down and placed a hand on my shoulder. "Just go toss them in the dirty bin, 'k?"

I made to leave but her firm grip held me in place. She was still smiling, but her eyes were steady.

"And don't even think about sneaking out tonight. Got it, Jake the Snake?"

She then squeezed my shoulder so hard I winced. I nodded so she'd let me go.

That night I had to pee worse than ever. But I stayed in my sleeping bag, squirming like a worm on a hook, as A.J. snored in the bunk below me.

Tomorrow would be my birthday, and I'd get thrown in the lake. Everybody would be watching. I imagined diving down and coming back up with a warm coil. I'd be an Unterlaken legend.

The next day it rained. And not a pleasant summer drizzle that just dampens your towel on the line and makes Frisbees harder to catch. This was a monsoon. Rivers flowed down the pathways between the cabins and, even indoors, the air felt charged with muggy electricity.

They announced over the loudspeaker that all activities were cancelled for the day, and that the campers had to stay in their cabins. I wasn't getting thrown in the lake after all.

Our cabin counselor Woody ran out into the rain below a plastic tarp to get our breakfasts from the cafeteria. He returned, soaked to the bone, with an armload of oranges and single-serving cereals we ate dry, straight from the box. I went for Frosted Flakes, as usual, and tossed them in my mouth one by one, like they were townspeople in a Godzilla movie.

After we ate, someone broke out a deck of cards, and we played Egyptian Rat-Screw as the rain grew heavier and the cabin creaked and groaned. I was distracted thinking about the heating coils, so I missed all the best slaps. Plus, my shoulder still hurt from where Becky had squeezed it.

Just as everyone started to go stir crazy — Randy and A.J. both slapped the card pile at exact same time and almost got into a fight over the length and grossness of A.J.'s fingernails — Woody got a call on his heavy black Walkie-Talkie. He plugged his ear and listened to a string of muffled buzzes. When they stopped, Woody clicked off the device with a pip, and turned to us.

"Rain gear!" he shouted.

Within the hour, all the campers had gathered in Shafrin Hall, and found spots on mats next to their friends. We all tossed our rain stuff in a huge wet pile in the corner, and if there was a plan for getting each kid back his or her own jacket, I couldn't figure it out.

Some of the kitchen guys wheeled around carts heaped high with bag lunches.

"We got tuna and PB and J!" one of them called. "Raise your hand if you want tuna." I did.

Shafrin Hall was where we put on the talent show at the end of the summer, and where they set up games and stuff for carnival night. All along the walls hung wooden boards with drawings and counselor signatures from every year the camp had been open, going all the way back to 1963. There was one I liked from '74 that had a funny old guy in a blue suit waterskiing and holding up two peace signs. Behind him trailed a banner with the Unterlaken motto: *Live This Summer Like It's Your Last.* All the boards had it.

I didn't know if it was the tuna, or the mildewy smell of the floor mats, or the huge crowd of campers screaming and laughing and farting, but my stomach felt uneasy. Something big was about to happen.

That's when the chanting started.

It was only a few kids at first, but it spread quickly: "Mo-vie! Mo-vie! Mo-vie!"

Even I joined in, forgetting for the moment about the heating coils and that everyone had forgot my birthday.

They rolled out the projection screen behind Marla, one of the girls' counselors, who raised her hand and put a finger to her lips. She stood there like that, slowly twisting back and forth like one of those oscillating fans until everyone quieted down.

"Ok, Unterlakeners!" she announced over the dying whispers. "Our movie this special rainy day is..." she paused so we could all do a drumroll on the floor. "The Princess Bride!"

There were cheers and groans. The counselors seemed more excited than the kids.

"Remember to be respectful," said Marla. "And if you have to use the bathroom, just raise your hand, okay? Enjoy!"

The lights came down, and we started watching. There were still some boos, but they stopped after the first part with the kid and the grandpa. Soon the only sound competing with the movie was the rain, which was tapping at the walls and windows like it wanted to come in.

It was during the part where Princess Buttercup escapes into the water and gets attacked by the Shrieking Eels that I started thinking again about the lake. The docks and swimming area would be empty now, I realized.

I knew I was supposed to stay in the hall, watch the movie, and finish my sandwich. But I'd already seen Princess Bride a million times. And the soggy clump of bread, mayo, and fish made my stomach turn.

This wasn't the birthday I wanted.

I wanted the counselors to carry me around and throw me in the lake as everybody sang and cheered. At least that's almost like a real party, which I never got, because my parents sent me to Unterlaken every year while they went on vacation. And I wanted to dig up the heating coils and show everybody, so I'd have the camp story to trump all camp stories. Maybe then Becky would see that I wasn't just another camper to smile at, then boss around.

I raised my hand and Marla gave me a nod to go to the bathroom. It was around the corner and away from everyone, next to a backdoor leading outside.

The walk to the docks was miserable, with the water on the path rushing over my ankles. I slipped and hit my knee hard on the ground, and said *Shit,* but no one was around to hear. Which was good, because I was probably in enough trouble already.

By the time I got there, it was pouring so hard I could barely see the end of the dock. A figure stood on the edge, like a shadow half-hidden among the raindrops. I knew right away who it was.

As I headed carefully down the slippery dock, I saw that, instead of her usual jean shorts and loose tank top, Becky was wearing a long white robe, which was soaked from the rain. I don't think she was wearing anything underneath.

It didn't seem to bother Becky one bit when I came and stood beside her. In fact, she looked happy to see me. More than happy. With her too-wide smile and tender eyes she looked...relieved.

"What are you doing?" I asked.

"Witnessing a birth," she said like she expected me to understand.

"Isn't it dangerous to be out here in the storm?"

A laugh broke from the back of her throat and came out ragged and sort of mean. It was a laugh you'd give a stupid kid for asking about monsters under the bed. Instead of answering, Becky purred and turned her face up to the sky to let the rain smack against it. She was being weird, and I didn't like it. I wanted to run back to the lodge and see Inigo and Westley sword fight. But I stayed.

"What were you doing here the other night?" I asked. "Are there really heating coils in the water?"

Becky laughed again and wiped her face. Her long arm snaked itself around my shoulder, and she pressed me to her side so that I could feel her body through the wet robe.

"Not exactly," she said, without letting me go. "I guess you could call them feeding coils. They store energy from movement in the water. It's taken more than fifty years, but they're finally ready..." she trailed off when she saw my confused face.

I didn't know what to say, so I blurted out the first thing that came to mind.

"It's my birthday."

Becky gasped. "How perfect! It's a sign."

"Of what?" I asked. "And what about the coils? I want to know."

"You will. Just watch."

I looked out at the gloomy water, which was bubbling and alive with the fat droplets of rain that pounded it from above. The air smelled clean and new, and as I breathed it in, I felt a tingling in my nose, like when you're about to cry.

Then lightning struck the lake.

I'd never seen it so close before. Not even fifty yards away flashed a thick pillar of blue light. It was as loud as a bomb going off in my ears.

"Jesus Christ!" I yelled, the wide bolt still burning in my vision.

Becky squealed.

"I can't decide if you're right, Jake o' Lantern. Or really, really wrong."

Becky turned me to look me in the eyes. Hers were blue and raw, like she'd been crying. She stroked the back of my soaked hair, which sent a tingle down my spine and made me feel uncomfortable.

"I'm so glad you're here," she said. "I really am. When the others chose me as the first sacrifice, I was so honored. But now..." She let out a deep sigh. "I don't think I can do it. I want to see the new world, not just usher it in. But she won't rise without a proper welcome. And someone has to do it."

I didn't like the way Becky was looking at me. "I think I should go back," I said.

But Becky just shook her head. "It's super awesome that you showed up, Jake in the Box. You're really doing me — everyone — a huge favor."

Before I could say anything else, Becky leaned down and kissed me. It stung, which was weird, but then I realized it was just the static pop jumping from her lip to mine. The kiss lasted only a split second, like something she'd give a baby brother.

"Happy birthday," said Becky.

She then dug her purple fingers into my sides and hurled me into the lake.

This wasn't like before. It wasn't a friendly prank where you just splash down a few feet away.

Becky skipped me like a stone.

I knew she was strong, but this was impossible. I must have bounced at least twice before I landed, far beyond the swimming area and almost to the middle of the lake where the pontoon boats go. Where the lightning struck.

Water was all around me, and I clawed and kicked for an eternity before I was rightside up with my head in the air. Even then there was water in my lungs, and I coughed and gasped and coughed again. I was breathing in and out so fast that my bottom lip sounded like a helicopter. So hard that my chest hurt.

I was scared and crying. Why did Becky throw me in? And how? What if the lightning struck again and I got electrocuted?

Everything was wrong. Even the water was too warm. Almost like a bath. And it smelled funny — like rotten eggs or the bathroom after my uncle Jerry.

This was unfair. All of it was unfair and stupid, and I didn't understand why Becky would pick on me. I would tell my dad, who was a lawyer, and he would sue Unterlaken. I'd never go back, and just stay home all summer and watch TV on the carpet with my dog Lambchop, who was getting old, but still liked to wrestle sometimes. I'd tell everybody how cursed this camp was, and no one would go, because they'd close it.

I tried to slow my breathing and tread water liked I'd learned — arms swing side-to-side, legs scissor.

Slowly, I started to calm down. It would be fine, I knew. Weird stuff happened at Unterlaken, but nothing too bad. It wasn't that far back to the dock. I could totally swim it. I was a good swimmer.

And then this would be one of those dumb camp stories that people tell. Like Backwoods Jones, who lives in the abandoned shed behind the ropes course and chops up kids with a chainsaw. Or that kid in Vermont who died from a peanut. Except my story would be true.

I began to swim back. I'd tell everybody about Becky. About how weird and mean she was, and probably on steroids. Then she'd go to jail. I just had to make it back to land.

Then something grabbed my foot from below. Then my other foot. And before I could even gasp, it pulled me under, and a thick, wriggling mass of muscle slid all over my body, like giant tentacles.

I just needed to wiggle out and come back with army guys, and they'd kill this thing, which was now coiled around me so tight.

Deeper and deeper it pulled me.

My last thoughts weren't about my parents or my friends. They weren't about Unterlaken or Becky Landers, or all the campers in Shafrin Hall and what would happen to them.

All I could think about was the water.

It had gotten so hot.

It came from Eugene Morgulis

The setting of the story is based on Camp Interlaken in Northern Wisconsin, which I attended every summer as a boy. The lake was freezing, so the counselors would joke that there were motion activated heating coils beneath the surface, and we had to jump in so they could warm up the water. The story takes that rumor, as well as other trappings and rhythms of camp life, and twists them into an adolescent horror tale that's moody, mysterious, and shocking.

A question for Eugene Morgulis

Q: Do you read more fantasy or SF (hard or soft)?
A: I tend to more fantasy and soft sci-fi.

About Eugene Morgulis

Eugene was born in Ukraine and immigrated to the U.S. as a child. He was raised in the Midwest, schooled on the East Coast, and currently resides in Los Angeles. He is likely at this moment stuck in traffic, missing the snow.

Pandemonium

Allison Epstein

Belial sighed as the Brown Line clattered overhead, sending aftershock tremors through the tracks to the pavement. He kicked a stray chip of gravel ahead of him as he walked, his hands pressed deep in his pockets.

"I hate this city," he muttered, mostly to fill the nearly deserted street with the sound of his own voice. "Too much fucking iron."

The woman walking behind him slackened her pace, widening the distance between them. He smirked, sensing her apprehension. A six-foot slouch in a knee-length woolen coat, he turned heads with his dark skin, broad shoulders, and untrustworthy air—and that without his habit of talking to himself. No doubt she considered him a walking public service announcement against talking to strangers.

Belial looked over his shoulder and grinned at her, teeth flashing TV static–white. The woman flinched and quickly crossed to the other side of the road.

He chuckled to himself, kicking at the gravel chip again before he hung a left onto Damen. He hadn't come to Chicago to frighten middle-class pedestrians, but if the shoe fit.

Belial paused in front of a mixed-use building sandwiched between two unremarkable freestanding homes. The usual array of businesses beneath: a used bookstore, a coffeeshop where the only thing more bitter than the espresso was the price, a Chinese restaurant called "Wok Like an Egyptian." Above, four levels of red-brick condos, black-painted balconies overlooking the street. He raised an unimpressed eyebrow. He'd visited this condo in Ravenswood before, of course. But he'd never used the front door.

As if sensing his hesitation, the thin iron rings around Belial's wrists seared white-hot, the pain brief as a blink. Lucifer, like a sharp elbow to the ribs, snapping at him to get on with it. Belial swore through gritted teeth, rubbing his wrists.

"You didn't have to do that," he said, though Lucifer could not hear. "I promised I'd serve."

Had promised, centuries ago, before the Fall, with knee bent and head bowed. And continued to promise, as days became centuries and millennia stacked neatly one atop the next. Still, Lucifer embodied the damage a right-hand man with his own agenda could do. He knew how easily promises broke. There was more security in iron than in words.

Better a bound, broken shadow than a threat. At least Lucifer had retained enough grace to look apologetic, at the time.

Belial stepped into the foyer, leaving the background noise of the neighborhood behind. The sage-green carpet absorbed the sound of his footsteps. Almost like walking on grass. He almost smiled. But there was no time for small pleasures. He took the stairs two at a time, sparks of anxiety shivering through his palms.

Yes, this is beneath you. An errand for a third-class spirit, not for an archdemon, for Lucifer's lieutenant at the Fall. But he asked you. And if you fail, you'll lose his respect, his trust, his smile. And you'll never get another chance to win them back.

No. Stop that.

He forced the thoughts aside, banishing the iron to the back of his mind. He did not need self-pity.

He needed this to *work*.

Belial paused on the landing and closed his eyes. An onlooker might have thought he prayed for strength, if that onlooker were devoid of any sense of irony.

You won't get another chance.

Collecting himself, he knocked sharply on the door of number 319.

After a moment, a man's voice came from the other side of the door. Nervous. Well enunciated. The repressed hint of a once-thick Southside accent.

"Who is it?"

"Open the door, Senator," Belial said.

"You didn't answer the question." The man's terror blazed clearly through the door.

The demon rolled his eyes. "You know who it is."

The door opened just a crack, revealing a sliver of the silver-haired, navy-suited man standing inside—Senator Roger Gatwood (R-Chicago 7th). Eyes wide, he attempted to shut the door, but Belial shot one foot forward, wedging it open. He grinned, displaying the full dazzling whiteness of his teeth.

And to think I was worried.

"That's not very nice, Senator," he purred. "What about that famed Midwestern politeness?"

Belial swept into the condo, ignoring the senator's obvious discomfort. He sprawled into a wing-backed armchair, a player king luxuriating on his throne. The senator sat rigid in another armchair opposite.

"I thought you couldn't come until I summoned you," Gatwood said, voice tight.

"Believe me"—Belial had a cigarette between two long fingers where moments before there had been nothing, and lit it with a vague gesture of his left hand—"I wish I could have left you alone until you did."

"Then why are you here?"

It was a reasonable question, but not one conducive to a short answer. Belial took a long drag of his cigarette and closed his eyes. Saw the corner of the Archregent's beautiful mouth curl into a sneer, his long fingers tapping against the arms of his throne, drumming out an impatient cadence. Felt Lucifer's mistrust darken Hell's shadows inch by inch, into something more complete than darkness, more final than eternity. The smoke from Belial's cigarette seeped into the chair's fabric. Stronger than nicotine, undertones of cloves and patchouli and the heat of a smelting-room floor. A scent that lingered.

"Collecting." The word undulated from Belial's lips on a wisp of smoke.

"Collecting?"

"Senator, you know who my master is," Belial said, dripping condescension. "Why did you think I came? To borrow a cup of sugar?"

The cigarette was done for—he ground it out casually against the knee of his creased black pants. Gatwood stood, alarmed, but when the demon pulled his hand back again, there was no ash, and no scent of burning flesh.

"Twenty-five years," Gatwood said, and closed his eyes, looking ill. He had paced to stand in front of the window, and seemed to be weighing the pros and cons of throwing himself out of it. The Southside accent grew stronger in proportion with his nerves. "I had twenty-five years with you first. That's what you said."

"Oh, I never forget anything I say," Belial drawled. "I love hearing myself speak. My services are at your disposal for a certain duration, provided you cooperate with my master's agenda. That was our deal. But your cooperation has scaled back, Senator. So, of course, the duration scales back, too."

"How long?" Gatwood's voice was a death rattle.

"Six weeks."

The senator's knees buckled. He caught himself heavily against the windowsill, breathing hard. "Six weeks?" he repeated.

Belial, without flinching, lit another cigarette. His eyes flickered toward the door, clearly implying this would be a two-cigarette conversation. "Time enough to set your house in order. As it were."

"I'll…I'll cooperate." By now, Gatwood's accent was out full force. His vowels were stretched to the breaking point. "What do you want me to do?"

Belial smiled. *Just like that.* If everything hadn't depended on his success, he might have mourned the lack of a challenge. "As soon as you return to Springfield after the holidays, you'll introduce a new piece of legislation."

"What kind of legislation?"

"Stop looking at me like that," Belial said, with an impatient wave of his hand. "I'm not asking you to carpet bomb Lake Shore Drive. You'll introduce a bill transferring management of urban water utilities to third-party corporations, which will perform the work at a fraction of the cost of a municipal department. Springfield will hail you as a hero. Maybe you'll actually pass a budget before next summer."

Gatwood's suspicion did not lift. Neither did his death grip on the windowsill.

"What will happen because—"

"Senator, you're a university man, right?" Belial asked.

Gatwood blinked at the non-sequitur. "Northwestern. MBA. '87."

"Then don't act like an imbecile. You know what will happen."

Gatwood did, and Lucifer did too. The number of souls a bill like this could catch. Every lie and bribe, every cover-up and deflection. So many souls damning themselves as silent poison seeped from crumbling pipes. A rich addition to any kingdom. And a rich gift from a servant under suspicion.

"People will die," Gatwood said at last.

"People die all the time."

"I…I can't, I, my constituents, they'll never accept…"

"Looking for a third term?" Belial asked, with a laugh that was not a laugh. "Be careful, Senator. The longer you drag this out, the more I'll start to feel like you're using me."

"I…I…"

Belial had every intention of twisting the knife further, but he was not given the chance. The rings around his wrists tightened their grip, as did the identical chains circling his ankles, waist, and the base of his throat. The pain punched the breath from his lungs, ripped sharp through his belly. He snarled a curse, fingers curling into unconscious fists.

Summoned both to Hell and from it. At least the Archregent kept his sense of humor.

"I'll give you time to decide, Senator," he said, rushing through the words as the summoning's corrosive tug blurred his body's borders, edging him out of being. "Give me a call tonight. Say, midnight. You know how to reach me."

And before the stunned, horrified expression left the senator's face, Belial flickered, and was gone.

Belial found himself at the doorway of a vast, underground chamber, two hundred yards long by seventy-five wide. The vaulted cathedral ceiling curved upward a hundred feet, meeting in gothic-pointed arches evoking the ribs of a sea monster. The demon straightened to his full height, a contrived air of unstudied confidence swirling from the set of his shoulders.

He'd done everything Lucifer had asked. He would simply tell the king what had happened, how faithfully he'd followed orders, and all would be well again.

Right. Because honesty has always served you so well in the past.

He crossed the hall, the military click of his polished shoes echoing through the empty room. With each step, the pain from the iron rings sharpened its focus.

The Archregent himself lounged across the throne at the far end of the hall. An utterly unsurprising state of affairs. Lucifer had a way of not so much occupying furniture as making it a part of himself. Belial doubted whether Lucifer even knew how to sit in a chair normally. The Archregent had assumed his workaday shape: a broad-shouldered man, pale and bright-eyed, *memento mori* cheekbones and a beard cut close as a shadow. He wore a narrowly pinstriped vest over a close-cut silk shirt, a dandified aesthetic Belial would have mocked in anyone but his master, whom it seemed to suit—as all things seemed to suit him. Even as a refraction of his former self, Lucifer commanded a room as only an angel could. Belial did not know whether to venerate him or curse him.

Beside Lucifer, in a low chair to his left, sat his wife. Persephone barely broke five foot four when standing, mousy-brown hair curled upward into a tidy bun, wearing a blue-gray wool sweater and loose, dark jeans. She watched Belial with an expression that did not connote worry precisely, more an apprehensive curiosity.

As Belial reached the throne, fighting to stand against the pain, Lucifer leaned to take Persephone's right hand in his left. She squeezed it, not taking her eyes off Belial, and in that moment he knew he could expect no support here. Away from her husband, Persephone brought a breath of something as close to Heaven as Belial had known in years. Only last spring, she had felt grass. Smelled rain. Seen stars. But this was not Persephone. This was the Queen of Hell. And Lucifer would have his way.

Lucifer glanced sideways toward his tall servant and smiled.

"Well timed, silvertongue," he remarked. "As if on cue."

Belial bowed low. Another sharp flash of pain seared his body as Lucifer shifted to look at him directly. The iron rings contracted further, burning as they did. The demon gritted his teeth but refused to cry out.

"You know I come when you call." Hell had taught Belial one thing to be proud of: how to keep your voice level, no matter what.

"True. Reliable as a dog. If not so obedient."

With a flick of his wrist, Lucifer snapped his fingers. Instantly the ring around Belial's neck flared hot and closed tighter, jerking him upright. He stood with the unnatural straightness of a hanged man, chin forty-five degrees up from the floor.

"What did the senator say?" Lucifer purred.

Belial paused, gathering his breath—not an easy task, as the iron tightened with Lucifer's growing impatience.

"He is...considering his options."

The pressure on Belial's throat vanished, as though an invisible hand had flung him aside. Air rushed through his lungs, and he dropped to his hands and knees, trembling. He did not dare look up to judge Lucifer's expression.

The tone was enough.

"Considering," Lucifer repeated. He released Persephone's hand and stood, pacing slowly to stand before Belial. When standing, the Archregent and his demon would be within an inch of one another's height, but Belial did not dare rise. "I don't recall sending you after the senator to win his *consideration*. Do you?"

Belial rose to one knee, keeping his gaze lowered. The demon spoke with the molasses-smooth rhythm of a master rhetorician. Persuasive. Making the simple words sing. If anyone could win the Archregent's favor with words, Belial was the one.

"No. Of course not. But for the contract to remain intact, he must agree to the plan without my interference. Which he is minutes away from doing. When I visit him at midnight, he will be yours, as you commanded. I swear it."

Lucifer smirked. Like a blackjack dealer who knew what card came   next.
"You swear it? What would you swear by, old silvertongue, to make me take you at your word?"

Belial glanced up. Lucifer stood six inches away, arms folded loosely over his chest, a note of dry amusement in his impossibly bright eyes. Blink, and there he was again, Lucifer the angel, as he had been before the war. The trusted friend, with sage advice and seraph's wings. The angelic politician, who could persuade a man to do anything at all with a smile, a word, a gesture. Blink again, and it had passed, but not without leaving its traces. Even now, even kneeling, fallen from grace and falling further by the second, Belial could not regret the moment of rebellion. Not when he followed a general like this.

"What do you want me to swear by?" he asked.

The corner of Lucifer's mouth nudged toward a diagonal smile. Unfolding his arms, he reached his left hand forward and took Belial by the chin, tilting his head up, raising him to his feet. In that moment, Belial could see nothing but Lucifer's face. The light in his eye. The uneven curve of his smile.

To be his again, entirely. What would I not give?

"Nothing at all," Lucifer answered, in that voice still carrying echoes of spun gold and trumpets. "You are a liar."

Persephone half-rose from her chair. "Darling, wait—"

"The best." Lucifer ignored her. "That's why I chose you for my lieutenant. But there are ways of keeping you honest."

Belial screamed, bloody and raw. Pain like this did not exist between Heaven and Earth.

The iron rings contracted bone-crushingly small, their throttling grip searing with a white-hot flame. He crumpled to the floor, slender limbs writhing. Nerves flayed with pain, decomposed muscle unthreaded and tangled in a useless, agonizing knot. Though the demon's flesh was made of pure spirit and suggestion, still the dark skin beneath the rings bubbled to a pink-yellow pustule, the bilious morass of third-degree burns. Burning, burning with the corrosive poisonous stink of iron. Charred, smoking remains. His body a scorch mark on stone. His fingers clawed the air, he could not silence the scream that echoed from the high vaulted ceiling like a cloud of Furies overhead—

And then it was over.

Belial curled into himself, motionless and trembling. The stone against his cheek brought cold relief to his burning skin. Though the rings cooled, he could still sense the latent, shadow pain. Each breath caught with a soft whimper at the back of his throat. The photo-negative of a scream hovered in the silence.

When Lucifer stood over him and drove his heel into the demon's fingers, Belial barely felt it.

"I sent you with the expectation you would finish the business." The Archregent's words landed cool and level. "I get what I expect. Do you understand?"

Belial said nothing. It did not matter.

"Go when he summons you," Lucifer said. "Show me you can deliver, silvertongue. Convince me." He turned back toward the throne, to the chair where Persephone sat, her hands gripping the arms until her knucklebones shone lighthouse-bright. Lucifer trailed one hand along the side of her face with anachronistic tenderness.

"You know, Persephone," he said, "when my kingdom was smaller, no one served me as well as he did. And yet I can't remember the last time he delivered me a soul. How long has it been?"

"Centuries, I think," she replied, breathless. "He smooth-talked the Athenian girl. Pandora. She was the last."

"That long? From the leader of my army to a master of delegation. How the mighty fall. Of course..."

He paused, raised a hand. Belial cringed as if hit. A slow smile inched across Lucifer's face.

"We never reach the lowest point, so long as we can still say 'this is the lowest.'"

The Archregent turned his back on Belial, toward the set of high double doors behind the throne. His long legs made short work of the distance.

"I have business, Persephone," he said, turning to grace her with a falling-star smile. "But I'll come tonight, when I'm finished. If you're asleep, I won't wake you."

"You can wake me," she said, and smiled back. To all appearances, genuine. "Or delegate what you can to Hecate and come sooner. It's been too long."

"Agreed. Until tonight."

The door closed behind him, echoing through the empty space. For a long moment, only the hitch in Belial's breathing could be heard, a ragged metronome through the quiet. Somewhere far off, a dog barked.

Persephone rose, crossing to where Belial lay curled on the floor. Bending to a crouch, she took the trembling demon's hand and helped him to sit up. Her cool palm sent a shiver through his burning skin.

"I thought the plan was to make him trust you," she said. "Not make him angry."

Belial tilted his head back and closed his eyes. His breathing still came too fast, but slowed by the second. "I didn't plan to. Roads paved with good intentions. You know."

"You ass."

"Incorrigible." Belial ran the back of his hand across his mouth, then turned to look at her. "Be honest. Can I...can I win him back, do you think?"

"Let's not have this conversation here." Persephone glanced at the door. "If it's all the same to you."

A fair point. Despite the empty room, the feeling that someone still listened from somewhere in the shadows persisted. Belial gave a grim nod.

"Lead the way." He warily pushed himself to standing. His knees shook, but he waved off Persephone's offer of help.

"My rooms?" she offered.

His laugh sounded like dirt striking a coffin lid. "Right. Because what I want right now is for Lucifer to find me alone with his wife in her rooms."

She rolled her eyes—in Belial's opinion, a disturbing show of naiveté. One did not thrive in Hell thanks to overly generous assessments of other people's character.

"My apartment isn't far," he said.

"I'm not the one worried about distance." Persephone sighed and slipped the tall demon's arm around her shoulder, keeping him upright. His mouth narrowed in irritation, but he voiced no protest. "Come on. We'll get some liquor in you, and you'll be as good as new."

Logically, Belial reasoned, pure spirit could not get drunk. But then, logically, pure spirit could not feel pain, either. Perhaps he'd never drunk enough to find out.

A science experiment, then, after a fashion.

He collapsed in the corduroy armchair in the corner, stretching his long legs in front of him. Centuries ago, when Lucifer would still visit Belial's rooms, the Archregent would make gently cutting remarks about his lieutenant outfitting the apartment like a tweed-jacketed university professor. But Belial did not care. The wood paneling, the corduroy chairs, the low coffee table spread with maps and astronomical charts, it comforted the demon. He found it familiar, somehow. And in Belial's opinion, a place in the Archregent's inner circle earned him the right to a few eccentricities of interior design.

However tenuous that place now seemed.

At the credenza near the door, Persephone filled two glasses brim-full with scotch, passing one to Belial. He'd downed half of his by the time she sat down.

She curled her legs beneath her in the chair like a cat settling into a window seat. Her hair had begun to escape its bun. She balanced the glass on the arm of the chair, hand hovering nearby a moment to see if it would fall, then shook her hair loose and wound it atop her head again.

"Tell me the truth," she said, taking up the glass. "Do you think you can get him the senator?"

"I told him I will, and I meant it," Belial said. "And his pet project in the Senate, I'll get him that too. Gatwood doesn't have the balls to say no," he added, grinning. "He almost pissed himself when he saw me."

She rolled her eyes. "Don't you think you'd finish the job quicker if you didn't have quite so much fun?"

"I don't, actually," he replied. His voice was stronger now, using the scotch as a crutch. "Showmanship's how I get through the day. Even your husband likes a little panache. The serpent's fangs and the brimstone, it's all window dressing."

"He doesn't use the fangs anymore," Persephone said wearily.

"Lucky for you. Can't imagine they were much fun in the bedroom."

"They weren't."

He sighed, looking down into his glass. "Tell me," he said, as if they'd spoken of nothing else all this time, "has he said anything to you?"

She raised her eyebrows. "He says a lot to me."

"But if he said anything about what made him doubt me, you'd tell me."

"Would I?"

He leaned forward, holding the scotch between his knees. "We're friends, aren't we?"

"Are we?"

He stared, black eyes wide. "When Lucifer first brought you here. You spent three months crying. Wouldn't get out of bed. Who talked you around? Not your husband."

Persephone looked down. Suddenly she appeared much younger.

"I think you remind him of the war," she said. "He doesn't like to think about it. He told me..."

Belial waited, regarding her like a complex math problem. She did not go on. His hands gripped the glass tighter.

"He told you what?"

She still would not meet his eye, but she couldn't avoid finishing the sentence, not now. She took another sip of scotch.

"He says you talked him into it. That he would have apologized. Taken it back."

The glass in Belial's fist shattered into a thousand dagger fragments. He leapt to his feet, amber scotch dripping down his arm, staining the carpet.

"Shit," he snarled, shaking his arm, raining droplets of scotch. "Fuck. Shit."

Persephone started to rise, either to deal with the mess or get him another glass, but Belial began to pace, a tiger prowling a cage. She tightened her lips and stayed put.

"Apologized? He would have apologized. Do you hear yourself? *I made him* King of Hell. I gave him everything." Belial's mouth twitched slightly, restraining words he did not dare speak. A long moment passed. Finally, arriving at some conclusion, he shook his head and laughed, quietly, to himself. "I should've known."

"Known what?"

Belial hopped up to perch on the credenza—high enough so his feet dangled a foot off the floor. He removed the stopper from the decanter of scotch, looked thoughtfully at the crystal glass beside it, then raised the decanter to his lips and drank deeply.

"That he'd outgrow me," he said. "I wish you'd known him then. The way he was. The golden child."

Persephone twisted the ring on her left hand, wringing it in a tight circle. White gold. Not iron. "I know him better than you think."

"No. Fuck, he was beautiful then."

"He's beautiful now," she protested.

Belial laughed, too loud for the room. "Not like that. Me, talk him into anything? He smiled at me and I turned my back on God."

He drained the rest of the decanter, winced at the burn along the inside of his throat. When he set the decanter beside him on the credenza, his hand was perfectly steady. So far, this science experiment was proving an abject failure.

He arched his back, feeling the lack of wings like a toothache. Sometimes he still dreamed of them, the black-pinioned feathers unfurling from his back, shrouding his limbs in light-rippled darkness. Could see angelic Lucifer's tawny falcon feathers silhouetted against the sun, more beautiful than any god. The wings, of course, had been the first to go. When he closed his eyes, he could still remember grasping for consciousness after the Fall, crumpled blood-slick and broken beside Lucifer in the darkness. The taste of Heaven still on their tongues, the raw wounds rotting their shoulder blades, as if their limbs had been ripped out at the roots. Which, in a way, they had.

"I'll miss you, come spring," Persephone said, breaking the silence.

He laughed and twisted his spine to one side, then the other. Useless—the dull ache would not release.

"Believe me, I'll—shit," he snarled, and slammed his fist against the credenza. "Goddamn fucking shit."

He'd already begun to fade, blurred around the edges. He fought the summoning, but some forces were too powerful, some codes too unbreakable, even for an archdemon.

"He's early," Persephone said.

"Son of a bitch must have—"

And he winked out of view, like a firefly at dawn. The faint scent of burning iron lingered above the credenza.

Midnight, Belial thought, cursing himself ten kinds of idiot. *Why did I say midnight?* This was what he got for not thinking fast enough, for assuming nothing would go wrong.

After all this time, you'd think I'd learn.

He had just enough time to cast the faintest of glamours, smoothing the creases from his clothes and his forehead, masking the pink-sick burns across his skin. Nothing more elaborate. If the senator wanted fire and brimstone, he'd have to provide more warning.

The iron rings jerked him forward like a hooked fish, and he stood again inside the Ravenswood condo, within the chalk circle on the kitchen's tiled floor. They stood facing each other silently. In one circle, the nervous senator, cracking his knuckles in anxious succession. In the other, the impassive demon, watching the senator like a wolf. Belial glanced over his shoulder toward the microwave, suspended over the smooth-top stove.

"Eleven fifteen," he remarked. "You're early."

"Underpromise and overdeliver." Gatwood had not changed clothes since their encounter earlier that afternoon.

"Not exactly the Politician's Code, is it?" Belial watched the sad little man squirm.

Is that what I look like to Lucifer? A quivering insect crushed on the pavement?

No. A reminder, of the view from below someone's heel.

Even so. He would never have apologized. He has a whole world now. He knows there's no going back.

He doesn't want Heaven, any more than I do. But a better kind of Hell…

If he would smile at me again.

"Well, Senator?" he prompted, when Gatwood's continued search for words came up empty. "You called. I came. What can I do for you?"

What wouldn't I do, to win his smile?

Nothing he hadn't done before, or wouldn't do again, for the right price.

The senator opened his mouth, closed it again, watched the demon watching him. He swallowed. Bit his lip. Nodded.

Belial's smile broadened.

A thick snowfall swept up the steps outside, white on white against marble. On the desk, standing like an altar in front of the window, two sheets of paper, an absurd number of pens. Across the paper, the bold-faced title: "SB1764: Municipal Utilities Privatization Act, Sponsored by Sens. Harrison (D-Peoria) and Gatwood (R-Chicago)."

State lawmakers milled about, drunk on the afterglow of legislative victory. In the center, Roger Gatwood accepted praise, cracked barely funny jokes, shook an infinite number of hands. Paler now than in November. Thinner. A persistent cough, some kind of infection.

Unseen by the horde of public servants, Lucifer perched on the desk, one leg folded beneath him, sitting on his heel. Belial stood nearby, arms crossed over his suit jacket and one foot propped on the wall. Lucifer watched Gatwood, eyes narrowed in thought. Belial watched Lucifer.

Finally, Lucifer turned to Belial, head tilted slightly to the side.

"Do you feel that?" he asked.

Belial nodded. "Soon."

And it would be soon. Belial knew how Lucifer's mind worked, and had designed the legislation to match. Pipes exhaling clouds of crumbling dust. The blood-rust taint hanging in a desert reservoir, like the crimson shadow of sunrise over a black ocean. Poison spreading, luxuriating, expanding to fill the space available.

"Thousands of souls," Lucifer said. The Archregent looked at the paper on the desk, not at his servant. He spoke so softly Belial had to lean forward to catch the words. "That's what you've gotten me. Thousands. And every soul in this room."

Pushing himself away from the wall, Belial took a step toward the desk. He paid no attention to the senators filling the room, nor to the way Roger Gatwood stared in mounting horror in their direction, as if he had suddenly noticed the Senate had company. Belial had eyes for nothing but Lucifer. Nothing but this.

Belial would have bowed, but no ready-made rules of etiquette existed for what he meant to accomplish. His black eyes locked on Lucifer's. When he spoke, the words sounded uncharacteristically plain, direct.

"If I could give you ten thousand more, I would."

Lucifer reached out to brush a hand against Belial's cheek, long fingers trailing to the base of the demon's throat. Belial shivered as the Archregent circled the pad of his thumb along the iron, slipping under the metal to caress the sensitive skin beneath.

Lucifer's soft smile did not quite convey regret.

Belial's clear gaze did not quite convey forgiveness.

"Well, old silvertongue?" Lucifer said. His hand lingered, before slowly returning to his side. "Shall we?"

Belial cleared his throat, brushing the dust off his words. "Shall we what?"

"Get back to work. The world is wide. And to make my way in it, I could use a good liar."

Belial grinned. "You've come to the right place."

Lucifer nodded. "I know."

A better kind of Hell...

Lucifer snapped his fingers, and both the Archregent and his lieutenant were gone.

A balding, blue-eyed senator from La Salle glanced toward the desk and frowned. "Did you hear something?" he asked.

Gatwood shook his head. "No. Nothing."

A question for Allison Epstein

Q: Do you use critique groups or other resources to polish your writing?

A: I swear by critique groups—my writing output would probably decrease by half without them. When you're writing by yourself, it's easy to get discouraged and think no one's ever going to read your work-in-progress. But when you know your critique group is going to read it, plus it has to be ready in three days, it's serious motivation to get off Twitter and back to work. I belong to a stellar writing group in my neighborhood, where writers of various backgrounds and genres meet up weekly to talk craft, navigate plot holes, and drink too much wine. I'm also notorious for running story ideas past friends with no invitation whatsoever. My friends are used to getting phone calls that open with "Hi, so, question: octopus-people. Yea / nay?" I have very patient friends.

About Allison Epstein

Allison Epstein is a writer, editor, marketer, and words person living in Chicago. She studied creative writing at the University of Michigan, and currently writes both historical fiction and what could be called urban fantasy if you squint. She is the grammar nerd your high school English teacher warned you about.

allisonepstein.contently.com

Hearts and Roses

Kathryn Yelinek

Every morning at exactly 8:47, three things happened: a swallow fed three nestlings in the eaves outside the mistress's bedchamber, a rabbit nibbled grass beside the white stone driveway, and a crow pecked at something that caught the morning sun on the perimeter wall. Leaving her feather duster on the dressing table, Rosa opened the window and leaned out to watch. The breeze smelled of honeysuckle and blew warm over her light green skin, rustling the scarlet petals that grew around her face.

Only within the perimeter wall did the morning progress like clockwork. Beyond the wall, the world changed daily. That morning, rain fell thick and gray, blotting out distant roofs and spires. Rosa wondered what rain tasted like. She had just wet her lips with her tongue when Heartwell strode into the room, his bow tie askew.

"I received another letter." His voice rumbled even lower than usual, betraying his nerves.

"From the master?"

"I wonder what we did wrong this time."

Rosa longed to touch him in reassurance, had wanted to ever since they woke, newly made, in this house. But in the month since then, he had never so much as let his fingers brush hers, and she couldn't bring herself to make the first move. Perhaps he didn't want her touch. While she was a gangly stem of a woman with stick limbs and leafy vines for hair, he was a solid muscle in the form of a man. The giant, pulsing heart that made up his body and head beat steadily beneath his black-and-white uniform. Its thump-thump, thump-thump filled the room, a commanding, comforting sound.

She dared not touch him, so instead she took the cream-colored letter from his hand.

"Is it bad?" he asked. In the month since their awakening, he'd started bringing her the letters that the master materialized beside him, so they might share whatever news they contained. It was, she thought, a small sign that he enjoyed her company.

As always, the master's penmanship was fastidious. She read quickly and gasped.

"What's he angry about now?"

She shook her head. Scarlet petals waved at the edge of her vision. "He's bringing our new mistress. They should be here around eleven o'clock."

"This morning?" Heartwell rocked back on his heels.

"Yes, in two hours."

"Heaven help us now he's coming back." Heartwell straightened his livery. "I'd better see that the stables are in order."

After he left, Rosa buried her trembling hands in her apron. The master had explained that the impending arrival of their new mistress was why he'd created them. Tending to his bride was to be their life's work. Yet Rosa felt nothing but dread.

During his previous visit, he'd flown into a rage when she placed lilies in a vase in the front hall. He'd demanded she create a bouquet, yet never said what kind. Infuriated by the lilies, he'd ripped a handful of petals from around her face and turned them into a rose arrangement. Only within the last few days had her scars stopped aching.

What sort of a woman would wed such a man?

Rosa shuddered at the thought. Then she squared her shoulders. She had work to do.

A cream-colored letter tucked in the top dressing table drawer laid out the master's directions for how to prepare for the mistress's arrival. She reviewed the list carefully before beginning. First she set crisp linens on the bed, sprinkled with lavender water. Then she laid out a gaudy amethyst necklace on the dressing table. Finally, she smoothed the bedspread and centered a heart-shaped pillow on it.

As she did, two robins fighting on the manicured lawn caught her eye. How odd. At 9:32, the robins should be bathing in the fountain, water glinting off their dark backs.

Instead they boxed with claws extended, their wings buffeting the air. The rabbit, usually grazing near the holly bushes, stared. Its delicate pink ears pivoted as if alarmed by what it saw.

A chill slid down Rosa's back. The last time something unexpected had happened on the estate was after the lily incident, when the master's anger caused the fountain to erupt like a geyser and pockets of dandelions to pimple the yard.

She rushed across the room and down the servants' stairs to the kitchen. Heartwell should be there, back from the stables by now. "Heartwell! The outside's changing again."

There was no answer. The kitchen stood empty, the hanging pots and pans gleaming in the light from the small, high windows. She frowned. She didn't know why the house had a kitchen, since all food materialized like the master's letters. Still, the room smelled of cinnamon and cloves, and she and Heartwell found it a cozy place to chat.

She crossed to the back door. Before she could open it, Heartwell barged inside. With one hand he carried a large bouquet. With the other, he rubbed the blood streaking the arteries and aorta on top of his head.

"The birds are acting up." He dropped the flowers on the table while Rosa wetted a dish rag. "I hate to think what this means."

"What happened?" She held the dish rag out to him.

Instead of taking it, he dropped into a chair and bent over, soliciting her help with a nod of his head.

Her breath caught in her throat. Cautiously she put one hand on his head. He was warm and surprisingly soft, like satin. She felt the blood circulating under his skin, and for a moment she froze, caught up in his coppery smell and the softness of his skin under her palm. Then she dabbed at his scratches.

He hissed. She paused, but he waved her on. He sat very straight and still under her care.

"Two swallows flew at me outside the stables," he said. "You'd think I was egg poaching."

"The master can't be angry again. What could we have done?" Although, she never knew what would anger him. He'd once stabbed Heartwell with a fork because Heartwell blinked at him while serving dinner.

"I don't know. I don't know how he created this place or why it would respond to him, when he's not here."

"What if something's gone wrong with the mistress?"

"Then we'll face it together." He rubbed his cleaned-off head and smiled shyly. "With all we've been through, we make a good team."

She felt her face warm. Suddenly shy, she hurried to discard the rag. When she returned, he had brought a vase and was snipping the ends of the flower stems on the table, a task he knew she disliked. He moved over to make room beside him at the table.

"Maybe the mistress will know a way we can escape." He handed her a rose.

Fear made her clutch the stem. Such dangerous words. "There isn't one." She focused on arranging the rose in the vase. "He swore he'd track us down and hurt us if we tried."

"There must be a way. He can't be all knowing."

"Even if there were, would she tell us?"

He worked in silence, his bottom lip between his teeth, his body pulsing with anger at the wretchedness of their situation. She felt anger, too, that the master would cause him such anguish.

"I'm going to get you away from here," he said suddenly. All at once, he dropped his shears and cupped her face in his hands. "Someday, somehow, we'll find a way out."

Now she held very still, amazed at his face so close to hers. It seemed impossible that finally he was touching her, speaking words that maybe meant more. "You—you fancy me?"

Color came to his cheeks. "Of course I do." He grinned nervously. "Your fingers, they're so slender. I can't stop watching them. And the way your petals flutter in the breeze..."

She was sure he could hear her own heart, beating to echo his. She covered his hands with hers. "Heartwell—"

"No." He pulled away. "Don't say anything else, not until we're free."

"But—" His sudden withdrawal confused her. She took a step closer, not wanting this moment to end. "What would we do out there? We don't know anything of the outside world." Just thinking about leaving the house, however wretched, sent a shiver of fear down her spine.

"Anything must be better than here," he said, though his voice rumbled low with nerves. He picked up the shears and severed a stem. It sounded like a bone snapping. "I could have killed him when he tore out your petals."

"He'd have killed you first." She gripped his wrist. "Promise me you won't do anything rash."

He sighed. "You're right. Now isn't the time, not with her coming. I promise."

"Thank you."

"But," he said, "I won't woo you here, in this prison."

She stared at him, aghast. "Why not?"

"Because I'm going to get you out. Maybe you'll prefer someone else then."

"That's a stupid thing to say."

He smiled a sad little grin. "What sort of man would it make me, to pursue you in this hell?"

"The kind that I'd like to woo me?"

He just shook his head and handed her another rose. With that move, he seemed to open a rift between them.

Stung, she dropped the rose into the vase with the others. It was a lighter shade of red than the rest. Even in the vase, in the middle of a bouquet, it looked lonely.

Would it have been better if he hadn't spoken? She didn't know. All she knew was that she'd remember the feel of his hands on her face for as long as the master let her live.

She worked in silence until a quarter to eleven, when Heartwell swept away the severed stems, and she spoke to the air: "A tea service for two, please."

A moment later, a silver tray appeared on the table. On it sat a silver teapot and two teacups with saucers, sugar and cream bowls, and sandwiches and biscuits. The aroma of mint and cucumber wafted up.

"We'll get through this," Heartwell said as he lifted the tea tray. Rosa merely nodded and followed him up the stairs to the parlor, carrying the vase of flowers. She set it on a pedestal table in the entry hall.

"The mistress will help us," Heartwell said, but his entire body beat at an anxious tempo, and when Rosa tried to take his hand, he closed his fist. Side-by-side, yet separate, they waited for the carriage to come.

It came at 11:12. Horse hooves and carriage wheels crunched over the gravel drive. Heartwell opened the carved front door. Through it, Rosa saw sunlight, the broad expanse of the lawn, and a wet black carriage with a gold embossed fist on its side. The carriage door opened, and she heard voices—a man and a woman's sharp, raised tones. The master emerged first, jumping down from the carriage and pulling their new mistress by the wrist behind him. He barreled up the front steps, tugging her along, and Rosa dropped into a courtesy, her eyes downcast.

"Welcome, m'lord, m'lady," Heartwell said.

"Let me go!" the mistress cried, and Rosa, startled, looked up.

"Hush, my dear," the master cooed to the mistress. He was as thin and pale and prissy as before. His hair was parted precisely down the middle; creases ran sharply up the fronts of his slacks. Even the wrinkles on either side of his mouth and the gray in his manicured beard were perfectly symmetrical. "Just a few more steps."

The mistress strained away from him, her left wrist imprisoned by his grip. She couldn't have been more than eighteen, a thin slip of a woman, with brown curls that fell to the waist of her polka-dotted dress. This, Rosa thought in dismay, was Heartwell's longed-for rescuer?

"Here!" In the center of the entry hall, the master released her. Immediately she darted for the door. With a snap of his fingers, it slapped shut. The mistress skidded to a halt and spun around, a look of panicked horror on her face.

"Well," he asked, spreading his arms to encompass the house, "isn't this better than what your beau could provide?"

She eyed the black-and-white tiled floor, the dark wood of the staircase, and the glittering chandelier. She glanced at Rosa by the parlor with an imploring look, but Rosa dared not respond. In the center of the hall, the master watched the mistress, his head cocked, breath held as he waited for her answer.

The mistress marched to the pedestal table by the base of the staircase, grabbed the vase with Heartwell's flowers, and hurled it at the master.

Rosa gasped, but the master easily sidestepped. The vase smashed on the floor, spraying flowers and water and china pieces over the tiles. The stink of newly broken stems filled her nose. The master blinked at the broken vase then at the mistress. The hint of a shadow passed over his face. A wave of his right hand caused the vase pieces to float up from the floor until the vase with its flowers stood undamaged on the table. "I thought you said you adored flowers?"

The mistress hurled it again. It shattered anew to the master's left.

Rosa caught Heartwell's shocked look. She must appear just as bewildered. She knew little of human society beyond the perimeter wall, but surely this was not normal. Could this be why the birds had attacked? Because the master's orderly world had encountered an obstacle?

This time the master did not repair the vase. For a moment he stared, stricken, at the mistress. Then his face smoothed over. He pursed his lips. "It won't work, my dear. I won't exhaust my power fixing doodads so you can escape."

"You're a monster and a cad."

"I'm your friend. Soon I'll be your husband."

"Geoffrey will come for me. The whole town will. You've gone too far this time."

He shook his head, grave. "Nothing goes in or out of my gate without permission. And behold this lovely house I made for you."

Again, the mistress glanced at Rosa. Now Rosa chanced a smile. The mistress might not be a powerful magician to counter the master, but surely she was on their side. And that meant escape might not be so impossible.

"You're sentient?" the mistress asked tentatively, looking from Rosa to Heartwell and back again.

Rosa nodded. Heartwell said, "Yes, m'lady."

"And you were made? From a rose and a heart?"

Yes, Rosa meant to say, but the master spoke first.

"Of course they were." He placed a hand over his own heart. "Roses and hearts—they symbolize love. My love for you. They'll tend to your every want and need."

"But—" The mistress wrapped her arms around her waist. Even at a distance, Rosa could see her shaking. "Did it hurt them? What if they didn't want to become people?"

The master's lips thinned. "If they don't please you..."

"I didn't say that," she said quickly.

"It's obvious they don't." He looked at Rosa then at Heartwell with his cold, cold eyes. "I can fix that." His right hand twitched.

Whether to blast them or change them into something else, Rosa didn't know.

She did know that she would not stand for it. Not again. Not in front of the mistress. Certainly not in front of Heartwell.

She lifted her skirts to flee, just as Heartwell shouted, "No!" and the mistress threw herself in front of Rosa.

The blast exploded to Rosa's right, where she would have been had she run. Tile pieces flew past, and smoke wafted acrid up from a dark spot on the floor. Her knees felt like they'd turned to sap.

The mistress, trembling, stood in front of her. The master glared at both of them, his gaze cold.

"Don't try to run," he said, and Rosa wasn't sure which one of them he spoke to.

Across the entry hall, Heartwell pulled on the front door, but it refused to open. A commendable effort, except that the master could destroy them before they crossed the hall.

She noticed a rivulet of blood running down the mistress's wrist. An idea blossomed.

"M'lady," she whispered and dared to touch the mistress's elbow. "You're bleeding."

"I am?" The mistress lifted her arm, never quite looking away from the master. "Oh, the tiles must have cut me."

The master paled. "You're hurt? The house hurt you?"

"Come on." Rosa tugged her arm. "I know where we can patch you up."

By the door, Heartwell nodded. He understood she meant to go to the kitchen, with its secondary door. As she backed towards the parlor, the mistress in tow, Heartwell joined them. "I'll get the bandages," he said.

The master watched them go, his face still pale. "You make sure she's well cared for. Arianna, I'll make sure this never—"

The mistress slammed the parlor door on the master's words. At once, Heartwell turned the lock and Rosa shoved a chair under the doorknob.

"That'll slow him a little," the mistress said.

The master banged on the door. "Arianna?"

Only a little, Rosa worried as she raced towards the kitchen. When she looked back, the door bowed in as if a giant hand pressed on it. The master screamed, "You think you're clever?"

The mistress shuddered. Rosa took her hand and held tight. Even three against one felt like poor odds.

The kitchen stood empty, a welcoming expanse smelling of cinnamon and cloves. Rosa pulled the door shut and helped the mistress shove the table across it as a barrier while Heartwell strode to the back door.

He was still tugging on it when Rosa turned around.

"It won't open." He smacked it with his palm.

"Oh gods," the mistress said. She tied a napkin around her scratched wrist. "Phineas must know we're down here."

Phineas? Rosa thought, before she realized the mistress meant the master.

"Most likely, m'lady," Heartwell said. He waved Rosa over to help drag a hutch in front of the back door.

The mistress said: "Please call me Arianna."

"Most likely, Arianna."

She flashed him a grin. She stacked chairs atop the table. Between them and the hutch, the kitchen felt oppressive, foreboding, not at all a good place for a chat.

"Is there another way?" Arianna asked.

"The windows." Heartwell pointed.

They looked so small, up by the ceiling. Rosa shook her head. "You won't fit."

"I'll fit. I have to." He dragged a chair to the counters underneath the closest window.

Rosa steadied the chair while he climbed up. "Where will we go once we're out?" The thought of leaving still chilled her to the core.

"You'll stay with me and my family," Arianna said.

"Would they let us?"

Arianna paused in stacking chairs. "Why wouldn't they?"

"The ma— Phineas. He said if we left he'd find us and hurt us."

"The town will protect you. He's made his last mistake."

"The town would let us stay?"

Again, Arianna looked puzzled. "Of course. Did you think you wouldn't be welcome?"

Rosa's petals ruffled as she glanced at Heartwell. His body pumped a rapid thump-thump. "We're, you know, different."

Arianna's face softened. "You're certainly unique. But you're lovely in your own ways. I'll see you find a place."

It wasn't a complete surety of acceptance, but it was better than Rosa had expected.

Heartwell seemed ready to take the risk. "Let's go then." He peered out the window. "It's sleeting."

"Here? At the house?" Only now did Rosa notice the rattle against the glass.

"But it's August," Arianna said. She touched Rosa's arm. "Will you freeze?"

Rosa startled. "I don't know. I've never been in the cold before."

"Put this on." Heartwell handed down his black jacket. "And stand back."

His jacket smelled like he did, coppery and sweet. She stepped away, shrugged into it, and shrieked.

Phineas stood inside the kitchen door. He smirked. "Arianna, come back. Whatever these two have told you, don't believe them. Come back, my love, so I can treasure you."

"Don't believe him," Arianna whispered. "It's just a projection. He's not really there."

"He looks real." Rosa inched away from him.

"Of course I'm real." His smile didn't reach his eyes.

Overhead, Heartwell yelped. Rosa spun. Heartfelt had pulled one of the pans from the wall and swung it at the window pane. Only, the pan dissolved in his hands, turning to mist and leaving the window unharmed.

"See what I can do?" Phineas said. "Come out, all three of you, and I'll be lenient."

"Liar," Arianna said. She threw a salt shaker, which passed through him.

Rosa had a moment to feel better. Then Heartwell yelped again. He scrambled off of the counter as it crumpled to the floor like a piece of paper. At the same time, the table against the kitchen door collapsed, sending chairs crashing to the floor.

Rosa pressed a hand to her throat. She felt like she couldn't catch her breath. Phineas might not be physically in the room, but his magic was, and now she knew how easily he could dismantle the chairs, too.

"Why doesn't he just make the door and chairs disappear?" she asked.

Arianna's face was grim. "He's toying with us."

Rosa's throat closed up. Then an idea surfaced. It might not work, still she whispered, "A tea service for two, please."

A laden silver tray appeared on the ground before her. The smell of mint and cucumbers wafted up.

She bit back a grin and crossed her fingers. "A chest of drawers, please."

A massive, five-drawer chest with claw feet appeared behind the tea tray. Heartwell skidded to a halt in front of it, a bench to put across the door in his arms.

His face lit up. "You're a genius."

Arianna whooped. "Let's see how long he can sustain this before his power runs out. A corner cupboard, please."

One popped into existence by the collapsed counters, complete with decorative plates.

"A king bed," Heartwell said. "A sofa, a loveseat."

"A secretary's desk," Rosa added. "A bookcase, a dining room table."

"Another chest of drawers, please," Arianna said.

Furniture crowded the kitchen. Phineas scowled impossibly from the middle of the sofa. "Your games won't work." But his image went out. They stood alone in an oddly furnished kitchen.

"Is his magic exhausted?" Rosa asked. She stood sandwiched between the loveseat and bookcase. The quiet felt ominous.

"I think he's modifying the spell so we can't create anything else." Arianna hugged a pillow from the loveseat. "But he must be weakened."

"Look out," Heartwell said. Glass shattered behind them. Rosa turned, shielding her face. Heartwell balanced on top of the corner cupboard. He wielded another pan from the wall, which he ran around the window frame, knocking out the remaining glass.

He held out one hand. "While we can. You first, Arianna."

She lifted her skirts and climbed up. "Modifying the spell won't distract him for long."

"So we'll be quick." He made a step with his hands to boost her up to the window, his movements steady and sure. Rosa watched with equal parts fear and pride.

Without a word, Arianna slid through the window. Heartwell leaned down to give Rosa his hand. "Your turn."

She climbed on top of the cupboard. His accelerated thump-thump, thump-thump sounded so much louder this close to him.

He pressed her shoulder. "You saved us just now."

She shook her head. "We're not free yet."

"But now we have a chance. Thank you."

She wanted to stay longer by his side, but they didn't have time. He cupped his hands, she put her foot into his grip, and he boosted her up. She grabbed the window frame, balancing against it at her waist. The window seemed smaller and Arianna a longer way down than she'd expected. Cold air chilled her face and hands. She swallowed, wondering if she could really jump.

Behind her, there was a thud and a grunt. Alarmed, she glanced back. Heartwell lay on the kitchen floor, the cupboard disappeared.

"Heartwell!" Was he dead? "Are you all right?"

He stirred, and she sagged against the window frame in relief. Beside him, the chest of drawers disappeared. Before Rosa could shout, all the furniture vanished in a single puff, and the door flew open.

Phineas strode in.

"Go!" Heartwell pushed himself up.

Hating herself for it, Rosa shimmied out the window.

She hit the ground hard enough to knock the air from her lungs. The cold wormed under her jacket and down her socks. Sleet drummed against her face and hands. It smelled sour and tasted bitter and reminded her of Phineas. That gave her strength to sit up, even as she gasped for breath.

"Heartwell," she wheezed.

Arianna pulled her to her feet. Her beautiful brown curls lay plastered to her face. "We have to go."

Rosa shook her head. "Won't leave him."

"We can't do anything for him except get help."

"But—" Darkness showed behind the kitchen window. What was Heartwell facing? He could never have fit through that window, and he must have sent her and Arianna away knowing this. She couldn't abandon him.

"Help him by getting yourself out. We'll come back for him. I promise." Arianna pulled her away from the house.

With one look back, Rosa followed her across the slick lawn. Sleet dripped off her nose and chin. She hunched her shoulders, feeling chilled and sluggish, desperate for Heartwell to be beside her. They should be watching robins pull worms from the grass. Instead the lawn was empty, and the sharp patter of sleet dulled all other sounds. Even with Arianna in front, she felt alone under the gray sky.

If Phineas changed Heartwell back to a heart, would he remember who he was?

The solid wood gate stretched dark across the white stone drive. Beyond it, the rain had stopped, and tendrils of afternoon sun shone down. From the street beyond, a clamor rose up, as if a mass of people assembled there.

Rosa shied away, but Arianna broke into a grin. "The town's come for us!" She tugged at the gate's handle. "It's locked." Her disgust made the words into curses. "Can you go under?"

The gap was so narrow. "I don't think so."

Arianna pounded on the gate. "Help! Can you hear me?"

"Arianna?" A voice shouted from the other side. "Is that you?"

"Geoffrey?" She pressed her hands to the gate.

"Yes! Are you all right?" The noise of the crowd lessened, as if all quieted to listen.

"Yes, but there are other people trapped in here. We have to get them out."

"Half the town is here, including the witches. We can't get the gate open. He's magicked it up, down, and sideways. Can you find the key?"

Arianna searched all around the gate. "It's not here." She spun around to Rosa. "Where would he hide it?"

"I don't know! He always magicks the gate open. The key's only a failsafe—" She stopped. Her brain whirled, and she turned, surveying the length of the wall.

Arianna looked from the wall to her. "What?"

"Every morning, I see a crow pecking at something." She squinted, imagining how the wall looked from the mistress's bedchamber. "There!"

She raced across the grass to a crack high in the wall. On tiptoes, she reached over her head.

A black ball of feathers struck her hand.

She snatched it back as a crow dove at her again. Panicked, she ducked, her hands over her head. Beak and claws and wings scraped her scalp.

"Leave her alone!" Arianna swatted at the bird as it swooped again. It reeled up, screeching.

As quickly as she could, Rosa reached up, only to have the crow sink its beak into her skin. Pain shot through her hand, but she grabbed something metal out of the crack.

"Got it!"

Arianna took another swing at the crow as Rosa opened her hand to reveal a small bronze key.

"Go try it." Arianna pushed her towards the gate. "I'll distract the bird."

Rosa scrambled towards the gate. The key had to work. Arianna's beau and the townspeople would take care of Phineas, and she would rescue Heartwell. It didn't matter how cold she was or that her hand stung. The gate lay just ahead, and the key would fit.

Phineas stepped out of thin air, with Heartwell beside him.

Rosa froze, fear squeezing her throat. The gate was perhaps twenty feet away.

"Give me the key." Phineas held out his hand.

"You're not real." Rosa inched forward. The sleet didn't touch him. "You're an illusion."

"Not this time." He flicked his fingers, and sleet pelted his palm. Rosa backed up. Another flick of his fingers, and his palm was dry. "I don't like getting wet."

Beside him, Heartwell shivered. Bruises dotted his face, and sleet dripped from the loops of his arteries and the tip of his nose. He mouthed something, but she couldn't tell what. Anger churned in her belly at those bruises.

"This is very simple," Phineas said. "Give me the key and come back to the house, or I cut him right here." He grabbed the top of Heartwell's head.

His aorta. He'd bleed out before Rosa could stop him. She felt cold all over.

A touch on her arm said Arianna leaned in close, offering support without words, although she didn't know how Arianna could help.

Don't do it, Heartwell mouthed. He winced as Phineas yanked his head down by pulling on his ear.

"On the count of three," Phineas said. "One." A knife appeared in his hand. "Two." He held it to Heartwell's head. Rosa felt her stomach clench. "Three—"

With a cry, Heartwell shoved Phineas. Phineas stumbled, falling to one knee.

In that moment, Rosa did the only thing she could think of. She threw the key over the wall.

It flew up and caught a glint of sunlight. "Stop!" Phineas cried and pointed, no doubt summoning a spell. Too late. The key fell over the other side. For one long, agonizing moment, nothing happened. Rosa feared she'd doomed them all.

Then the gate boomed open, and a stream of people poured in.

"No," Phineas said. He scrambled to his feet and no doubt would have disappeared, but at a shout from three women at the head of the villagers, he froze in place. Immediately the sleet stopped, and a ray of sunshine pierced the clouds. A robin sang from its perch on the fountain. Phineas stood frozen, mouth agape.

Heartwell rushed over to Rosa. "Are you all right?"

"Yes. I think?" She felt trembly. It seemed impossible that the ordeal was over. "Are you?"

He smiled, a bit lopsided with the bruises. "Nothing time won't heal, thanks to you."

Rosa felt her heart swell. Beside them, Arianna was in the arms of a sandy-haired young man. Beyond that, the witches muttered charms that wrapped Phineas in thick rope. The rest of the villagers swarmed the grounds, whispering about what grisly fate awaited him.

The sandy-haired young man turned to Heartwell and Rosa, his arm firmly around Arianna's waist. "Arianna tells me how brave you two were. Please, come to my house. We'll get you patched up, and you can stay until you decide what you want to do next."

"Please do," Arianna said, beaming.

"What do you think?" Heartwell asked Rosa. He touched her elbow.

Rosa studied the sandy-haired man's face. He seemed earnest enough. A few of the villagers threw her and Heartwell sidelong glances—as she had feared—but this man and Arianna seemed nice.

"I don't know what I want to do next," Rosa confessed.

"Neither do I." Heartwell grinned. "Maybe I'll become a doctor."

Through the gate Rosa could see small, tidy houses. Their window boxes held pink and purple blossoms. The breeze smelled of cut grass and baked bread. A rabbit loped across a lawn. That, at least, didn't seem too scary.

"Maybe I'll be a veterinarian," she said.

"You'd be a good one." He tucked her hand into the crook of his elbow. "Let's go find out."

Together they walked into the world beyond the gate.

It came from Kathryn Yelinek

"Hearts and Roses" came about by merging two different ideas, as so many of my stories do. First, I've always enjoyed stories about individuals who have been turned human from something else, e.g., *The Shape-Changer's Wife* by Sharon Shinn. I'd been wanting to write a story like that for some time but couldn't find a hook for this idea. Then I was talking with my boyfriend about strange things (as we often do), and I got the idea for a human heart with agency. Suddenly, Rosa and Heartwell were born, and the story followed after that.

A question for Kathryn Yelinek

Q: Do you live near where you were born? Have you traveled much?

A: I live about 2.5 hours from where I was born. This is close enough to visit family on a somewhat regular basis and to make it into New York City when I want (a necessity since I adore Broadway musicals). As to if I've traveled much… How do you define "much"? I've traveled to South America and to Europe several times. The farthest south I've been is Venezuela. The farthest east I've been is Poland. The farthest west is California (although I was very young then and don't remember much). The farthest north I've gone is Pond Inlet, on the northern tip of Baffin Island in Nunavut, Canada. That trip was devoted to seeing narwhals, the unicorns of the sea. It's still one of my peak life experiences.

About Kathryn Yelinek

Kathryn Yelinek works as a librarian in Pennsylvania. In addition to the required hobbies of reading and writing, she enjoys bird watching, star-gazing, gardening, and going to see Broadway musicals. She shares her home with two parakeets, who she is actively striving to make into the most spoiled birds in the Western Hemisphere. They don't seem to mind.

www.kathrynyelinek.com

December

The World's Secret Heartbeat

Aatif Rashid

Blake tried once again to start his car, a mustard-yellow vintage two-door from back when companies still made gasoline cars — but the engine only sputtered and groaned. It sounded to Khalid like a dying person, coughing and wheezing through its final moments of life with a few last and naive gasps of ill-conceived hope.

"I told you we should have taken the electric," Khalid said.

"Don't worry!" Blake called from the driver's seat. "It'll work!"

Blake tried the car again, and Khalid sighed and turned to look across the bay. From here, he could see the full extent of the sprawling, ruined city where they were set to rendezvous with the Movement's two local contacts. Cold glass towers rose into the dark sky, and in the distance lay the broken bridge, its red frame collapsed into the gray water. White, cubed houses were scattered like dice across the surrounding hills, and the setting sun reflected off their hollow, uncurtained windows. Meanwhile, the ash-strewn road where Khalid stood wound its way around the bay, through the dusty fields, and up into the city, cutting through the warm haze that hung around it all like a shroud.

"I think we're out of gasoline," Celine said.

"The meter says it's still half full," Blake said.

"Half empty," Khalid corrected. "And maybe the meter's broken."

Blake ignored him and tried the car again. Celine leaned in through the driver's door and put her hand delicately on Blake's shoulder, though Blake as always remained unresponsive. Khalid wanted to tell Celine to give it a rest. Blake obviously didn't go in for that sort of thing, at least not with her. She should have known this by now, having worked with him in the lab for almost six years. But as the Movement's only historian, Khalid noticed certain human subtleties that scientists like Blake and Celine did not. It was possible that Celine understood the truth of Blake's feelings and was attracted only to the tragic romanticism of it all, of being emotionally invested in something that could never work out. But Khalid felt a part of her probably still held out hope. Humans were after all so easily deluded into optimism.

The car sputtered and groaned once more, but still didn't start. Blake stopped for a moment and then tried it again, with the same predictable result.

Khalid found it ironic that they might have run out of gas on this particular mission, to track down that rumored old source of sustainable energy, "the world's secret heartbeat" as it was referred to in the records of the board meeting at Gold Man Investments. "It might just be a rumor," he had cautioned Blake, when Blake brought them in front of Erin to propose the mission. "These old corporate documents are filled with false starts, projects that never got the funding or that never panned out."

But Blake had argued his case effectively and convinced Erin to authorize the mission. "It's worth chasing even a rumor," he'd said. "We all know that shale and oil won't last forever, a few hundred years more at most, and as long as the Domes are profiting year to year, they're not going to be the ones to look for a long term solution. It's up to us. And, I mean, think of how everything will change when we have long term, sustainable energy. We can finally break the Dome Corporations' monopolies and end the long years of economic stagnation. And then we can rebuild everything, our cities, our farms, our whole society. We can make the world like it used to be."

More convincing than his actual words had been the way he'd said them, purposeful, confident, his voice rising at the end with passion. This had always been what drew Khalid to Blake, this depth of feeling, this soul-stirring resonance that only he could create. It was how he'd convinced Khalid to join the Movement during University and it was why for the past eight years Khalid had never quit, despite his growing pessimism about their cause. Blake was like a source of energy all by himself, charging everyone around him with his own optimism, making them believe in the utopian future he envisioned for humanity, which to his physicist's mind was a simple equation, one that by necessity had a solution that would bring the world into mathematical balance. Khalid envied the world view that allowed Blake to believe in such a thing, and perhaps that was why he always found himself following Blake, no matter how outlandish his goals. Deep down he really wanted to see the world that Blake saw.

Overhead, the sun beat down from the cloudless sky, and Khalid felt sweat building up on the back of his neck (they had plenty of sunscreen, but even so, he'd read enough stories about the long term effects of direct sun exposure outside a Dome to be worried). Blake stepped out of the car and went around the front to pop open the hood, as if the answer lay there. He took with him the battery pack, a small device he'd brought that could jumpstart electronic devices, though even a non-scientist like Khalid could tell the car's issue was more than just a simple electronic malfunction. The battery pack had a limited charge, and Khalid didn't want Blake to waste any of it, as he assumed it might be necessary somewhere on their mission, in the ruined city still filled with old electronic infrastructure with residual power. But Blake's eyes gleamed with characteristic hope as he looked under the hood and across the car's vast and complex inner workings. Celine leaned next to him, placing her hand a few inches from his, her eyes moving wherever his did. Khalid turned away to scan the horizon.

Where they'd come from was just a grimy haze, miles and miles of flat earth, the road just a thin black strip crumbling to ash under the harsh climate conditions. As it wound its way across the parched land, it passed the occasional gas station or road sign or other remnant of the old world — all now a kind of museum, or mausoleum, of the history of mankind's folly.

As Khalid stared at the brown land around him and then back at the haze-shrouded glass and metal city across the bay behind him, he remembered what he'd read in the histories at University, about how all this had once been beautiful, green fields and rolling hills that turned gold in the summer. Things had grown here, a quarter of the world's food — strawberries, garlic, avocados, foods that now existed only in literature and fading collective memory. He'd tasted a strawberry only once, back at the University, when a rich friend's parents had purchased a frozen crate of them (for the price of a nice house in one of the Domes) and shipped some to her. She'd let him try one, and the taste had been sweet, but in a different way from the processed sugar he was used to. Now, gazing around the scorched earth, he couldn't imagine anything had ever grown here that didn't taste like ash and dirt.

Khalid knelt and ran his hands through the dust at his feet and wondered if the earth remembered the strawberries like he did. More than that, he wondered if strawberries would really ever grow here again. If Blake was right, and at the end of this road lay a heartbeat that would power the world, could everything really change? Would there really be a better future for humanity, and would these hills really be green and golden, like they once were?

Blake never got the car to work, and they had to abandon it on the road. They finished circling the bay on foot and it was evening by the time they reached the rendezvous, an abandoned metro station on the outskirts of the city proper. There they found their local contacts, who waited for them against the concrete wall, under the peeling letters of the sign ("BART," an acronym whose meaning had, like so much, long since been lost). One of their contacts was a man, older than them, 40s Khalid guessed, though it was hard to tell with his bushy beard.

His companion was a younger woman, their age (late 20s) but nevertheless looking far more weathered and seasoned than the three of them. They both wore gray, hooded cloaks, black boots, and brown bullet-proof vests, and carried large packs on their back. Despite all the gear, they possessed an enviable grace, especially when compared to Khalid, Blake, and Celine, trudging with tired steps up to the station past the broken freeway ramp.

"Are you Miles and Julia?" Blake asked. He smiled and extended out his hand out. "I'm Blake, from headquarters."

The bearded man, presumably Miles, frowned and didn't shake Blake's hand.

"Next time instead of telling me your name and where you're from, trying waiting till I've confirmed my ID," he said. "What if I'd been Santa Clara police undercover?"

"So, are you police?" Blake asked, nervously, yet still with his smile.

Miles didn't respond and looked across them with displeasure. Celine and Khalid shared a nervous glance. They'd been briefed only a little on Miles and Julia — hard, no-nonsense types, with years of experience running missions in the Santa Clara Dome, the kind of foot soldiers who would probably resent escorting three intellectual types from headquarters with little field experience. The only other operatives Khalid had ever met were trainees, and they were fresh faced recruits who looked up to even Khalid, Blake, and Celine as the older, more experienced members of the Movement. Miles and Julia, with their dirt-smeared faces and calloused hands, reminded Khalid just how far from home they really were.

"Which one of you's the historian?" Miles asked. "The one who found out about this rumored energy source?"

"I am," Khalid said, stepping forward.

"And it's not just a rumor," Blake added, stepping forward too. "Based on the documents, Gold Man investments poured considerable money into this, a few hundred billon dollars, which at pre-war currency rates comes out to—"

"Erin said you have an address," Miles interrupted. "For Gold Man's corporate offices."

His voice was a low growl, and Khalid could barely see his mouth move behind his beard. Blake frowned but didn't speak. Khalid noticed then the pistol tucked into Miles's leather belt, and he understood suddenly that neither he nor Celine nor even Blake was in charge of the mission anymore.

"The document said California Street," Khalid said. "555."

Miles turned to Julia, who pulled out a phone and typed in the address. Khalid and the others had a crude map of the city, which they'd used to get to the rendezvous, but not one with street names of anything in the city center. He watched as Julia loaded up a GPS map on her phone.

"You have access to a network outside the Dome?" Celine asked.

"I've hacked the Santa Clara Police," Julia said, without looking up. "They patrol through here pretty regularly, and their SUVs have mobile access."

There was silence as Julia thumbed across the map of the city. Celine looked nervously around them, as if a police patrol might suddenly appear. Above them the sun was setting, but to Khalid the air felt no cooler than it had before.

"None of these maps have street names either," Julia said finally. "The signs might still be there, though, if we get close."

"Do we know where we're headed?" Miles asked.

"If it was an investment banking company, then probably the old financial district," Julia said.

"OK then. Let's move."

Without waiting, Miles turned and moved up the road, towards the distant towers. Julia gave Khalid and the others a brief, terse glance and then followed.

Khalid looked at Blake and then at Celine and saw in their eyes the same fear he felt himself. But Blake looked resolute too, and Khalid knew his mind was still firmly in the future, on the energy source that he believed with an almost religious conviction would be humanity's salvation.

As they made their way through the desolate streets, Khalid ran through in his head the catalogue of dangers Erin had wanted them about, from Santa Clara Dome police patrols (citizens were forbidden from venturing this far out) to National Government agents on a mission (though in recent years, with the Domes growing more autonomous and the Capitol lowering taxes, it was unlikely that the Government could afford to send people to this coast) to Naturalists who'd lived their whole lives outside a Dome and who killed and ate anyone they came across (in truth, Khalid had never heard a confirmed report of a Naturalist and assumed they were just a ghost story designed to frighten any rebellious children who thought about venturing outside the Domes). The greatest danger, though, was the city itself, the crumbling overpasses and fallen streetlamps, the buildings on the brink of collapse, the sections of concrete road that could at any moment cave in, the volatile gas stations and abandoned cars that needed only a wayward spark, and the potentially toxic fumes from the old tech sections of the city. That was where the former inhabitants had once believed they could conquer nature through silicon and other elements, and where nature was now reclaiming those very elements, the sun's deadly rays breaking down the hardware humans had synthesized and releasing cancerous fumes into the air — another reminder of humanity's hubris.

To the group's left, the sun was setting over the hills and what Khalid knew were the stormy oceans beyond, once the source of mankind's power and industry, now poisoned liked the rest of the environment. And yet Khalid felt that this city, even in its shattered state, was much more alive than a Dome's pristine, immaculate streets (the products of the unartistic and uniform corporate vision that had taken power since the war). Here the apartments were varied, a brick facade followed by a stucco one, a pointed roof followed by a flat one, and the abandoned cars that lined the streets were all of different makes and models. Even the empty storefronts suggested their former vivacity, many with glass doors and windows looking in on broad, open, high-ceilinged spaces, some still with letters from their former lives, "La Boulange" and "Blue Bottle" and a place with missing letters called "____a Republic."

"So why bother to study something like history?" Julia asked him. "Why not science or business or soldiering?"

Khalid could tell in the way she walked, upright, shoulders back, eyes alert and looking in every direction, that she had studied soldiering.

"Well I used to think," he said, "that in times like these, history was everything. Studying the old world, I thought, might help us rediscover some old technologies, some old ideas, help us rebuild the world, maybe even help us figure out what went wrong and why everything fell apart. I thought that maybe knowing the truth would keep us from doing it all over again."

"But you don't think that anymore."

"No. But I don't regret studying what I did. Reading all the histories, all the mistakes people have made, all the ways they've failed — that's made me who I am. I've learned to see the world a certain way."

Khalid could see in the way she looked at him that Julia understood what he meant. Blake could keep his scientific optimism, his commitment to progress. As a historian, Khalid knew better than to trust in humans' capacity for goodness, for redemption. Julia, the soldier, had clearly learned the same, sad, human truth.

And yet, Khalid couldn't help but recognize that, despite their cynicism, here they were, members of the Movement, an organization committed to overthrowing the Domes and the current, corrupt government and ushering in a better world, trekking across the ruins of an old world city, hoping to find a rumored source of sustainable energy. Ultimately, it was a testament to just how powerful Blake's optimism was — the beating heart at the center of their group that powered them all and kept even the most cynical of them moving forward.

As they walked, Khalid wondered what lay at the end of their road. In University he had studied some of the final pre-war attempts at more renewable energy. At first, scientists believed they'd found a breakthrough, a way to convert plant life into energy at a vastly more efficient rate than the ethanol of the time, and there had been talk across the internet about a possible future of unlimited energy, where humanity could grow all the plants it would need to power the world. But as the climate change grew worse and crop failures increased, the idea was abandoned. For a while after that, scientists' experiments grew bolder, attempts to convert everything into usable energy — trash, fecal matter, even the human power generated at a gym. This last avenue Khalid found most intriguing, and he'd read with morbid fascination documents detailing strange experiments, labs with humans running on treadmills for hours while hooked up to machines, advertisements asking for volunteers to donate large amounts of blood for "experiments in human energy." But in the end, these experiments had been only society's wild, desperate flailing at the clear signs of worldwide decline, the last spasms of what was already a corpse, and when the Dome Corporations consolidated their hold over the remaining oil and shale reserves, the experiments were all shut down. So what then was this early blip they were following? Had Gold Man really had the foresight to prepare for the world's energy woes? There were a thousand reasons to doubt that they would find anything — the fact that there weren't any other records of this source, or that despite being developed so early, in 2016, it didn't prevent the impending war and collapse — but Khalid couldn't help but feel a stirring in his heart as he thought about the possibility, however faint, of what they might find. Maybe Blake was right, and it would indeed lead to a better future.

Behind Khalid and Julia, Blake was lecturing Miles, seemingly against his wishes, on the larger importance of our mission. "Imagine what we could do with unlimited energy! If we end the Corporation's monopoly, we could free their technology. The domes, so limited right now, could be expanded across the whole country, possibly even over the seas and across the world, and it could all be protected from the sun, all connected no longer so provincial. We could rebuild this city too. Open up the storefronts again, settle these apartments, fill up those empty glass towers. Make it like it once used to be."

Blake's eyes were shining, and Celine was gazing adoringly at him, and Miles's gruff exterior too was cracking a little. As Khalid gazed forward, at the glass towers towards which they walked, even he saw reflected on their surface all the possibilities of Blake's grand vision.

To their left, meanwhile, the sun finally set below the horizon and plunged the city in a quiet but welcome darkness.

It was a few hours later, after they'd turned right onto a diagonal street ("Mar__t Street" was what they pieced together based on a few signs), a street which according to the map on Julia's phone would be a straight-shot to the financial district, that they heard and felt a strange rumbling beneath the ground.

"An earthquake?" Celine asked, her voice quivering with the ground.

"Get off the road!" Miles shouted.

He pointed to a large concrete building, part of which had already fallen in on itself. Julia was already racing to the door, a crowbar in her hand ready to pry it open. Khalid imagined it collapsing onto them as soon as they stepped inside.

"That place won't survive an earthquake!" Khalid said. "We have to stay in the open—"

"It's not a fucking earthquake!" Miles growled, grabbing his shoulder.

The authority in Miles's voice compelled Khalid more than the grip on his shoulder. Julia pried open the wooden door and they crouched inside by the cracked window, staring out at the dark road.

From the far end of the hill came a gradually brightening set of white lights. The ground shook even more and the building rattled dangerously. Khalid heard the whir of electric engines now, and after a moment, a convoy of five police SUVs rattled past, down Mar__t Street and in the direction of the distant towers, their massive tires crushing the gravel of the uneven road. As the lights flashed by, he made out the logo of the Santa Clara Dome on the side of each of the vehicles. Celine moved close to Blake and held onto his arm. Khalid felt his own heart beating in fear.

After a moment, the lights were gone, and the sound was receding into the distance. The ground and the concrete building slowly sopped shaking. Silence settled around the group, save for the wind which whistled through the broken window. They looked uneasily at each other.

"That's too many to be an ordinary patrol," Julia said.

"Why are they here?" Celine asked.

"They're looking for it too," Miles said, glaring at Khalid as if it was his fault.

"The documents aren't hidden," Khalid said. "I found them in the corporate archives, at the National Library. It's not impossible the police did too—"

"They might have tracked your research history," Julia said. "Followed your online footprints."

Miles shook his head and let out a steady breath.

"We should abort," Julia continued. "Report back—"

"No," Blake said. "We can't let this energy source fall into Dome hands."

Blake was right of course, but Khalid could see that this wasn't the only reason he wanted them to push forward. In Blake's wide-open eyes and rapid breathing, Khalid noticed another, more primal need to keep going, a need that went beyond Blake's utopian dream. The rational vision of a balancing some abstract equation seemed imbued now with something more human and desperate, as if Blake needed them to succeed not just for some grander future but also for his own private one, so that he could validate the optimism he'd felt all his life. It was a side of Blake Khalid had never seen before, something darker and more intense.

Miles looked out the window, down in the direction of the SUVs, where undissipated smoke lingered in the air in a strange layer, a trail beckoning them to follow. Khalid saw in his eyes the same dark gleam that was now in Blake's, as if finally Blake had broken through to him and charged his spirit too.

"We're not aborting," Miles said.

The buildings of the financial district glowed with an eerie brightness under the stars and moon, the white light reflecting off their glossy glass exteriors. Parked in a cluster at the base of one of these buildings were the five SUVs. Their lights remained on, illuminating a group of about thirty police officers, all dressed in kevlar, helmets, and boots and carrying large rifles on their backs. One of the officers was directing the others, who were fanning out in pairs into the nearby buildings. To Khalid they looked like black cloaked ghosts, laying claim with their presence to an already dead city.

"They're checking each one," Khalid said.

"Maybe they don't have an address like we do?" Blake said.

They were waiting down the street around a nearby corner, looking out over the tops of a line of parked cars. Over their heads, the faded white sign read "K____ Street" and across from them was the sign for the cross street, one whose letters were this time all preserved: "California Street".

A little ways down this street was a large, dark brown building, not glass but granite, rising into the sky and looking to Khalid like some kind of crenelated castle tower. The plaza before it was tiny, dwarfed by the sheer size of the buildings on each side, which blocked out all but a few of the overhanging stars. Large, silver letters on one of the building's facades read "Giannini Plaza." In the center of the plaza was a misshapen black stone sculpture, over six feet in length, and a few feet high, as if a piece of the building had fallen into the ground. The plaque at the base with the name of the artist and the work was too small to read from this distance, but across the front of the stone was spray-painted a large, white graffiti inscription reading "The Banker's Heart." Two police officers slowly made their way past the sculpture and through the glass door of the granite building, the lights on their helmets illuminating the silver numbers hanging over entryway of the tower: "555."

Miles studied the length of California Street. The police SUVs were about a block away, and in between the group and the building.

"We could go around," Julia suggested.

"It'll take too long," Miles said. "And they'll still be there when we come out. We need to get them to move away."

Blake then leaned forward, his eyes glowing with purpose. "I have an idea."

Julia, Celine, and Khalid stood on the opposite side of K_____ Street, with a clear view of the plaza of 555 and the police officers grouped nearby in the middle of the street. Across from them, the corner they'd come from was shadowy and quiet. Khalid stared at the line of cars and waited, unsure what Blake was planning. He was still unsettled by what he'd seen earlier, that new and intense gleam across Blake's eyes.

After a moment, a glowing shape emerged from around the corner, crackling and whirring: a car, engulfed in flames, drifting ghost-like and steady down the street towards the gathered police, its engine quietly whirring. The officers turned at the noise and quickly raised their guns, surprised, tensed, and looking around for danger. Khalid at first thought the car was only a distraction to lure the officers away from the building. But the car's hood was slightly open, and oil dripped from the front. Under and behind the car, meanwhile, was a thin trail of fire. Khalid understood then what it was meant to do. After a moment, the officers suddenly seemed to understand too and tried to disperse — but before they could, the car reached their cluster of SUVs and exploded.

The fireball engulfed the entire group of officers. Even before the sound died down, Khalid could hear their pained screams. One officer ran from the site, his body lit up like a candle wick. Another was crawling on his hands and knees across the asphalt — his legs had been ripped clean off and his body left smears of blood and fire in its wake. Khalid's stomach churned and he tasted bile in his mouth. Beside him, Celine turned away in horror.

The Movement had never been a peaceful organization, and Khalid knew that. Their spies and soldiers often killed police officers during missions and sometimes even conducted targeted assassinations of the Domes' Corporate Executives. But he had never seen the cost of their war up close. He thought again of the dark gleam in Blake's eyes. Was Blake so committed now to achieving the mission that he was willing to accept any cost? The police might be their enemies, but to kill them like this, in such a brutal way? Khalid wondered whether Blake felt any horror at all at what they now saw, any sympathy in the sight of these shadows suddenly become human, flesh and blood now scattered across the concrete.

Julia maintained her soldier's composure and ushered Khalid and Celine forward. As they ran down the street towards the plaza, Celine covered her nose with her shirt. The air smelled of burning rubber and meat sizzling on a grill. Khalid looked up briefly to the sky and saw to his surprise that the stars had vanished, the fire's light pollution blocking them from view.

They crossed the plaza quickly, hugging the far side of the building on the left. At the entrance to 555, they found Blake and Miles waiting. Miles looked excited, and his body was tense and agitated, no doubt filled with adrenaline. Blake too looked energized, his face and hands smeared with grease and oil, his eyes wide and gleaming, the hint of a smile on his lips. But as soon as he saw the sickened looks in Celine and Khalid's eyes, his excitement faded, as if he suddenly realized what he'd done. Behind them, Khalid could still hear the screaming and crackling. One of the officers had pulled an extinguisher from the one untouched SUV and was trying in vain to contain the blaze. Another officer was shouting out orders, and two more were racing towards the corner where the car had come from, guns up. The awful smell of sizzling flesh drifted over on the wind, and Blake put his hand to his mouth and turned away.

Miles quickly ushered them into the building.

"Come on," he said, looking directly at Blake. "You did well. No time to get sentimental now."

The main offices of Gold Man Investments were on the top floor. At first Khalid thought they'd have to take the stairs, as the police who'd entered before them were no doubt doing. But Blake and his battery pack only needed a moment with the elevator to tap into its residual power supply and get it going again, and soon they were hurtling upwards at a dizzying speed. The elevator periodically passed glass windows, and through them Khalid could see the fire, blazing silently in the street below. Blake avoided looking out and stared firmly at the doors.

At the top, Miles cautioned them to be silent, in case the police were already in the building. He and Julia overturned a wooden bench by the entrance and knelt behind it to guard them all while the others worked. Celine, Blake, and Khalid used Blake's battery pack on the computer behind the reception desk. The network was long defunct, but the computer still had files stored directly on its hard drive, files carefully hidden but which Celine was able to pull up.

Khalid searched for references to project number but the only documents that came up were the ones he'd already found in the National Library's archives. They were all from the same year, 2016, and around the same months, and though they confirmed the idea of a renewable energy source and a large sum of money, after them the project seemed to vanish entirely.

"Maybe they never went ahead with it," Khalid said.

"Or they erased all references to it," Blake said. "Try this."

He leaned over Khalid and typed in "the world's secret heartbeat." In addition to the one document where the phrase was first mentioned (and several other random ones which happened to contain those individual words) one email came up, one that Khalid hadn't found in the archives. It was dated 2026 (well after the project was proposed, and only a few years before the war) and contained only one, enigmatic line: Gentlemen. The world's secret heart, now beating. The warehouse, Pier 15.

"It's a location," Blake said.

"It could be anything," Khalid said. "This is ten years after any other mention."

But even Khalid was tantalized by the possibility. He told Julia to pull up an address for Pier 15. Blake watched her and waited, his eyes wide open. Khalid was relieved to see the dark gleam was gone and the old, dreamy optimism had returned.

"It's nearby," Julia said. "Twenty minutes."

Khalid let out a slow breath and looked at Blake, feeling energized by what they'd found. He wondered if this was how Blake felt all the time, always powered by some sense of possibility. It was an exhilarating, addictive feeling.

Celine shut down the computer and removed the battery pack. When its hum stopped, Khalid noticed how quiet and eerie the offices behind him were. He looked over his shoulder and at the rows and rows of long-deserted cubicles.

The door to the stairwell suddenly creaked.

Celine and Blake tensed. Miles and Julia raised their pistols towards the darkness.

"Police!" called a voice. "Who's there?"

Miles didn't respond, and instead opened fire. A second later, Julia did too. Blake, Celine, and Khalid ducked, and for a moment all Khalid could hear were the sounds of the firefight, the screaming of someone in pain, the echo of gunshots against plaster. Then the fighting stopped, and he heard footsteps scrambling down a tiled floor.

"He's coming to you!" Miles's voice called.

Khalid looked up, around the reception desk, in time to see a police officer darting towards them, crouched low, using the nearby cubicle as cover against Miles and Julia's fire. The officer had a pistol in one hand while the other clutched at a wound in his side. The bright flashlight on his helmet lit up the office, and suddenly he turned and pointed it directly at Khalid. The light was momentarily blinding, but when it faded Khalid saw that the officer was scrambling to raise his pistol. Khalid looked around for something to grab, for something to stop him — but before he needed to, Celine hit the officer in the side of the face with the battery back. The impact made a strange, sickening, wet thud, and the officer slumped quietly to the floor. His pistol clattered to the ground at Khalid's feet. The battery pack, meanwhile, was destroyed, now just a mess of circuit boards and metal, and Celine let it clatter to the ground.

Miles and Julia approached them, breathing hard. Their faces were sweaty, but they were unharmed. Miles looked down at the body slumped at his feet. Khalid could see the pulse beating faintly in the vein on the officer's neck. He was still alive, despite the bloody gash in the side of his head and face. Miles lifted his pistol towards the body, but Celine grabbed his arm.

"He'll wake up," Miles said, eyes narrowing. "And he's seen Khalid."

"We can tie him up," Celine said.

"The other officers will find him."

"We can lock him up then, in one of the rooms."

"So he'll starve to death? Kinder to shoot him now."

Celine looked with anguish down at the body. Miles laughed suddenly, a sharp, strange laugh that echoed across the dark office.

"You didn't say anything when your boyfriend built that car bomb."

Celine didn't reply but looked up at Blake, pleadingly. Khalid looked at him too, wondering what Blake would do. Blake looked uncertainly between Miles and the body on the floor.

"He's right," Blake finally said, looking up at Celine. "We have no choice."

Celine stared at Blake in horror, and for the first time since Khalid had known them, she looked angry and disappointed in him. Blake looked away, avoiding her gaze. She stepped out into the hallway and back towards the elevators.

Miles smirked and held out his pistol to Blake.

"You want to do it?" Miles asked.

Blake frowned and looked up at Miles. Khalid watched them, hoping Blake would change his mind, would tell Miles no and tell him to put the pistol away. But instead, Blake slowly took the pistol, aimed it at the guard, and fired once, into the officer's head. Somehow, the gunshot didn't echo, but instead hung in the stale air of the office before fading to silence. The officer's body twitched briefly, and then settled into the ground, as blood pooled slowly around it. With a condescending smirk, Miles turned back to the elevators. Blake remained staring at the body. Khalid saw that the dark and desperate gleam had returned to his eyes.

They had to take the stairs back down, since the battery pack was now broken. The second officer's body was slumped in the doorway, holding the door ajar with an awkwardly extended foot. His eyes were open and terrified, and his head was covered in blood from the bullet hole between his eyes. Khalid stepped gingerly over the body and tried to not to look at it as they entered the stairwell.

Outside, the remaining SUV and the surviving police were gone, save for two who crouched behind a makeshift barrier of abandoned cars.

"They're waiting for reinforcements from the Dome," Miles said. "We have to move."

In front of the two officers, in the middle of the street, were the bodies of their fallen comrades, piled up and set alight in a hurried, unceremonious pyre. The flickering flames illuminated the burnt out husks of the destroyed SUVs. Blake stared directly at the burning bodies, and Khalid saw that he didn't look disturbed at all, only resolute.

Wordlessly, they moved down California street, in the other direction, towards the bay and the piers. They walked silently through the quiet blocks, zigzagging through the smaller streets via the map on Julia's phone, now in Miles's hand, and making their way towards the location of the Gold Man warehouse on the pier. Blake walked steadily ahead of Khalid and Celine, at the head of the group, and didn't once look back, moving with a desperate, relentless pace. Ahead of Blake, Miles walked with a similar intensity. He seemed changed since Khalid had met him only hours before, though more likely Khalid had misjudged him then. It was clear now that Miles wasn't just a soldier, like Julia, pushing onward out of a sense of duty, but a visionary much like Blake, powered by a similar energy, and possibly even a similar moral code.

They soon emerged from the tangle of streets and towers onto a broad boulevard that bordered the bay. The water glistened under the stars and moon, and Khalid's eyes had to adjust to the sudden, almost harsh reflected light. Remnants of the white and yellow lines were visible on the crumbling asphalt. Ahead of them was the warehouse, a large, light gray, concrete building sitting squat along the stone pier, with an arch at the front which still read "Pier 15" in white letters. The large windows were smeared with grime, and a few abandoned cars and trucks stood in the small parking lot. Behind it was a large glass building, surprisingly clean and beautiful in contrast to the dirty, crumbling stone of the warehouse. It was too dark too see inside, but as they crossed the road and approached the warehouse, Khalid noted the sign by the glass building's entrance, a sign that read in vividly clear letters, "Exploratorium: Museum of Science and Technology."

Inside, the warehouse was dark, and the group's flashlights did little to illuminate the large, open space. The ceiling was high and arched, and over their heads ran a metal catwalk that looked unsteady and threatened to come down at any moment. They were standing on the warehouse's upper level, which ran around the perimeter of the room and looked down onto a large, open main floor, with only a flimsy, corroded metal railing for protection. At the far end of the warehouse were a few offices with smashed in windows and broken doors, as well as a staircase that led down to the main floor. It took a few minutes of shining their lights around for Khalid to piece it all together, and it was only then that he realized that on the floor of the warehouse, stretching from one end to another, was a large, monolithic machine, made of glass and steel. At first it looked like a replica of a building, a kind of miniature version of the towers outside. The machine reflected the group's lights, like the bay outside, and unlike the grimy walls and windows of the factory, it was clean and unblemished, as if it had never been dirty. A small computer console was linked to the machine nearby.

They stepped slowly down the staircase and fanned out around it, all unable to speak. Khalid could see the wonder in Blake's eyes, the possibilities whirring through his mind. Even Miles and Julia looked amazed and for a moment let their guards down, their sharp, tensed bodies relaxing in the presence of this majestic thing. Celine and Khalid stepped over to the computer console, and Khalid noted a label on the bottom of the flatscreen monitor: "Property of Gold Man Investments."

Celine placed her hand on the CPU.

"There's residual energy," she said, eyes lighting up.

Without waiting for the others, she reached down and pushed the computer's power button. The machine began to hum, a sound which shook the walls and the ground and rattled the catwalk above. A white light turned on inside the glass and steel of the monolith and filled up the warehouse, as if it were daytime and the machine an artificial sun. Khalid stared through the glass walls but couldn't see past the light. Blake reached out and touched the glass and closed his eyes and smiled, as if he could feel something stirring. After a moment, the light faded, and the machine ceased its whirring and grew quiet and dark once again. The computer monitor remained on, however, humming steadily with energy. Celine stepped to it and started clicking through what was to Khalid an unfamiliar screen of code.

"What does it run on?" Khalid asked.

"I'm checking the application code," Celine said.

Miles and Julia were with them looking over Celine's shoulder. Khalid could see a gleam in Miles's eyes, reminiscent of the one he'd seen in Blake. Blake remained standing next to the machine, his hand still held to the glass, as if he could power it with his own beating pulse. All five of them were at that moment a little more alive, brimming with excitement, as if the machine had powered them too. Khalid felt a surge of hope, and he saw that Blake felt it too, along with a sense of relief, that everything they'd done to reach this point, the long trip, the car bomb, the dead officer amidst the cubicles, had all been necessary, and that here was the solution to that equation in his head, humanity's future and his own vindication. Khalid watched Celine's sparkling eyes, listened to her typing and clicking as she moved through the streams of code. But after a long, agonizing minute, her eyes dim and her brow furrow.

"Strange," she said.

"What?" Blake asked, turning from the machine.

"The inputs. They're..." Celine clicked around, and Khalid watched the lines of code appear drift down the screen, ghostly white letters floating across a black background. "They're biological," Celine said.

"What do you mean?" Miles asked, eyes narrowing.

"The inputs for the machine. It's like it takes..." As Celine stared at the code, flowing like it was being pumped through a bloodstream by a beating heart, she seemed to suddenly understand something. She stepped away from the computer, holding up her hands.

"What?" Blake pressed.

"It takes people," Celine said.

Khalid looked at Julia and saw the horror seep into her eyes. Miles slowly leaned his head back. Only Blake failed to see what the rest of them saw.

"So then let's bring the dead officers in here," Blake said. "Use them to power it—"

"They need to be alive," Celine said. "It... sucks all the life out of them to make energy."

Blake looked at her and then over at the screen, and Khalid could see the circuits whirring behind his eyes. But for some reason, perhaps a willful denial of what was now obvious, he clung to the idea that the machine was something other than what it clearly was.

"So the inputs have to be alive," Blake said, repeating Celine's pronouncement. "Let's find something living then. There's probably rats somewhere in these warehouses—"

"Blake, no," Celine said, quietly. "The machine was built to take humans."

The air in the warehouse grew still as the five of them remained fixed where they were, paralyzed with understanding. The computer continued its incessant humming, oblivious to the change in the room. Miles's bearded face remained expressionless, but Khalid saw his jaw clenching. Blake was dumbfounded and stared at the computer, but even he finally seemed to understand. Here before them was mankind's salvation, a source of renewable, sustainable energy. Yet Khalid now understood that they weren't looking into the future, but rather into the past. Despite all their money and visions of a better future, those bankers had done nothing more than build a sacrificial altar — just another example in the long history of human self-delusion.

Blake was standing by the machine now, with his hand on the metal hull. Khalid wanted to yell at him, to tell him that he should have expected nothing less, that he was foolish and naive to have been so optimistic. But he couldn't bring himself to say anything, because he too had been deluded. Despite everything history had taught him, he'd let himself believe in Blake's vision and be charmed by Blake's soul-stirring voice proclaiming vague utopian futures. Khalid hated himself for being so carried away, but he ultimately felt only pity for Blake, whose eyes now looked empty and hollow. Khalid imagined how in the machine's incessant humming Blake could hear the hiss of gasoline streaming from a tube, the crackling of a flaming car, the repeated, punctured cries of dying men, the sharp, sudden sinking of a bullet into bone and flesh, and the crumpling of a body against tiled floor echoing down through empty cubicles.

Miles finally turned to Celine. "So where do we put the people, then?" His words, coming after long minutes of silence, were sharp and loud and echoed through the warehouse.

"You're not thinking of using it?" Celine asked.

"The Movement will want to test it on one their prisoners," Miles said.

"You can't tell the Movement about this!" Celine said.

"Why not? Why else did we come all this way?" Miles eyes narrowed. "So it's not as moral as we hoped! But it is what we were looking for. An energy source. And we've discovered it for the Movement. What more could we have wanted?"

He stared around at the others, but specifically at Blake. Blake was still in a daze, but when Miles looked at him, his features sharpened into a focused look.

"No," he said, shaking his head. "No, it's wrong."

"Oh, don't you get all hung up on right or wrong, you hypocrite!" Miles said, his voice rising and echoing off the overhanging catwalk. "We've all done plenty of wrong for the sake of the Movement. At least

now if we need to kill a police officer, we can get something in return
—"

"We have to destroy it," Blake said, in a quiet, measured tone.

The others stared at him. Khalid was surprised at how suddenly sure Blake sounded, how quickly he'd gone from despair to a new resolve. Miles, however, started to laugh.

"Don't be an idiot. We can use this, to win the war, to change the world like you said—"

Blake stepped towards Miles, with the dark gleam returning suddenly to his eyes.

"We're not using it," Blake said.

"You're not in charge here."

Miles folded his arms across his chest. They faced each other, in silence. The machine continued to him. Khalid saw now that even Julia was worried as she gazed at Miles. Slowly, her hand moved down her holster. Underneath his beard, Miles's jaw twitched.

Then suddenly, Blake and Miles were moving. Miles went for his pistol and Blake lunged for it too. There was a struggle and the sound of fumbling. Julia put her hand around her pistol, and Khalid wondered whether to rush forward to help — but before anyone could move, Miles's pistol went off with a flash that lit up the darkened space. Miles cried out and fell to his knees, clutching at his side, and Blake stumbled back. In the confusion, Khalid thought Blake had the pistol. But Miles aimed it up at Blake and fired twice, and Blake crumpled to the ground.

"Blake!" Celine cried.

Miles spun to aim at Khalid, but Julia was quicker. She lifted her pistol and fired one shot, hitting Miles between the eyes and sending his head careening back against the computer console. As he fell to the ground, a smear of blood streaked across the screen and the lines of ghostly code. Khalid felt his heart beating wildly, and he half expected Miles's body to move again and another shot to ring across the cavernous space. But slowly, silence descended onto the warehouse.

Celine rushed forward to Blake's side, to her knees, and cradled his head in her hands. Khalid looked at Julia with a wordless, numbed look, half of thanks, half of shock. She lowered the pistol to her side, but kept her eyes fixed on Miles's body.

They stood like that for a long moment, a strange operatic tableau in that grand, open space, the only sounds Celine's punctured sobbing and the machine's indifferent humming.

Back at headquarters, Khalid stared at the two new stars on the wall. The day before, the Movement had put them up in a small ceremony honoring Blake and Miles for "valiantly giving their lives for the greater good," as Erin had put it. As far as she knew, they'd been killed in a shootout by the police. The stars were only the latest in a long column of several hundred, tiny flashes of light against the wall's vast, dark concrete.

Khalid felt lonely as he stood in the cold, empty corridor. Julia had already returned to the Santa Clara Dome, after only a day of rest, now with a new trainee who'd be her new partner. Celine was back in the lab, already at work on a new coding project. She'd seemed sad the last time Khalid had seen her, though not like he was. Though she found Blake's death tragic, it fit with her romantic vision of their doomed relationship. Khalid, by contrast, was profoundly shaken, and not just because his old friend's resonant voice no longer echoed down the halls of the Movement's headquarters. To him, a whole dream had died along with Blake, a dream he never knew he'd secretly harbored. When they'd burned the warehouse and everything in it, the machine and Blake and Miles's bodies, Khalid had felt that on the top of that pyre he'd left the last optimistic remnant of his cynical, historian's heart, the part that had still beaten despite everything with a quiet energy, charged by Blake's vision for a better future. Now, life would have to go on as it always had. As far as Erin knew, they'd never found anything on their mission — and so the Movement would keep on fighting, and the Dome's would hold onto their monopoly, all while the world clung to the last dregs of its slowly depleting energy. But Khalid felt like nothing would ever be the same. For a moment he'd let himself believe that there might be strawberries again on the hills outside the ruined city, and the knowledge that they would likely never grow back left him empty and depleted, a battery drained of all power.

He thought of Blake's yellow two-door, still sitting there by the side of the road. As with all abandoned cars, it would seem to be just an empty shell, and no one who passed by would realize that there had once been a bold spirit within it, misguided perhaps but full of energy nonetheless, willing it down the road and towards some distant and more perfect future world. Now, that car would never run again.

It came from Aatif Rashid

The story actually began as a simple 2-page writing exercise for a creative writing class. The assignment was to write a scene with a few characters, a car with no air conditioning, and a hill. I hadn't written that much science fiction, but I found myself creating a vaguely post-climate-change world where the central character reminisces for the disappeared past. At the time, I'd been reading *Annihilation* by Jeff VanderMeer, and so I was also interested in writing something using the framework of a quest into the periphery, into ruins on the outskirts of civilization. I'd also always been interested in the idea people of living in a time of decline and decay. One of my history professors from college always talked about the Middle Ages this way, asking us to imagine living in a world where all around us were ruins of a civilization greater than our own. How would living like that affect people, I wondered? What would it do to their ambitions, to their faith in humanity, to their sense of history? Eventually, with those thoughts on my mind, I turned the exercise into a full length story.

A question for Aatif Rashid

Q: What is the most effort you've ever put into making dinner?

A: I'm actually a pretty lazy cook and I go out to eat way more than someone of my income-bracket should — but one time in college I did attempt to cook chicken tikka masala. I spent over an hour trying to buy all the ingredients, which involved trips to two separate grocery stores, since Trader Joe's didn't have everything I needed. Then, because I'd never actually cooked chicken before, I had trouble figuring out what to do. Was I meant to wash it first? To cut it? Eventually, with my laptop on the counter displaying step-by-step instructions, I managed to prepare the chicken and the marinade and put it in the fridge. I then had to prepare the masala, which was also challenging. The spices came in plastic bags with the labels stapled to the top, but when I opened them and threw out the labels, I had trouble remembering which spice was which, and had to smell them and then google-search what coriander was supposed to smell like and what cumin was supposed to smell like to differentiate them again. I also had difficulty deseeding the jalapeños and once touched my eye with my finger and had to go splash water on my face until the stinging went away. Finally, I had it all ready, and the spices and garlic and tomato sauce were simmering nicely in the pan — but then I remembered that the chicken had to sit in the fridge for at least another hour. So I turned off the heat and just let the masala mixture sort of sit there, congealing in the pan, and I watched Battlestar Galactica on Netflix while I waited. After a few episodes, I turned the heat back on and put the marinated chicken in. I had to let it all simmer for 10 minutes or so, so I went back to watching Battlestar.Unfortunately, I lost track of time, and a whole episode passed before I realized the chicken was still cooking. I turned it off and tasted it tentatively. It seemed fine, and not overcooked, though I wasn't really sure what overcooked chicken tasted like. I then slowly added the cream and watched the masala turn the familiar orange color. It was now past 8:00 and I had gone out to buy the ingredients before 4:00. But there it was, sitting in the pan, a meal I'd actually cooked for myself. I'd forgot to make rice or buy naan but that was OK. I spooned some chicken tikka masala into a bowl and ate it like soup while I sat in front of my laptop and watched another episode.

About Aatif Rashid

Aatif Rashid is a writer living in Los Angeles.
www.aatifrashid.com

The Nature of Glass

Sandi Leibowitz

Whispers from the Jewish quarter about the raising of a golem. A clock where every hour Death pursued sins and set them quaking. Astronomy, botany, art. Bohemia in the days of Rudolf II was famed for many things. Among them was the making of glass.

Zoja was a master glassblower who lived in the outskirts of Prague. In her youth she had married Jozef, learned his trade and worked alongside him. What greater happiness than to find pleasure in your work, shared with the one you love? Perhaps that was why their glass had been so beautiful. Sometimes, Jozef would send the apprentices home early. Locking the door after them, he would steal behind Zoja and, breathing warmly upon her neck, place his hands upon hers as she dipped the blowpipe into the sand. Together they rolled it back and forth upon the metal plate. They took turns blowing their breath into the blowpipe, as if it shared their kisses. Together they would shape the glass, the furnace glowing as hot as their desire. They would retreat to their little house beside the studio and consummate what they'd begun. Even now, years after Jozef's death, Zoja trembled to remember the fervor of their lovemaking.

Their life had been complete except for one thing—they could not conceive a child. When years passed and it grew clear no child would come to them, Zoja and Jozef threw themselves even more ardently into their work. They eschewed the new-fashioned method of cutting into the glass to embellish, instead creating inventive shapes that made their work well prized. Their fluted pine-green glasses rose in supple forms, opening like rare blossoms. Liqueur flasks in the shape of cavorting lions or savage griffons delighted anyone who saw them. Cabbage leaves with finches perched on the rim were barely recognizable as bowls. The longer Zoja remained without a child, the more imaginative her work became, for if she could not create new life from her womb, she would do so with her hands. Emperor Rudolf himself had once sent an emissary to inspect their work and purchased their most spectacular piece, a glass Triton blowing a glass conch-shell from which the emperor might drink his wine.

Before Zoja attained middle age, Jozef died, leaving her desolate. To still her grief, she labored longer hours in her studio. Years passed. The glassblower never took another husband, although from time to time she sought comfort in the arms of Jarmil the innkeeper, who would have wed her, or shared a sweet night in the bed of Milos the cooper, whose invalid wife left him almost a widower.

The pain of Jozef's death eventually became a bearable ache, but Zoja's desire for a child intensified. And now, gray hairs streaking her temples and lines etching the edges of a mouth that once laughed in love, her longing was a persistent torment. It greeted her faithfully as a dog each morning, and stalked her dreams like a starving wolf each night. Her life felt as cold and dead as the ashes of the great furnace days after firing. It was the loving she desired, not merely the idea of seeing her own image repeated in another; she had a silvered mirror for that. If only she could discover a foundling! But no miller's wife with too many brats came calling. No king's child draped in brocade and dire prophecies floated down the Vltava to her door.

One day, Zoja's longing became unbearable. *Glass may take the form of anything one wishes. A vessel may hold water, wine or ale— why not dreams?* She shooed the young men from the workshop, as she and Jozef had so often done long ago in happier times, and set to work to make a child of glass. Madness had not seized her; she knew it could never be a real child.

The furnace roared beside her, its flames less hot than her own passions. Sweat pouring from her, her lips set in a scowl as she focused all attention to her task, she spun the glowing mass of molten glass into the likeness of a baby. A bit of cobalt added to a mixture of sand created blue glass for the eyes. The purest gold, such as had gone into the Triton fountain for the emperor, was used to make the precious ruby-glass, called aventurine. Molded separately into the familiar valentine-shape, a crimson heart of glass was plunged into the transparent breast while the infant-form had not yet hardened. What little of the aventurine was left formed lips that parted in a charming moue.

Zoja set the glass child into a cooling oven and waited. She did not mind; had she not waited all these years? When making anything —a figure of glass, or a story, or a child—one must have patience.

Hours later the glassblower removed her creation from the oven. Zoja examined the tiny fingers and toes, like any other mother, relieved to find no flaws.

She hugged the glass babe to her breast. "Ah," she crooned. Her arms felt complete with this weight in them.

Tears, clear as crystal, slid down her face. "You are not a real child, just a lonely woman's doll. If only you could become real, my beautiful glass daughter." Zoja covered the figure in her apron and took it home. She hid it in the old chest at the foot of her bed, wrapped safely in winter blankets.

Every night, when the day's work was done, she held the glass child close and imagined the cold, hard form was warm, soft flesh. Her face gathered lines, cut deep as patterns on a pair of wedding goblets, new grief engraved upon old.

One morning, while Zoja swept the dust from the workshop floor, an old woman visited. Radka served as housekeeper in the house of Count Vitkovc, and frequently came to order fine glassware and exchange gossip. It was rumored that Radka dabbled in alchemy, and had even had dealings with the emperor in this capacity.

Radka scrutinized Zoja's face. "I do not know what sorrow eats you," she whispered, her leathery hand grasping Zoja's, "but perhaps you may find some ease in this news. Edward Kelley, the Emperor's English astrologer, has told me that on the night of the next new moon, a star will fall from the sky, glowing red as one of your globules of molten glass—a comet he calls it. When that star falls into the Vltava, those who witness may ask a wish and the gods will grant it. Or so he says."

On the night of the new moon, Zoja wrapped the glass child in a blanket, and wended her way through the dark, cobbled streets of Prague. She stopped at the Stone Bridge. Here and there stood hunched figures, still as statues in the shadows.

At last the comet appeared in the sky, flaming like long-thwarted desire. Zoja uncovered the blanket from the glass babe's face. In the comet's red light, she lifted the child to the heavens.

"Quicken my glass girl," Zoja husked. "Give her breath."

The comet fell into the river. The embers made the Vltava shiver and glow. When the last was extinguished, the figure of the child stirred. The glass chest rose and fell. The heart of ruby glass beat. Eyes of cobalt glass blinked and, seeing Zoja, the glass lips parted in a smile.

How Zoja's heart swelled with joy! She wanted to skip her way home, but instead she walked slowly, carefully, with her precious bundle. "I name you Bozena, my daughter," she whispered, "for you are my divine gift."

Motherhood granted Zoja greater happiness than she had even imagined it would. For more than a year the glassmaker guarded her secret well. She left most of her work to the apprentices and assistants. Bozena needed no food, but, like any other infant, she cried from time to time, quieting when rocked and sung to. And she laughed, and oh, when the mother saw that glass nose crinkle and the red lips smile, a comet blazed in her chest.

One question consumed Zoja: *What is the nature of glass?* She feared that the answer was: *to break.* The child grew, and became ever more curious about her world. The little one needed to walk, and every toddler is prey to tumbles. But Bozena could not afford to fall—she could well lose a limb or even her very life, for who knew how the comet's power worked? Perhaps a single crack could end the spell. So Zoja cleared the little one's path of all obstacles, hovering a breath behind so she'd be certain to catch her if she should stumble.

Eventually the mother had to concede that if her daughter were to lead a full life, she must meet other people and take part in the wide world. She feared how others might react to Bozena's strangeness, and set aside a few essential belongings in case the worst happened, and they needed to flee and begin a new life elsewhere. One day she held Bozena's hand and led her through the streets of the village to do her errands. At first those who saw the girl drew back in horror. *What sorcery is this?* they murmured. But like any happy child, she smiled and gurgled so adorably that they could not help but smile back, though her cooing had a fey, hollow sound, like wind blowing through a crystal flute.

For several days, other children remained wary of Bozena. How could they trust one who was not allowed to play like everyone else? But they were lured to her side by the combination of her gentle friendliness and her unearthly beauty. Zoja begged them to refrain from roughhousing near her. They learned to stand still in her proximity, making up songs and quiet hand games to please her. Soon she was the village favorite.

When Bozena grew older, Zoja allowed her to travel on her own like any other girl, as long as she promised to stay within the village limits and avoid dangers, especially horses and carts and rambunctious dogs. Bozena moved with a measured gait, always scanning ahead. Strangers to the village would pause to stare at the child to admire her gracefulness before they noticed her peculiar transparency. She was precious in every beholder's eyes. Prague was a proud city, and Bohemia did not mind, even celebrated, its reputation for outlandishness.

Now that Zoja could relax her guard somewhat, she renewed her attention to her work. Happiness sparked a new phase of creativity in her. Even her assistants grew astonished at the colors she could coax from mere sand and mineral, and at the intricacies of her invented forms. To delight her daughter, Zoja conjured from molten glass all kinds of animals and hybrid creatures—mice with hummingbird wings, foxes that pranced on stallions' legs, tiger-headed whales. That playfulness spilled over into all her work, so that the studio took on the look of an enchanted forest made of glass.

Years passed. The glass girl became a woman. What kind of future could she expect? Would she find someone to love her? Would a husband care for her the way her mother did? Men were such careless creatures. *She is still young,* Zoja counseled herself; *there is time to worry about that.* But she worried any way. *The nature of glass is to break*, she kept remembering. Many of the village boys courted Bozena but these were only innocent flirtations.

Eventually, however, Bozena fell in love with a boy who loved her in return. Every evening she ran to meet him in a meadow just outside the village, where they could be alone together. Should Zoja counsel Frederick on how to care for the girl? Should she intervene at all?

One summer evening, Bozena failed to return home for dinner. Zoja grew frantic. She searched throughout the village but no one had seen the girl. She rushed to Frederick's home. Wild-eyed, she flung open the door.

"Where is she? Where's my daughter?"

"I haven't any idea," he said. He wouldn't meet her gaze.

"Frederick has been home for an hour," his mother said. "It's not his fault if you can't keep track of your girl."

Zoja continued to press him.

"I didn't mean it!" he cried at last, his face flushed red. "I've grown tired of having to clear the path for Bozena to walk. When I put my lips to hers, how cold they are, as if kissing ice that refuses to melt. I have to close my eyes when I embrace her. It's too disturbing otherwise! On cloudy days, her greyness makes me sad. On stormy days she's dark and churning like the ocean. On blue and cloudless days, she bores me. When we're indoors, I find it so confusing, I don't know where to look. My gaze drifts through her from the chair to the kettle to the door...

"So I turned to another girl. Danika is plump and vivacious. She blushes when she sees me—Bozena's body never changes. Danika's hair blows in the wind, while Bozena's always stays in place. Danika's flesh warms when I touch her. Today, I foolishly told her to meet me in the meadow where I go with Bozena. I thought we'd be done by the time Bozena got there. But I lost myself in her arms, forgetful of the time, of everything else, when I heard an odd noise—*Crkk!*

"I never meant to hurt her!"

Zoja's heart almost ceased to beat. "Show me."

Frederick led Zoja to a field where blue cornflowers and red poppies bloomed amidst the grass, and sparsely spaced elms offered shady bowers. Behind one such elm, inanimate as a statue, stood the maid of glass. Her hands were raised to her mouth, which was opened wide. Zoja thought she could hear her daughter's gasp of surprise and pain, though it must have been only the wind whistling past the glass lips. She caressed the girl's hands and arms. She pulled down the edge of Bozena's chemise to find what she had suspected. The ruby heart had cracked in two, shattering the magic that had brought the girl to life.

Zoja sank to her knees in grief. She didn't know how long she wept there. When she raised her head at last, Frederick still waited with her. The sun was setting.

"Bring her to my house. She will serve as her own monument."

Frederick did her bidding. Days later, Zoja learned that he ran away that night, never to return to Bohemia.

Visitors came to see the grieving mother every day, bringing her meals she refused to eat. They spoke in glowing terms of the glass maiden, many weeping at her loss. The village maidens wove a chain of white flowers and draped it around the glass figure.

Zoja sent away her workers; the furnace was as cold as her heart. A month or more passed. One day she opened the door to her studio. Old habits die hard; she found the broom and got to work. Her eyes swept over the rack of finished glassworks, waiting to be sold. Her wares had never before been rimed with dust. She passed a finger over a sea-green pitcher with mermaid handles.

What is the nature of glass? The familiar question came to her mind unbidden. *It is alchemy, the harnessing of three elements—earth, air, fire—to become a transcendent fourth. If the glassblower is alchemist, can she perform other magicks?*

Zoja stoked the furnace. She struggled to carry the statue to the studio, careful not to damage it any further. She prepared a batch of aventurine and thrust the molten glass into the glass girl's chest. How it hurt to do that! As if she stabbed her own daughter in the heart. But Bozena didn't cry out or move; she remained a statue. Slowly Zoja worked, fitting the two pieces of the ruby heart back together. She could not help but cry. She did not notice the single tear that fell and entered the ruby-glass heart. She closed up the chest. A tiny seam, barely detectable, was the only testament to the repair.

Zoja sat beside the cooling oven, waiting, much as she had done eighteen years before. This time there was so much more at stake. Then, she had only sought to create a glass statue. Now, she meant to bring a daughter back to life. Would it require the magic of another comet? Exhaustion forced her eyes closed and she slept.

"Mama?"

Zoja looked up. Bozena was rising from the table.

"My precious child!" She ran to her and clasped her.

"Mama, you're holding me too tightly," the girl complained, laughing. "You'll break me." She pushed her mother away.

Zoja held Bozena's hand and examined the ruby-glass heart. It beat steadily. The only flaw that she could see was a tiny bubble. It was her tear, which had been captured in the glass. It sparkled like a diamond in the rich crimson of the heart.

Joyfully, she brought her daughter home. If Bozena smiled less, found fault in little things, and seemed less affectionate than she had been before, perhaps that was to be expected, as one who undergoes a deadly illness becomes irritable for a while, angry at all they've undergone. *Or*, the mother thought, *she still rankles at Frederick's infidelity and mourns her first love. She will recover from both maladies in time.*

How the village rejoiced at the glass maiden's return! A feast was prepared. Since the honoree herself could not partake of it, the women brought her gifts of new gowns and aprons, as if she were a bride. The men brought her ribbons and other trinkets. The girls wove garlands for her hair and waist, this time red lilies to symbolize her renewed life.

After the initial jubilation, life returned to normal. The assistants and apprentices were summoned back to the studio. Although Zoja resumed her work, she spent more time with her daughter, keeping a careful eye on her, almost as protective as she had been in Bozena's infancy. The girl chafed at the restraint.

"You must take care, my child. You're not like others."

"Mama, I'm a grown woman, I can walk by myself!"

Bozena sulked. She disappeared for hours at a time, disobeying her mother's injunctions and growing negligent of her chores. Zoja hated to scold the girl—she was so grateful to have her back. Instead she pleaded. But Bozena did as she wished. Even Zoja's most fanciful gifts of glass figures failed to please her.

Boys became attentive to the glass maiden once again, more so than they had been before her calamity. The air of tragedy about her excited their curiosity. The cruelest and vainest of them secretly hoped to find out if he had the power to render her inanimate again.

"Please be careful," her mother begged. "Don't let another boy break your heart."

"No danger of that," Bozena scoffed. The sound of her laugh was sharp as shards of broken glass.

And indeed, it seemed the girl was in no danger of breaking her own heart; she was too busy breaking others'. She did not care to see one young man very often, but preferred a constant stream of suitors. If any wooer became too passionate, she spurned him at once.

Zoja and her daughter argued constantly. A new bone of contention became Bozena's demand to help in the studio.

"I want to learn how to make glass," the girl insisted. "I need a trade. I don't want to merely sweep and wash and cook."

"How many times must I tell you? It's too dangerous for you in there. The studio is a bustling place, full of workers intent on their tasks. You're too fragile! One shove against a rack of glassware, one slip, and that could end your life! Besides, there are savings enough for you to live on after I die. The house and the business are yours. You need never marry."

But Bozena grew more and more discontented, more and more neglectful, more and more angry. Zoja seldom knew where she was at any given time. The girl remained obstinate and unreachable, no matter how lovingly her mother treated her.

One day a knock came at the studio door. Zoja opened it to find a velvet-clad gentleman outside. Three other men stood behind him, before a well-appointed carriage led by a pair of matched chestnuts.

The gentleman bowed. "I am the Curator of the Emperor's Wunderkammer. Word has come to Emperor Rudolf that you have created a maiden of glass that lives and breathes and walks like any person born of a woman and a man. These are the royal glassmakers who shall examine her."

Zoja could do nothing but step back as they made their way inside. She had heard of this Chamber of Wonders, where the emperor collected beautiful and strange objects for his sole delight. He had amassed rare stones, model ships carved from coral and jasper, the jaw of a mermaid, clocks that sang, golden serpents with real sharks' teeth, skulls of amber and no fewer than three unicorn horns.

"I'm afraid I do not know where she is," the mother stammered. "She is a bit—willful. But until she returns, I would be glad to show you my studio and my other work."

The men murmured unhappily together, but they followed her through the studio, shaking hands with the workers, observing them create new pieces, examining completed objects. The Curator yawned throughout the tour but the glassmakers frequently expressed their admiration.

Soon dusk fell. The visitors retired to Zoja's home, where she served them tea and medovnik. Bozena had baked it that morning, and the cottage was still warmed by the aromas of honey and cinnamon.

At last Bozena arrived. The gentlemen rose the instant she walked through the door.

"These men," Zoja explained, "have come from the Emperor to see you. You must do as they ask."

The girl frowned, but made a perfunctory curtsey.

"A wonder!" one of the glassmakers exclaimed.

"Come here, girl," the Curator commanded. Bozena walked toward him with her usual careful tread.

"Can she run?" He addressed Zoja, as if the maiden of glass could not answer for herself.

"Of course I can!"

"Bozena! Be polite!" Zoja remonstrated.

"Let us see," the Curator said.

"She is *capable* of running," the mother explained, "but then she might break and shatter. That would be the end of her. So she *must* not run."

The curator tsked.

"Can she perform only tasks that you set her?" the first glass-blower asked.

"Oh, no," Zoja said. "She's not an automaton, but a real person like you or I. It is only her—material—and the way in which she came into being that make her different from us."

"Priceless!" the Curator gushed.

The second glassmaker went up to the girl and looked her up and down in such a way that would have made a maiden of flesh blush. He touched her arm, fingered the mass of her hair, poked at her nose. "Such workmanship," he assessed.

The third glassmaker stood utterly silent throughout this process, hands folded, gazing at Bozena intently.

"Do you have a favorite color?" he finally asked her.

The glass maiden stared at him in surprise. "That blue that comes at dusk just before the darkness falls, that has both night and day in it."

Zoja had thought her daughter loved red best; that was the color of her favorite dress, and she loved poppies. Why didn't she know this?

The visitor smiled wide. "That's my favorite color, too. And my favorite time of day. It feels so full of magic and possibility. And what is it that you like to do best of all?"

Ruby-glass lips responded with a shy smile of their own. "Although my mother worries I'll get hurt, I prefer to be outdoors, walking in the woods—in spite of the treacherous tree roots—or in a meadow full of wildflowers. If I were like any other young woman, I would love to run across a field, faster than the wind. Or climb a mountain. Maybe even swim in the sea." Bozena frowned. "I can never do any of those things."

Swim in the sea? Zoja bit her lip at the thought.

The other glassmakers continued to prod the glass maiden, and demand that she do this task or that. The third glassmaker, however, asked nothing more of Bozena. At last the examination was done. The men conferred with each other. The third glassmaker argued quietly with the others.

"It is decided," spoke the Curator. "We would like to purchase your glass maiden."

Zoja gasped. "Purchase? She is my daughter!"

"We will give you four hundred tolars."

"She is not for sale!"

"Six hundred tolars! A thousand!"

"Never! Bozena is my child, not an object. There is no price you could name that would make me change my mind. Not even if the Emperor himself begged for her. Or demanded her."

Hands clenched into fists, Zoja stood with her legs spread wide, her eyes flashing like those of a tigress defending her cub. The Curator opened his mouth to argue but shut it at once. Zoja opened her door. The gentlemen entered the carriage. All but the third glassmaker, who remained in the courtyard, plumed hat in his hand, while the carriage clattered back to Prague.

"My name is Matthias," he told Zoja. "Forgive the rudeness of my colleagues. They sometimes forget their manners in their singlemindedness of purpose. May I have your permission to speak with your daughter? I will not insult you or her by suggesting that you sell her; I would not cheapen the miracle of her existence. I should like to be considered—an admirer."

Zoja softened toward him. But she remembered what had happened with Frederick. Could she allow Bozena to entertain the possibility of love again? If another man broke her heart, she might not be able to bring her back to life. Before she could state her objections, Bozena answered for herself.

"I would be delighted to speak with you. One of the benefits of walking so slowly is that you get to notice little things that others pass by. The lady's-smocks are blooming in a quiet place I know. Come, let me show you."

Before Zoja could protest, the couple went off.

Shortly after dusk, they returned, hand in hand. The young man placed Bozena's hand in her mother's, as if he were returning her to her care. He bowed solemnly and walked off in the direction of Prague.

"Please don't see him again, Bozena!" the mother begged. "Surely so important a gentleman—and a master glassmaker at that, one who is only interested in how you were made—has no good intentions toward you." Zoja liked Matthias, and sensed no ruthlessness in him, but she had her girl to think of.

Bozena gave her a wicked smile and went off to her room, shutting the door. The mother stood helplessly behind it. *No doubt my daughter will outgrow this cruel stage,* she thought. But she worried.

Matthias called on Bozena the following Sunday. And every Sunday after that. And soon more often. In the interest of peace, and the hope for a good outcome, Zoja held her tongue.

One day, when Matthias returned the glass maiden to the cottage, he held Bozena's hands for a long time and sighed. He bowed deeply before her when he made his adieus and walked out to the courtyard whistling. Bozena watched him disappear down the road.

"Matthias has asked me to marry him," she announced, "and I have accepted."

"No!" Zoja cried. "You cannot! He will hurt you! Break you! You must refuse him! Men cannot be trusted—remember what happened with Frederick! Stay a maiden. Let me care for you."

"And who will keep me company when you die?" Bozena swept her hand across her face, just under her eyes, as if to wipe away a tear, although the maiden of glass could shed no tears. "I wish to love and be loved, and not just by you, Mother. How can I live a full life if I do not love?"

Zoja begged and pleaded but the girl covered her ears with her transparent hands and closed her eyes. Bozena fled to her room. Under other circumstances, Zoja would have cautioned her to move more carefully.

There is time, the mother thought. *Surely, I will be able to convince my daughter that it is not so terrible to live alone. She will always have friends to love her. Many have to find that sufficient. Perhaps I can win Matthias to my cause. If he truly loves her now as he claims, he might see things reasonably, agree to nip their passion in the bud.*

In the morning, Bozena was silent and resentful. Her charming red mouth formed a scowl her mother had never fashioned there. Zoja thought she would have gone off on her own early that day, but instead the glass maiden turned resolutely to domestic chores. She scrubbed the hearth with an almost brutal energy. *Perhaps she seeks to make amends,* the mother thought, *but is too proud yet to admit I'm right.*

The suitor returned that evening, flushed with the elation of the recently betrothed. As always, he was friendly and polite to his beloved's mother, and veered between tongue-tied and gushing with his intended. Zoja attempted to speak with Matthias alone, but at every turn Bozena intervened. Before her lover departed, the glass maiden whispered something in his ear. He blushed. She threw her arms around him and kissed him. When he bid Zoja goodnight, he would not meet her eyes.

Zoja lay awake for hours that night. *Is it wrong for me to deny my daughter love?* For the first time in many years, she thought of Jozef. The yearning for him had ceased to plague her years ago, all the years in which she had been filled to the brim, like a great glass bowl, with her love for Bozena. She realized that it had been a long, long time since she had felt the touch of flesh—not merely during love-making, but any kind of ordinary human contact. She had grown used to the feel of cold glass against her skin; her daughter's was the only hand she ever held, the only cheek she ever kissed. *Have I become so diminished a person,* she wondered, *a vessel empty of everything but a mother's devotion?*

The lasts stars had faded away before she fell asleep. No doubt that is why she did not rouse at the sound of glass breaking. It was the smell of smoke that wakened her.

"Bozena!" she shrieked, no matter that an ordinary fire could never harm the glass maiden; it was a mother's instinct to worry for her child first. It did not yet occur to her that Bozena should be seeking to save her mother as well.

She ran through the cottage. No sign of fire or smoke. Or of Bozena. She banged open the door to the street. The studio had been set ablaze.

"Fire! Fire! Help!" she called.

Neighbors rushed to her aid. The villagers formed a line snaking from the well to the studio, buckets rushed forward from hand to hand.

Hours later, the fire was extinguished. It had destroyed one section of the studio, the racks that held the glasswares, part of the floor, some of the beams. Much would need to be rebuilt, but the building still stood. The villagers had prevented the flames from spreading to the cottage or any of the surrounding houses. Blackened with soot, Zoja sat wearily on the stoop to her house. Numbly she accepted the hugs and shoulder-pats of each rescuer as they murmured kind words and offered to help in any way they could, before they trudged their way home. Bozena was nowhere to be seen. But her work was everywhere.

Some willful hand had smashed each piece of glass to splinters. The furnace had been put out by the apprentices, and the mistress of the studio had checked it again, as she did every night, before she went to bed. Besides, it was the coldest thing there. The flame had been carried in from elsewhere. Zoja had no enemies. Bozena's absence suggested her guilt. But why? Why?

"Come, you will eat with us tonight," Lenka said. "And sleep in Kamila's old room. This is no time to be alone."

Zoja shook her head. She had no appetite. "No. Thank you. No."

Lenka returned home, leaving the glassmaker staring blankly at the burned studio door.

Someone sat down beside her. A man, she could see from the boots. She didn't feel like looking up at the face.

"We were going to run away," he said quietly. "Elope to avoid your disapproval. I told her I would take care of her forever, just as you had done."

Zoja raised her head. Matthias had lost his plumed hat. His jerkin was black with soot, the once brilliant white ruff ruined. Ash dusted his handsome brown curls, turning him prematurely gray. But it was his expression that had undergone the greatest change. *He is a vessel filled with loss,* she thought. She wondered if her own eyes looked like that.

"I rose early this morning," Matthias said. "We were to meet at the stables at the foot of the Castle. I wanted to make sure all was ready, furs and rugs to cushion Bozena's ride so she would suffer no injuries. I carried the damask gown and the cask of jewels I had bought to adorn my bride. But my carriage and horses were gone. Bozena had come in the dead of night, the ostler said, telling him I'd sent for her. She whipped the team into a gallop and set off laughing."

Zoja stifled a whimper. She crushed Matthias' hands in hers, attempting to comfort the abandoned groom. They had little more to say to each other.

"Let me know if you hear from her," Zoja said before the young man departed. He swore he would do so, and she promised she would send him word if Bozena returned. Both knew she wouldn't.

Zoja entered the ruined studio. Since she could not sleep, she would sweep. So much shattered glass.

Stories circulated, a few years later, about a female pirate who, masked and gloved, terrorized the seas. Some claimed they'd caught glimpses of a wolf's snout or a scaled hand or even a barbed tail. It was the story of the transparent face, which some claimed belonged to a ghost but one man swore was made of glass, that caught Zoja's attention. The glassmaker suspected that the truth lay in that last rumor. She didn't know whether to mourn or rejoice at what had become of her daughter.

All the times I worried over the problem, she mused, *I never considered that the nature of glass is also to cut. That was the wrong question in the first place. I should have asked, what is the nature of a human being?* In many respects, she had treated Bozena as merely a vessel for her love. If she had a second chance—but there would be no second chance. She could only wonder how her daughter would fare out in the wide, dangerous world where breaking and cutting both come so easily.

A question for Sandi Leibowitz

Q: What is your favourite part of writing?

A: My favorite part of writing is polishing. I do love the initial fervor of the onset of idea—but I struggle (usually) with working out the whole story. That's where the hard labor comes in. But once I have my "skeleton draft," as I call it, I love to see how the story fleshes itself out, often in ways I never dreamed. And I love to edit, but especially the part beyond mere copy editing, which is where the metaphors turn more apt, or interesting names are conjured up, etc. Then the story ceases to be just a skeleton, even a fleshed out one, and gains a personality, maybe even a soul.

About Sandi Leibowitz

Sandi Leibowitz lives in a raven's wood next door to bogles, right in the middle of New York City. After a variety of careers and jobs (including ghostwriting for a monsignor and working behind one of the caribou dioramas at the Museum of Natural History), she is now an elementary-school librarian, which enables her to hook kids on reading, tell stories, and occasionally use puppets and funny voices. She also sings classical and early music and plays recorders and other non-orchestral instruments.

www.sandileibowitz.com

The Stars are Tiny Lights on a Perfect Black Dome

Simon Kewin

"Chancellor, it's Zend, at the University. One of your research students. I think you should come and see something."

The voice on the other end of the line was groggy. The Chancellor didn't bother to keep the irritation from his voice. "Are you aware what hour it is, Zend?"

"Sorry, yes, it's late, I know. Or I mean early, depending on how you look at it."

"Have we inadvertently fabricated another black hole in Astrophysics? Has the Bio lab released a pathogen capable of eliminating all known life in the galaxy? Because if it's anything less than either of those things I'm not going to be pleased, Zend. Not at all."

"It's ... it's nothing like that, Chancellor. Something rather more ... philosophical has cropped up."

"*Philosophical!* At this time in the morning?"

"Yes, Chancellor, I'm sorry, it's just ... it's The Experiment."

"Which experiment? There are hundreds of experiments. What are you talking about?"

"*The* Experiment. You know, the big globe in the faculty lobby. *The Experiment.*"

There was, finally, a pause from the other end as the Chancellor grasped what Zend was talking about. His voice was noticeably more shaky as he replied. "Are you saying something has happened after all this time?"

"There are lights on it. Flickering electric lights. I don't know what they mean but they look like alarms. They're flashing in a way that suggests ... urgency."

"What colour are these lights?"

"Red. Is that bad, Chancellor? They look bad."

"I have no idea! The Experiment hasn't done anything for a hundred years. No one has any clue what flashing lights mean. No one knew it even had flashing lights."

"There's also a sort of mechanical buzzing sound, like a clockwork alarm bell ringing."

"I'm coming in, Zend. Tell nobody else and keep the doors locked until I arrive. No one else is to know about this, understood?"

"Understood, Chancellor."

Within the hour, four of them stood in a circle around the shining, ten metre sphere that had dominated GalTech's lobby for as long as anyone could remember. Normally the high hall echoed with a thousand conversations, with footfall and skitter and slither. Now it was filled only by an eerie, echoey silence. Zend could see his own distorted reflection in the coppery surface of the orb above him. It gave off its familiar smells of oil and grease and steam. The red lights continued to flicker in rings.

The orb was a remarkable device, a feat of early metaphysical engineering, although the jets of steam that occasionally whooshed out of it always alarmed Zend. There were plenty more advanced micro-universes these days, but the huffing, rumbling original fascinated him. He'd been studying it for two years, topping it up with water and oil, tapping it, peering into it. Partly because no one else in the University seemed interested.

Next to him stood the Chancellor, the Archdean herself, and also Professor Overarch, GalTech's Head Philosopher, called in especially for the crisis.

"Are you sure it isn't merely a malfunction?" asked the Archdean. She was, Zend knew, a historian by training. She could probably drone on for hours about the significance of the Experiment to the development of galactic scientific culture, the breakthroughs it had heralded. She probably had little idea how it worked.

Which, to be fair, was probably true for most of them.

"Let me show you," said Zend.

A movable flight of five wooden steps gave access to the various spy holes and scopes distributed around the sphere. Zend wheeled the steps into place so that the aged and somewhat shaky Archdean could ascend to peer through one of devices.

Her voice was muffled by her billowing sleeve as she adjusted the tiny focus wheels. "It looks the same as ever. The same tiny blue planet, the oceans, the clouds. Remarkable, truly. I'd forgotten how beautiful it was. The life forms on it survive?"

"Try adjusting the focal length and you'll see," called up Zend. "That scope is positioned very precisely but you'll need to use maximum magnification."

There came a series of muffled sounds as the Archdean battled with the controls on the unfamiliar contraption. "Ah. Yes. Of course. Um. Ah! My word, I see now. There's definitely ... something."

"You can see a tall stone tower? There's a man on top, yes? Peering into a contraption? It's night so it's hard to see but the man has little candles by his books. I'll brighten the moon a notch for extra illumination and send a few fireballs across the sky."

"Yes, I see him! So tiny and sweet!"

"The beings are, of course, only small with reference to our frame of existence," said the Chancellor, doing his best to sound like he knew what he was talking about. "If we could ask them, they would think they were the same size as us. In the same way that their time appears to move normally to them but from our perspective..."

The Archdean ignored her Chancellor, as she so often did. "That device the little man is looking at. It's almost like ... like a telescope." Her face reappeared from the folds of her voluminous gown, eyes wide in an expression of astonishment. "He was looking upwards at me! Could he see me? Have they worked out the truth after all this time?" She looked genuinely alarmed, wobbling slightly on top of the little flight of steps.

The Chancellor's grey, thinning fur bristled. "No need to worry yourself. They've made a remarkable invention, but it's still crude; they can only see what they've always been able to see. The stars as tiny points of light, the sphere slowly rotating. The planets and moon and sun projected across it. Everything is under perfect control. In many ways this is a triumph for GalTech. Not only did our forebears create the first viable micro-universe, but now the life forms evolving there have shown glimmerings of genuine intelligence."

Professor Overarch shook her head, horned brow wrinkled with anxiety. She was the youngest professor in GalTech, her skin still a delicate, spring-bud green. "It should never have been allowed to get this far. We should have terminated the Experiment when the first single-celled creatures appeared."

"As I recall," said the Chancellor, "it was your faculty that argued against that proposition, claiming the absolute right to life even if you happened to exist on a manufactured planet housed within a steam-powered brass sphere."

Professor Overarch's eyes narrowed very, very slightly. "Philosophy has moved on a lot since then. Destruction of a monocellular life form is surely morally preferable to wiping out a complex and intelligent species."

"Is it?" asked the Archdean. "You must explain the thinking to me. Some other time. The issue we have now is what are we going to do?"

"Why do we have to do anything?" said the Chancellor. "Everything is ... contained."

"But for how long?" said Zend, finally speaking up. "Don't you see? Not so long ago the beings in there were sharpening stones to kill each other more effectively. Suddenly they're building telescopes and staring into the night sky wondering about the nature of reality. And that's not all."

The Archdean looked suspicious, as if, somehow, all this was Zend's fault. "What do you mean *that's not all?*"

"It's not just telescopes," said Zend. "It's microscopes, too."

"Well, yes," said the Chancellor. "Very similar mechanisms. That's hardly a surprise."

"But they'll *see*," said Zend. "They'll see the gaps and the flaws. All the details that were left out two hundred years ago. The beings were never supposed to get to this point of technological development."

"Wait, *gaps?*" said the Archdean, peering down at them all. "Flaws?"

"I've studied the Experiment in great detail," said Zend. "Our forebears didn't ... fill in all the details of the physics of the universe when they built it. They didn't think it would be worth going to so much trouble. The Experiment was rather, well, cobbled together. Once the beings' lenses are a little better they'll see that the stars are tiny lights on a perfect black dome. They'll see that the sun is a small but bright yellow circle. Through their microscopes they'll see that everything is made of tiny dots of stuff but that no one has worked out what the dots are made of. The beings will realise they live in a fabricated – a rather poorly fabricated – universe."

The Archdean's voice was sly. "So, why, exactly should that matter? I mean, who's to know?"

"They also have these writers and inventors with big ideas of building spaceships," said Zend. "I've seen them. Give them time and they'll succeed, I know they will. They'll blast off into space and puncture the black sphere and they'll be *here.*"

The Archdean studied Zend for a moment as she absorbed his words. "The effect on the reputation of GalTech would be terrible. An escape like that would contravene all galactic statutes. People would *laugh.* We have to do something."

"We could just, you know, quietly switch the machine off," said the Chancellor.

The rest of them looked at him, not speaking. "What?" he said. "I'm just saying, who'd know?"

"Well, *they* would," said Professor Overarch. "The beings in there."

"No they wouldn't. Their whole universe would have just stopped."

"No, it's unthinkable," said the Archdean. "We have a clear duty of care to any universes we construct. There must be another way."

In the silence that followed, Zend cleared his throat and spoke again. "Erm."

"What is it?" asked the Chancellor, once again not bothering to keep his irritation in check.

"Well, it's just, I have been sort of fooling around with plans for an expanded version of this micro-universe. Thinking we might need it one day, sort of thing. It's still not infinite, but it's a lot larger."

"Ah," said the Archdean. "An expanded universe? Now that sounds splendid."

"I haven't finished some of the trickier calculations," Zend continued. "I've got a problem with missing matter at the macro level and some of the subatomic particle interactions are frankly a bit hazy. Plus I haven't yet worked out a way to reconcile quantum effects with gravitational..."

The Archdean waved these reservations away with a dismissive pincer. "But it will work?"

"Well, it's a mock-up. I've had to limit the speed of light to make everything hang together and the transferral process might be a bit bumpy. But it should function for now."

"Excellent!" said the Archdean. "Then let's do that. We'll transfer the beings over and they'll never know the difference."

The Archdean, Chancellor and Professor prepared to leave, nods of congratulation passing between them.

"But eventually we'll be back to square one," objected Zend. "The beings in there will notice the new flaws, the things that don't make sense."

The Archdean reached the bottom of the stairs and smoothed down her gowns. "And how long will that take?"

"Centuries in their terms. A lot less for us, obviously."

"Well, then," said the Chancellor, "that's all fine. We can go back to bed and worry about the Experiment in the morning. Or next week. Or some other time."

The three filed out, laughing together, leaving Zend alone with the warm, gently humming sphere.

Frowning, he climbed the steps and peered through the scope the Archdean had used.

It was day down on the planet now, but the man with the telescope was there again, staring upwards to the sky. He had some sort of sketchbook in his hand. Fitting a stronger eyepiece, Zend could just discern that the man's eyes were narrowed, his expression puzzled. After a moment he began to urgently scribble something in his tiny book.

Zend swallowed and looked away. Sooner or later there was going to be trouble with these beings. He couldn't contain them forever, even in version two of their universe. They'd work out the

truth and then they'd break free, out into real reality. Demanding answers and, quite possibly, angry at being imprisoned for so long.
    And when that happened no one at all was going to be safe.

It came from Simon Kewin

This was a story that grew from its title. I'm not sure if I heard the phrase somewhere or it simply came to me, but I liked the sound of it and set about wondering why the stars might only be tiny lights upon a perfect black dome. I also liked the idea of a hissing, smoking, steam-powered universe. Plus, the universe mark 2 allowed me to work in a few slight jokes about theoretical physics, which is always good.

A question for Simon Kewin

Q: If you could have any super power, what would it be?
A: The ability to travel instantaneously to any point in the universe. Despite all its riches, the Earth is obviously only a tiny, tiny portion of reality. What other wonders are out there? I'd love to be able to find out...

About Simon Kewin

Simon Kewin is the author of over 100 published short and flash stories as well as several novels. He writes fantasy, science fiction, and some stories that can't make their minds up. He lives in England with his wife and their daughters.
    simonkewin.co.uk

The Doctor's Mask

Taylor Hornig

I let Cameron take me to him, but I already knew where he was. I smelled him as clearly as I smelled old Barty's woodsmoke. He had a bad scent. Sweet and sick, like rotting flowers.

"Did you touch him?" I asked. It was a frigid afternoon, the sun clear and bright, the air frosty and still. When Cameron spoke, his breath bloomed in a cloud of white.

"No, Dr. Slatewall." The boy clambered onto a snowdrift and pointed at the squat stony water mill. It perched next to the frozen river, its curved walls dusted with snow. "He's behind the mill, on the ice."

I inhaled. The scent was potent and foul. I looked at Cameron's unperturbed face and felt a pang of jealousy. He did not have the *vasku;* the air might have been scentless, for all he knew. But I was used to hiding jealousy, and the *vasku* too. When I faced him, it was with a doctor's smile—calm, reassuring, competent. "Thanks. Stay here while I take a look."

He nodded, his eyes shining in the winter light. I couldn't make out the color, but I knew they were blue. Everyone had blue eyes in the lands north of Havenstok. A curious genetic quirk, those eyes. Sometimes I wondered where it had come from. Most likely a reduction in genetic diversity following the Last War. But I could only guess. Havenstok had trained me as a doctor, not an historian. I knew even less about this place than the townspeople, who themselves knew next to nothing.

I turned and trudged toward the mill. Last night's sleet had left the snow shiny and slick. It was all I could do to keep my footing as I made my way to the river, where the snow gave way to a vast sweep of glittering ice.

On it lay a man. A small man, his limbs splayed in an awkward X. He wore leather breeches, sheepskin boots, and nothing else. His gleaming back was sickly white, his shoulders a darker shade that looked like green.

The diagnosis should have been easy. His photosynthetic shoulders marked him as a man of Havenstok. A man of *Homo herba,* we doctors would say. And his symptoms—excessive sweating, overheating, unconsciousness—were standard in *herbas* who suffered from mutant-herbal fever, the terrifying plague that had swept the region during the past several months.

A *Homo sapiens* doctor would already be gathering a disposal team. Townspeople armed with leather gloves, cloth masks, and an impressive amount of courage. They would drag the body far into the snowy woods, far enough to keep it from contaminating town property. Then would come the quarantine. The waiting. And, possibly, the death. Unlike *herbas, sapiens* never survived MHF. They just boiled with fever until their organs shut down. A fact the townspeople knew too well.

But I was not *sapiens.* I was *herba.* And I knew the scent of MHF. It had a sharp odor, sour and acrid. This disease smelled softer. Almost cloying. I sniffed again. The scent poured into my nose, intensely putrid—and completely unfamiliar.

This wasn't MHF.

This was something else.

"Dr. Slatewall?" Cameron's words, reedy with distance. "Is he going to make us sick?"

"No," I called back.

"Will you make someone get rid of him?"

A note of fear in that boyish voice. Or maybe anger. Since the outbreak they'd become almost the same.

"Yes," I told him. But I ached when I did it. And when I looked back at the man, I seemed to see the vine-wrapped towers of Havenstok, circling the Great Tree that gave them life.

Havenstok, which I had abandoned.

Havenstok, which I had betrayed.

A cold wind blew across the river, scattering snow across my goggles. I wiped it away. My gloves smudged the tinted lenses, turning the man into a blurry brown smear. Still I regarded him for a long moment, my sleeves rippling in the last of the wind, before I returned to the road.

"You'd better go home," I told Cameron. "It's getting dark."

He blinked nervously. "You'll make someone get rid of him. Won't you?"

"Yes. Now go."

After he left, I returned to the river. The man still lay on the ice, motionless. I climbed over the bank and crouched next to him. There was no sound but the empty whistle of the wind. But I checked behind me anyway, ensuring no one had followed, before I heaved his body over my shoulder.

I carried him home in the chill evening light. In summer the streets would have been thick with workers returning from the fields; now, in the dark depths of winter, there was no one but the occasional dim figure glimpsed through a curtained window. Normally that would have bothered me. Even after so long I missed the biolumes of Havenstok. How they hung from every tree, banishing the shadows with gentle golden light. But this time I gave silent thanks to the darkness. If anyone saw me with a sick *herba,* I would be chased out of town.

No. I corrected myself. *If anyone saw me with any herba, I would be chased out of town.* MHF had originated in Havenstok, and the *sapiens* thought we were all carriers. Even those of us who were healthy.

I had never told them what I was.

I knew better than that.

I brought the man into my office and laid him on my examining table. His head lolled on a burlap pillow stuffed with down. His limbs were limp, his skin bloodless. I held a hand in front of his blue lips. No breath. I pulled off my gloves and touched his chest. A long moment passed. Then his heart beat once. I waited ten seconds. It beat again.

I withdrew my hand. So my odd patient had gone dormant. Exactly what I would have expected from a sufferer of late-stage MHF.

But he didn't *have* MHF.

Frowning, I began to strip off my clothes. The fleece-lined jacket I would sterilize with heat and disinfectant. Good jackets were hard to come by, and I would be no use to anyone if I froze to death. Everything else I would burn.

I dropped the contaminated clothes in a basin and went to the sink to wash my hands. As I scrubbed my palms with a lumpy bar of soap, I stared at my reflection in the mirror: black hair, mussed from my heavy leather cap, and a white face half-obscured by those ever-present goggles. The townspeople thought I wore tinted lenses to protect my light-sensitive eyes. That was true, in a sense. They did protect me—but not from the light.

I pulled the goggles off. The world filled with color, and nothing was brighter than my own reflected eyes, staring back at me as clear and green as fresh leaves.

My secret *herba* eyes. My secret *herba* patient.

I was so tired of secrets.

I turned to the man. He lay still as a corpse, his pale skin shining in the lamplight.

I wondered if he would live. I wondered if the townspeople would learn what I'd done. I wondered why I felt so guilty.

I wondered when I'd felt anything else.

For the next several days I saw patients in my sitting room. "I'm renovating the office," I told them. "We can't use it for a week or two."

Most of them didn't mind. They were happy as long as I kept treating their cuts and sore throats. Only Jake Clearsoil seemed suspicious. He was Cameron's father, a huge man with arms as thick as the logs he cut for a living. He eyed me from beneath bristling brows as I cleaned a burn on his hand.

"Cam said he found a greenie," he informed me. "Near the mill." I dabbed the burn with herbal antiseptic. "Yes. But I took care of it."

"Haven't heard of anyone in quarantine."

"Some traders were passing through. I asked them to take him."

"And they agreed?"

"For a few furs."

He frowned, flexing his calloused fingers. "You gave them our furs?"

"It seemed worth it to avoid a quarantine."

"True." But he didn't sound convinced. I pretended not to notice as I bound his injury in a clean cloth bandage. I made my own bandages, woven using the traditional methods of Havenstok. They usually pleased the townspeople, who'd wrapped their wounds in rags until the day I'd stumbled onto their land. Jake, however, seemed unimpressed.

"The medicine stings," he muttered as he got to his feet. "Is it supposed to do that?"

"It isn't supposed to. It just does."

He squinted at the bandage. "Are you sure?"

"Mr. Clearsoil, I've been treating injuries for a long time. I know what I'm doing."

He gave me a long hard look. Then he glanced at the door to my office. For a heart-stopping moment I thought he smelled the sick man within. I'd grown used to my strange patient's scent, but anyone else with the *vasku* would have been coughing the second they entered the house.

Of course, Jake Clearsoil was not an *herba*. He did not have the *vasku*. And he could not smell anything.

But I was frightened all the same.

"Strange folk." Jake was looking at me again. "Those greenies. Sometimes I think they're trying to kill us off."

I rolled up the extra bandages and stowed them in my satchel. "Why do you think that?"

I sounded perfectly calm. I'd developed a remarkable talent for calmness, or at least the appearance of it. Jake studied my face a moment more, then lowered his eyes.

"The Fever kills us." His fingers went to his bandage, tugging at a loose corner. "They just sleep it off. And they have all that pre-War gene stuff. They can probably make any disease they want."

That was untrue. If we could control pathogens so easily, we'd have obliterated MHF a long time ago. Even a non-fatal disease could destroy a community. A subtle destruction, not a shatter but a warp. Havenstok lived, but it had changed. The thought came with a flare of anger, and for the first time in months I felt my mask crack.

Relax, I told myself, willing my twitching cheeks to smooth. *Relax.*

Calm won out, as it always did. I smiled at Jake, all kindness and concern, and offered my hand. "I wouldn't know. Thanks for stopping by, Mr. Clearsoil. I hope the burn heals quickly."

He clasped the hand in a grip like a clamp. "I hope it does too. Thanks for the help, Dr. Slatewall."

But as he left, slipping on his deerskin jacket, his eyes darted again to my office. As if he'd heard a sound he could not quite place; as if he'd smelled a scent that did not quite belong.

The lie about renovations was only partly a lie. After I'd brought the ailing man home, I'd turned my office into a Havenstok-style sickroom. Bags of dried manure lay stacked in one corner with buckets of snowmelt clustered around them. A makeshift filtration apparatus fashioned from mesh sheets and scraps of wood bubbled softly by my desk. Across the room, the examining table stood beneath the single high window, bathed in winter sunlight.

The man never moved. At least not of his own volition. I'd repositioned his limbs so that I could place his hands and feet in tubs of effluent—nutrient-water strained from crushed manure. His heart still beat slow as a summer stream, and he still stank of sickness.

But he did not die.

Sometimes that scared me. More than once, as I stood over him in the unsteady lantern light, I thought about dragging him into the woods. Leaving him to rot beneath the spindly, leafless trees.

I could have done it.

I wanted to do it.

But I did not.

And one day his cheeks flushed a bright, clear pink.

He would be awake soon. Awake—and aware.

I went to my desk, tripping a little on the feet of the filtration system, and unlocked the smallest drawer with a brass key I kept on a chain around my neck. It was empty but for a huge book bound in leather—*The Havenstok Encyclopedia of Medicine, 14th edition,* read the faintly bioluminescent title—and a dusty glass bottle half-full of amber liquid.

I withdrew the bottle and squeezed the rubber bulb near the neck. Pungent mist burst from the nozzle, scalding my sinuses with the spicy scent of cloves. I'd never been an innovative doctor—the treatments the townspeople found so miraculous were some of the most basic in Havenstok—but this reeking concoction was all my own. Steeling myself, I sprayed great clouds of it over my neck, my arms, my chest. It felt like thrusting my nose into a bottle of smelling salts. I coughed, gasped, and shoved the bottle back in its drawer. Then I put on my goggles. My heart was beating fast, much too fast.

I ordered myself to relax. The spray would mask my *herba* scent; with luck, the man would attribute the stink to the primitive medicines of a *sapiens* doctor, and think little of it. Either way, I had to seem calm. If he saw my fear, he might wonder what I was hiding. And if he wondered what I was hiding, he might even suspect that—

A sound interrupted my thoughts. A soft sound, like the rustle of leaves.

A breath.

I went to the examining table. The man lay perfectly still, his hands and feet afloat in their metal tubs. I lowered trembling fingers to his chest. His heart throbbed under them. Seven seconds between each beat. Then six. Then five.

I stepped back as a shudder ran through him. His hands twitched, splashing water on the floor. He opened his mouth and sucked in a great gulp of air. His eyelids fluttered as if he were dreaming, and all at once I wondered if *I* were the dreamer—if this were nothing but a freakish nightmare. I couldn't have been so foolish, could I? Foolish enough to bring an *herba* into my own home?

Then his eyes opened. I knew their color, though I could not see it: a beautiful green, clear as fresh leaves.

"Where am I?" he whispered in a tired voice.

I smiled my best doctor's smile. "In the town of Clarity Falls."

"On the Great Northern River?"

"Yes."

"Ah." He sighed. "And you saved me?"

"I did."

"I appreciate it."

I shrugged. "I'm a doctor. It's my job."

"Most of your doctors won't touch us." He nodded at my gloved hands. "Even with protection."

"Most of our doctors lack my confidence."

I'd prepared that answer, as I'd prepared all of them. To my relief he seemed to believe it. With a feeble grin he said, "Then I'm a lucky man. May I ask your name?"

"Nadia Slatewall." I'd picked it for its averageness. It sounded like someone you'd pass on the street. Someone you'd wave to, and forget. "May I ask yours?"

"Lavr of Havenstok-East."

"Nice to meet you, Lavr." I pretended to study the tubs. "I need to change your water. I hope you don't mind."

"Not at all."

He closed his eyes, and his breath grew slow. I busied myself with the tubs, knowing he slept, fearing he would wake. His eyes had unnerved me. They were sleepy now, unfocused with fatigue, but who knew when they would sharpen?

And what they would see when they did?

The day after Lavr woke, a storm rolled in from the west. It dropped a foot of snow on the town's tiled roofs before dissipating into shreds of dense wet cloud. I spent the afternoon outside, clearing a path to the unplowed road.

When I was done I leaned on my shovel, listening for the rattle of wheels, the clatter of hooves. But the town was as silent as the frozen river. The plow must have been delayed—unless it had found its own trouble. Broken axles and lame horses were all too common in the lands north of Havenstok.

I returned to the house. I'd made a fire that morning; its heat forced sweat from my skin and fogged the lenses of my goggles. I took off my hat and jacket but left the goggles on. I didn't dare take them off. Not with Lavr awake.

I stood in front of the fire until they cleared.

Then I went to my office.

Lavr lay on the table. His eyes were shut, his breath imperceptible. A strip of sunlight splashed across his naked chest.

I did not want to disturb him. I feared those green eyes, that too-sensitive nose. I'd reapplied my scent that morning, doused myself in huge stinking clouds of it, but I still felt uneasy.

I also had to talk to him, whether I liked it or not. I'd spent most of last night poring over my *Encyclopedia,* trying to diagnose his condition. But the book had been useless. Nothing matched his symptoms except for MHF. Which, of course, he didn't have.

I needed more information. More specifically, I needed to question him. With luck, I would learn enough to make a diagnosis. With a little more luck, I would be able to cure him. Then I could release him, and free myself of his all-too-dangerous presence.

I coughed lightly. "Lavr?"

His eyes slid open. They blinked slowly, then rolled towards me. "Dr. Slatewall. Nice to see you."

"Nice to see you, too," I said. "How are you feeling?"

"Much better." He lifted a wet hand, then let it fall back in its tub. "Which isn't saying much. But your nutrient baths are a big help. I never thought a *sapiens* doctor would be so well-versed in Havenstok medicine."

The implicit question made my skin tingle. "My predecessor treated one of your people," I lied. "He taught me his techniques." Then, changing the subject: "If you can, I'd like you to tell me what you know about your illness. The more I know, the better I can treat you."

A strange expression pinched his face—a quick wince, as if I'd pricked him with a needle. "You can only do so much. All of this—" He waved a hand at his chest, dripping effluent on his pallid skin. "—it's just a symptom of something else. Something you can't cure."

That made me anxious. I needed to cure him. Otherwise I'd have to choose between throwing him out and keeping him here indefinitely. Neither option was appealing. I forced myself to speak steadily. "What would that be?"

"It's hard to explain." He shifted a little. "You see, Havenstok has a sort of core. A Great Tree that sustains the entire habitat. And something's wrong with it. We're not sure, but we think it has a mutated version of MHF."

He closed his eyes. He looked suddenly weak, as weak as he'd been the day I brought him home. I felt weak myself. I had never thought MHF would mutate. Or maybe I just hadn't cared. Because I was a hypocrite. Because I was a liar. Because I had hidden so well behind my doctor's mask. And I kept hiding even as he opened his eyes and said, "Dr. Slatewall, the Tree is going to die. And when it does, so will Havenstok. The habitat is already contaminated. There's poison in the air, the water. Most of us are already sick. If we don't find a cure soon...our own Tree will kill us."

"Then why are you here?" I asked. Now I sounded concerned. Detached. The small-town doctor, soothing her anxious patient. "Shouldn't you be in Havenstok?"

He gasped, coughed. His hands spasmed. Cloudy water sprayed across his thin chest.

"We had someone special," he whispered finally. "Someone who could help us find a cure. But we lost her months ago. We've been searching for her. We—"

His words dissolved in another coughing fit. I took the opportunity to pick up a pair of empty buckets. I hoped he couldn't see my face. My mask was cracking again, and I had no clue what lurked behind it.

Still I managed to speak gently. "Don't worry. We'll figure something out." I lifted a bucket. "I need to refill these, but I'll be back in a minute."

I went outside and scooped fresh snow into the buckets. Then I set them down and put my hands on my knees. I felt like I couldn't move—like I'd just aged a century.

I stood there for what felt like eons, the wind blowing my hair, swirling the fresh snow in great clouds of white.

Thinking of Havenstok.

Thinking of a young doctor waking healthy next to her sick family. Of Havenstok's medical elite arriving at her door. Of a white sterile lab where pathologists prodded her skin and sampled her blood. Of strange experiments that intensified as whole communities fell dormant. Desperate experiments. Dangerous experiments. She was immune to MHF, and her immunity was killing her. If she ran away from those experiments—if she refused to sacrifice herself—was that really so wrong?

Was it?

After a minute, or many minutes, I was shaken from my thoughts by a high voice calling my name.

I looked up. In the street, up to his knees in snow, stood Cameron Clearsoil.

"Cameron," I said. "How can I help you?"

He stepped into the path I'd cleared. Snow scattered around his booted feet. "Daddy sent me."

Jake Clearsoil. My heart sank another notch. "Why would that be?"

Cameron glanced at my little house. "He wants to look in your office. He thinks you might be keeping the greenie in there. He says maybe you're a traitor and you want to kill us all."

The boy announced this matter-of-factly, as if he were reading a list of medicinal ingredients from my *Encyclopedia.* I wondered why Jake Clearsoil hadn't told me this himself. Probably because a child seemed more innocent. And harder to deny.

"How could I do that?" I asked. Perfectly calm, as usual. "If I exposed myself to the Fever, I'd die."

My hundredth lie. Or my thousandth. But I'd become a skilled actor, and my words seemed to reach him. Doubt flickered in his eyes as he stepped back, frowning at his scuffed boots with what looked like guilt.

"I guess," he said slowly. "Maybe I'll talk to Daddy again."

"Please tell him I won't hurt anyone."

He nodded and started back down the road. I watched him push through the snow, and wondered when Jake Clearsoil would show up at my door.

Probably soon.

Probably very soon.

I ran up the path and into the house. I had to get Lavr out of here. Where I would send him, I had no idea. The forest, maybe, with a bundle of firewood and enough effluent to keep him awake. Not that that would save him. But at least it would protect him from the wrath of a furious *sapiens*.

But did I really want to save Lavr?

Or did I only want to save myself?

The fire's heat washed over me as I slammed the door shut. My goggles fogged, reducing the familiar furniture to a wash of blotchy gray. I pulled off my gloves and rubbed the lenses with clammy fingertips.

They refused to clear. I swiped at them once more; then, in frustration, I tore them off. The warm air felt strange against my eyes, so unused to being exposed. The world burned with strange colors, and I ran through their brightness until I reached the office door and flung it open.

Lavr lay sprawled on the examining table. At the sound of my entrance he glanced up.

"Dr. Slatewall," he began. "What—"

Then his green eyes met my green eyes. For an instant they narrowed in confusion.

Another instant, and they lit with recognition.

I had no time to be afraid. I strode to the table and leaned over him, planting my hands next to his tubs. "I'm not Dr. Slatewall. I'm Denr of Havenstok-West."

I expected anger. Rage, even. But he only laughed a weak laugh and said, "Denr. I should have known. Those goggles, that smell...the sickness must be making me stupid."

"It doesn't matter. Listen—a *sapiens* is coming. He knows you're here. You have to leave."

He smiled bitterly. "Because you care so much." He shook his head, rolling it back and forth on the pillow. "Why did you take me in? It would have been easier to let me die."

"I felt sorry for you."

"At home they say you never felt sorry for anyone."

I thrust buckets beneath the filtration apparatus, filling them with cloudy effluent. I wondered how to tell him that *sorry* and *sacrifice* were not the same. That I could be human without being a hero. That I loved Havenstok and feared it, just as I loved and feared my perfect doctor's face—the mask that had saved me and lied for me and made me someone I never should have been.

"Lavr," I said.

"What?"

"I feel sorry for all of you." I found lids and secured them to the buckets with sturdy clamps. "Take these buckets. I'll find firewood and clothes. If you wear enough, they probably won't recognize you."

He pushed himself into a sitting position. His damp hands clutched the table as he faced me. "I was looking for you. I'm supposed to bring you back."

"I know."

"So will you come?"

If I had been a hero, I might have said yes. But I was not a hero. I was Denr of Havenstok-West, and I would not let my people destroy me. Did that make me a bad person? Perhaps. And yet I wanted to save Lavr, whom I had already saved once. I wanted to save my home, which I hated and missed and loved.

Maybe I could find a way to save us all.

"No," I said. "I won't. But tell Havenstok I want to help. Tell them I'll come back if they promise not to hurt me. Tell them to send me a messenger with their decision." I fixed my gaze on his. "Tell them they only get one chance. That I escaped once, and if I have to, I'll do it again."

His shoulders tensed. I thought he might be about to rise; to try to seize me with those wet hands. But he didn't. He just looked at me, immobilized by his sickness, or maybe, just maybe, by his gratitude.

"You have to go," I said. "Now."

He let me dress him, load him with supplies, and hustle him out the back door. He hesitated briefly on the snowy path. Sunlight sparkled in his tinted lenses—*my* tinted lenses—as he glanced back at me.

Then he walked away.

I went to the sitting room and lowered myself onto the sofa. Through the window I watched Lavr walk, slowly but steadily, down the street. Just before the bend he passed another man. A burly man, with arms thick as logs.

They both looked bright. Vibrant. Colorful and alive. It was strange, how many colors I'd forgotten.

I wondered if I had truly wanted to save Lavr. His departure certainly made my own life easier. I doubted I could convince anyone to excuse my protection of a sick *herba*. But to excuse my own identity, after all the times I'd served the people of Clarity Falls? I thought I had a chance. Not a good chance, but a better one than I'd had with Lavr sprawled on my examining table.

Then again, it was nice to watch him walk away. Free and secure, like I wanted to be. Maybe I *had* tried to save him, in the only way I could.

Maybe I would never know.

Maybe it didn't matter.

I gazed at the street until my doorbell rang.

I rose and went to the door. Then I put on my best doctor's face. Smiling, pleasant, with eyes so very green.

It came from Taylor Hornig

I've always enjoyed writing about the woods, and one day I wondered if I could write a story that readers might classify as treepunk. It would look a bit like cyberpunk, I figured, but with technology that draws its power from the natural world. To make the concept more interesting, I decided to include two societies: one that uses this nature tech, and one that relies on more familiar resources. I also thought it would be fun—and unusual—to make the "natural" society the more technologically advanced of the pair. This basic dichotomy eventually evolved into Havenstok and Clarity Falls, and I was off and running.

A question for Taylor Hornig

Q: Are you an outline or discovery writer?
A: I'm mostly a discovery writer. I usually have a basic idea of the plot before I start writing, but it changes and grows as I work my way through the draft. I often realize that details I thought would be minor become crucial to the ending, or that I need to add a plot point I could never have imagined at the beginning of the process. I really like writing this way, but it does make my work days less efficient, so I've been trying to outline a bit more lately. Hopefully I can learn to have the best of both worlds!

About Taylor Hornig

Taylor Hornig is a speculative fiction writer based in New Hampshire. In her free time, she enjoys reading, playing video games, and hanging out with her very fuzzy dogs.

Never Miss: Moses Abebe is a Machine

J. T. Gill

"After just one year, undrafted rookie Moses Abebe has taken the league by storm, becoming the first player in NBA history to make every shot in a single season…"

"Moses Abebe continues to dominate headlines as well as opponents after his performance in game four of the NBA championship, making him the only player ever to complete two full seasons with an unprecedented one hundred percent completion percentage. But some do not agree with the native Somalian's spotless record, saying that he might be vamping — a method of genetic modification that enables users to increase brain efficiency. Commissioner Stern said if Abebe is found guilty of the accusations, he would be subject to disciplinary action…"

"The investigation on Moses Abebe was concluded today when doctors cleared the two-time NBA Champion of all charges related to vamping. However, the NBA is continuing to investigate, stating, 'despite Abebe's talent and work ethic, no player has ever maintained such a high completion percentage for so long.' The young star declined to comment…"

Never Miss: Moses Abebe is a Machine

By: Richard Gregory

June 1, 2052

The practice building was just outside of D.C. — Washington's new state-of-the-art facility where Abebe and I had arranged to meet. Fresh off a win in the Conference Finals and with less than a week until his third consecutive Championship appearance, it was a rare day off for the 23 year old superstar, and the only time that worked for us to get together.

I pulled in at the gate entrance and left my car to a parking attendant out front — a labeled copy unit, engineered to look like an attractive young female. It's ironic, actually. Even the low level copies are programmed with emotions now. Hers were clearly getting the best of her; she barely even looked at me when I handed her the keys.

After double checking that my lens-phone was recording, I headed inside. I didn't want to miss anything.

Moses was waiting in the lobby, dribbling lazy figure eights between his legs by rote. There was a glaring absence of the trappings I'd grown accustomed to in sports reporting: headphones, shooting sleeves, fancy branding. Not for Moses. Just shoes, shorts, and a shirt, all of which looked as if though he had dug them out of his closet and none of which were branded.

But the most surprising thing about him was his height. On the team's official roster he's listed as six four, but in reality he's no more five foot ten, if that. Being able to look an NBA player in the eyes without craning your neck is a rare treat.

"Moses," I said, extending my hand. "Good to meet you."

He cradled the ball with one arm and smiled broadly — a white slice of moon against his midnight skin. "Richard Gregory," he said. "It is nice to meet you as well."

We shook hands. Most players enjoy the attention of a sports interview, but Abebe seemed almost awkward, nodding curtly.

"You got to sleep in today, huh?" I joked.

"Yes," he said. I think he thought I was being serious.

I gave the lobby a quick scan and nodded approvingly. "I haven't been out here yet," I said. "This is nice."

"Come," Abebe said. "I will show you around."

Three dimensional mock-ups can't compare with the immersive experience that is Washington's new practice facility. Not when you're walking beneath cathedrallike ceilings, basketball courts on either side — empty, expansive. Everything is bigger, wider, built to accommodate the physically gifted.

Moses wasn't an initiator when it came to conversation, though he was quick to respond to every question I asked. Still, the burden was on me to keep a dialogue going. I kept things light to start.

"What time did you show up this morning?" I asked.

"On the team we have a game," he said. "Who can show up the earliest. If I tell you what time, the others will read about it and try to beat me."

"Your secrets are safe with me," I said. I couldn't help it.

He gave a kind of snort. "Because you want to know if I have been vamping. You do not believe that I could make so many shots and never miss."

I shrugged it off, a little taken aback by his directness. "I just want to get to know you, man."

He must have read my expression though because he said, "And I will be happy to answer whatever questions you might have."

I nodded, grinning a little. We kept walking.

Washington's facility represents the future of athletic training. I saw mirrorscreens displaying exercises to target specific muscle groups, based on a given week's game plan, holo courts programmed to mimic opposing players, and automatically restocking lockers — "stockers" Moses called them. He showed me the locker rooms, along with the swimming pool and saunas — for recovery training and aerobic exercises. We walked through the film rooms, big as movie theaters, footage from their early season losses playing on repeat. And finally we came to the gym, a three story tower with every type of machine you could imagine. Some sections — focused on team-specific strategy — were labeled off limits. Camo-blends had been installed, blurring the surroundings whenever I glanced in the direction of the restricted areas.

But no matter what we saw during our tour, it all seemed lost on Moses. He gestured vaguely to equipment I knew cost hundreds of thousands of dollars. And I wasn't even sure if he knew what some of the things were. It almost seemed like he was bored.

So I prompted him, asking if he wanted to shoot. He nodded, and I motioned for him to lead the way.

We headed for the courts.

Moses took one hundred and twenty three shots on the practice court — I counted.

He never missed. Not once.

Watching him up close was like watching a berserker, exacting his revenge on every person who ever told him he wasn't good enough to play. He breathed in and out in short bursts through his nose, slipping inside, then cutting out for the fade away, splashing the net with a ladylike whisper. Hunting down the ball after the bounce and sticking to the outside this time, nailing the three. Dribbling to the top of the arc, he jerked a head fake and then lofted it over the shoulder for a skyhook, dead on. More than once I caught myself breathing hard, my heart beating fast just watching him, almost nervous.

But no matter how graceful his performance, there was only one thing I could think: there's no way the guy isn't vamping. He's dodged a few investigations, maybe paid the doctors off to come out and say he's clean, but no human makes one hundred and twenty three shots in a row. At that point you're either vamping something or straight up inhuman.

When he finally finished, I was shaking my head, smiling. In some ways, it was impressive, but only in the same way Barry Bonds was during his prime, or Lance Armstrong. Only until you find out the rest of the story.

"Moses," I said, walking over. "I've never seen anything like that."

He nodded, hardly acknowledging me. "All right," he said. "You are here for an interview."

I followed him off the court and down the hallway.

The players' lounge was a sprawling expanse of wealth and entertainment — an adult's play room.

Easy chairs, TV's, a fully stocked arcade, with the latest RPG motion capture pods. The walls were all mirrorscreens, which came to life when we walked past. After a glance, I realized it projected my reflection to be about a foot taller than reality, and my frustratingly crooked nose was somehow straight again — a psychological confidence booster, I imagine.

There was a full-length bar at one end, shrouded in the shadows. The menu kicked on as we walked towards a booth at the far end of the room. I hunkered in, Moses opposite me, staring out the window, which must have recognized his face because it switched to show a heavy thunderstorm in the distance, rain spattering the window.

"You like the rain?" I asked, looking over the virtual menu floating in front of me.

"Yes," he said. "Very much."

I ordered a salad — something light so I could talk. Moses had a protein shake and fish, though he hardly touched either throughout our interview.

The remainder of our interview went as follows, as best as I can remember.

Richard Gregory (RG)

"So you grew up in Somalia," I asked. "What was it like as a child in one of the most dangerous places in the world?"

Moses Abebe (MA)

"Every day was a fight for survival. I saw terrible things. My heart breaks for those still there."

RG

"Did you ever have dreams of one day playing in the NBA?"

MA

"No. I never imagined this. I only hoped that I might be able to help those around me."

RG

"Expand on that. How did Moses Abebe get so good at basketball?"

MA

"There are things you cannot control. I will never be the tallest or the fastest, but what I can control, I work at. So I become the quickest, the most accurate."

RG

"Tell me about how you were discovered."

MA

"My friends and I would travel to Mogadishu, to play on the street courts against the bots. One day, a white man came to watch us. When the game was over, he asked me to continue taking shots. I showed him that I could shoot very well, that I could shoot even more accurately than the bots. At first he stood to the side and watched, smiling, but very soon he was watching me closely with his arms crossed. Then he said he was a recruiter, and asked if I would consider flying with him to America. I agreed, and here I am."

RG

"Do you like it in D.C.? Playing for the Wizards?"

MA

"It is a great city, and the team has been good to me. Everything is nicer in America, but the people do not understand."

RG

"What do you mean?"

MA

"In America, you have everything. Whatever you want, within an arm's reach. In Somalia, you have to fight. Every day, you must fight. Many die, all the time. No one seems to understand."

RG

"Do you have family back home?"

MA

"I brought my mother and sister here with me. There were many issues with visas and passports. The reporters and those with microphones, they shove them in my face and ask me about the records and the championships. No one has ever asked me about my family."

RG

"You would rather reporters ask you about your family?"

MA

"I only think it is wrong that so many are so concerned about money when people are dying. Basketball is not about the records. Basketball is not about wins. Basketball is not about championships. Not for me. For me, basketball is about protection, survival, you see?

Everything I do, I do for my mother and sister, and those still in Somalia."

RG

"Then why are you here on your day off? You already have two championships. I'm sure you have enough money to buy Mogadishu. Moses, if you keep playing this way, you could become the highest scoring player of all time. You have a very real shot at winning more championships than anyone else in the history of the game. You can't tell me that doesn't appeal to you."

MA

"My Father's last words to me were, 'Moses: Lead us into the Promised Land.' I care only to fulfill his dying wish."

RG

"Seems like your father had a profound impact on your life. Do you mind me asking how he died?"

MA

"He was killed. Our village was attacked and he died defending us. I was able to escape with my mother and sister, but he was killed."

RG

"I'm sorry to hear that. He didn't teach you basketball?"

MA

"No."

RG

"You've gone through multiple investigations now to determine whether or not you've ever vamped. Both investigations concluded that you're clean, but obviously we're still asking questions, so I've got to ask you face to face: have you ever vamped?"

MA

"Never."

RG

"And you've never gone through any sort of genetic modification?"

MA

"No."

RG

"How can you expect people to believe that when you've somehow made every shot you've ever taken? I just watched you take one hundred and twenty three shots and you never missed a single one. And that was practice. How do you justify that?"

MA

"Every shot I take is legitimate, every sho—"

RG

"But you can understand how someone might think it's not, right? You can understand that people see you as a kid who needed to get out, who would do anything to get away, and instead of just telling me that you've never cheated, you feed me a story about how basketball is about survival."

MA

"You think I am a cheater."

RG

"How else do you explain it?"

MA

"People assume my accomplishments are a result of dominance. But the truth is that when I make a three point shot, the only voice I hear is that of my father. The only faces I see are those of my mother and sister."

RG

"You're really sticking to that, huh?"

MA

"I can only tell you the truth."

RG

"Well, I guess I don't have anything else. Moses, thank you for your time."

MA

"Thank you, Richard."

He walked me out, down huge hallways and back into the lobby where he thanked me for my time.

I stood there motionless, my eyes slipping over the creases of his smile. "Come on, man," I said, leaning in. "I know you're running something. Just admit it."

"Running something?" he said, as if he didn't know what it meant.

"Vamping," I said. "No one makes—"

But I didn't have time to finish. He lashed out at me. Piston powerful. Python fast. I felt his fist connect with my eye and a shock of pain ripped through my cheek. I stumbled backwards, falling to the ground. At the same instant, I felt my lens-phone shatter, tiny glass shards sprinkling across the floor.

When I opened my eyes, something warm was trickling down my cheek. I patted my face, and my fingertips came away bloody. Moses was standing over me, the skin on his hand torn. And underneath, metal.

Metal.

"What are you?" I breathed.

"I suppose there is no turning back now," he said, stepping forward, crushing the shards of my lens-phone underfoot. "I am a copy unit."

I stared at him, stunned, half scared he was going to strike again. My cheek was throbbing.

"Many years ago," he said, kneeling beside me. "A man — my 'father' — stole me from a reseller on the streets of Mogadishu. As my programming is set to include a capacity for emotion, I found it only natural to protect his wife and daughter — my mother and sister — even after he died."

"But you were cleared in a medical investigation," I said.

"The doctors are, of course, aware of my situation," he said.

"Then why haven't they said anything?"

"Because I pay them well," Moses said. "And they would rather that no harm come to them."

"You're not even human!" I hissed. "You shouldn't even be in the league!"

He nodded. "Which is why I need you, Richard."

"What do you mean?"

"The only reason my mother and sister are here now is because of the fame of Moses Abebe. If I was exposed, their visas would come under scrutiny, and they would almost certainly be deported. Could you live with that, Richard?"

My mouth hung open. I struggled for words, but none came.

"But fortune favors the famous. If I continue never to miss, I remain in my current position, and I can continue to ensure they are kept safe. Here. In America."

"So what happens if I don't write anything?" I asked, my mind racing.

"I think you will," he said, nodding to my cheek. I swallowed. How many others had suffered the same thing? How many doctors, threatened and paid to keep quiet? And no one said a word. I was guessing he hadn't yet threatened anyone who actually cared.

"I am sorry about your lens-phone," he said, hauling upright. "My emotional programming sometimes overcomes me. Though, for obvious reasons I could not have you recording this conversation. I will ensure you receive a new one. Otherwise, can I trust you?"

He held out his hand.

I stared at it, then looked him in the eye, two thoughts running through my head simultaneously: the biggest scandal in the history of the NBA revealed, or two human lives kept safe, and a boatload of cash to keep quiet. It was the hardest decision I had ever had to make.

So lying about it came naturally.

"Yes," I said. "You can trust me."

It came from J. T. Gill

The inspiration for this story came when I was (shocker) playing basketball. There's a basketball court not far from our house, and I was out shooting hoops one night in December. It was freezing, and late, and dark, and honestly I don't know why I was out there except to think. This story is pretty much where my mind went. I was missing a lot of shots that night, so naturally I started thinking about how awesome it would be to make every shot...and then I carried that a little further. Specifically, to the NBA. One of my favorite things about having a story published is sharing where the inspiration came from, not only for others, but for myself as well. I have fond memories of this one, because it always takes me back to that freezing night in December, missing all those shots. Maybe not a great memory, but I think stories have a way of making un-extraordinary memories a little more meaningful. At least they do for me.

A question for J. T. Gill

Q: Have you ever consciously written a 'message' story? Was it easier or harder than usual?

A: When I first started writing, I think all my stories were "message" stories...and they were terrible. I learned very quickly that when the message drives the story, the story usually suffers. As I've continued to write (and learn), I think I've gotten better at navigating that balance, but intentionally working in a message is definitely difficult. Very difficult.

About J. T. Gill

JT Gill is a pianoman who enjoys sports of most any kind, spending time with friends and family, and savoring large bowls of cereal. He and his wife live in Fairfax, Virginia, just outside of D.C., where they are probably on an adventure.

www.jtgill.com

2015

Before *Metaphorosis* formally published, I posted one sample story so that curious readers would find something to look at along with our submission guidelines, etc. The story was, in fact, the source of the magazine's title.

Metaphorosis

B. Morris Allen

Like the sound of soft fingers on skin, green palm fronds whispered amongst themselves. Their soft breath caressed his cheek as he listened for the slight scratching of frond cilia against stiff palm trunks.

"Sam." The breeze was stronger, the fronds closer. He could almost feel them tickling his face.

"Sam. You'll be late for work." He stirred, allowed the cold waves to sift sand from underneath him. Gently, that was the way, no quick... A huge wave sucked him into the chilling surf.

"Give back the comforter." He opened his eyes, saw one vagrant palm frond floating nearby. It looked darker in the water. He reached out for it.

"Ow! Let go," she cried in pain. "Thank you. Now come on, get up."

Sam sat up, hugging his arms to his chest. "Sorry, hon. Thought you were a palm frond." The cold seeped in, forcing him to stand and head for the warm shower.

"Did you, now?" She smiled. "Agree to go to Jamaica for Christmas and I'll be a whole palm tree. But we're not going anywhere unless we both get paychecks. So get moving, or I'll abduct you as is."

Sam, already in the shower and turning the valve, ignored the threat. As the cold water struck, he forgot it entirely.

Cough. "Thanks, Franz." Sam coughed again as he took the proffered lozenge.

"No problem, Mr. Gregson. Always have a cough drop or two for just this purpose. NyQuil, DayQuil, aspirin, ... You got a cold, I'm your man."

Sam sucked the menthol-laced candy with relief, and looked over at the chubby night guard in his black and yellow sweater. "I appreciate it, Franz, I really do. Funny, though. Felt fine the whole damn day, then bang! The minute I'm ready to go home, I start coughing like crazy."

"Allergic to your wife?" Franz waggled fuzzy eyebrows to make clear that this was a joke. "Don't tell her I said that." The man bobbed from side to side as he chuckled.

Sam coughed. So much for trying to laugh. "Oh, I will. She'll probably come right down and stomp the life out of you. She's a vicious woman. Like a preying mantis." Sam smiled as he wrapped his scarf around his neck, though it was true that she was a little controlling. "Probably just cockroach dust, though. They're all over our building. Scared to death of the things myself." He offered his best self-deprecating grin.

"Oh, sure," smiled Franz. "Got them all over the city. Good thing this building has centipedes instead." He laughed.

"I'll see you, Franz. Thanks for the cough drop."

"No problem, Mr. Gregson. Wouldn't want you getting sick again, after all."

Sam pushed his way through the revolving door, steeling himself for the chilly night air. Like leaving your shell, he always thought. You go from the soft cozy cocoon of your bed to the hard warm casing of the office, then back again through intemperate climes between. Over and over, like an indecisive hermit crab, scuttling over the sand between homes. Eventually, the waves were bound to separate the choices too far, and you'd get washed away by the cold tide. One of your more evolved hermit crabs here, he thought, watching dark cars creep down the street, their glowing eye stalks waving slowly back and forth. *Next shell, please!*

He stumbled aboard a commuter bus. Did it seem like the steps were lower than they should be? Nothing had felt quite right recently. Ever since that flu episode last month; barely conscious for two days, all sorts of weird dreams, and he still felt disoriented. No depth of field, he decided, focusing on the window across the aisle. That beetle-browed black man in the tan suit, for example. *He* was in focus, when Sam looked just above him. They avoided eye contact. *Like all good commuters*, he thought, *since the first trilobites lined up to crawl down the beach*. The man was clear enough, but the woman beside him,... What color was her clothing, green? Grey, he saw, shifting his gaze nearer to her. Grey like a chrysalis. But now the black man looked kind of beige. He was wearing a tan suit, of course. Maybe it was nothing.

He'd have his eyes checked, Sam decided. Could the flu do something to your eyes? Probably. *Viruses. Little aliens crawling inside your body. Talk about probing.* But did they come in little UFOs? Was that how they got past security? All that hand cleanser being sold, and here little virus saucers were just flying right up your nostrils. He wrinkled his nose. No way to really get them closed. He was defenseless, he thought with a thrill. And loopy. Never really recovered from that flu, and now it had gone to his brain. Have to take some time off, recuperate.

When his stop came, he leapt off the bus. More aliens in a crowd, he thought. More chance of abduction. Best to steer clear of the teeming hordes. He watched the glowing tail of the bus roll out of sight. *Must be the season.* You only got that effect in the spring, when the buses were attracting mates.

As Sam walked slowly up the dark stairs to his flat, a door opened beside him. "Nice hat, Ms. Gordon," he called out as went past. Weird old thing. Always seemed to wrap up in grey fringe, like a moth. A gypsy moth, he thought with a giggle. Was he wrong, or had hats with big dangly feathers not gone out of style years ago? And she was so pale all the time. Needed makeup – a little cochineal red lipstick, maybe. Except wasn't it made from crushed insects? Disgusting thought, putting that near your mouth.

He stopped in front of his own door. *Alright, Sam. Time to get it together. In control. Serious, sober, successful, that's the way to go. A man's home is his shell.* He dug in his pocket for a key, and opened the door.

"Honey, I'm home!" He stepped into the hall, coughing again. It always seemed to smell a little off in this apartment. *Have to save up for a bigger place.* "Where are you, my little nymph?" He hung up his coat and hat.

"Oh!" he cried, as something touched him on the shoulder. He stepped back, rubbing his eyes. "Startled me for a minute." Was it his imagination, or was she wearing a dark, stiff suit, and a hat? Maybe feathers were back in style after all. And was there something different about her face? He shook his head, containing a sneeze.

"Oh, darling, you're sick again." She rubbed soft feelers down his cheek, and he flinched. "Come in and I'll make you a nice cup of tea."

"Sorry, honey," he said, opening his eyes again. She looked down at him with eyes so bright he could see his reflections in them. "Just a mite tired." He glanced at her shiny brown tunic. Some sort of synthetic, he supposed. "Thought you were wearing a suit of armor there for a minute."

"Armor? Were you going to attack me?" She twisted her thorax demurely.

"No. No, of course not. I just... I don't know." He smiled wanly. "I think I will take that tea. Maybe a hot bath, too."

"Like to be in hot water, do you?" Her spiracles winked as she laughed.

"There's something warming about it." It was a weak effort, but the best he could do. Definitely needed that time off. *Best to raise it right away.*

"Come on, then." She led the way to the kitchen, cerci waggling appealingly.

Cerci, he thought, following. Strange word for legs. A lot like "Circe". Wasn't she the one who'd turned Odysseus into a pig, or something? Not quite right, but something about transformation, anyway.

"Have a seat, while I get your tea ready." Her segments crinkled as she bent over an electric kettle.

He sat. "May be safer not to drink anything," he offered. "Don't want to turn into a pig."

"A pig? You really *are* sick." She turned to face him, a worried look on her face, and a teabag in each gripper. "Maybe something herbal? I'm pretty sure it'll just make you sleepy, not turn you into anything."

He gathered his resolve. "Honey, I've been thinking."

"Oh, I'm proud. You know how excited I get when you do that. And with you not feeling well!"

It stung, but he bored on relentlessly. "Let's take that vacation now. Let's get away from all this. From this city, this apartment. Somewhere different, ... Clean."

"Sam. You know we can't do that. We don't have the money. And I just took on this new research job at the lab. If I get it done quickly, they may promote me!"

"I just... I'm feeling strange, lately. Not myself."

"Don't be silly, honey. Who else would you be?"

"No, not... I mean, I'm starting to see things differently. They're not what they seem. Or, they are, but they seem like they're something different."

"That doesn't make sense."

"It's hard to explain."

She brought over a steaming cup. "Have some tea. I'm sure it'll all be clear in the morning, when you're rested. Probably just a midlife crisis." She flashed her maxillae. "Next thing you'll be working late with Jeannie in accounting. I hope it's Jeannie; she has such nice legs." She extended her own.

Hairy, he noted; *thick black hairs*. Strange how he hadn't noticed her having that unshaven look before. Not really to his taste, he decided. Time to put his foot down, to show who was in charge here.

"Well, we're going." He put as much determination as he could into the declaration. "We're going, and that's that."

Tea spilled as the saucer shook, and she quickly set it down before him. Her mouthparts worked rapidly.

The tension grew, and Sam felt himself weakening. It was important to hold on, he told himself. To stand up for himself. For himself, and for all men. At this crucial time, at this epochal moment, he must stand firm, forsake creature comforts (he looked longingly at the steaming tea) in favor of principle. The principle, he reminded himself, of self-determination. Of freedom. Of vacation.

But then her antennae drooped, and he felt his resolve slipping away, the moment fading. The cool breeze from her wings wafted a delightful scent his way.

"Sam, ..." She sniffed. "I've worked so hard for this opportunity; there's so much riding on this. Please. I'll finish this one project. Then we'll go wherever you want. But I have to finish this work; it means a lot to me. To both of us. Please."

She never pleaded, he thought. The scent of her was almost overpowering now, like a heady mix of nutmeg and ginger; and something more primal. He looked into her soft eyes, their facets glowing with concern, and gave up the fight for mankind. "I guess I'll have some of that tea," he conceded.

"I'll go start your bath."

Heck of a good wife really. He took a sip of chamomile. He'd been wrong about the tunic, too. That glossy brown really brought out her mandibles.

He drifted off quickly after his bath. His dreams featured ants and grasshoppers massing for battle. But then they just formed into a choir and a marching band, and deep sleep came at last.

Green palm fronds sighed with contentment. *A little like a wing.* A cricket wing. The palm fronds tickled his skin again, and the sound of crickets grew louder. Annoying things, he thought. And the noise! Not quite cricket, he smiled. That sound they make. *Strai... strei... stridulation!* He woke suddenly.

She stood beside the bed. *Funny*, he thought. *Funny that I know it's her, when she's dressed up as a giant cockroach. Doesn't look like her at all, really.* An angry buzz sounded by the bed as the cockroach rubbed two forelimbs together. "Yes, honey, I'm getting up." *Do cockroaches stand on their back legs? I thought there was more scuttling involved. Like ships. Flying saucers.*

"Get up," she cried. "You've overslept again. You're ruining my results!"

He blinked his eyes. She still looked like a cockroach, and an angry one at that.

With a violent motion, the giant bug ripped the covers off the bed. Exposed, he woke completely. He was on his bed, naked, with a monster cockroach leaning over him, mouthparts working side to side. Yellow slime dripped onto the bed by his side. It burned as it seeped into the sheet under his leg. With agility born of terror, he leapt from a supine position to a full sprint, heading for the bedroom door. His feet had barely touched ground when something long and sticky wrapped around his waist and brought him down. As his head slammed into the hardwood floor, he saw bugs of all sizes crawling from under the bed, from behind ceiling panels, behind outlets. Overwhelmed, his mind gave up its hold at last, and dropped him into a bottomless pit.

Beneath the tall palm trees, piles of dry fronds rustled in a fetid breeze smelling of decaying seaweed and coconut shells. The sound drowned out the voices of two sand fleas arguing over a piece of flotsam.

"Report."

"Its health is good, and the filters are back in place."

The larger flea prodded at the flotsam with a stiff foreleg. "You must be more careful. This is our only specimen. We paid dearly for it!"

Silly, thought Sam. Since when did beachcombers pay for flotsam? Of course, fleas might have different rules.

The small flea stiffened. "The nature of research is experimentation. I could not have anticipated that the sedative would counteract the sensory filters. But even this near-failure has taught us a great deal about human defenses."

The incoming tide, warm and salty, lifted the flotsam briefly before sucking sand out from under him as it pulled away.

"Very well," said the large flea at last. "Your data is crucial to the effort. But you could have set our plans back considerably. Penance is required."

"I will eat a hundred of my young."

"At *least* a hundred." The large flea paused. "Perhaps... Let me show you something. Our scouts get little information. But what little we have is frightening. The problem of scale, ..." It began to dig industriously, setting off a murmuring cascade of sand. They watched it fall. "You see? We must take them by surprise."

The fleas hopped up the beach as a tiny wall of white sea-foam washed over the sand. Like a bubble bath, thought Sam as the crinkle of popping bubbles drowned out the conversation. As the foam receded, the fleas were only faintly audible.

"I appreciate your trust. I will not disappoint you." The small flea folded its top arms in respect. "I will find a weapon."

"I hope so." The large flea shook its bristles free of sand. "You are dismissed."

"Thank you. May your eggs always have a warm depository." As the smaller flea passed near, Sam could hear her muttering "... clearly a virus won't work. Maybe a sterilant rather than a straight pesticide?"

Good choice, agreed Sam as soft waves pulled him slowly out to sea. *More humane that way*. Any further thoughts melted away in the warm salt water as a sea spider gently inserted its proboscis into a vein.

It came from B. Morris Allen

As you might expect, "Metaphorosis" is a simple inversion of the plot of Kafka's "Metamorphosis". I've always had a powerful fear of cockroaches (perhaps due to early exposure in the tropics), so it may be natural that one day when I happened to be thinking about Kafka, it occurred to me to wonder whether in fact perhaps everyone else was a cockroach in disguise. The story grew from that seed, though I turned the concept more to whimsy than the horror I would actually feel.

The title went through several fairly awful variants until I realized that I'd worked in a number of metaphors, and perhaps I should simply go with that. Given my love of metaphor, I stole the title for my new magazine.

About B. Morris Allen

B. Morris Allen is a biochemist turned activist turned lawyer turned foreign aid consultant, and frequently wonders whether it's time for a new career. He's been traveling since birth, and has lived on five of seven continents. When he can, he makes his home on the Oregon coast. In between journeys, he edits *Metaphorosis* magazine, and works on his own speculative stories of love and disaster.

Copyright

Metaphorosis Publishing

Metaphorosis offers beautifully written science fiction and fantasy. Our imprints include:

Metaphorosis Magazine

plant based press

Metaphorosis Books

Driftwyrd

Vestige

Help keep Metaphorosis running at
Patreon.com/metaphorosis

See more about some of our books on the following pages.

Metaphorosis
a magazine of speculative fiction

Metaphorosis is an online speculative fiction magazine dedicated to quality writing. We publish an original story every week, along with author bios, interviews, and notes on story origins. Come and see us online at magazine.Metaphorosis.com

Keep Metaphorosis running! Support us at
Patreon.com/metaphorosis

You can also find us at:
Twitter: @MetaphorosisMag, @MetaphorosisRev, @Metaphorosis
Facebook: www.facebook.com/metaphorosis

We publish monthly print and e-book issues, as well as yearly Best of and Complete anthologies.

**Metaphorosis:
Best of 2018**

The best science fiction and fantasy stories from *Metaphorosis* magazine's third year.

Metaphorosis 2018

All the stories from *Metaphorosis* magazine's third year. Fifty-two great SFF stories.

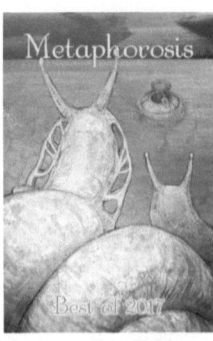

**Metaphorosis:
Best of 2017**

The best science fiction and
fantasy stories from
Metaphorosis magazine's
second year.

Metaphorosis 2017

All the stories from
Metaphorosis magazine's
second year. Fifty-three great
SFF stories.

**Metaphorosis:
Best of 2016**

The best science fiction and
fantasy stories from
Metaphorosis magazine's first
year.

Metaphorosis 2016

Almost all the stories from
Metaphorosis magazine's first
year.

Plant Based Press

plant
based
press

Vegan-friendly science fiction and fantasy, including an annual anthology of the year's best SFF stories.

**Best Vegan SFF
of 2018**

The best vegan science fiction and fantasy stories of 2018!

**Best Vegan SFF
of 2017**

The best vegan science fiction and fantasy stories of 2017!

Best Vegan SFF
of 2016

The best vegan science fiction
and fantasy stories of 2016!

Susurrus

A darkly romantic story of
magic, love, and suffering.

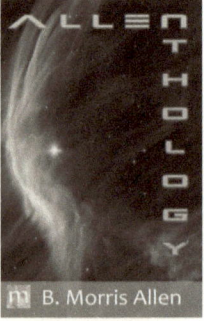

Allenthology:
Volume I

A quarter century of SFF,
including the full contents of
the collections *Tocsin, Start
with Stones,* and *Metaphorosis.*

Science fiction and fantasy books for writers – full of great stories, but with an additional focus on the craft of speculative fiction writing.

Score

an SFF symphony

What if stories were written like music? *Score* is an anthology of varied stories arranged to follow an emotional score from the heights of joy to the depths of despair – but always with a little hope shining through.

Reading 5X5

Five stories, five times

Twenty-five SFF authors, five base stories, five versions of each – see how different writers take on the same material, with stories in contemporary and high fantasy, soft and hard SF, and a mysterious 'other' category.

Reading 5X5

Writers' Edition

All the stories from the regular, readers' edition, plus two extra stories, the story seed, and authors' notes on writing. Over 100 pages of additional material specifically aimed at writers.